SKIP!

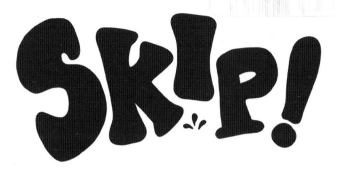

A GRAPHIC NOVEL

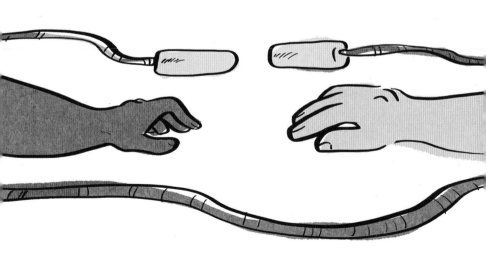

Andrews McMeel Publishing
a division of Andrews McMeel Universal
1130 Walnut Street, Kansas City, Missouri 64106

www.andrewsmcmeel.com

23 24 25 26 27 SDB 10 9 8 7 6 5 4 3 2 1

Paperback ISBN: 978-1-5248-7737-8
Hardcover ISBN: 978-1-5248-8454-3

Library of Congress Control Number: 2023933957

Editor: Erinn Pascal
Art Director: Tiffany Meairs
Production Editor: David Shaw
Production Manager: Chuck Harper
Cover Lettering: FYONAFINN

Made by:
RR Donnelley (Guangdong) Printing Solutions Company Ltd
Address and location of manufacturer:
No. 2, Minzhu Road, Daning, Humen Town,
Dongguan City, Guangdong Province, China 523930
1st Printing – 6/12/23

ATTENTION: SCHOOLS AND BUSINESSES

Andrews McMeel books are available at quantity discounts with
bulk purchase for educational, business, or sales promotional use.
For information, please e-mail the Andrews McMeel Publishing Special
Sales Department: sales@amuniversal.com.

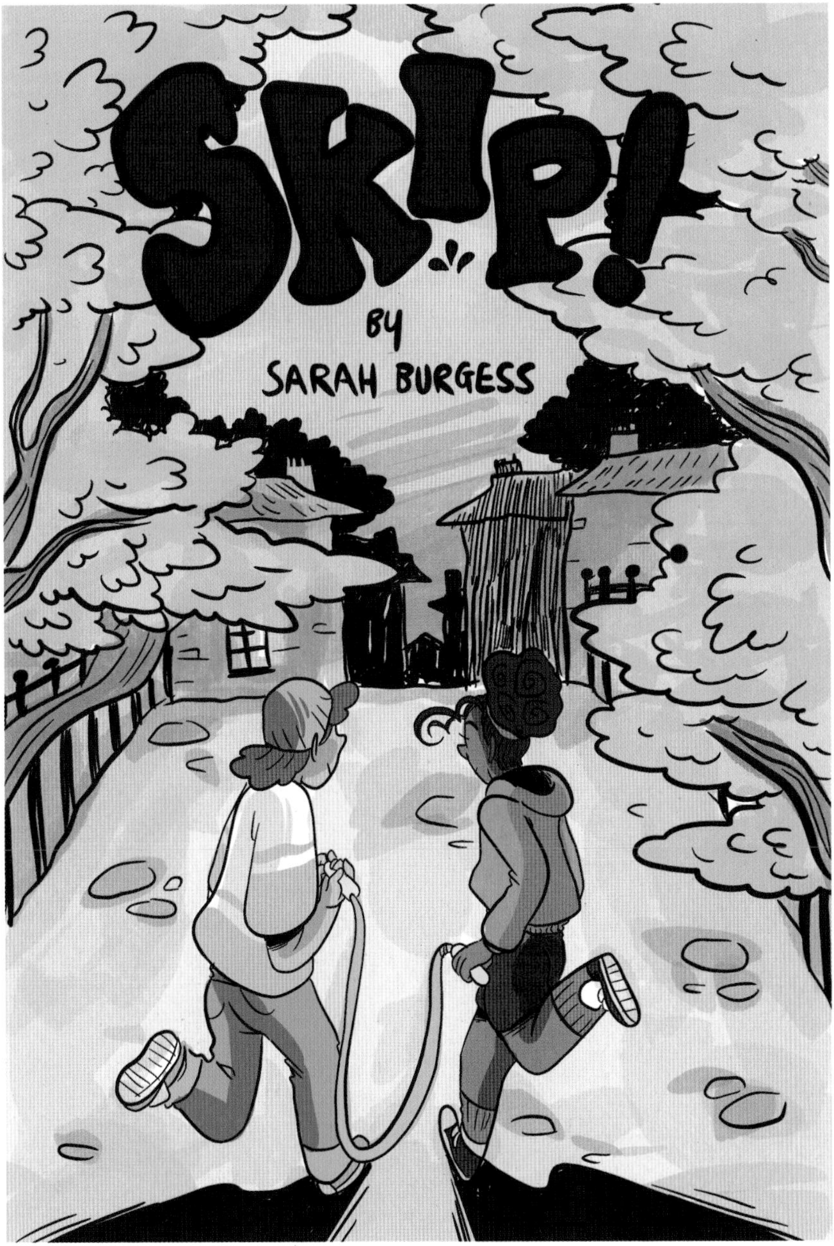
SKIP!
BY
SARAH BURGESS

Andrews McMeel
PUBLISHING®

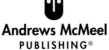

CHAPTER ONE

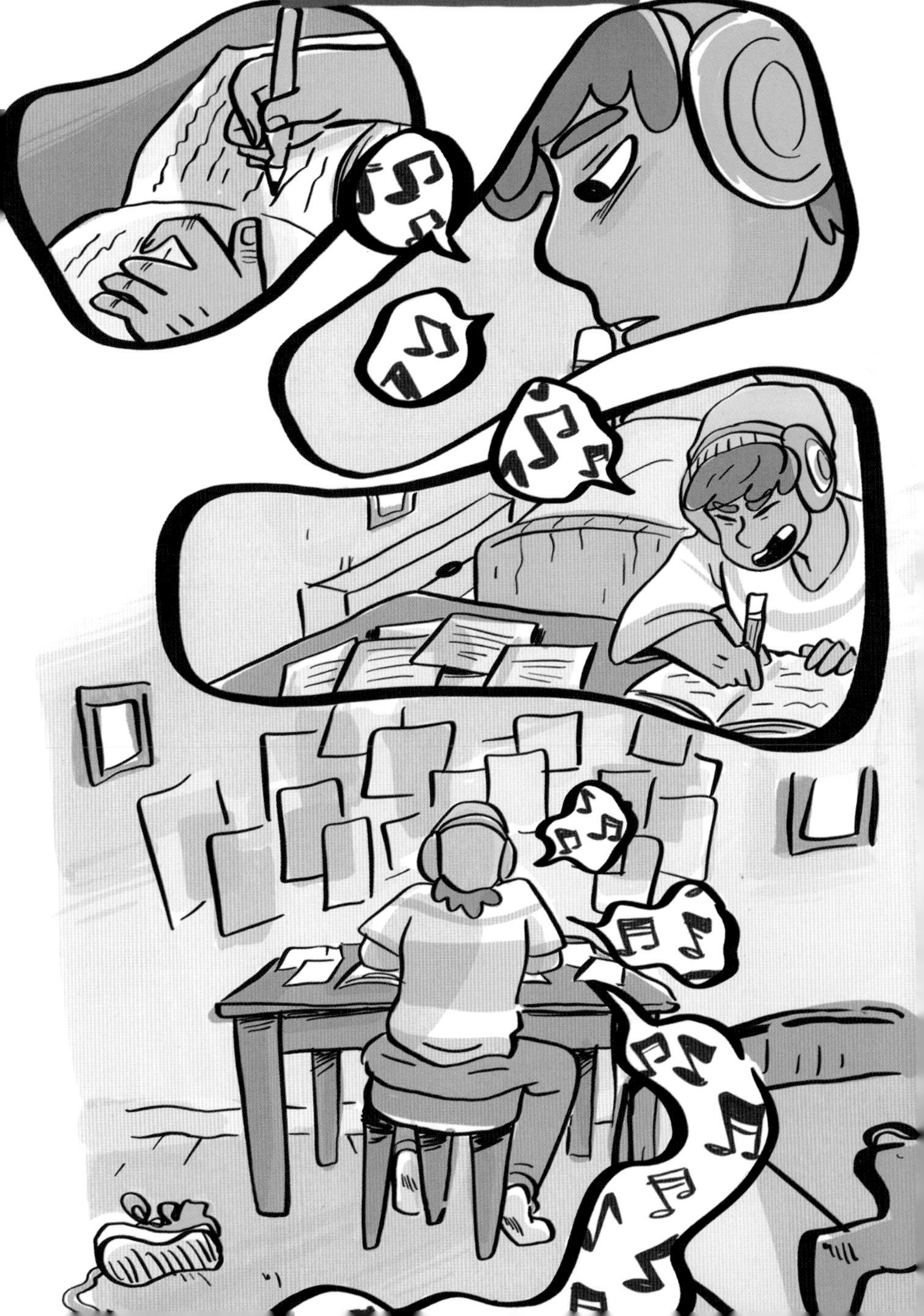

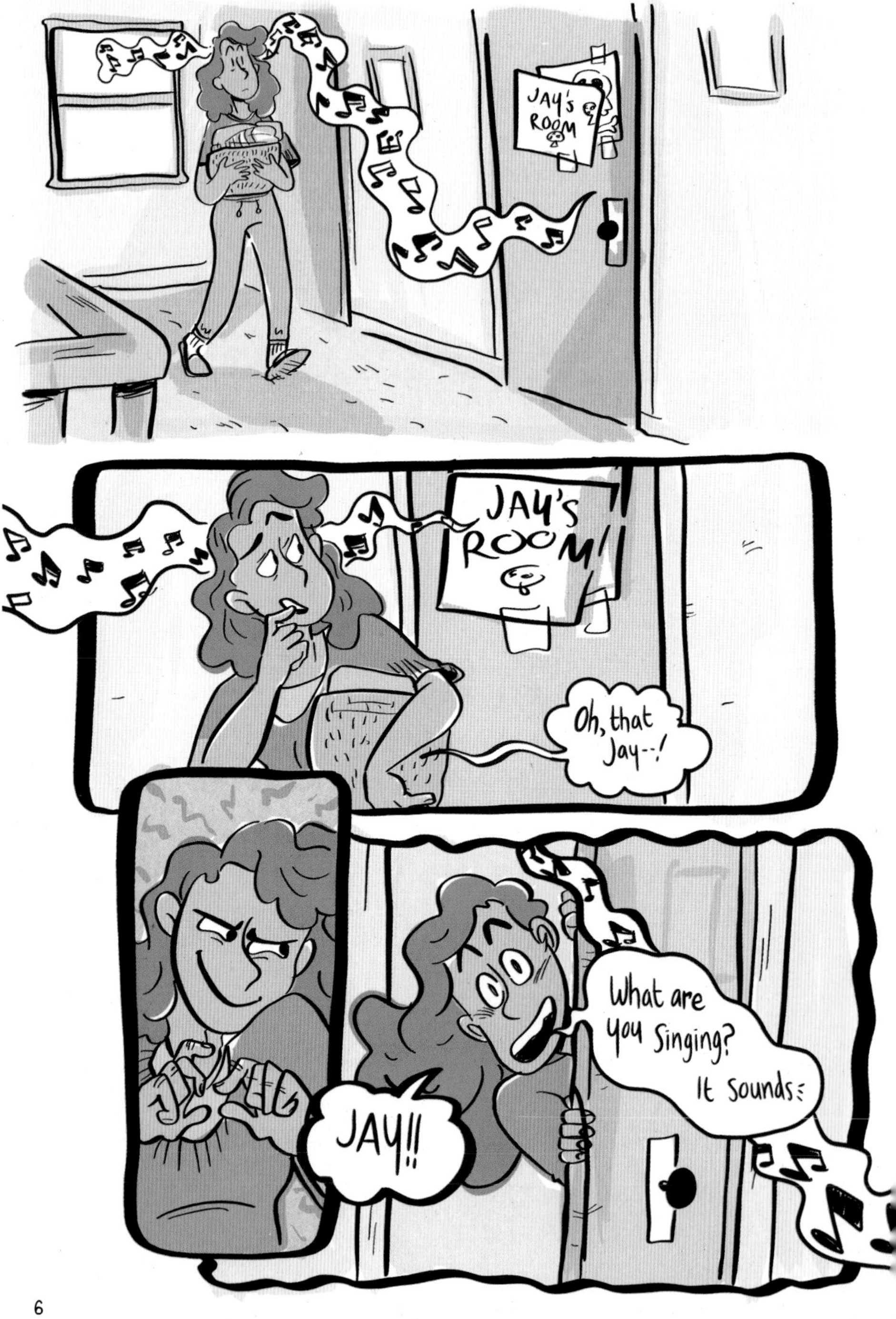
JAY'S ROOM
JAY'S ROOM
Oh, that Jay--!
What are you singing?
It sounds
JAY!!

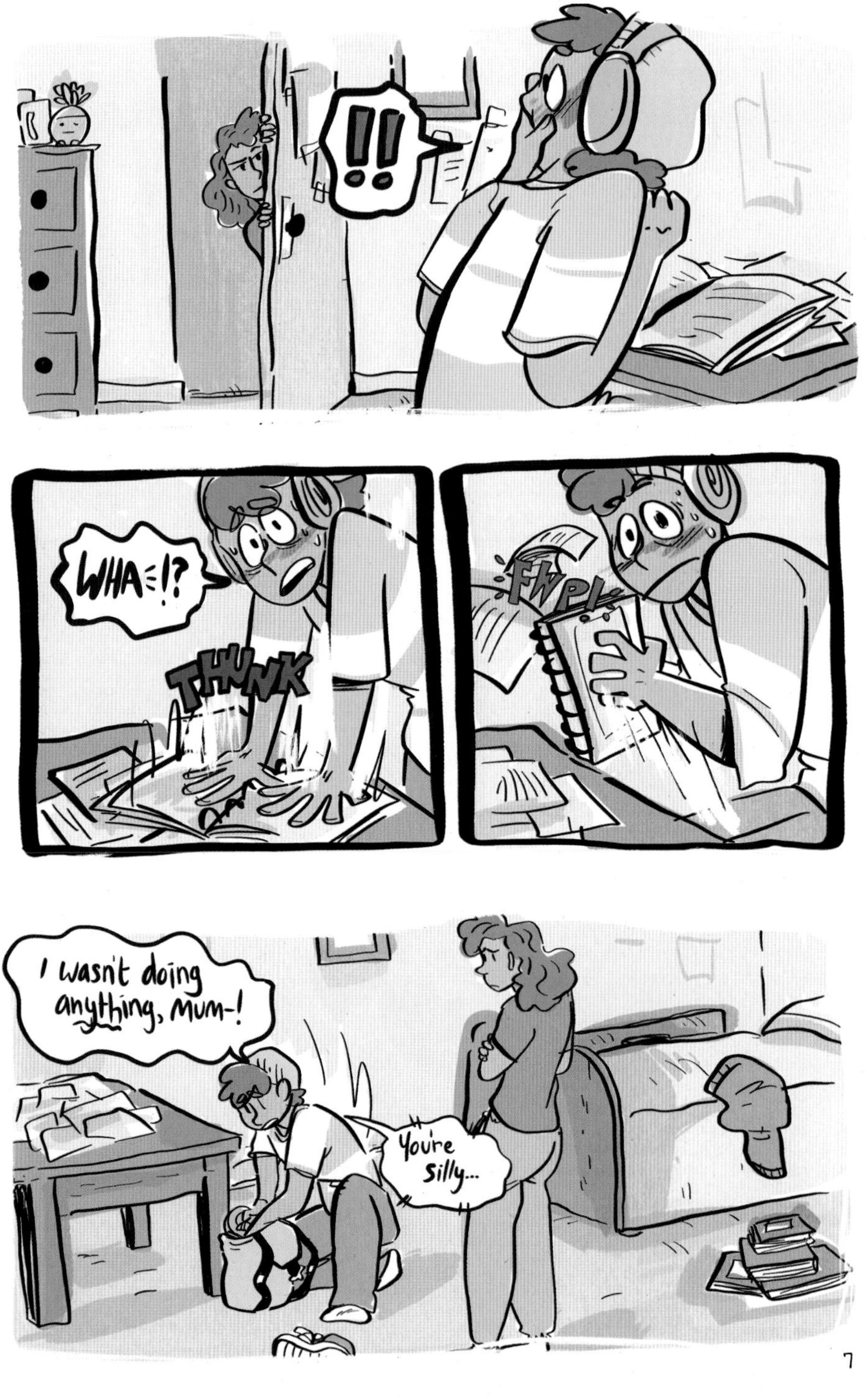
!!
WHA-!?
THUNK
FWP!
I wasn't doing anything, mum-!
You're silly...

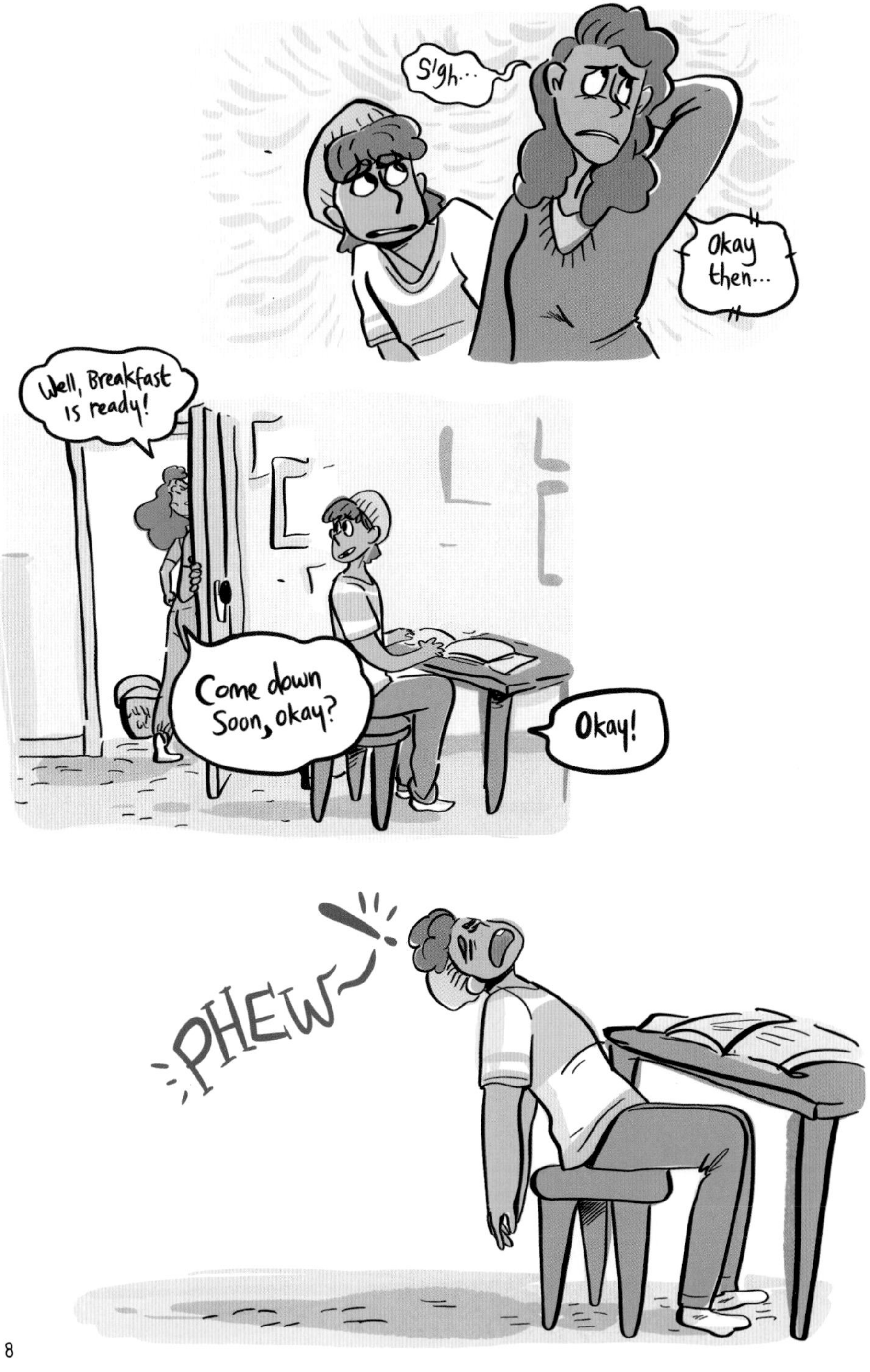
Sigh...
Okay then...
Well, Breakfast is ready!
Come down Soon, okay?
Okay!
PHEW~

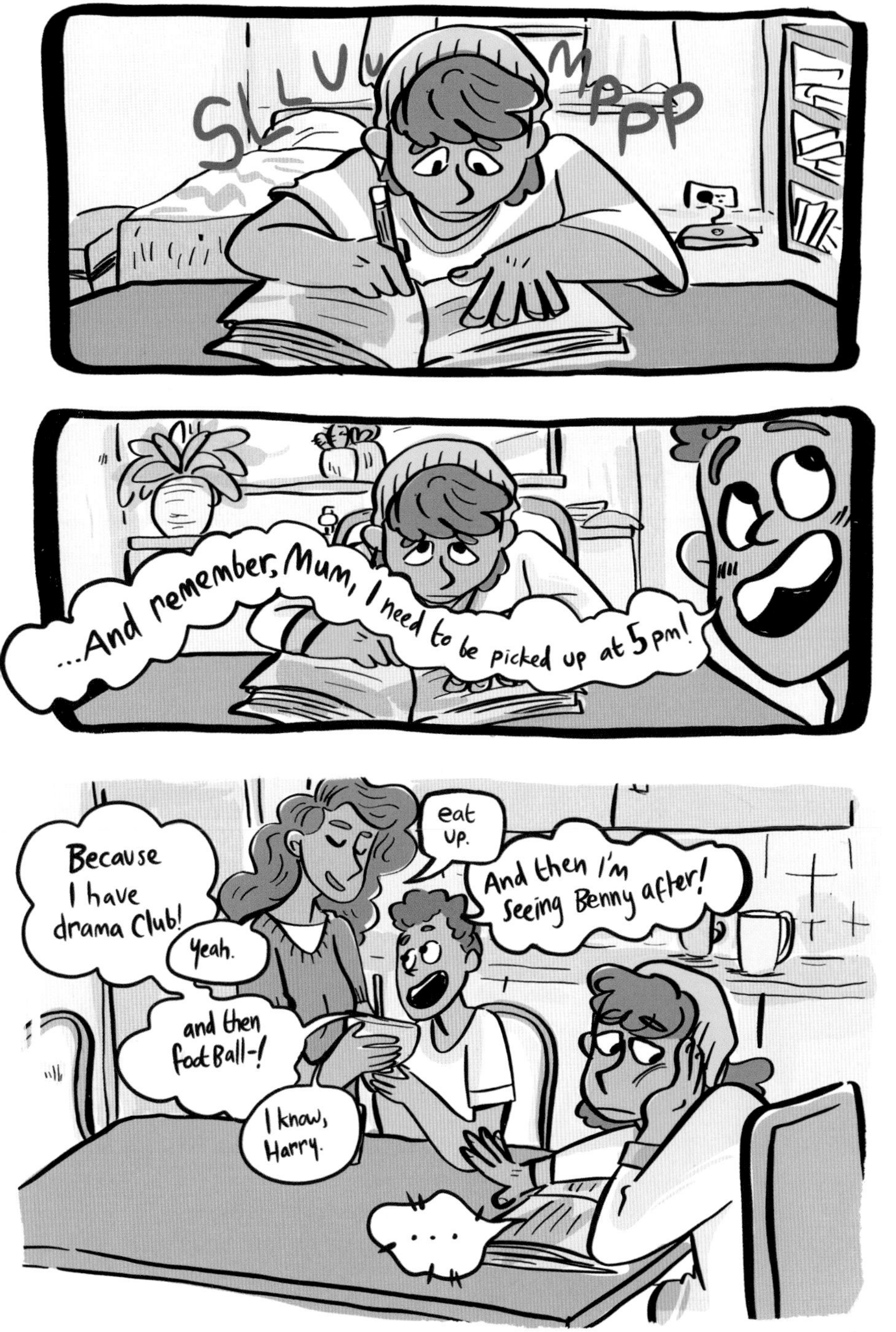
SLLUUMPPP
...And remember, Mum, I need to be picked up at 5pm!
Because I have drama Club!
Yeah.
eat up.
and then footBall-!
And then I'm seeing Benny after!
I know, Harry.
...

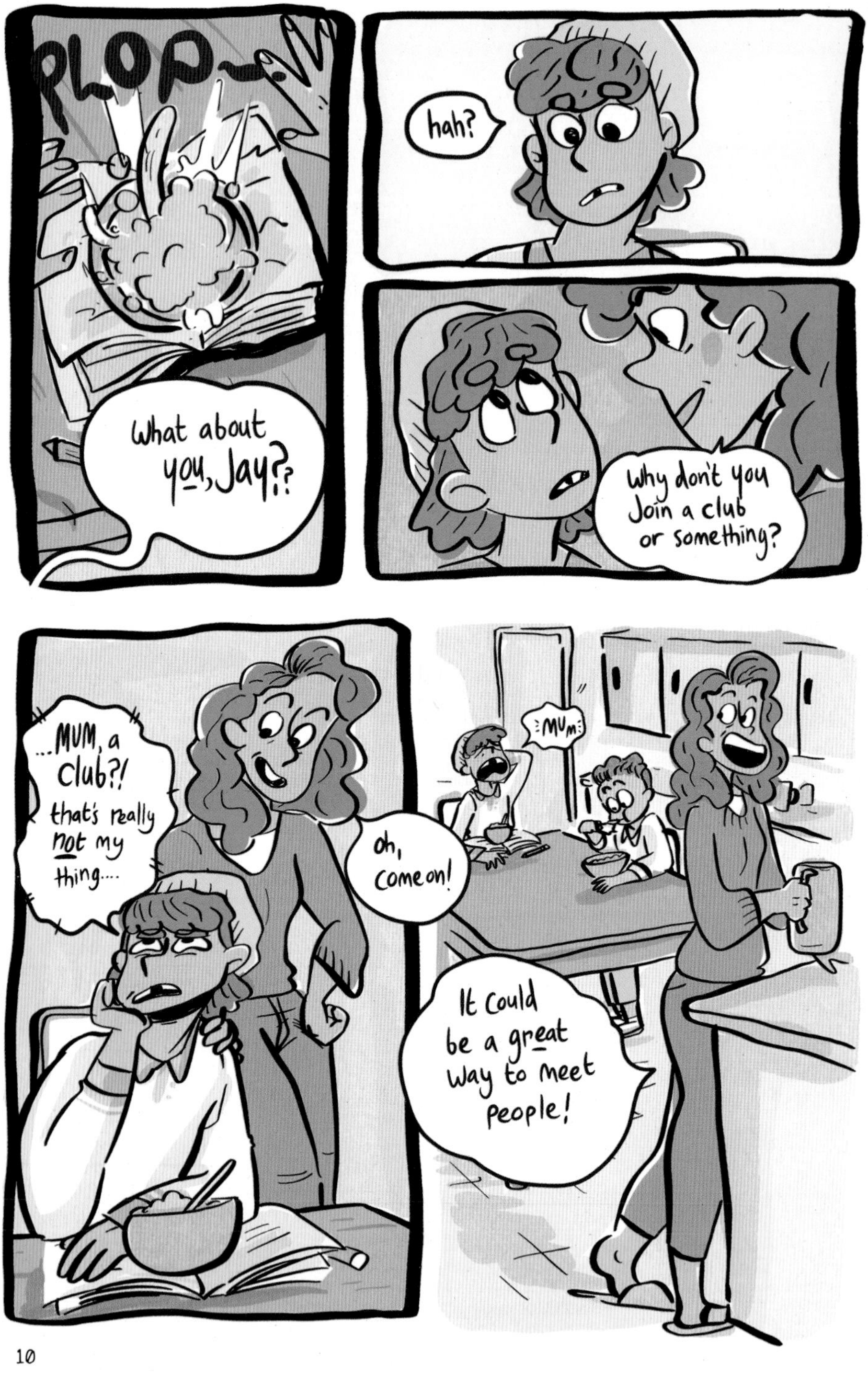
PLOP~
What about you, Jay?¡?
hah?
Why don't you Join a club or something?
...MUM, a club?! that's really not my thing....
oh, come on!
MUM
It could be a great way to meet people!

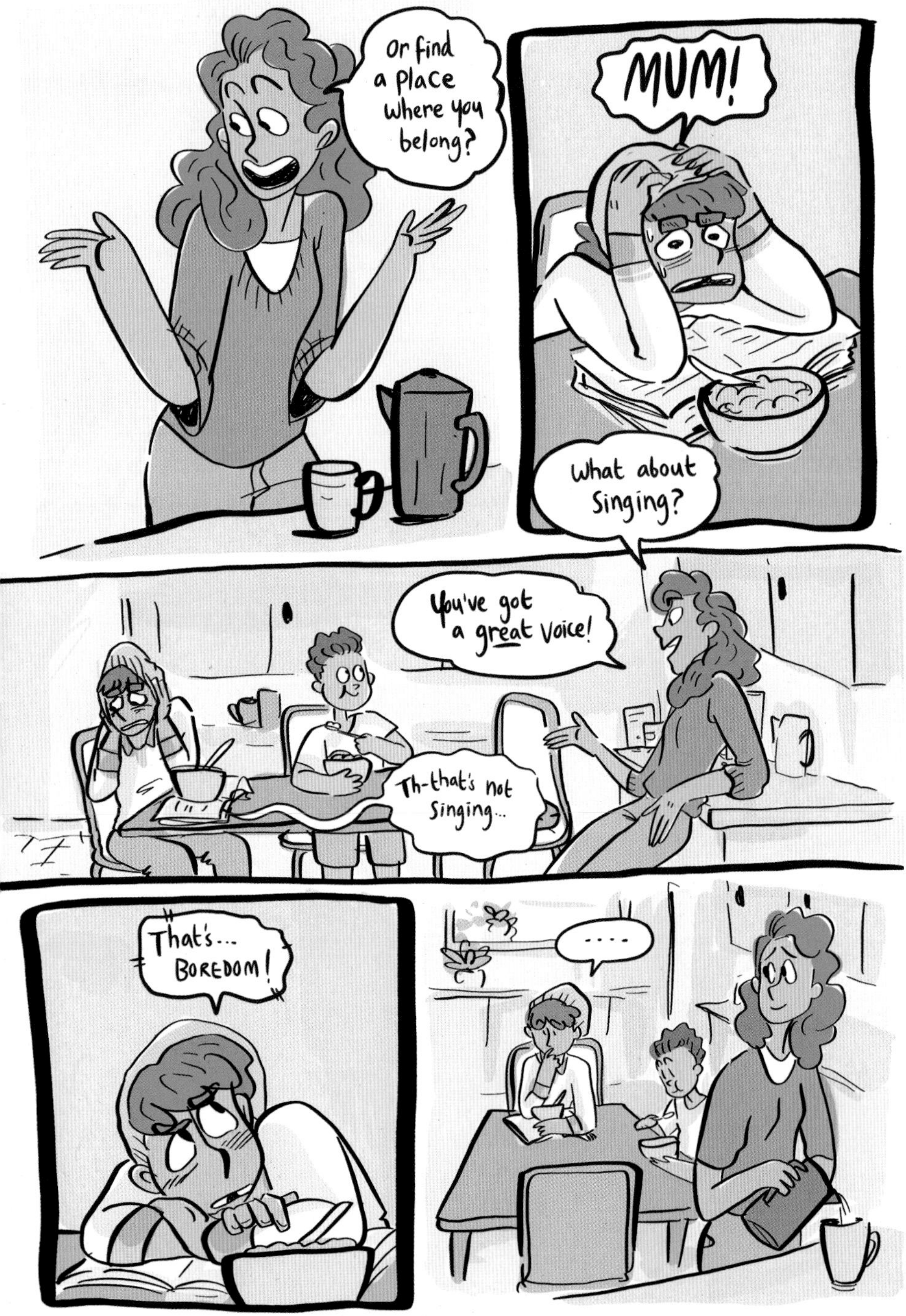
Or find a place where you belong?
MUM!
What about singing?
You've got a great voice!
Th-that's not singing...
That's... BOREDOM!
....

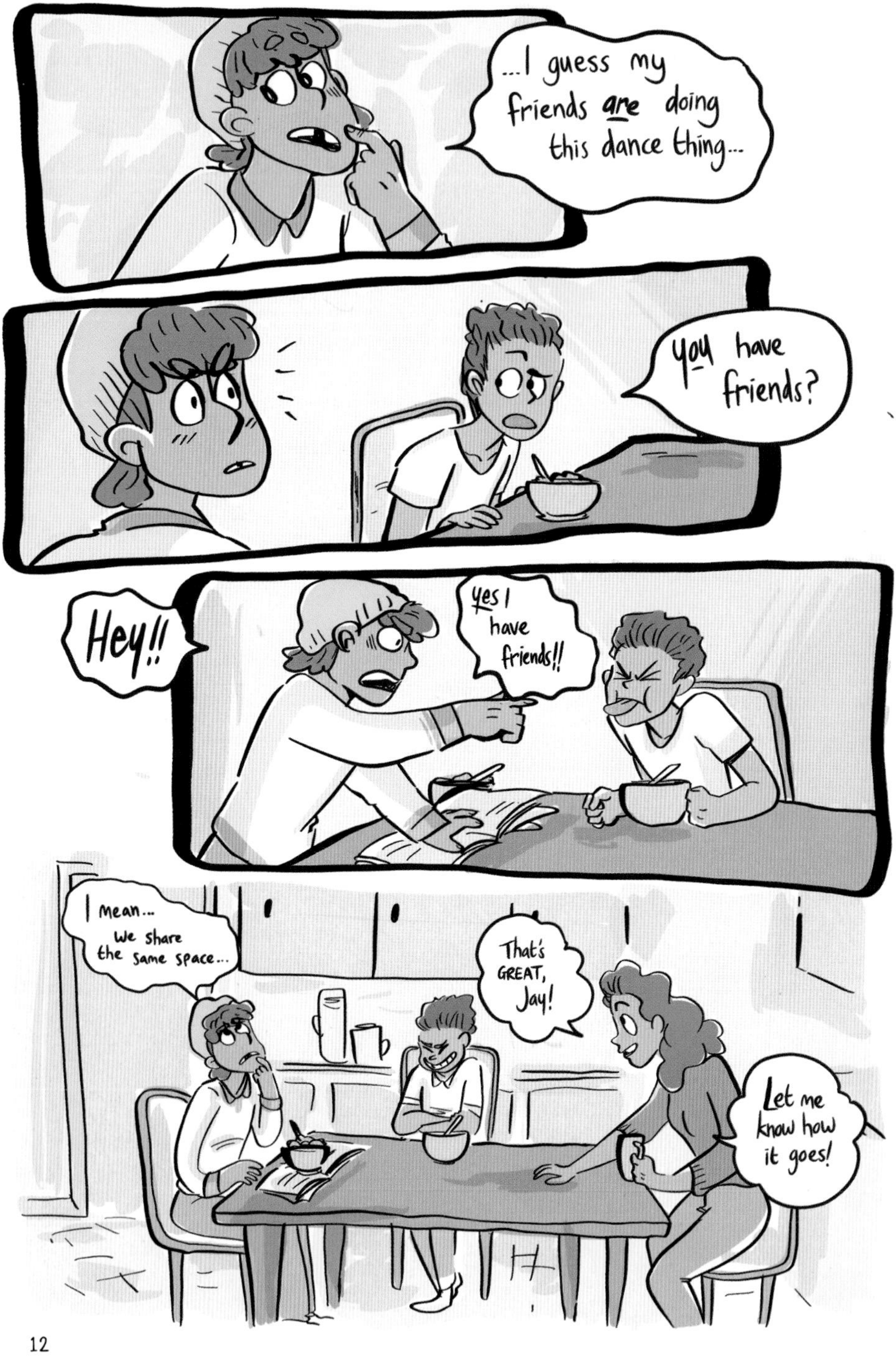
...I guess my friends are doing this dance thing...
you have friends?
Hey!!
yes I have friends!!
I mean... we share the same space...
That's GREAT, Jay!
Let me know how it goes!

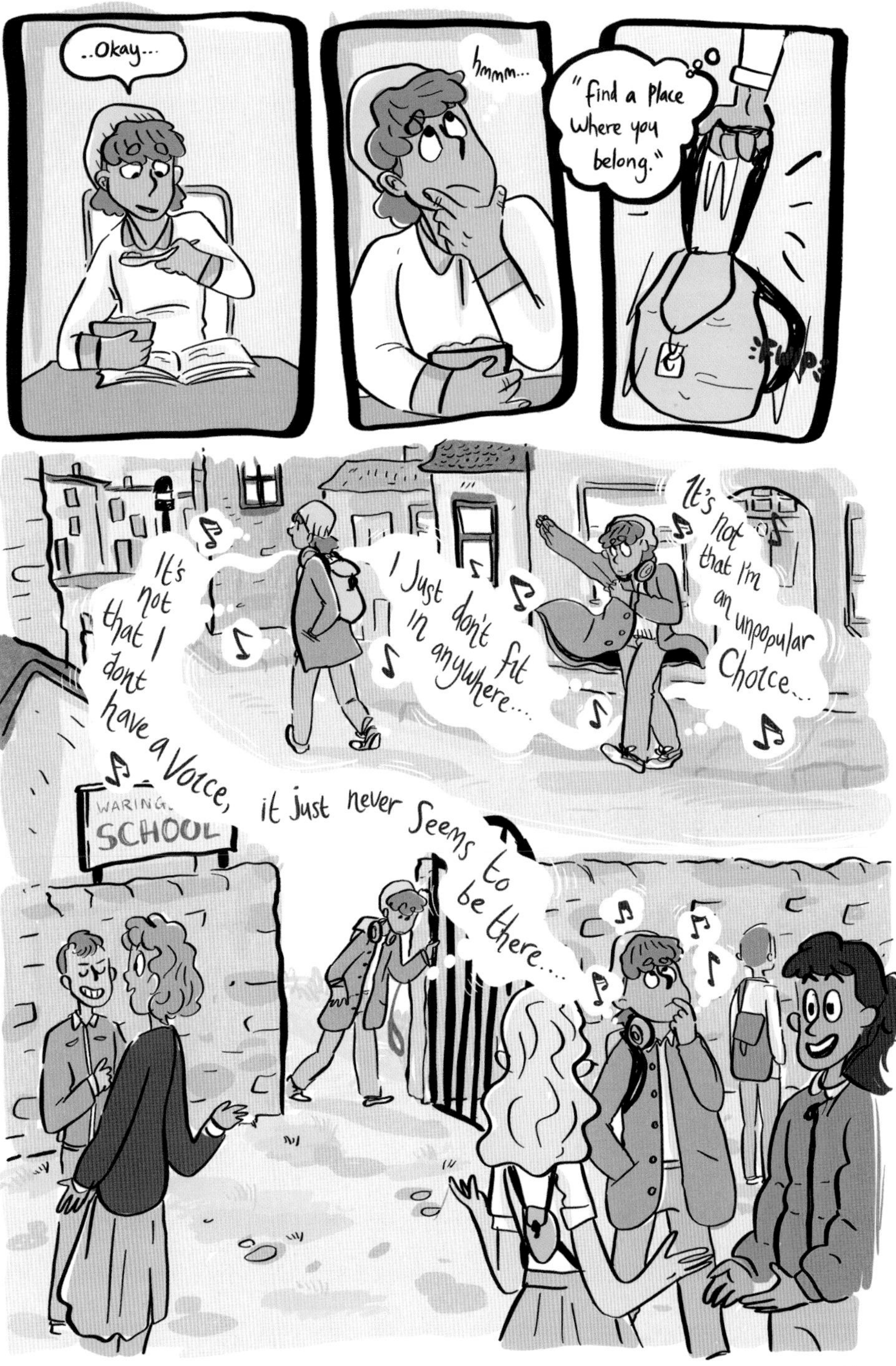
..Okay...
hmmm...
"find a Place Where you belong."
It's not that I dont have a Voice, it just never Seems to be there....
I just don't fit in anywhere....
It's not that I'm an unpopular Choice...
WARING
SCHOOL

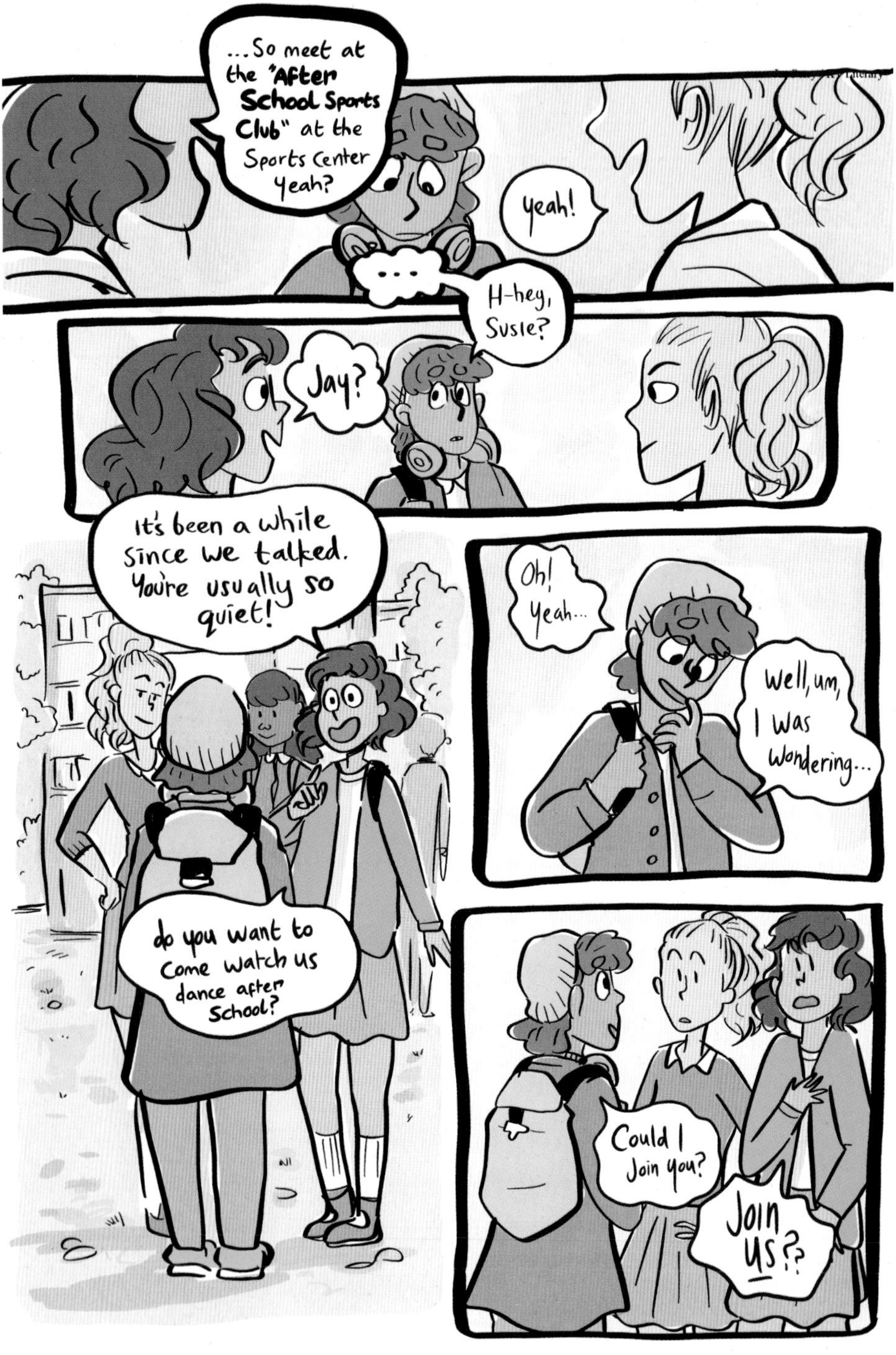
...So meet at the "After School Sports Club" at the Sports Center Yeah?
Yeah!
...
H-hey, Susie?
Jay?
It's been a while since we talked. You're usually so quiet!
do you want to come watch us dance after school?
Oh! Yeah...
Well, um, I was wondering...
Could I Join you?
Join us?!?

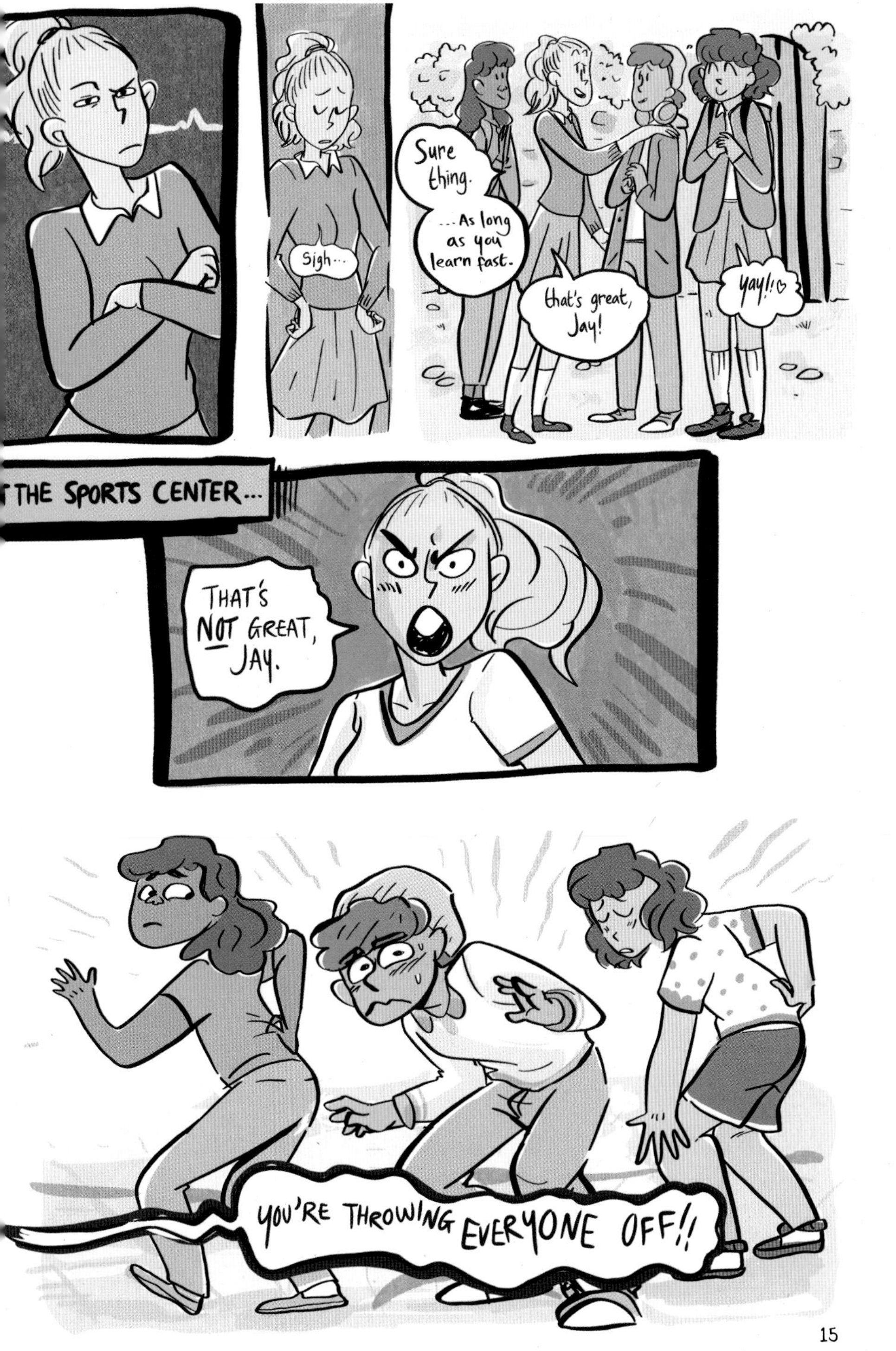
Sigh...
Sure thing.
...As long as you learn fast.
that's great, Jay!
yay!♡
THE SPORTS CENTER...
THAT'S NOT GREAT, JAY.
YOU'RE THROWING EVERYONE OFF!!

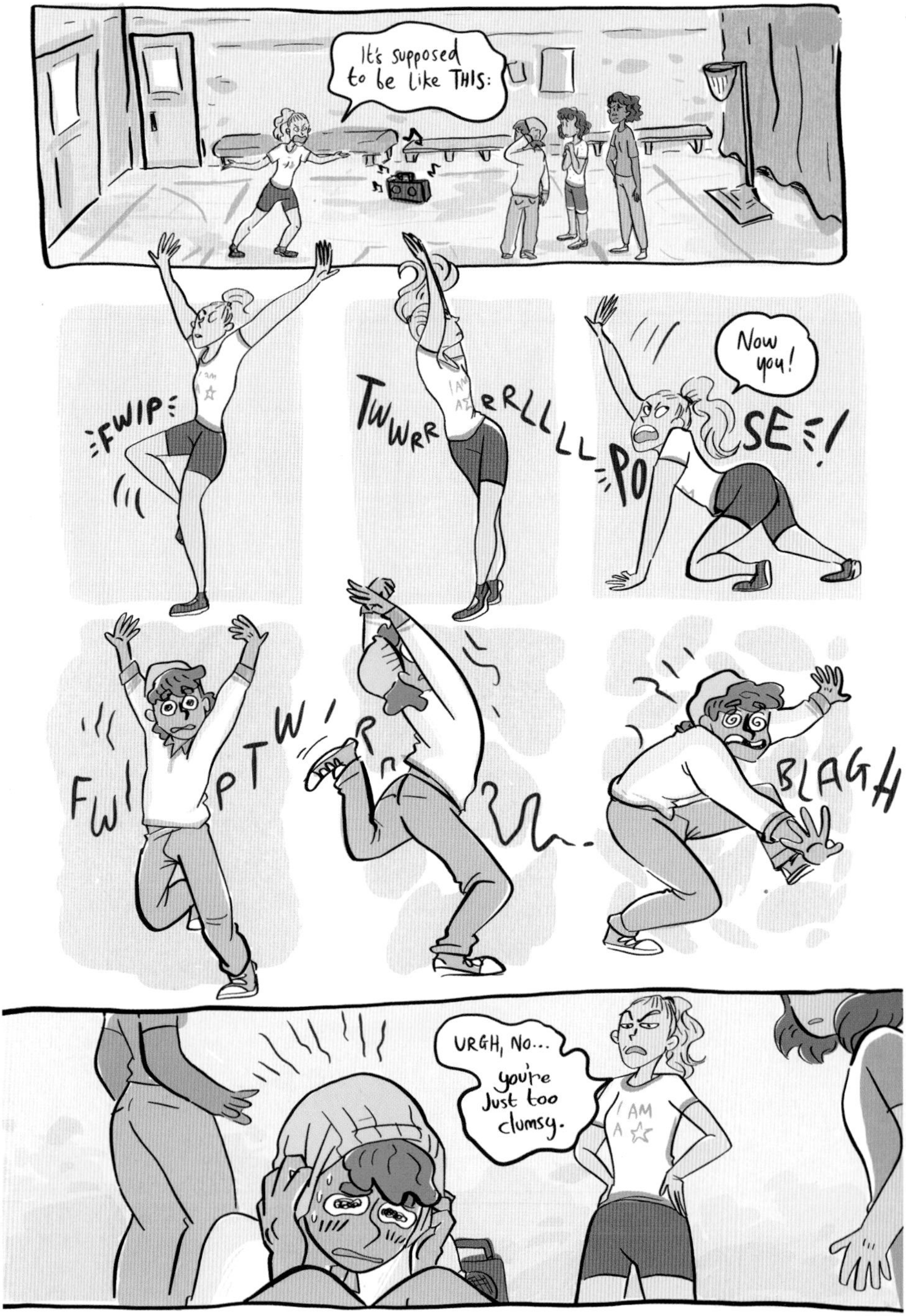
It's supposed to be like THIS:
FWIP
TWWRRRRLLLLL
POSE!
Now you!
FWPTWIRR
BLAGH
URGH, NO...
you're just too clumsy.

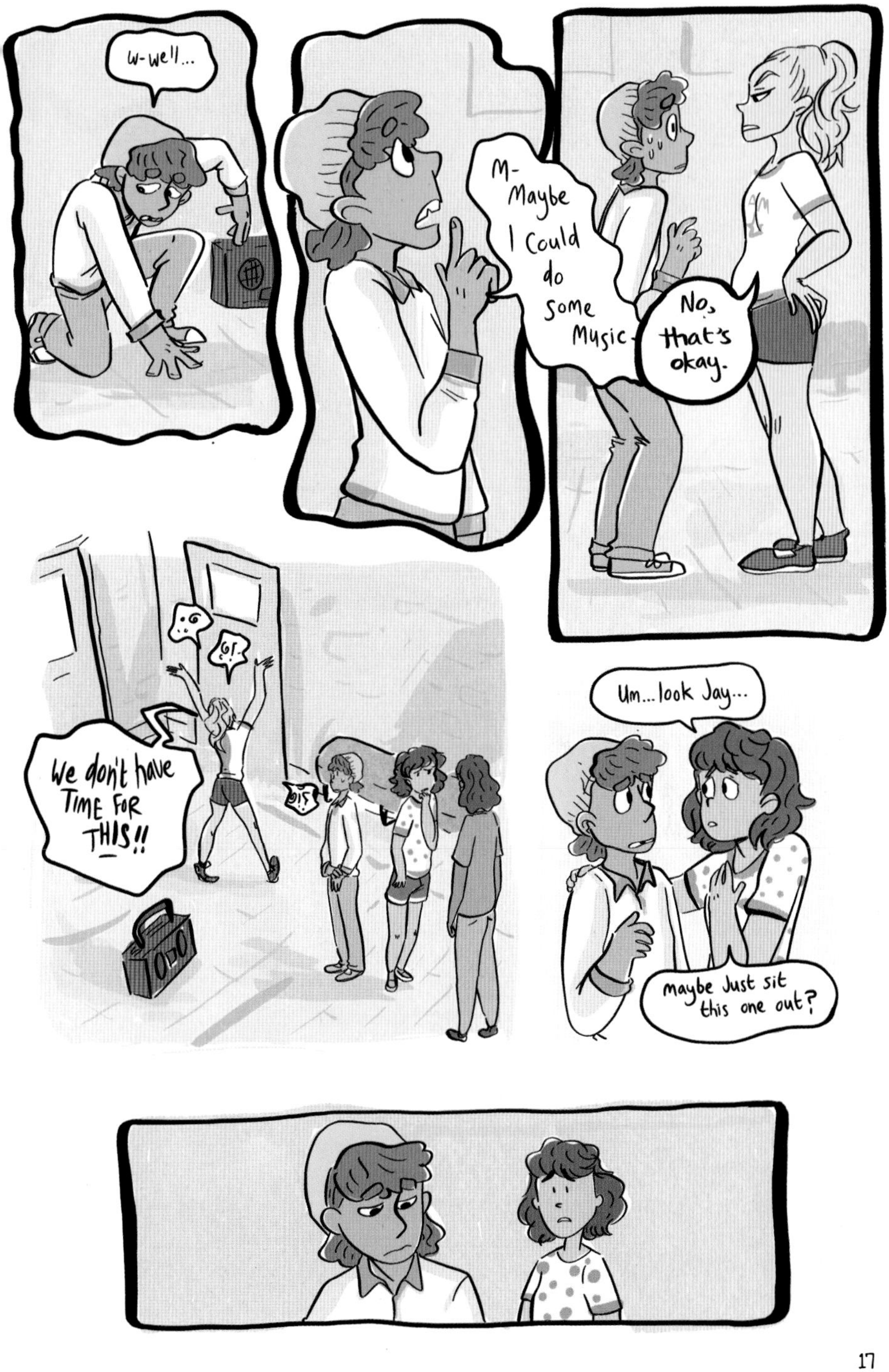
W-We'll...
M-Maybe I could do some Music-
No, that's okay.
We don't have TIME FOR THIS!!
Um...look Jay...
maybe Just sit this one out?

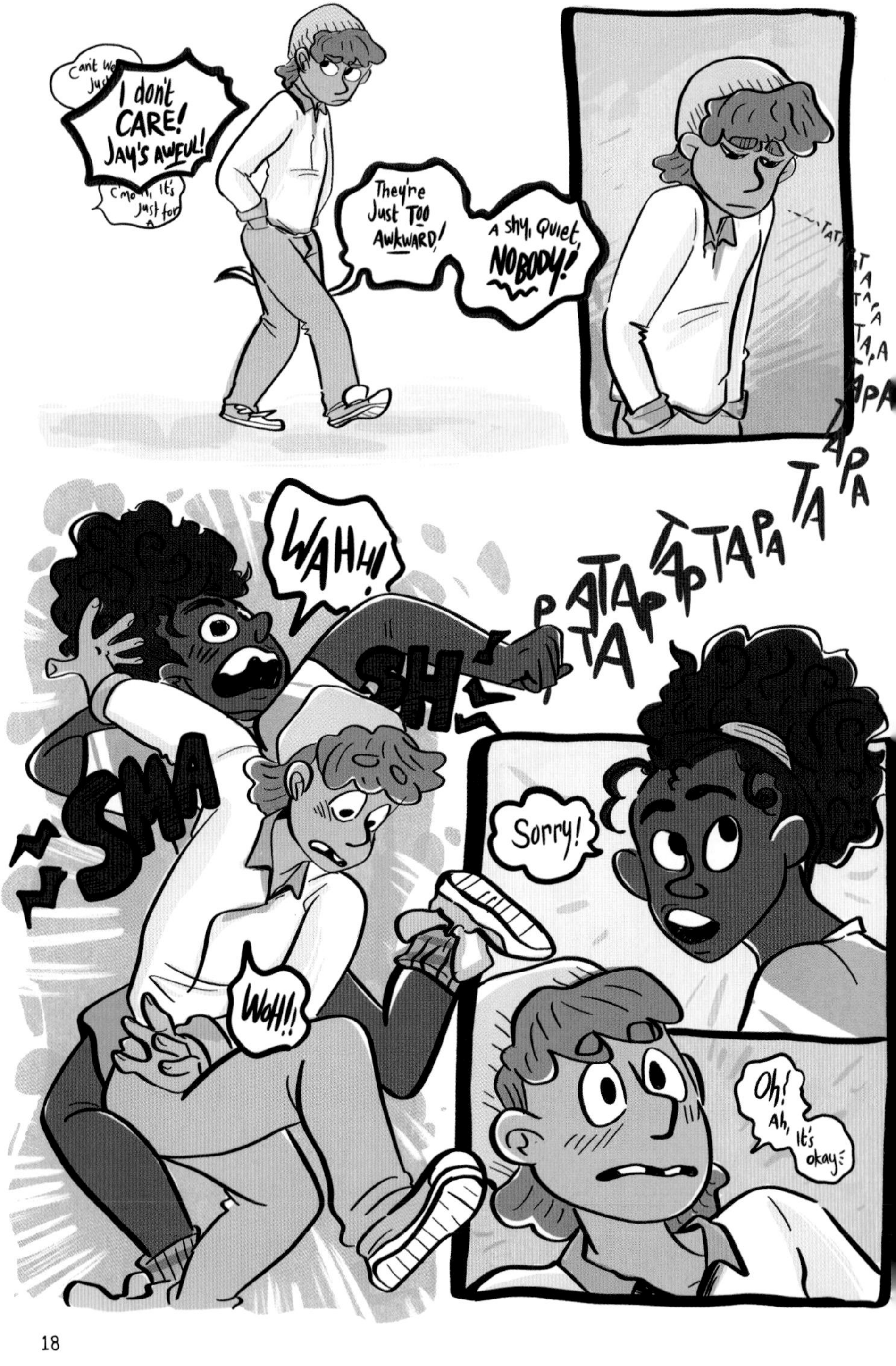
I don't CARE! JAY'S AWFUL!
They're just TOO AWKWARD!
A shy, quiet, NOBODY!
TATAPATAPA TAPA TAPA TAPATAPA TAPA
WAHH!!
SH
SMA
WOH!!
Sorry!
Oh! Ah, It's okay

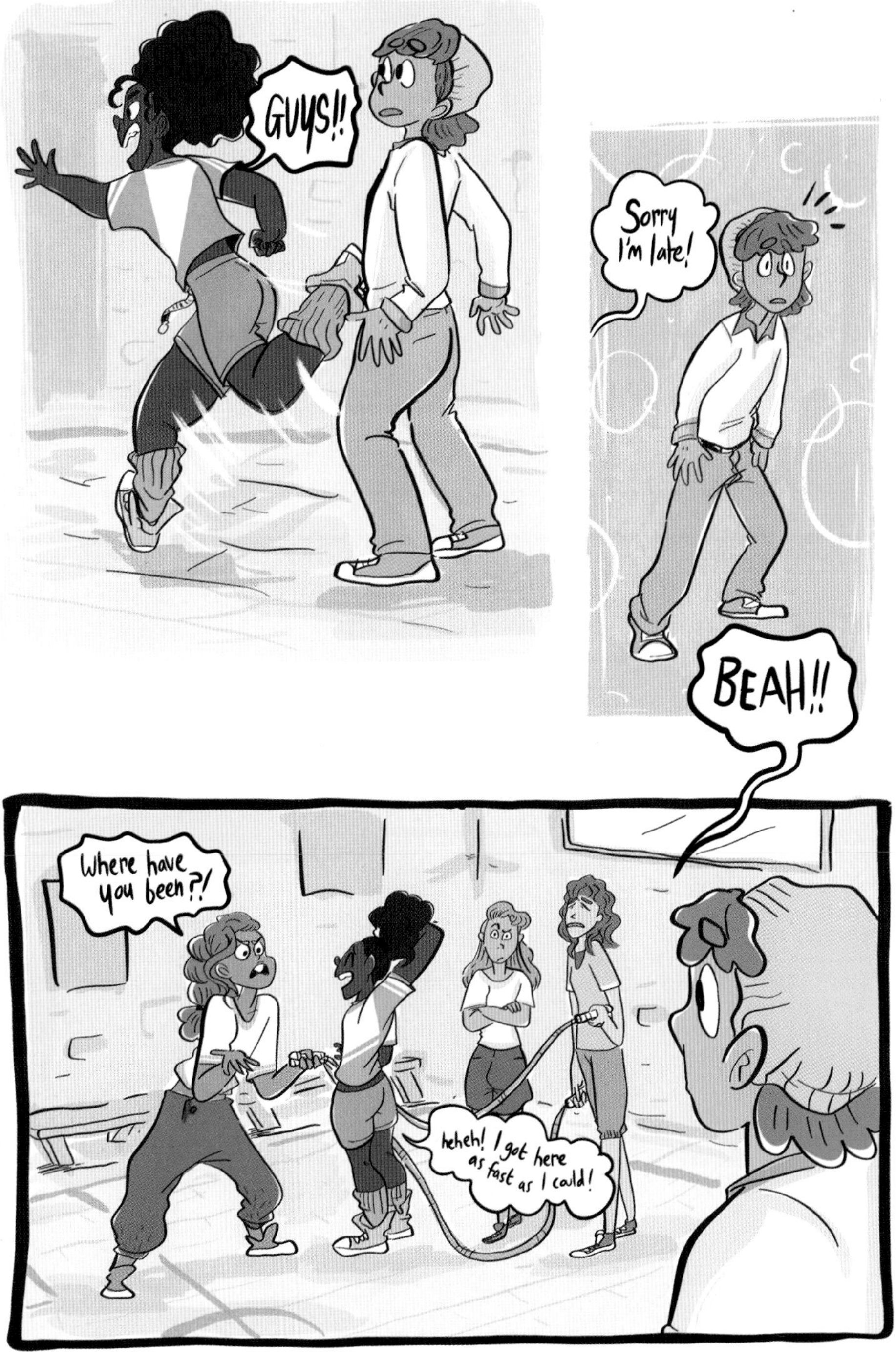
GUYS!!
Sorry I'm late!
BEAH!!
Where have you been?!
heheh! I got here as fast as I could!

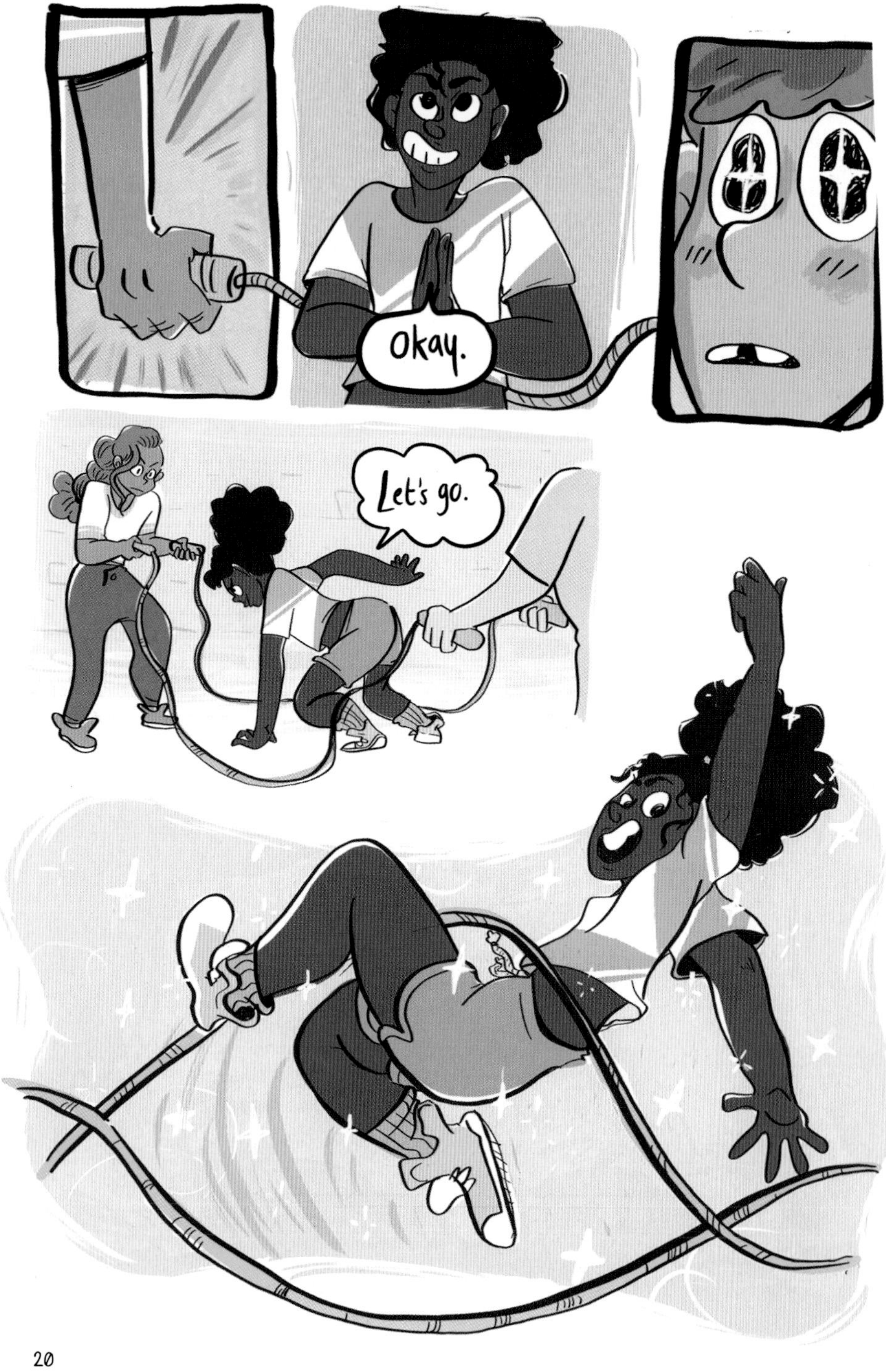
Okay.
Let's go.

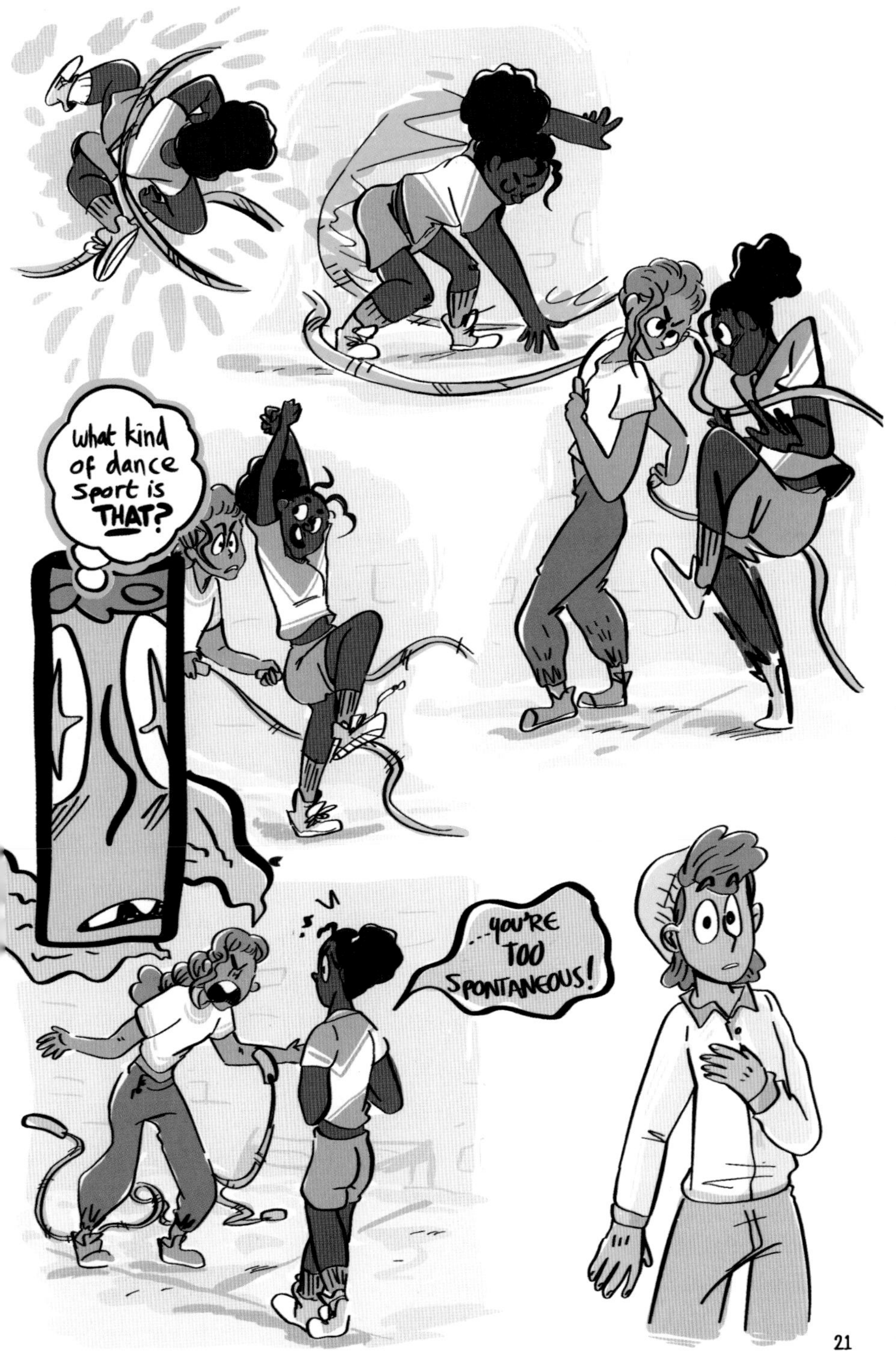
what kind of dance sport is THAT?
...YOU'RE TOO SPONTANEOUS!

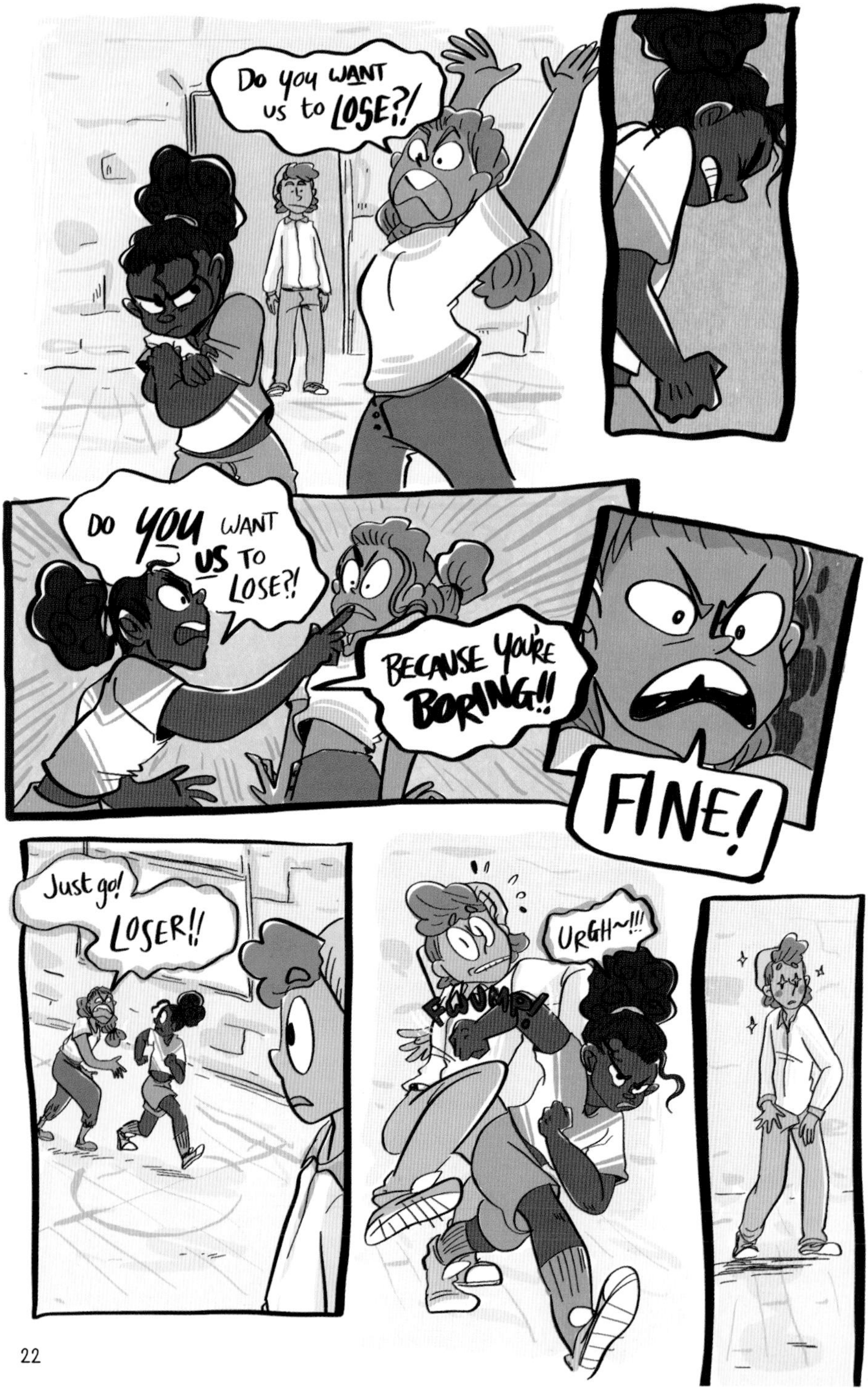
Do you WANT us to LOSE?!
DO YOU WANT US TO LOSE?!
BECAUSE YOU'RE BORING!!
FINE!
Just go! LOSER!!
URGH~!!!
FWUMP!

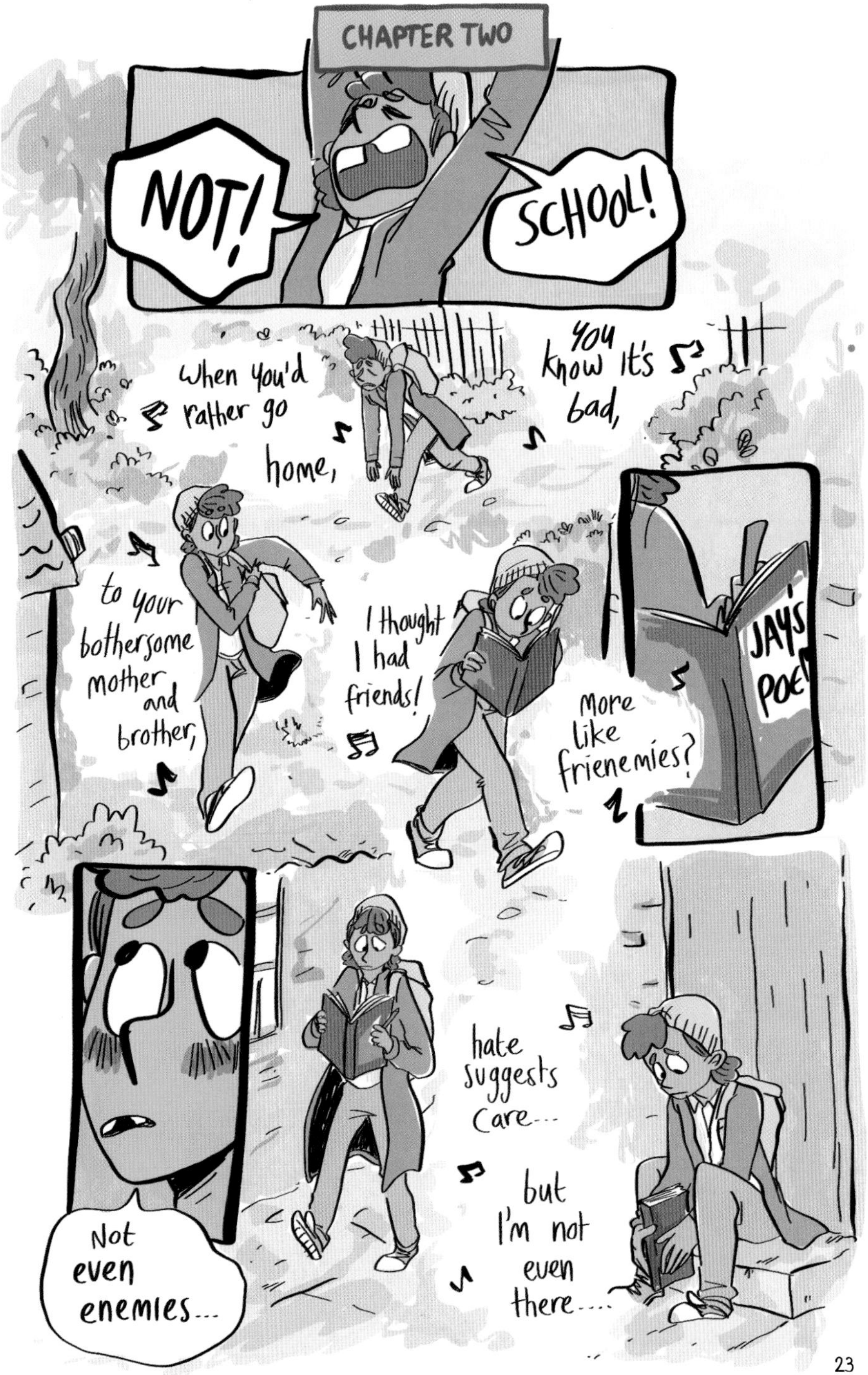
CHAPTER TWO
NOT!
SCHOOL!
When you'd rather go
home,
you know it's bad,
to your bothersome mother and brother,
I thought I had friends!
JAY'S POE
More like frienemies?
hate suggests care...
but I'm not even there...
Not even enemies...

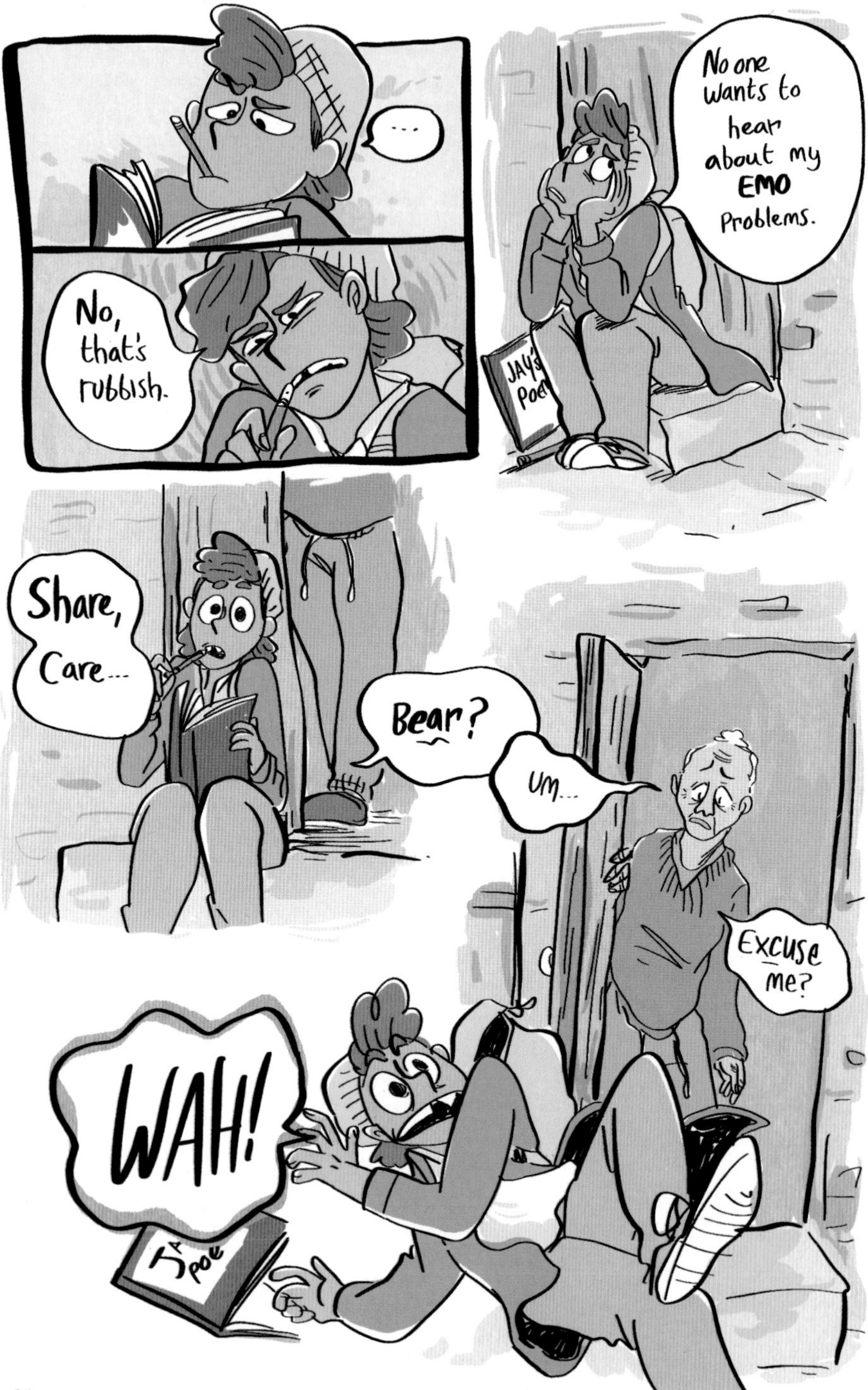
...
No, that's rubbish.
No one wants to hear about my EMO Problems.
JAY's POE
Share, Care...
Bear?
Um...
Excuse me?
WAH!
J POE

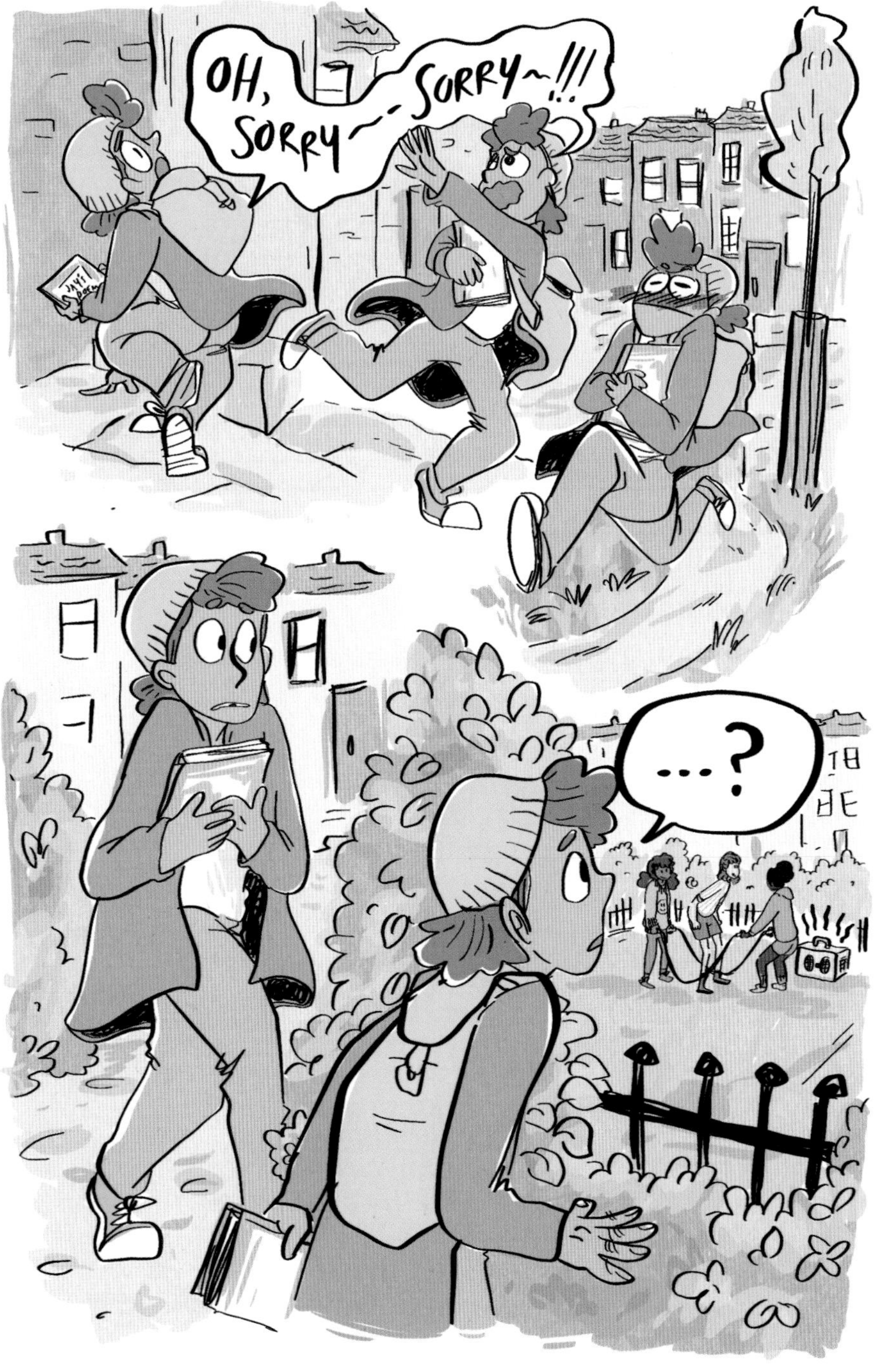
OH, SORRY~
SORRY~!!!
...?

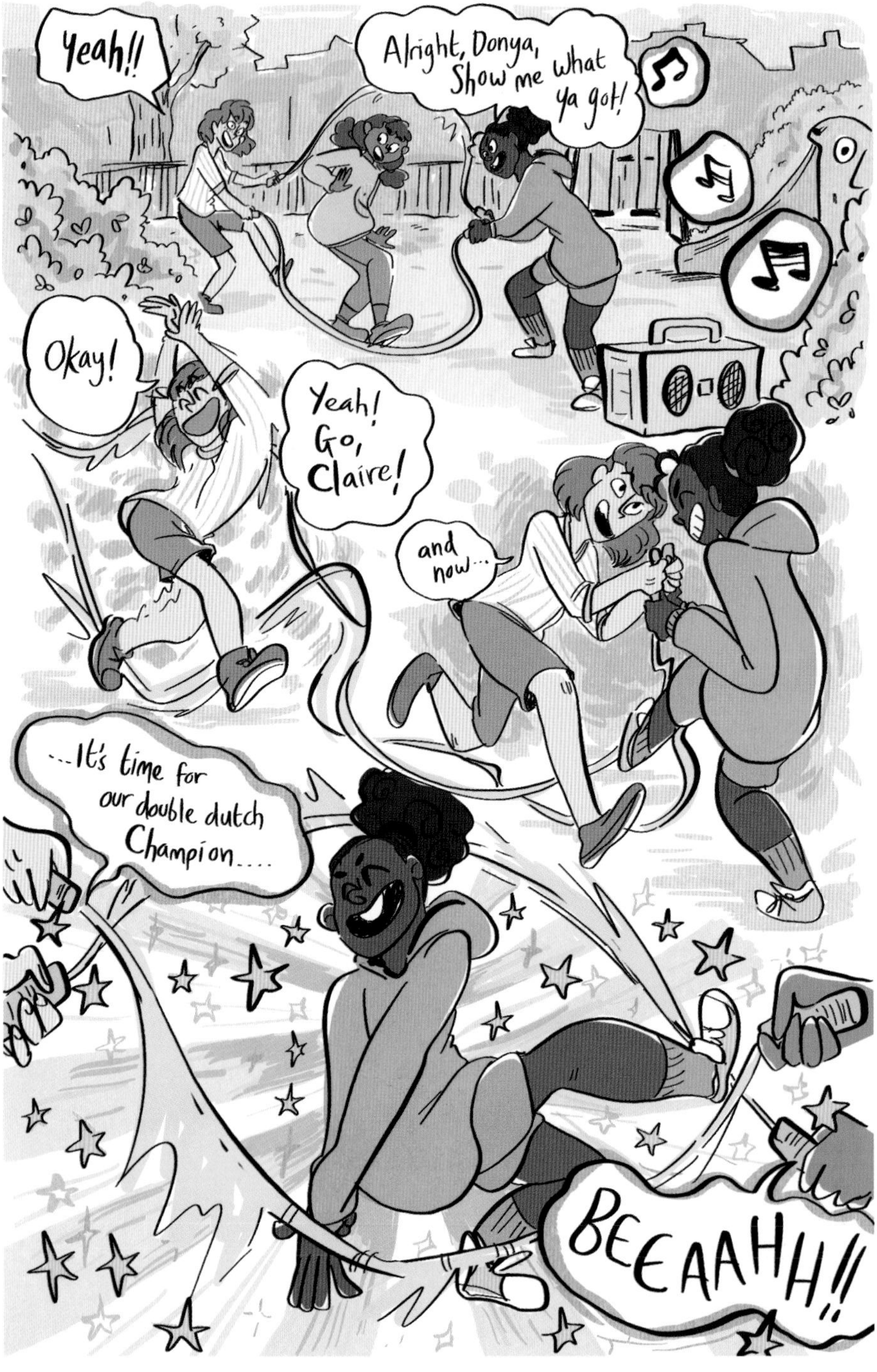
Yeah!!
Alright, Donya, Show me what ya got!
Okay!
Yeah! Go, Claire!
and now...
...It's time for our double dutch Champion....
BEEAAHH!!

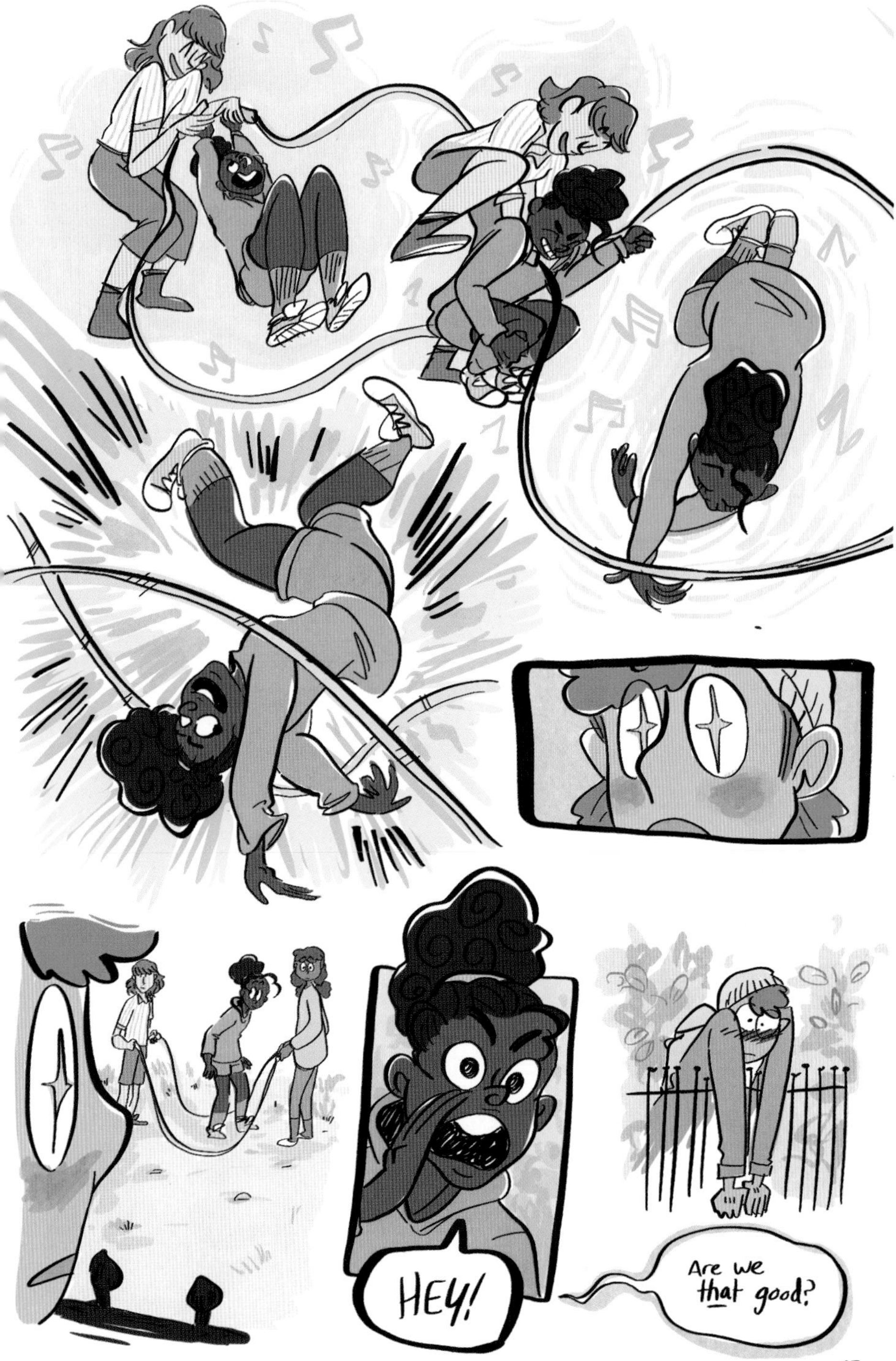
HEY!
Are we that good?

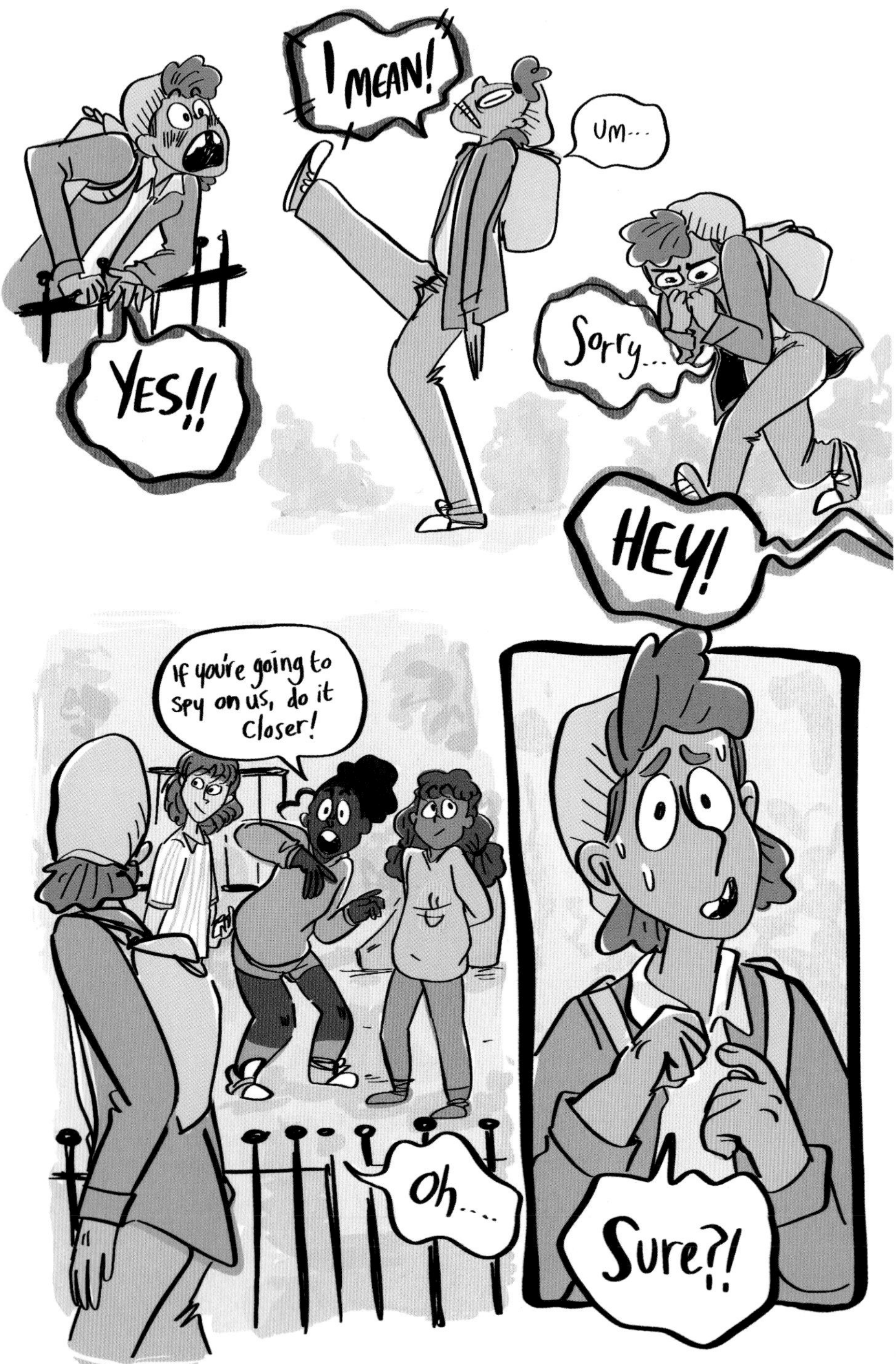
YES!!
I MEAN!
Um...
Sorry...
HEY!
If you're going to spy on us, do it closer!
Oh....
Sure?!

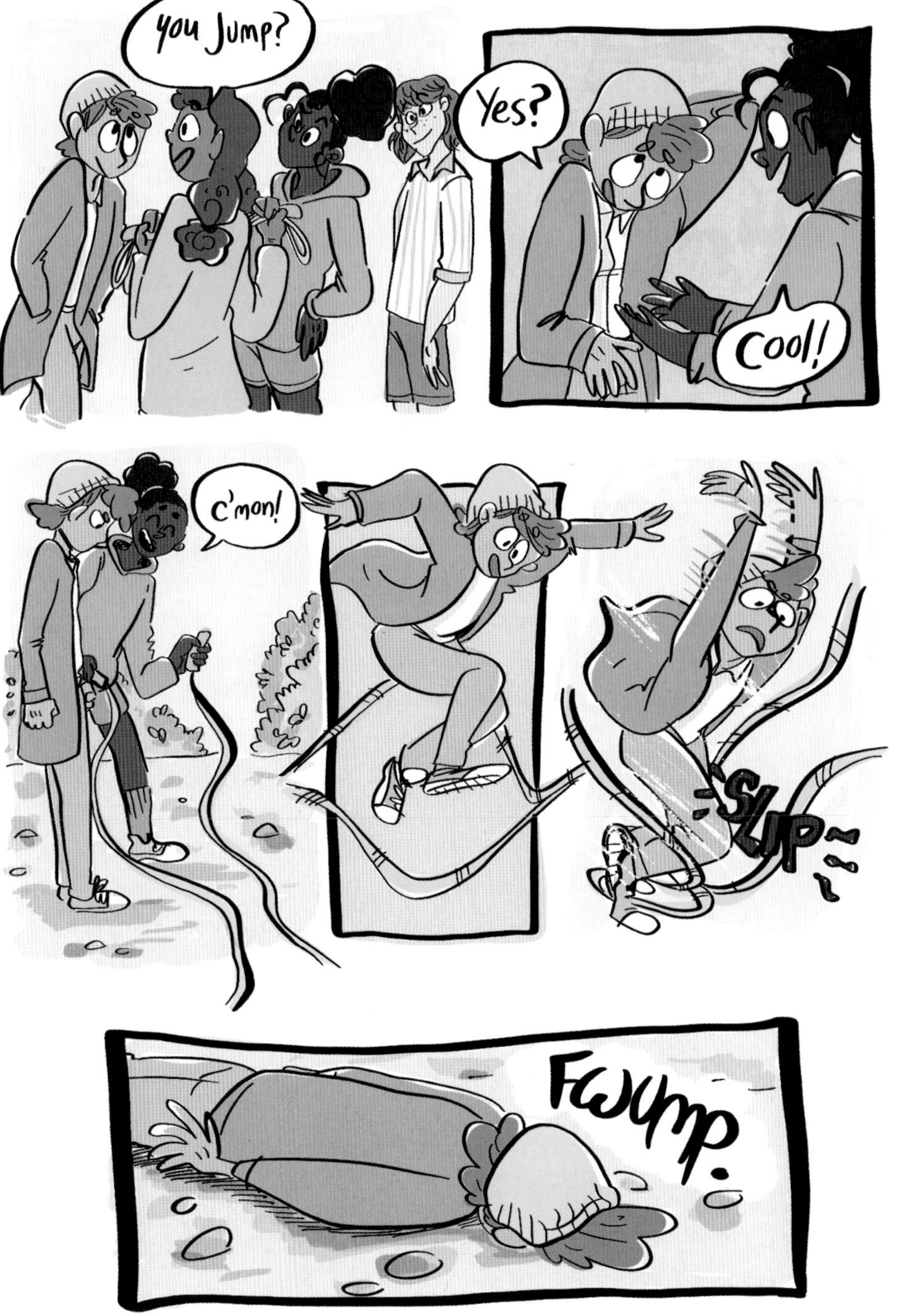
you Jump?
Yes?
Cool!
c'mon!
SLIP
FWUMP.

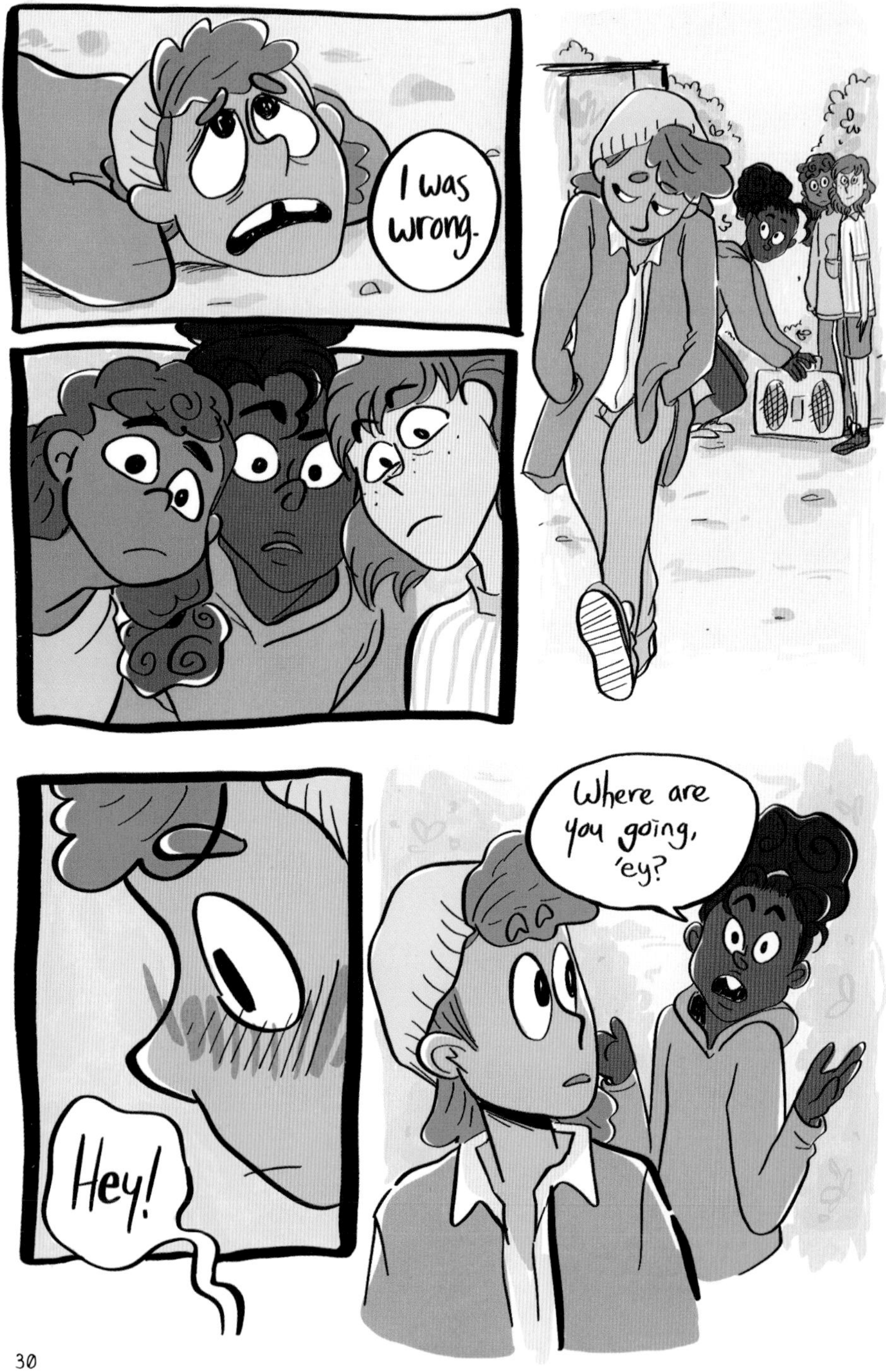
I was wrong.
Hey!
Where are you going, 'ey?

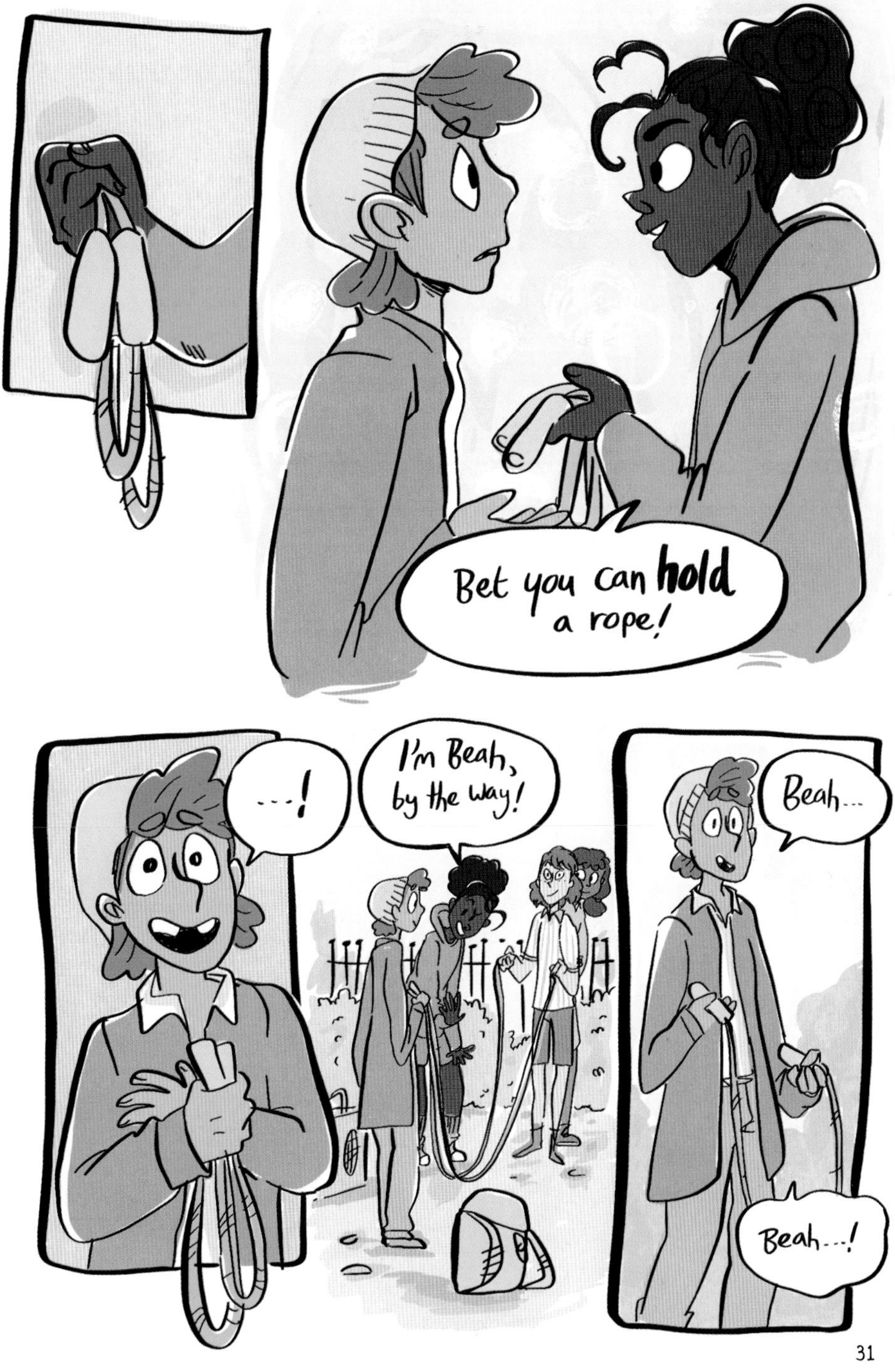
Bet you can hold a rope!
...!
I'm Beah, by the way!
Beah...
Beah...!

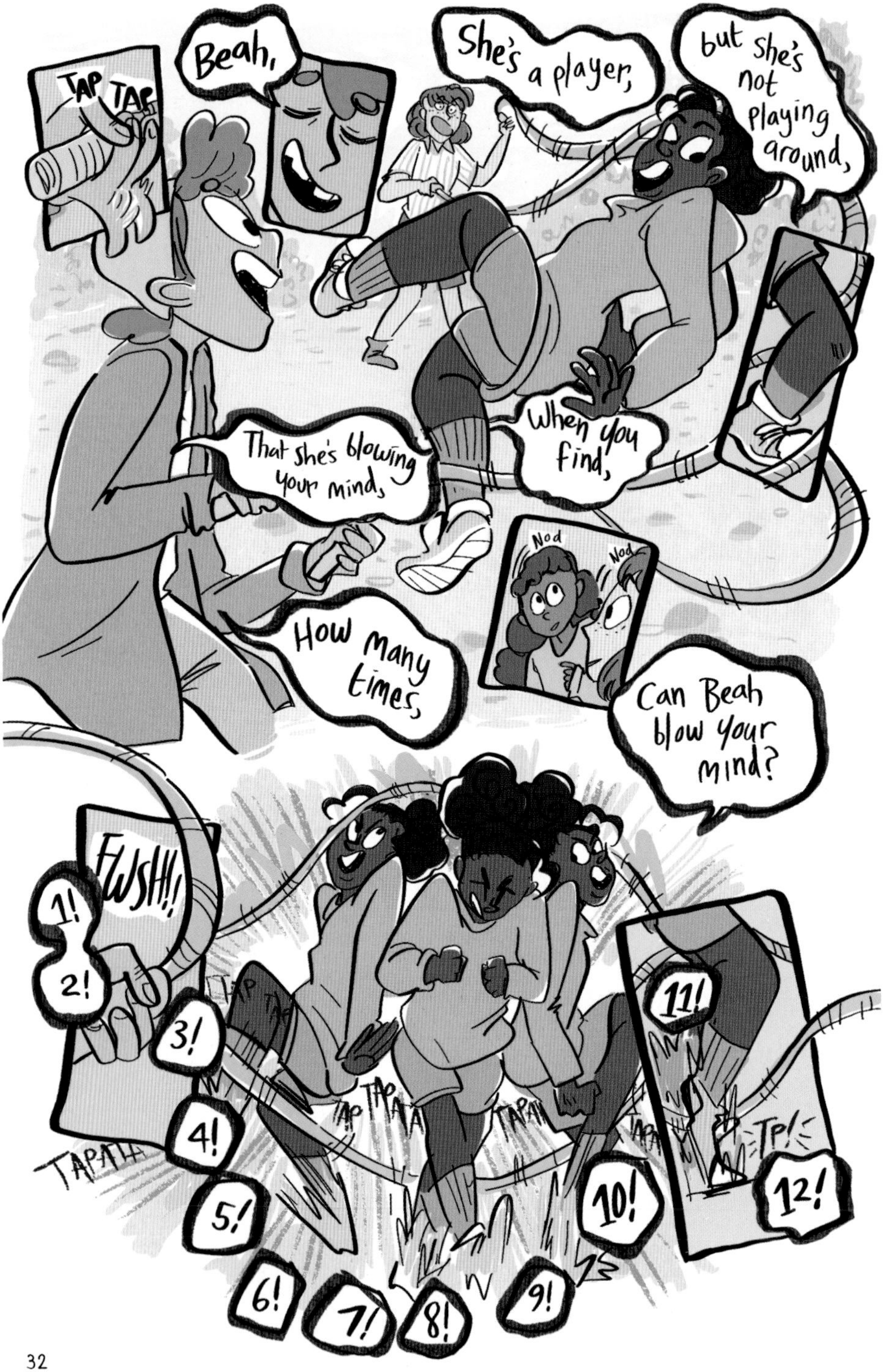
TAP TAP
Beah,
She's a player,
but she's not playing around,
That she's blowing your mind,
When you find,
How many times,
Nod
Nod
Can Beah blow your mind?
FWSH!!
1!
2!
3!
TAPATA
4!
TAP TAPAAA
TAPAA
5!
6!
7!
8!
9!
10!
11!
TP!
12!

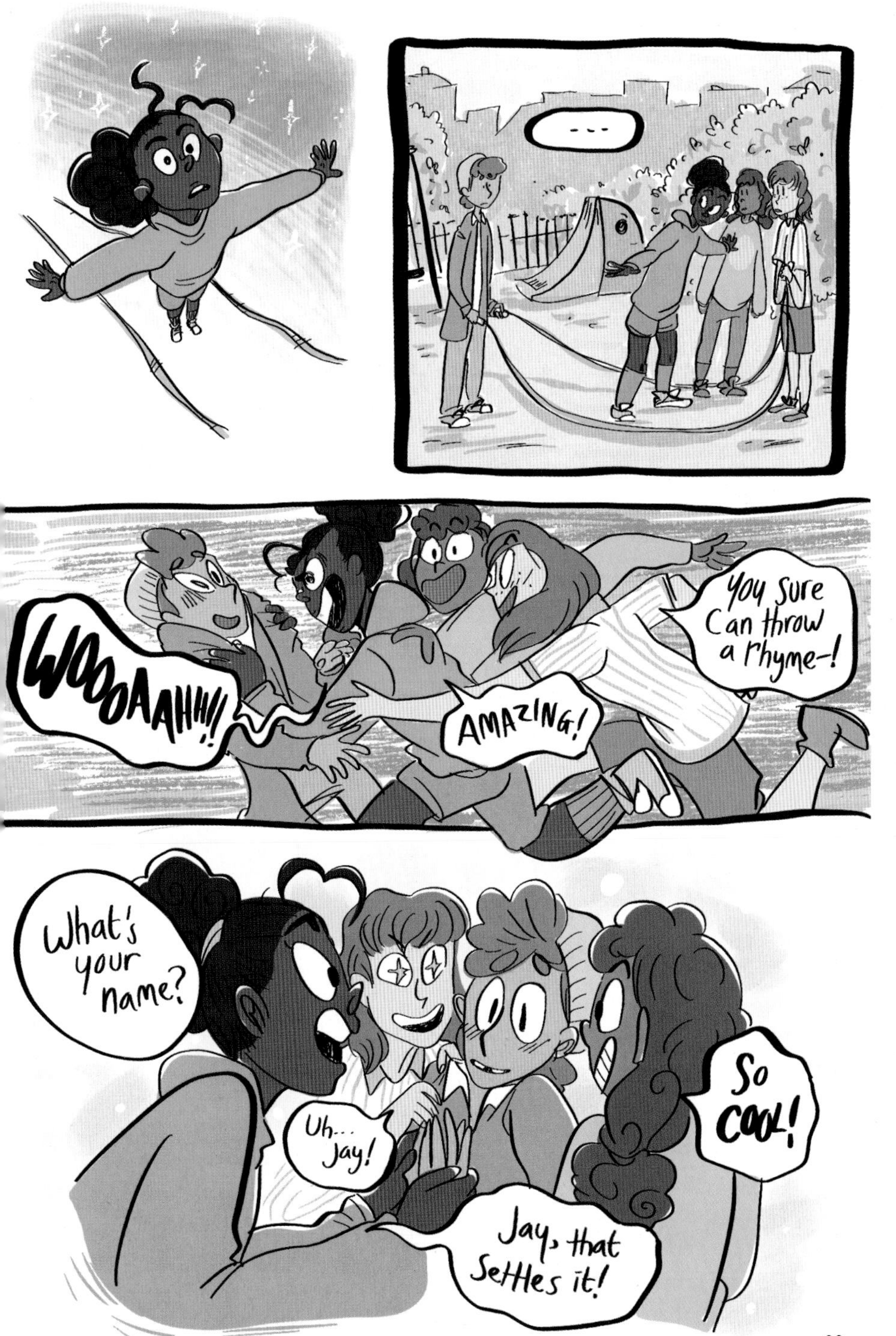
...
WOOOAAHH!!
AMAZING!
You sure can throw a rhyme-!
What's your name?
Uh... Jay!
So COOL!
Jay, that settles it!

CHAPTER THREE

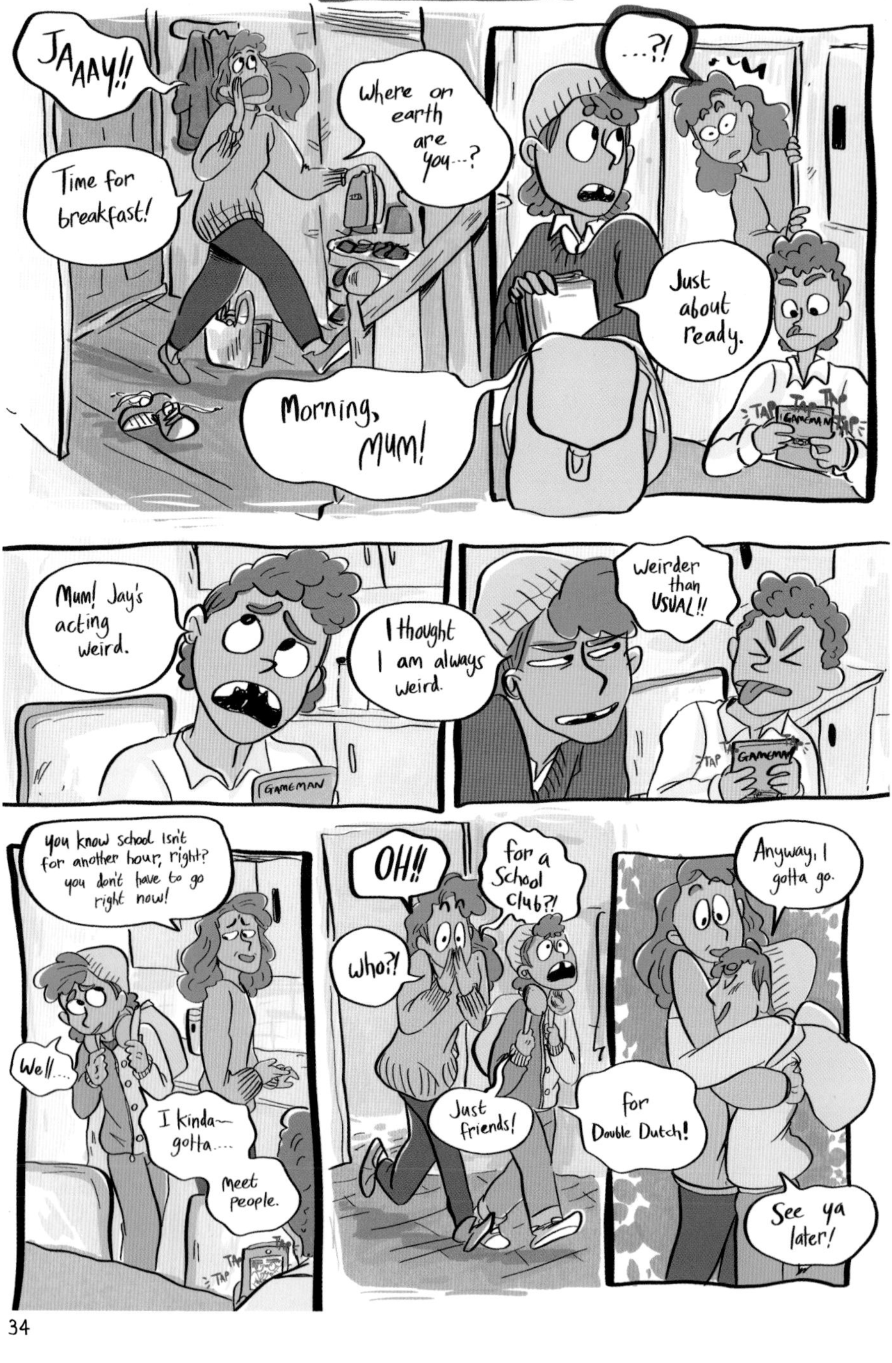
JAAAY!!
Time for breakfast!
Where on earth are you...?
Morning, MUM!
...?!
Just about ready.
TAP TAP TAP TAP
GAMEMAN
Mum! Jay's acting weird.
I thought I am always weird.
Weirder than USUAL!!
GAMEMAN
TAP TAP
GAMEMAN
You know school isn't for another hour, right? You don't have to go right now!
Well....
I kinda— gotta....
meet people.
TAP TAP
OH!!
For a School club?!
Who?!
Just friends!
For Double Dutch!
Anyway, I gotta go.
See ya later!

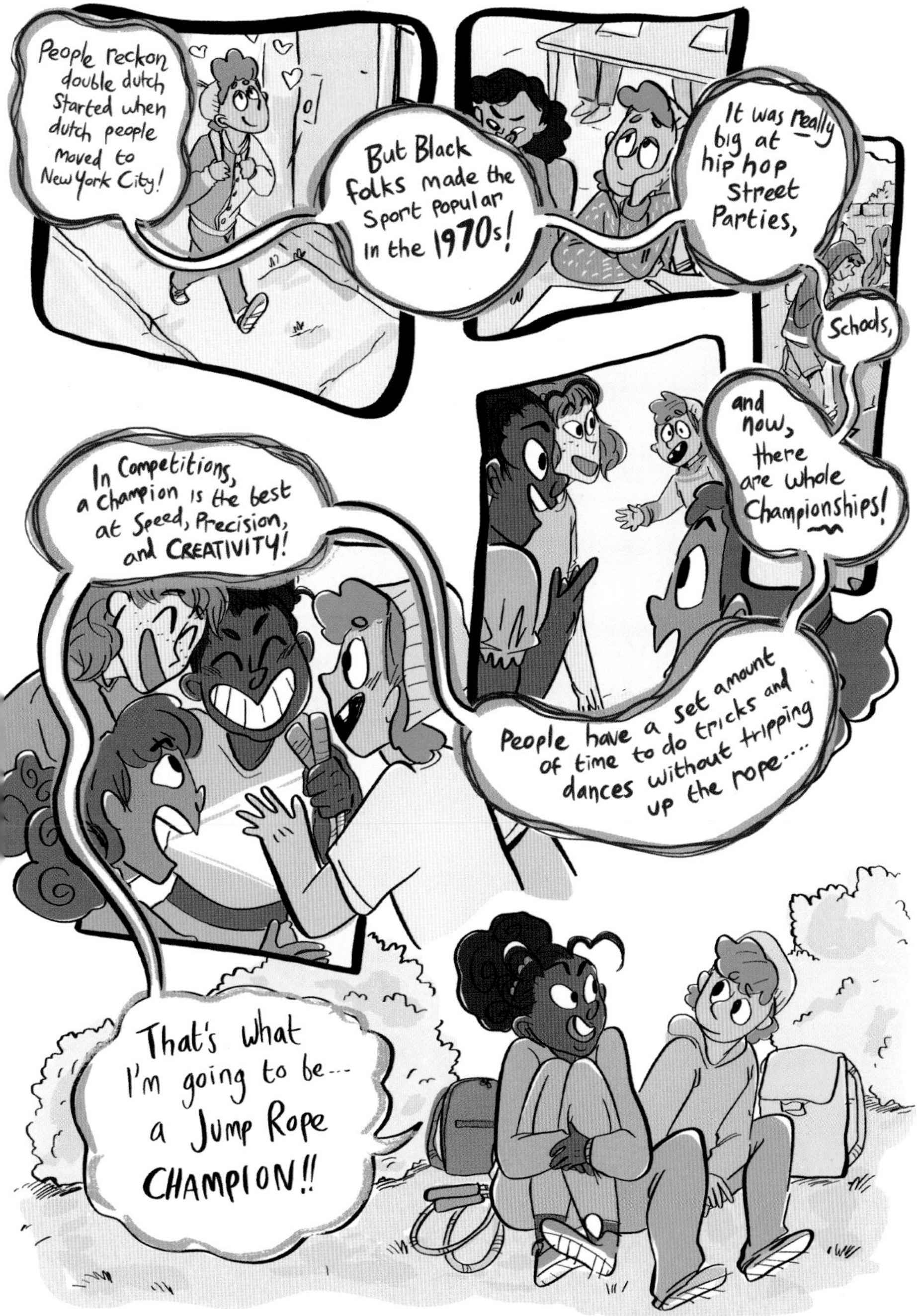
People reckon double dutch Started when dutch people moved to New York City!
But Black folks made the Sport popular In the 1970s!
It was really big at hip hop street Parties,
Schools,
and now, there are whole Championships!
In Competitions, a champion is the best at Speed, Precision, and CREATIVITY!
People have a set amount of time to do tricks and dances without tripping up the rope....
That's what I'm going to be... a Jump Rope CHAMPION!!

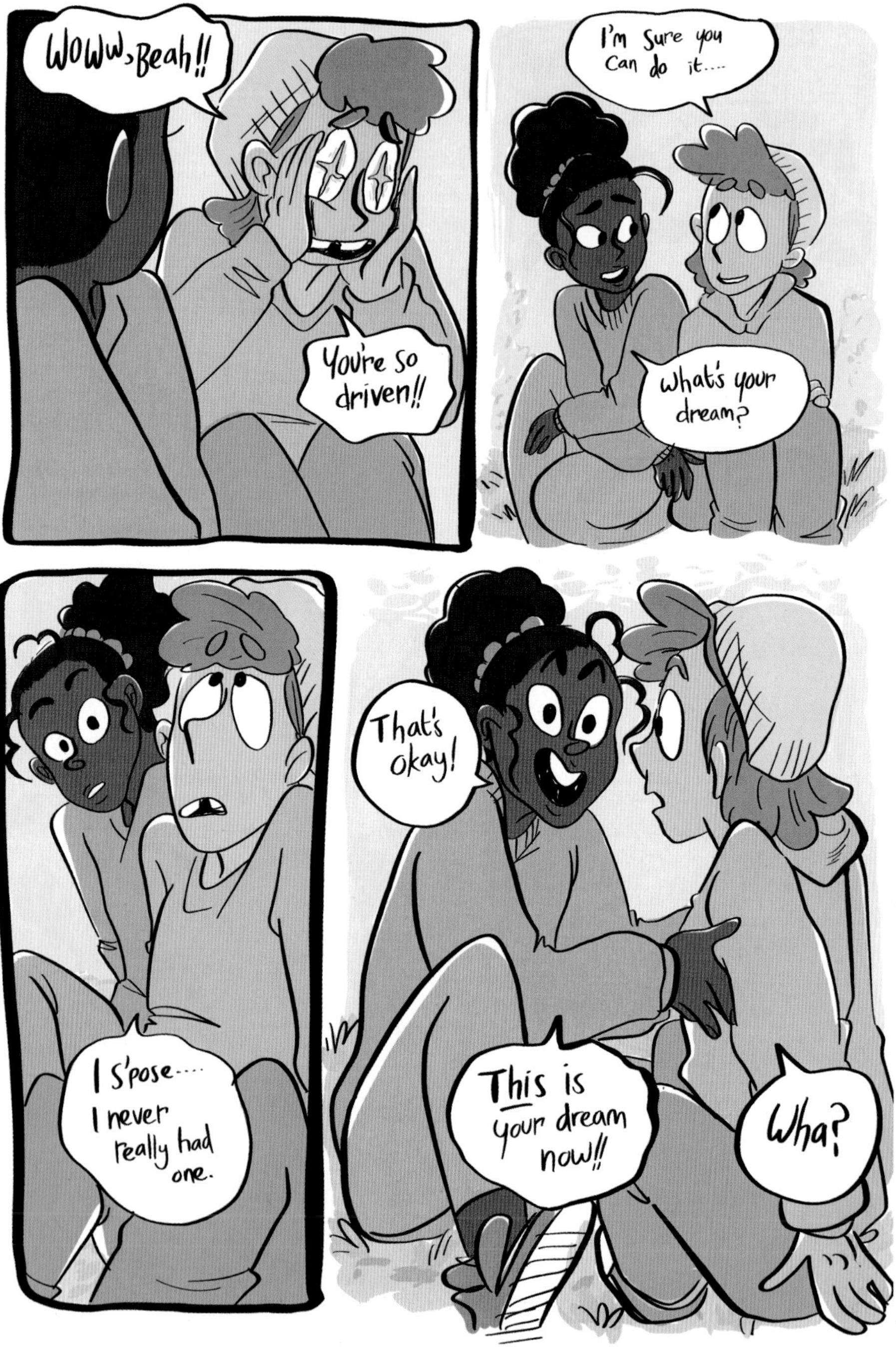
WOWW, Beah!!
You're so driven!!
I'm sure you can do it....
what's your dream?
I s'pose.... I never really had one.
That's okay!
This is your dream now!!
Wha?

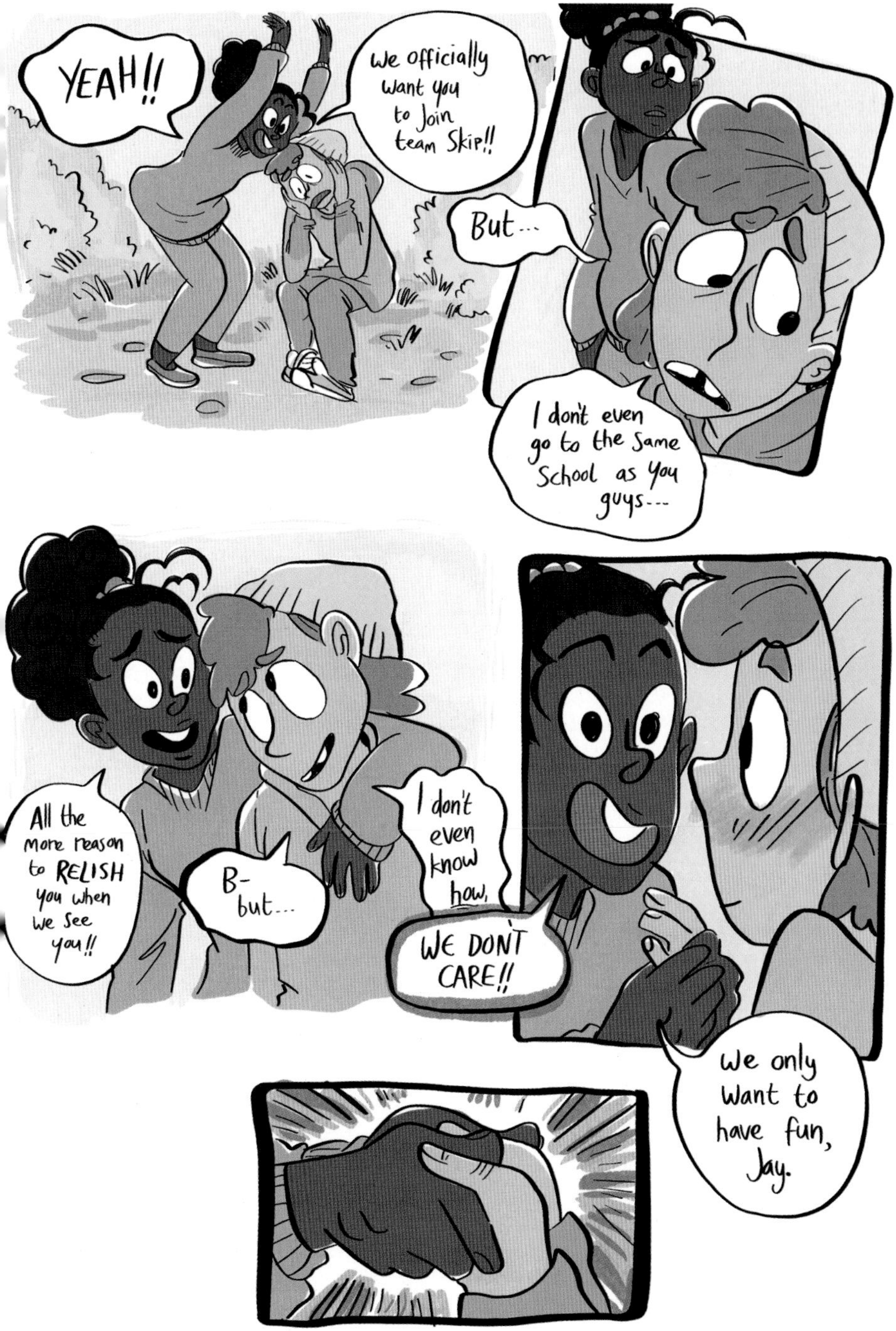
YEAH!!
We officially want you to Join team Skip!!
But...
I don't even go to the Same School as you guys---
All the more reason to RELISH you when we see you!!
B-but...
I don't even know how,
WE DON'T CARE!!
We only want to have fun, Jay.

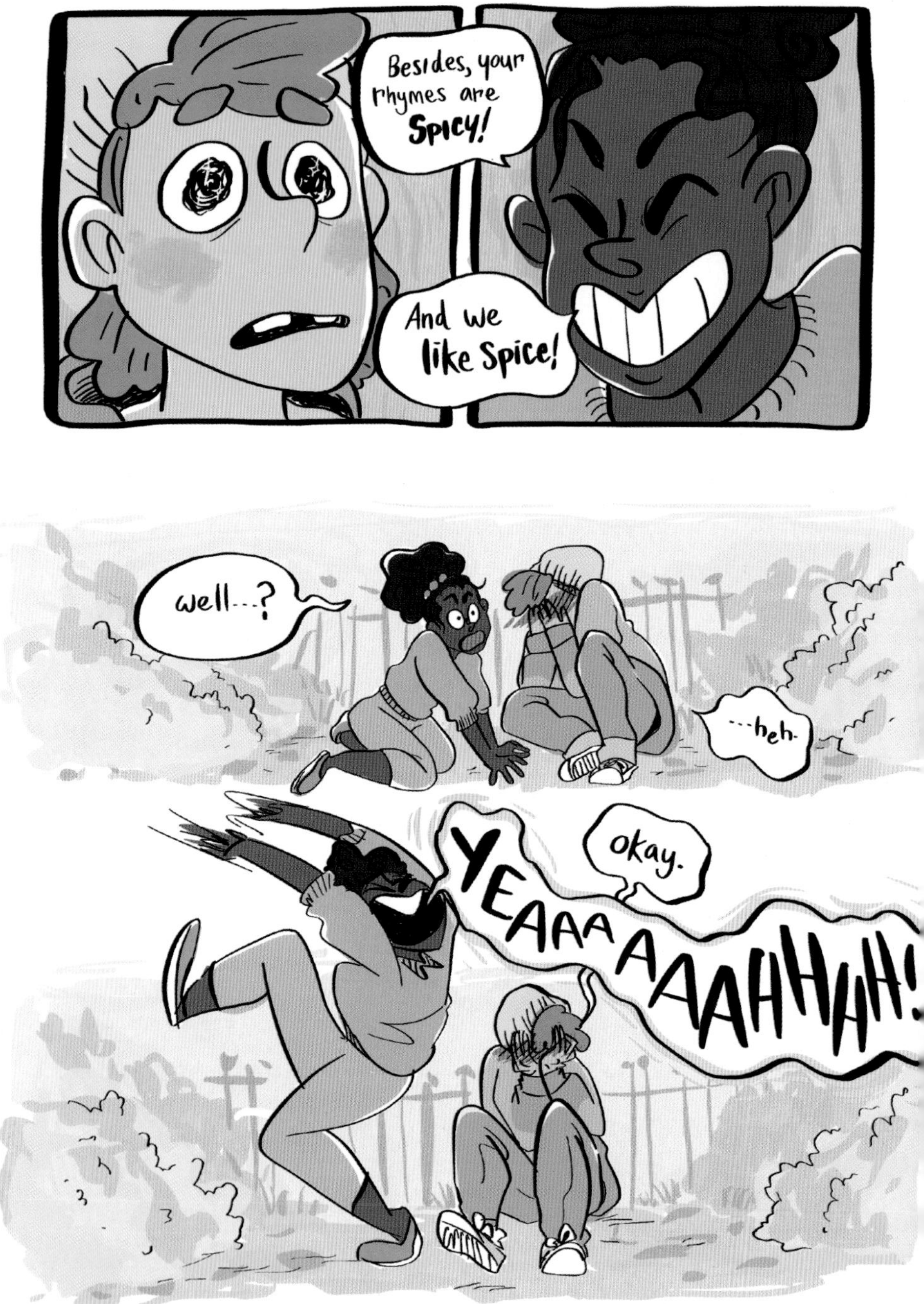
Besides, your rhymes are Spicy!
And we like Spice!
well...?
...heh.
YEAAAAAAAHHHHH!
okay.

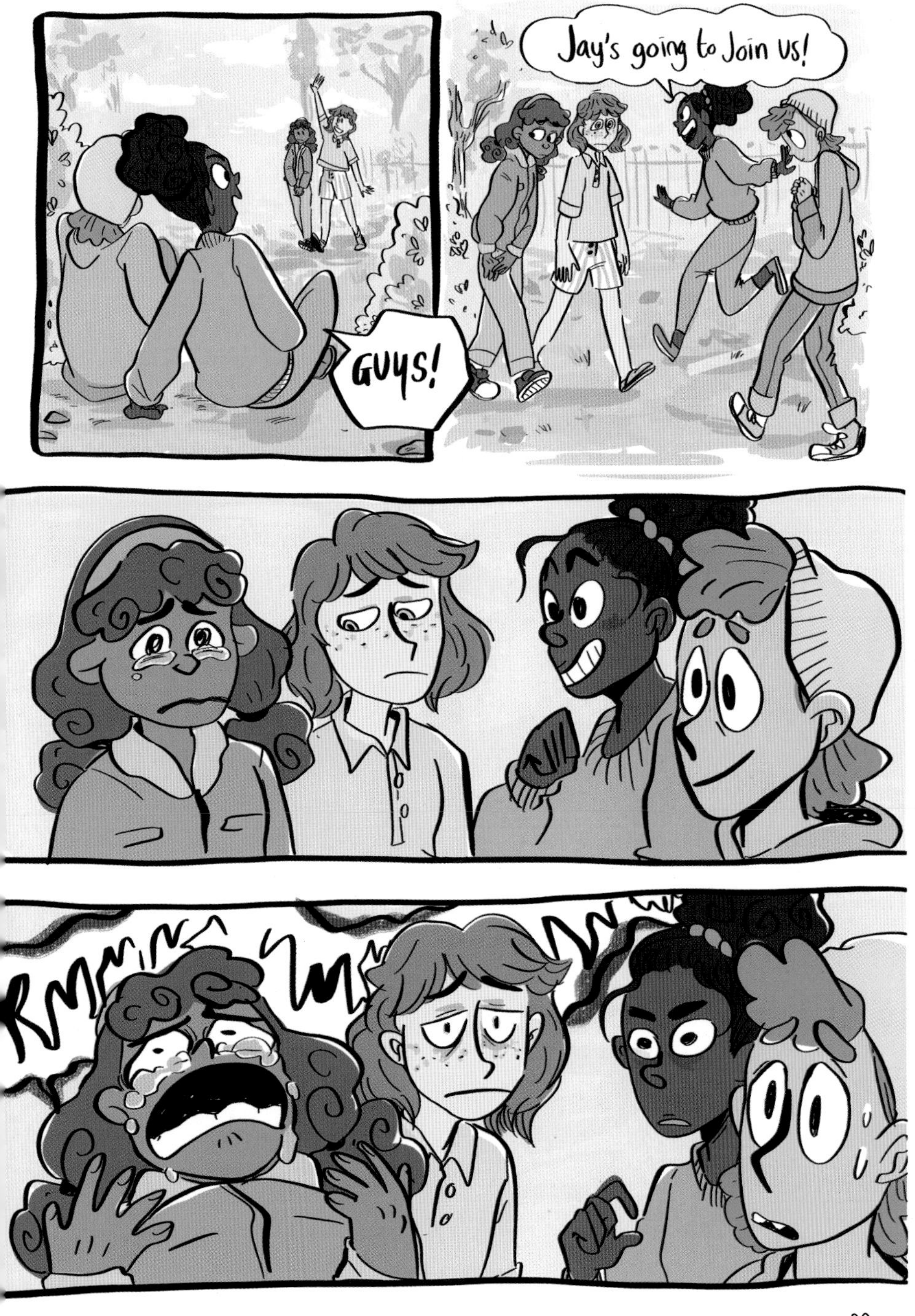
GUYS!
Jay's going to Join us!

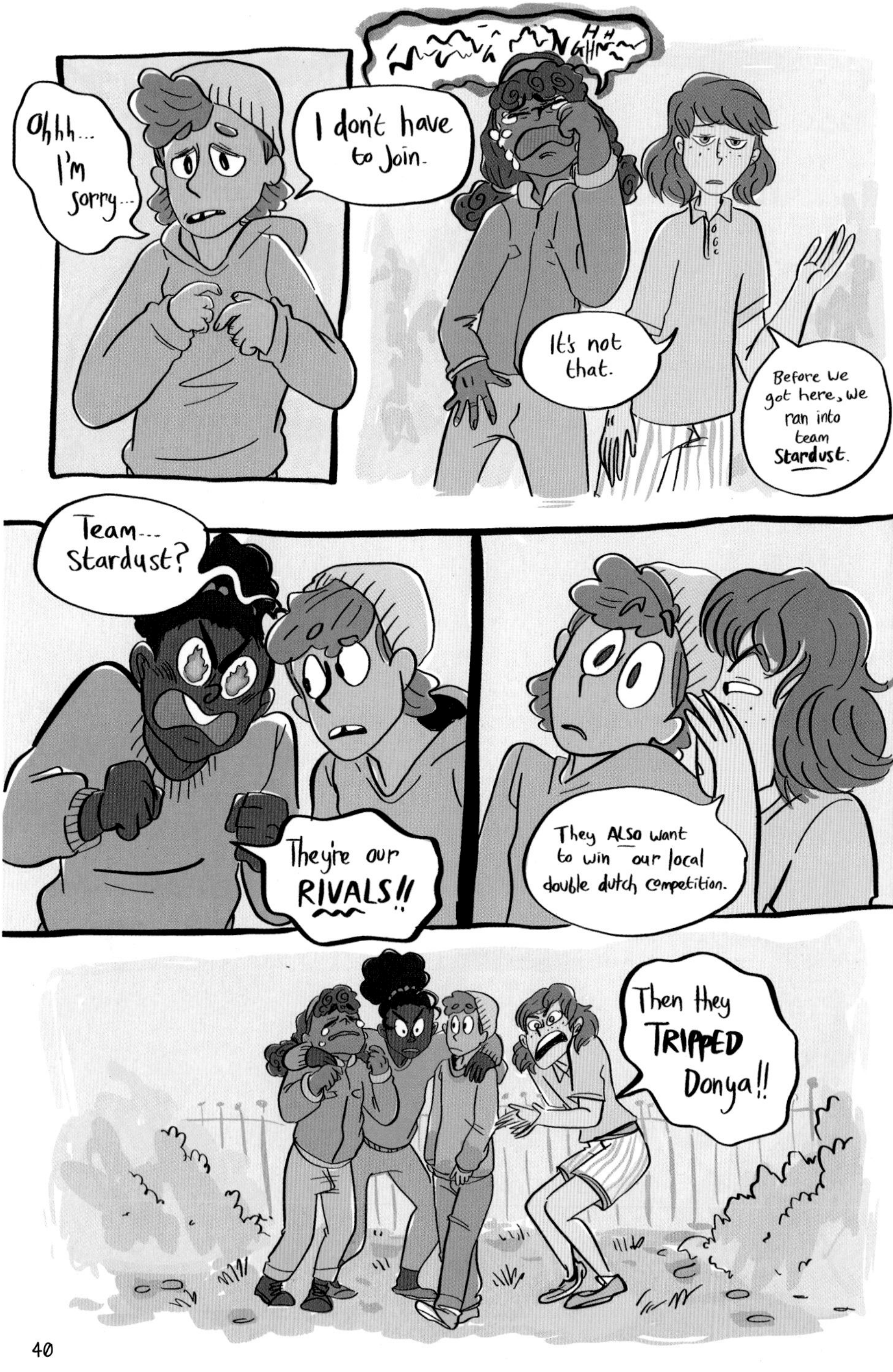
Ohhh... I'm sorry...
I don't have to join.
NGHH
It's not that.
Before we got here, we ran into team Stardust.
Team... Stardust?
They're our RIVALS!!
They ALSO want to win our local double dutch competition.
Then they TRIPPED Donya!!

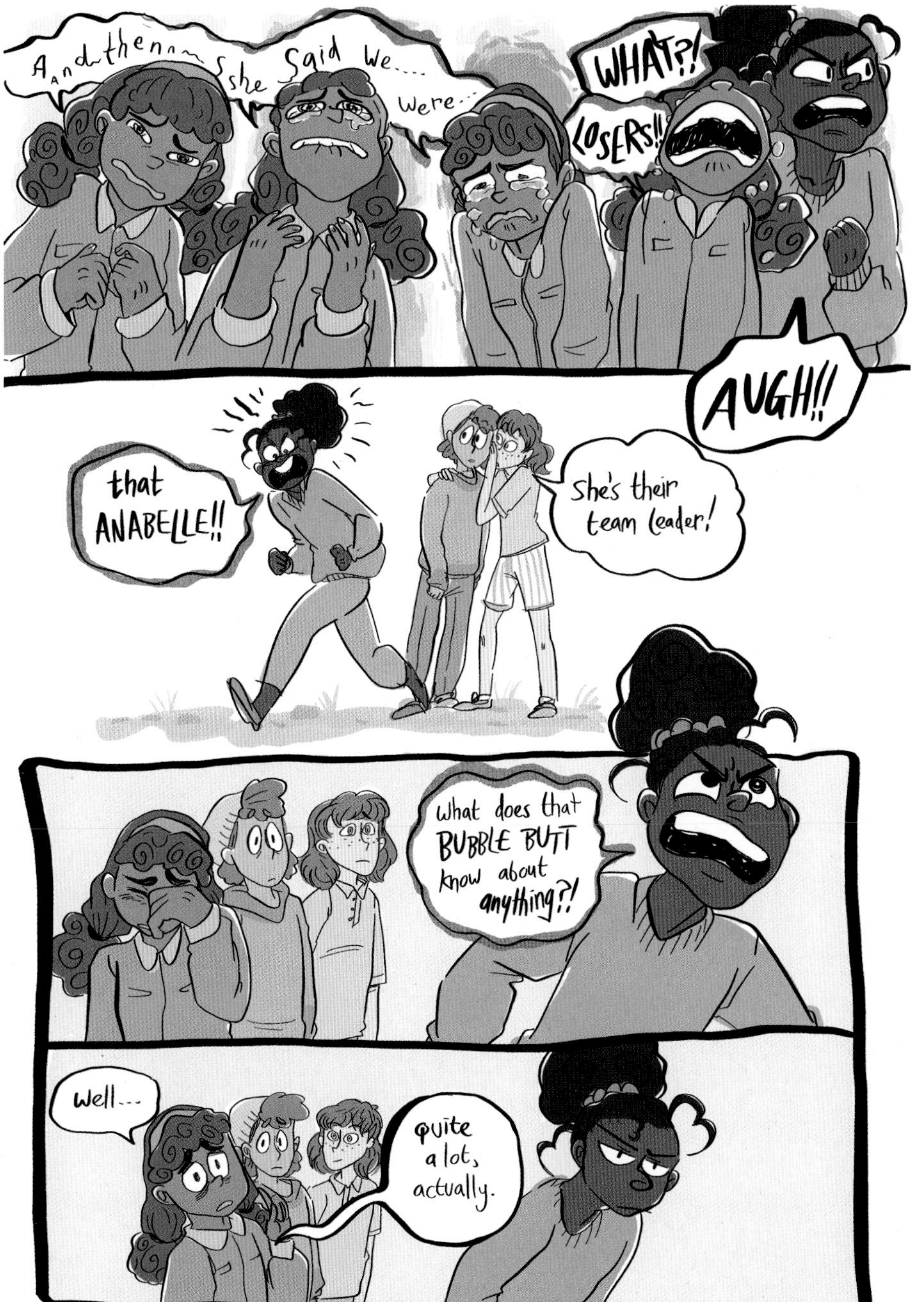
And then~~ she said we.... were...
WHAT?!
LOSERS!!
AUGH!!
that ANABELLE!!
She's their team leader!
What does that BUBBLE BUTT know about anything?!
Well...
quite a lot, actually.

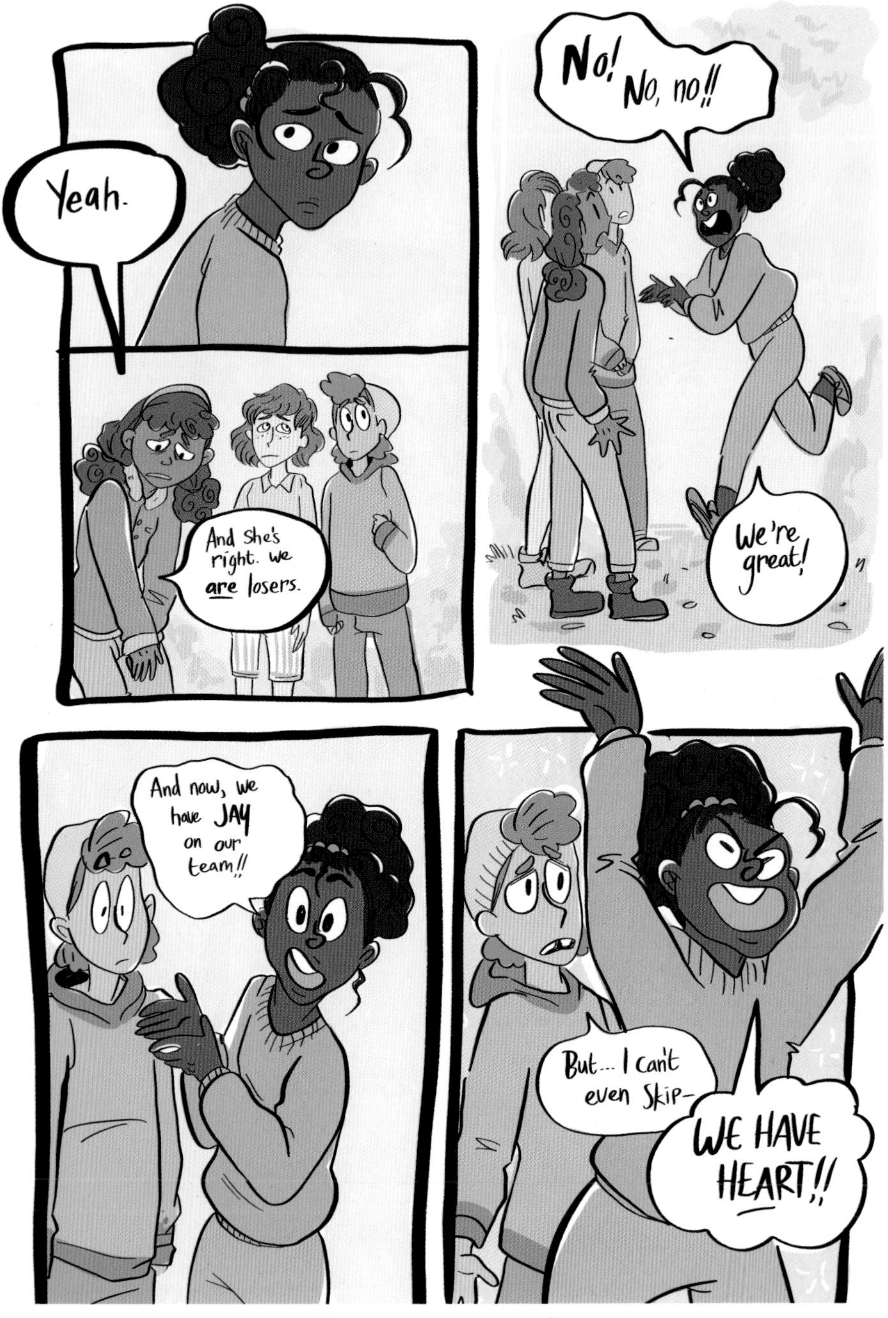

Yeah.
And she's right. we are losers.
No! No, no!!
We're great!
And now, we have JAY on our team!!
But... I can't even Skip-
WE HAVE HEART!!

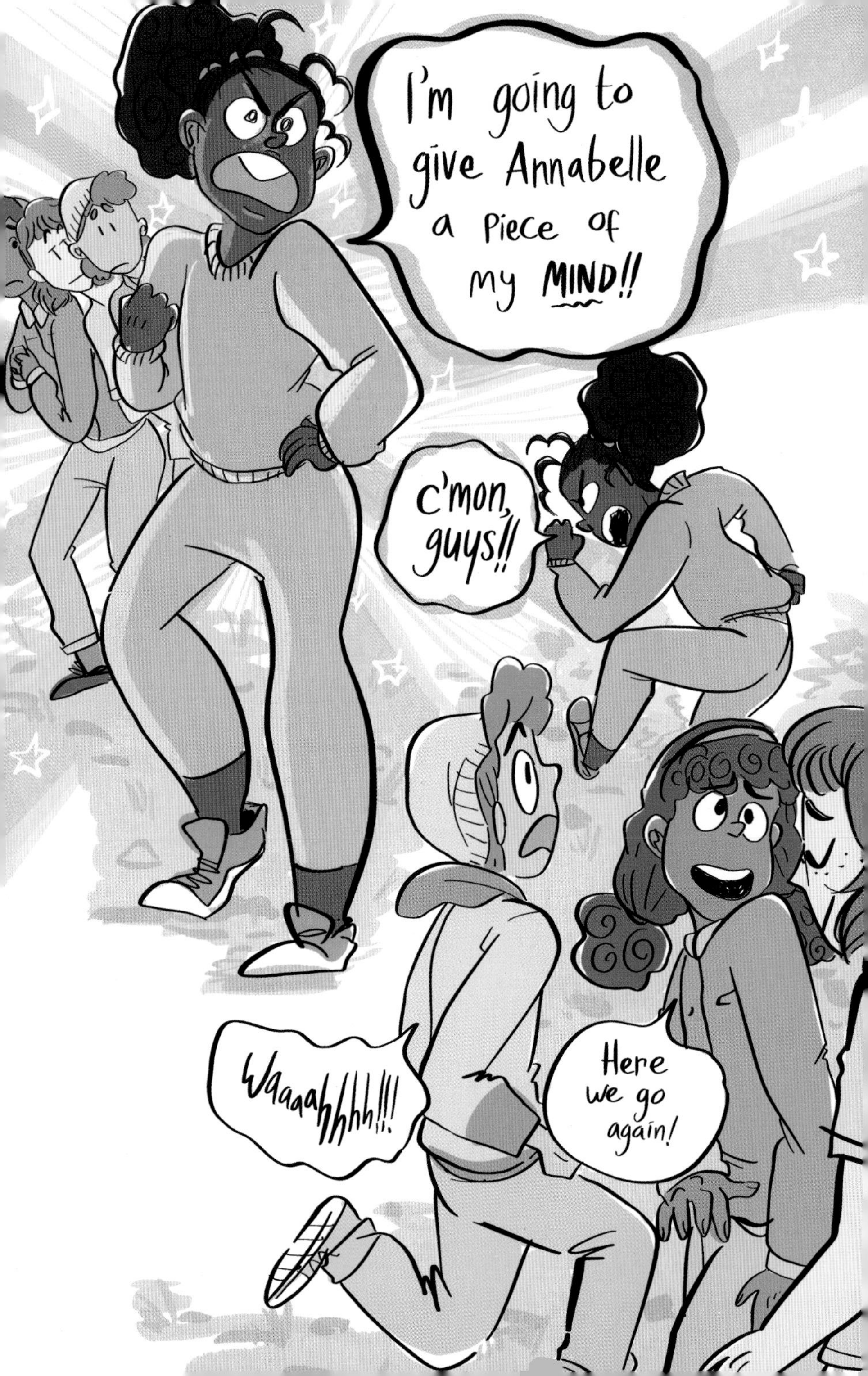
I'm going to give Annabelle a piece of my MIND!!
c'mon, guys!!
Waaaahhhh!!!
Here we go again!

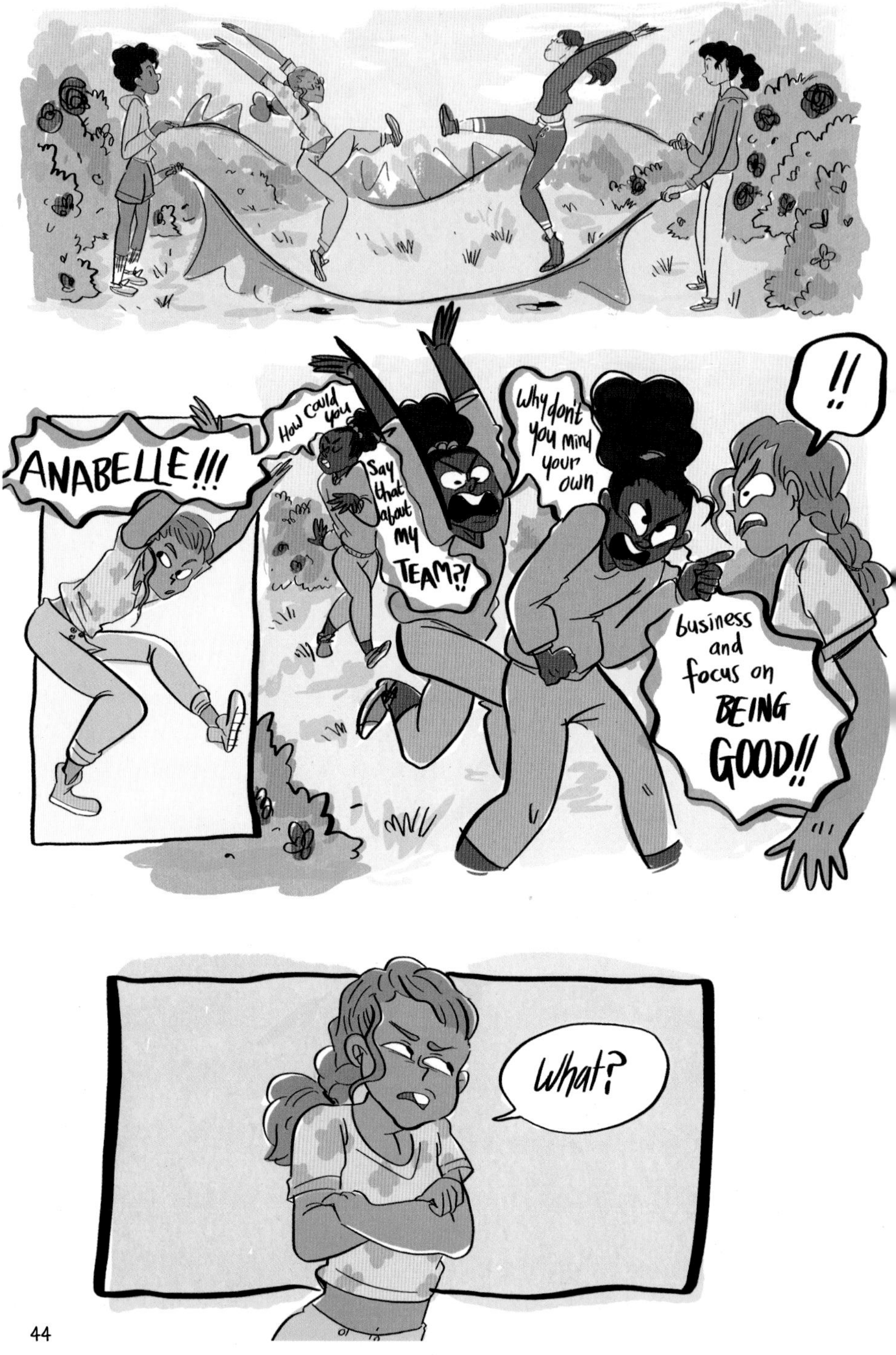
ANABELLE!!!
How could you
Say that about MY TEAM?!
Why don't you mind your own
business and focus on BEING GOOD!!
!!
What?

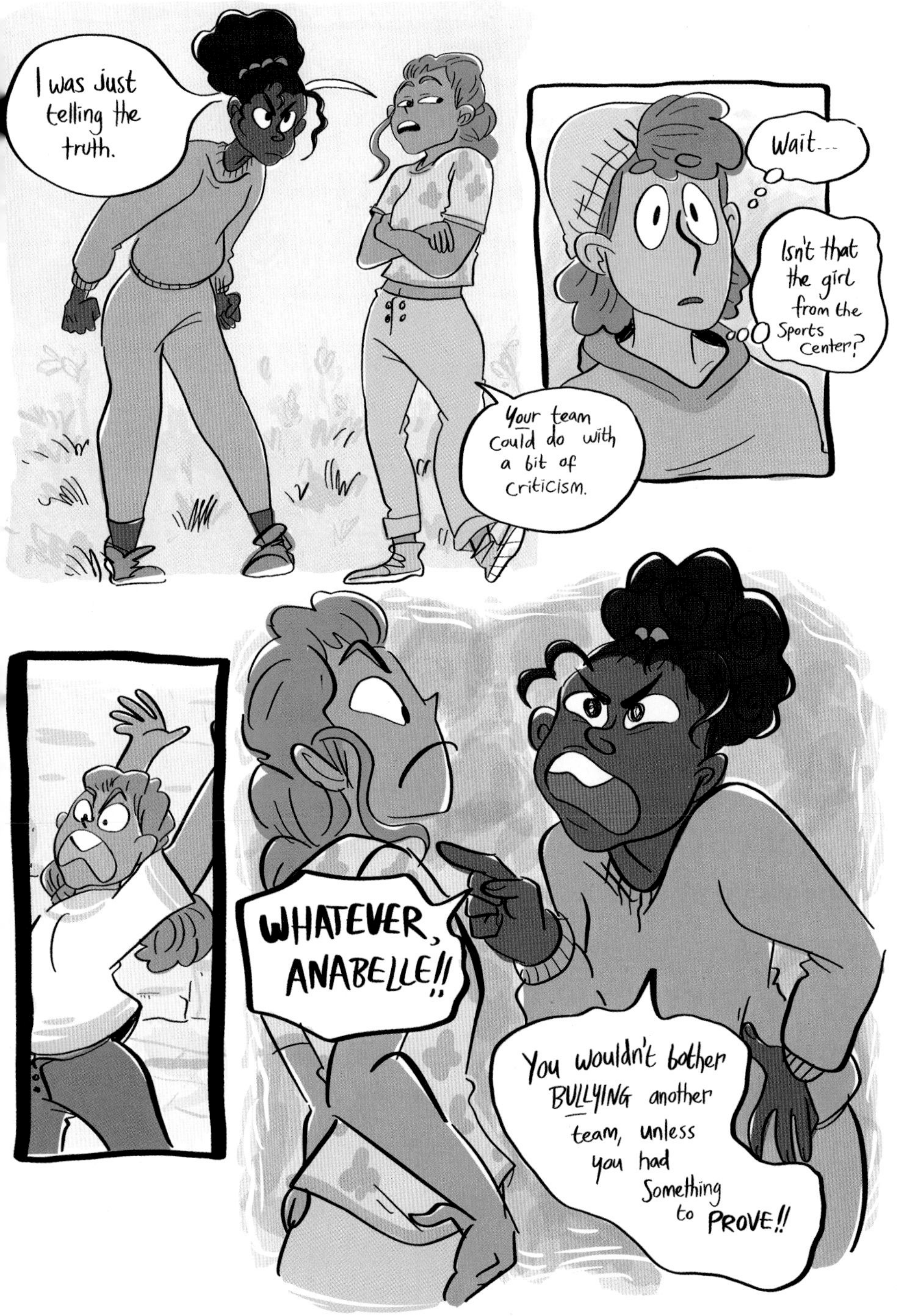
I was just telling the truth.
Wait...
Isn't that the girl from the Sports Center?
Your team could do with a bit of criticism.
WHATEVER, ANABELLE!!
You wouldn't bother BULLYING another team, unless you had something to PROVE!!

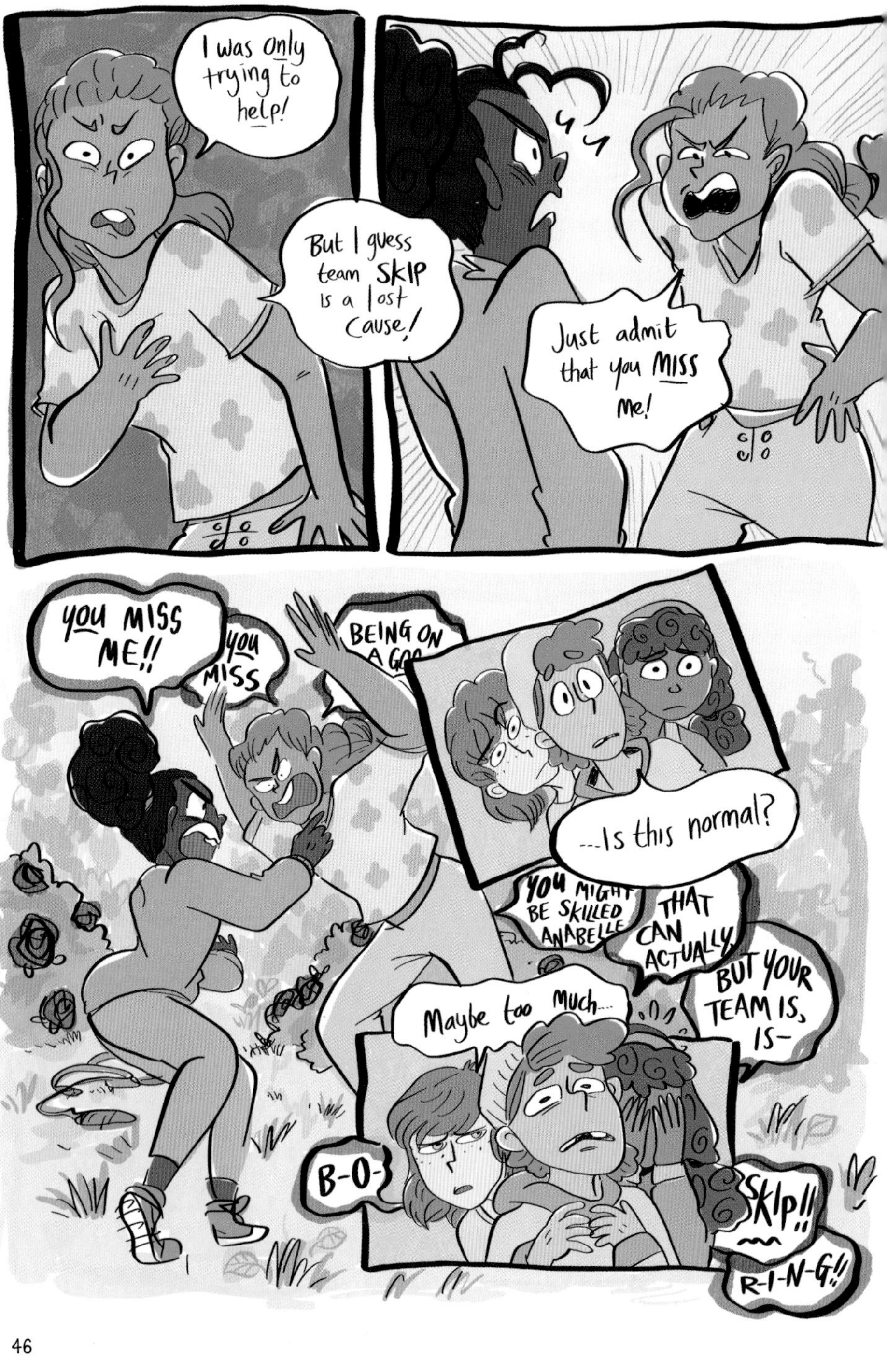
I was only trying to help!
But I guess team SKIP is a lost cause!
Just admit that you MISS me!
YOU MISS ME!!
YOU MISS
BEING ON A GOO
...Is this normal?
YOU MIGHT BE SKILLED ANABELLE
THAT CAN ACTUALLY
BUT YOUR TEAM IS, IS-
Maybe too much...
B-O-
SKIP!!
R-I-N-G!!

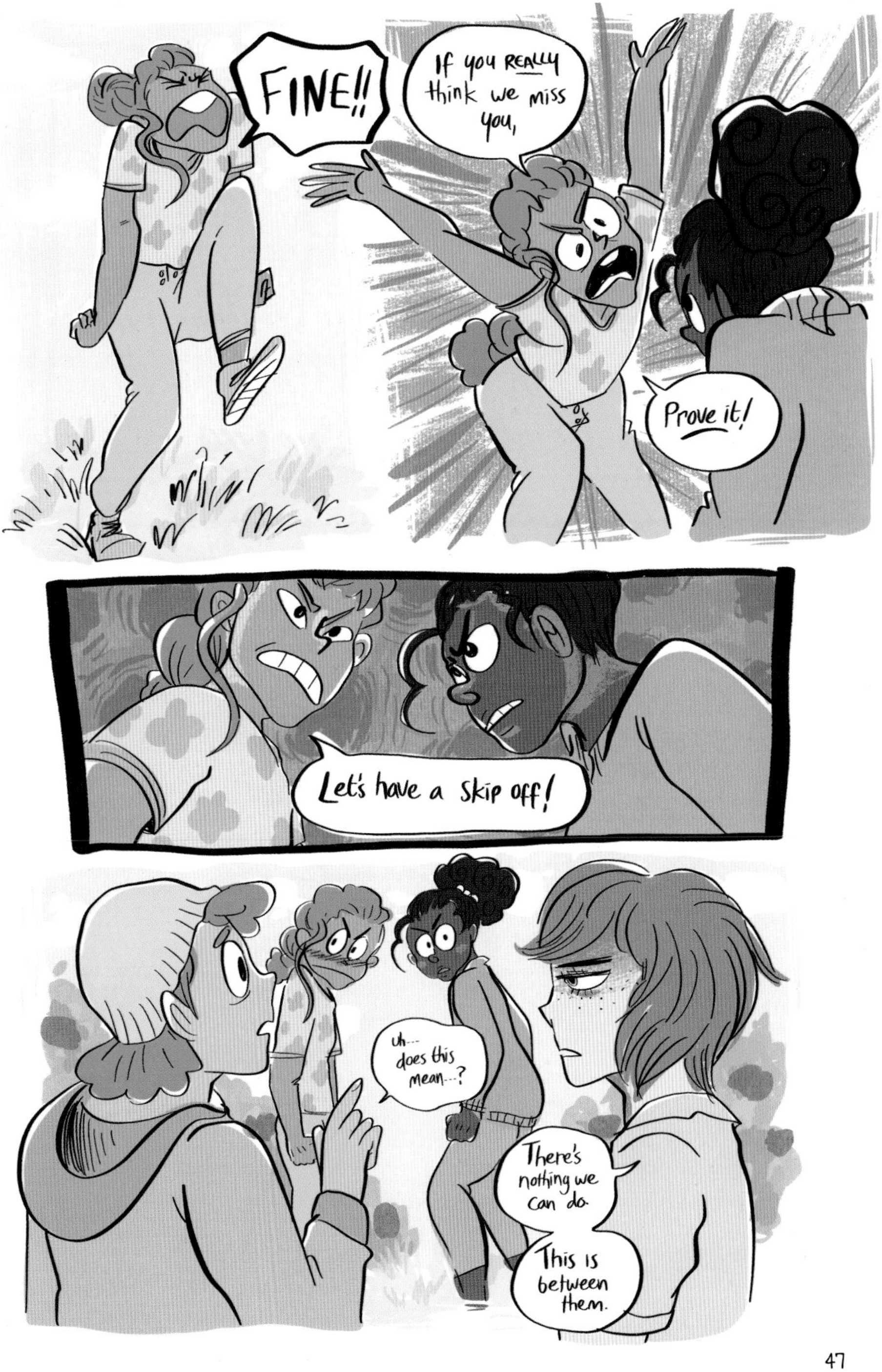
FINE!!
If you REALLY think we miss you,
Prove it!
Let's have a skip off!
uh... does this mean...?
There's nothing we can do.
This is between them.

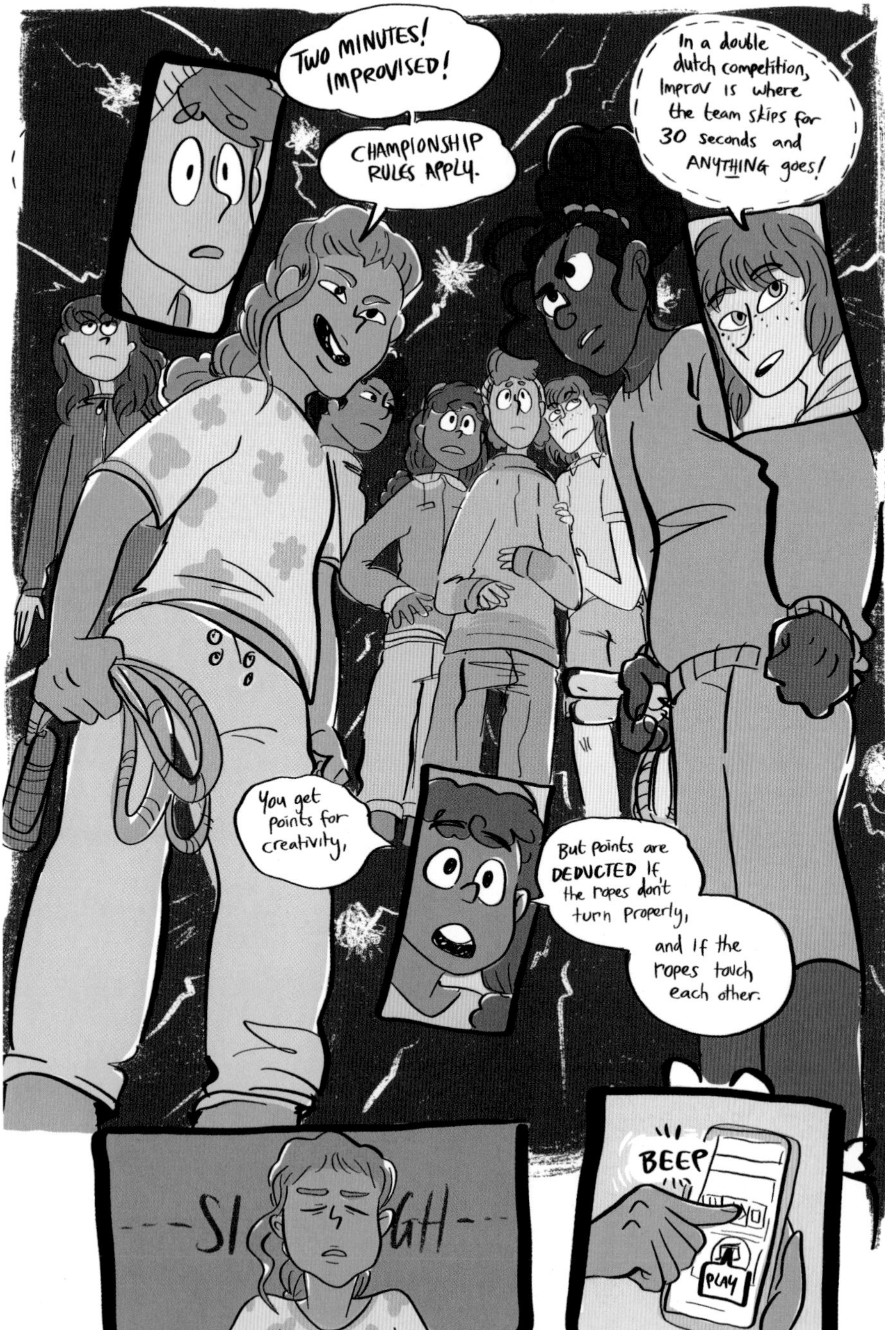
TWO MINUTES! IMPROVISED!
CHAMPIONSHIP RULES APPLY.
In a double dutch competition, Improv is where the team skips for 30 seconds and ANYTHING goes!
You get points for creativity,
But points are DEDUCTED if the ropes don't turn properly,
and if the ropes touch each other.
SIGH
BEEP
PLAY

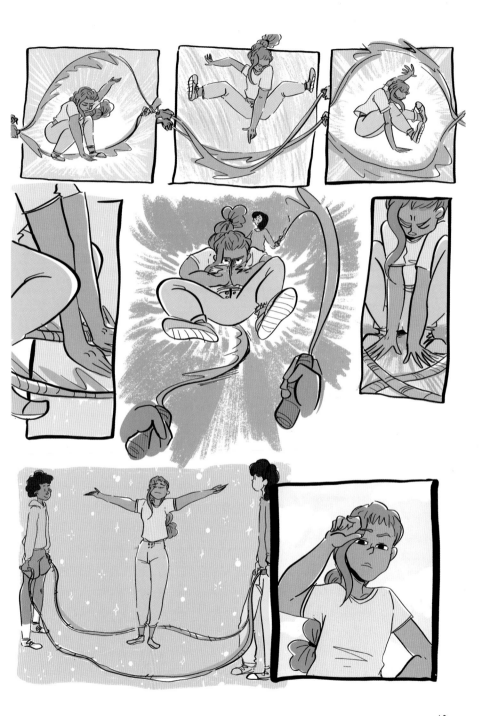

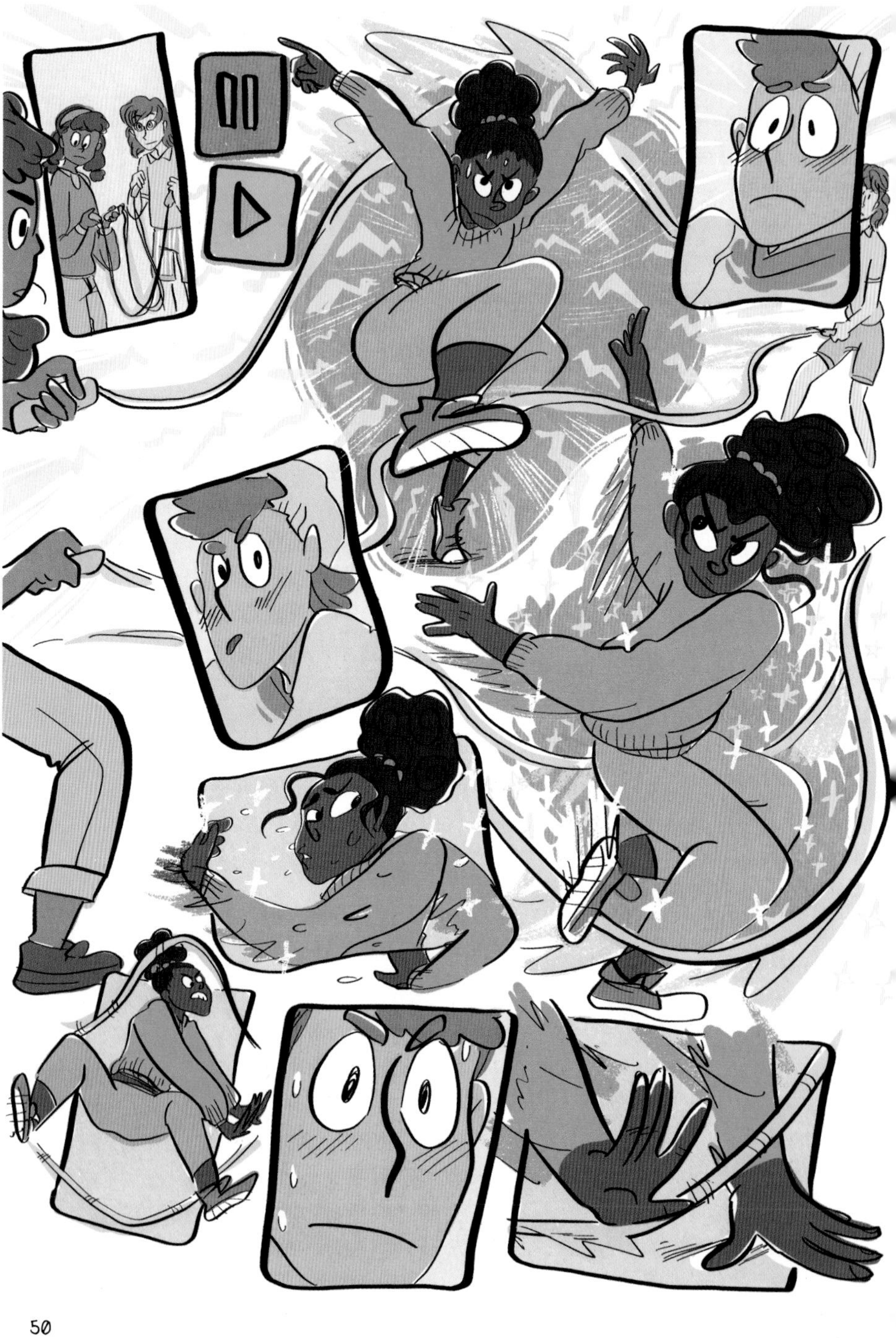

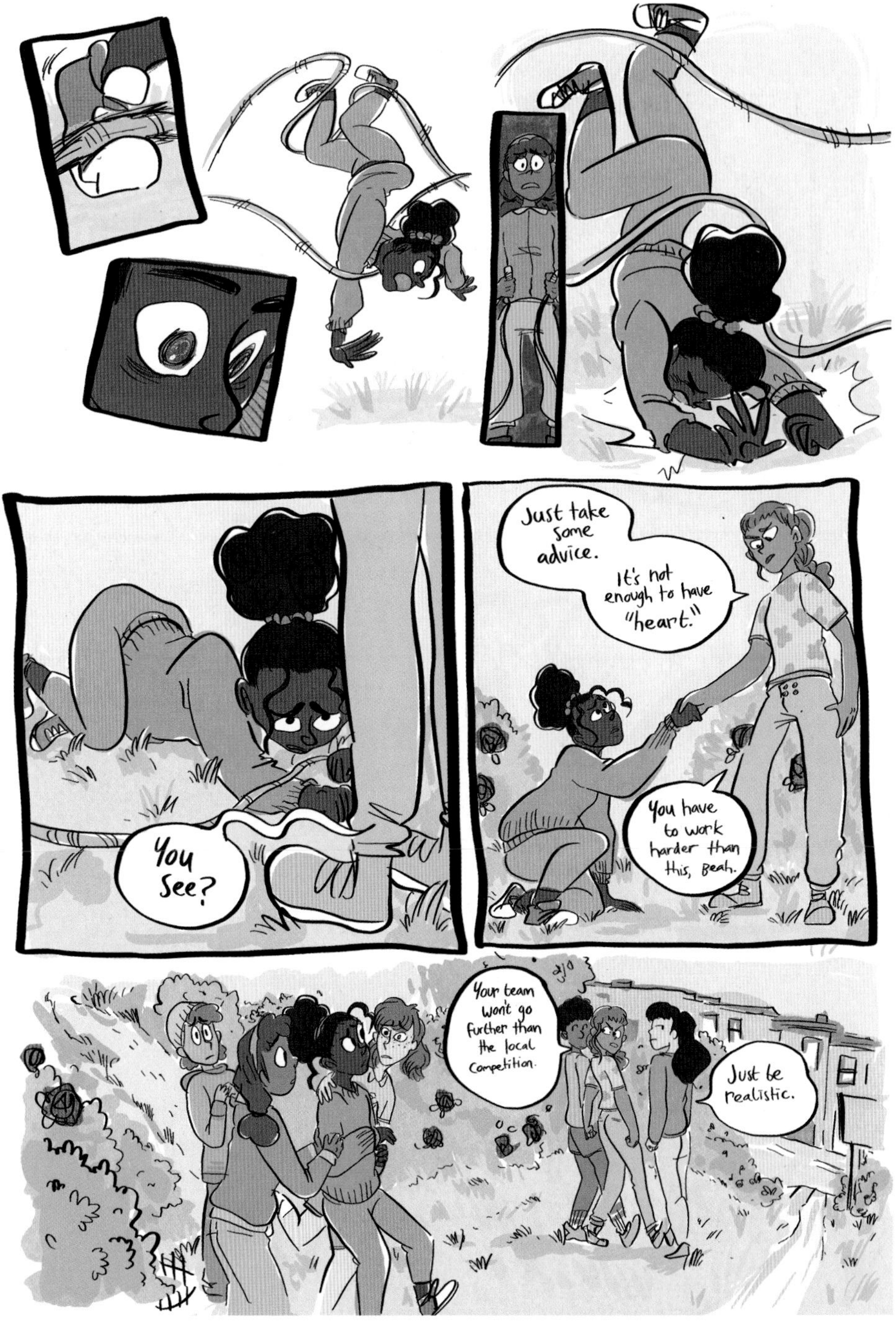
You see?
Just take some advice.
It's not enough to have "heart."
You have to work harder than this, Beah.
Your team won't go further than the local competition.
Just be realistic.

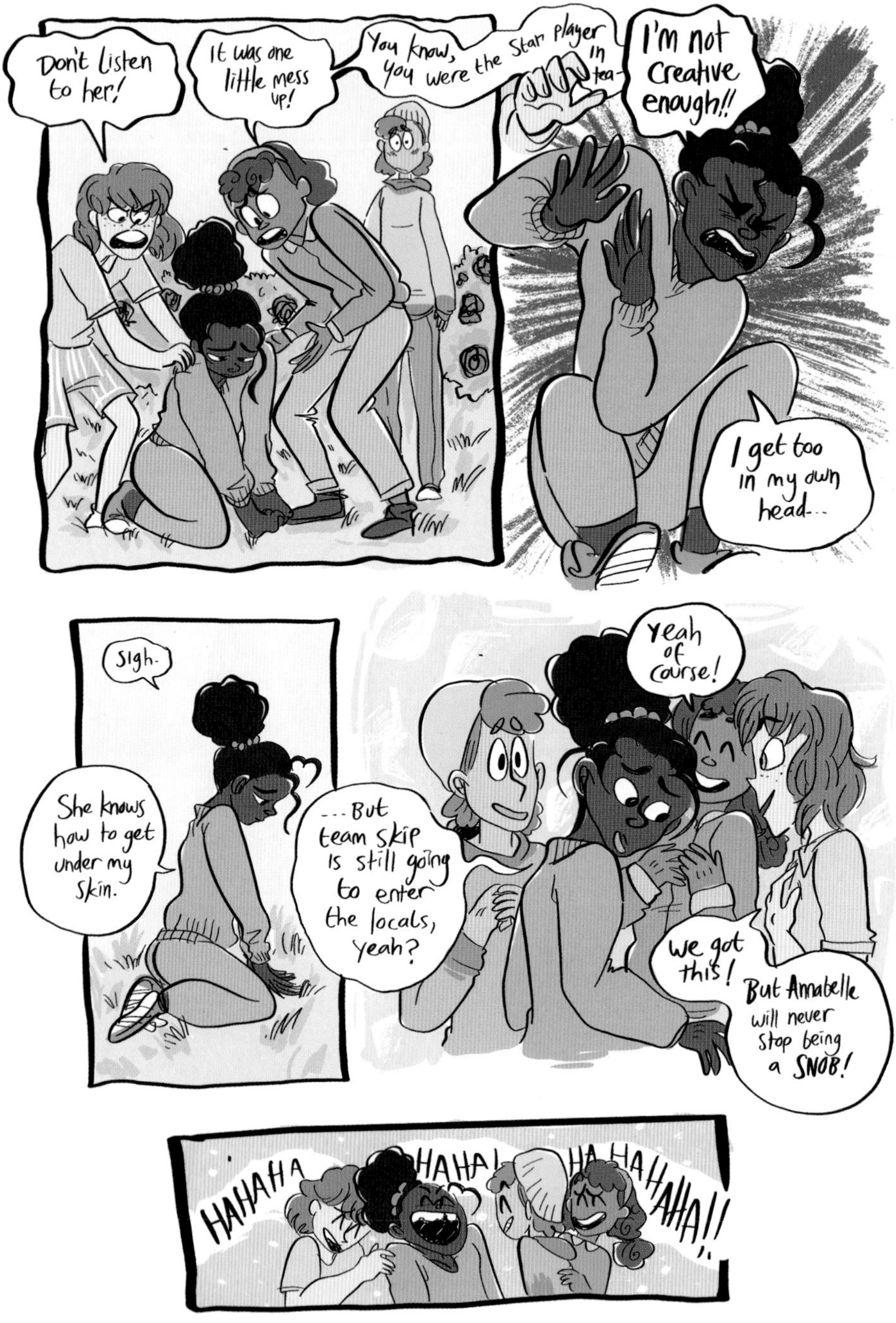
Don't listen to her!
It was one little mess up!
You know, you were the star player in tea-
I'm not creative enough!!
I get too in my own head...
Sigh.
She knows how to get under my skin.
...But team skip is still going to enter the locals, yeah?
Yeah of course!
We got this!
But Annabelle will never stop being a SNOB!
HAHAHA
HAHAHA
HAHA!
HA HA HA
HAHA!!

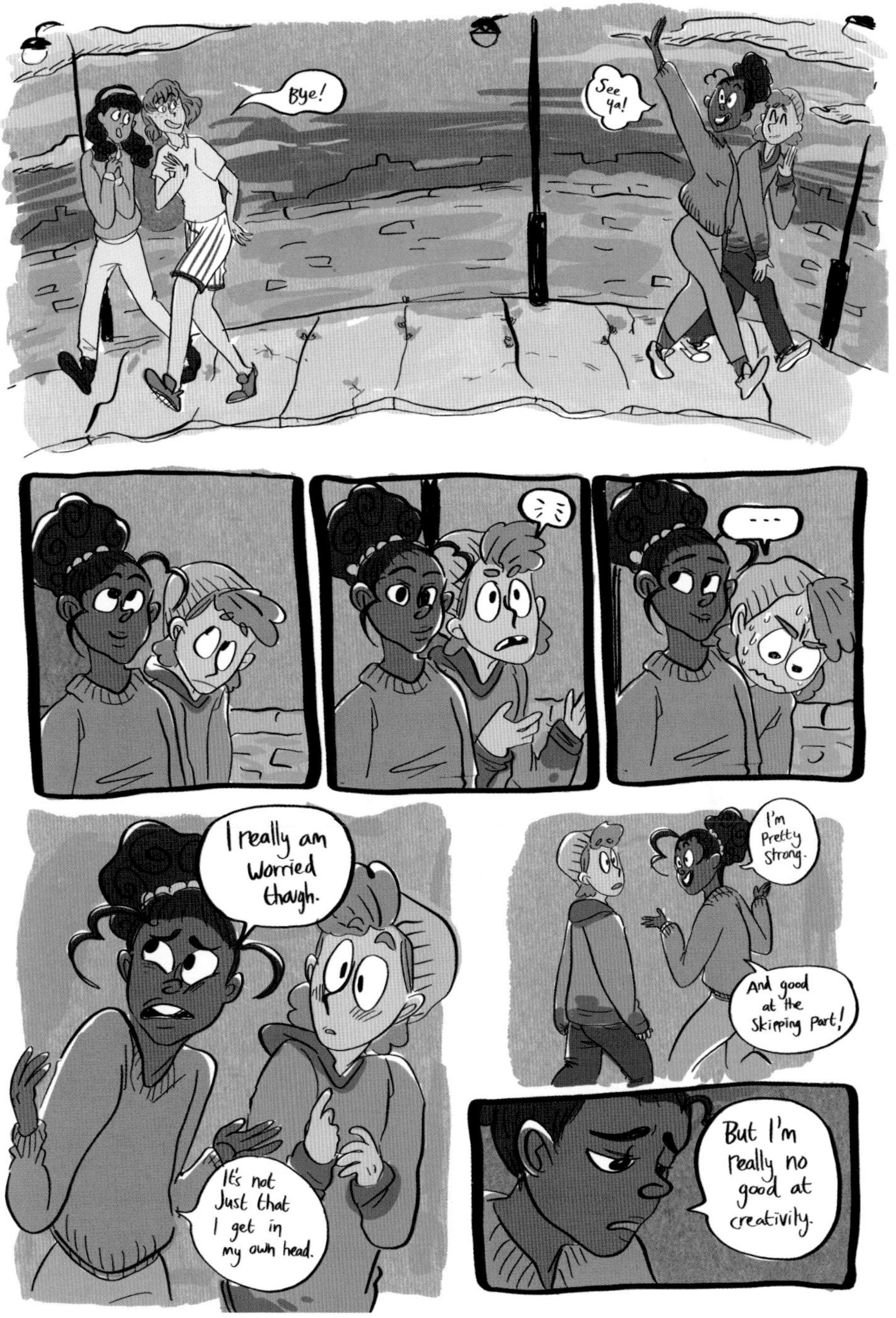

Bye!
See ya!
...
I really am worried though.
It's not just that I get in my own head.
I'm pretty strong.
And good at the skipping part!
But I'm really no good at creativity.

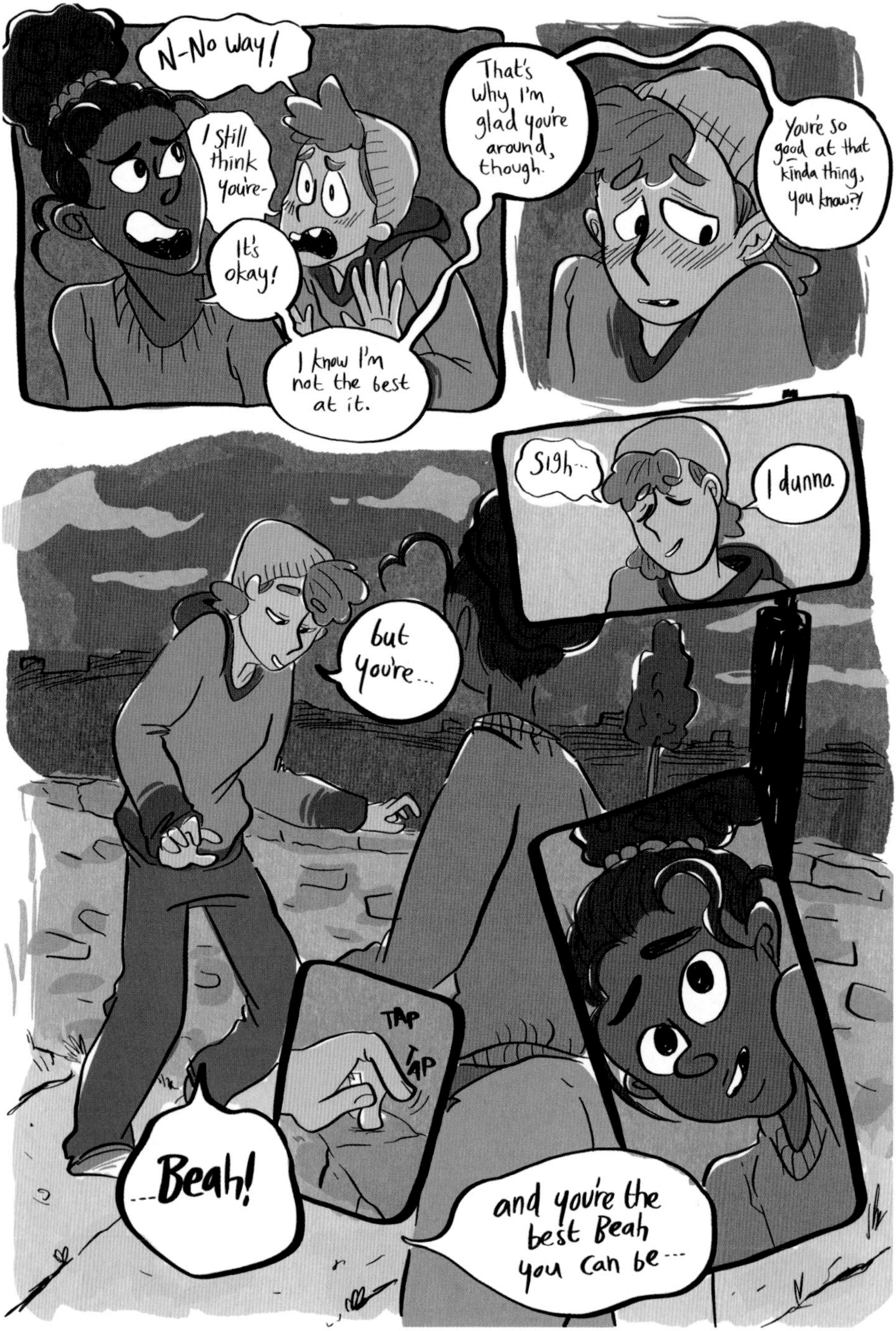
N-No way!
I still think you're-
It's okay!
I know I'm not the best at it.
That's why I'm glad you're around, though.
You're so good at that kinda thing, you know?!
Sigh...
I dunno.
but you're...
TAP
TAP
...Beah!
and you're the best Beah you can be...

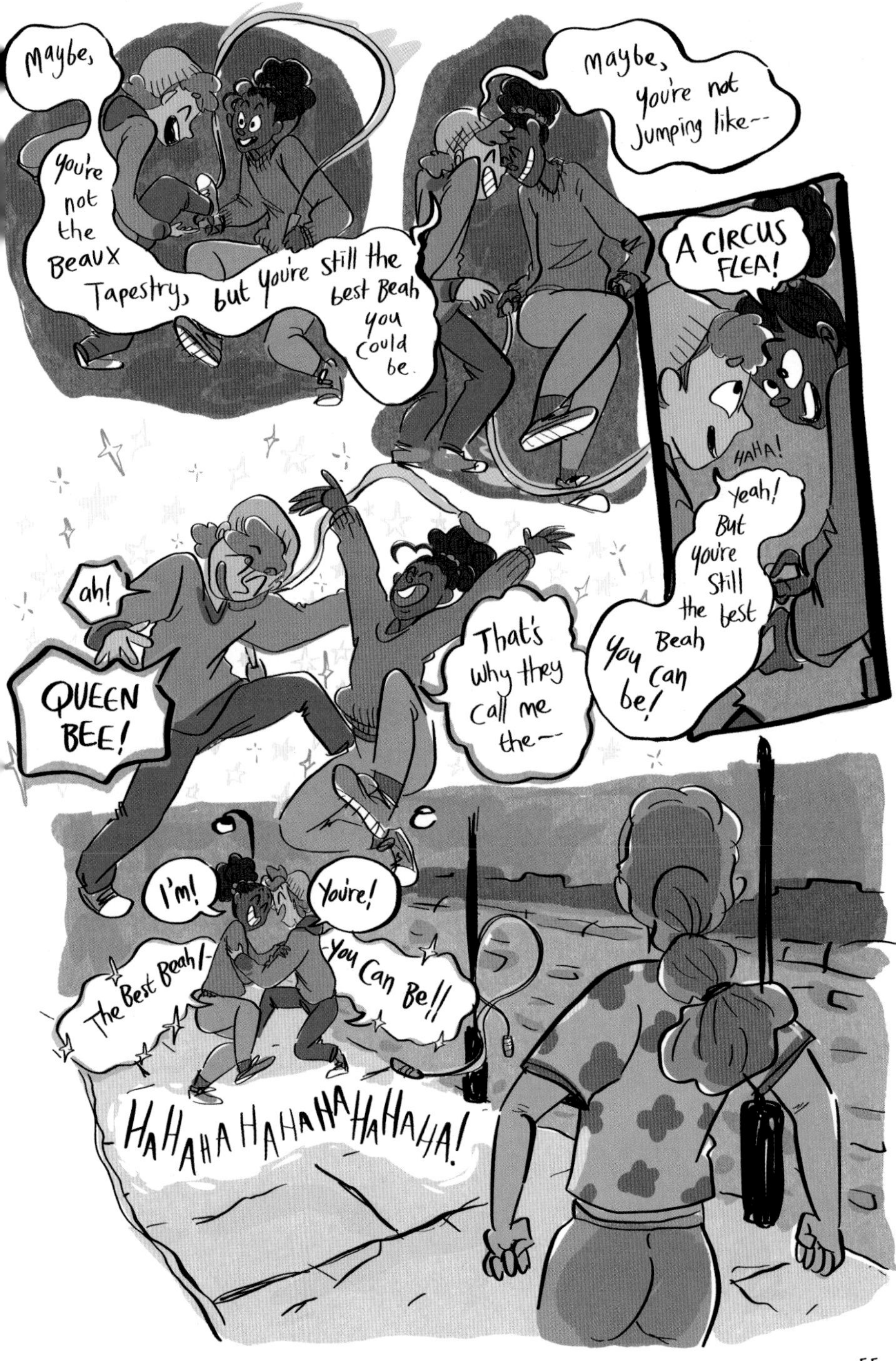
Maybe,
you're not the Beaux Tapestry, but you're still the best Beah you could be.
Maybe, you're not jumping like--
A CIRCUS FLEA!
HAHA!
Yeah! But you're still the best Beah you can be!
ah!
QUEEN BEE!
That's why they call me the--
I'm!
You're!
The Best Beah!-
-You Can Be!!
HAHAHAHAHAHAHAHAHAHA!

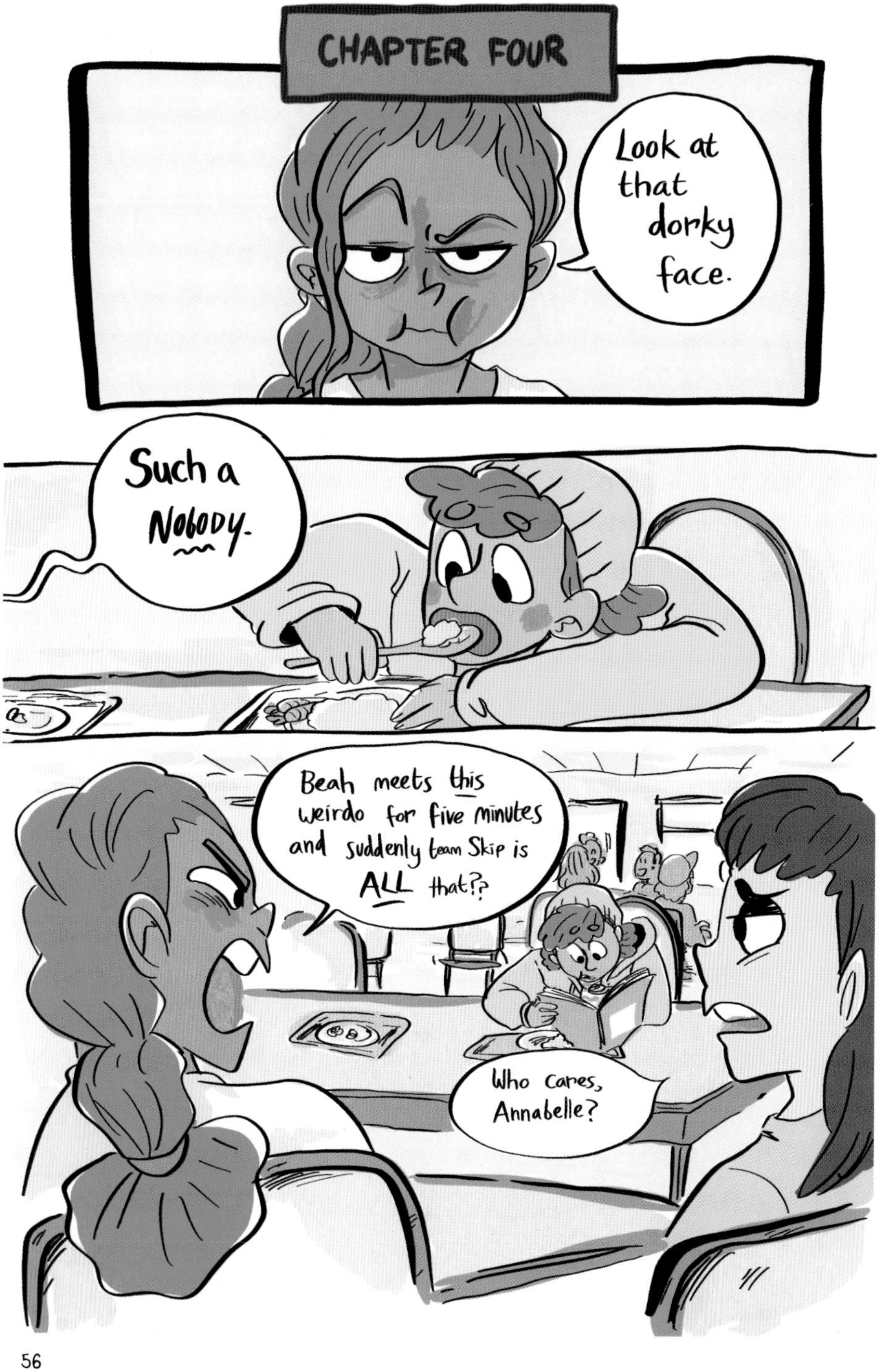
CHAPTER FOUR
Look at that dorky face.
Such a NOBODY.
Beah meets this weirdo for five minutes and suddenly team Skip is ALL that?!?
Who cares, Annabelle?

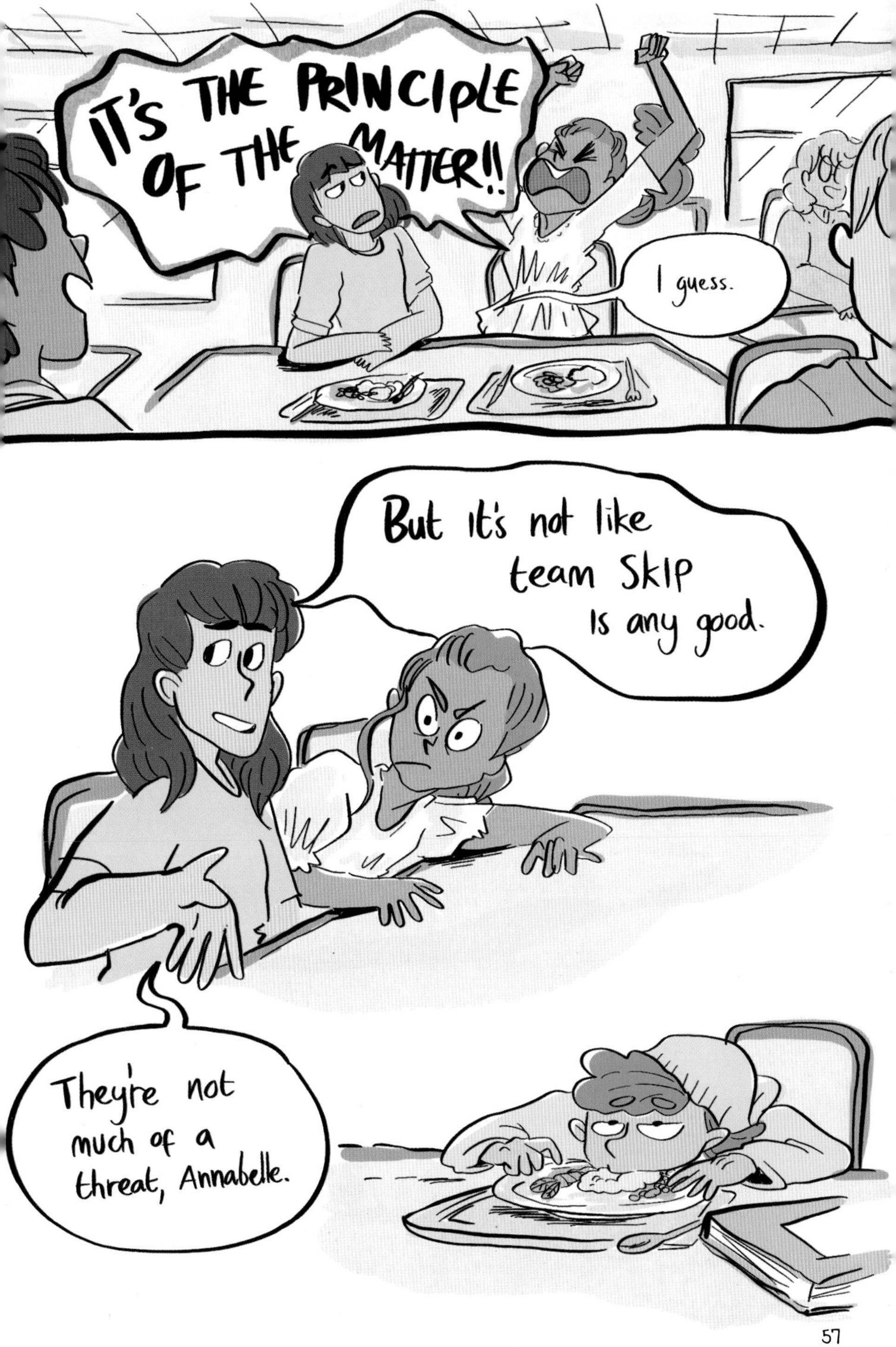
IT'S THE PRINCIPLE OF THE MATTER!!
I guess.
But it's not like team SKIP is any good.
They're not much of a threat, Annabelle.

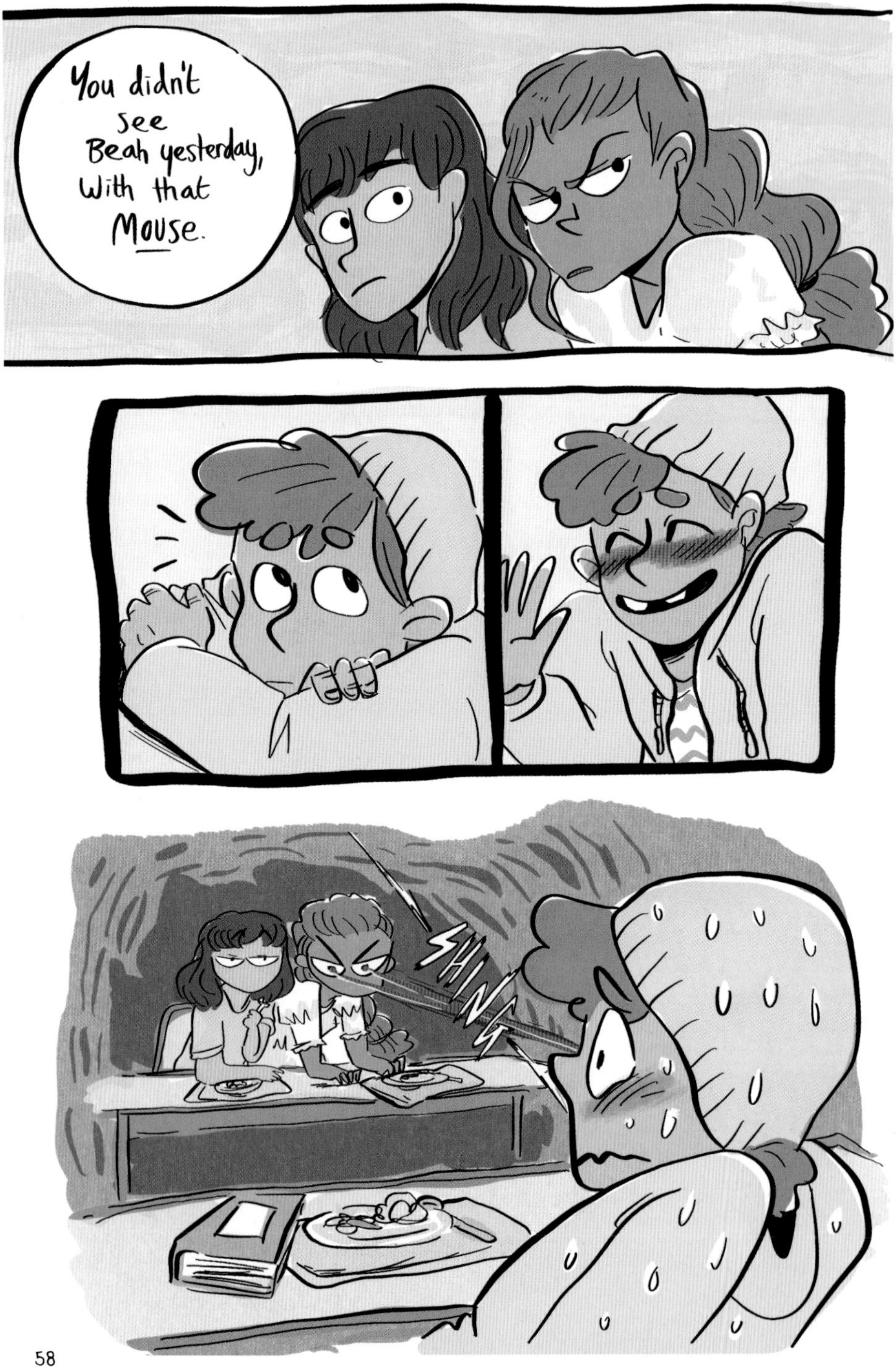
You didn't see Beah yesterday, With that MOUSE.
SHING

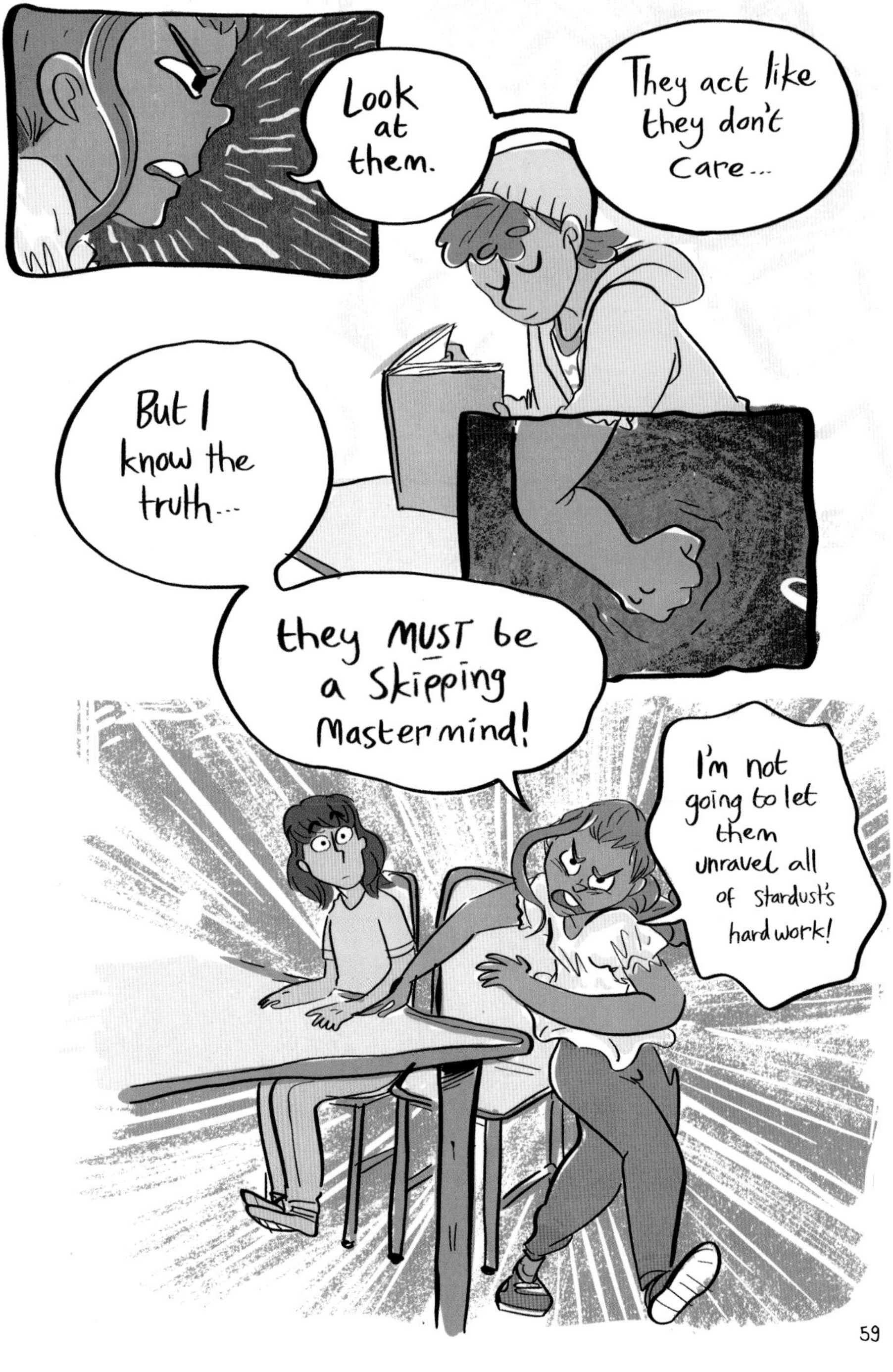
Look at them.
They act like they don't care...
But I know the truth...
they MUST be a Skipping Mastermind!
I'm not going to let them unravel all of Stardust's hard work!

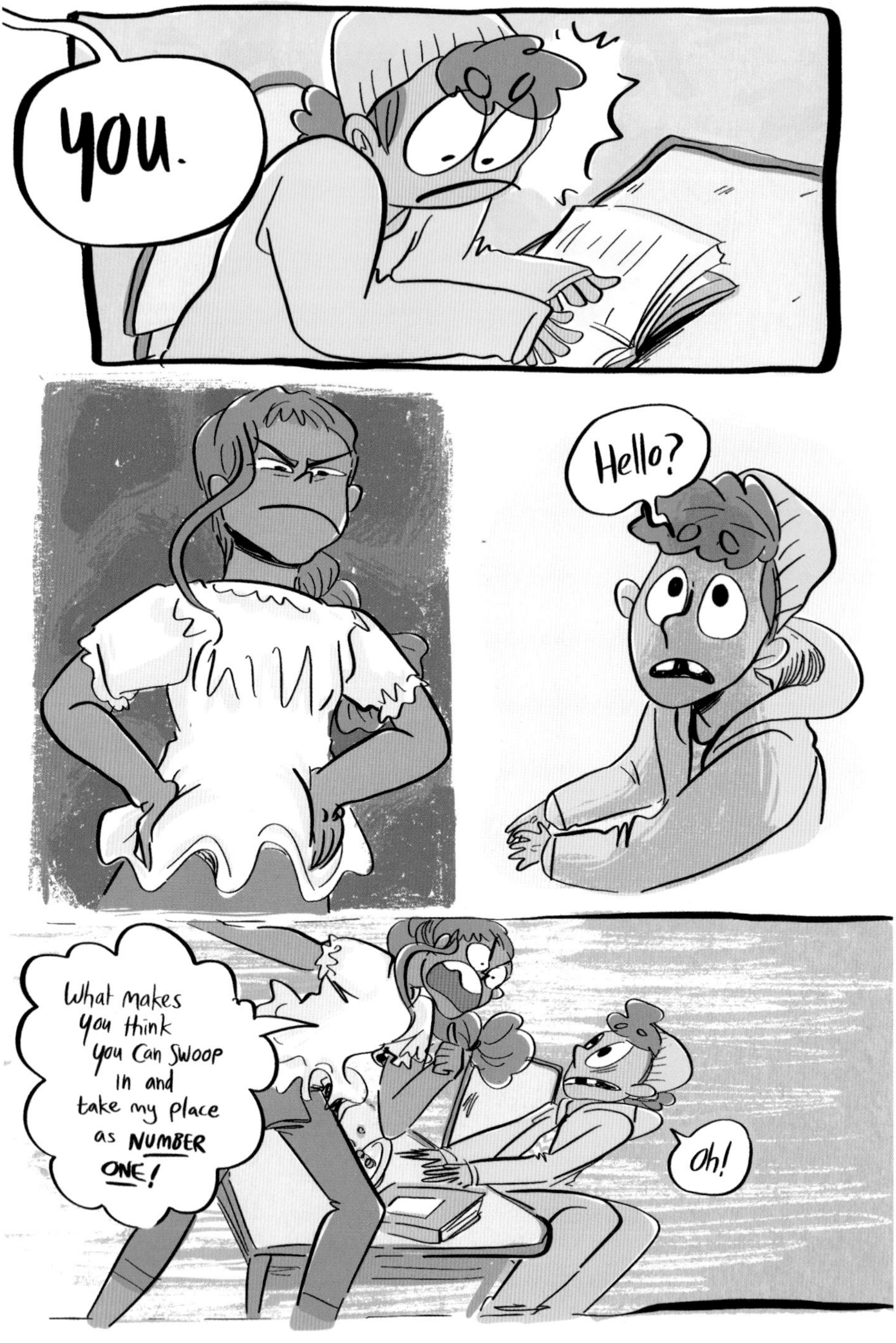
YOU.
Hello?
What makes you think you can swoop in and take my place as NUMBER ONE!
Oh!

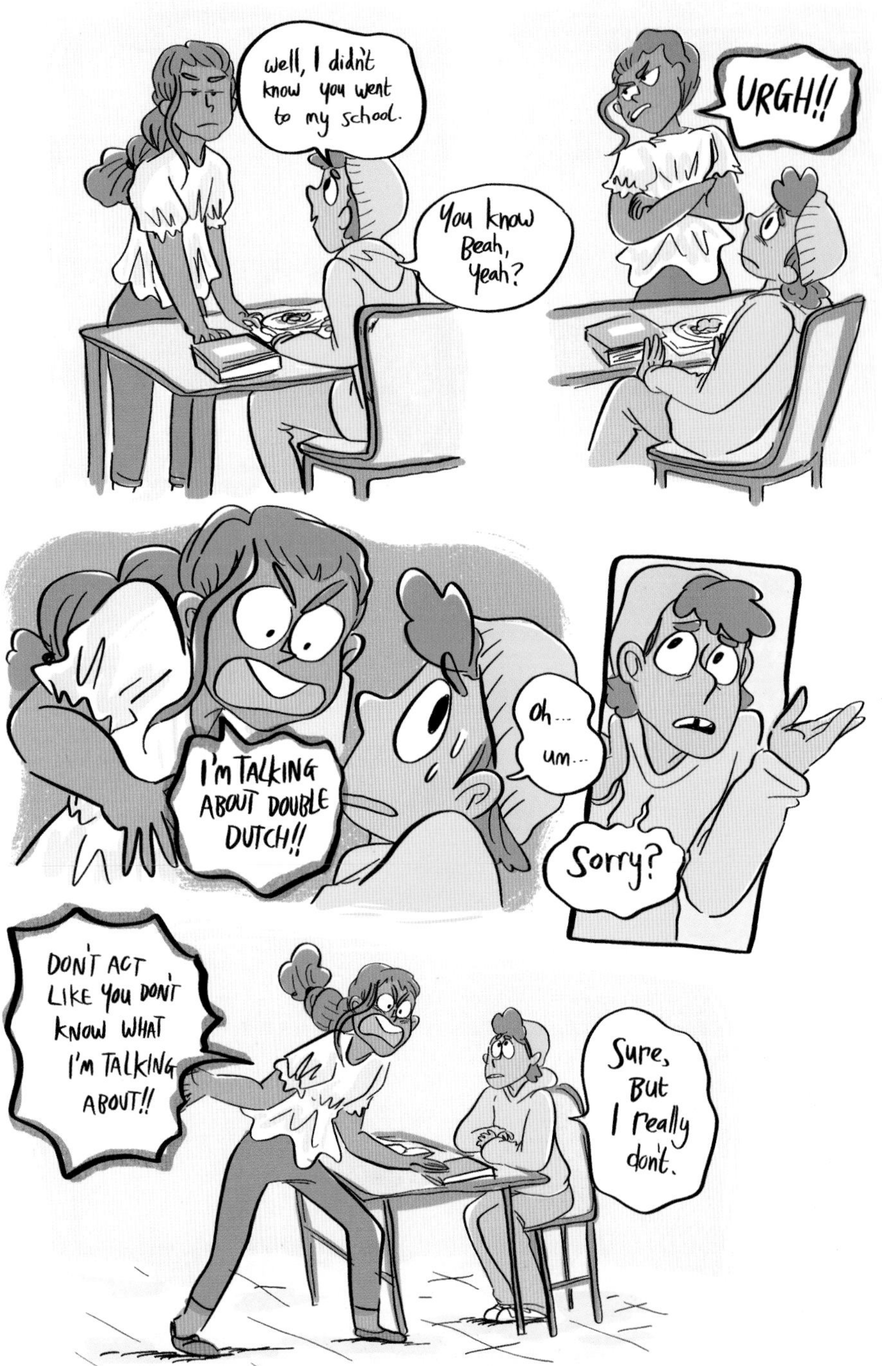
well, I didn't know you went to my school.
You know Beah, yeah?
URGH!!
I'M TALKING ABOUT DOUBLE DUTCH!!
oh...
um...
Sorry?
DON'T ACT LIKE YOU DON'T KNOW WHAT I'M TALKING ABOUT!!
Sure, But I really don't.

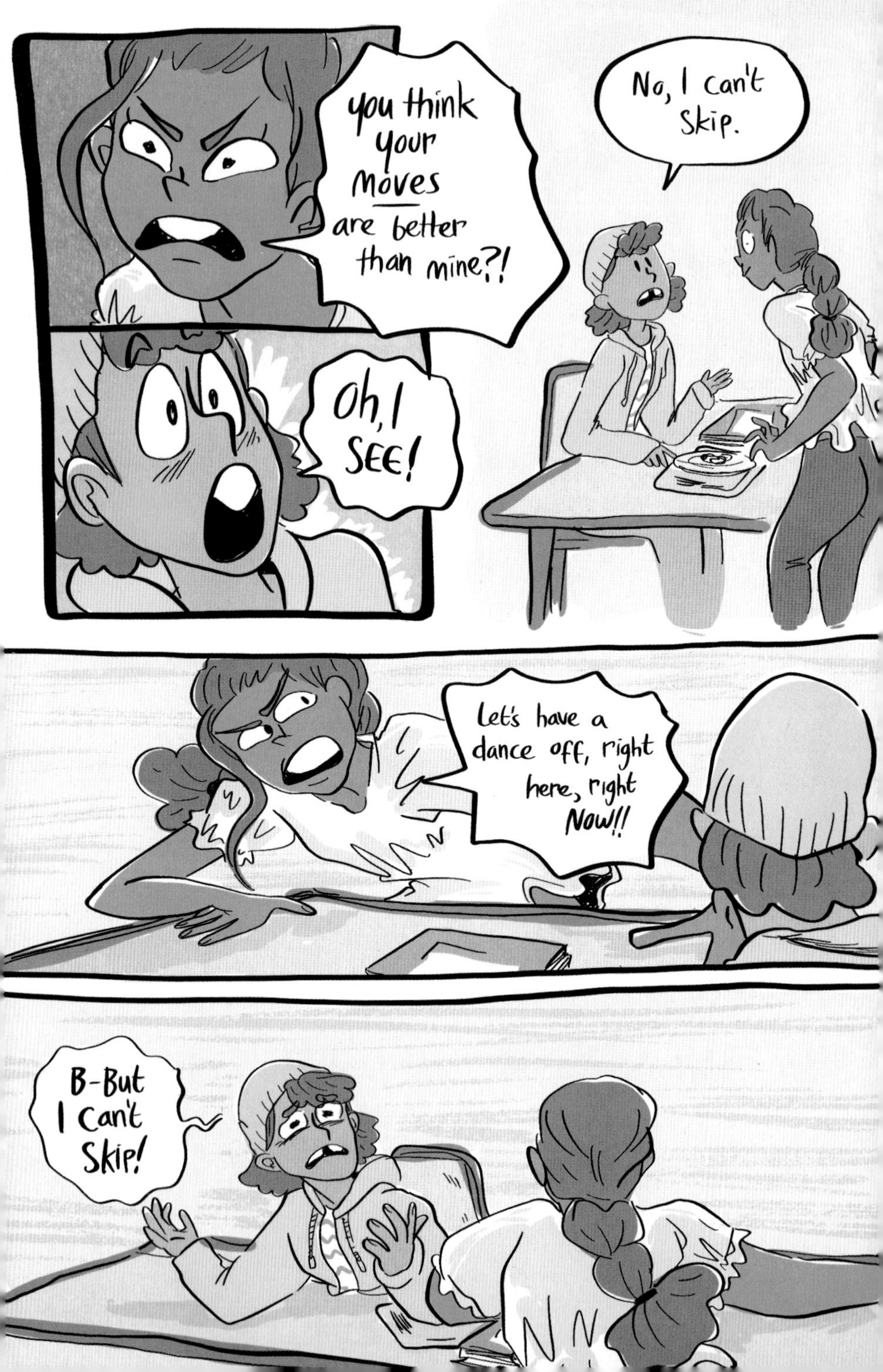
you think your moves are better than mine?!
No, I can't Skip.
Oh, I SEE!
Let's have a dance off, right here, right NOW!!
B-But I can't Skip!

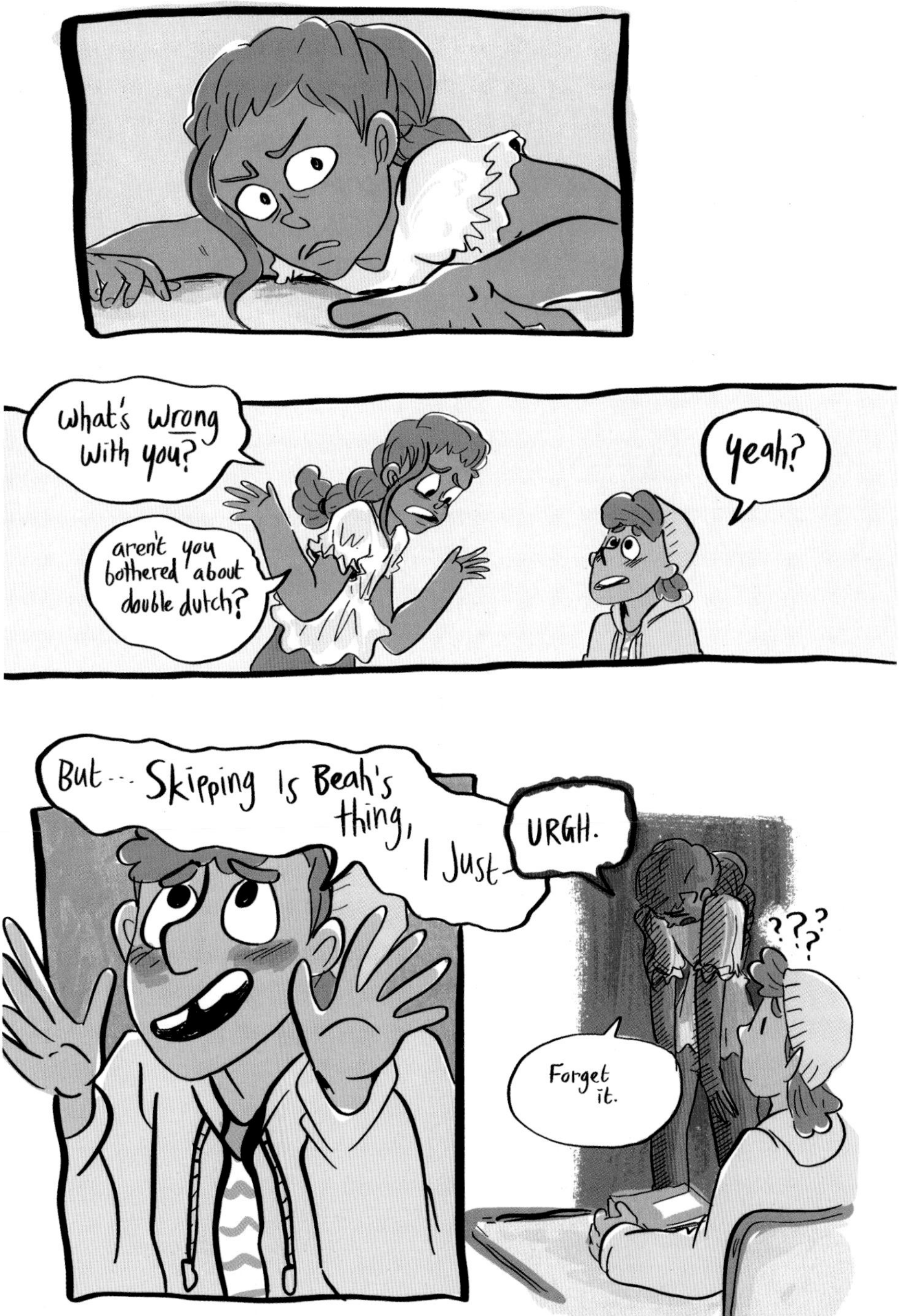
what's wrong with you?
aren't you bothered about double dutch?
yeah?
But... Skipping Is Beah's thing, I Just-
URGH.
???
Forget it.

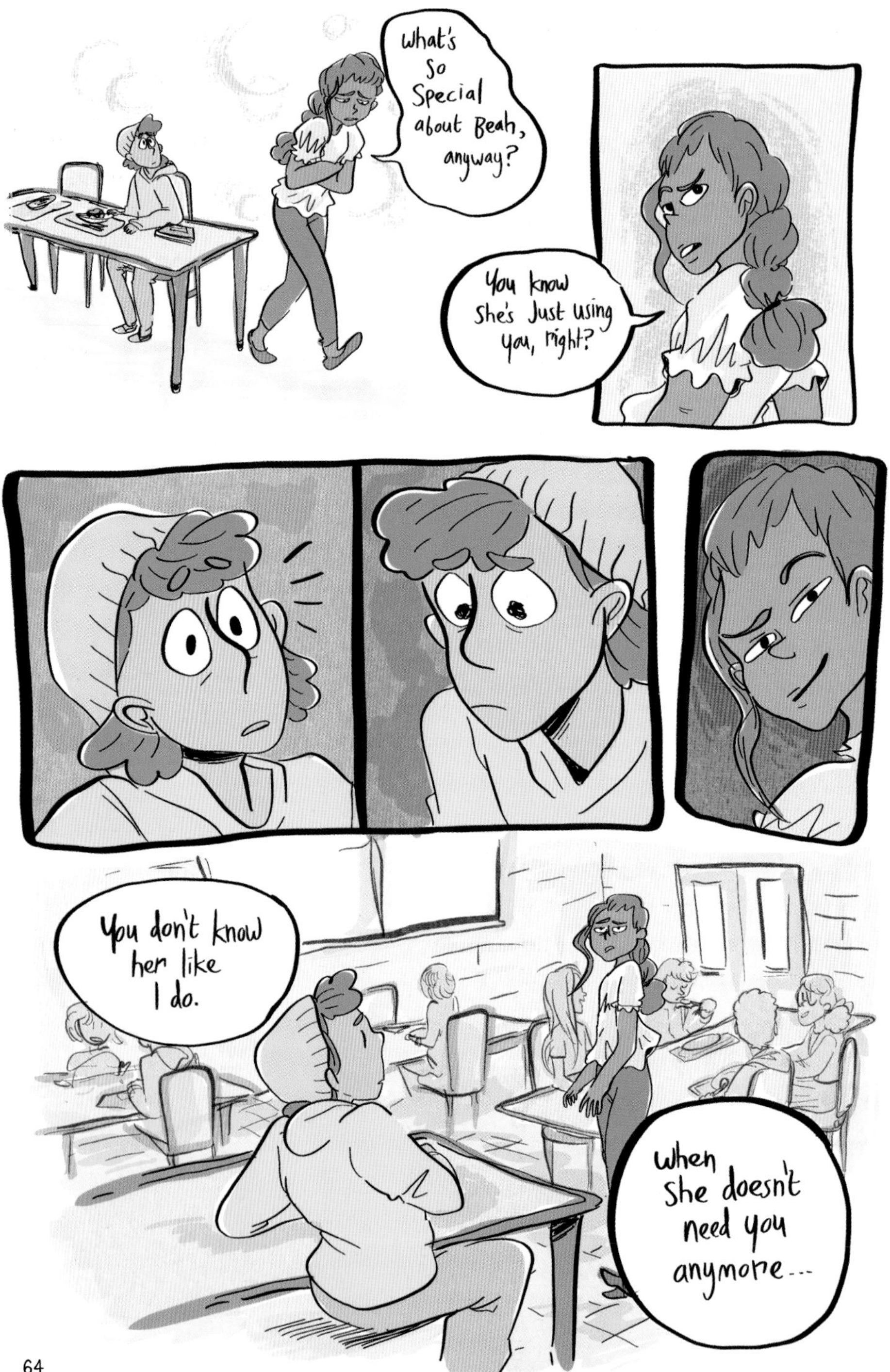
What's so Special about Beah, anyway?
You know She's Just using you, right?
You don't know her like I do.
when She doesn't need you anymore...

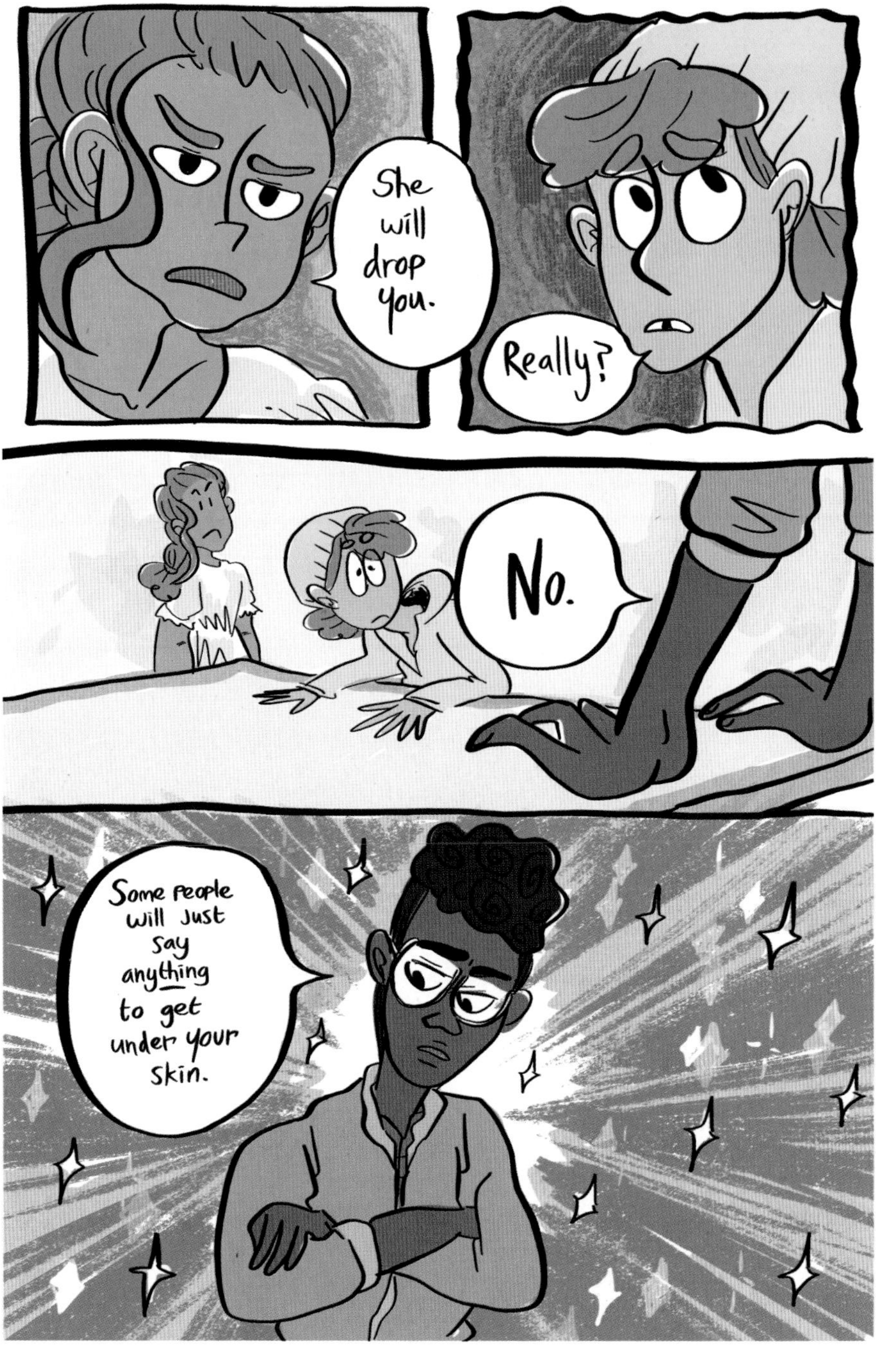
She will drop you.
Really?
No.
Some people will just say anything to get under your skin.

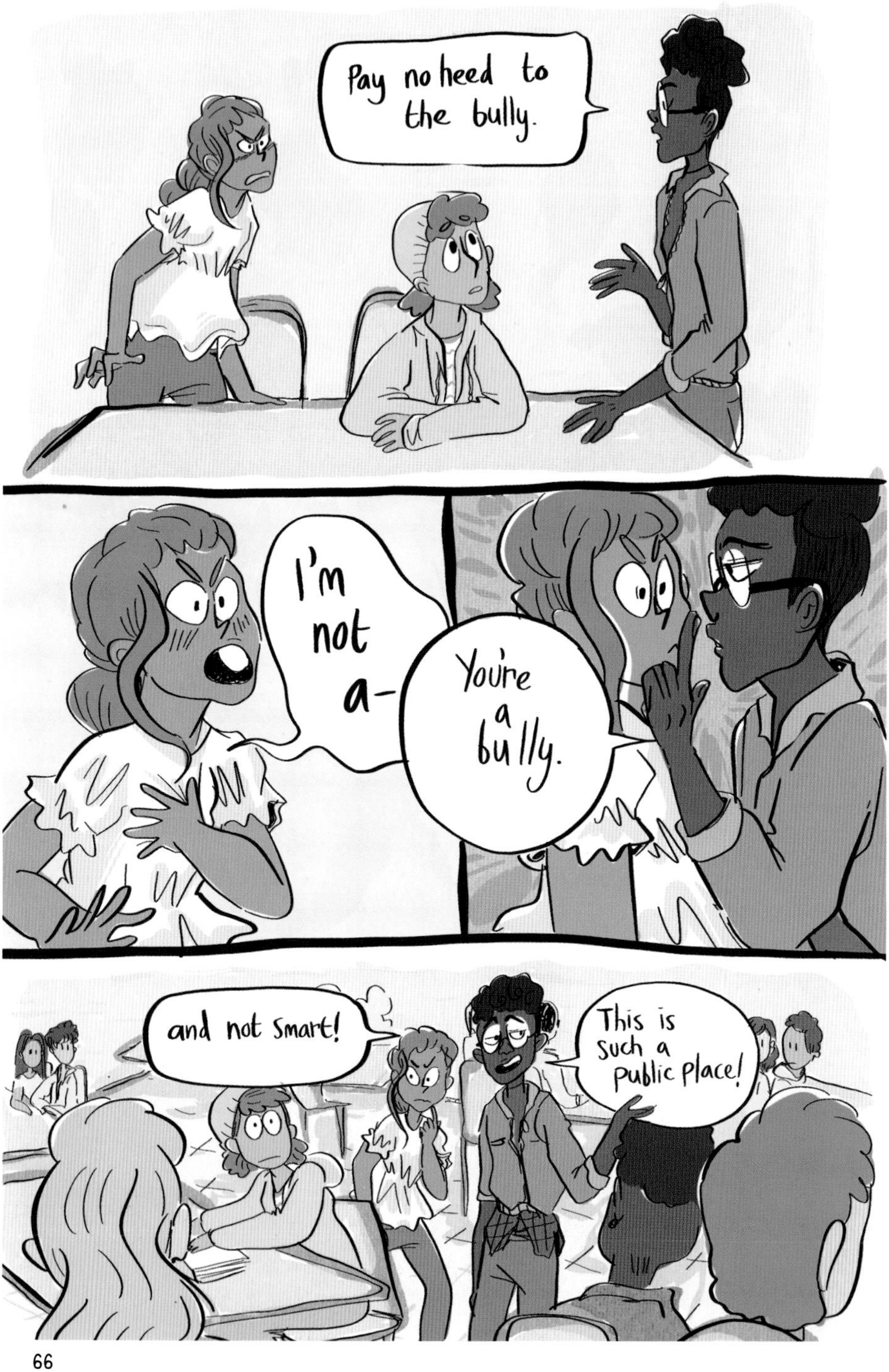

Pay no heed to the bully.
I'm not a-
You're a bully.
and not smart!
This is such a public place!

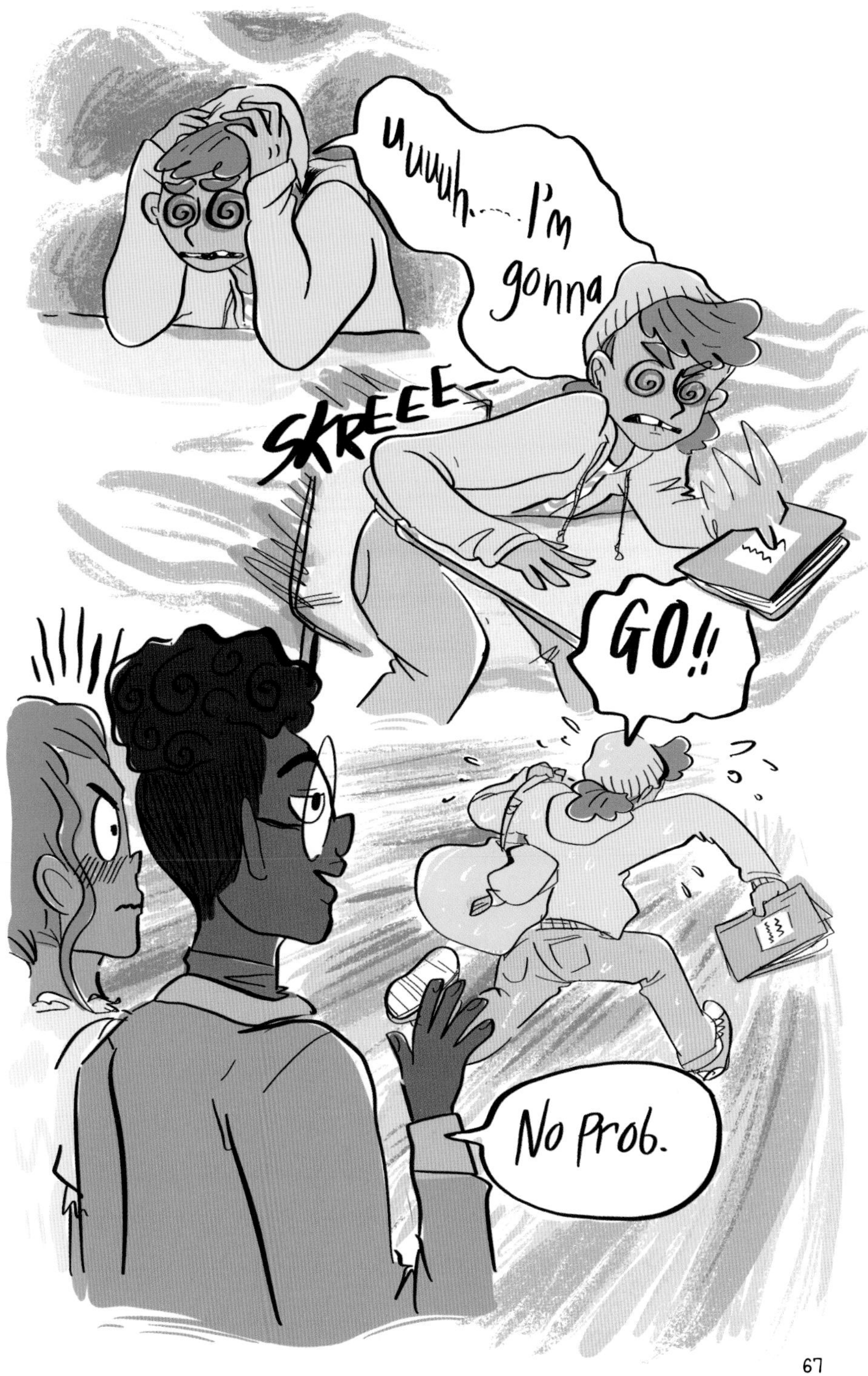
uuuuh.....I'm gonna
SKREEE-
GO!!
No Prob.

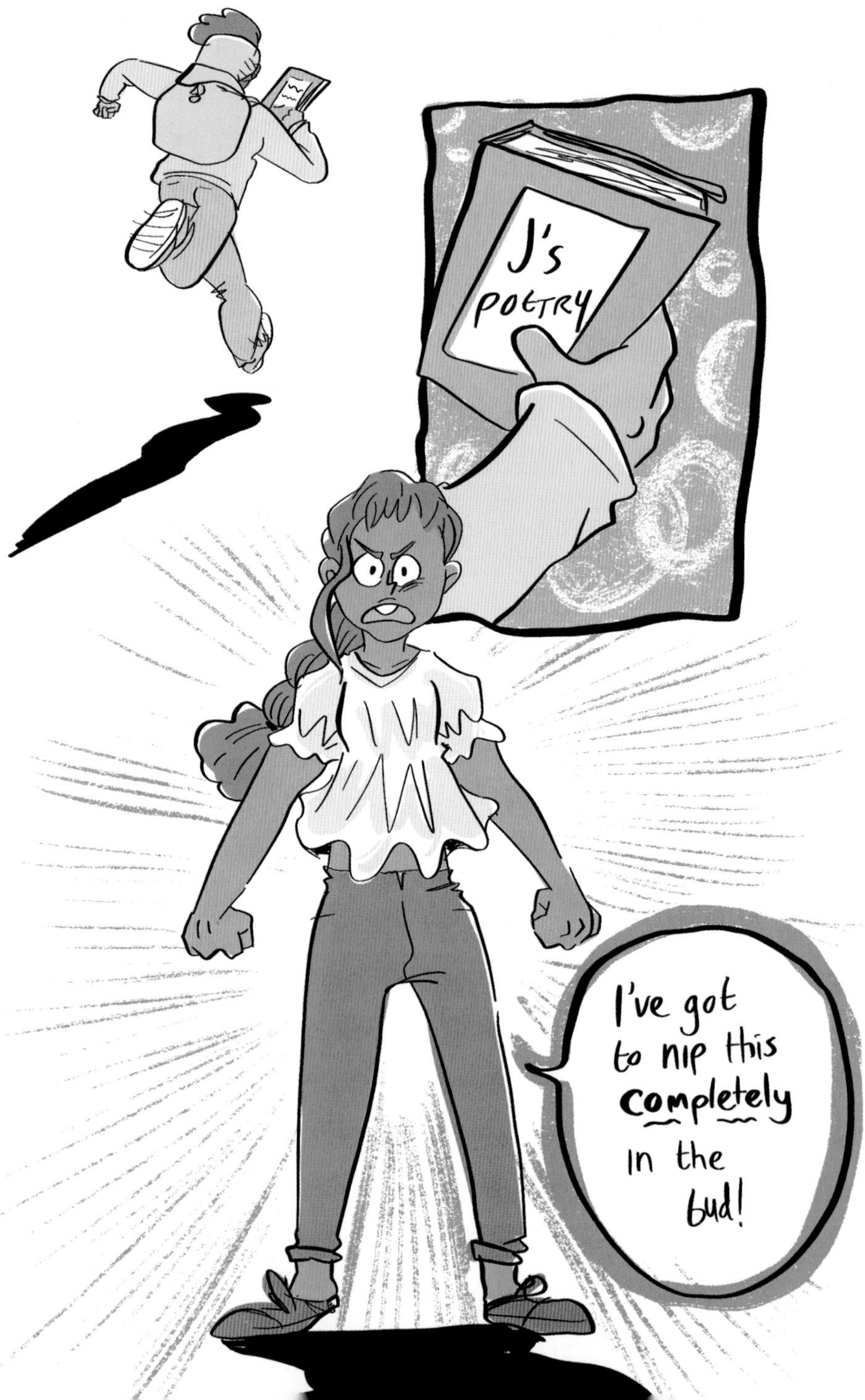
J's POETRY
I've got to nip this completely in the bud!

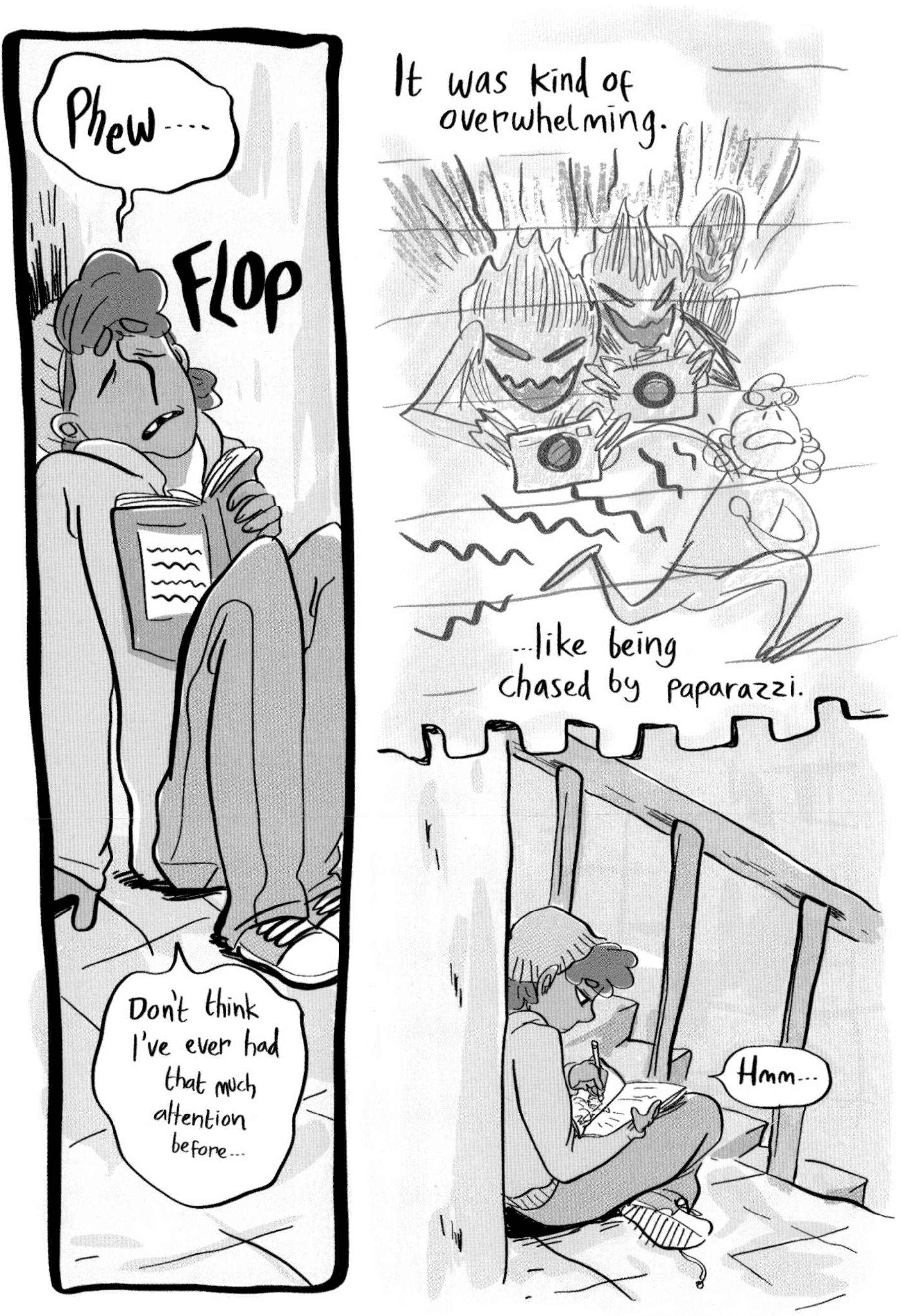
Phew....
FLOP
Don't think I've ever had that much attention before...
It was kind of overwhelming.
...like being chased by paparazzi.
Hmm...

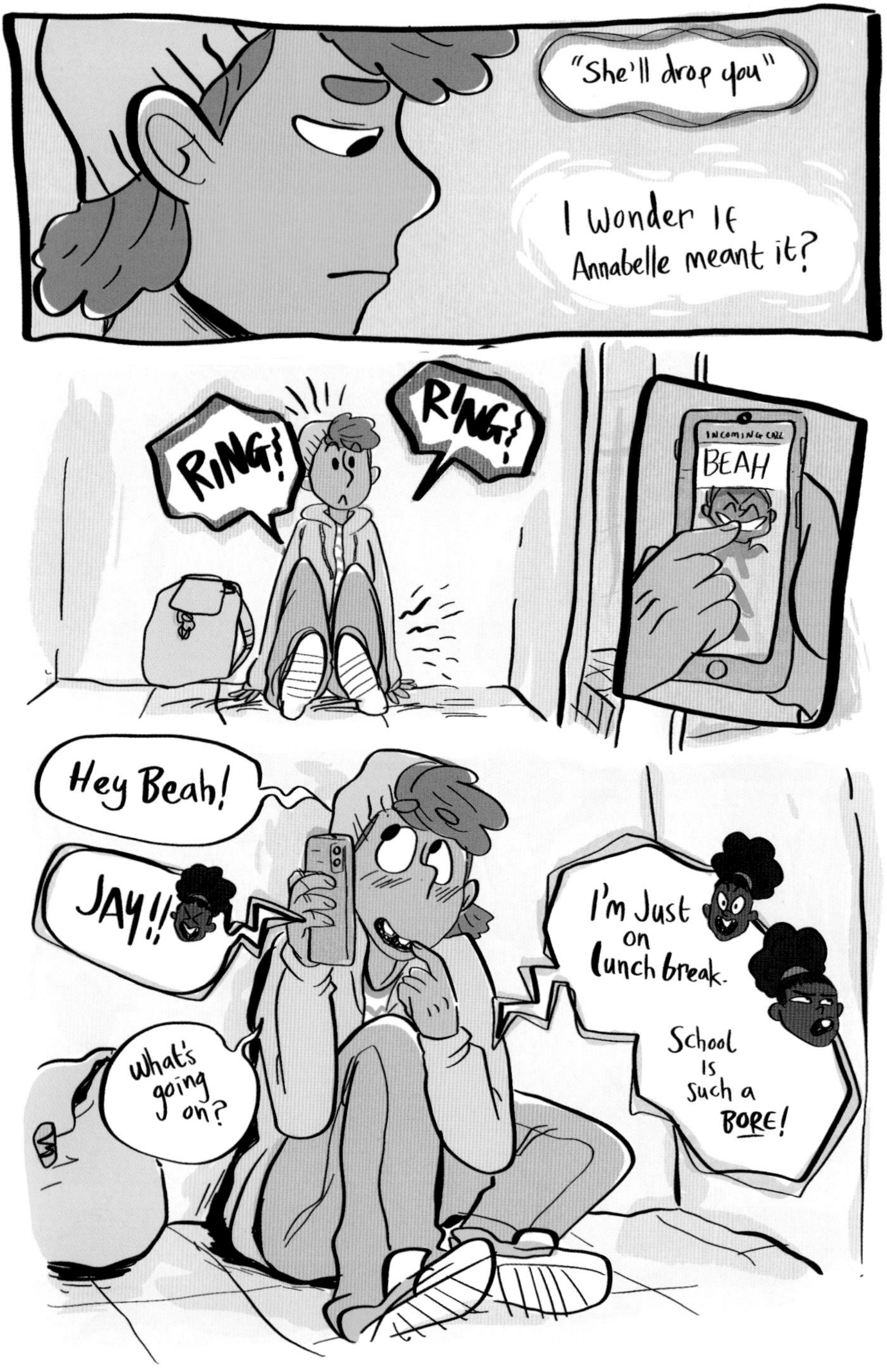
"She'll drop you"
I wonder If Annabelle meant it?
RING!
RING!
INCOMING CALL
BEAH
Hey Beah!
JAY!!
I'm Just on lunch break.
School is such a BORE!
what's going on?

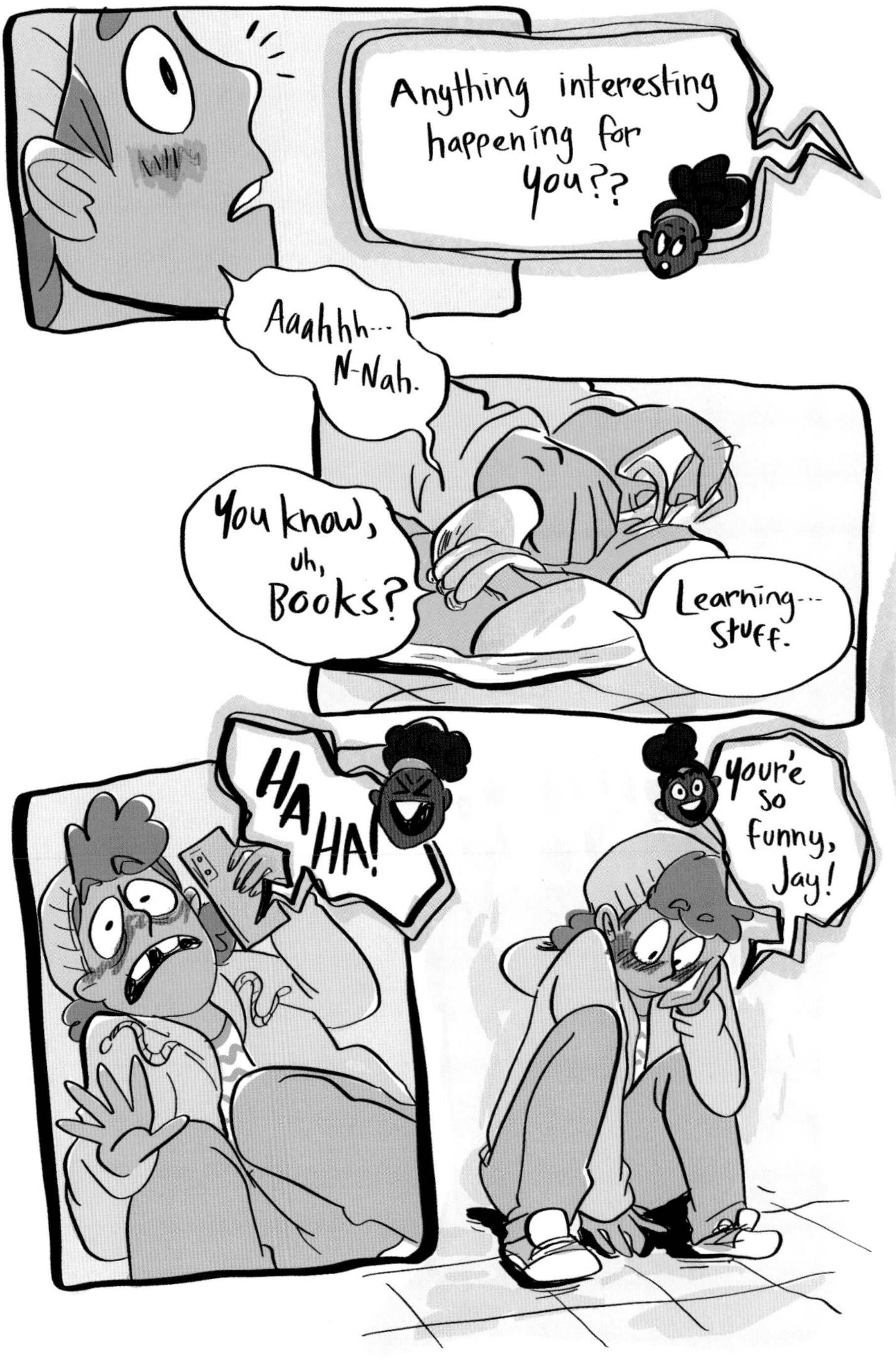
Anything interesting happening for you??
Aaahhh... N-Nah.
You know, uh, Books?
Learning... stuff.
HAHAHA!
You're so funny, Jay!

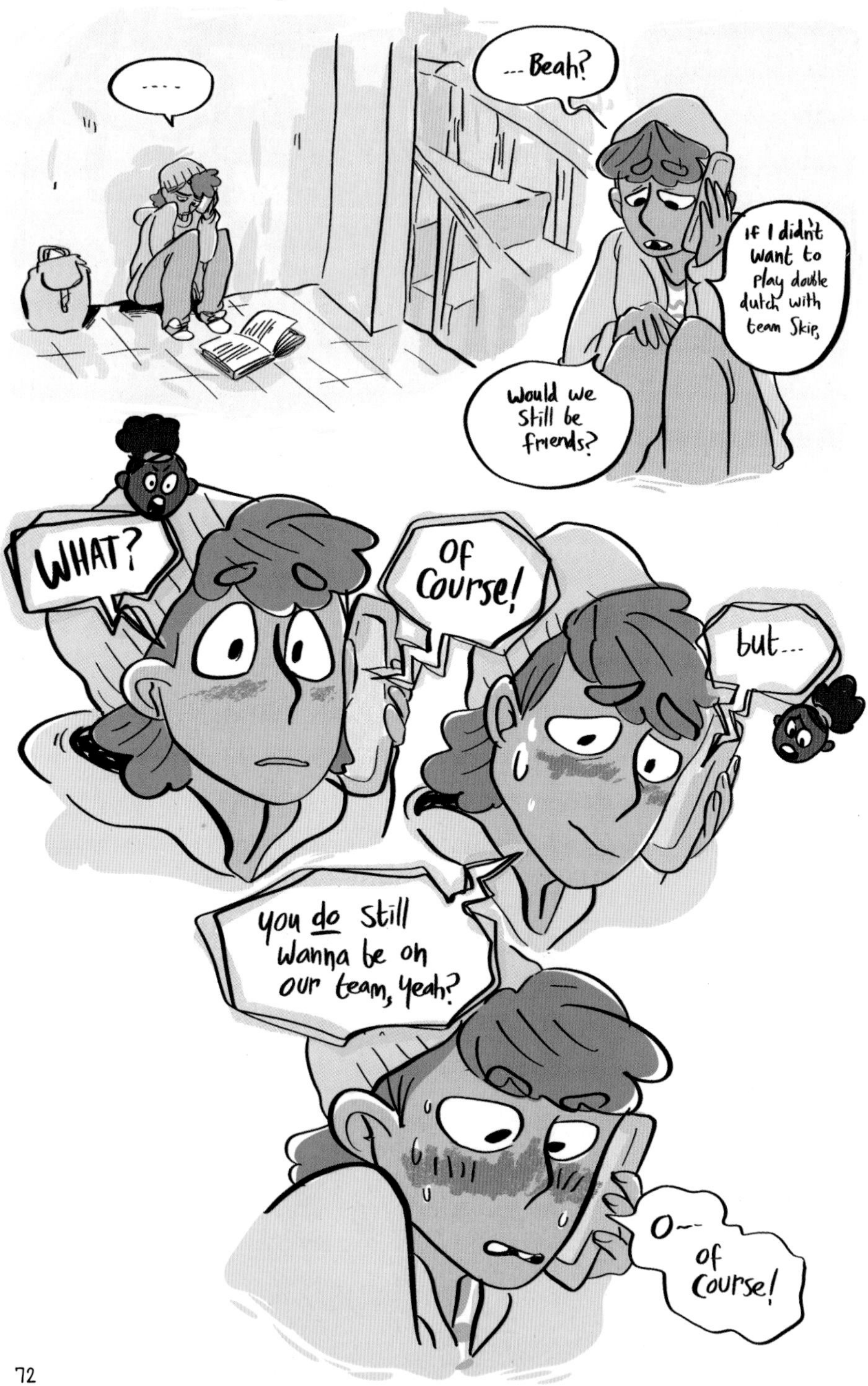
....
...Beah?
If I didn't want to play double dutch with team Skip,
Would we still be friends?
WHAT?
Of course!
but...
you do still wanna be on our team, yeah?
O--
of course!

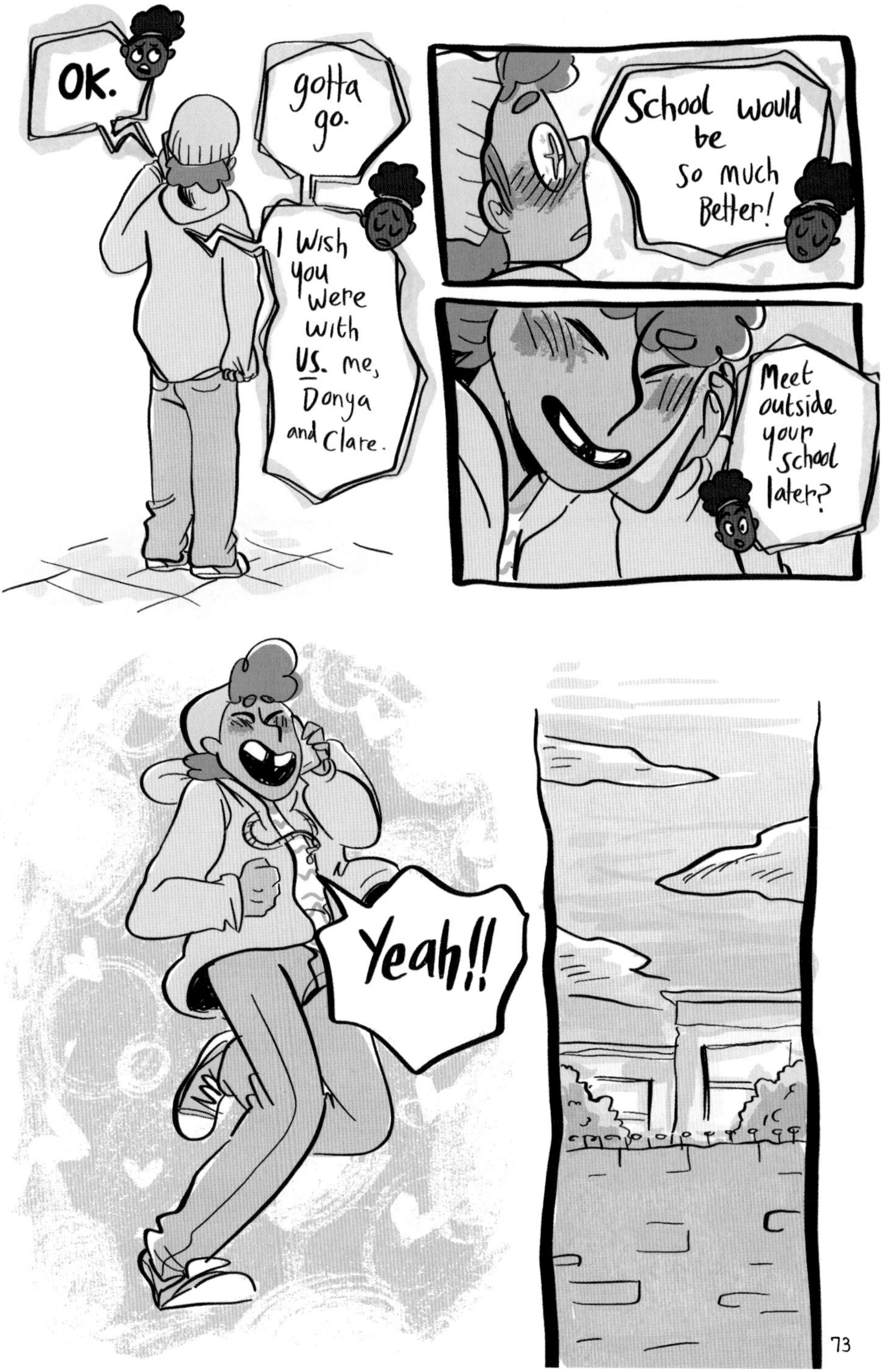
OK.
gotta go.
I wish you were with US. me, Donya and Clare.
School would be so much Better!
Meet outside your school later?
Yeah!!

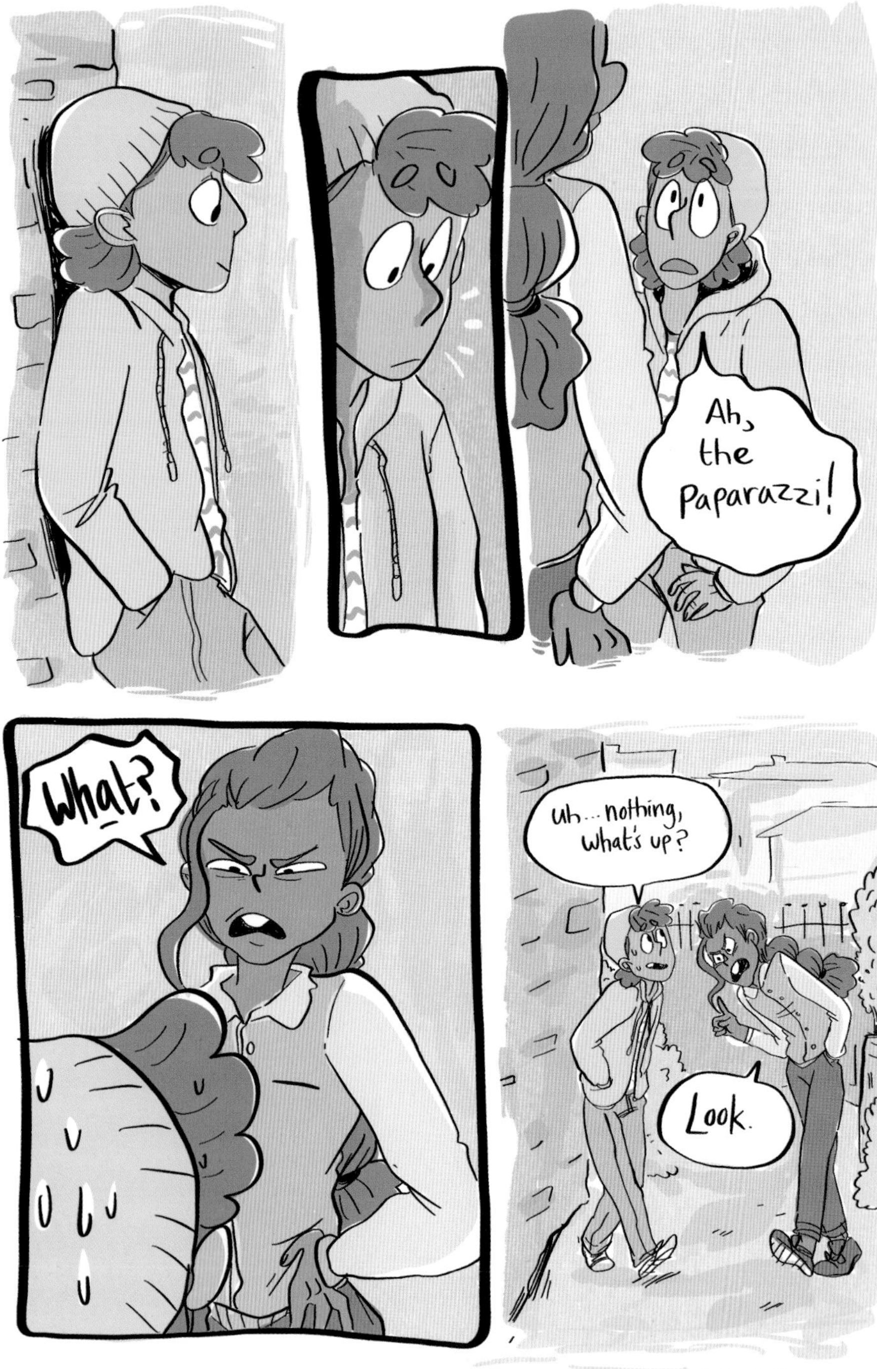
Ah, the Paparazzi!
What?
uh... nothing, what's up?
Look.

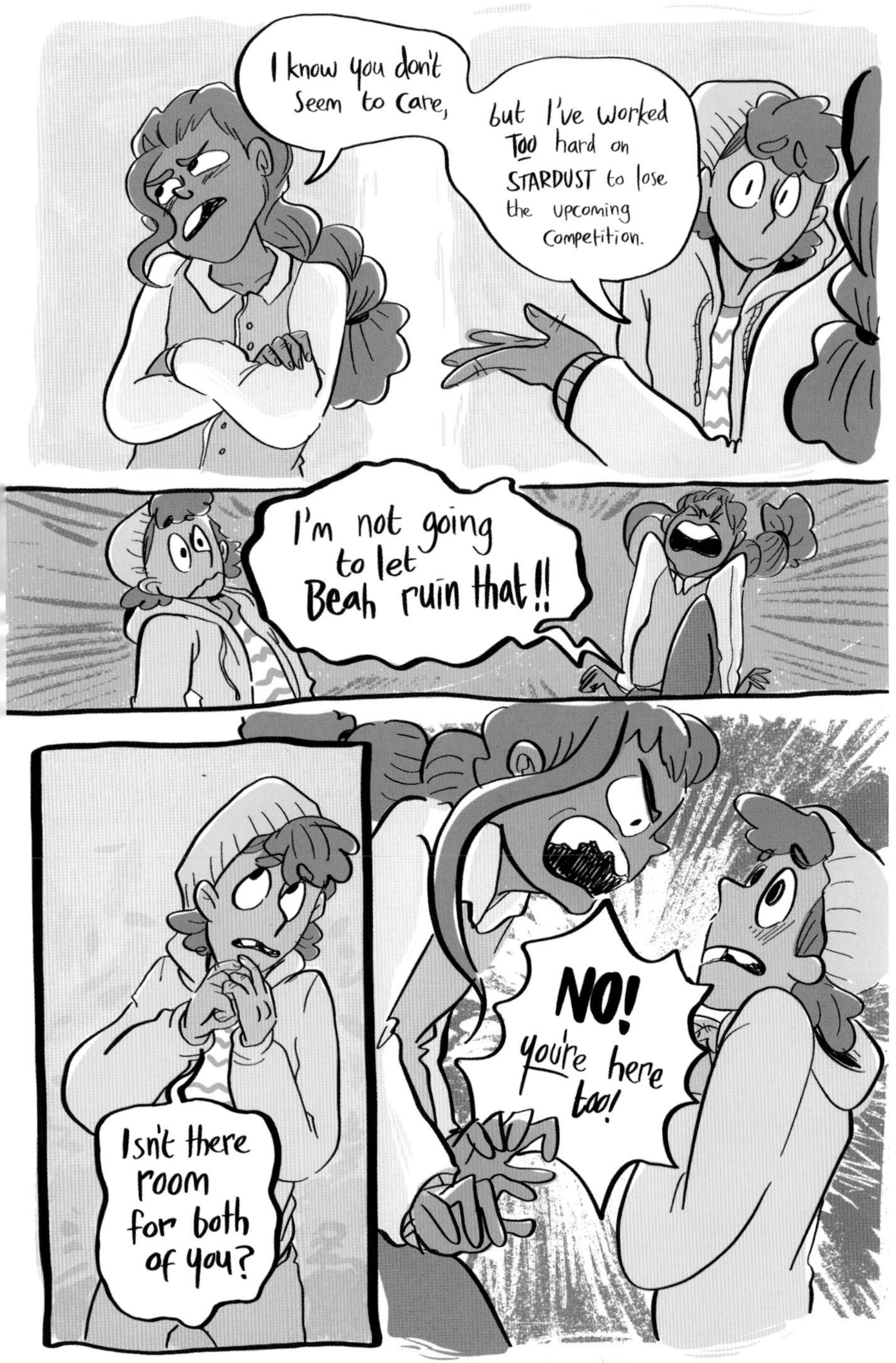
I know you don't Seem to Care,
but I've worked TOO hard on STARDUST to lose the upcoming Competition.
I'm not going to let Beah ruin that!!
Isn't there room for both of you?
NO! you're here too!

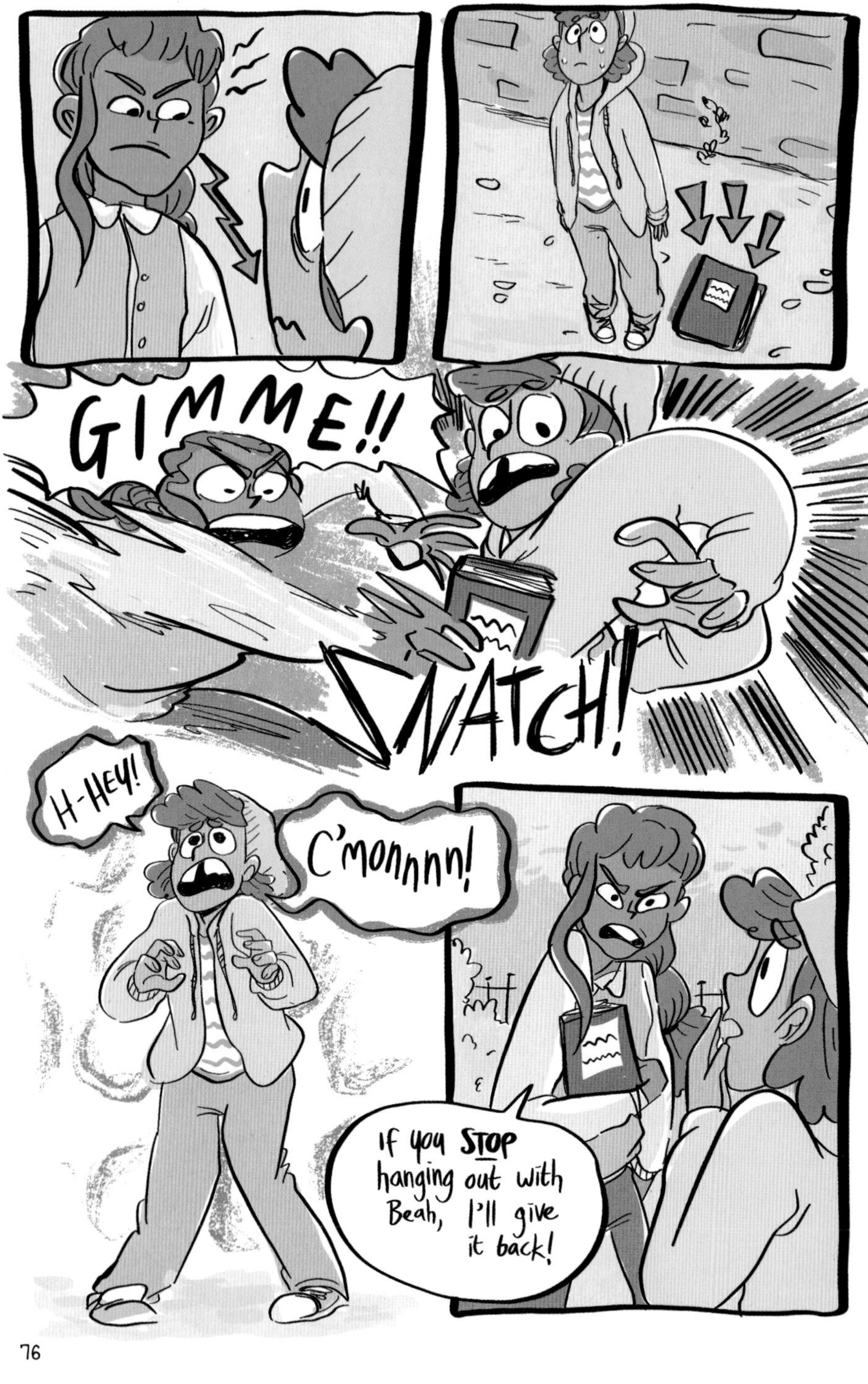
GIMME!!
SNATCH!
H-HEY!
C'monnnn!
If you STOP hanging out with Beah, I'll give it back!

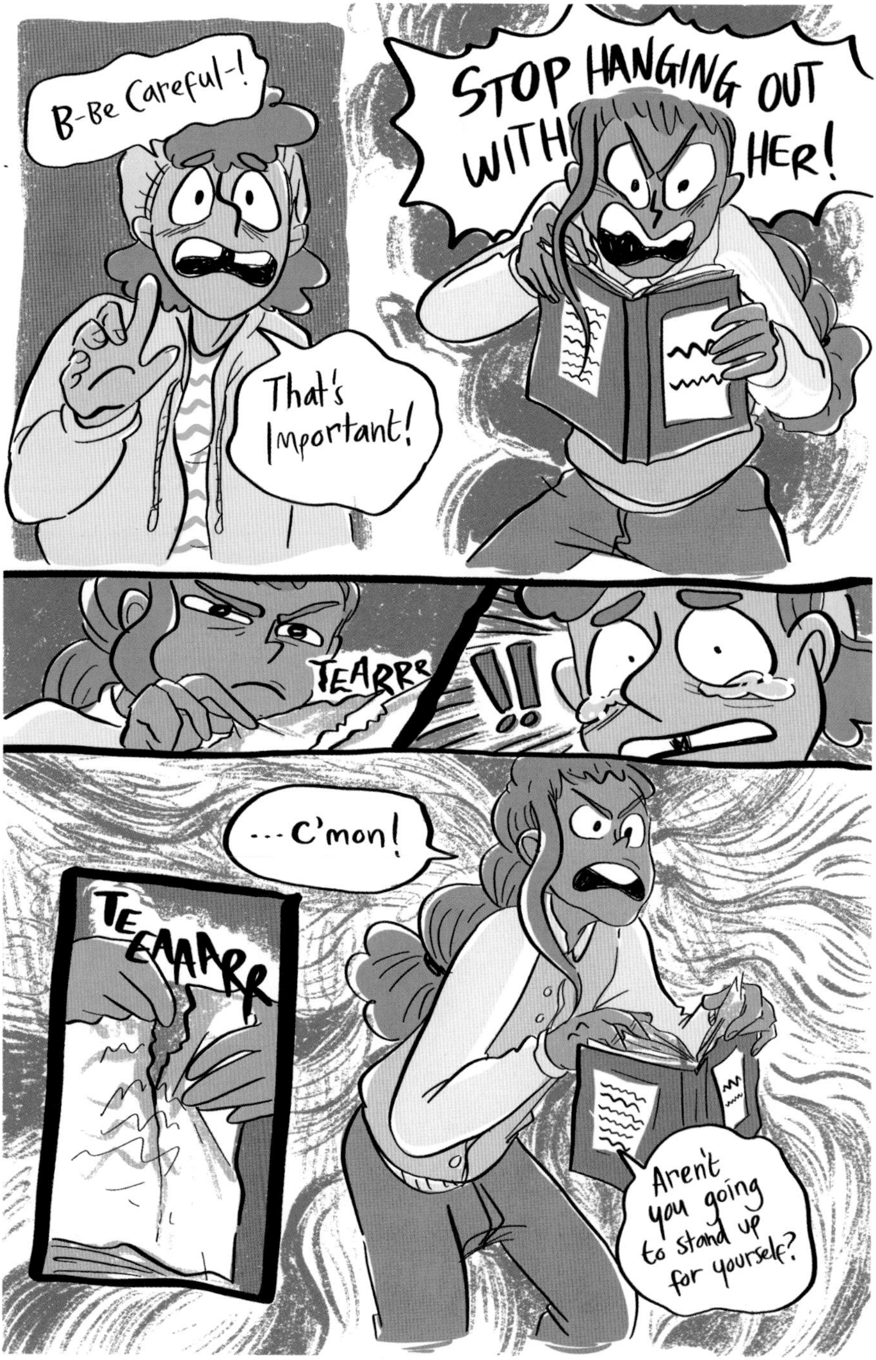
B-Be Careful-!
That's Important!
STOP HANGING OUT WITH HER!
TEARRR
!!
...C'mon!
TEEAAARR
Aren't you going to stand up for yourself?

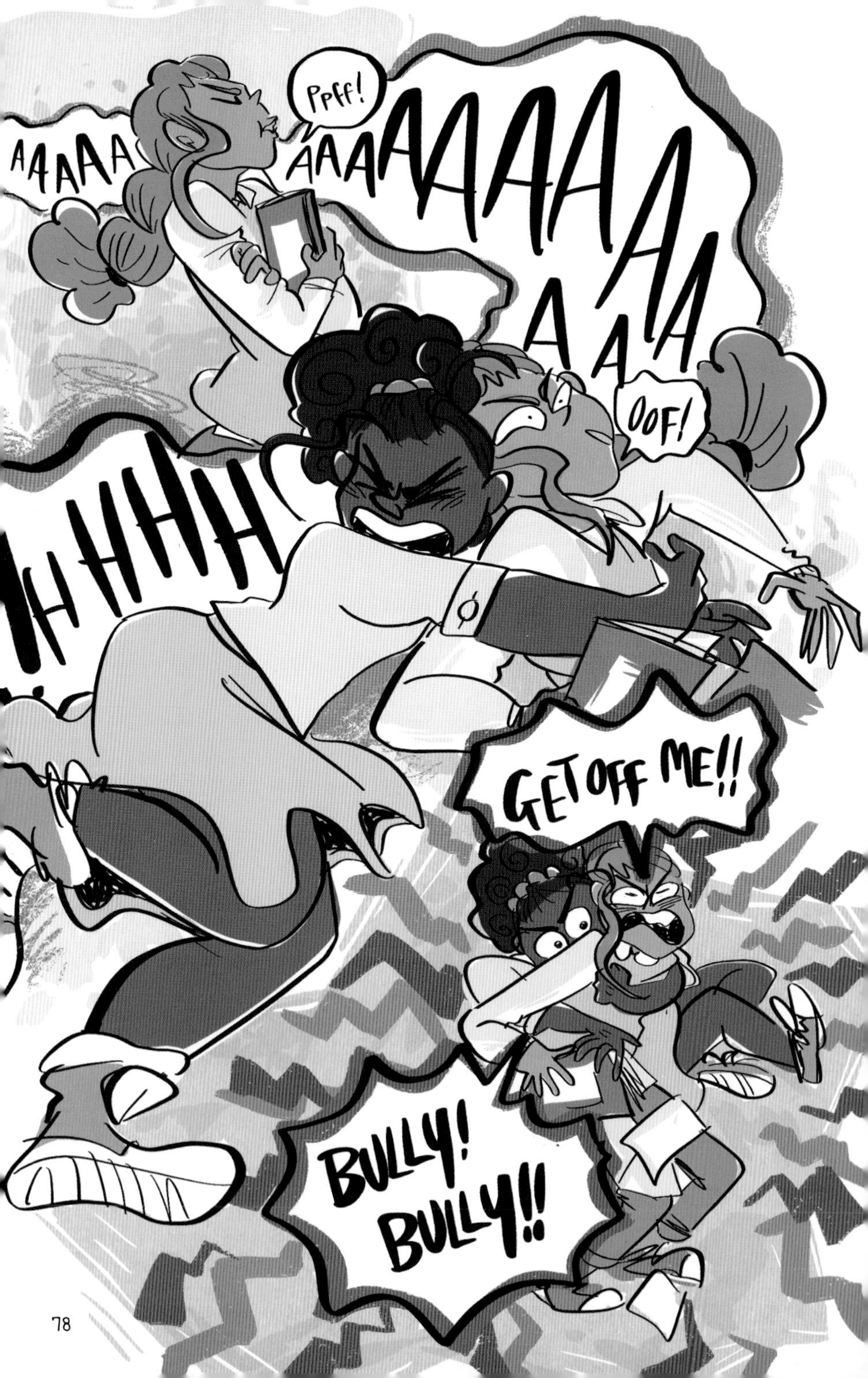
AAAAA
Ppff!
AAAAAAAAAAAAAAAA
OOF!
HHHHHH
GET OFF ME!!
BULLY! BULLY!!

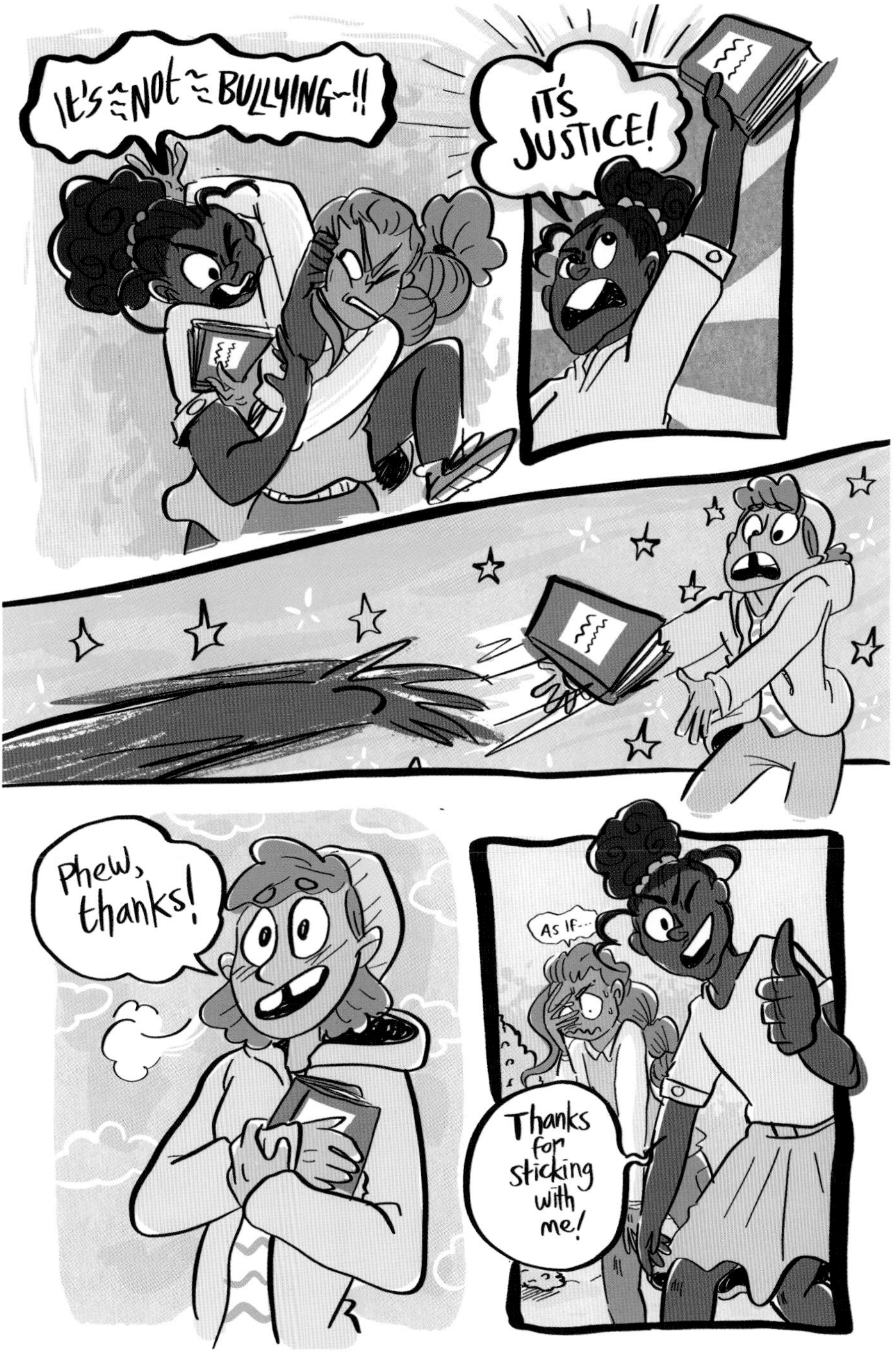
IT'S NOT BULLYING~!!
IT'S JUSTICE!
Phew, thanks!
As IF---
Thanks for sticking with me!

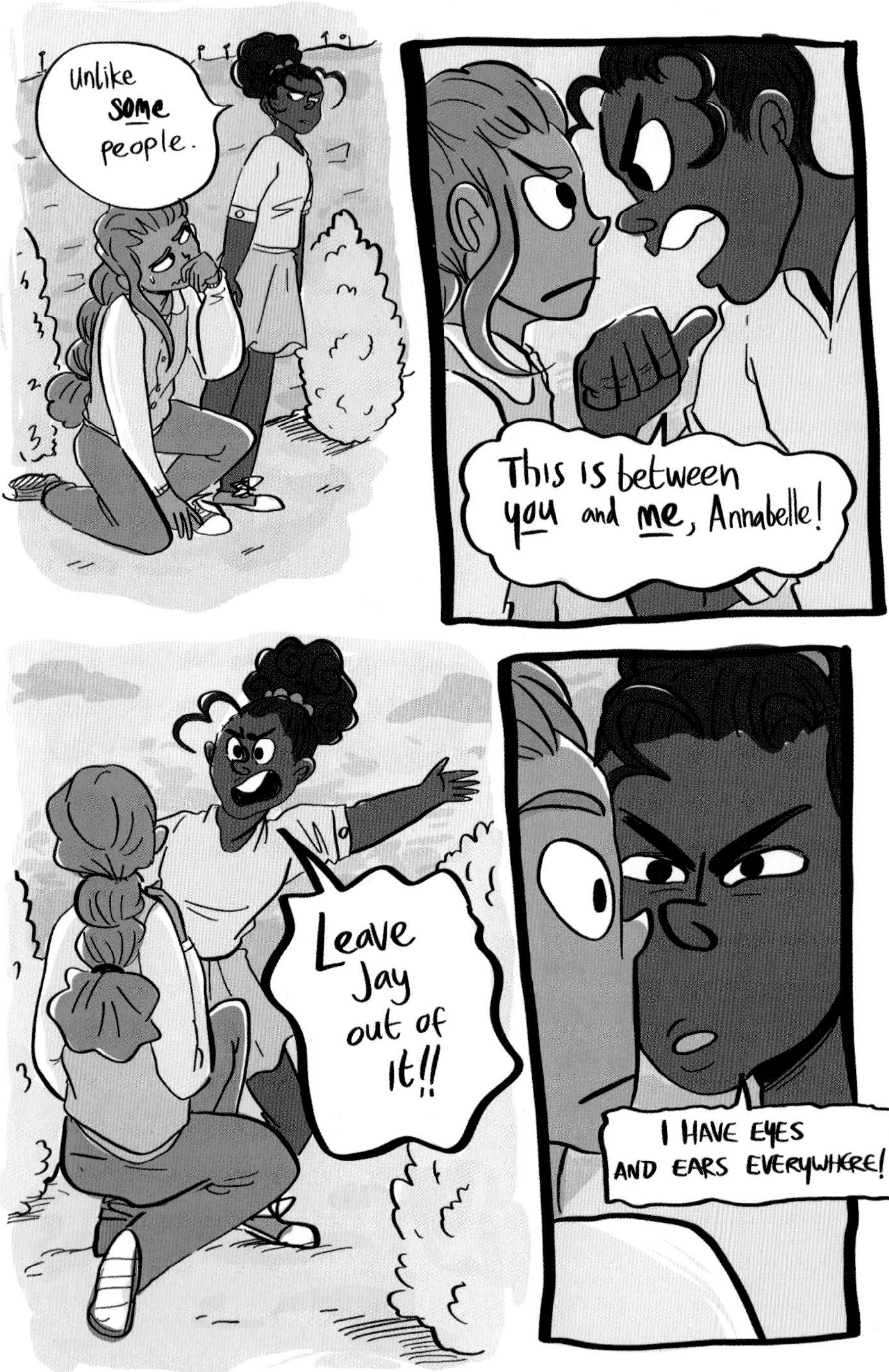
Unlike some people.
This is between you and me, Annabelle!
Leave Jay out of it!!
I HAVE EYES AND EARS EVERYWHERE!

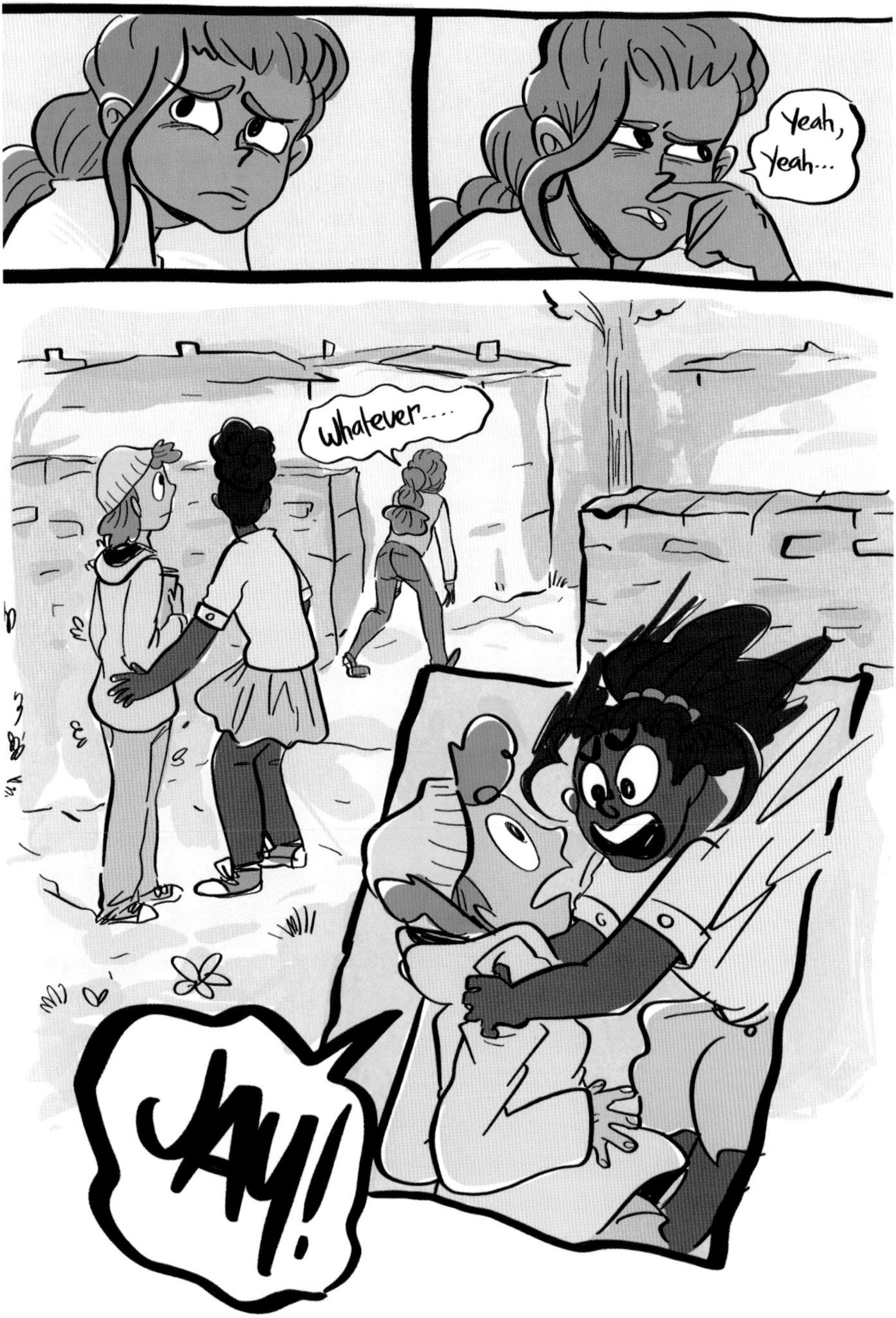
Yeah,
Yeah...
Whatever....
JAY!

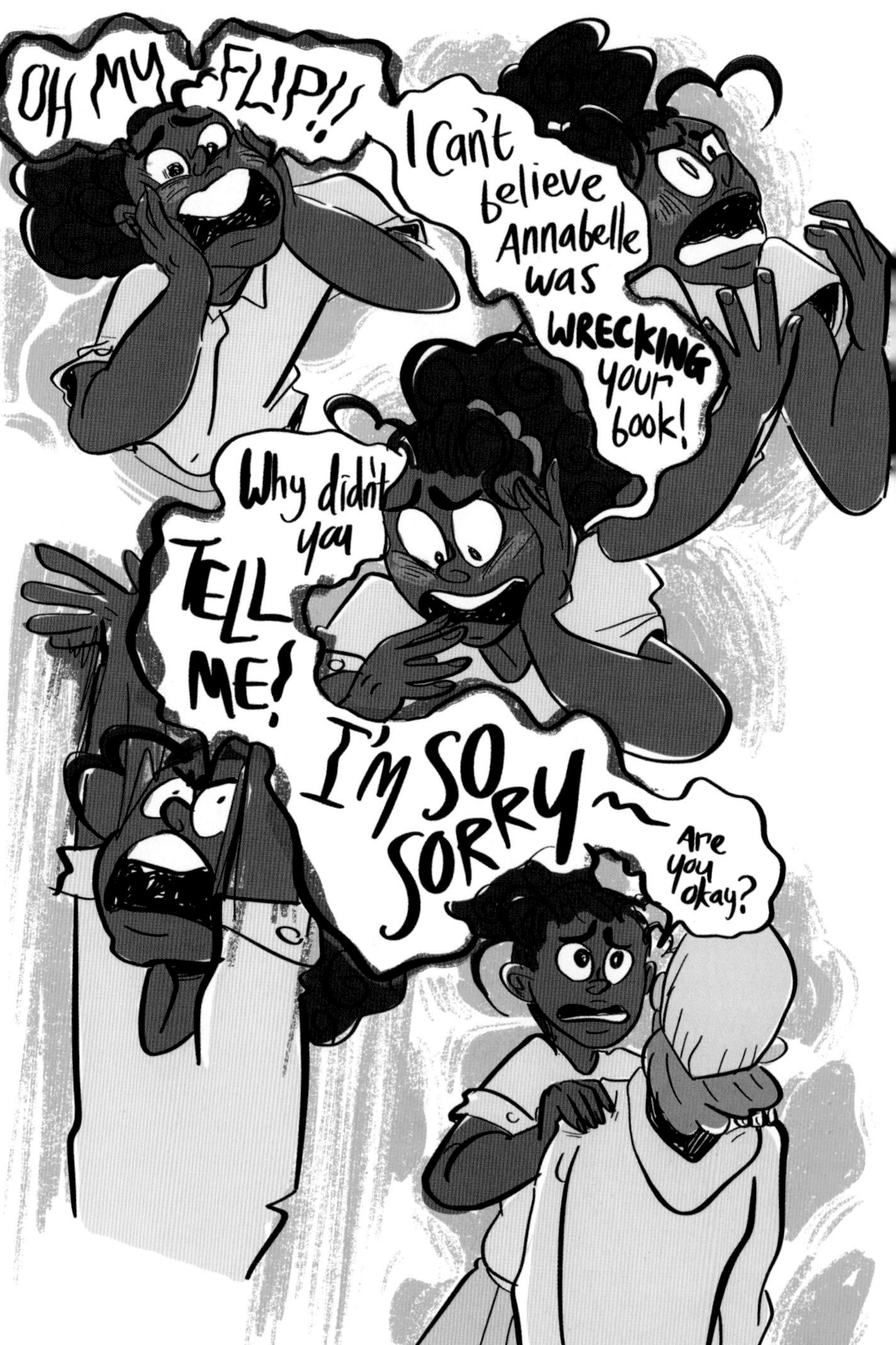
OH MY FLIP!!
I can't believe Annabelle was WRECKING your book!
Why didn't you TELL ME!
I'M SO SORRY~
Are you okay?

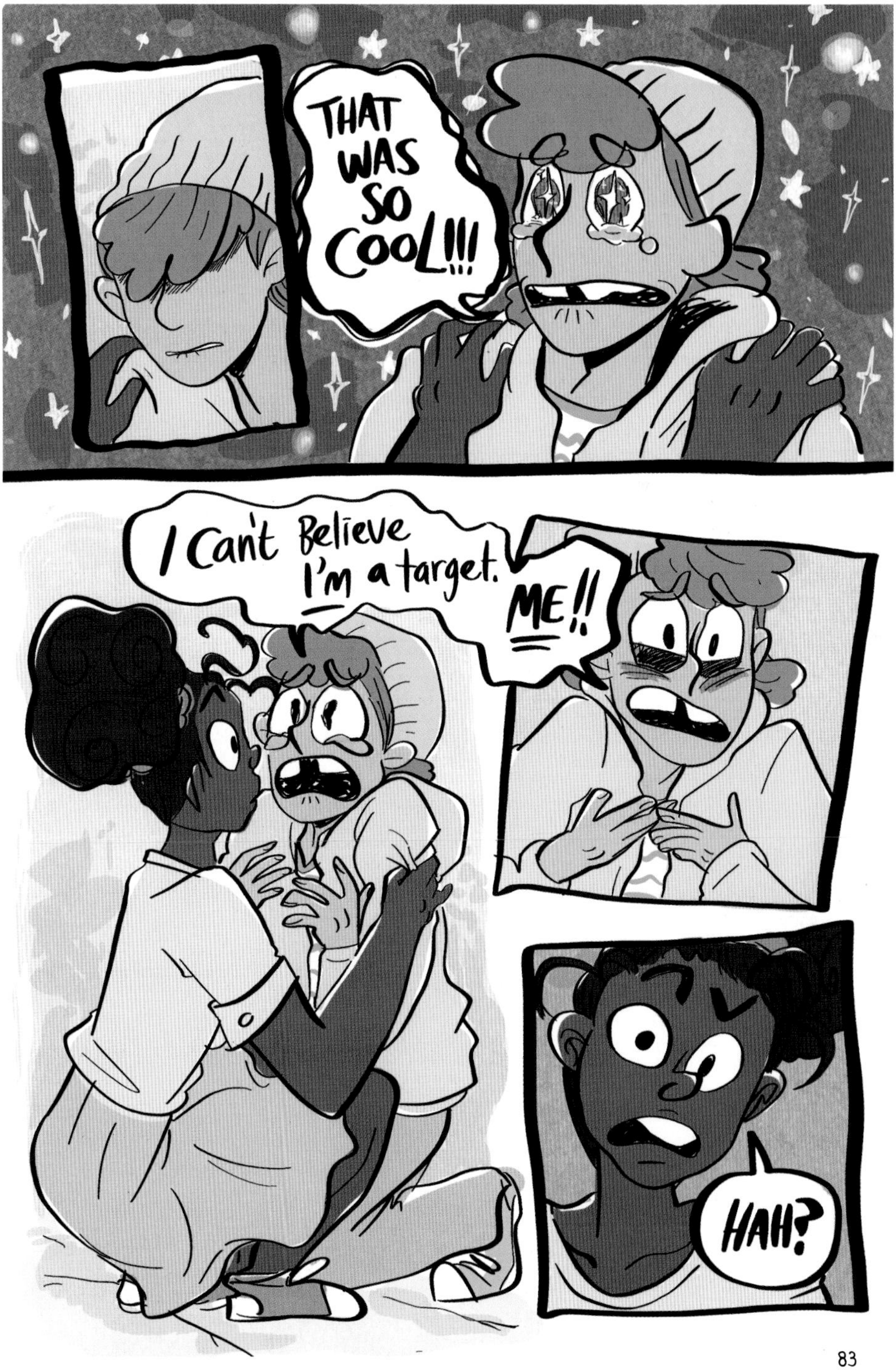
THAT WAS SO COOL!!!
I Can't Believe I'm a target.
ME!!
HAH?

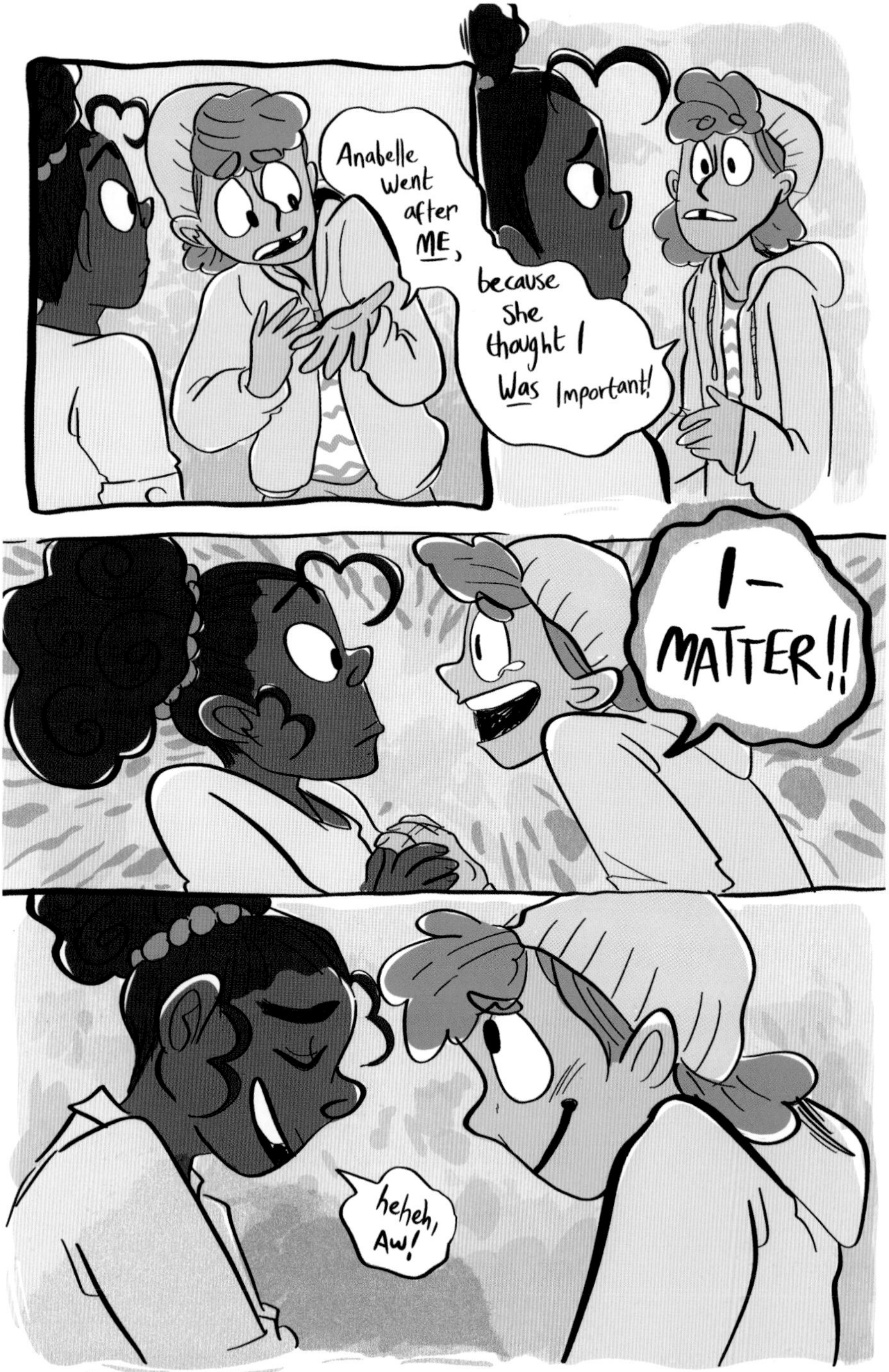

Anabelle went after ME,
because she thought I Was Important!
I— MATTER!!
heheh, Aw!

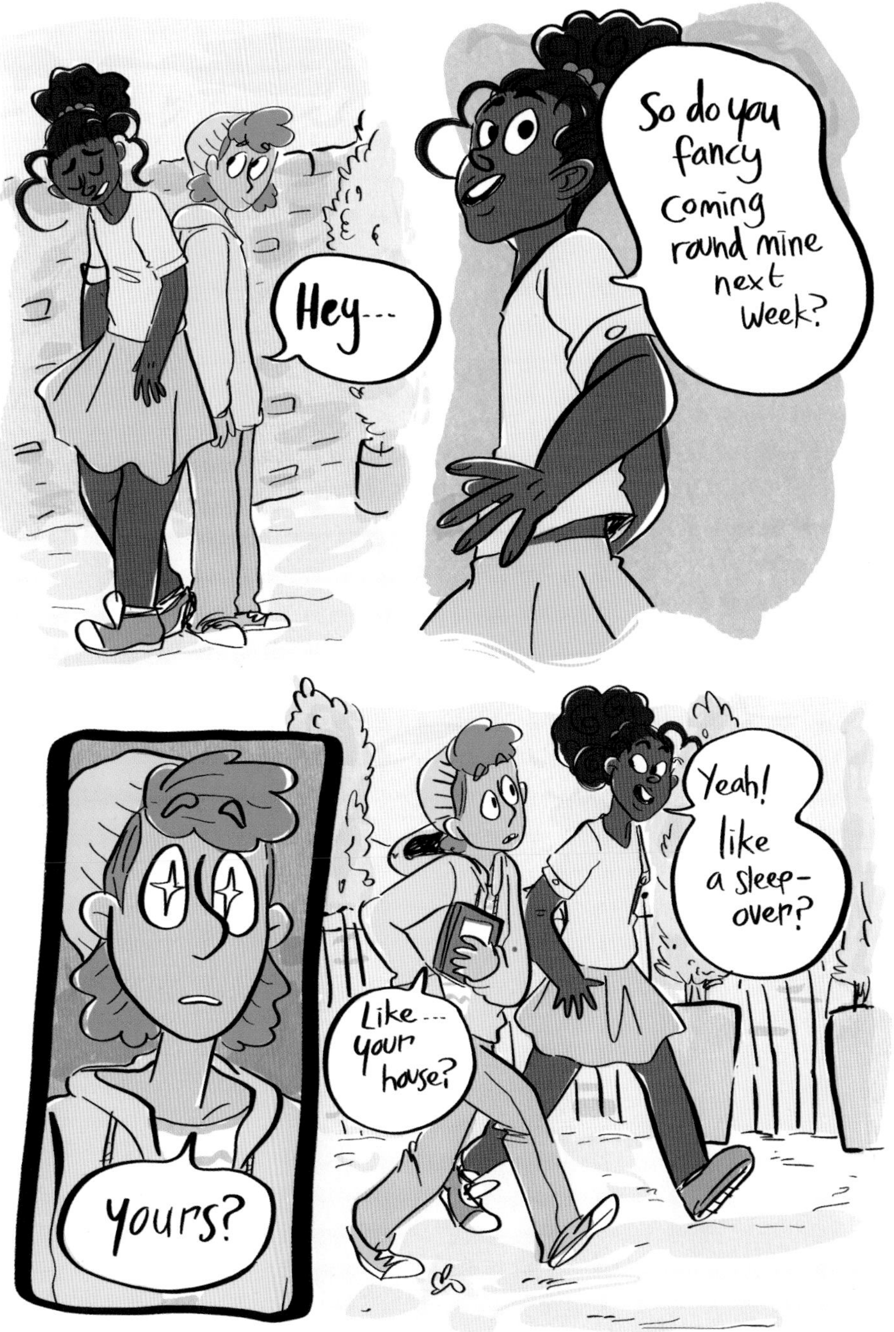
Hey...
So do you fancy coming round mine next week?
yours?
Yeah! like a sleep-over?
Like... your house?

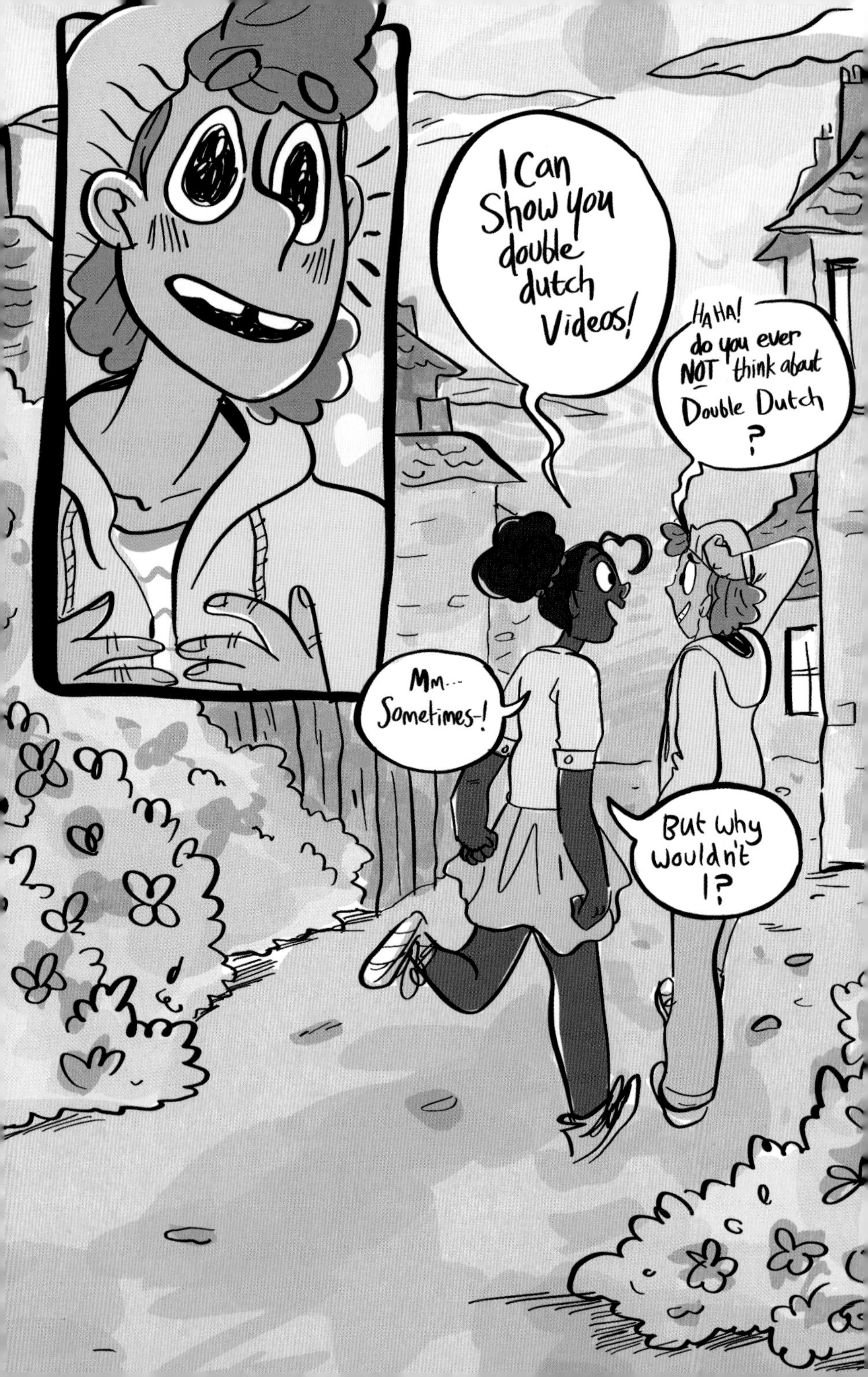
I can Show you double dutch Videos!
HAHA! do you ever NOT think about Double Dutch ?
Mm... Sometimes-!
But why wouldn't I?

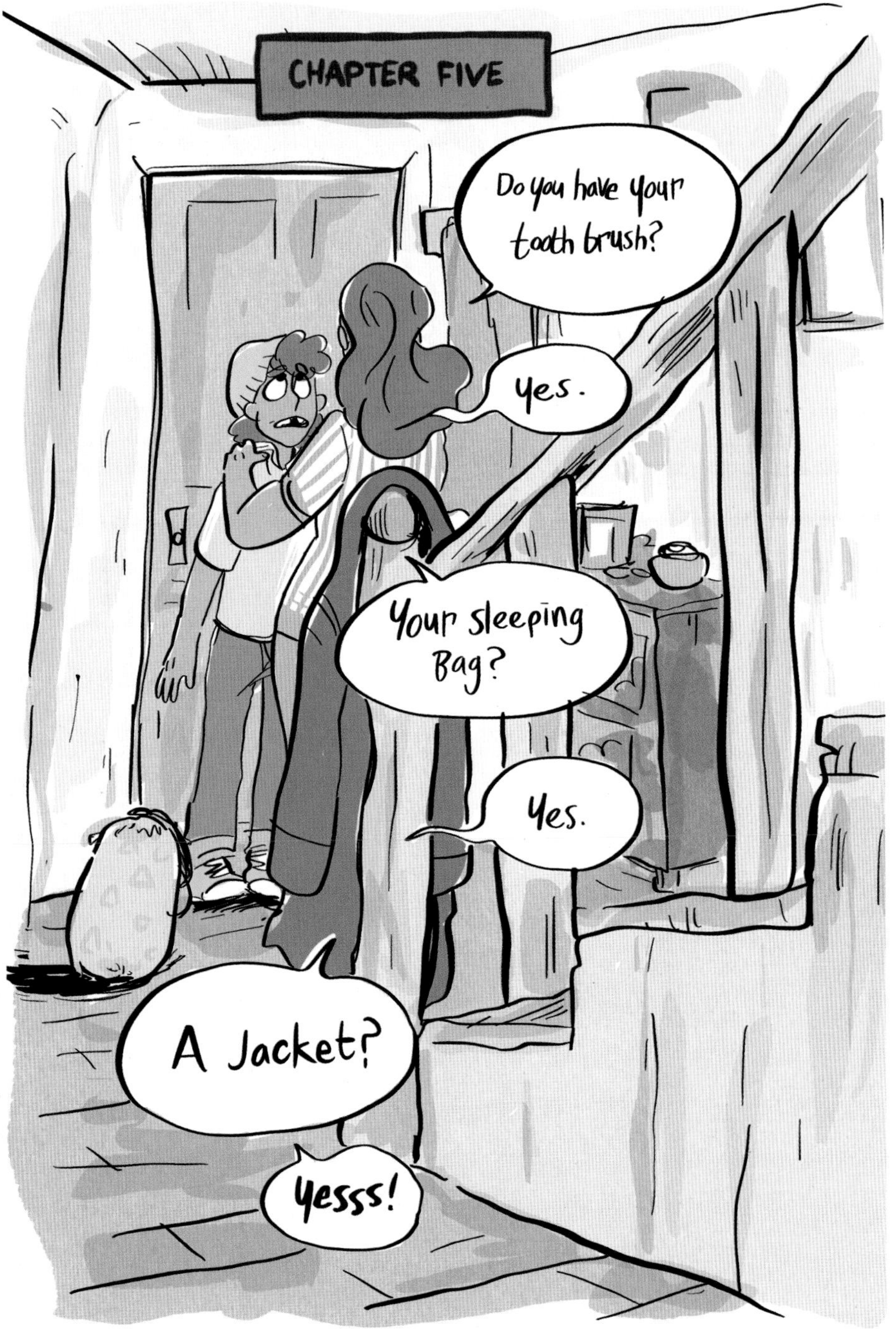
CHAPTER FIVE
Do you have your tooth brush?
Yes.
Your sleeping Bag?
Yes.
A Jacket?
Yesss!

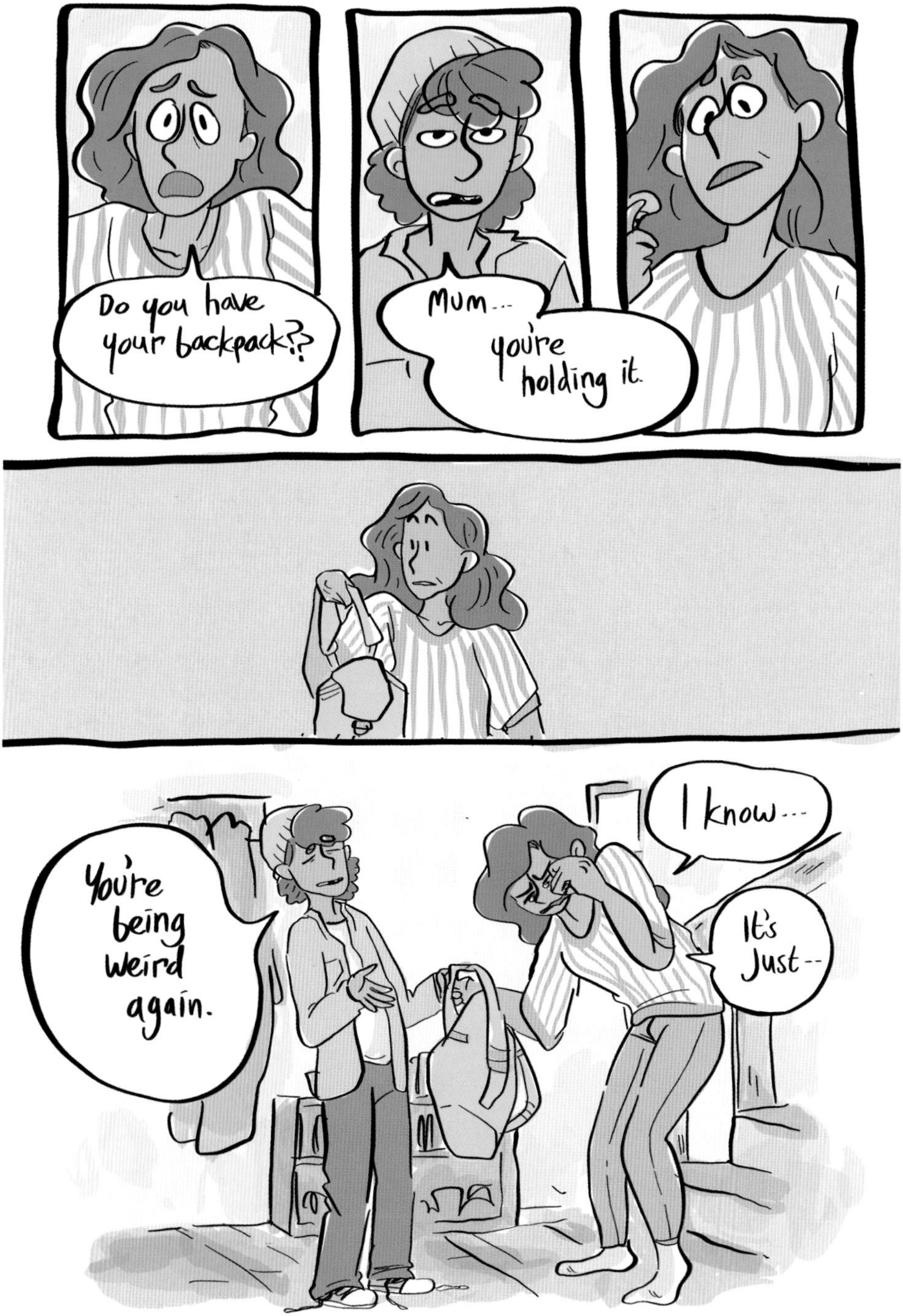
Do you have your backpack?!?
Mum...
you're holding it.
You're being weird again.
I know...
It's Just--

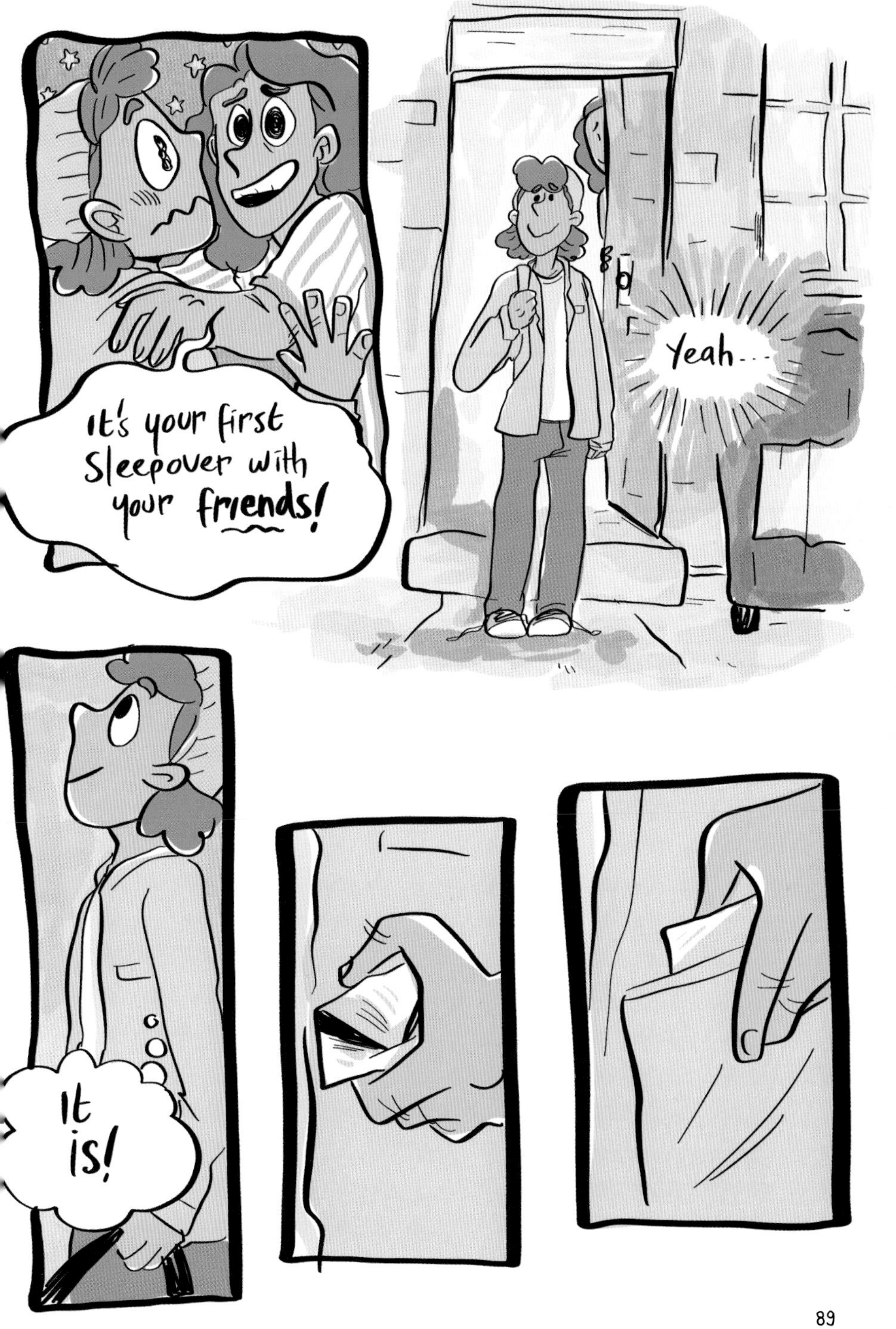

It's your first Sleepover with your friends!
Yeah...
It is!

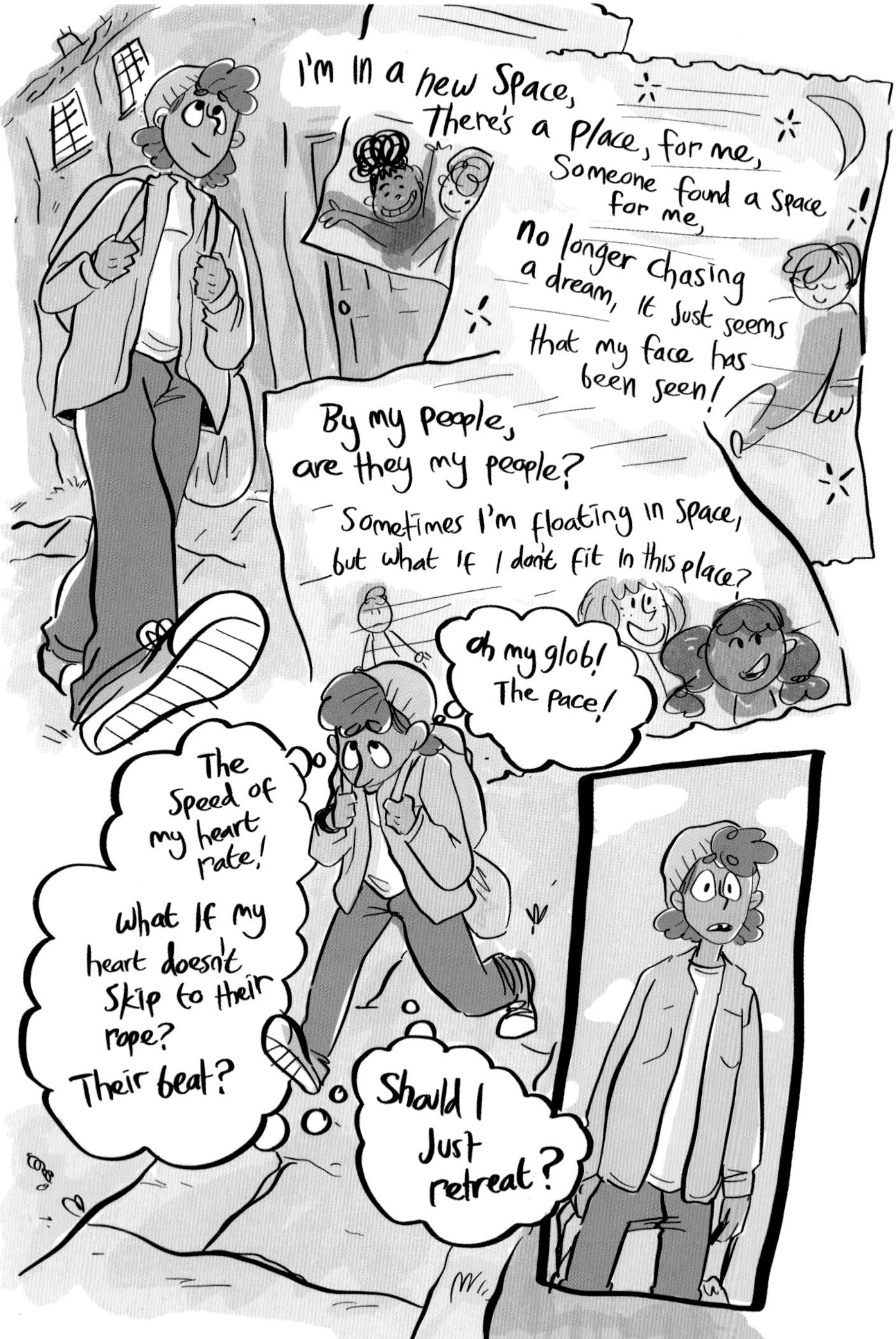
I'm in a new Space,
There's a place, for me,
Someone found a Space for me,
no longer chasing a dream, it Just seems that my face has been seen!
By my people, are they my people?
Sometimes I'm floating in Space, but what if I don't fit in this place?
oh my glob! The pace!
The Speed of my heart rate!
What If my heart doesn't Skip to their rope? Their beat?
Should I Just retreat?

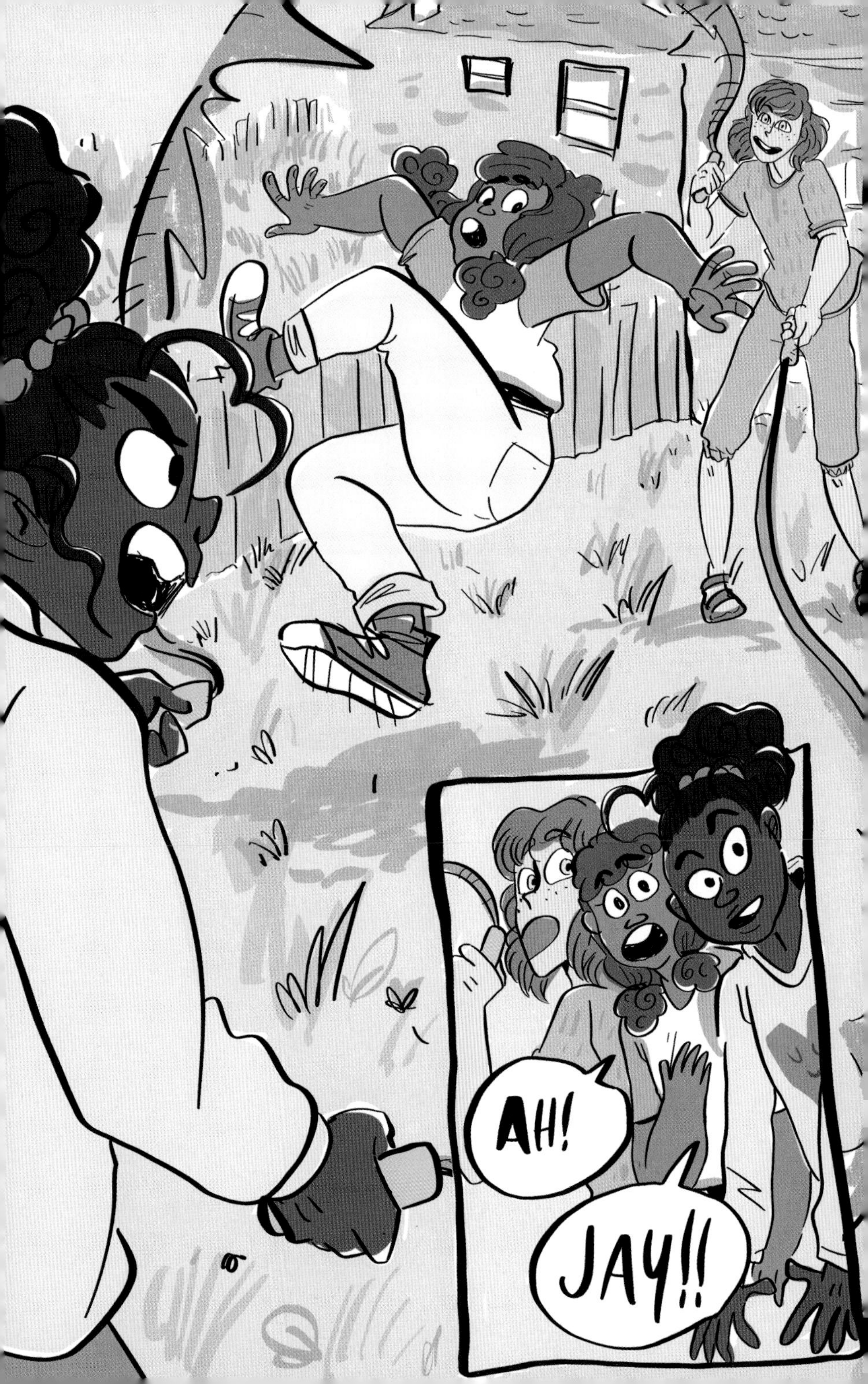
AH!
JAY!!

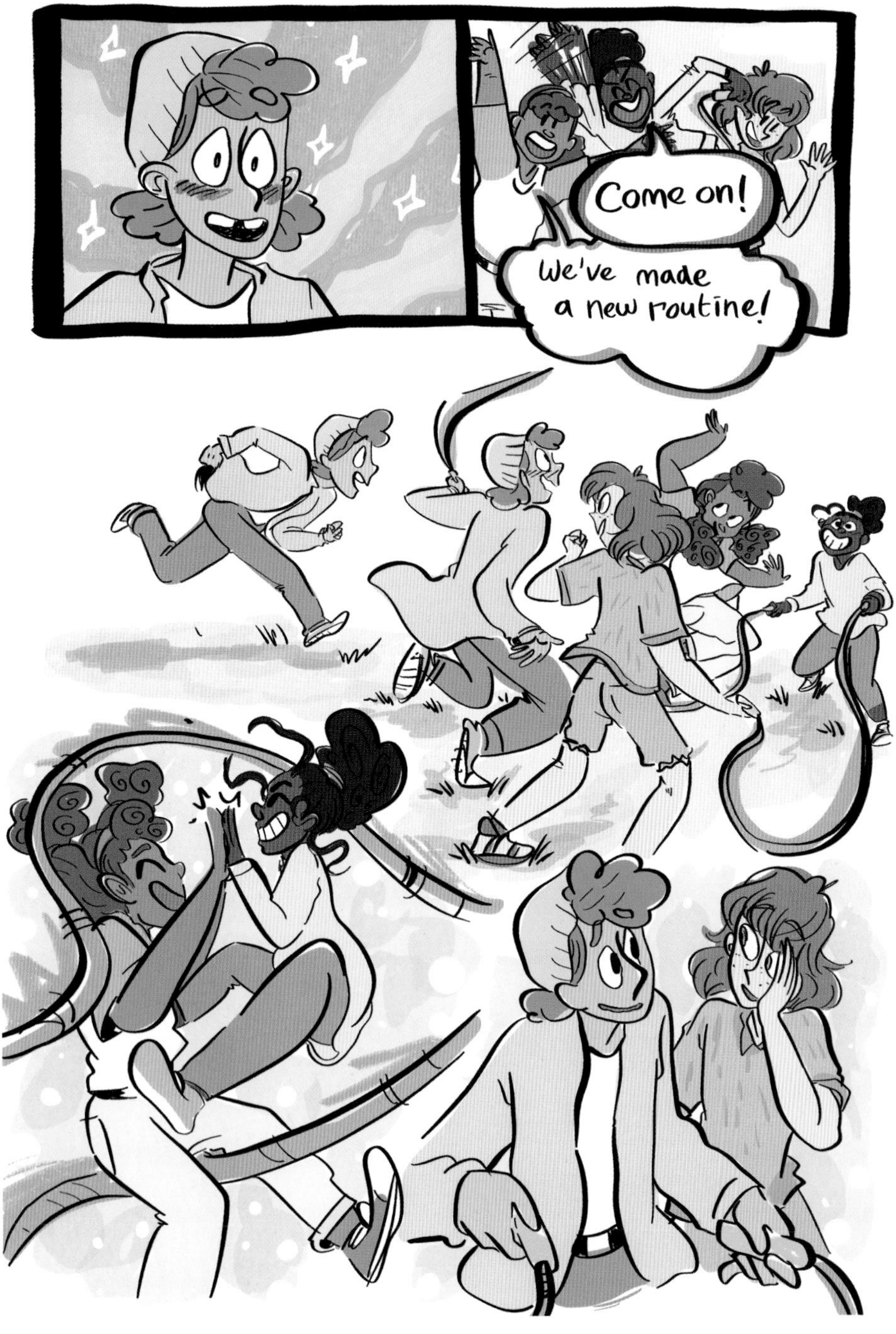
Come on!
We've made a new routine!

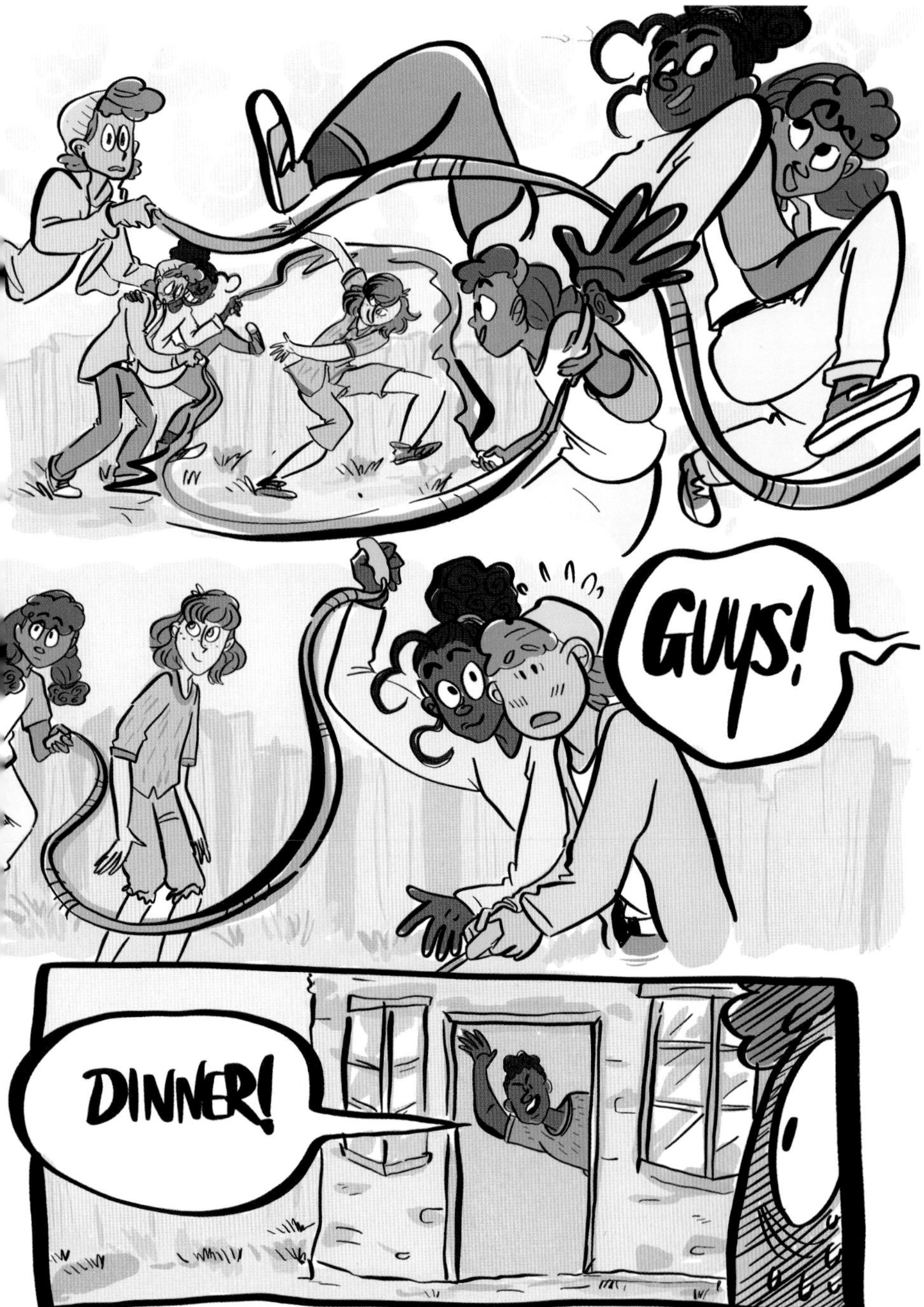
GUYS!
DINNER!

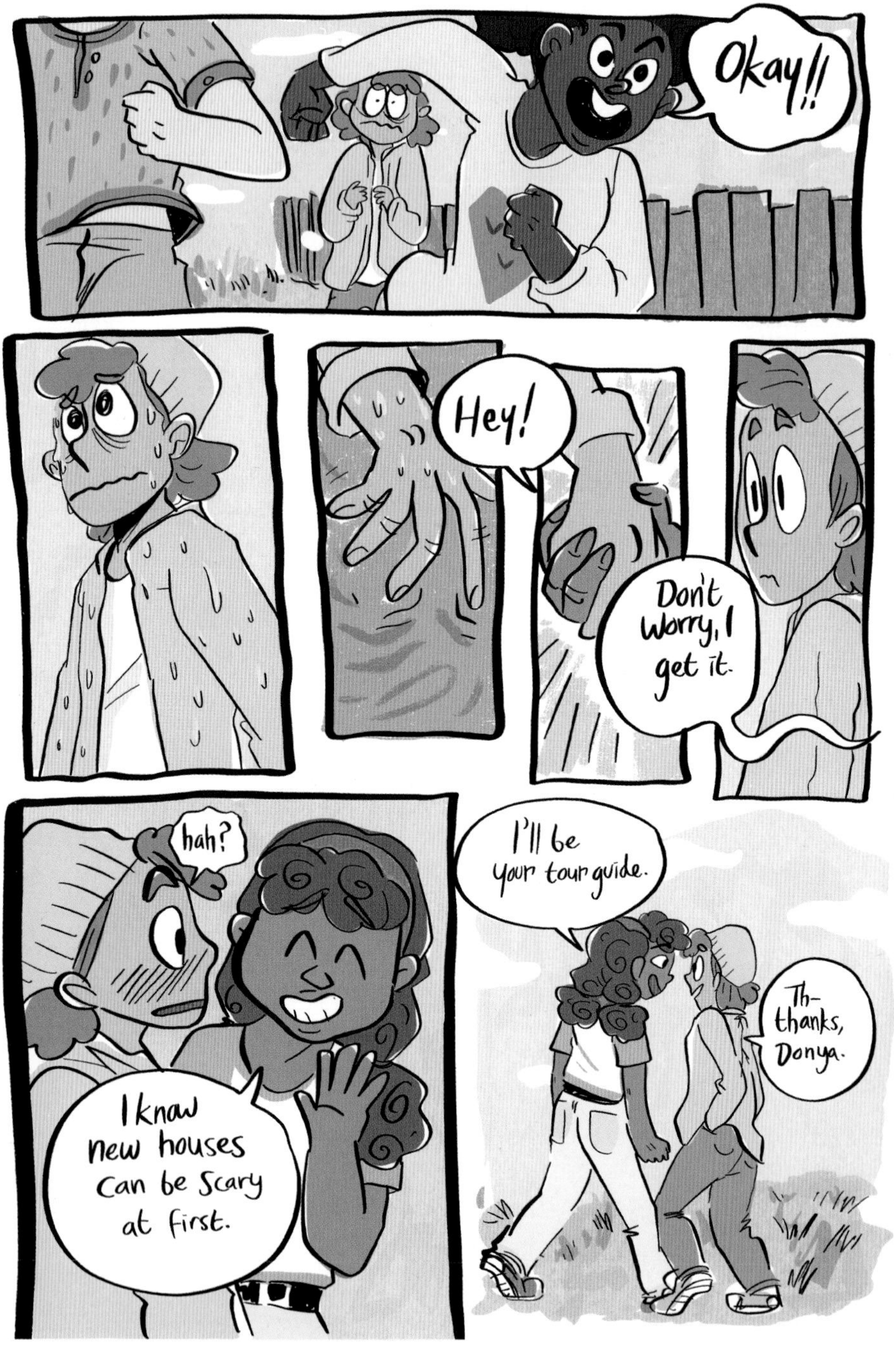
Okay!!
Hey!
Don't worry, I get it.
hah?
I know new houses can be Scary at first.
I'll be your tour guide.
Th-thanks, Donya.

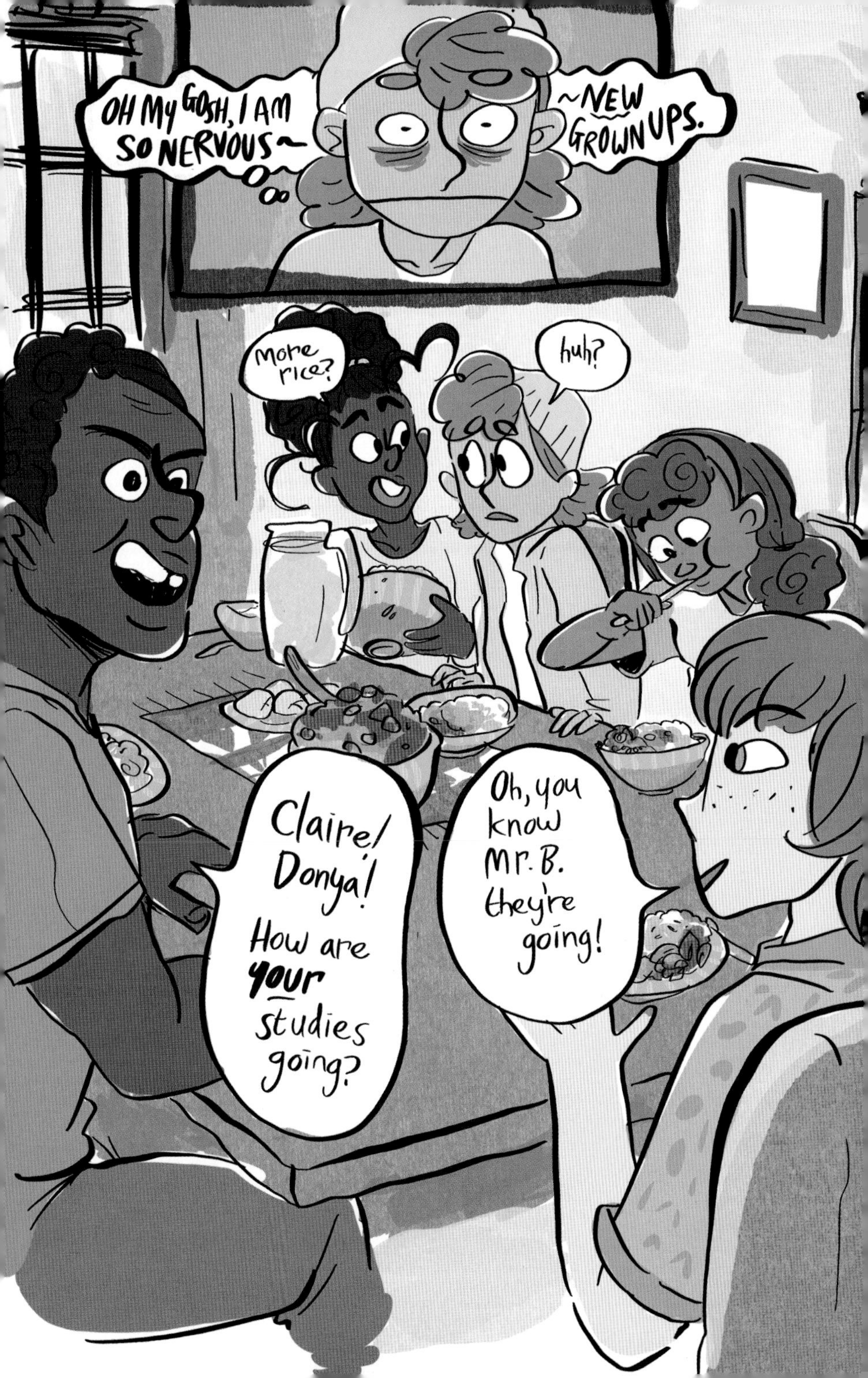
OH MY GOSH, I AM SO NERVOUS~
~NEW GROWN UPS.
More rice?
huh?
Claire! Donya! How are YOUR studies going?
Oh, you know Mr. B. they're going!

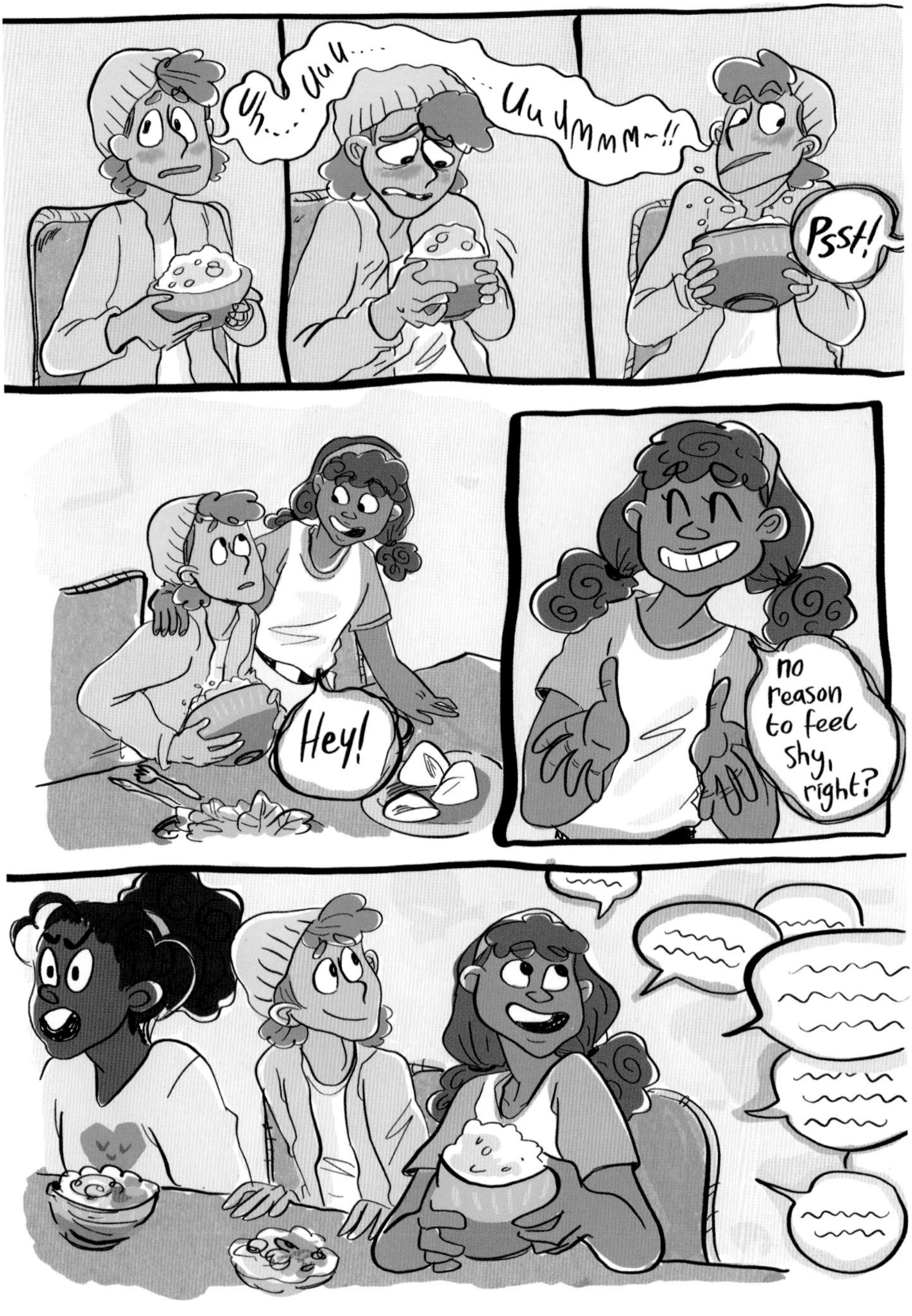
Uh... Uuu... ...Uuummm~!!
Psst!
Hey!
no reason to feel shy, right?

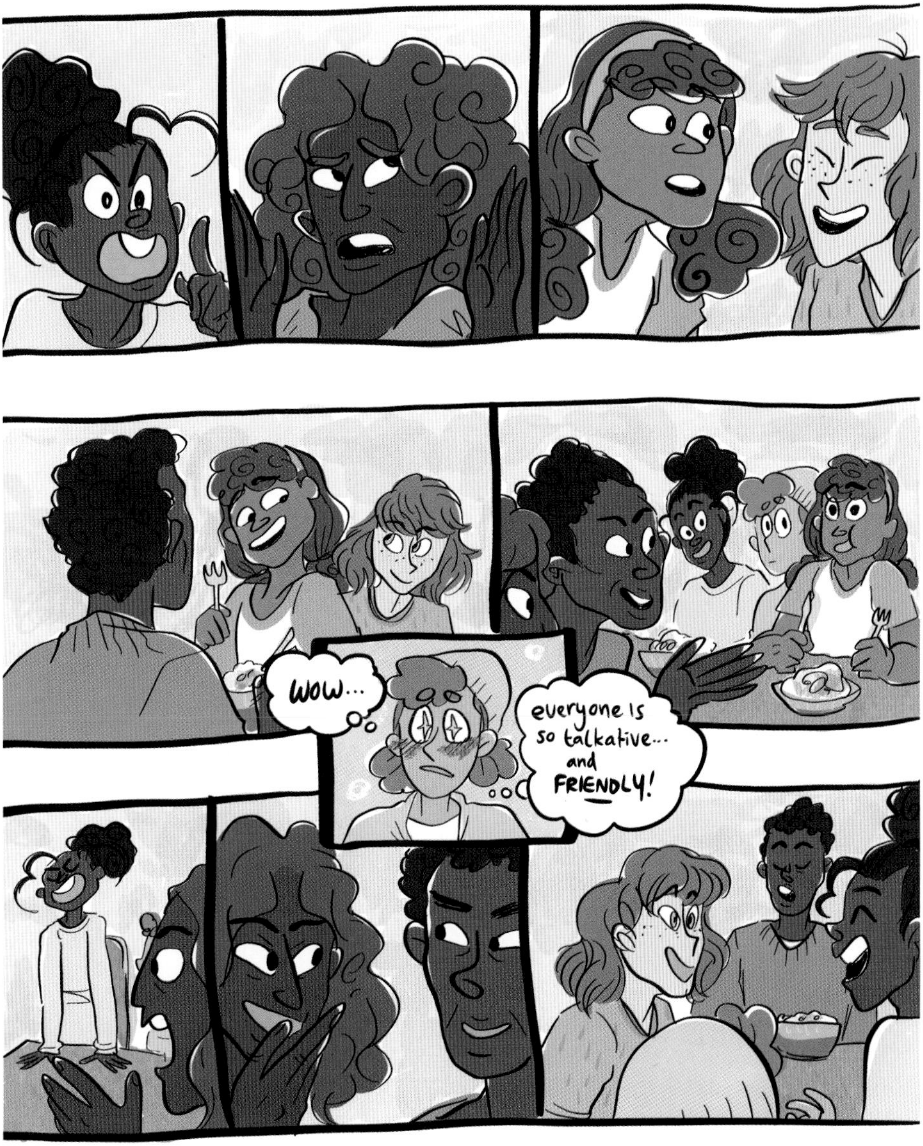
WOW...
everyone is so talkative... and FRIENDLY!

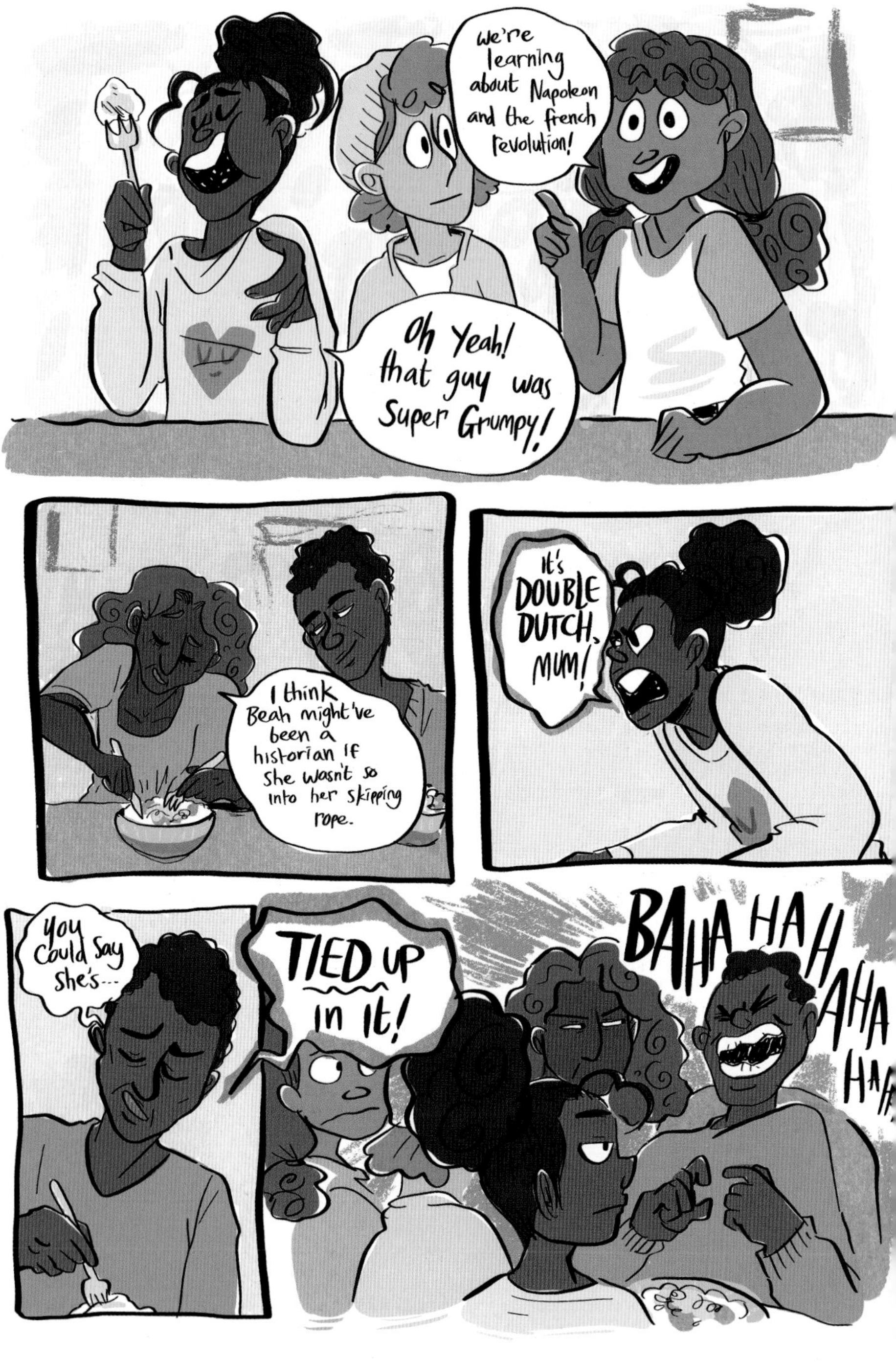

We're learning about Napoleon and the french revolution!
Oh Yeah! that guy was Super Grumpy!
I think Beah might've been a historian if she wasn't so into her skipping rope.
It's DOUBLE DUTCH, MUM!
you could say she's...
TIED UP in it!
BAHA HA HA AHA

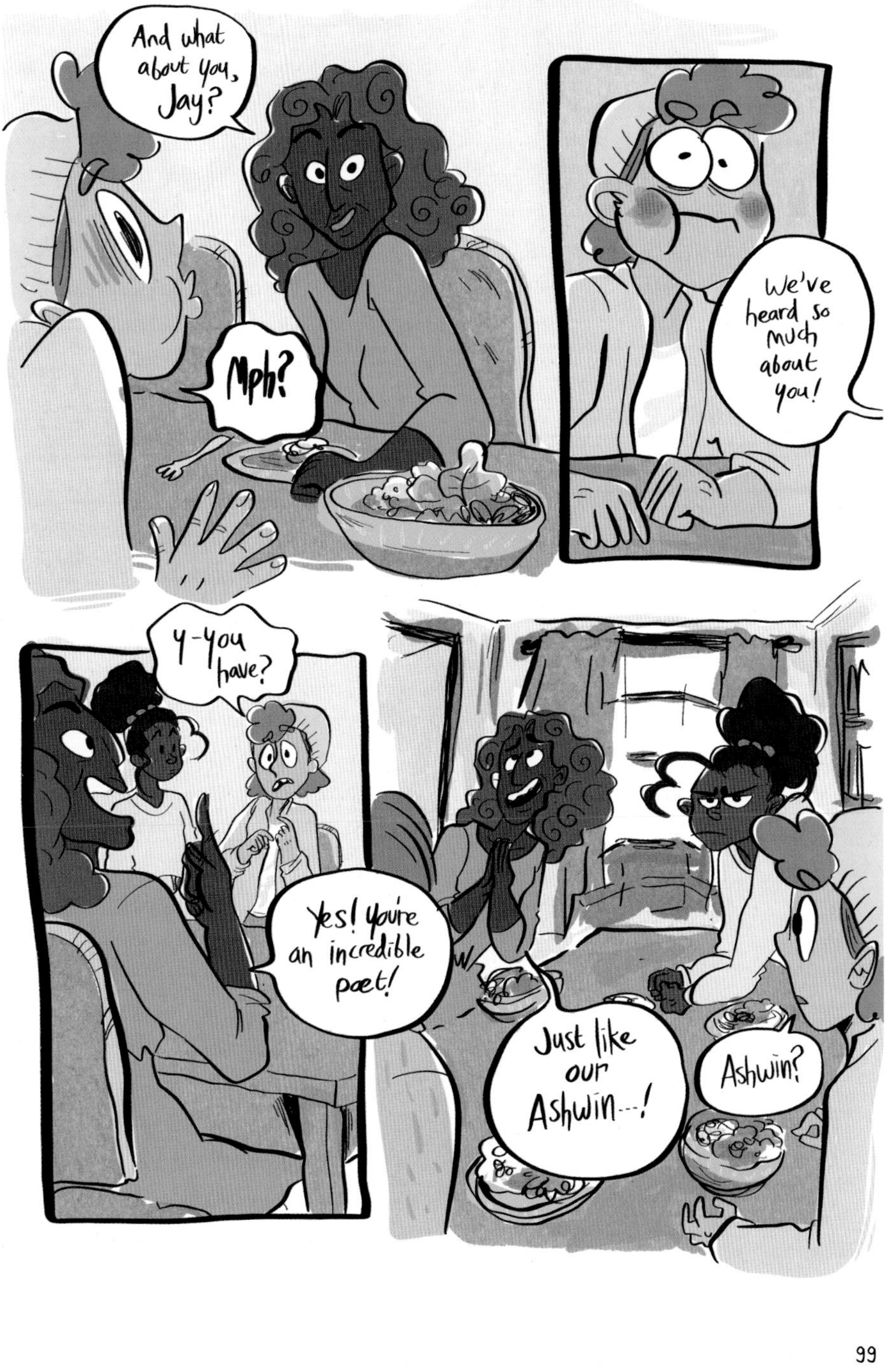
And what about you, Jay?
Mph?
We've heard so much about you!
Y-You have?
Yes! You're an incredible poet!
Just like our Ashwin...!
Ashwin?

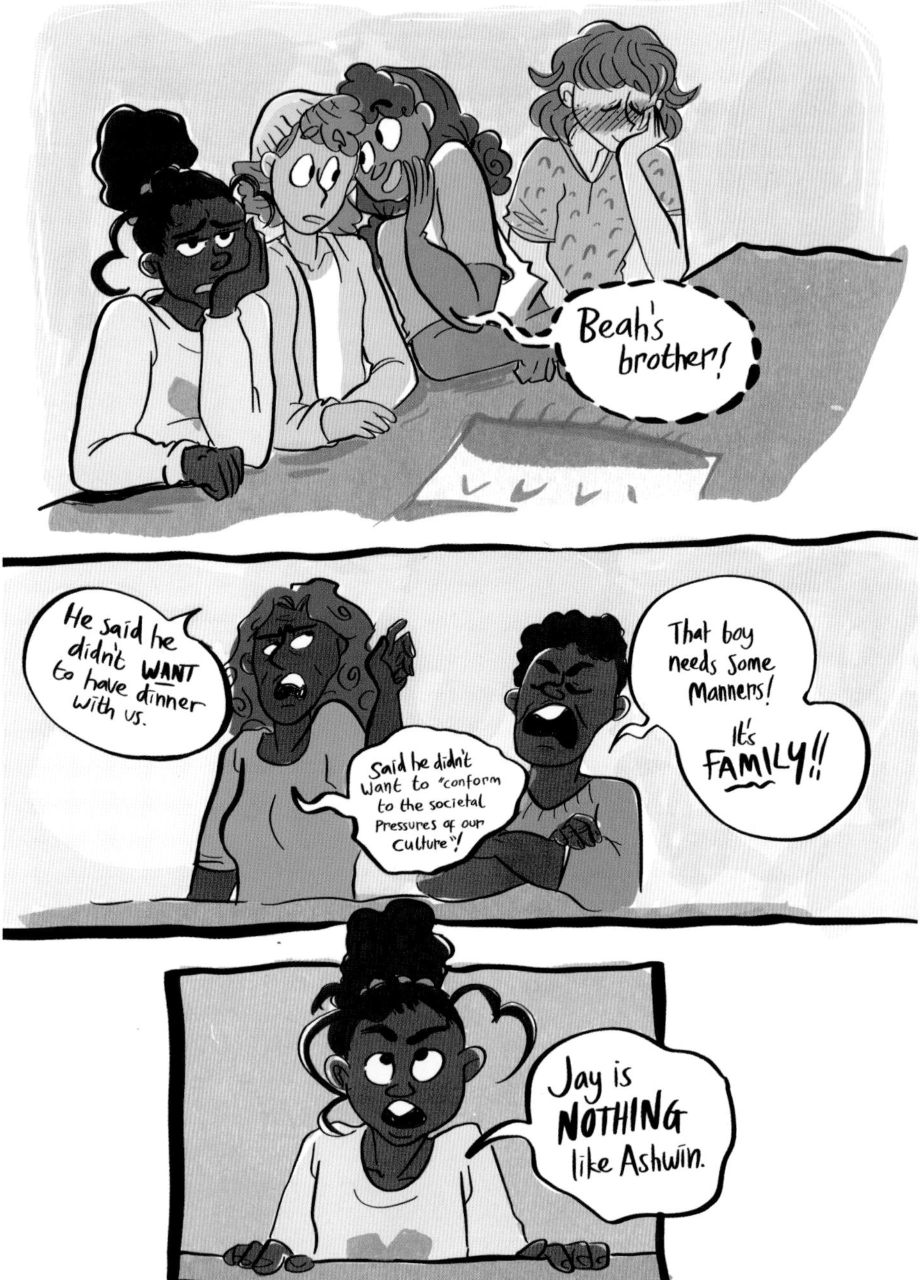
Beah's brother?!
He said he didn't WANT to have dinner with us.
Said he didn't want to "conform to the societal pressures of our culture"!
That boy needs some manners!
It's FAMILY!!
Jay is NOTHING like Ashwin.

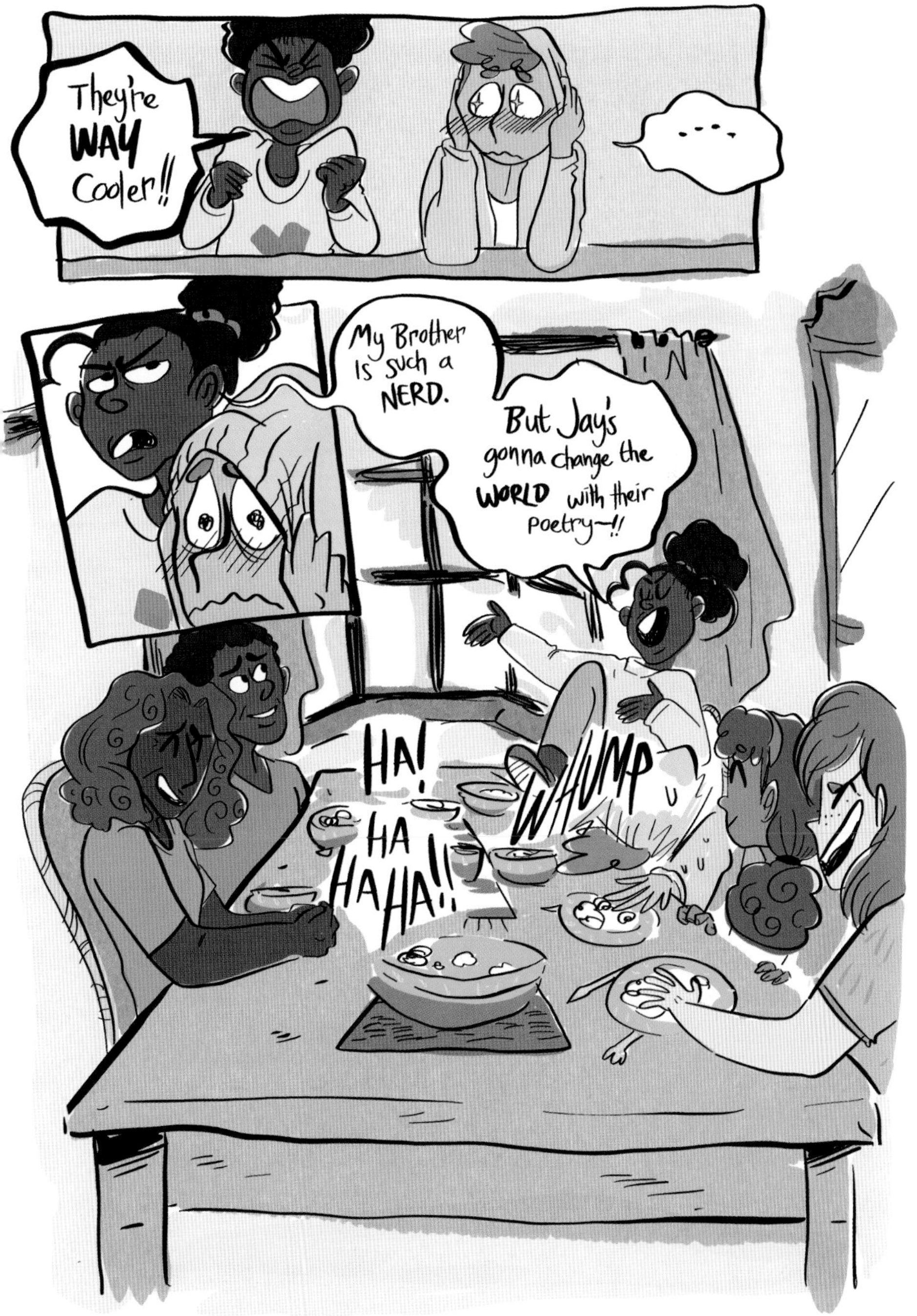

They're WAY Cooler!!
...
My Brother is such a NERD.
But Jay's gonna change the WORLD with their poetry~!!
HA! HA HAHA!!
WHUMP

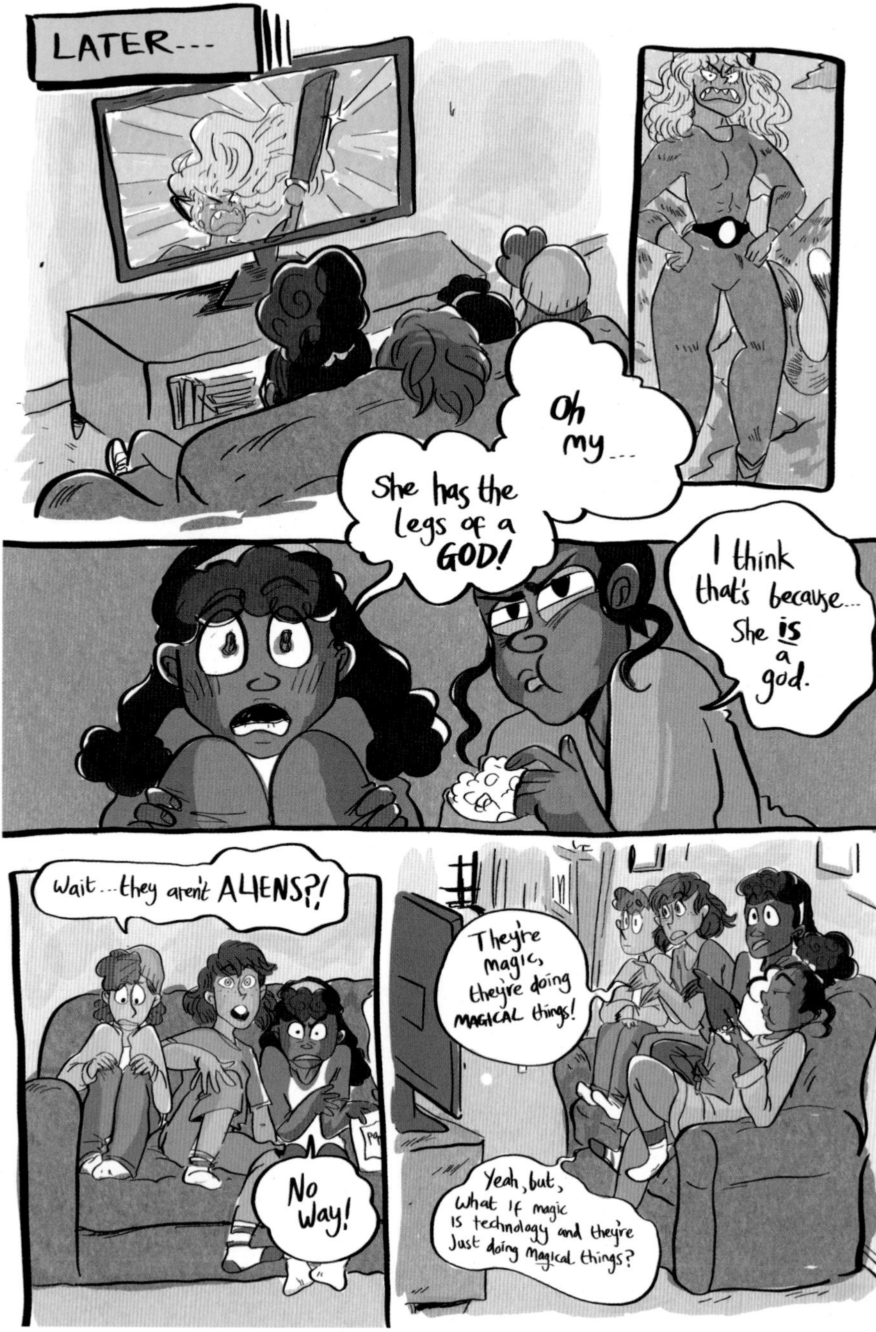
LATER...
Oh my...
She has the legs of a GOD!
I think that's because... She IS a god.
Wait...they aren't ALIENS?!
No way!
They're magic, they're doing MAGICAL things!
Yeah, but, what if magic is technology and they're just doing magical things?

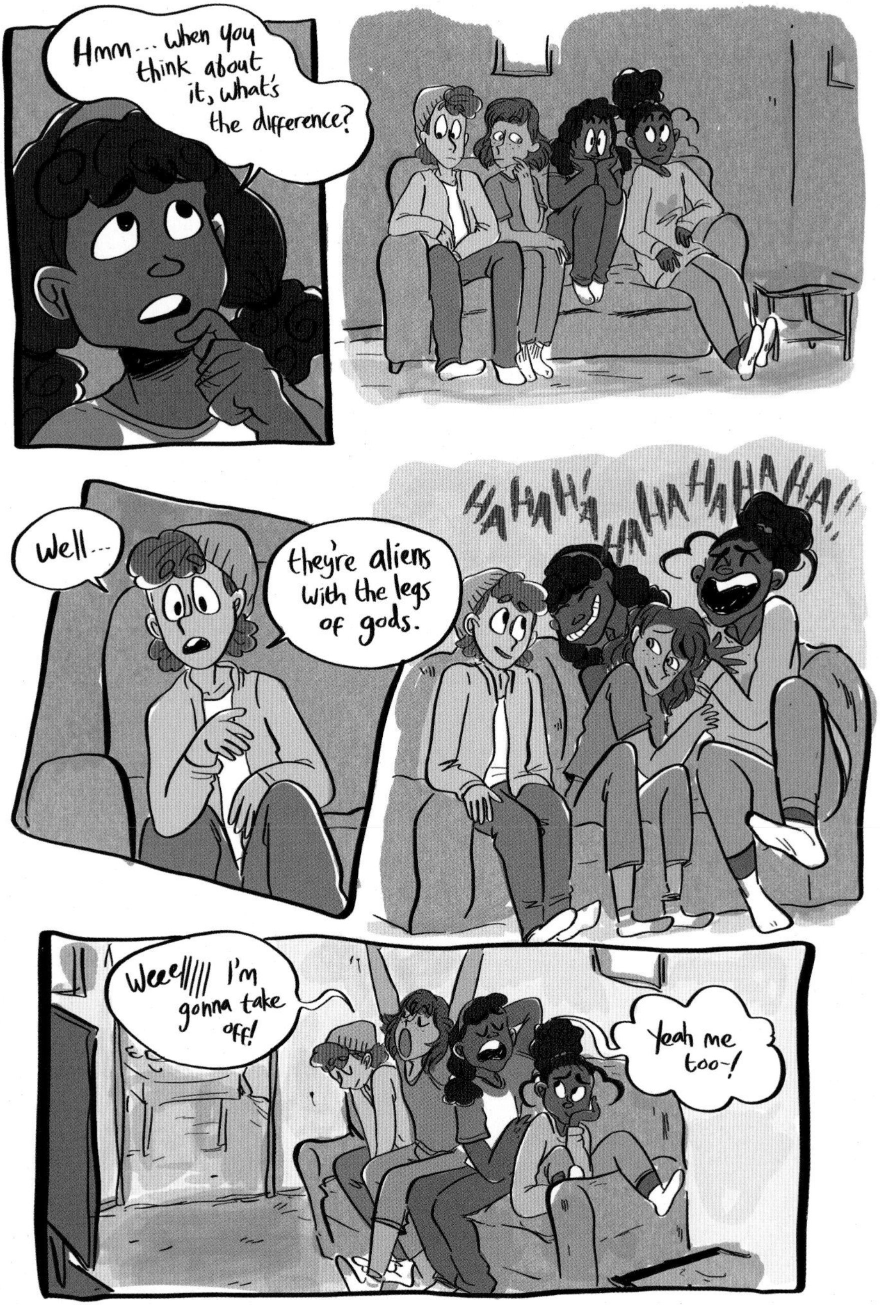
Hmm... when you think about it, what's the difference?
Well...
they're aliens with the legs of gods.
HAHAHA! HAHAHAHAHA!
Weeelllll I'm gonna take off!
Yeah me too-!

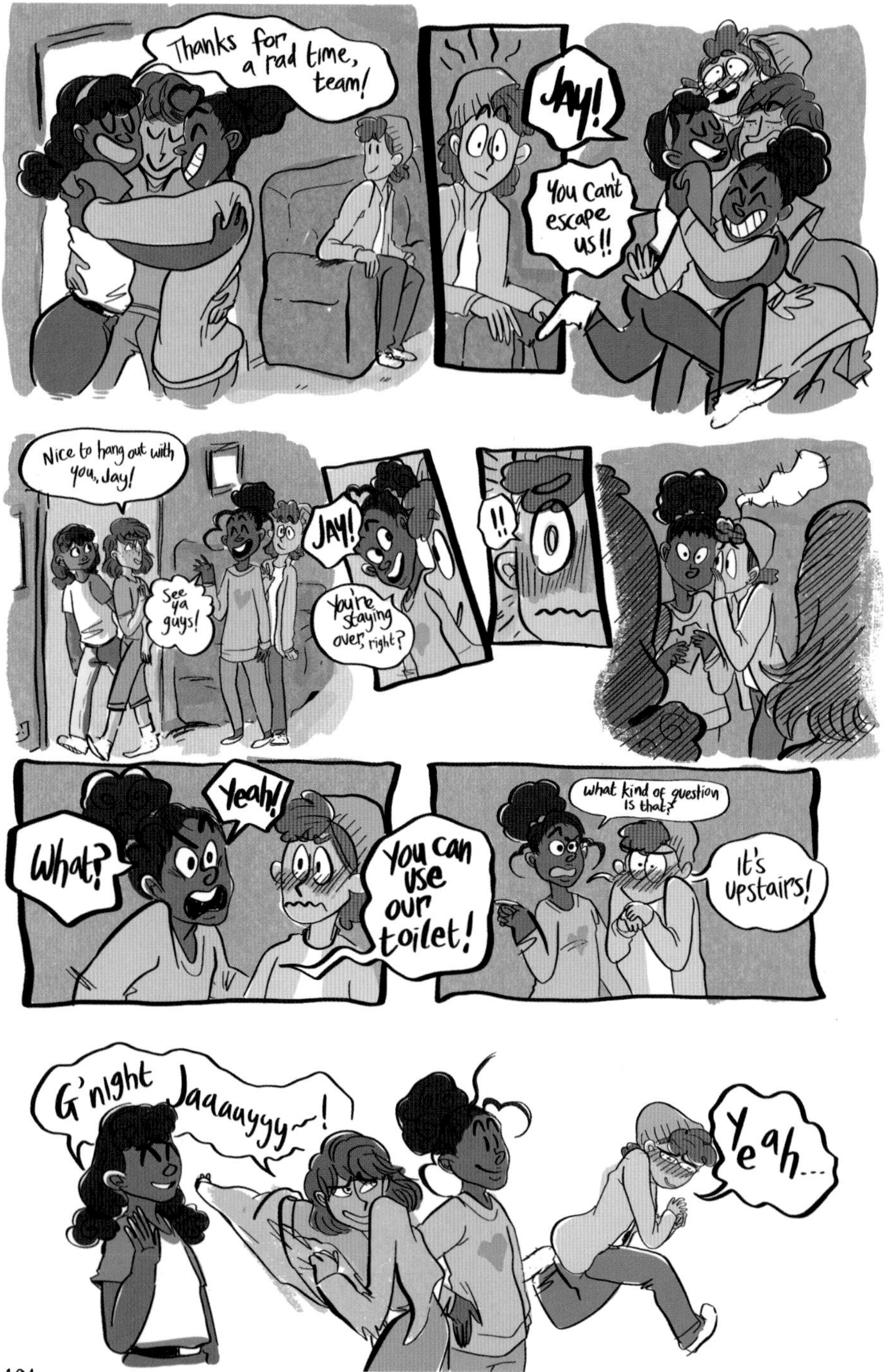
Thanks for a rad time, team!
JAY!
You can't escape us!!
Nice to hang out with you, Jay!
See ya guys!
JAY!
You're staying over, right?
!!
What?
Yeah!
You can use our toilet!
what kind of question is that?
It's upstairs!
G'night Jaaaayyy~!
Yeah...

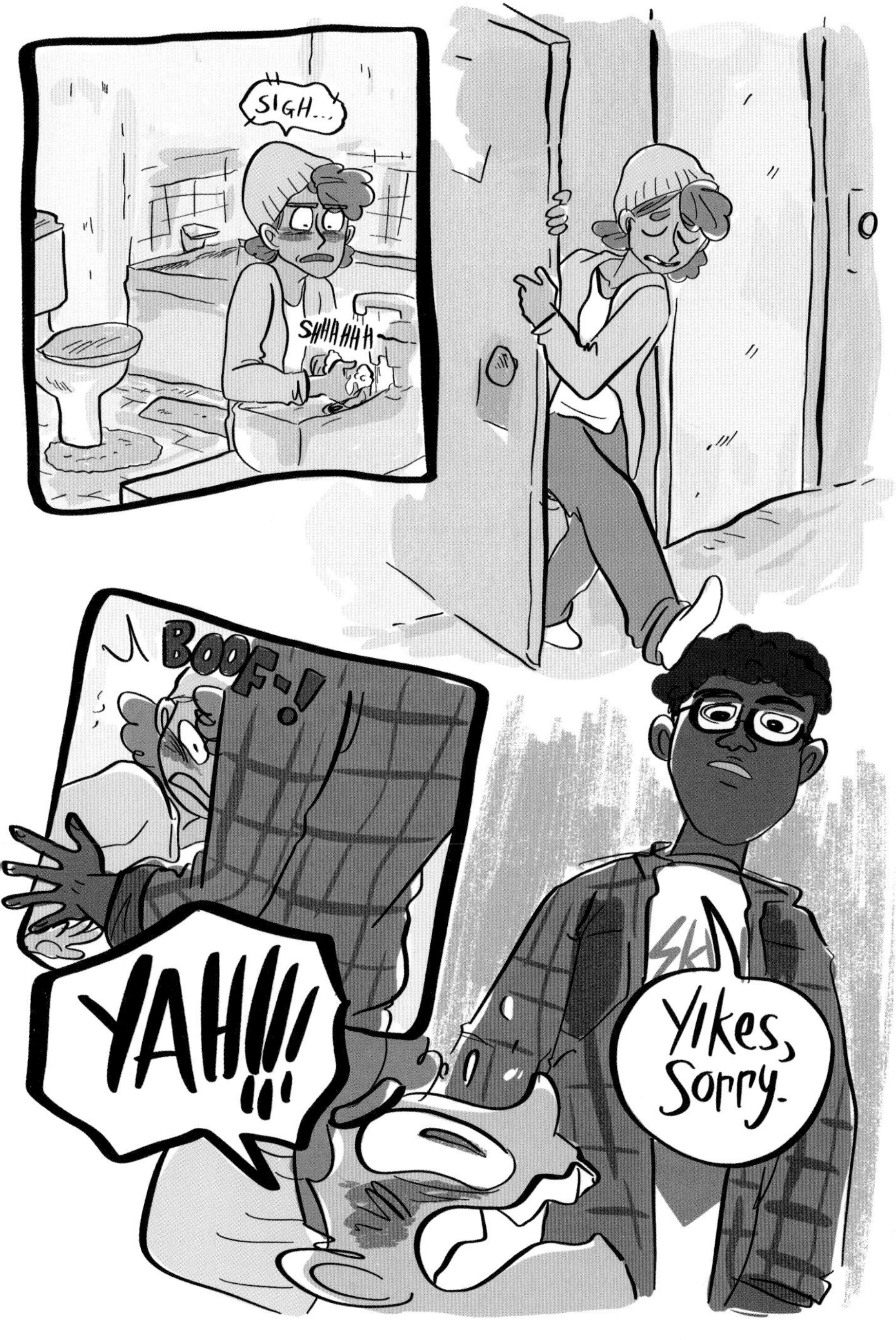
SIGH...
SHHHHHH
BOOF-!
YAH!!!!
Yikes, Sorry.

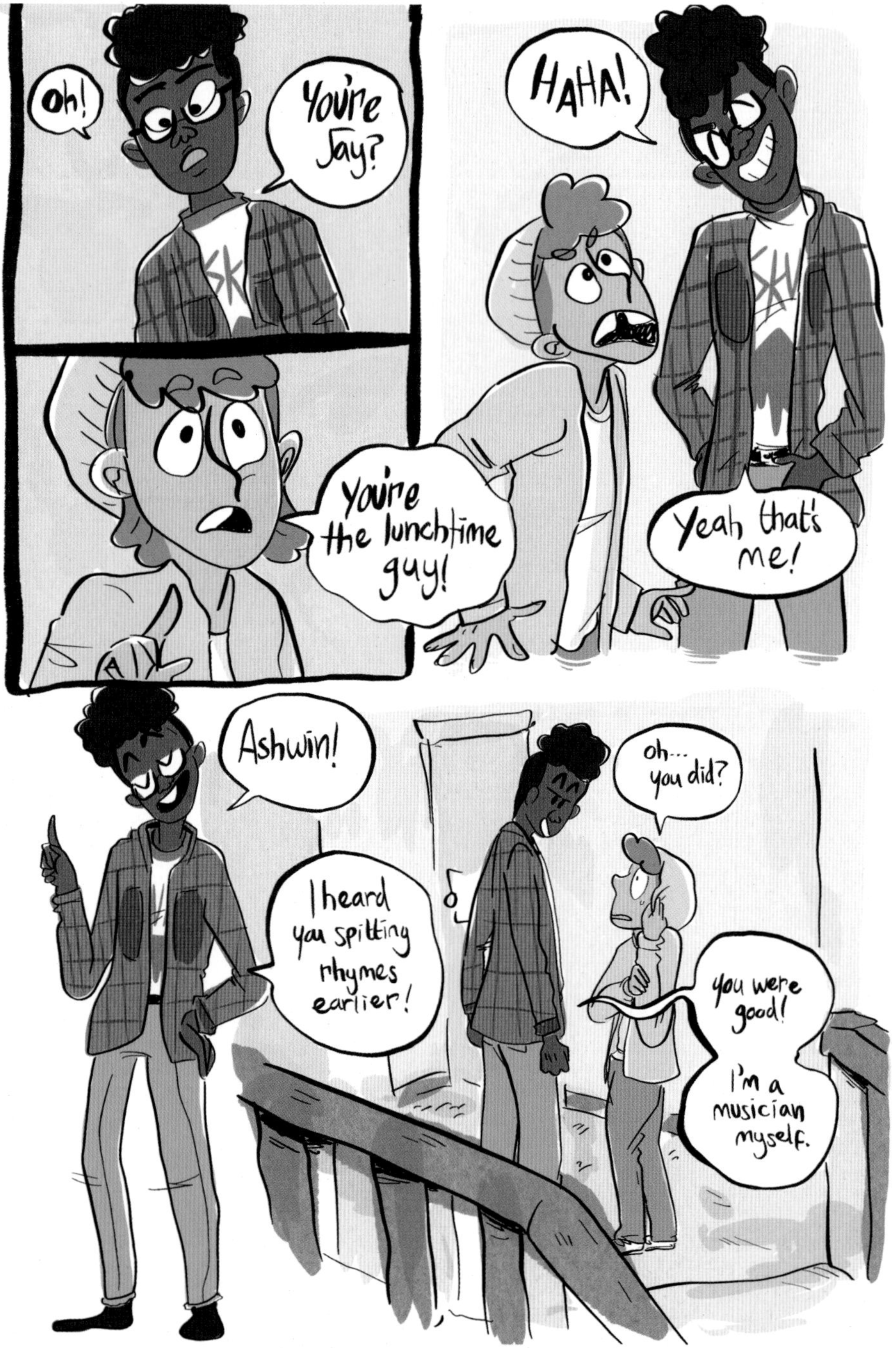
Oh!
You're Jay?
HAHA!
You're the lunchtime guy!
Yeah that's me!
Ashwin!
I heard you spitting rhymes earlier!
oh... you did?
you were good!
I'm a musician myself.

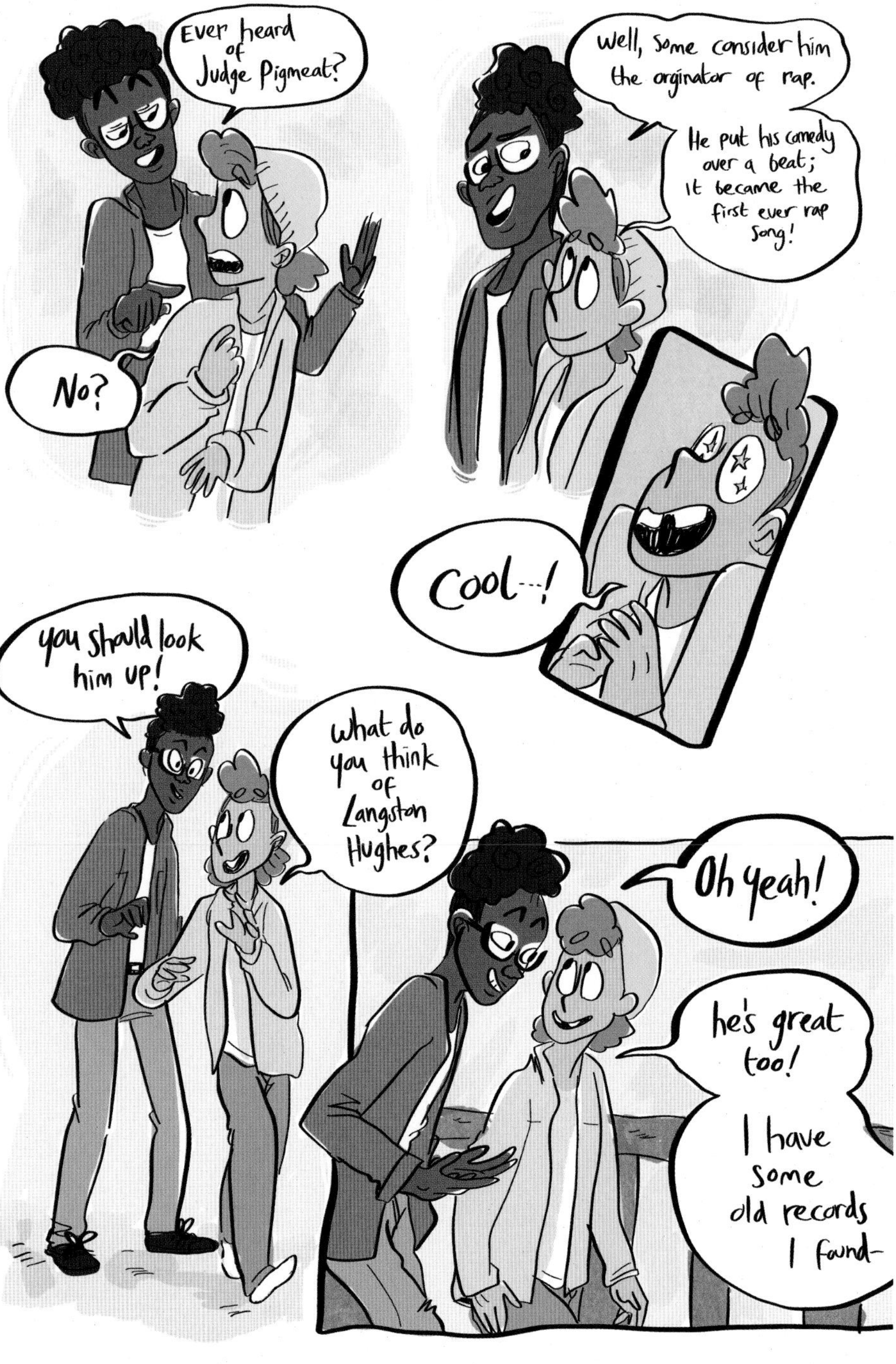
Ever heard of Judge Pigmeat?
No?
Well, some consider him the orginator of rap.
He put his comedy over a beat; it became the first ever rap song!
Cool...!
you should look him up!
what do you think of Langston Hughes?
Oh yeah!
he's great too!
I have some old records I found-

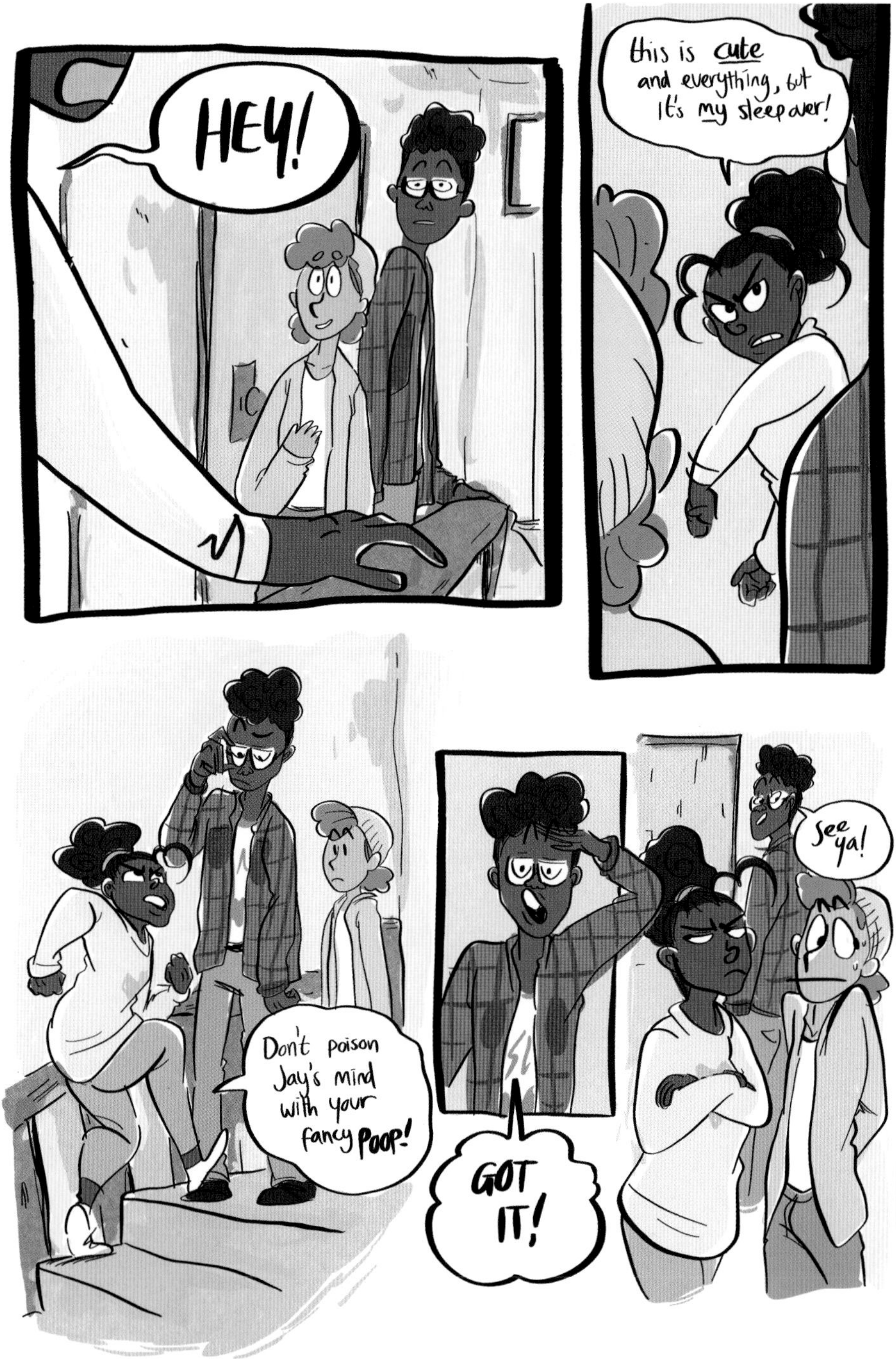
HEY!
this is cute and everything, but it's my sleepover!
Don't poison Jay's mind with your fancy POOP!
GOT IT!
See ya!

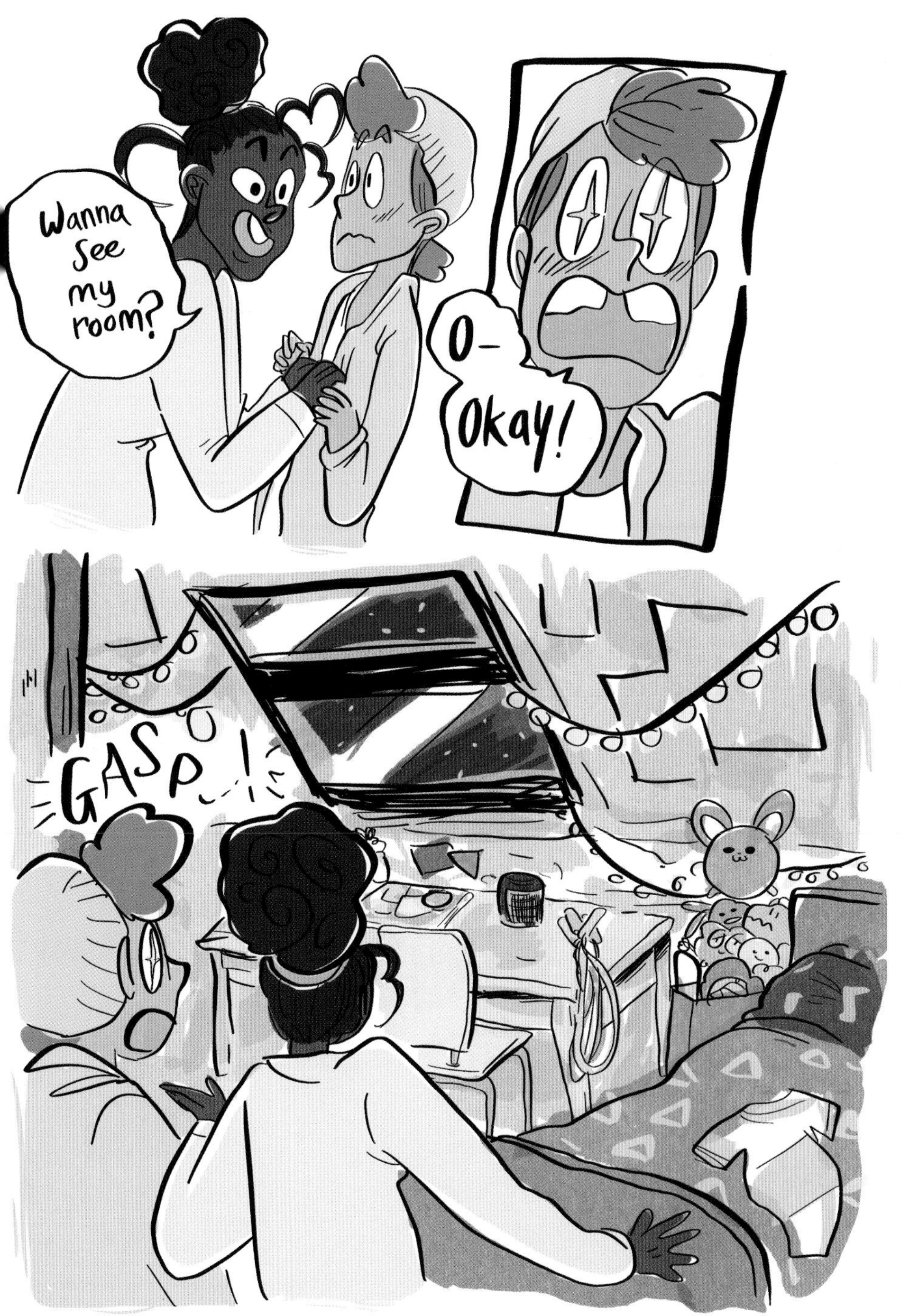
Wanna see my room?
O– Okay!
GASP...!

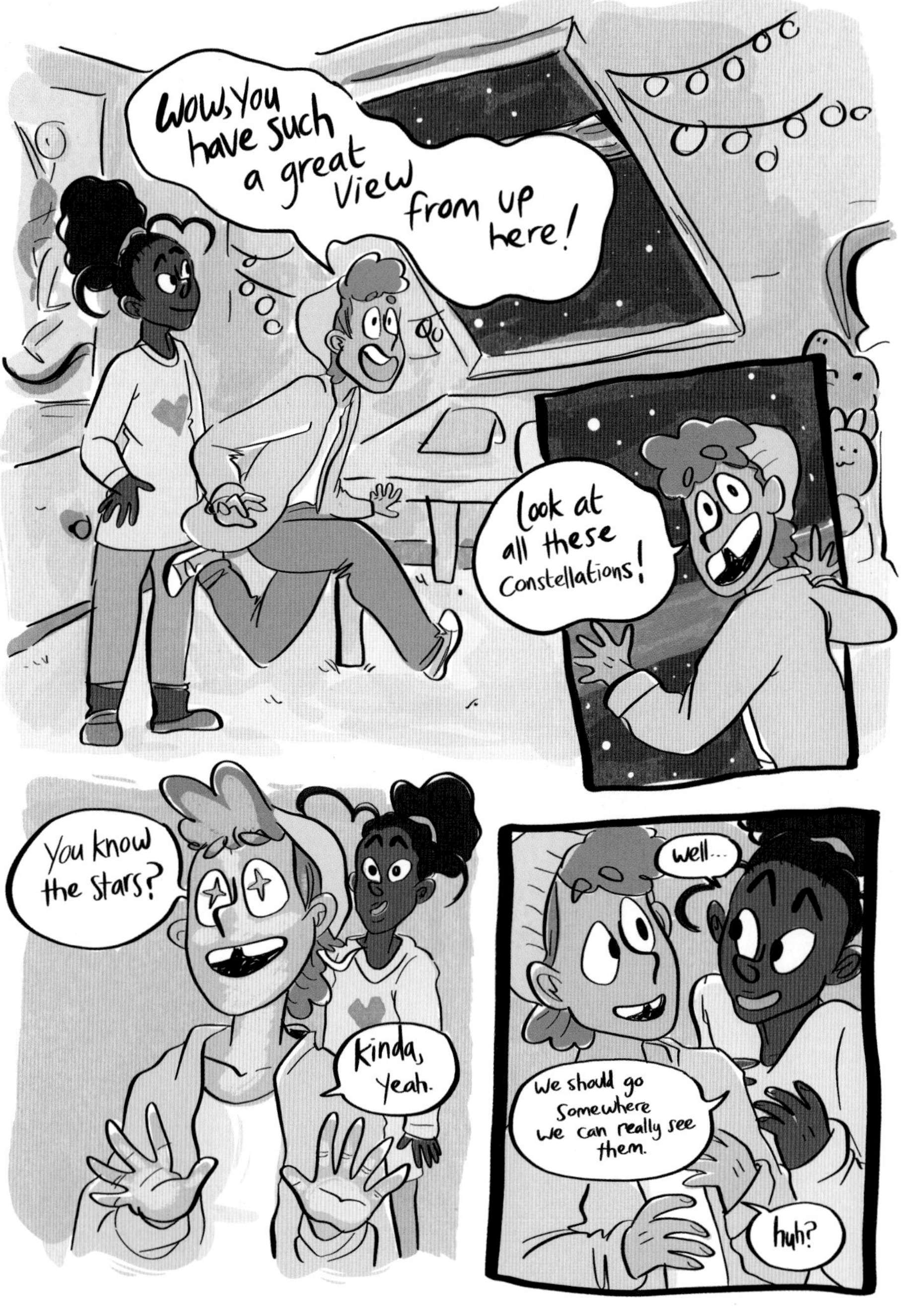
Wow, You have such a great View from up here!
look at all these Constellations!
You know the stars?
Kinda, Yeah.
well...
We should go somewhere we can really see them.
huh?

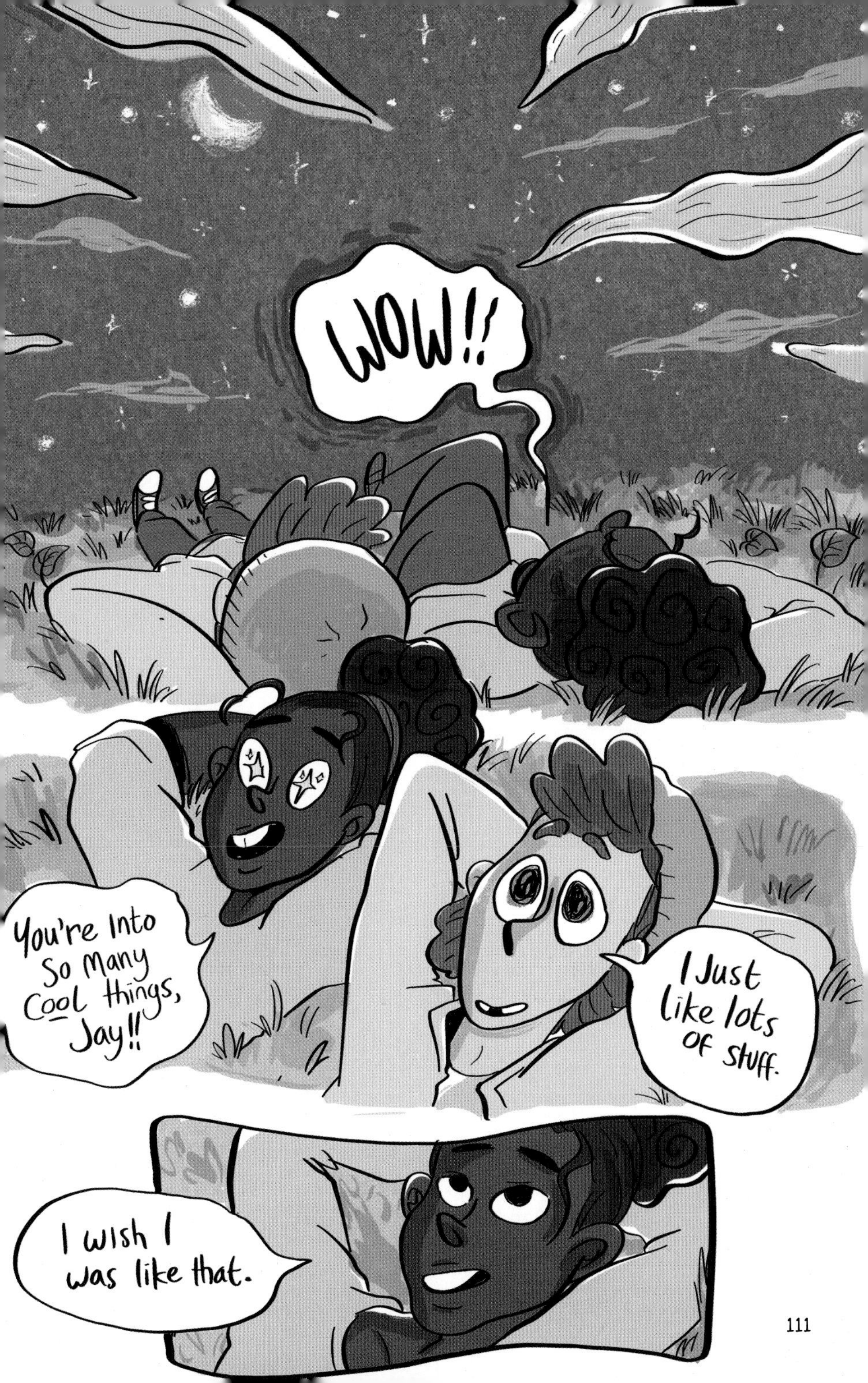
WOW!!
You're Into So Many Cool things, Jay!!
I Just like lots of stuff.
I wish I was like that.

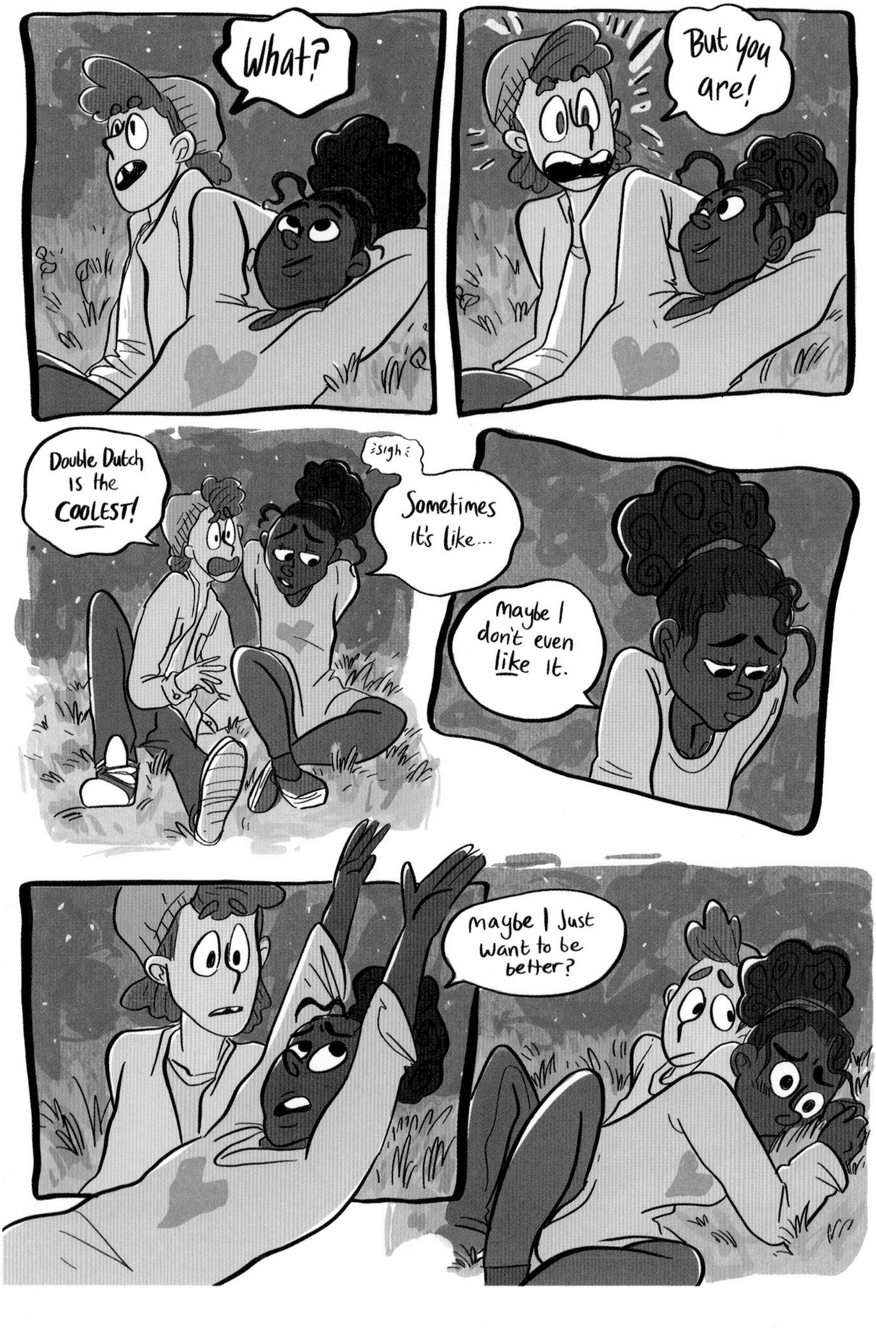
What?
But you are!
Double Dutch is the COOLEST!
sigh
Sometimes it's like...
maybe I don't even like it.
maybe I just want to be better?

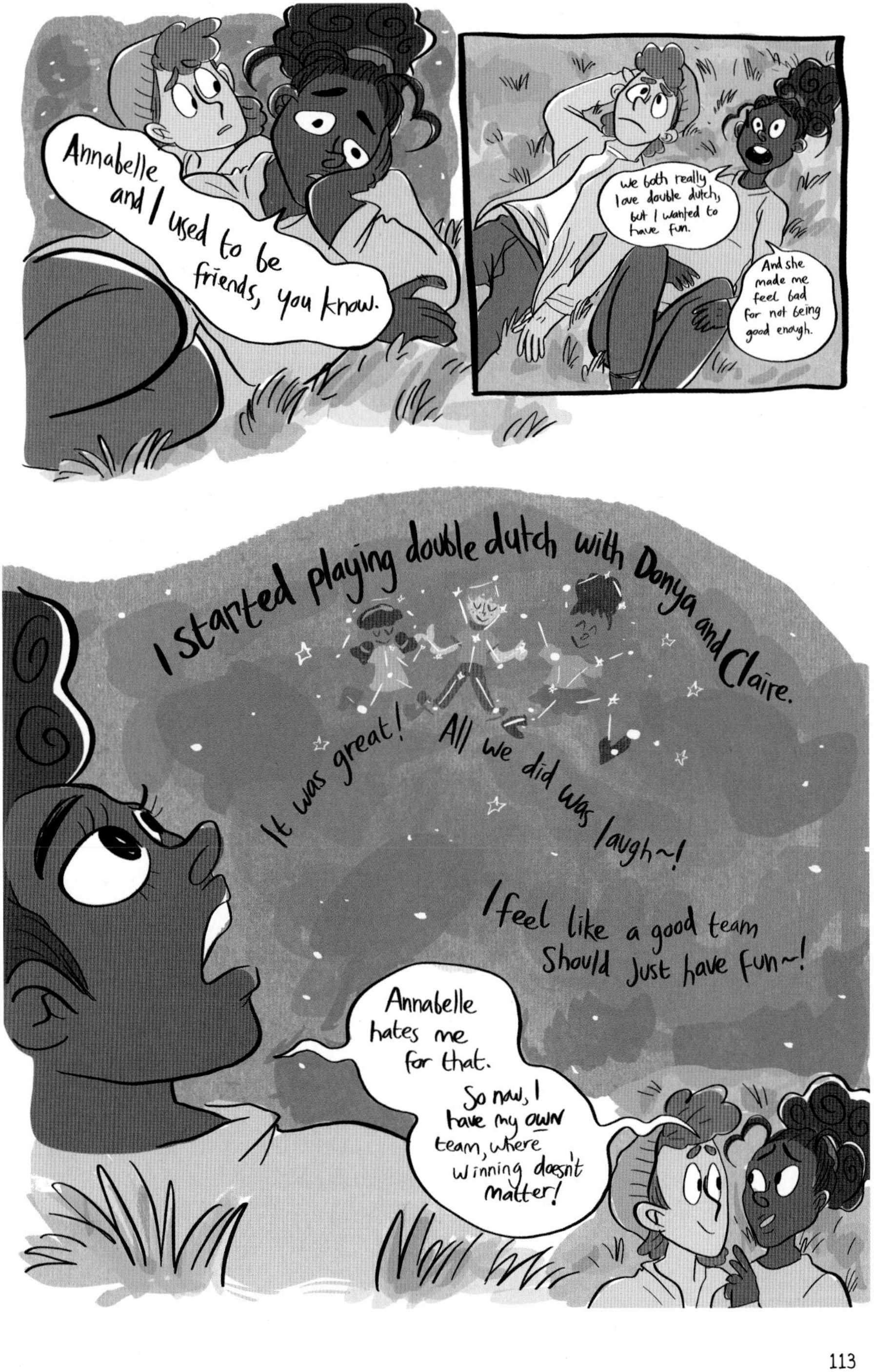
Annabelle and I used to be friends, you know.
We both really love double dutch, but I wanted to have fun.
And she made me feel bad for not being good enough.
I started playing double dutch with Donya and Claire.
It was great! All we did was laugh~!
I feel like a good team should just have fun~!
Annabelle hates me for that.
So now, I have my OWN team, where winning doesn't matter!

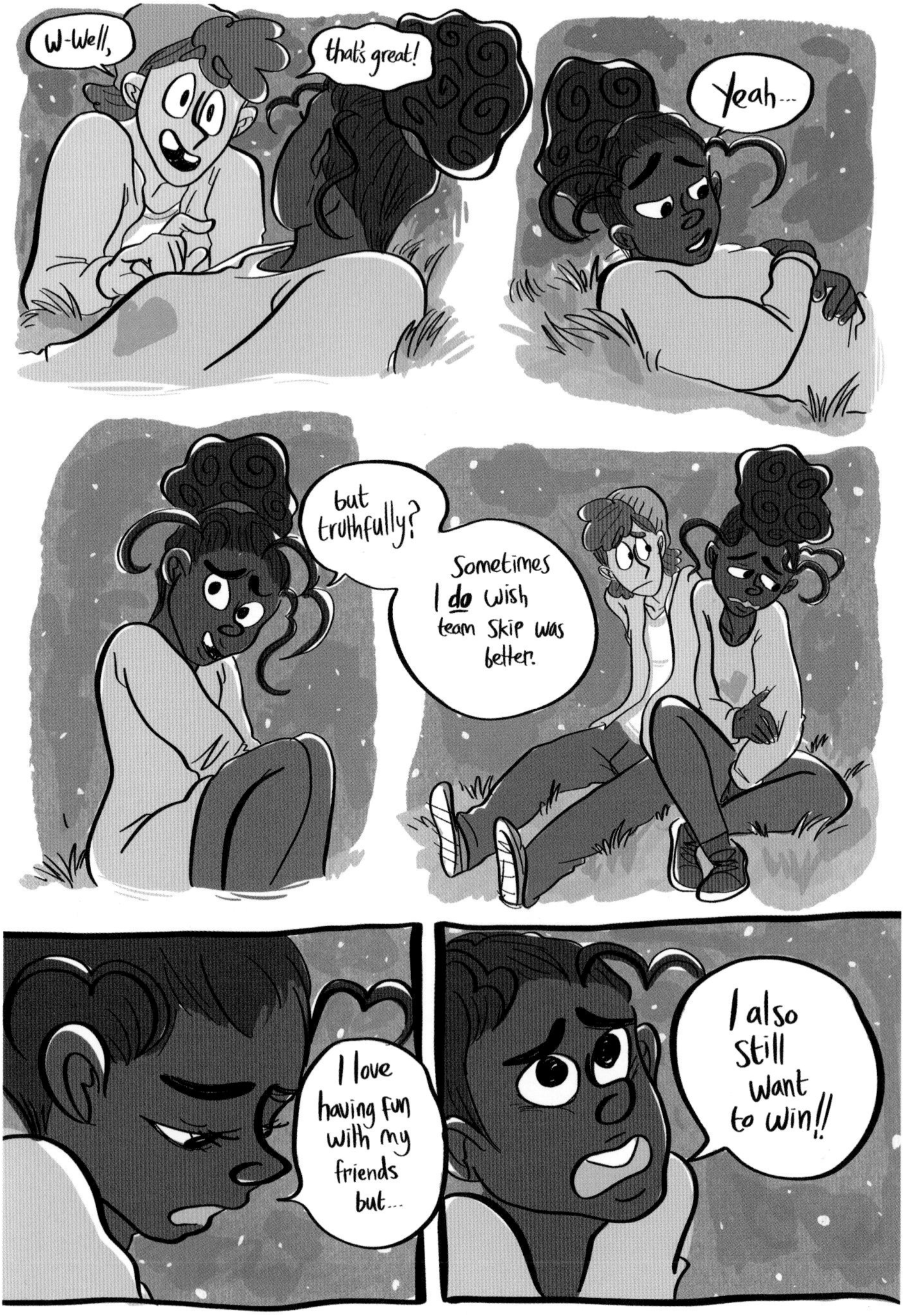
W-Well,
that's great!
Yeah...
but truthfully?
Sometimes I do wish team Skip was better.
I love having fun with my friends but...
I also still want to win!!

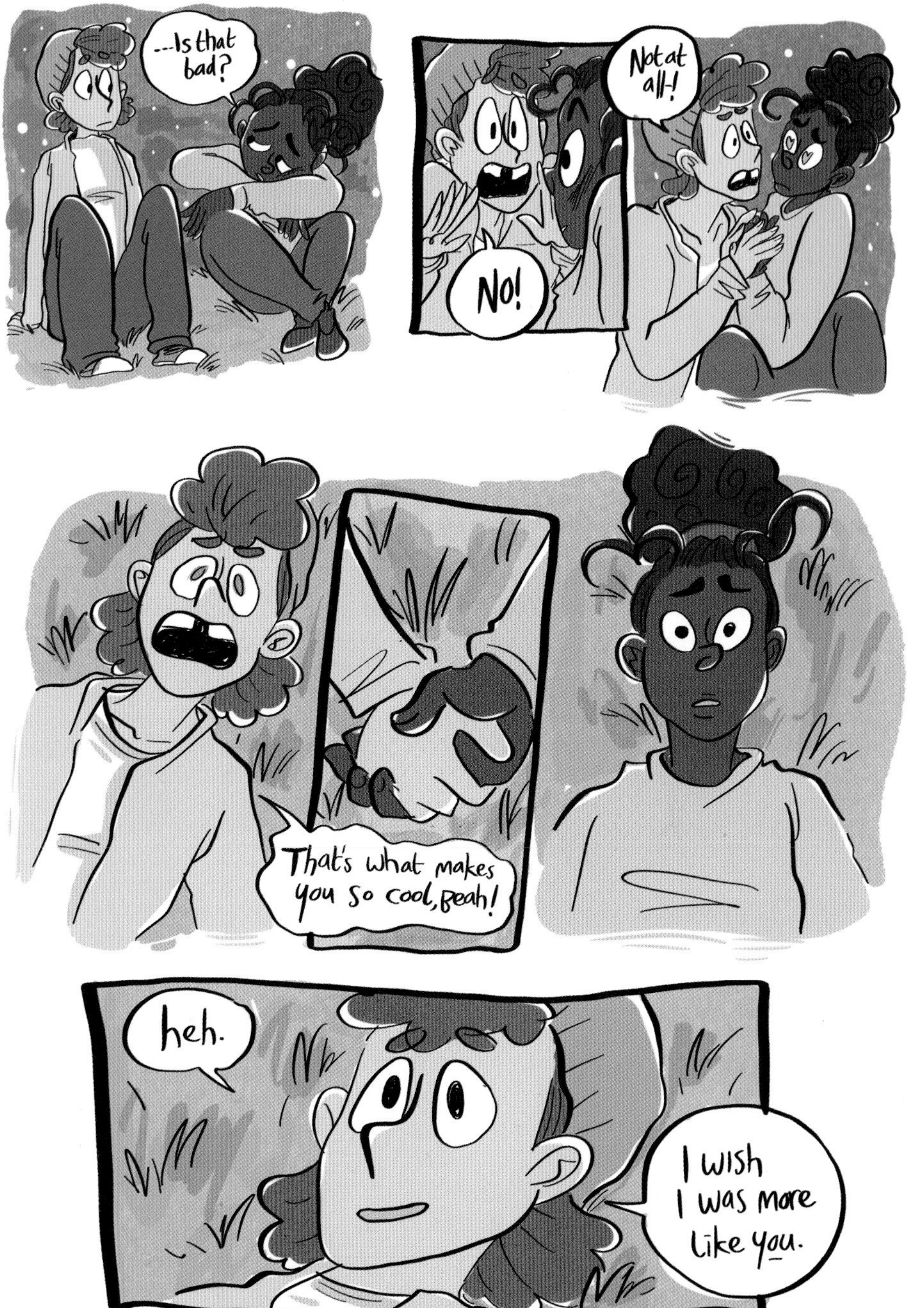

...Is that bad?
No!
Not at all-!
That's what makes you so cool, Beah!
heh.
I wish I was more like you.

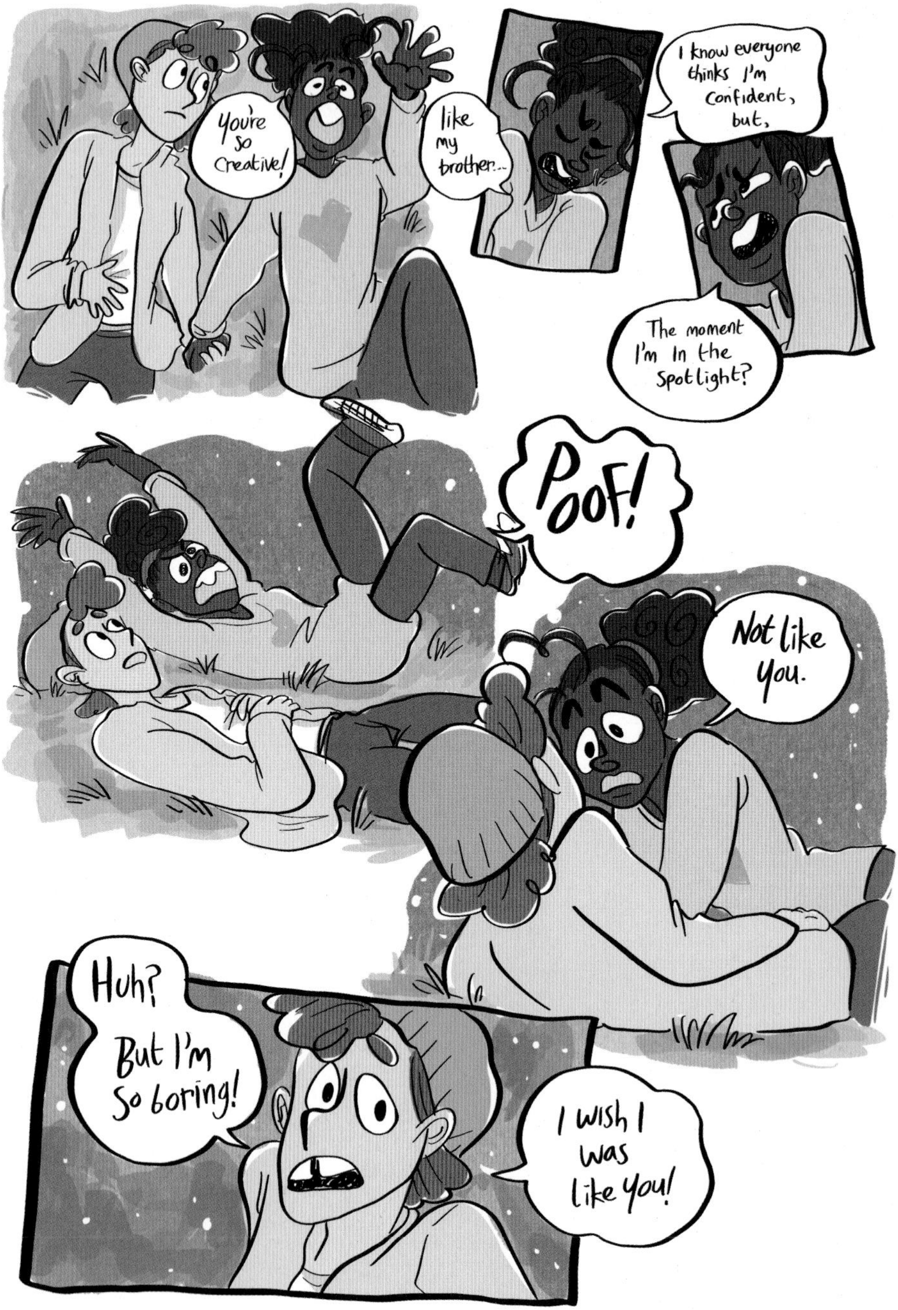
You're so creative!
like my brother...
I know everyone thinks I'm confident, but,
The moment I'm in the spotlight?
POOF!
Not like you.
Huh?
But I'm so boring!
I wish I was like you!

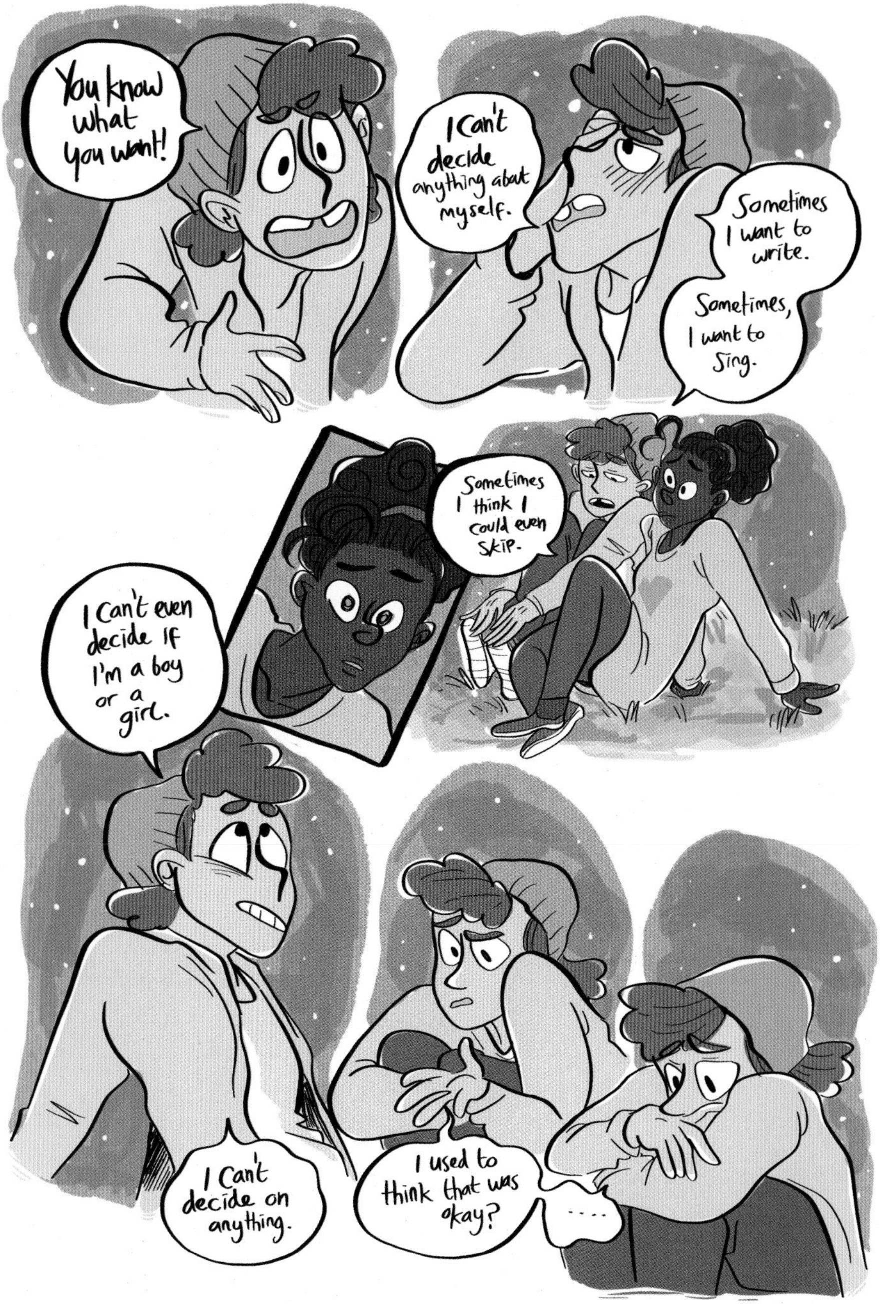
You know what you want!
I can't decide anything about myself.
Sometimes I want to write.
Sometimes, I want to sing.
Sometimes I think I could even skip.
I can't even decide if I'm a boy or a girl.
I can't decide on anything.
I used to think that was okay?
....

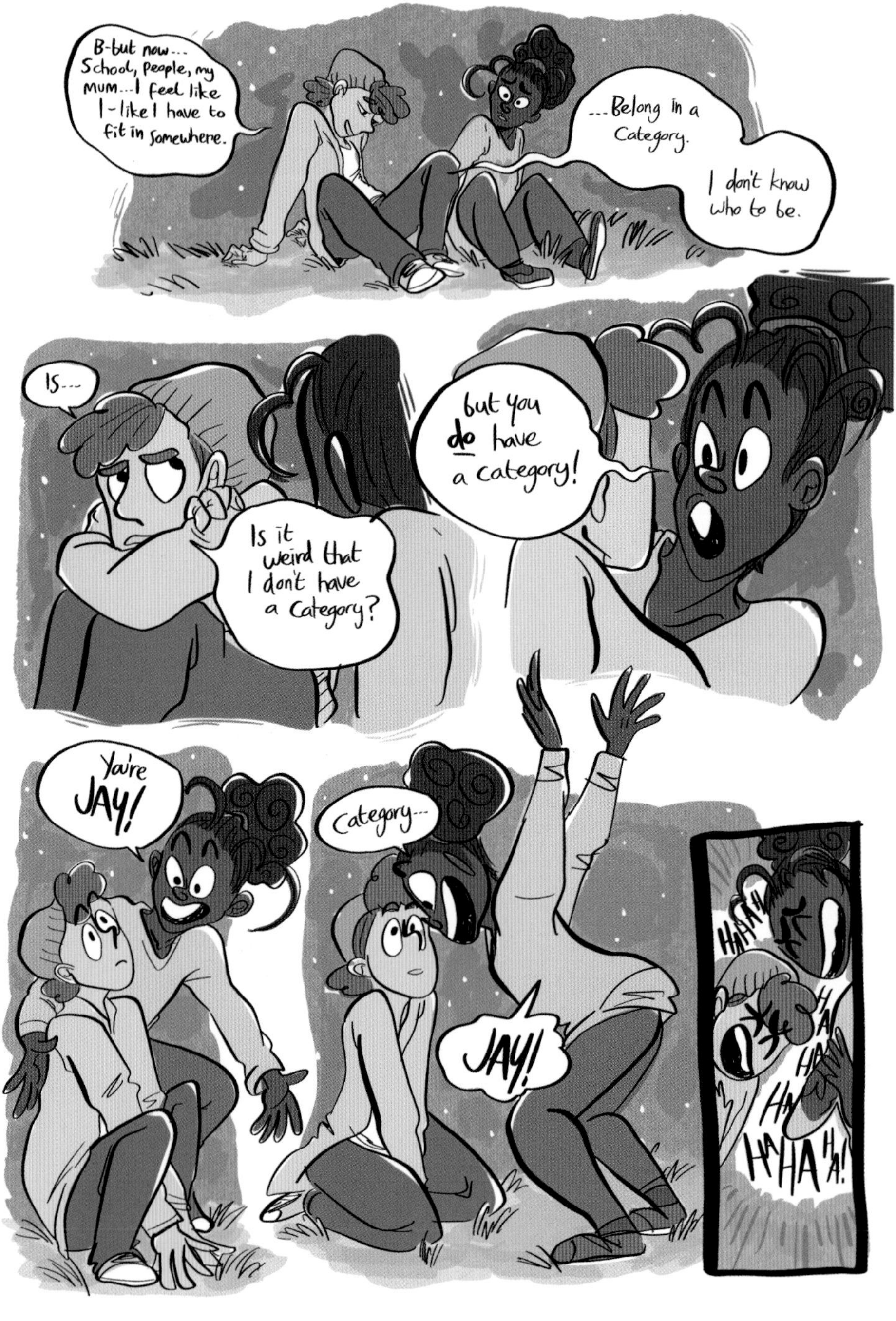

B-but now...
School, people, my mum... I feel like I-like I have to fit in somewhere.
...Belong in a Category.
I don't know who to be.
Is...
Is it weird that I don't have a Category?
but you do have a category!
You're JAY!
Category...
JAY!
HA HA HA HA HA HA HA HA HA HA!

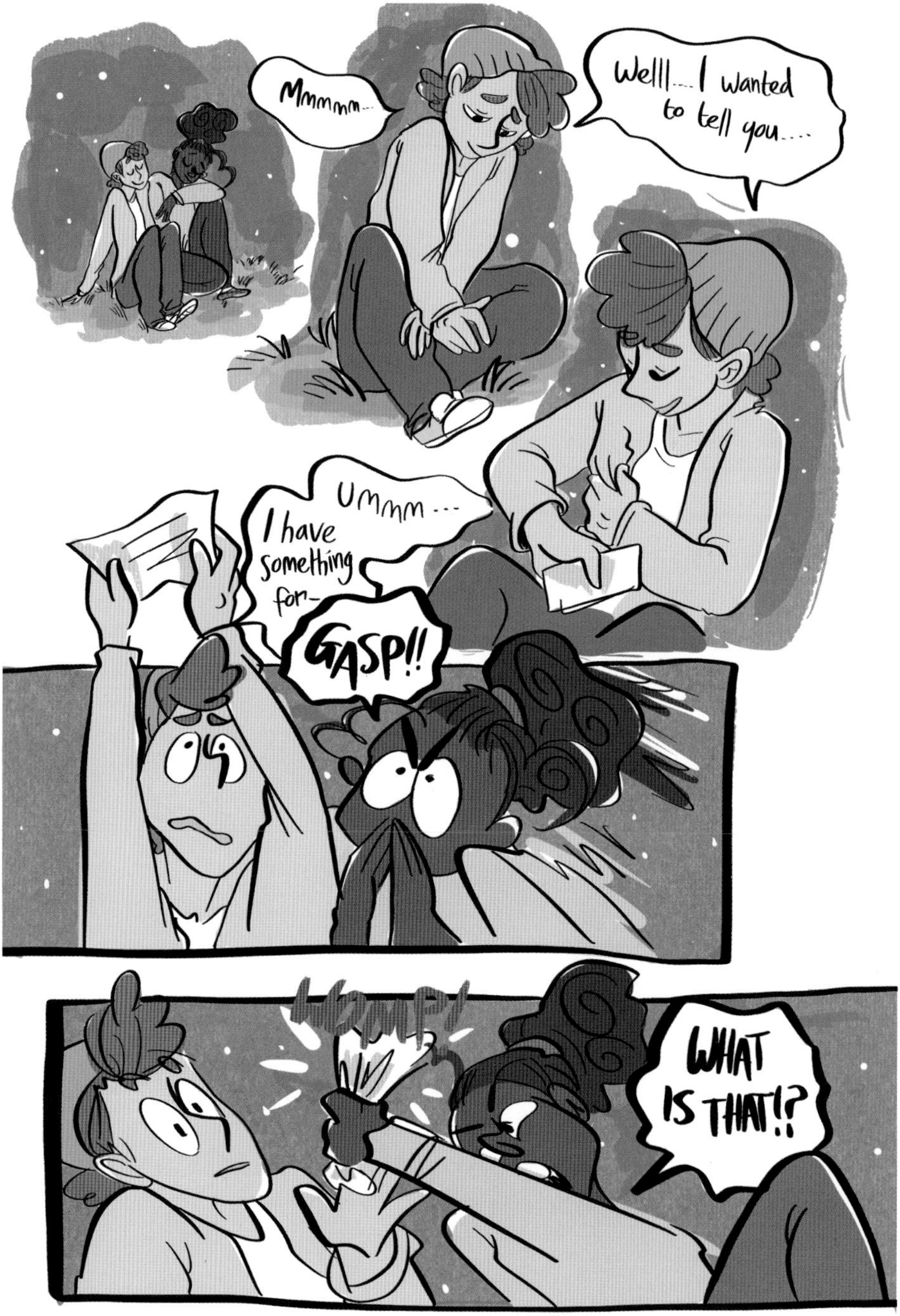
Mmmmm...
Welll... I wanted to tell you...
Ummm...
I have something for—
GASP!!
WHAT IS THAT!?

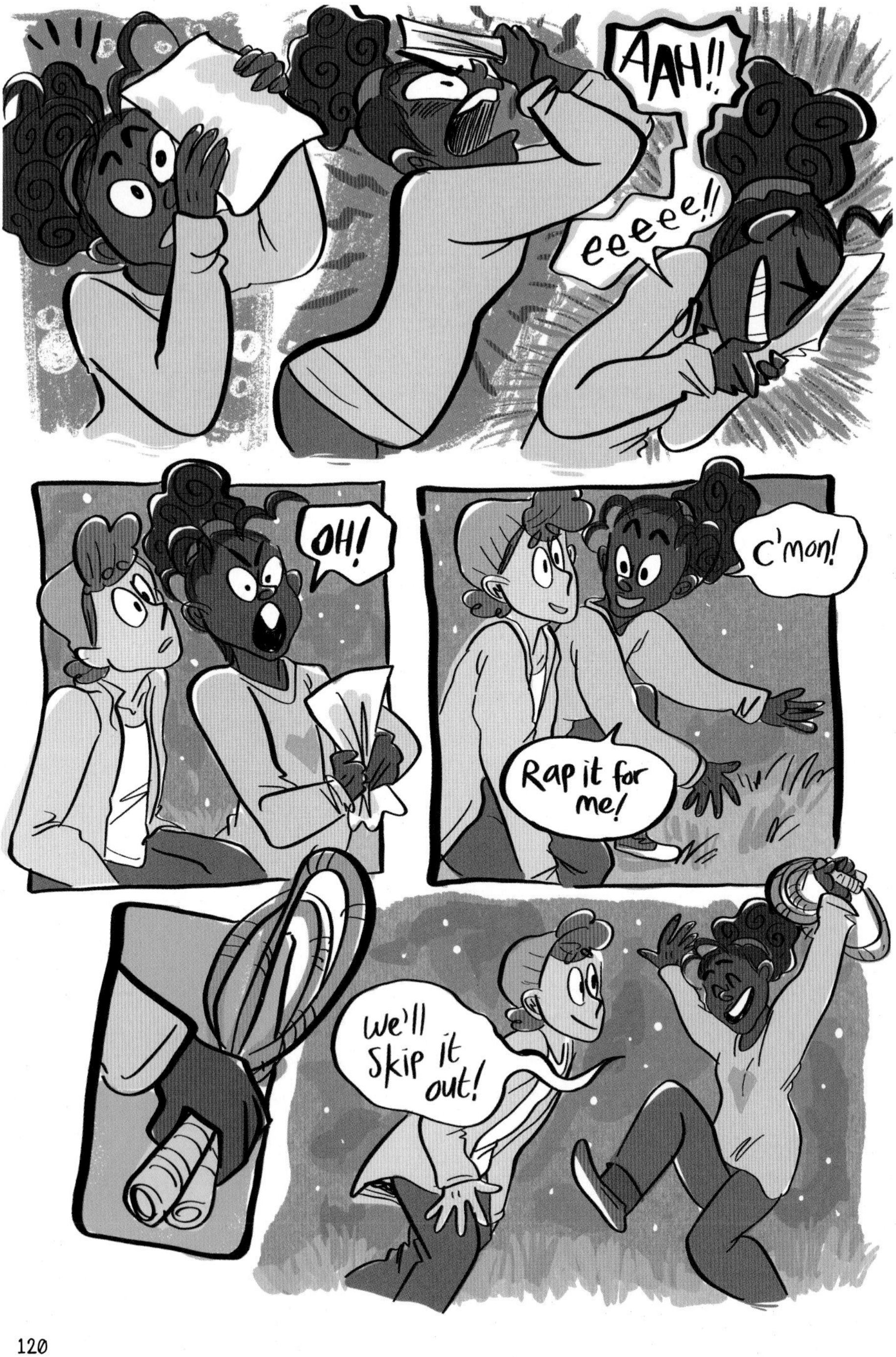
AAH!!
eeeee!!
OH!
C'mon!
Rap it for me!
We'll Skip it out!

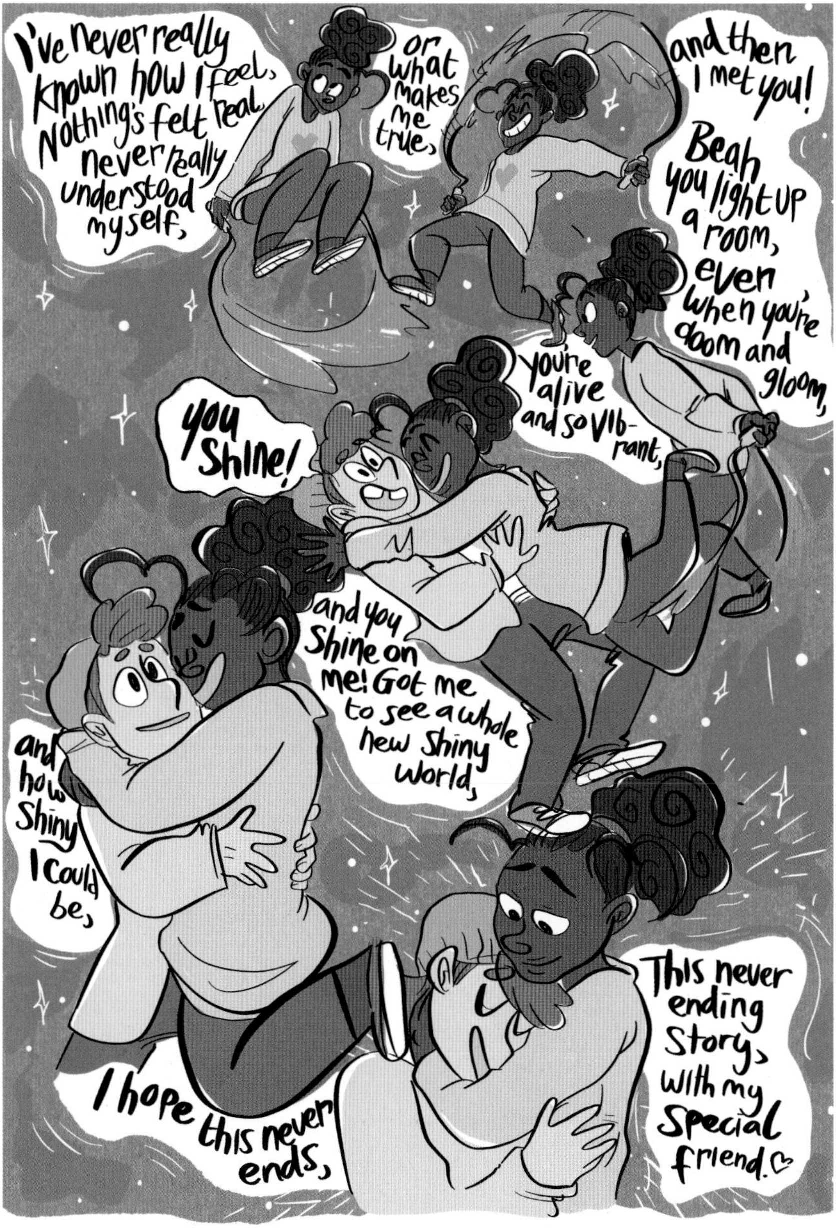
I've never really known how I feel, Nothing's felt real, never really understood myself,
or what makes me true,
and then I met you!
Beah you light up a room, even when you're doom and gloom,
you're alive and so vib-rant,
you Shine!
and you Shine on me! Got me to see a whole new Shiny world,
and how Shiny I could be,
I hope this never ends,
This never ending Story, with my Special friend.♡

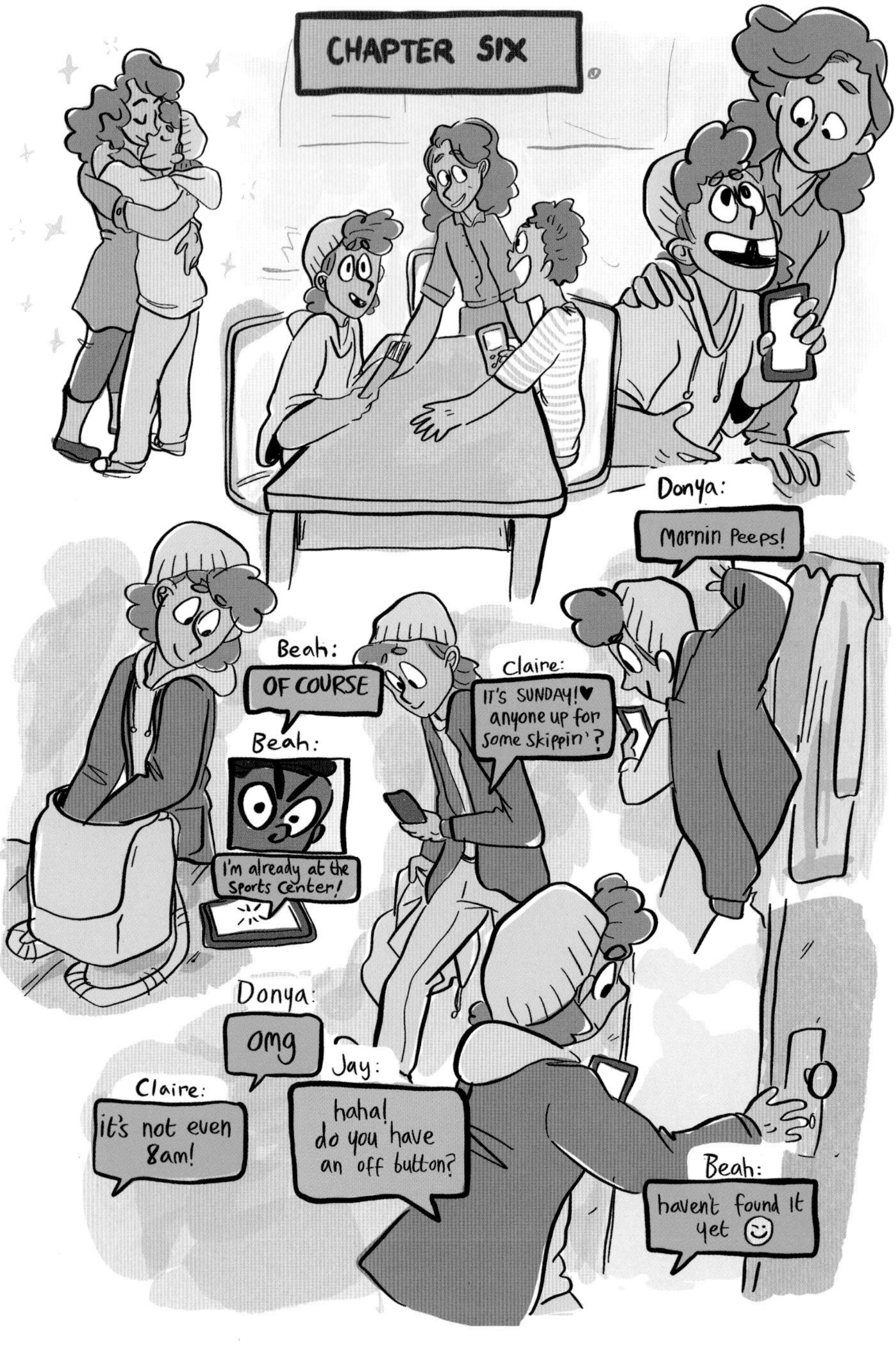
CHAPTER SIX
Donya:
Mornin Peeps!
Beah:
OF COURSE
Beah:
I'm already at the Sports Center!
Claire:
IT'S SUNDAY!♥ anyone up for some skippin'?
Donya:
omg
Claire:
it's not even 8am!
Jay:
haha! do you have an off button?
Beah:
haven't found it yet ☺

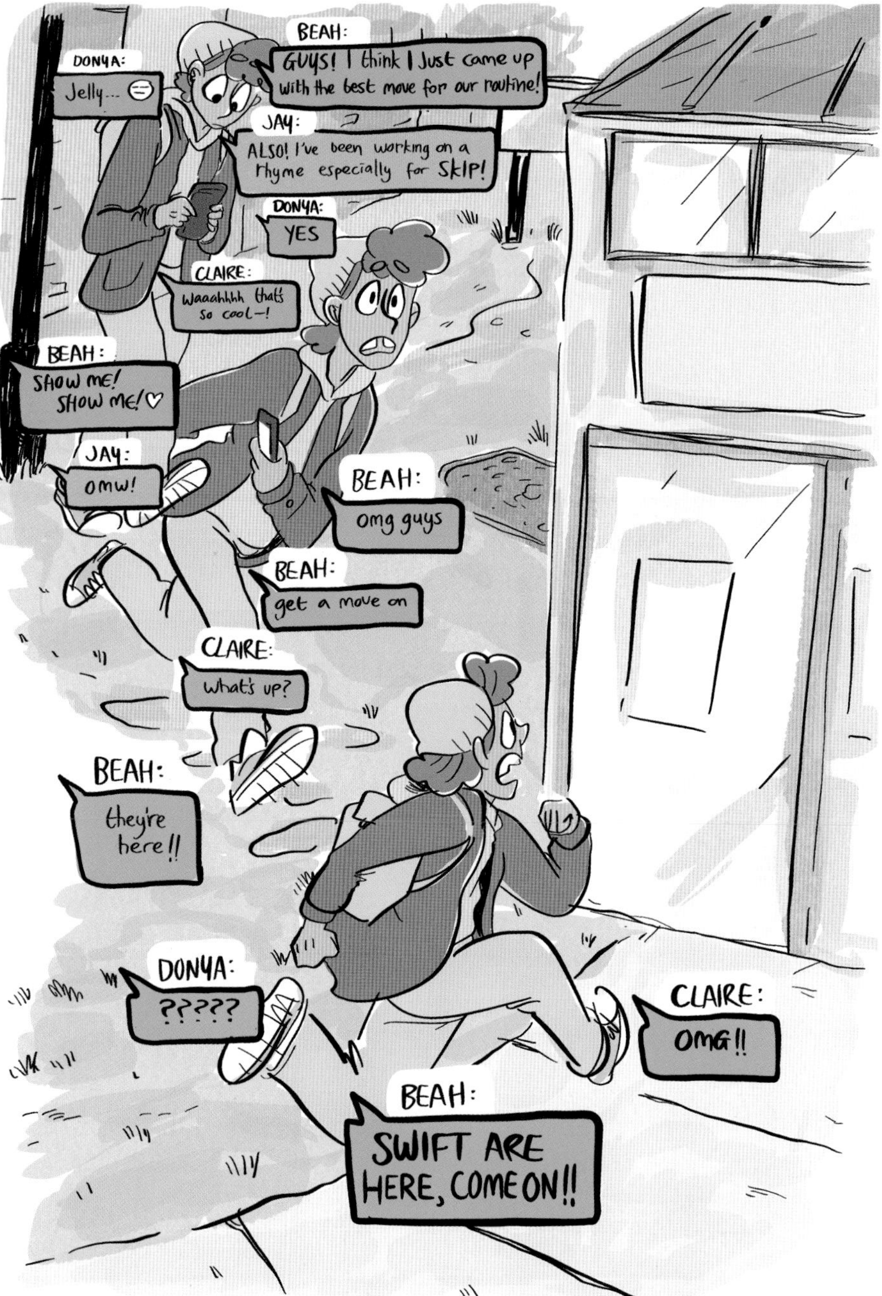
DONYA: Jelly...
BEAH: GUYS! I think I Just came up with the best move for our routine!
JAY: ALSO! I've been working on a rhyme especially for SKIP!
DONYA: YES
CLAIRE: Waaahhhh that's so cool—!
BEAH: SHOW ME! SHOW ME! ♡
JAY: omw!
BEAH: omg guys
BEAH: get a move on
CLAIRE: what's up?
BEAH: they're here!!
DONYA: ?????
CLAIRE: OMG!!
BEAH: SWIFT ARE HERE, COME ON!!

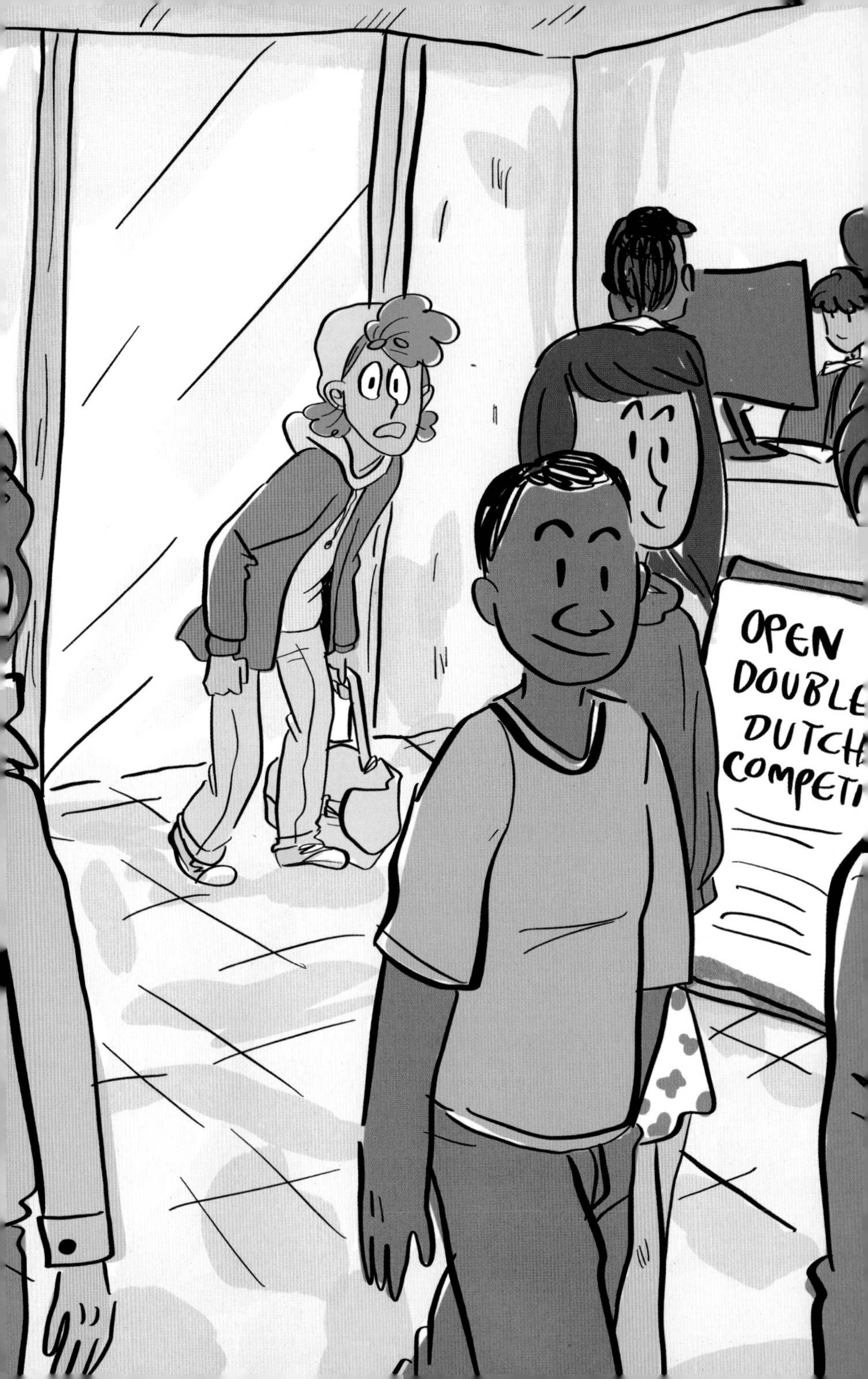
OPEN
DOUBLE
DUTCH
COMPETI

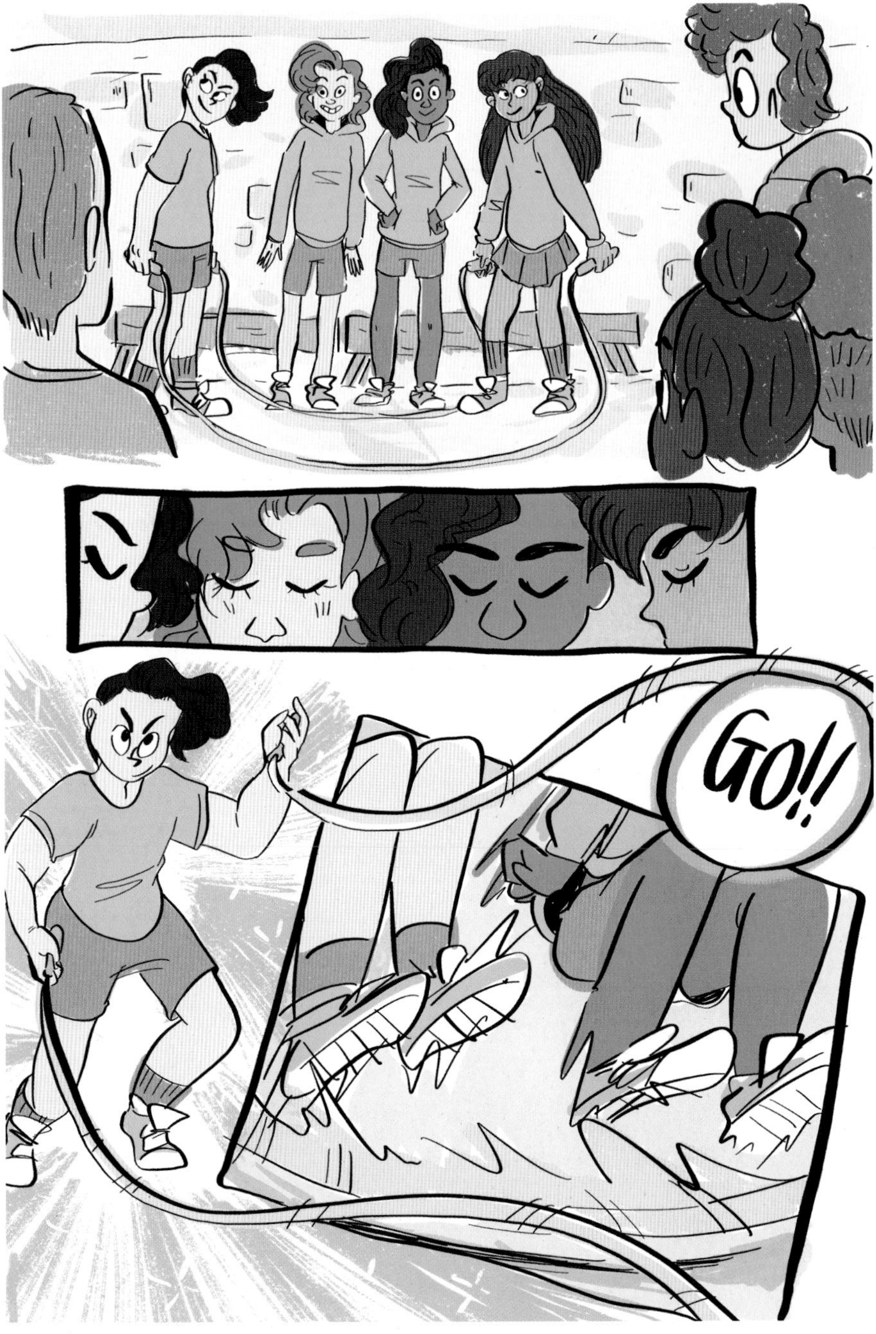
GO!!

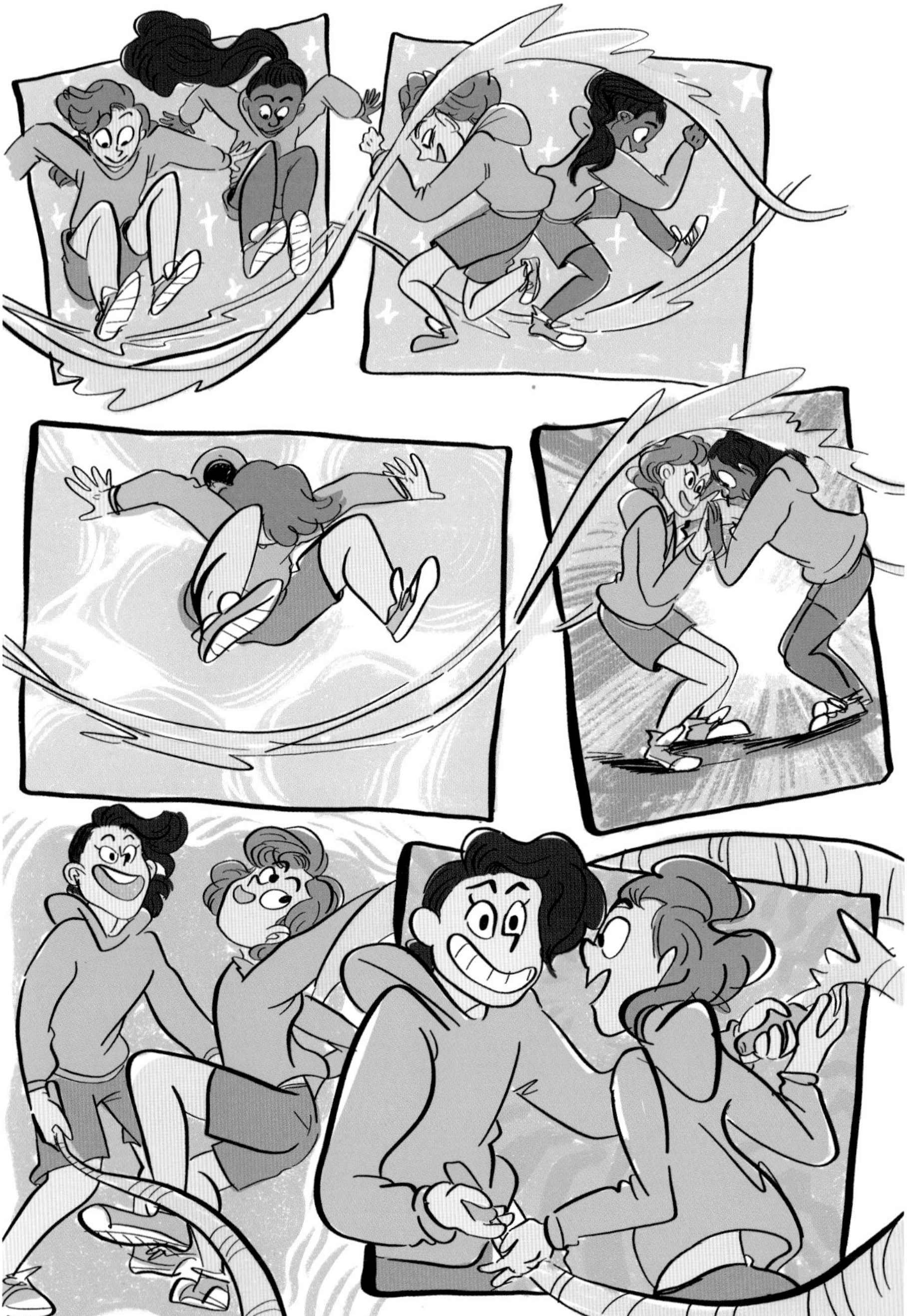

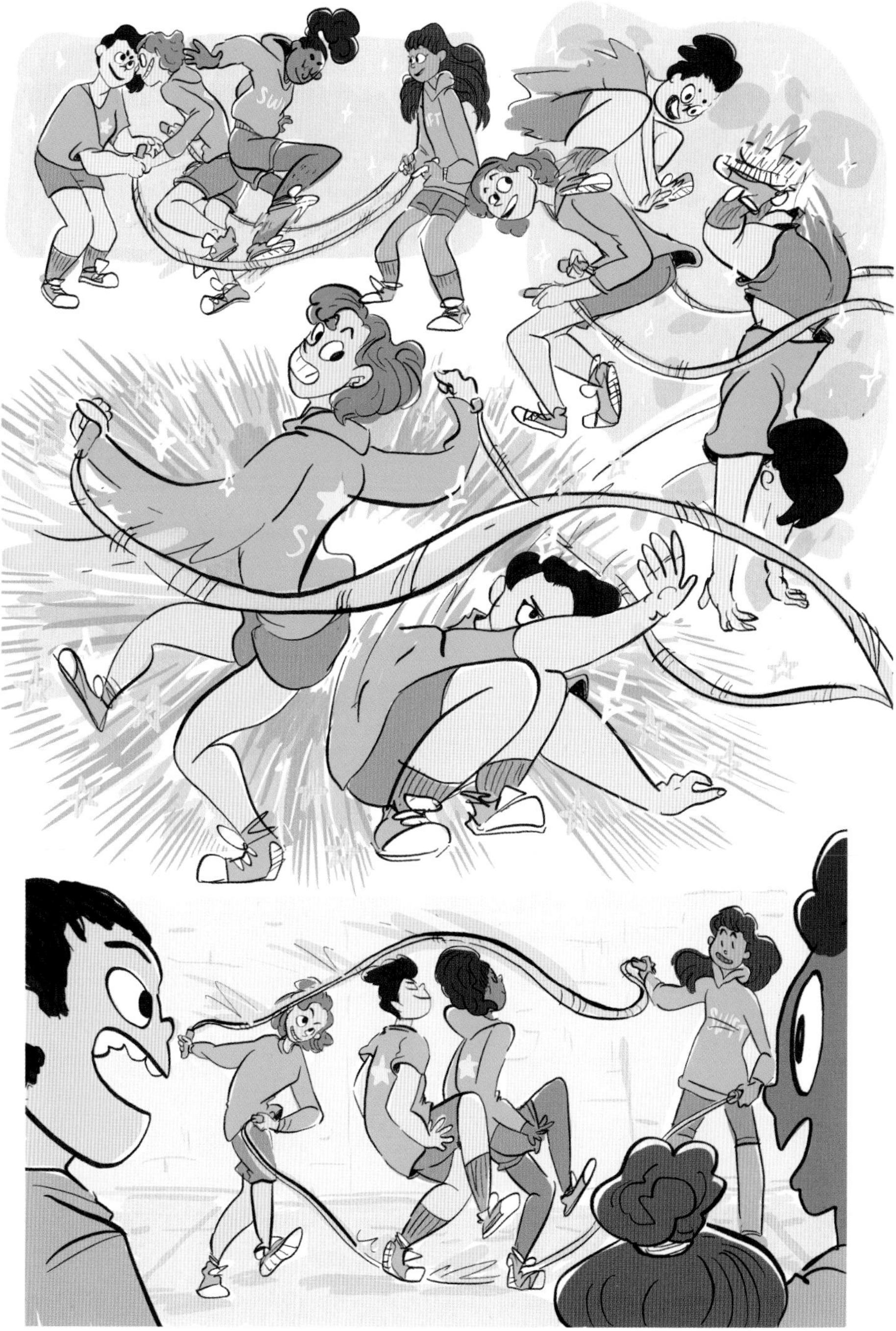

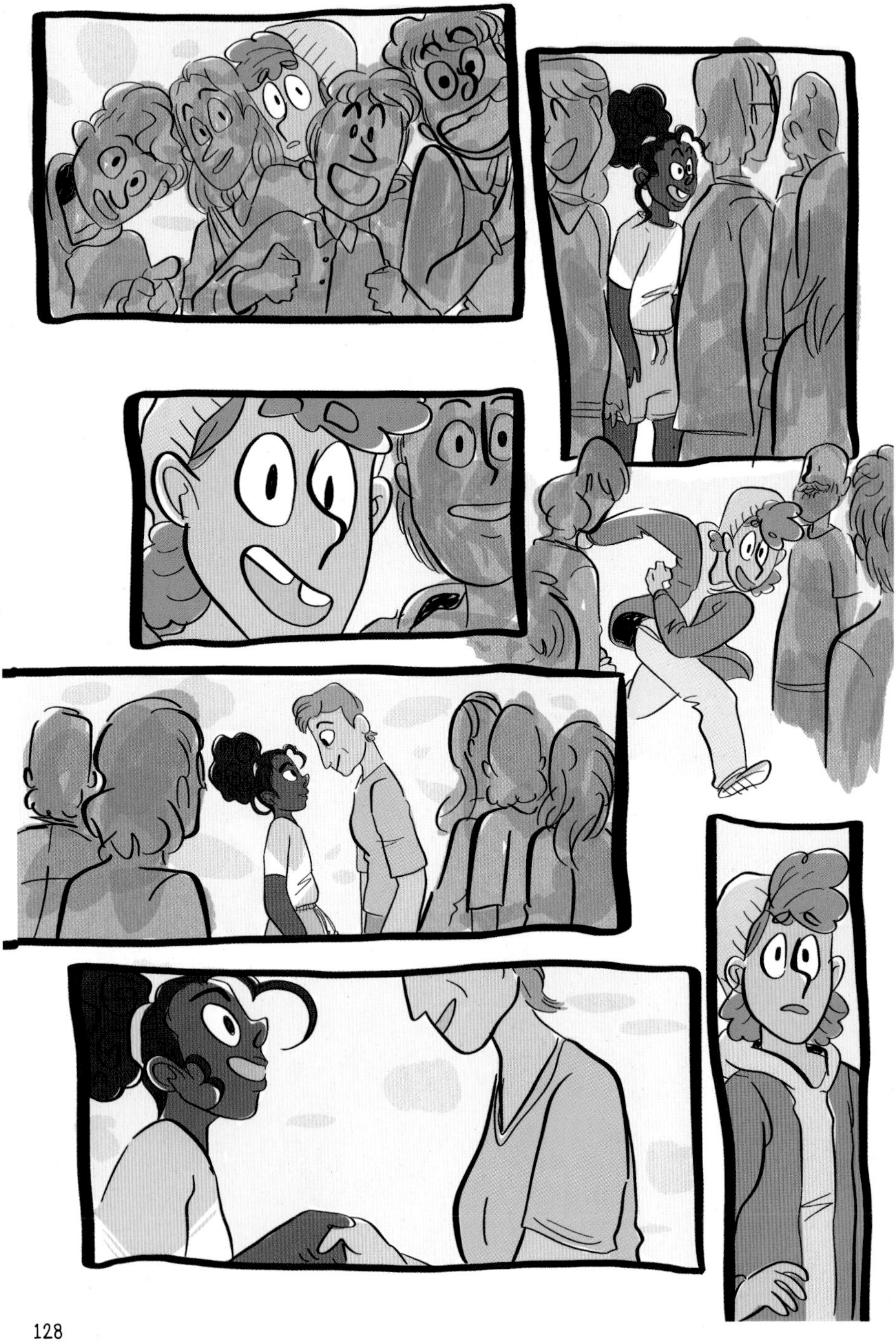

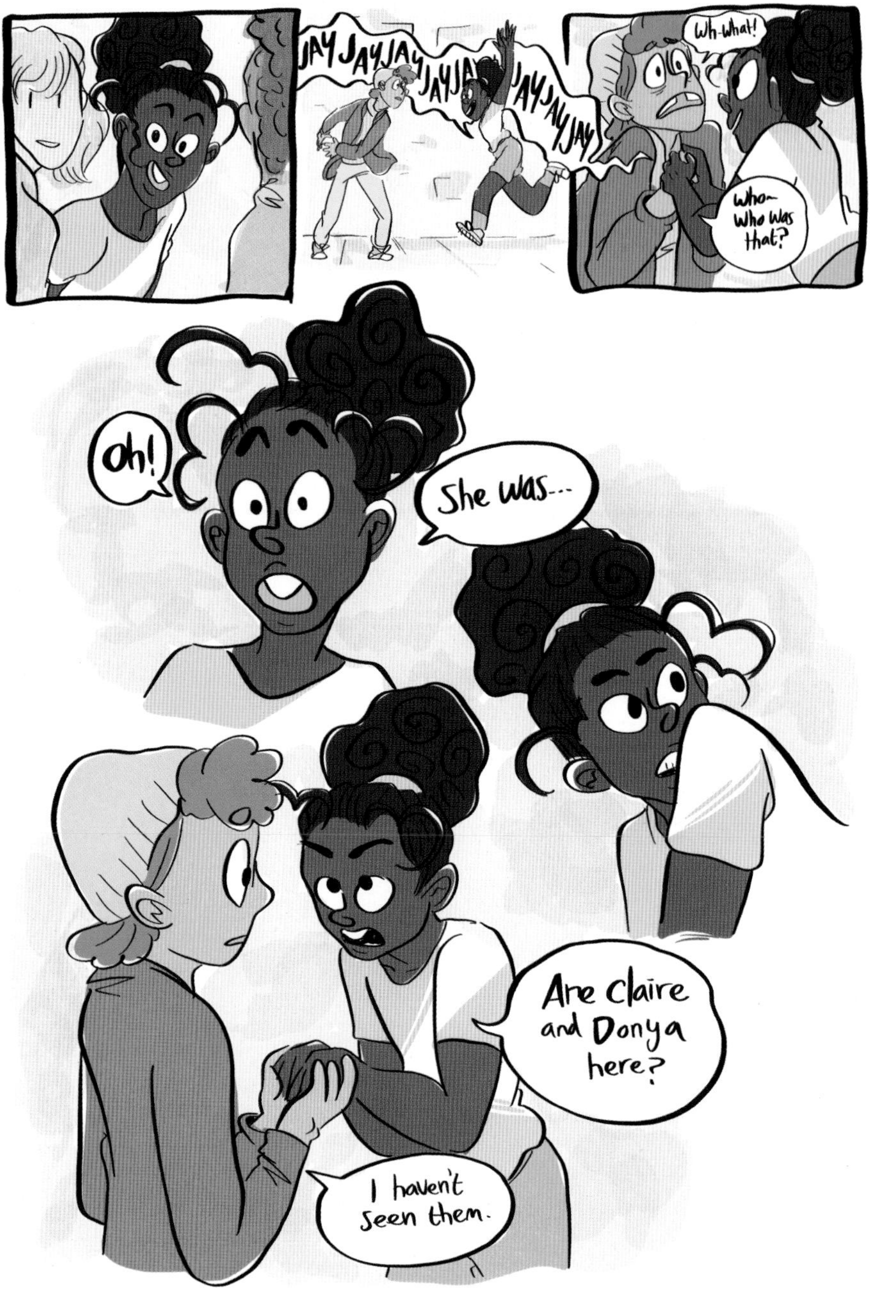
JAY JAY JAY JAY JAY JAY JAY JAY JAY JAY
Wh-what!
Who- Who was that?
Oh!
She was...
Are Claire and Donya here?
I haven't seen them.

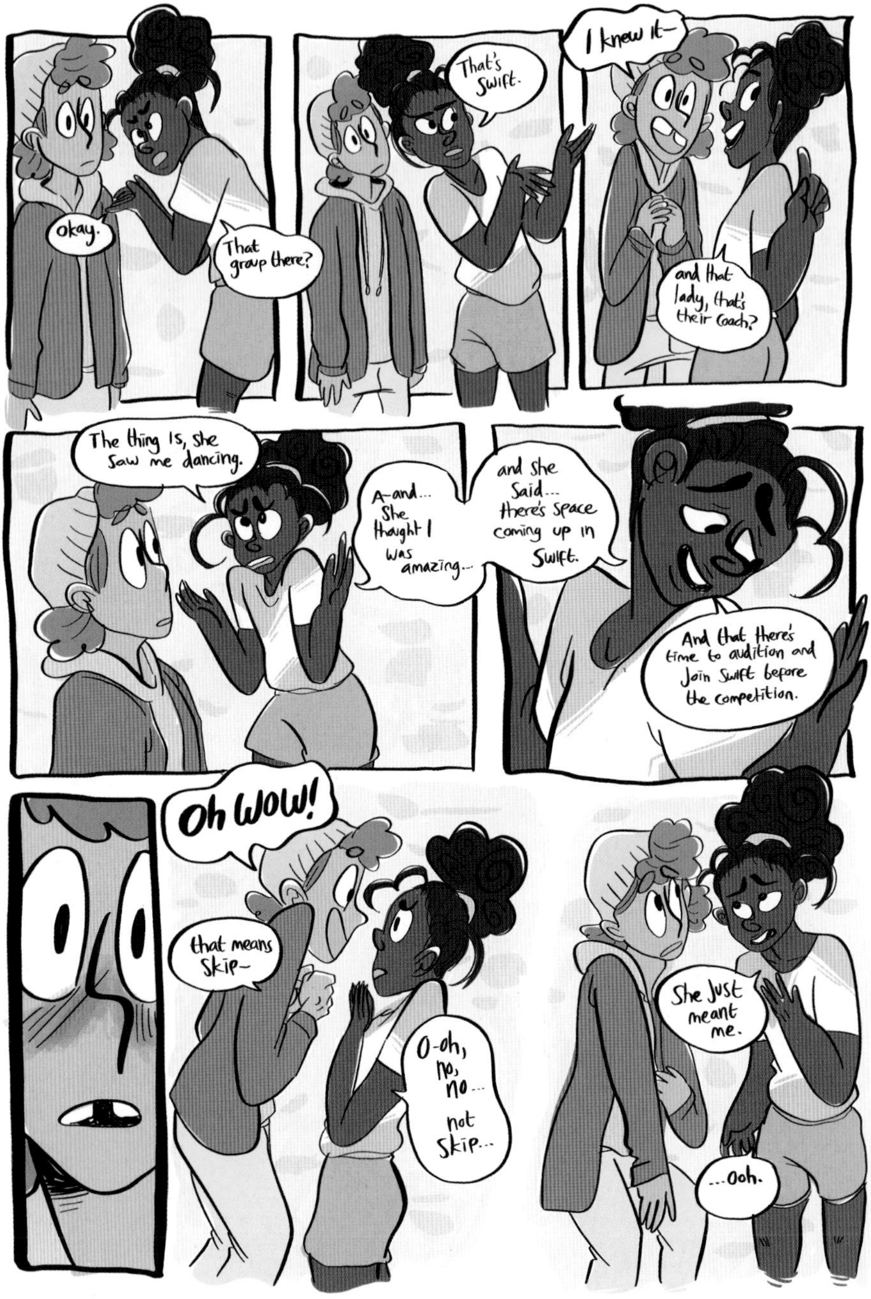
okay.
That group there?
That's Swift.
I knew it—
and that lady, that's their coach?
The thing is, she saw me dancing.
A-and... She thought I was amazing...
and she said... there's space coming up in Swift.
And that there's time to audition and join Swift before the competition.
Oh WOW!
that means Skip—
O-oh, no, no... not Skip...
She just meant me.
...ooh.

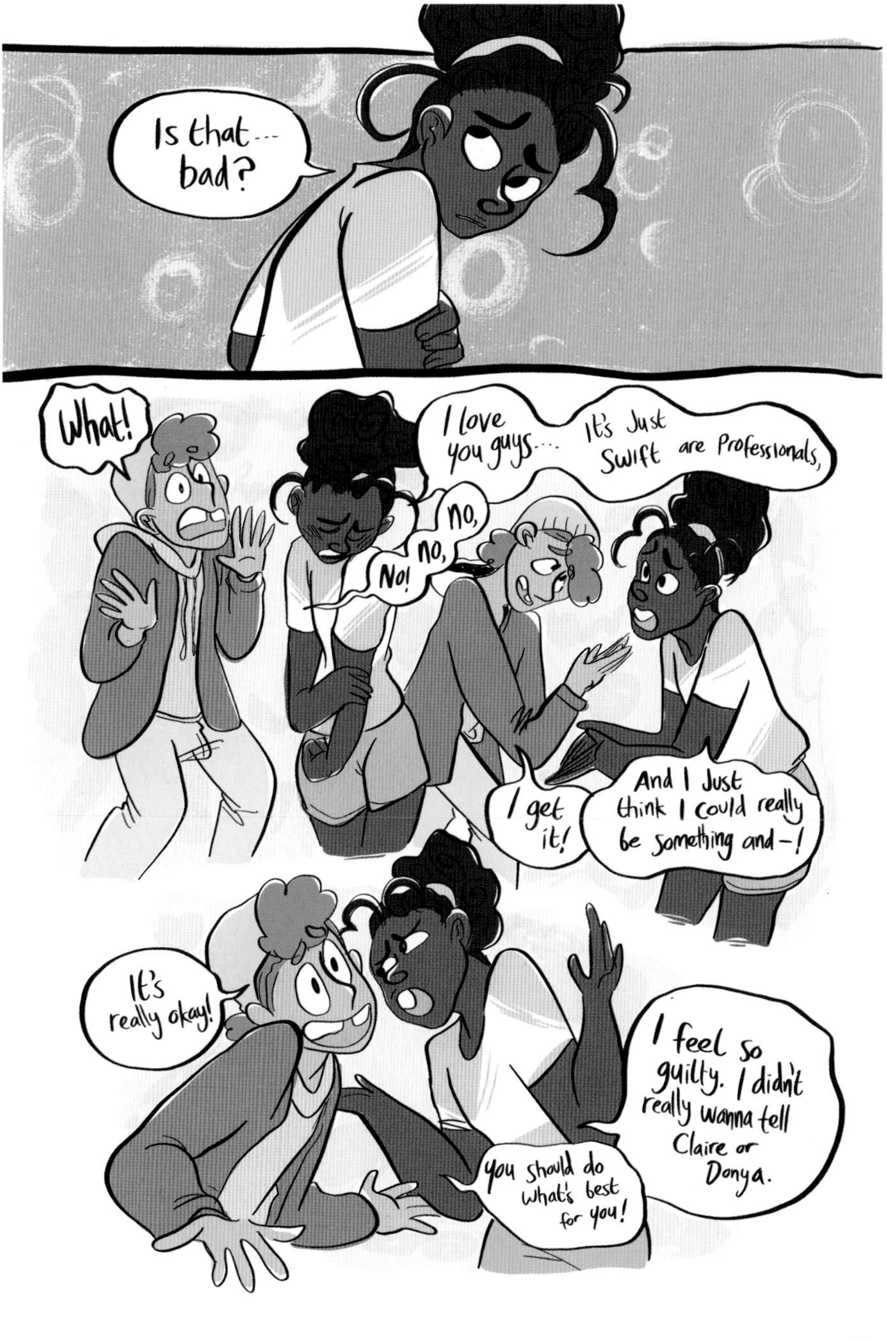
Is that...
bad?
What!
I love you guys... It's just Swift are professionals,
no,
no,
No!
I get it!
And I just think I could really be something and–!
It's really okay!
I feel so guilty. I didn't really wanna tell Claire or Donya.
You should do what's best for you!

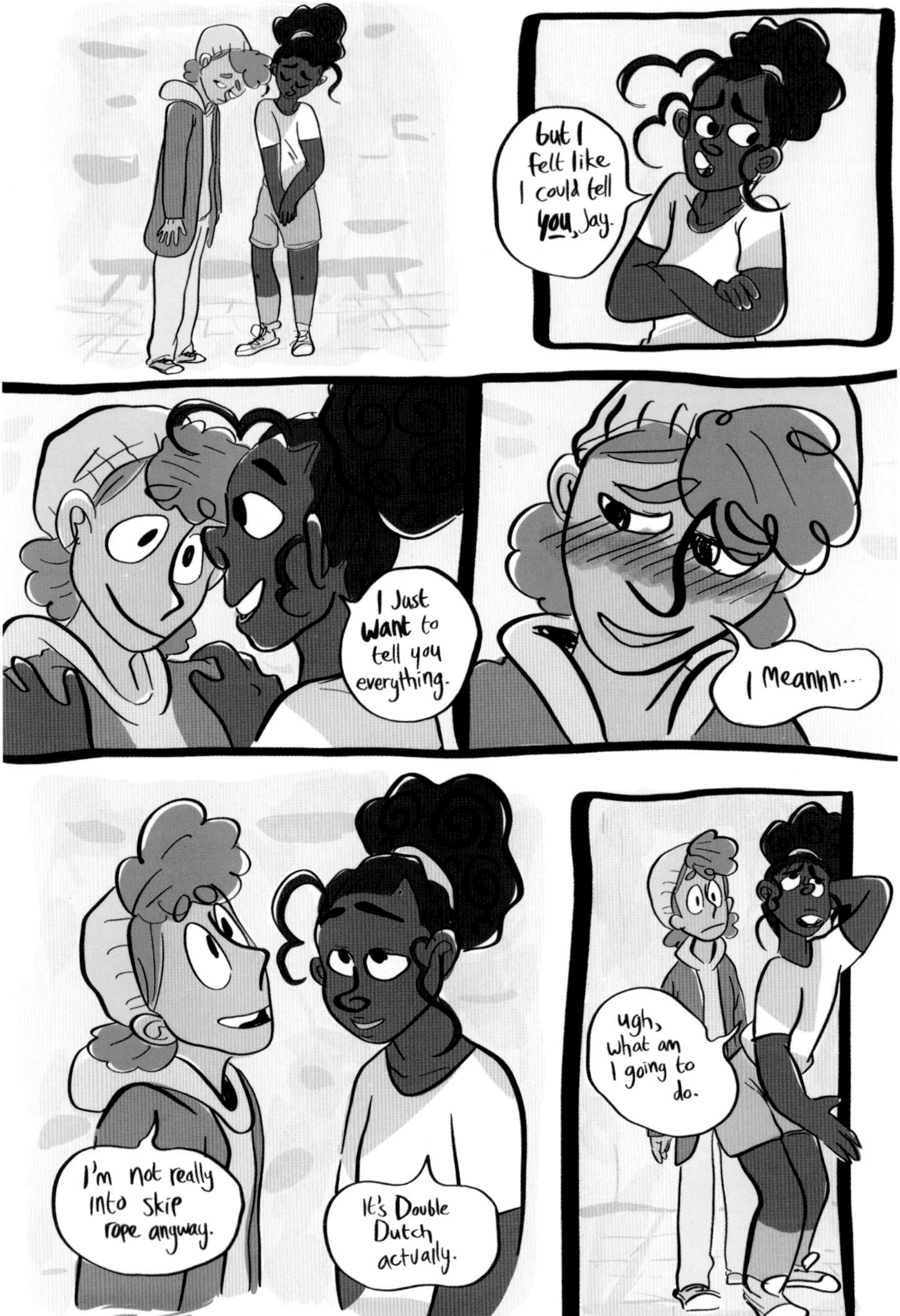
but I felt like I could tell **you**, Jay.
I Just **want** to tell you everything.
I Meanhn...
I'm not really into skip rope anyway.
It's Double Dutch actually.
ugh, what am I going to do.

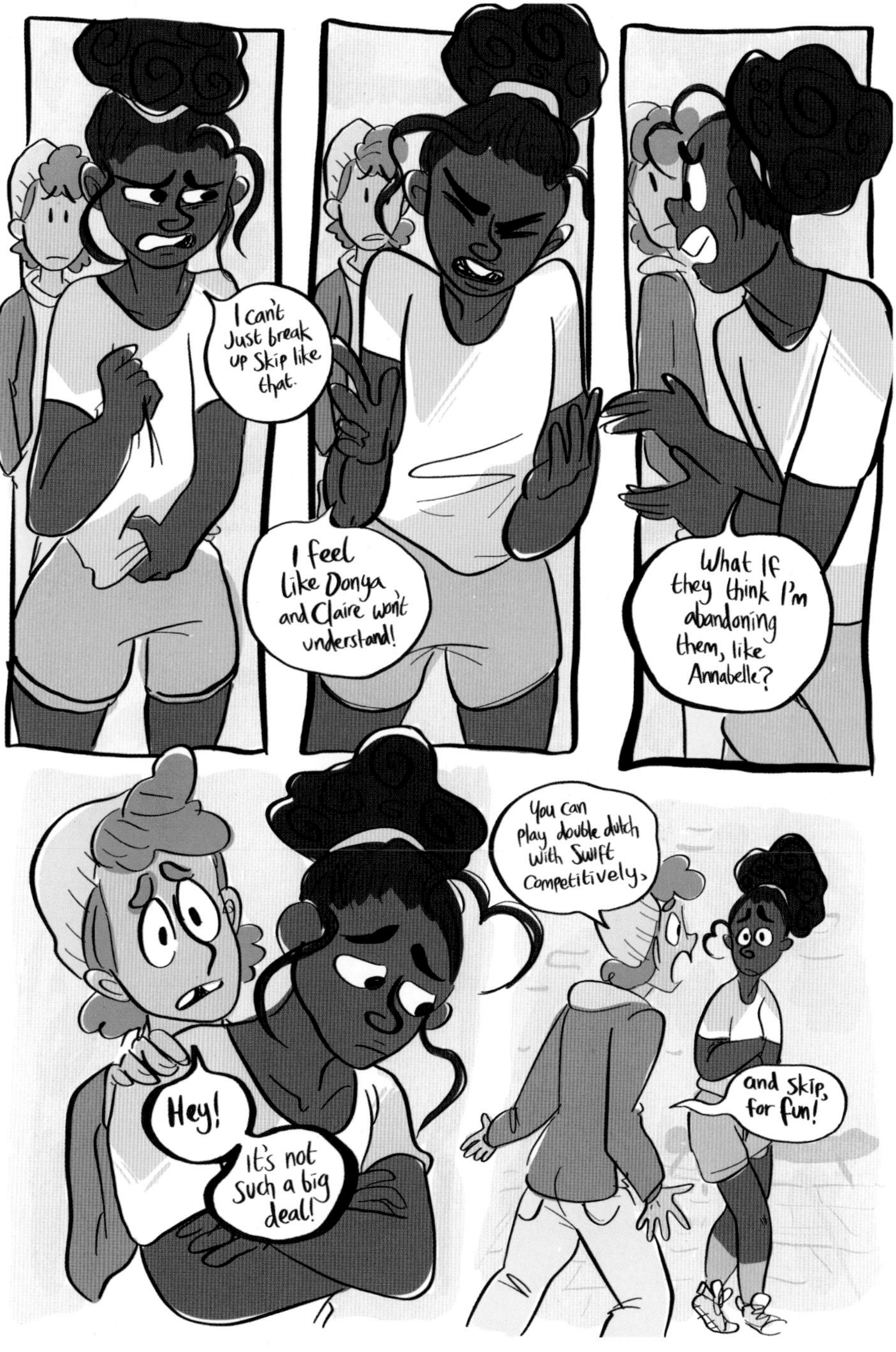
I can't Just break up Skip like that.
I feel like Donya and Claire won't understand!
What If they think I'm abandoning them, like Annabelle?
Hey!
It's not such a big deal!
You can play double dutch with Swift competitively,
and Skip, for fun!

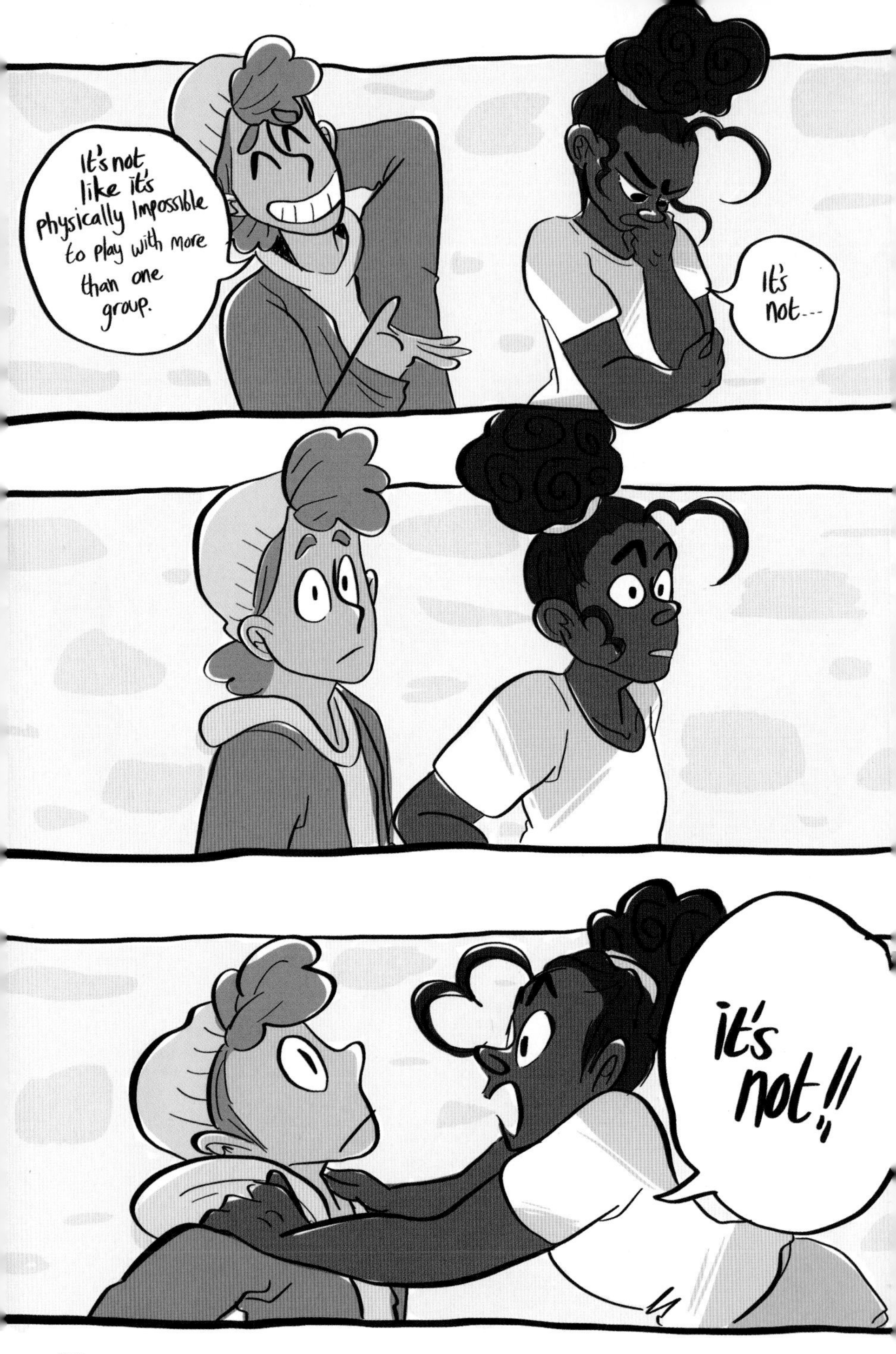
It's not like it's physically impossible to play with more than one group.
It's not...
it's not!!

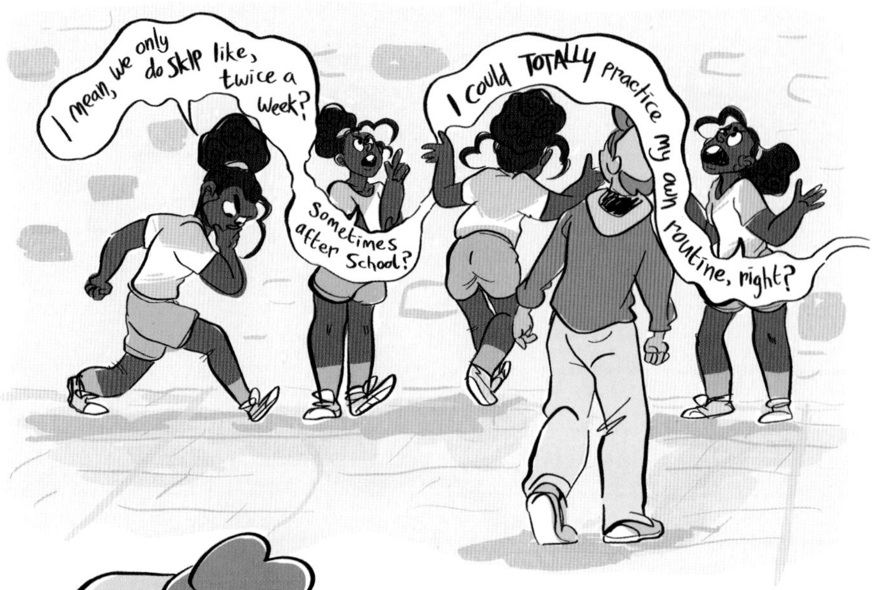
I mean, we only do SKIP like, twice a week?
Sometimes after School?
I could TOTALLY practice my own routine, right?

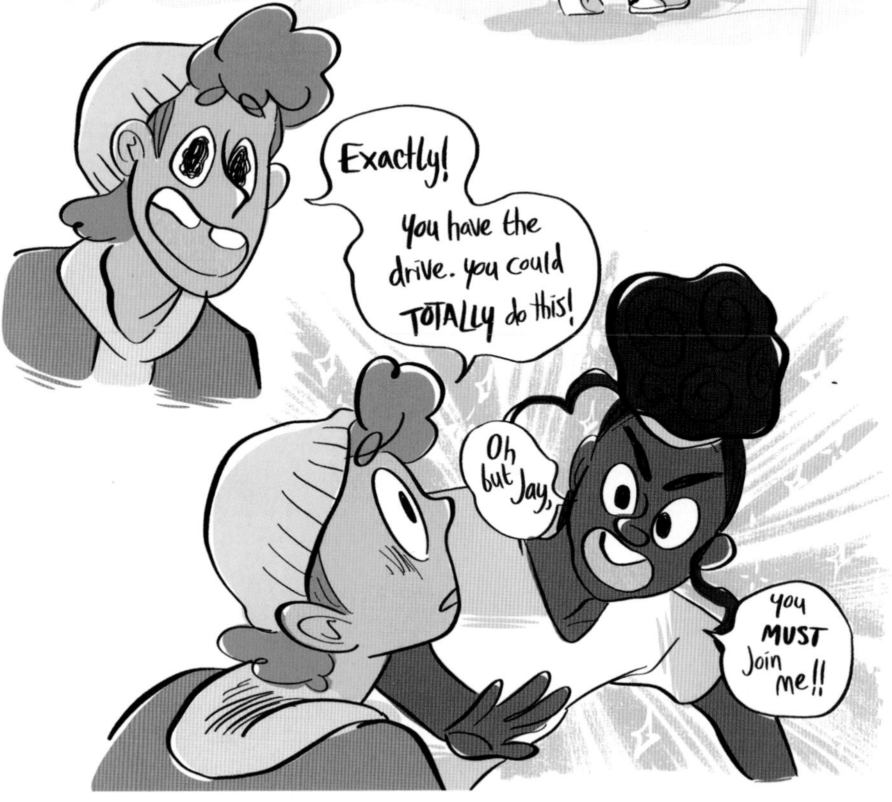
Exactly!
you have the drive. you could TOTALLY do this!
Oh but Jay,
you MUST Join me!!

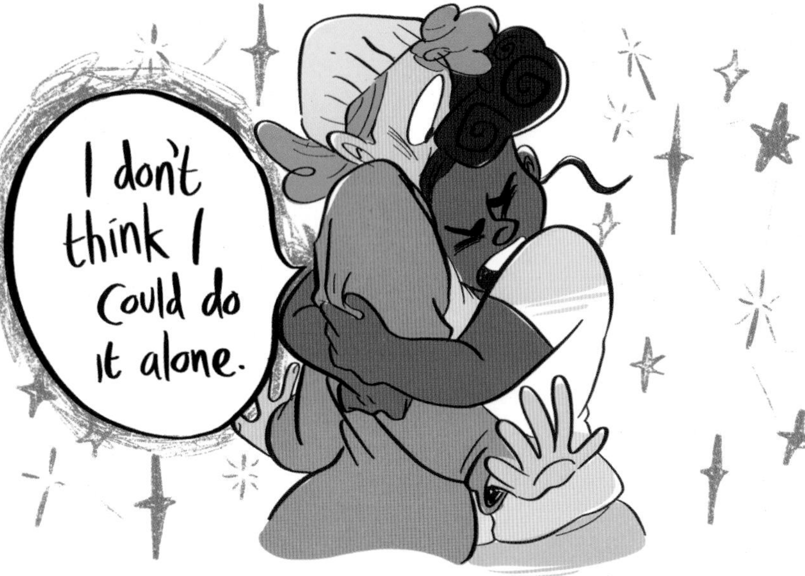
I don't think I could do it alone.

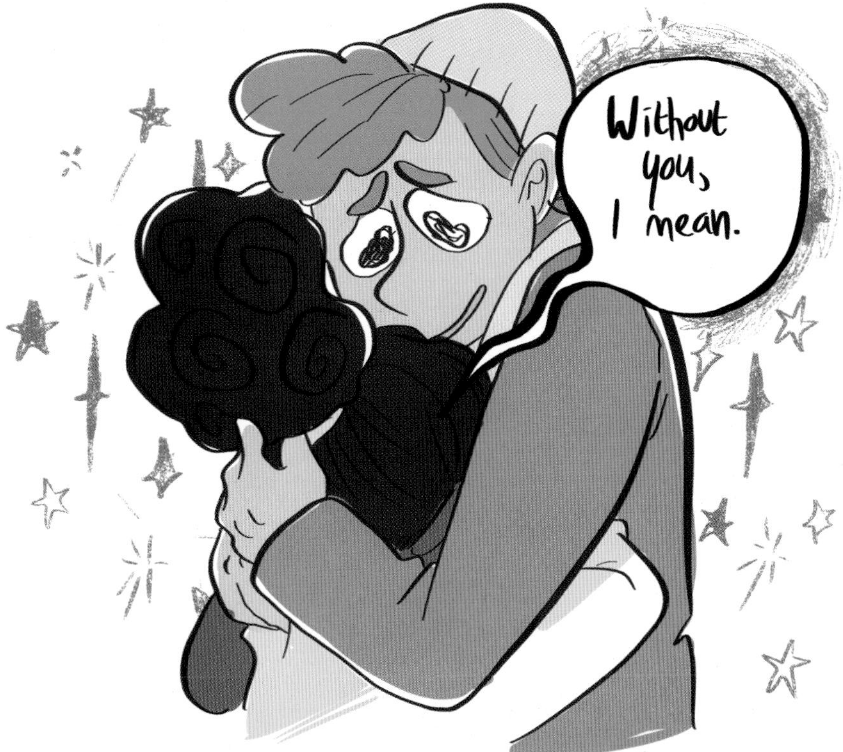
Without you, I mean.

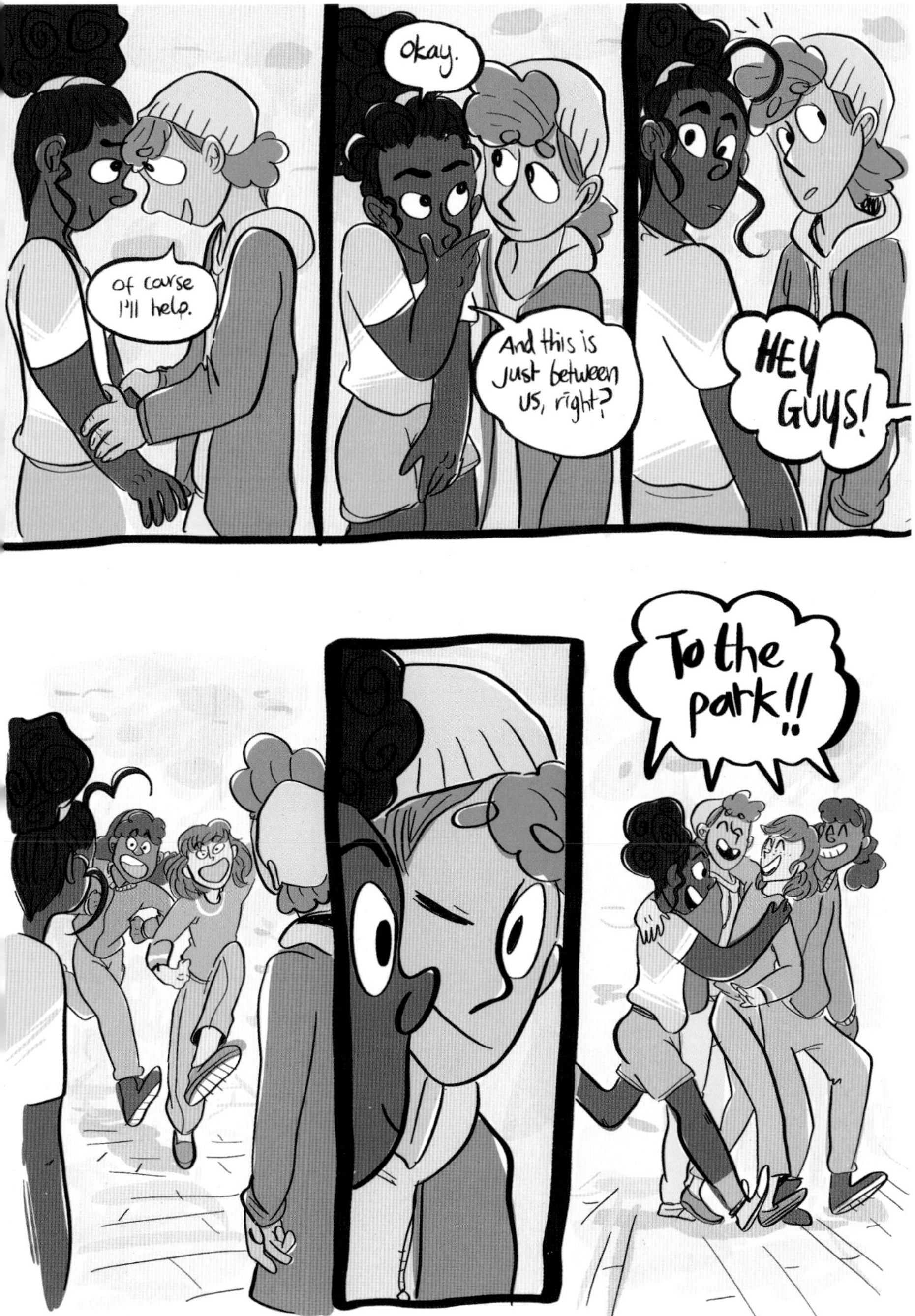
Of course I'll help.
Okay.
And this is just between us, right?
HEY GUYS!
To the park!!

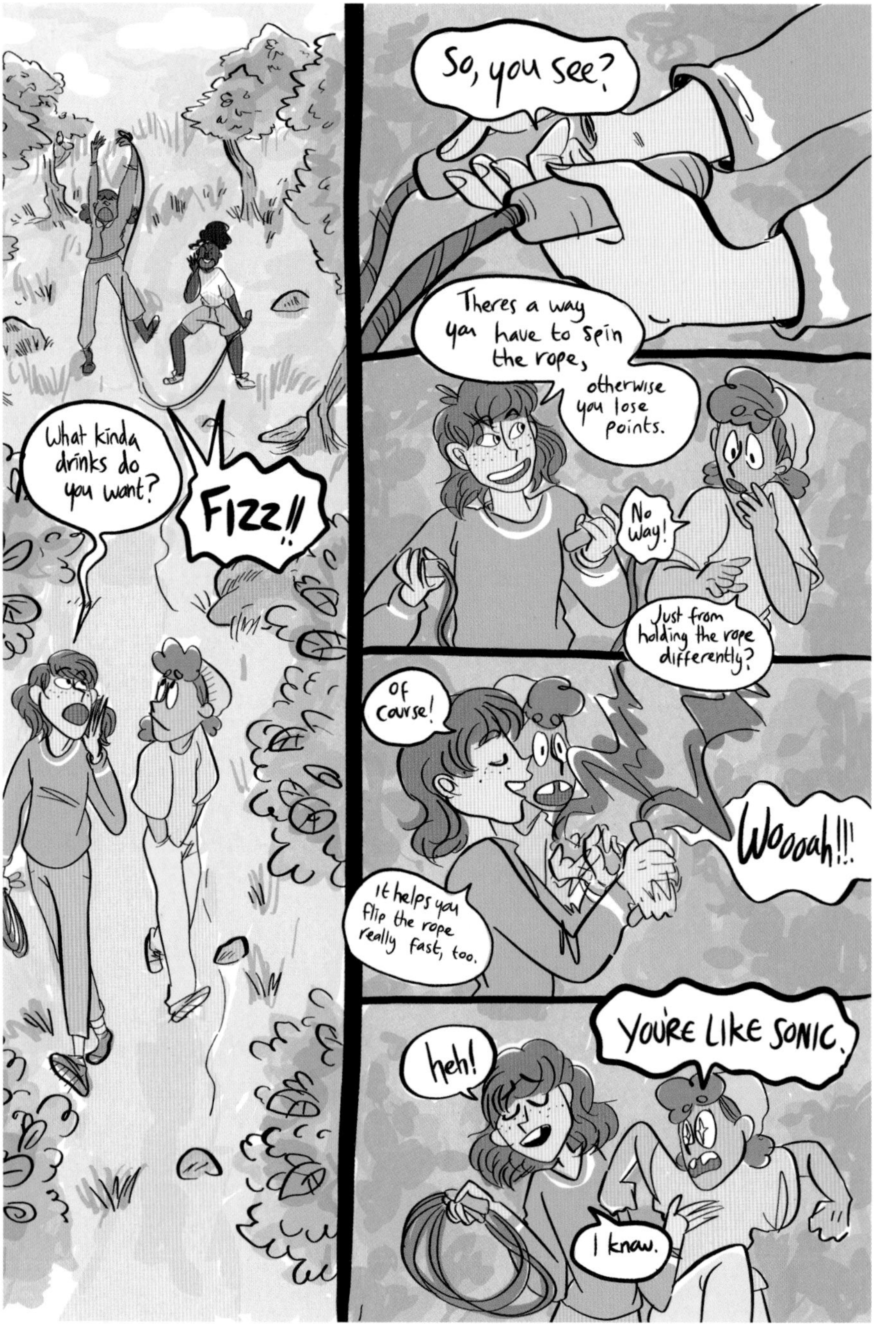
What kinda drinks do you want?
FIZZ!!
So, you see?
Theres a way you have to spin the rope, otherwise you lose points.
No way!
Just from holding the rope differently?
Of course!
Wooaah!!!
It helps you flip the rope really fast, too.
heh!
YOU'RE LIKE SONIC.
I know.

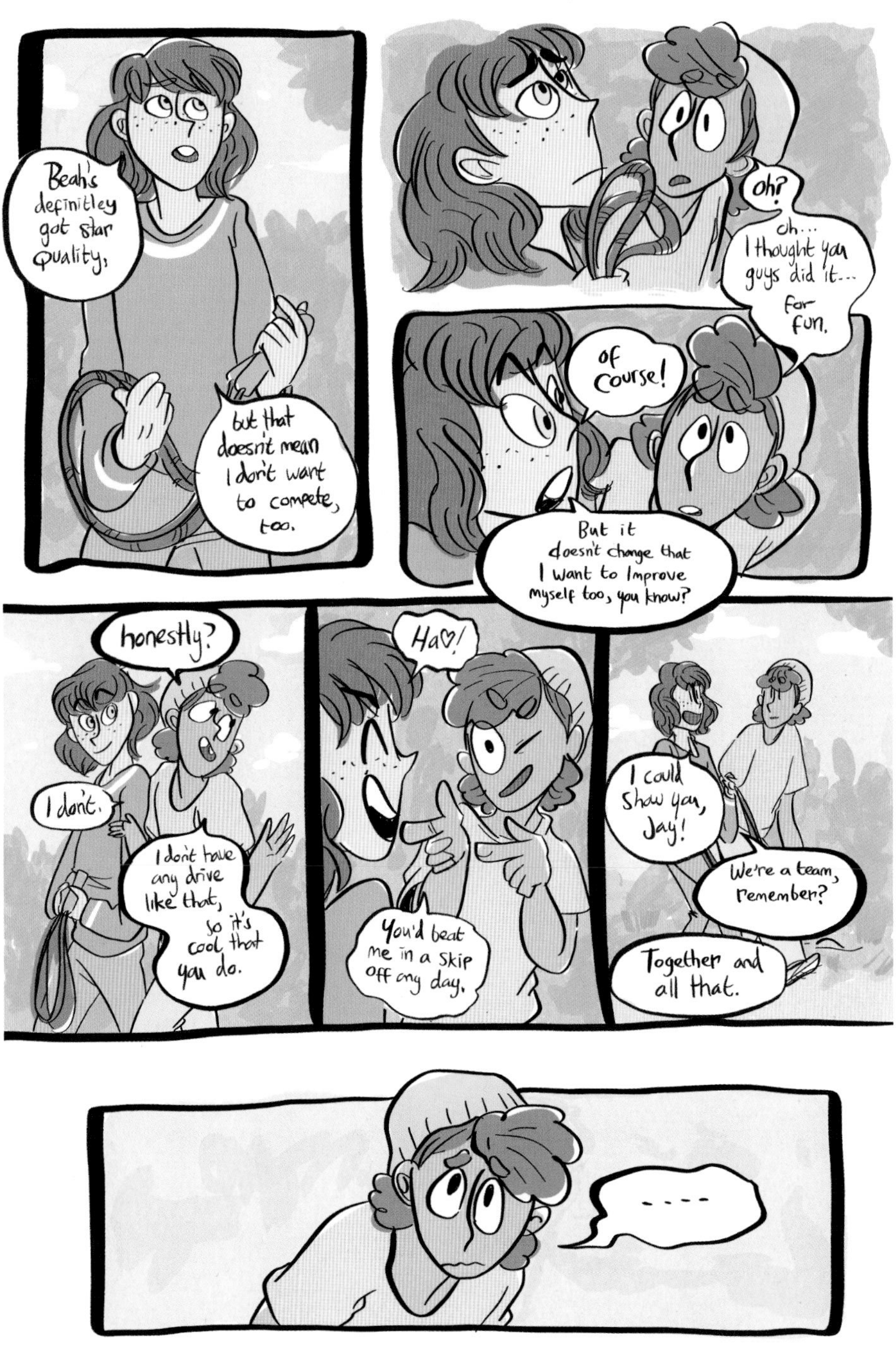
Beah's definitley got star quality,
but that doesn't mean I don't want to compete, too.
oh?
oh... I thought you guys did it... for fun.
of course!
But it doesn't change that I want to Improve myself too, you know?
honestly?
I don't.
I don't have any drive like that, so it's cool that you do.
Ha♡!
You'd beat me in a skip off any day.
I could show you, Jay!
We're a team, remember?
Together and all that.
....

CHAPTER SEVEN

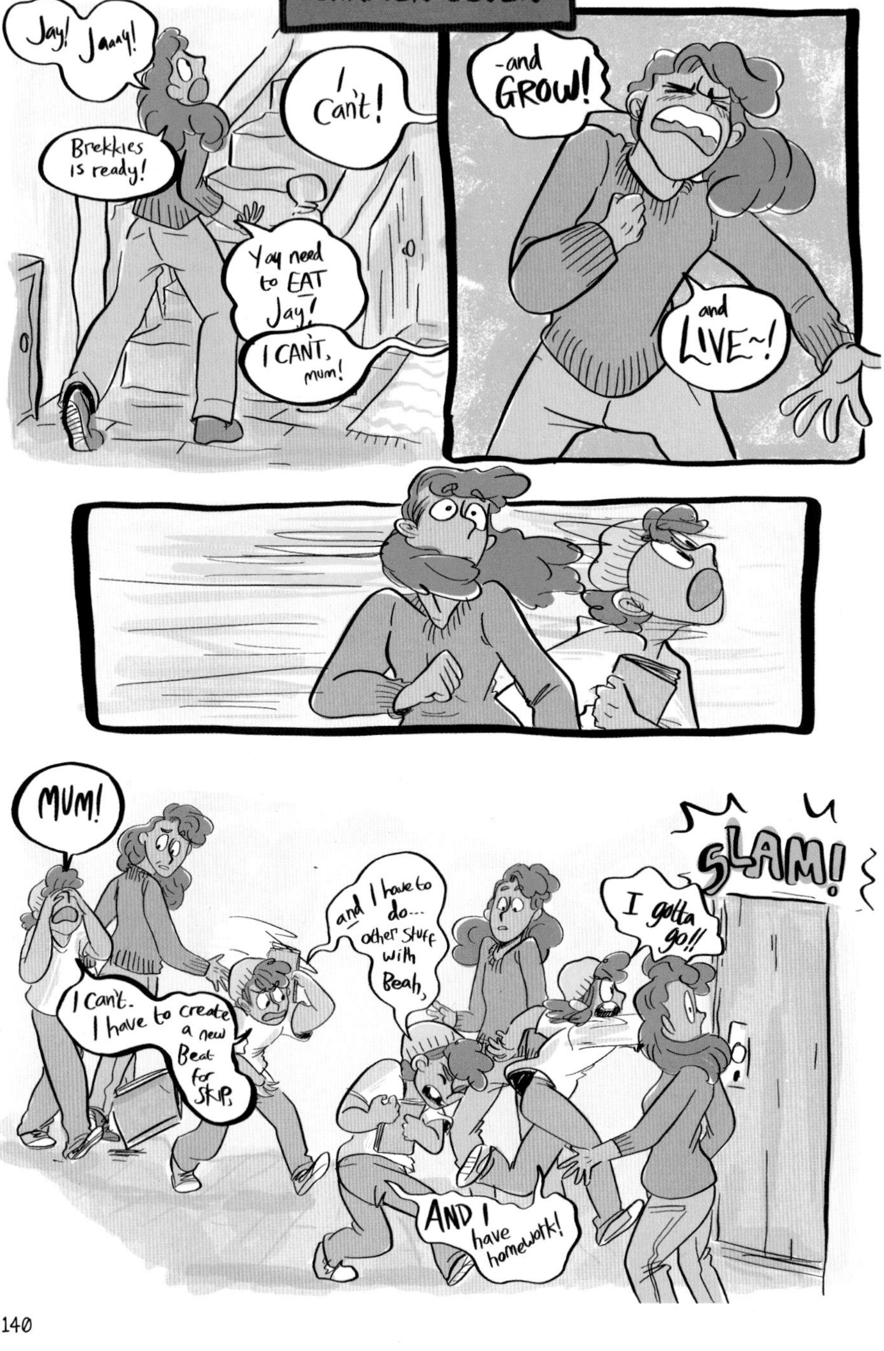

Jay! Jaaay!
Brekkies is ready!
I can't!
You need to EAT Jay!
I CAN'T, mum!
-and GROW!
and LIVE~!
MUM!
I can't. I have to create a new Beat for SKIP,
and I have to do... other stuff with Beah,
AND I have homework!
I gotta go!!
SLAM!

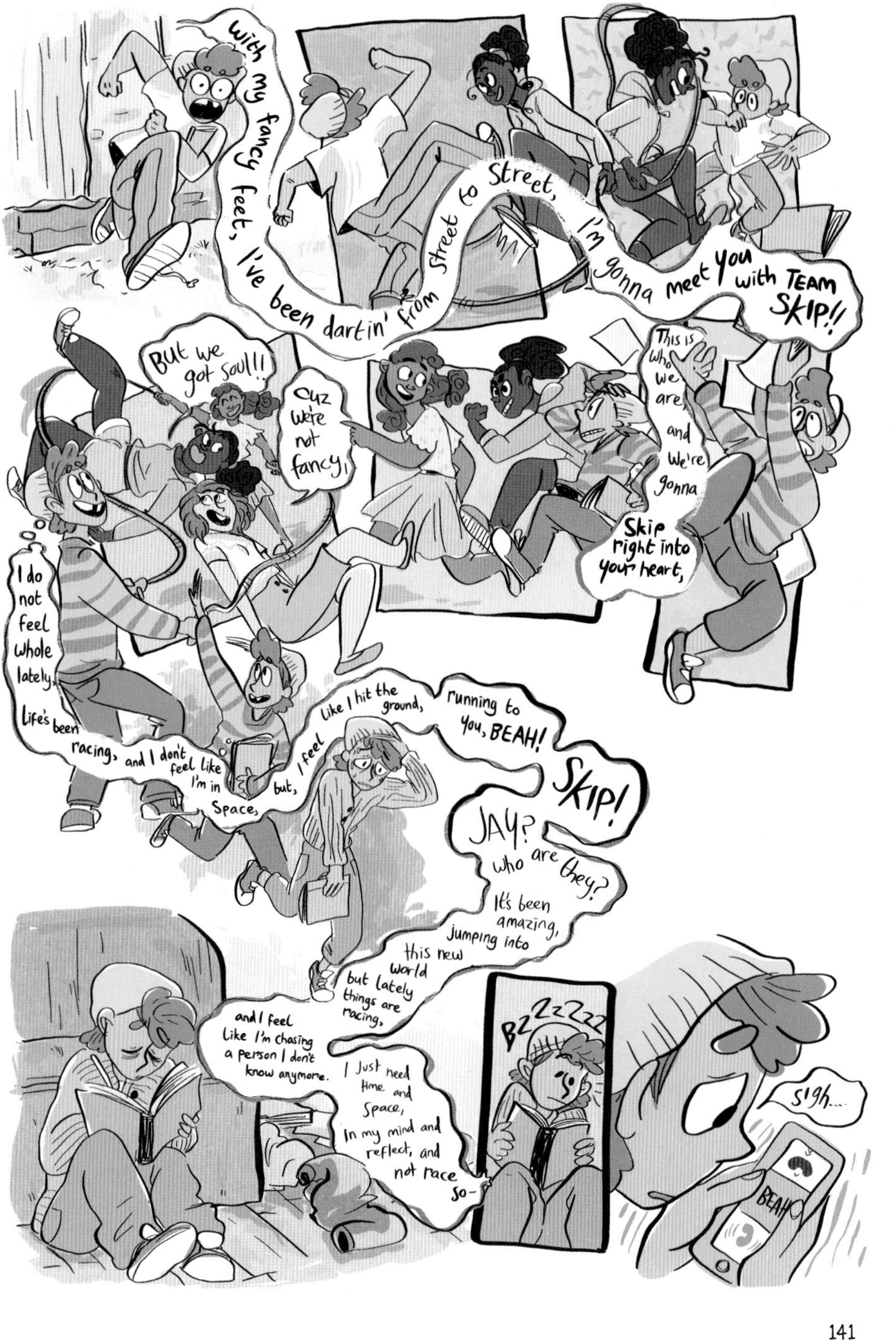
with my fancy feet, I've been dartin' from street to street, I'm gonna meet you with TEAM SKIP!!
But we got soul!!
Cuz we're not fancy,
This is who we are, and we're gonna Skip right into your heart,
I do not feel whole lately,
Life's been racing, and I don't feel like I'm in space, but, I feel like I hit the ground, running to you, BEAH!
SKIP!
JAY? who are they?
It's been amazing, jumping into this new world but lately things are racing,
and I feel like I'm chasing a person I don't know anymore.
I just need time and space, in my mind and reflect, and not race so-
BZZZZZ
sigh...
BEAH

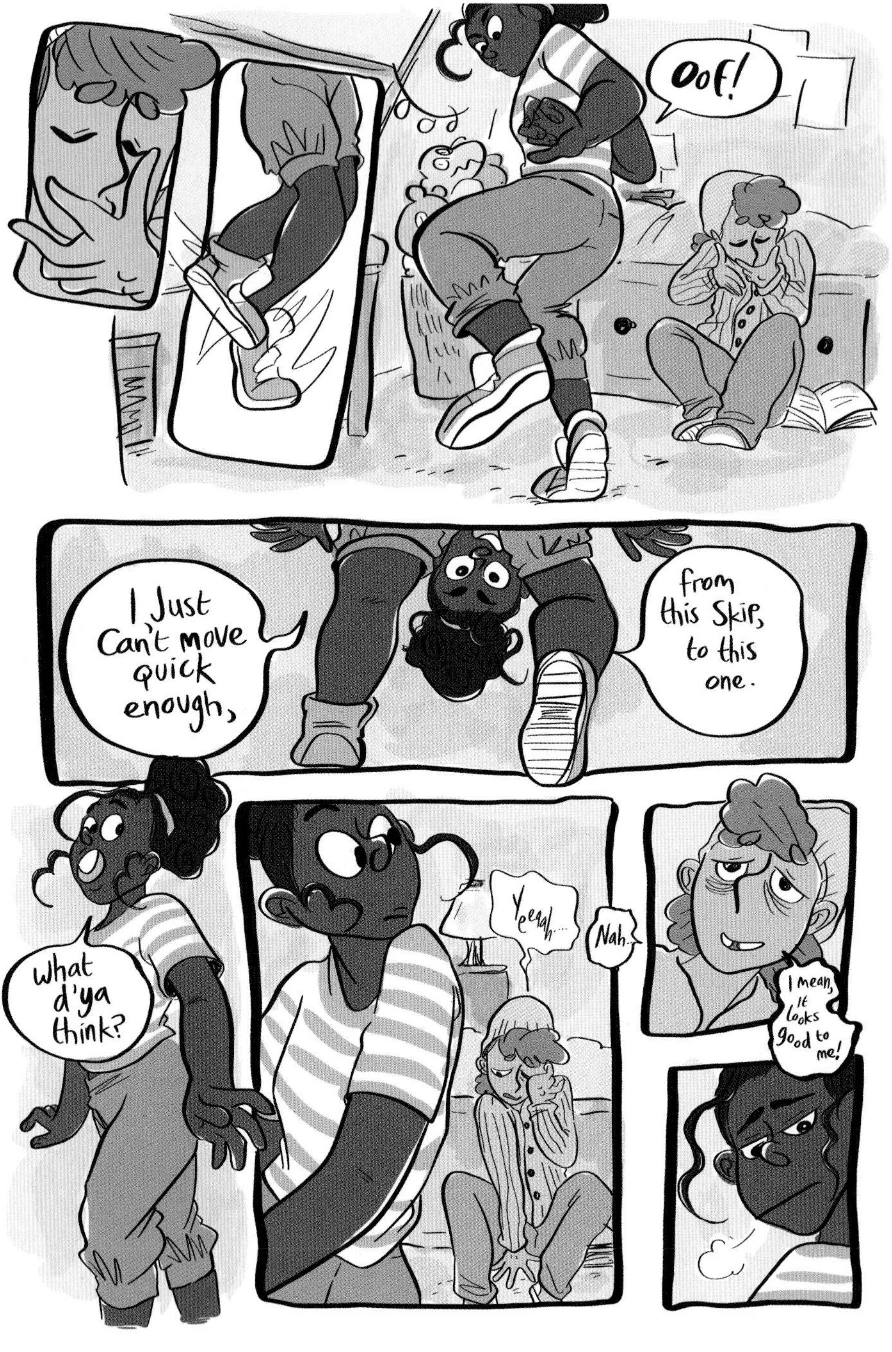
Oof!
I Just Can't move quick enough,
from this Skip, to this one.
what d'ya think?
Yeeaah....
Nah..
I mean, it looks good to me!

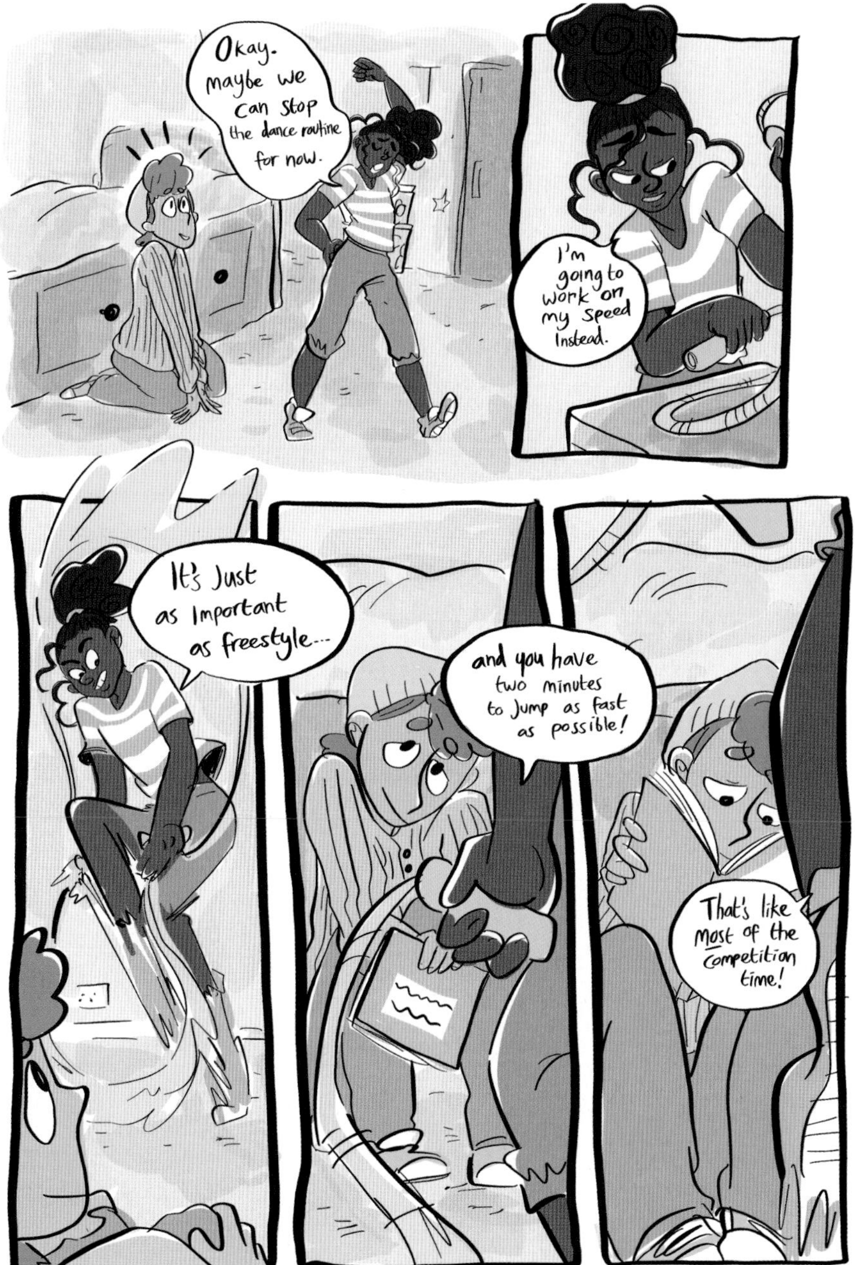
Okay. maybe we can stop the dance routine for now.
I'm going to work on my speed Instead.
It's Just as Important as freestyle...
and you have two minutes to Jump as fast as possible!
That's like most of the competition time!

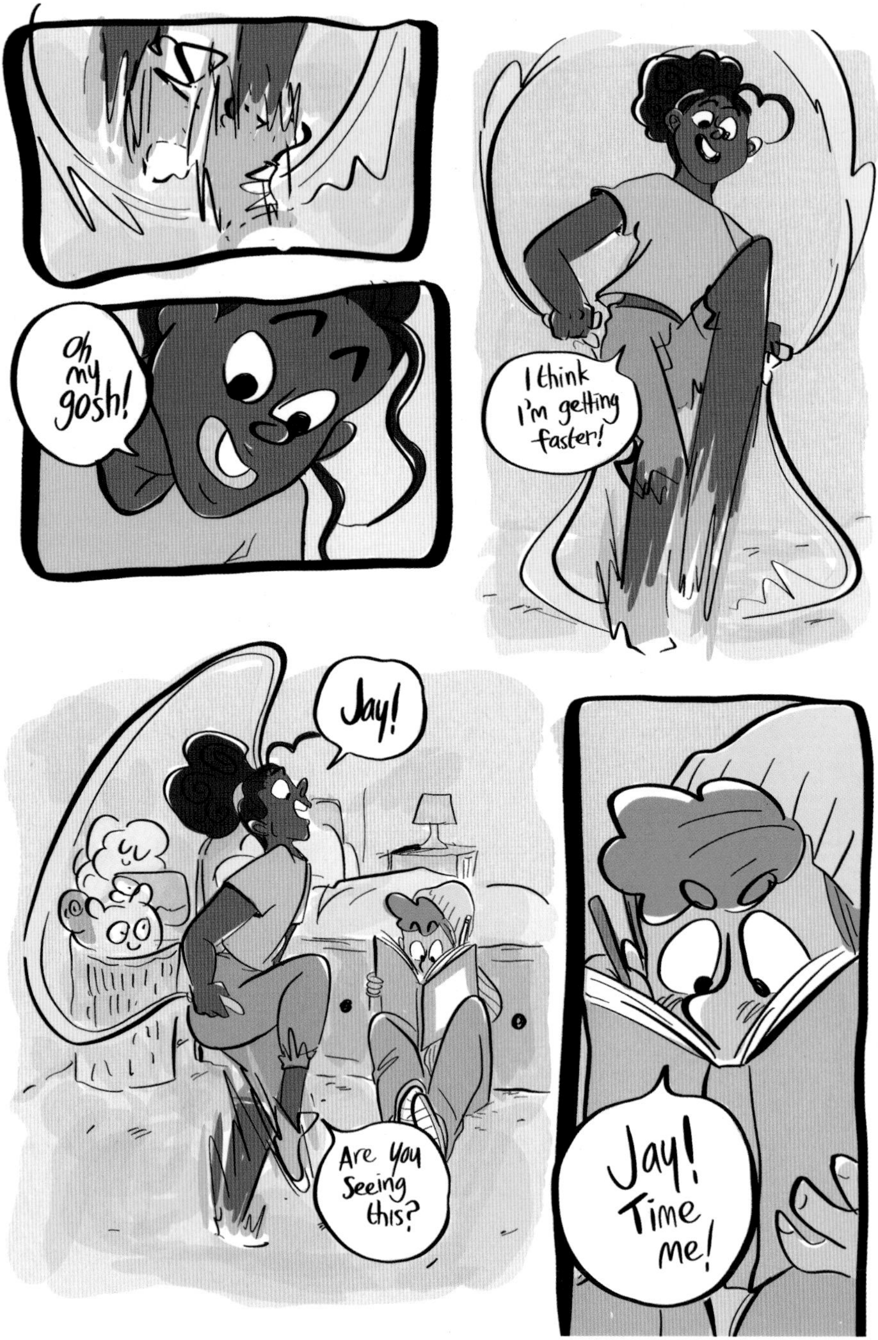

oh my gosh!
I think I'm getting faster!
Jay!
Are you seeing this?
Jay! Time me!

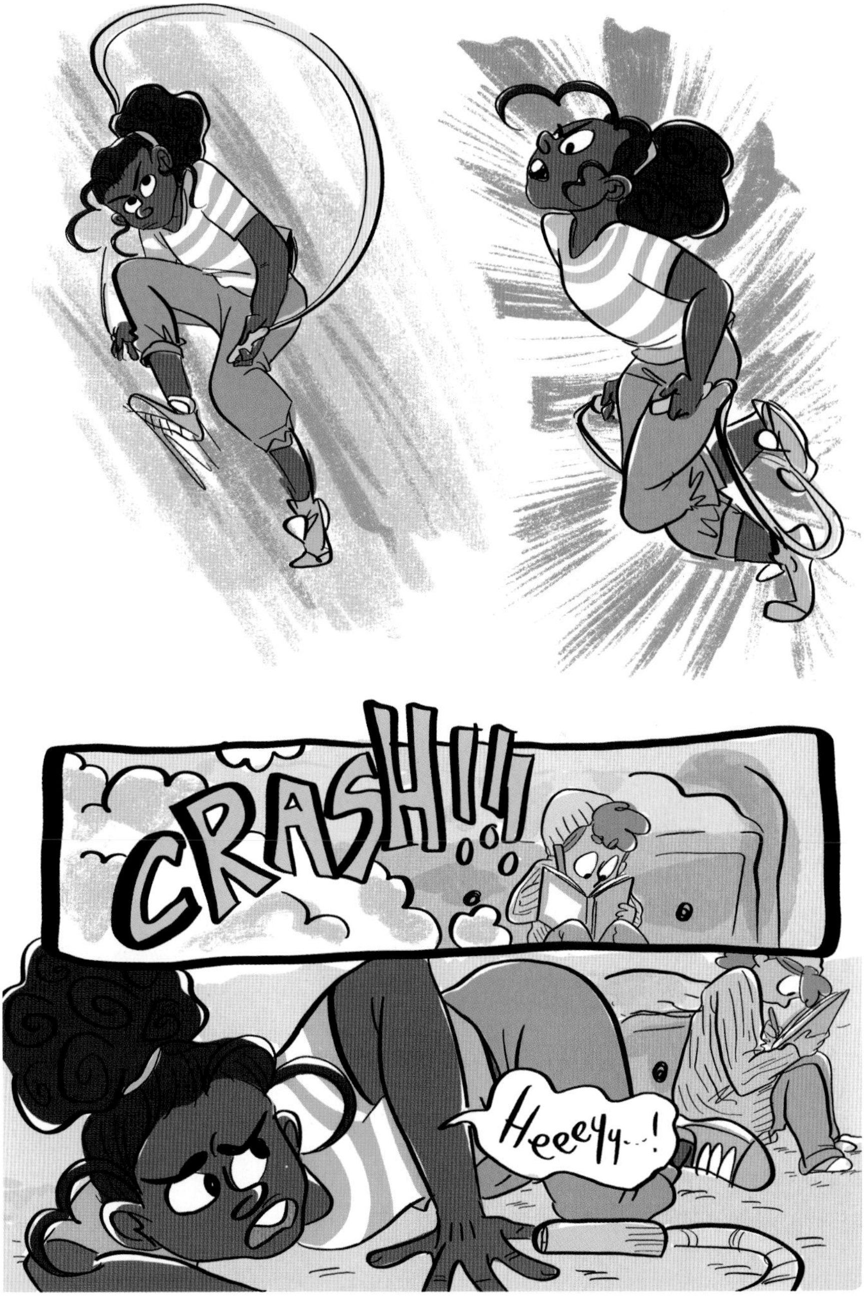
CRASH!!!
Heeeyy...!

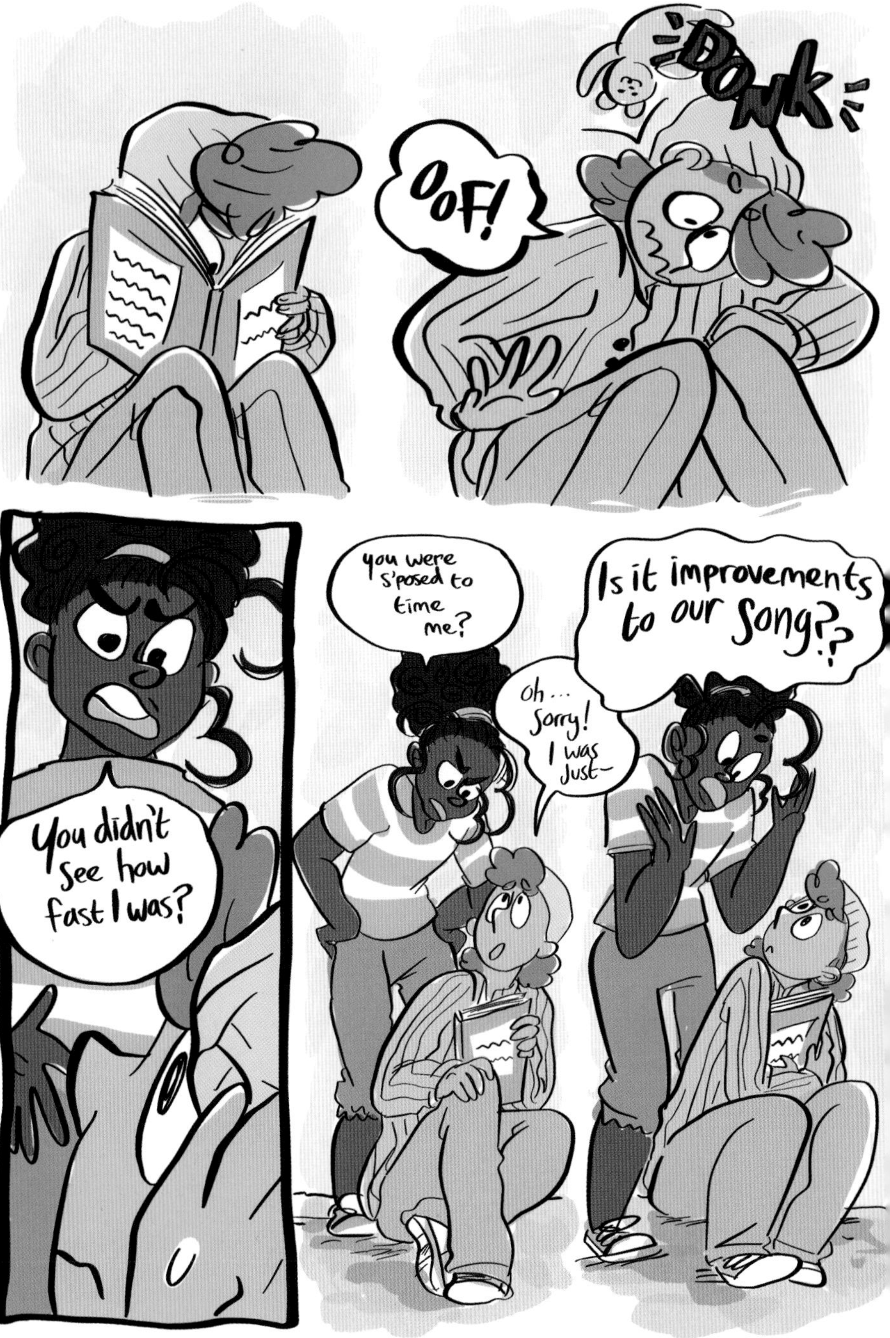
DONK
OOF!
You didn't see how fast I was?
you were s'posed to time me?
Oh... Sorry! I was just~
Is it improvements to our Song?!?

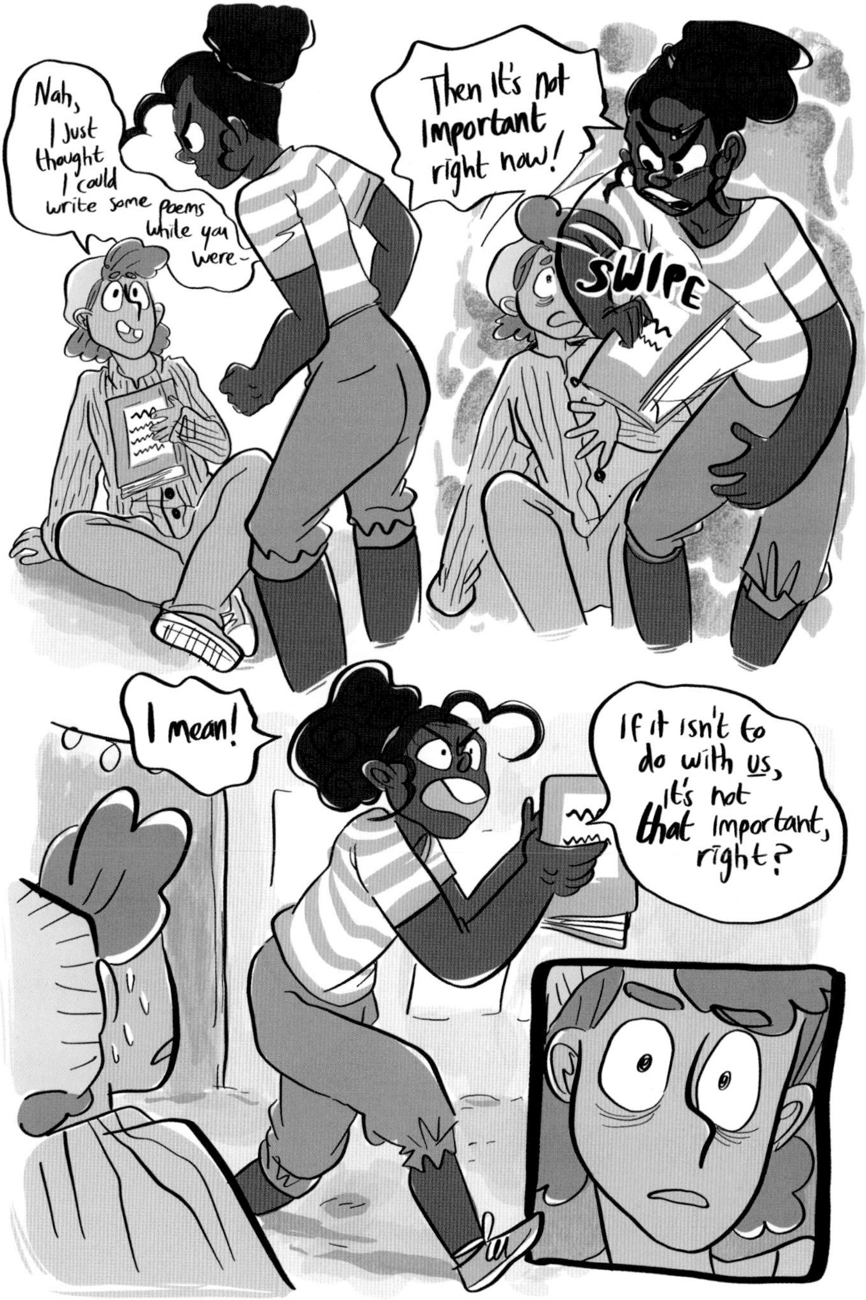
Nah, I just thought I could write some poems while you were-
Then it's not important right now!
SWIPE
I mean!
If it isn't to do with us, it's not that important, right?

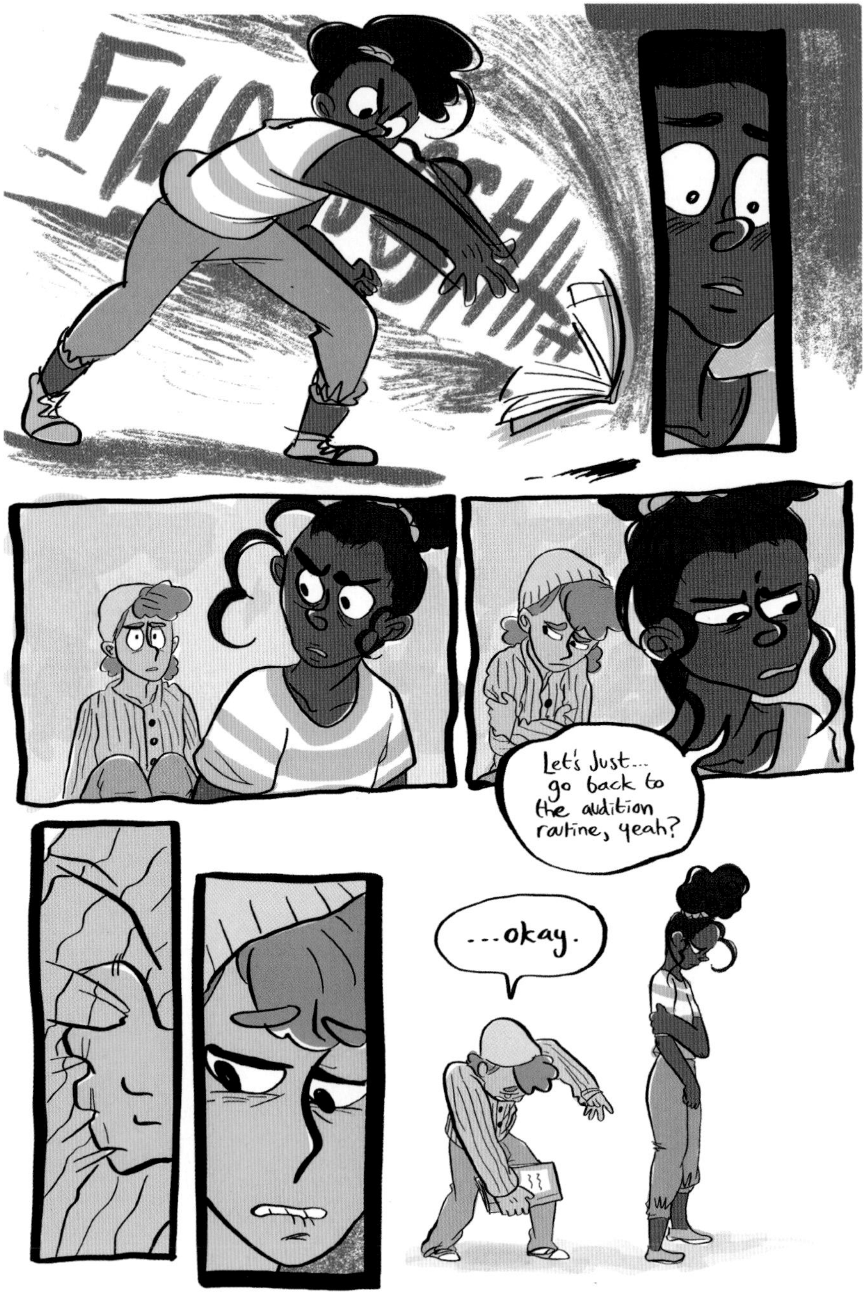
FWOOSH
Let's Just... go back to the audition routine, yeah?
...okay.

CHAPTER EIGHT

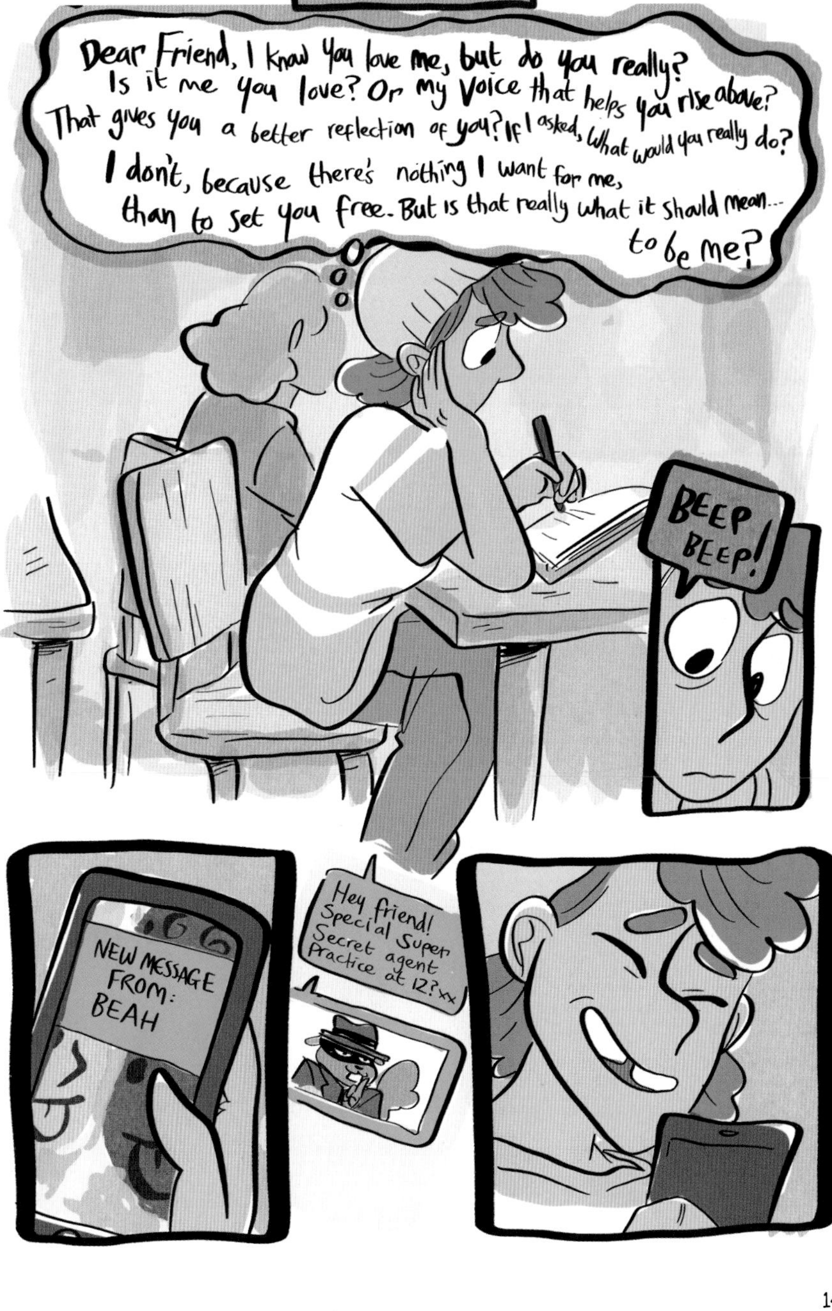

Dear Friend, I know you love me, but do you really? Is it me you love? Or my voice that helps you rise above? That gives you a better reflection of you? If I asked, What would you really do? I don't, because there's nothing I want for me, than to set you free. But is that really what it should mean... to be me?
BEEP BEEP!
NEW MESSAGE FROM: BEAH
Hey friend! Special Super Secret agent Practice at 12?xx

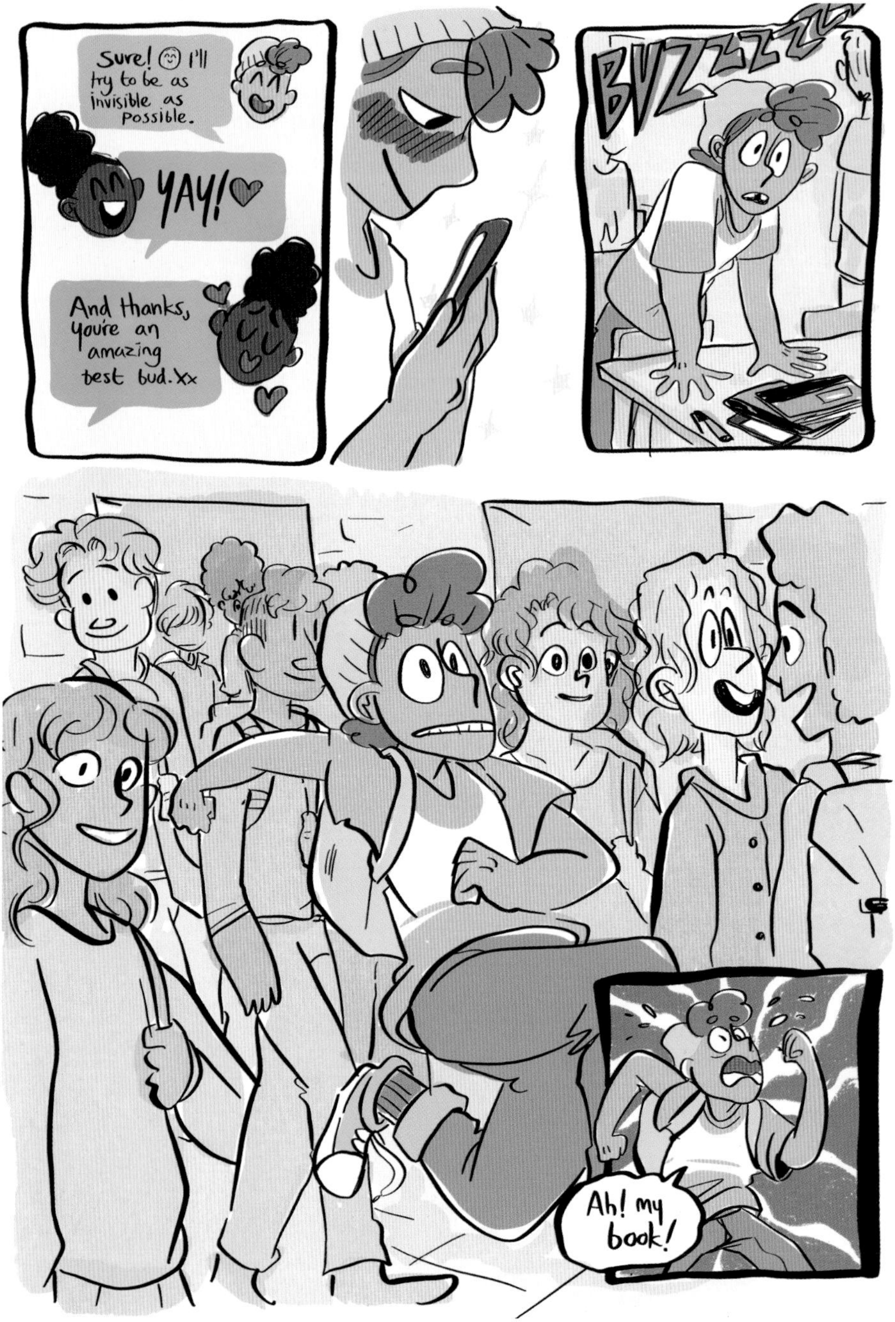
Sure! I'll try to be as invisible as possible.
YAY!
And thanks, you're an amazing best bud. Xx
BUZZZZZZ
Ah! my book!

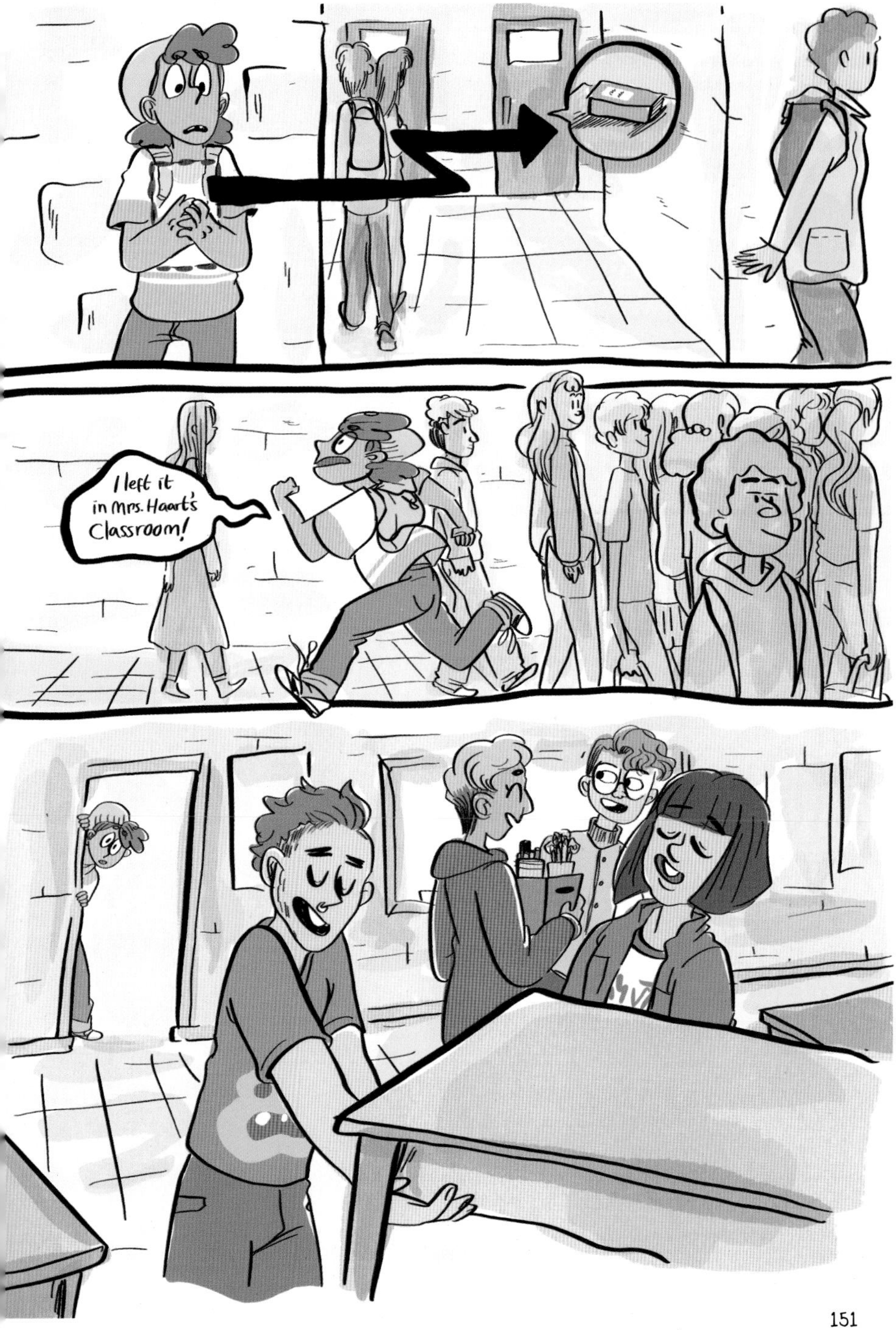
I left it in Mrs. Haart's Classroom!

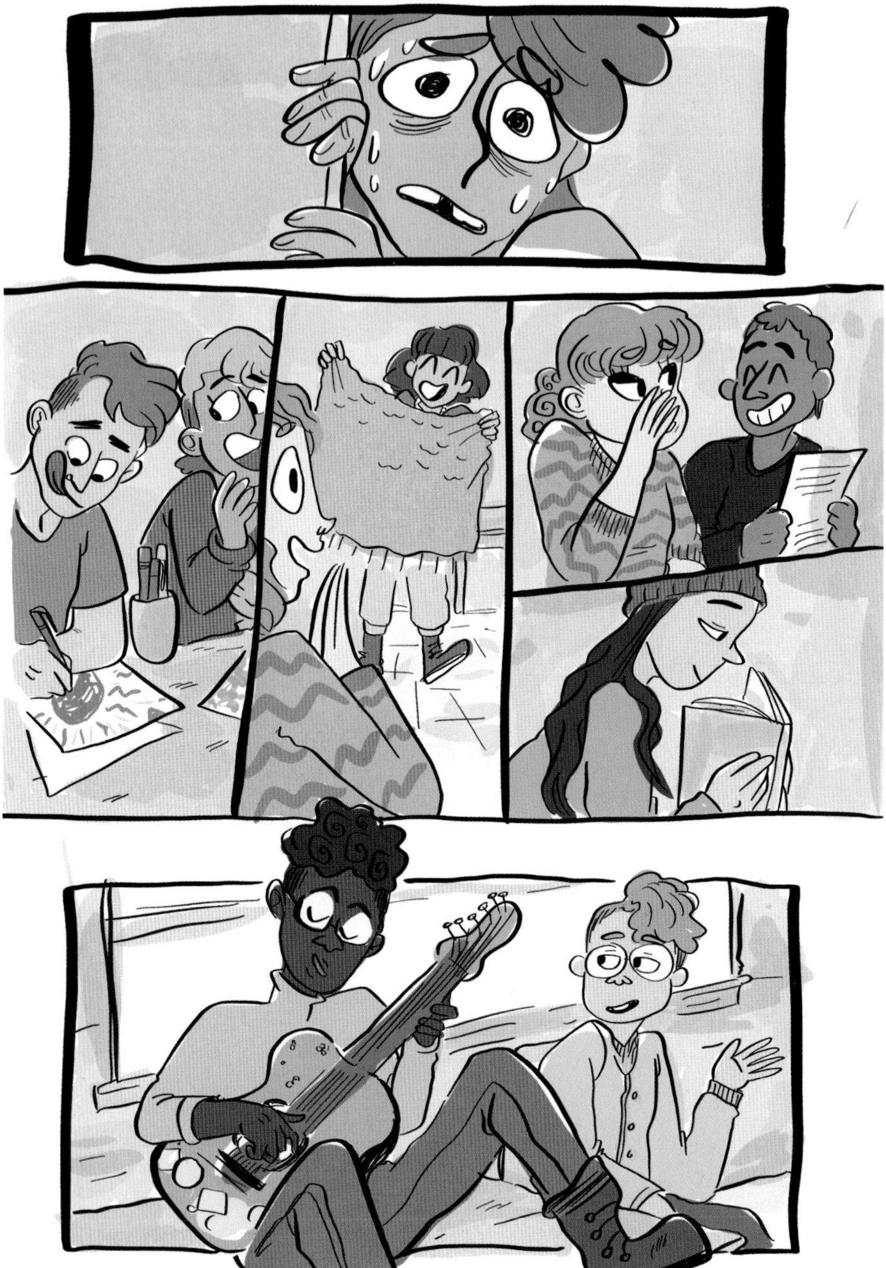

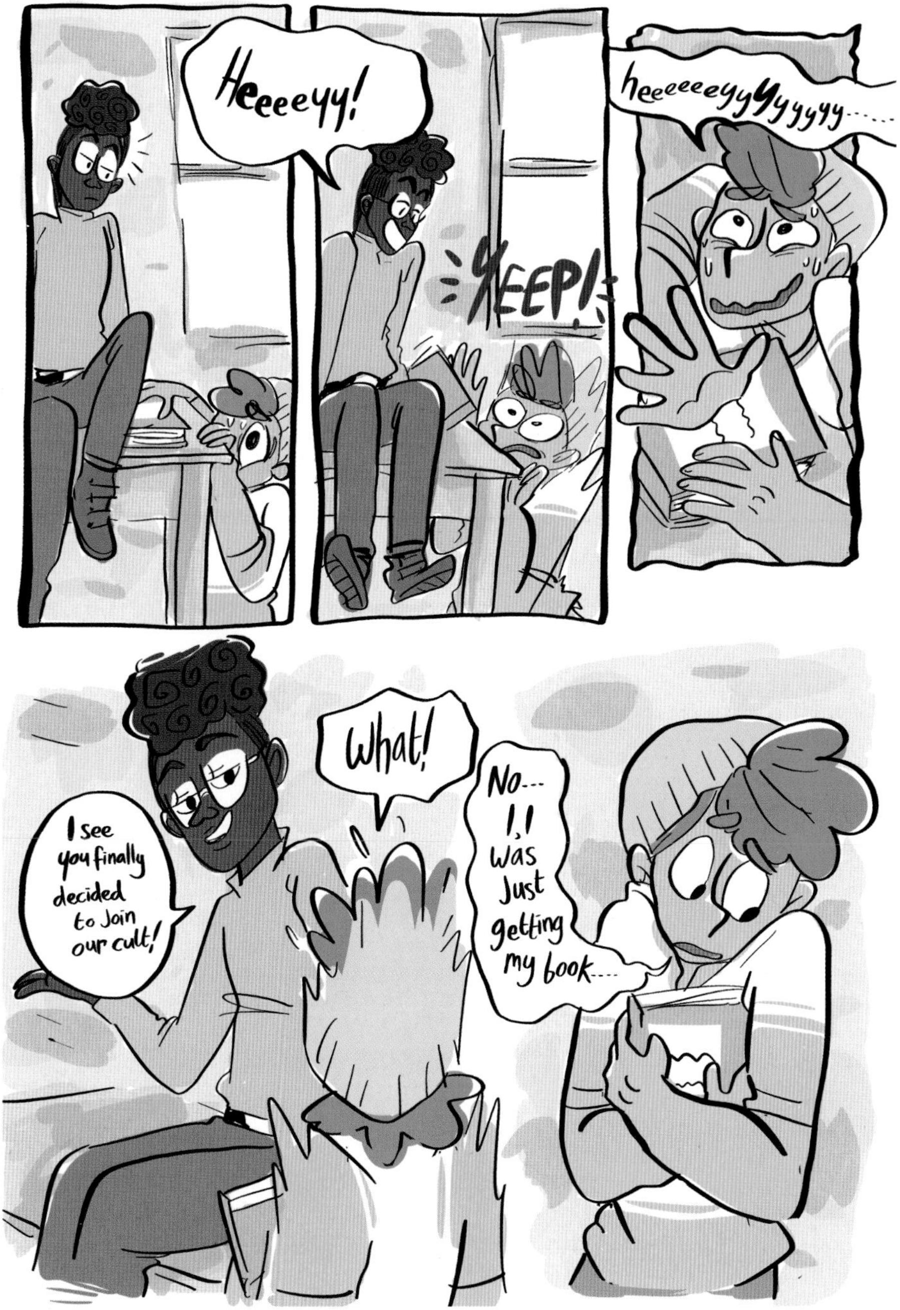
Heeeeyy!
YEEP!
heeeeeeyyyYyyyyy.......
I see you finally decided to Join our cult!
What!
No... I, I was Just getting my book....

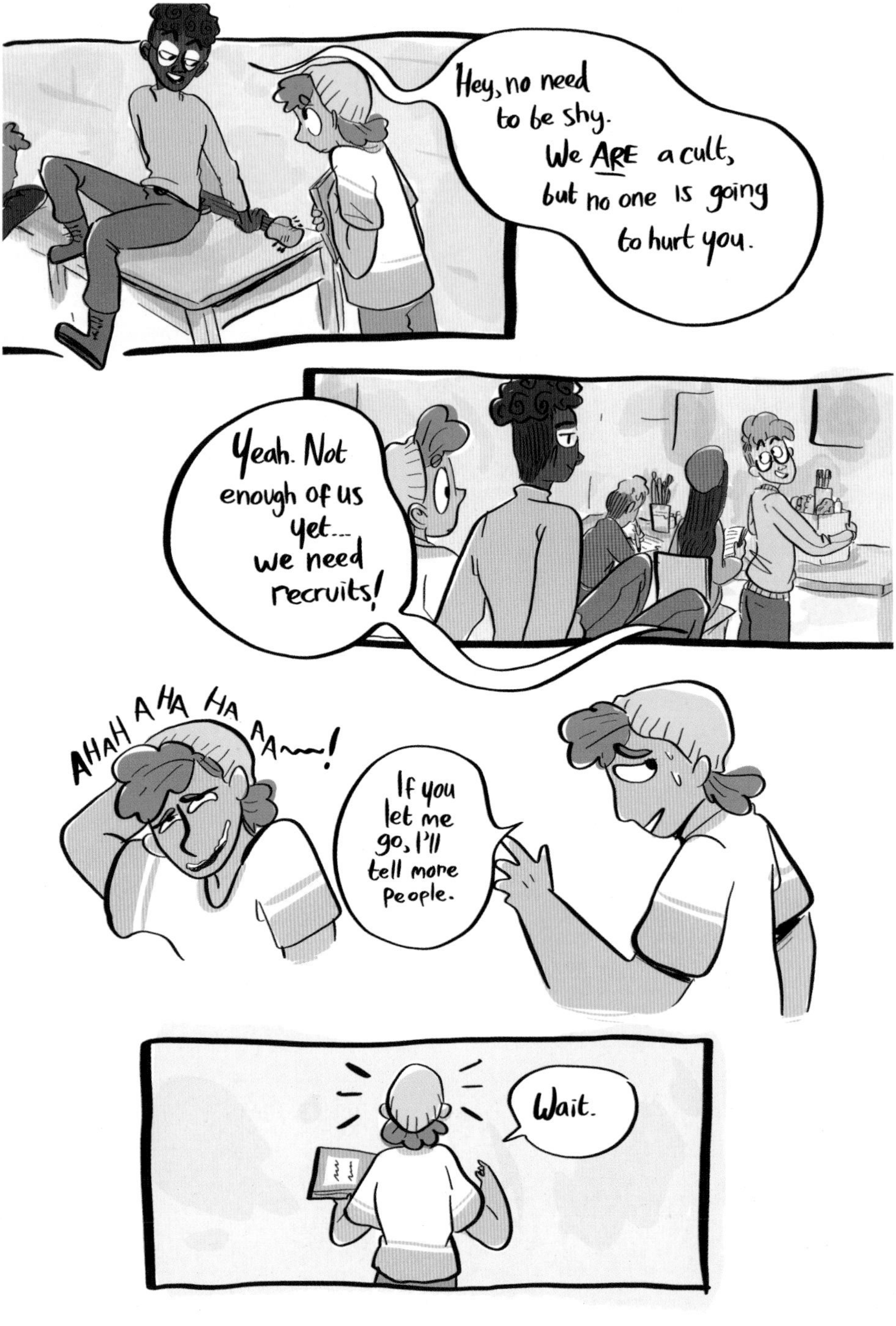
Hey, no need to be shy. We ARE a cult, but no one is going to hurt you.
Yeah. Not enough of us yet... we need recruits!
AHAHAHA HA HA AA~~~!
If you let me go, I'll tell more people.
Wait.

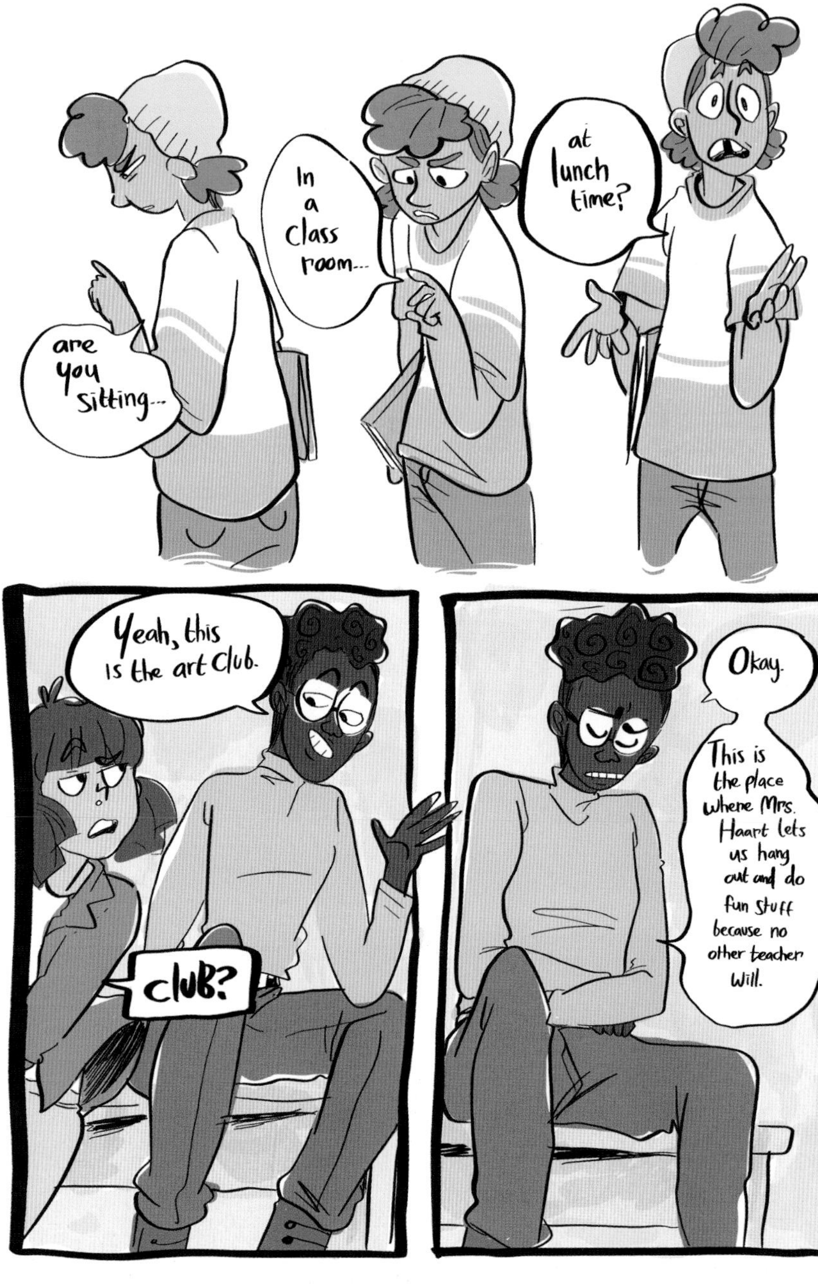
are you sitting...
In a Class room...
at lunch time?
Yeah, this is the art Club.
club?
Okay.
This is the place where Mrs. Haart lets us hang out and do fun stuff because no other teacher will.

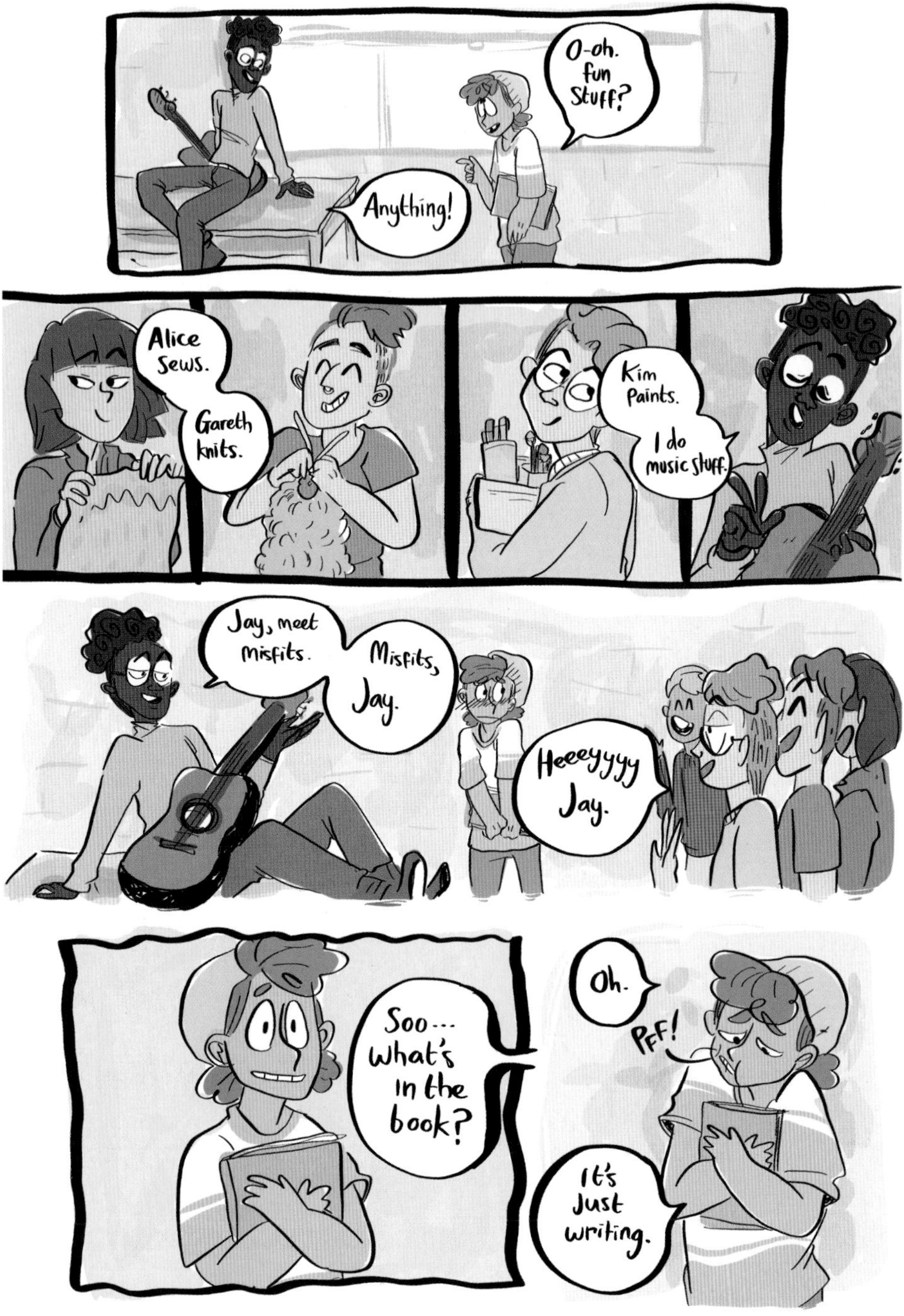
O-oh. fun Stuff?
Anything!
Alice Sews.
Gareth knits.
Kim Paints.
I do music stuff.
Jay, meet misfits.
Misfits, Jay.
Heeeyyyy Jay.
Soo... what's in the book?
Oh.
PFF!
It's Just writing.

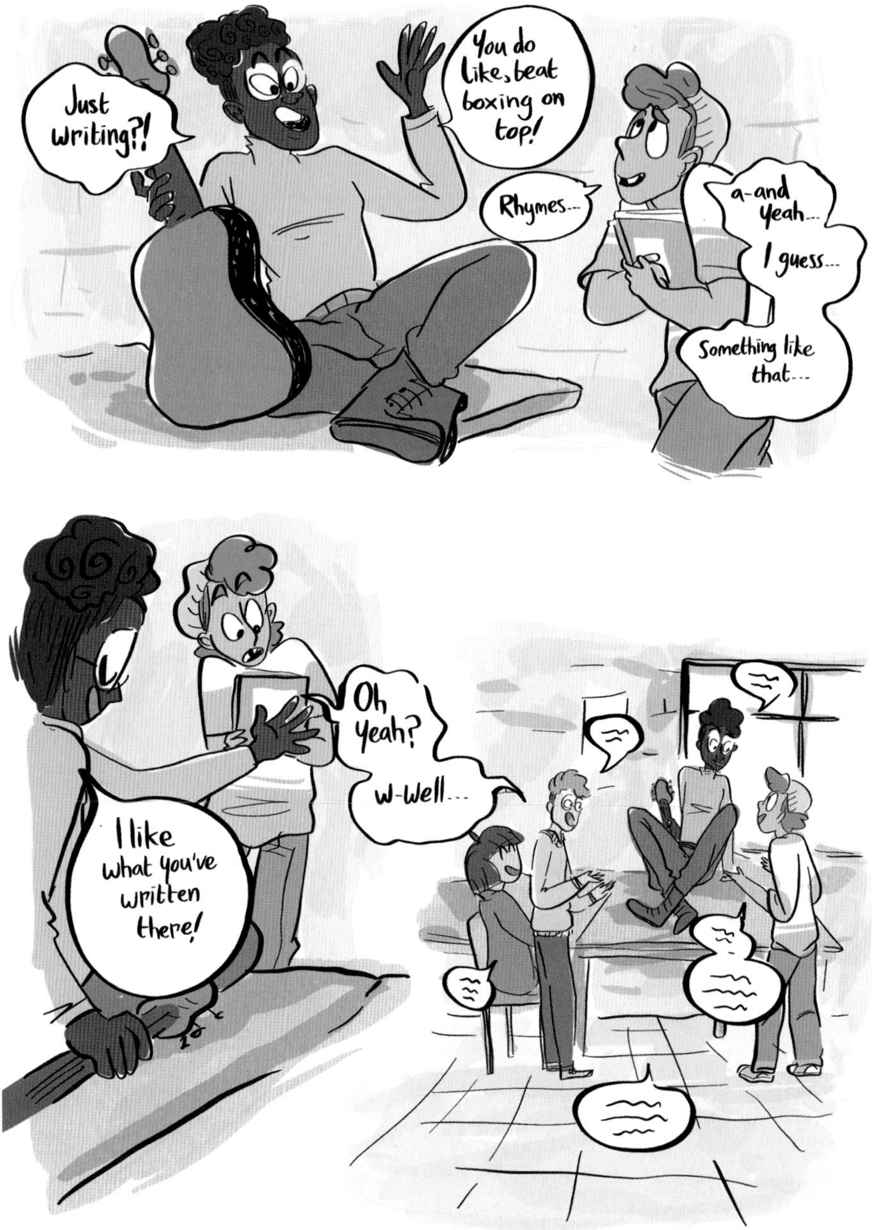
Just writing?!
You do like, beat boxing on top!
Rhymes...
a-and yeah...
I guess...
Something like that...
Oh yeah?
w-well...
I like what you've written there!

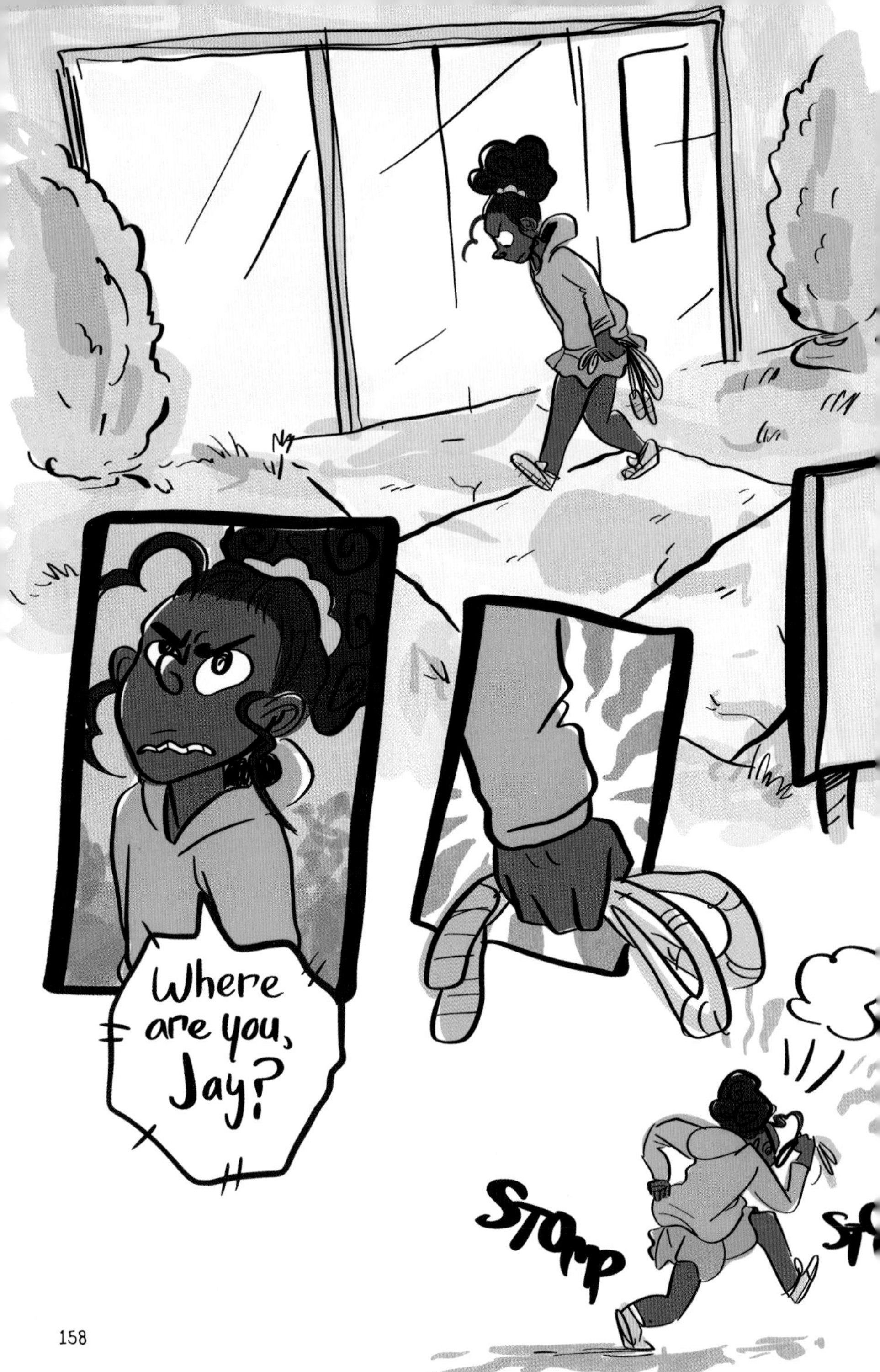
Where are you, Jay?
STOMP

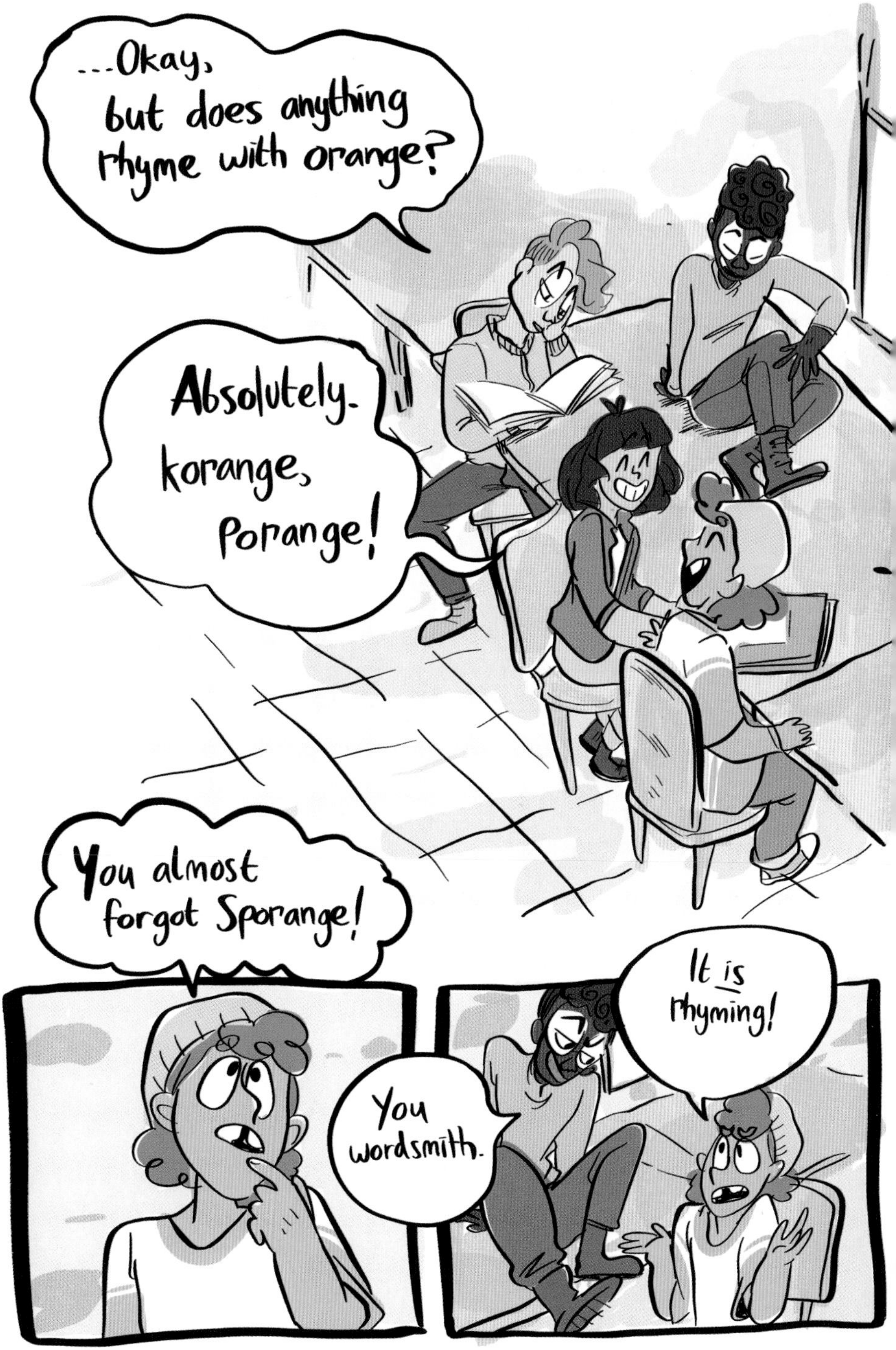
...Okay, but does anything rhyme with orange?
Absolutely. korange, porange!
You almost forgot Sporange!
You wordsmith.
It is rhyming!

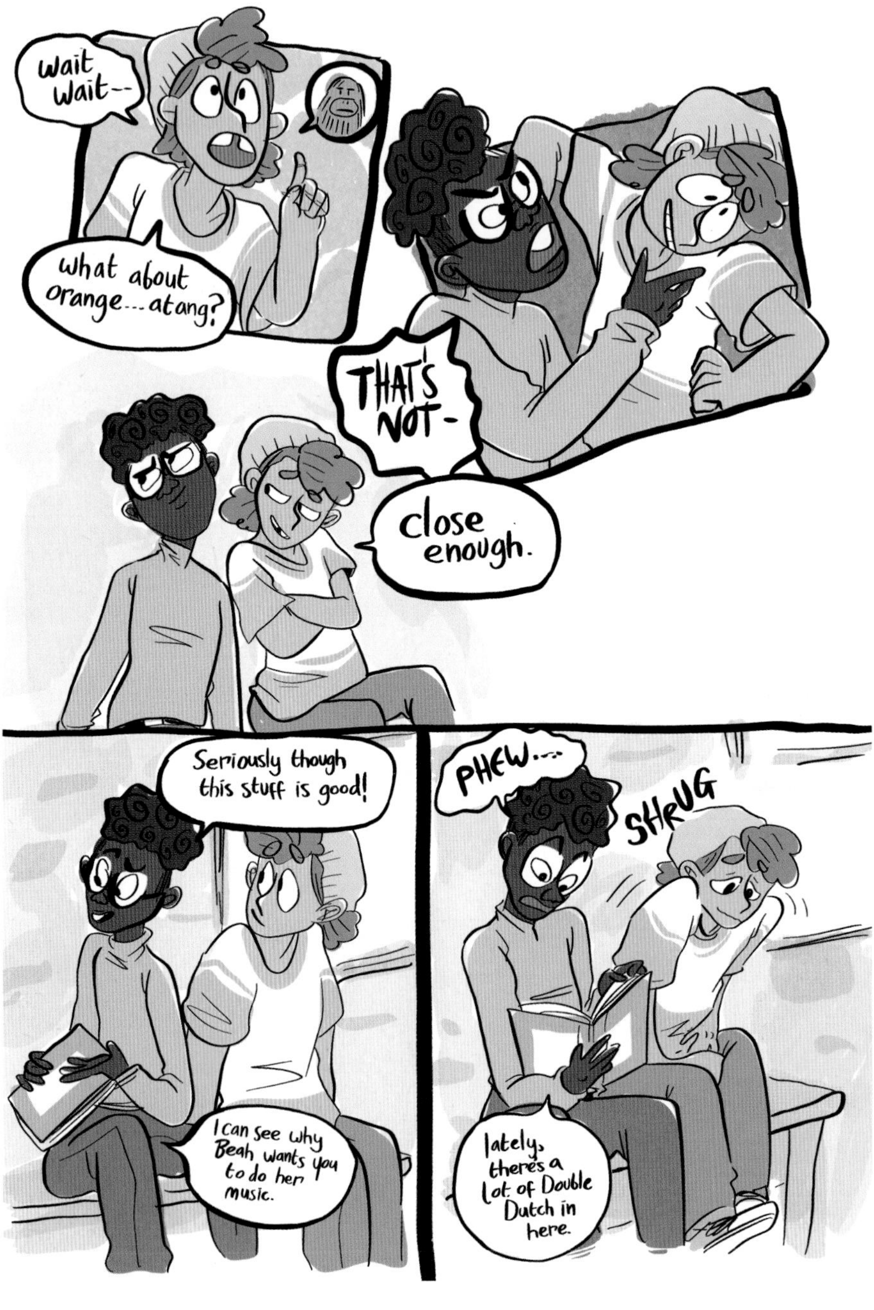
wait wait--
what about orange...atang?
THAT'S NOT-
close enough.
Seriously though this stuff is good!
I can see why Beah wants you to do her music.
PHEW....
SHRUG
lately, there's a lot of Double Dutch in here.

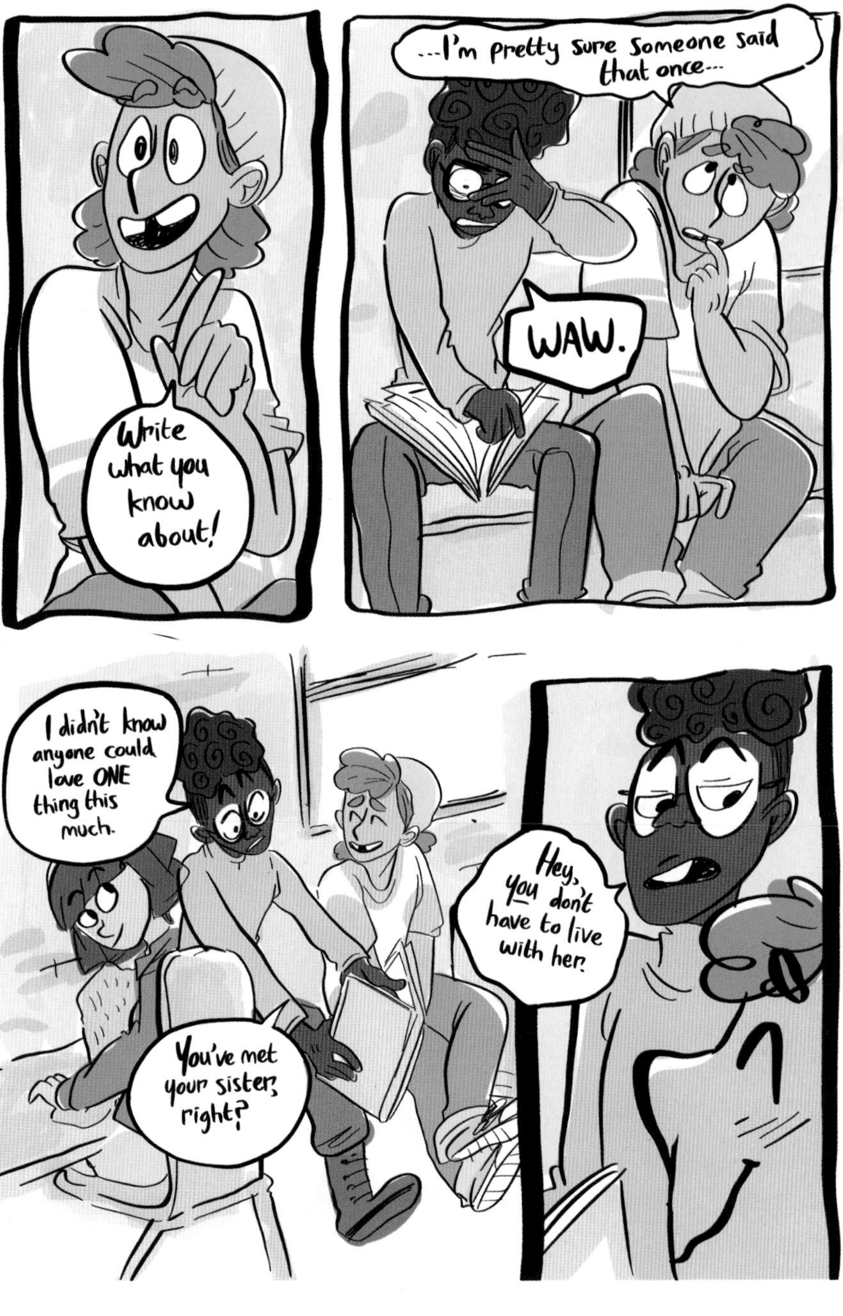
Write what you know about!
...I'm pretty sure someone said that once...
WAW.
I didn't know anyone could love ONE thing this much.
You've met your sister, right?
Hey, you don't have to live with her.

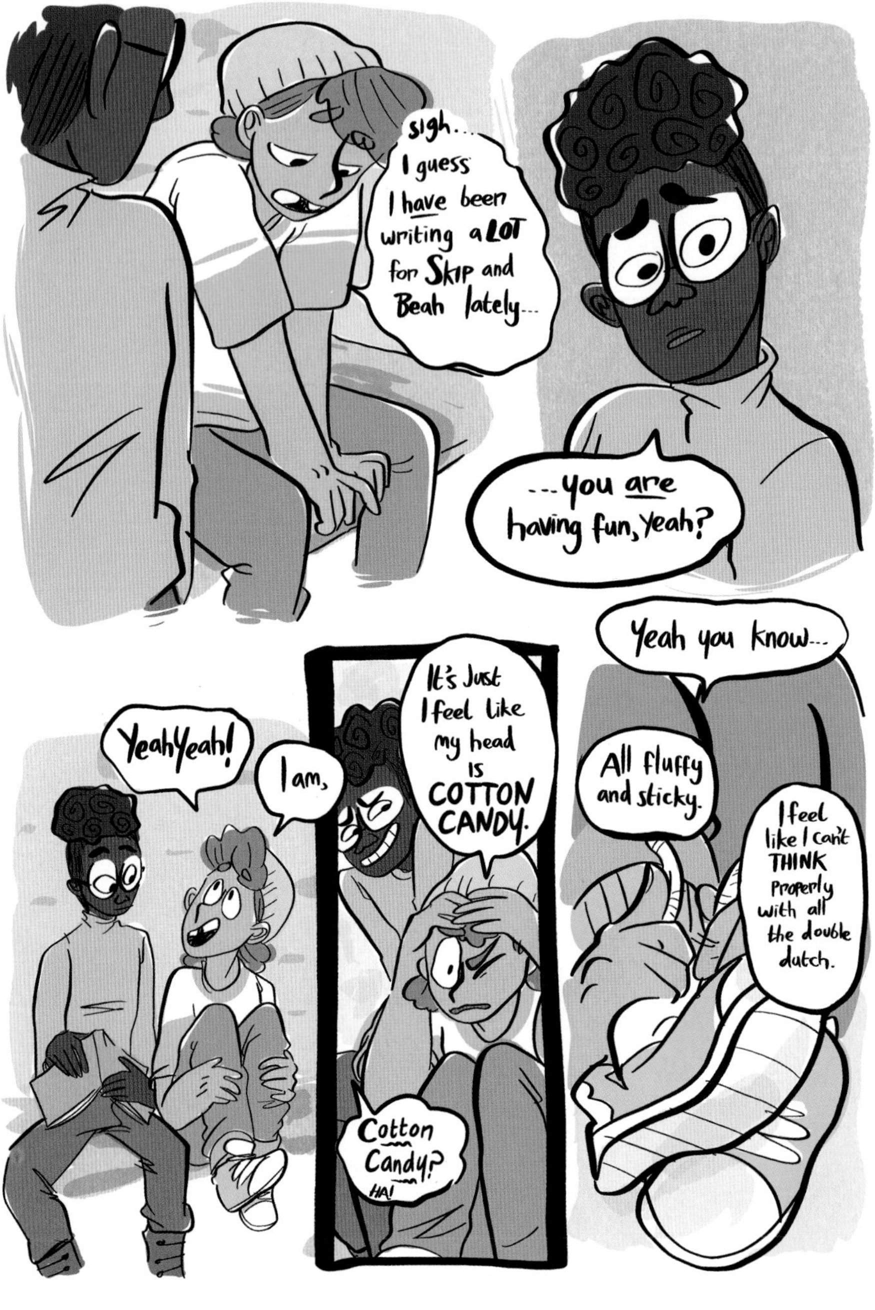
sigh... I guess I have been writing a LOT for SKIP and Beah lately...
...you are having fun, Yeah?
YeahYeah!
I am,
It's Just I feel like my head is COTTON CANDY.
Cotton Candy? HA!
Yeah you know...
All fluffy and sticky.
I feel like I can't THINK properly with all the double dutch.

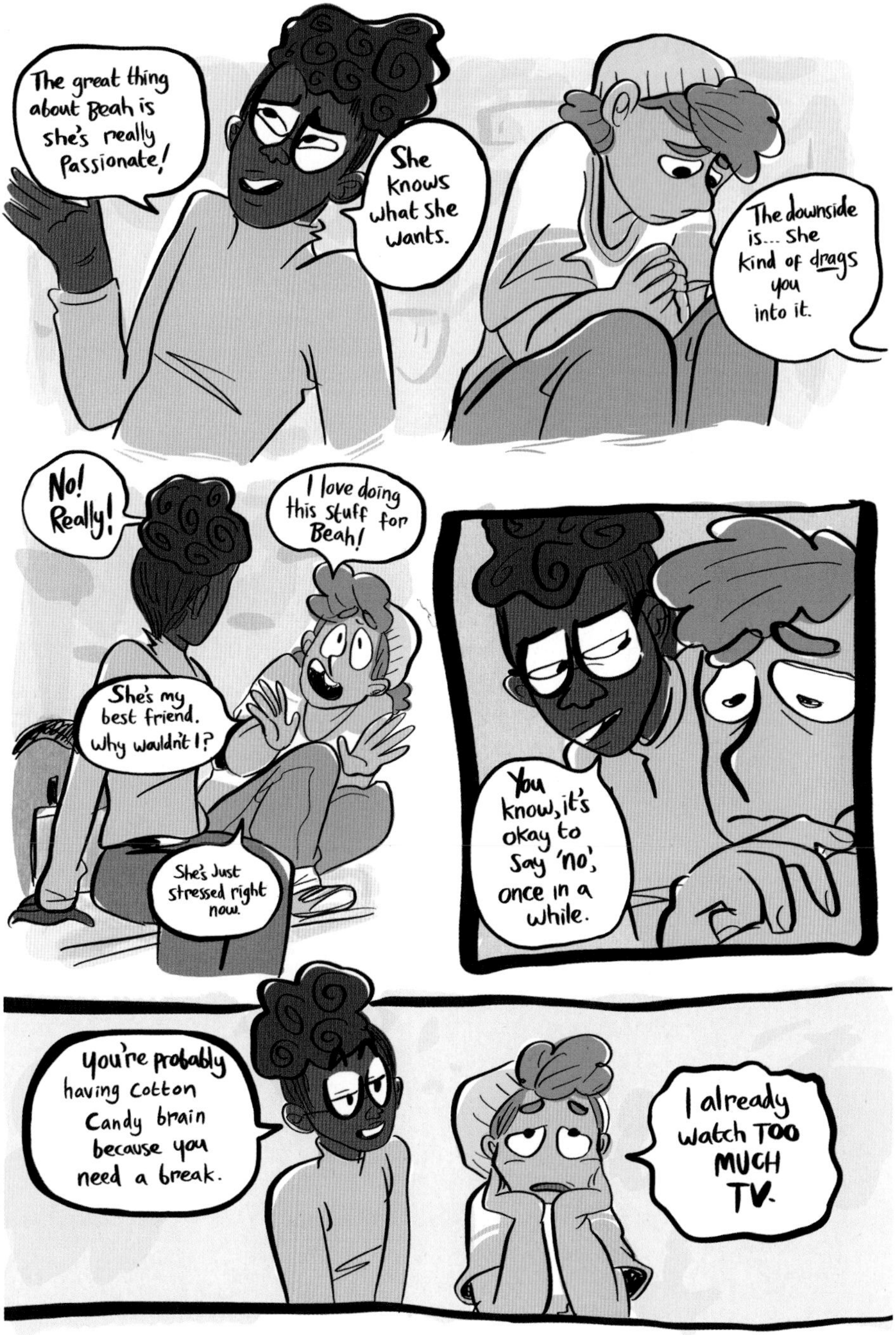
The great thing about Beah is she's really passionate!
She knows what she wants.
The downside is... she kind of drags you into it.
No! Really!
I love doing this stuff for Beah!
She's my best friend. Why wouldn't I?
She's just stressed right now.
You know, it's okay to say 'no', once in a while.
You're probably having cotton candy brain because you need a break.
I already watch TOO MUCH TV.

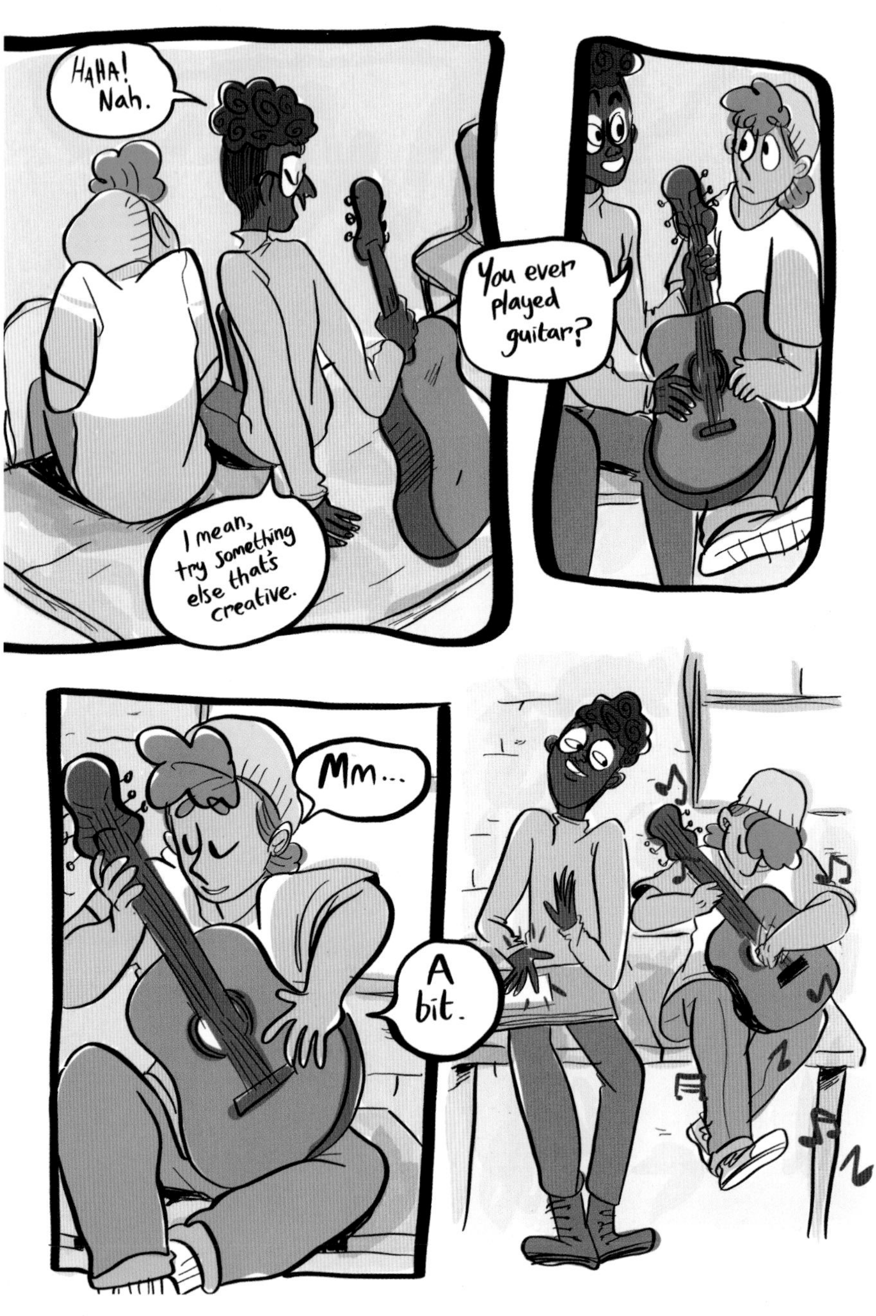
HAHA! Nah.
I mean, try something else that's creative.
You ever played guitar?
Mm...
A bit.

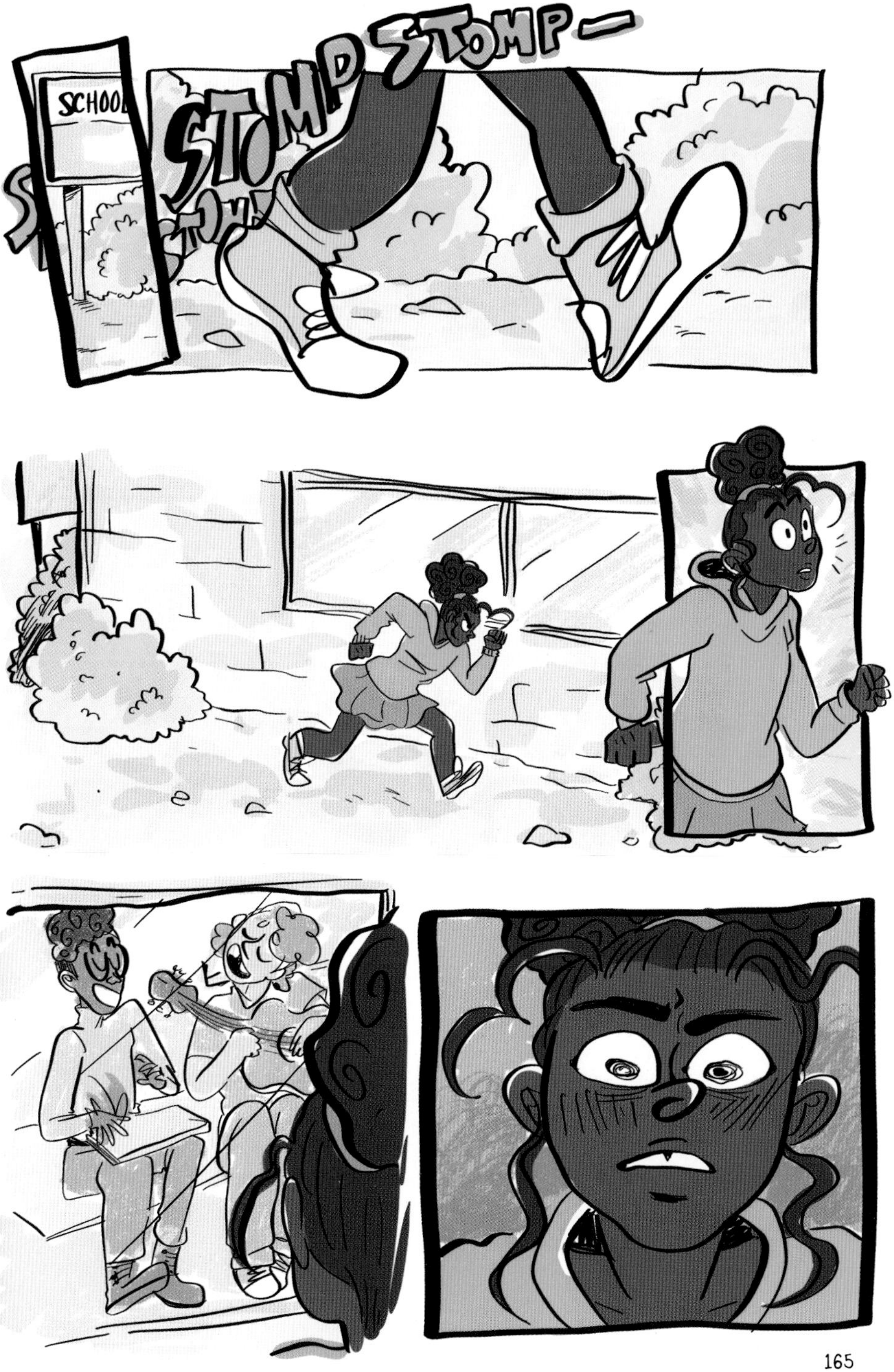

SCHOOL
STOMP STOMP STOMP-

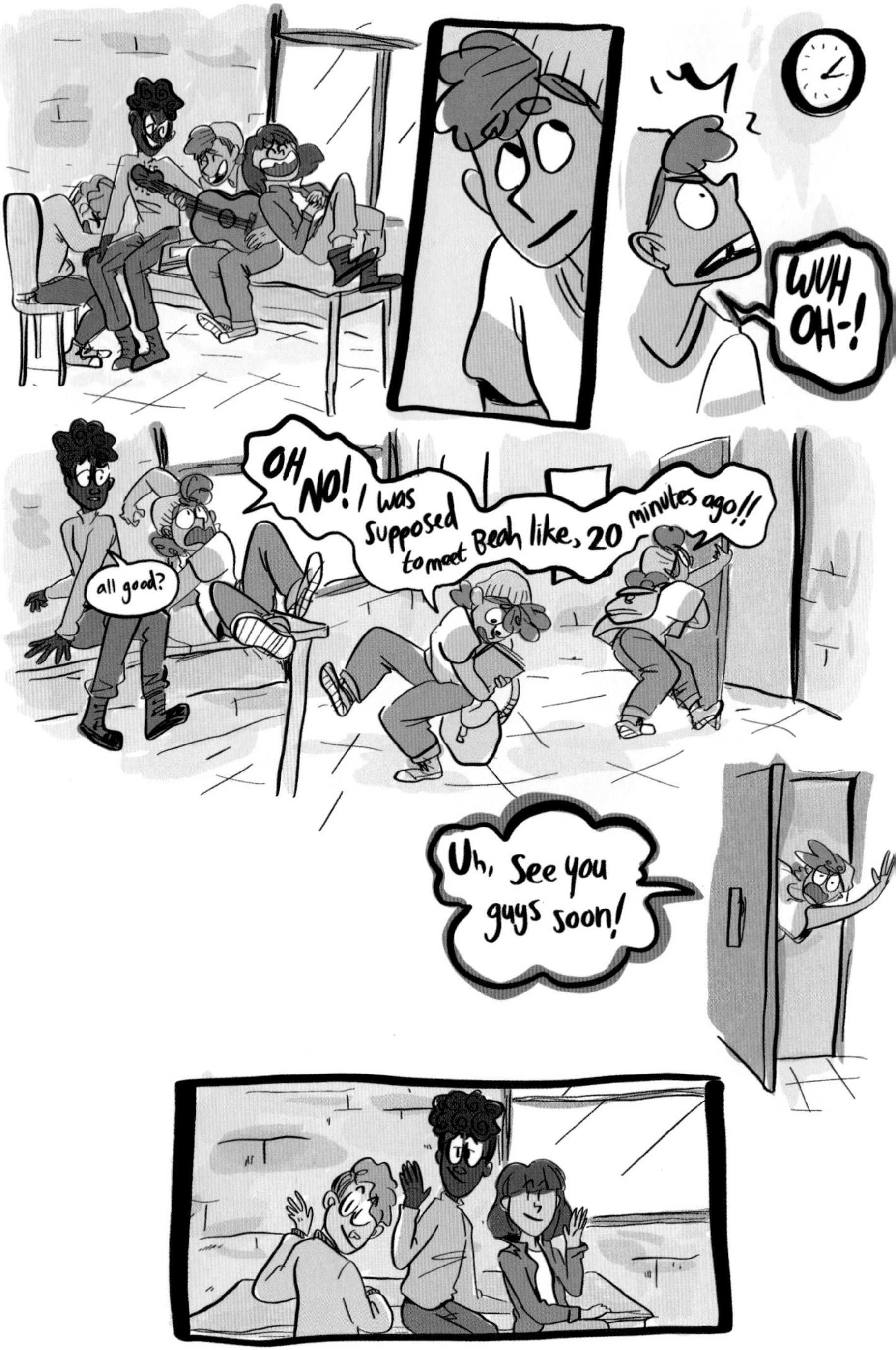
WUH OH-!
OH NO! I was supposed to meet Beah like, 20 minutes ago!!
all good?
Uh, See you guys soon!

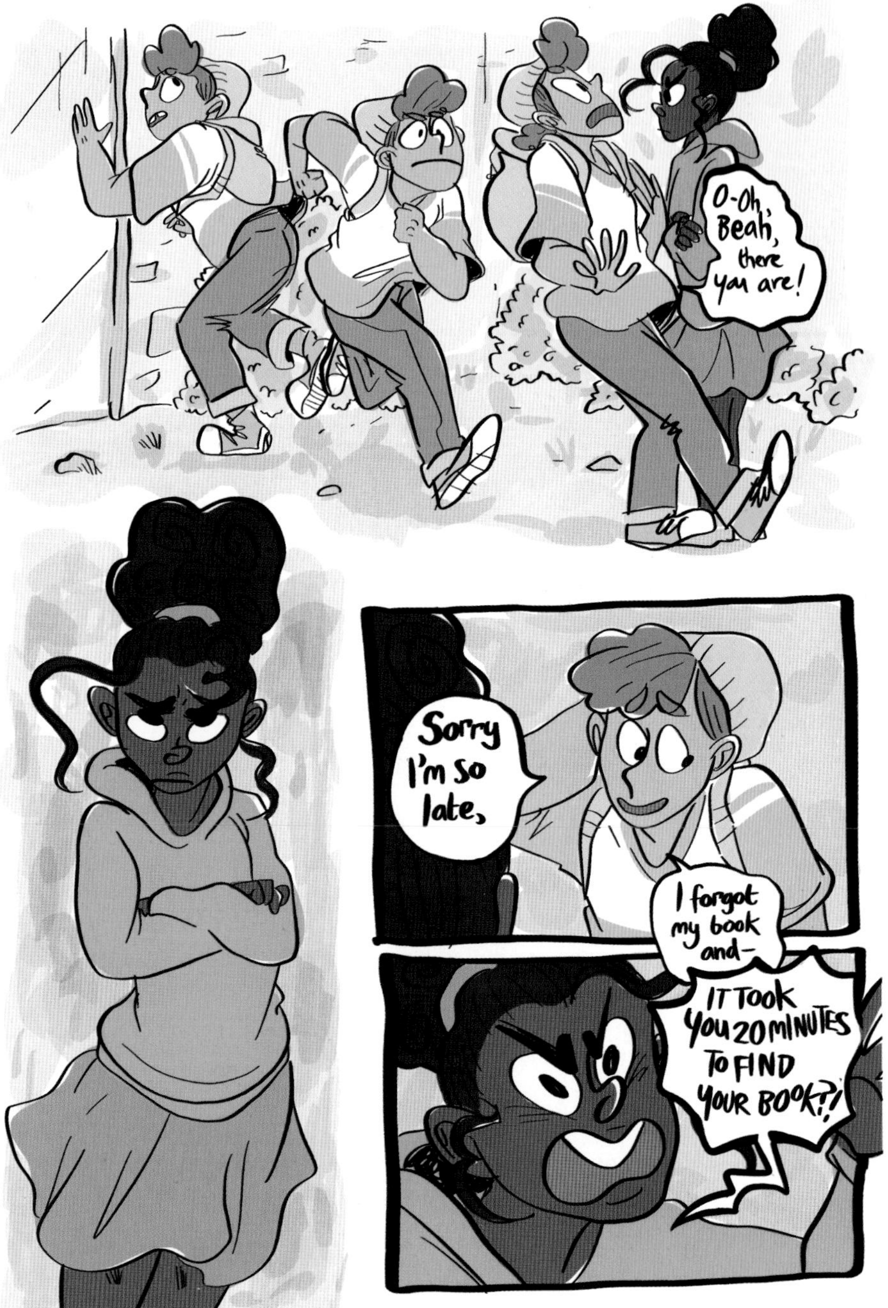
O-Oh, Beah, there you are!
Sorry I'm so late,
I forgot my book and-
IT TOOK YOU 20 MINUTES TO FIND YOUR BOOK?!

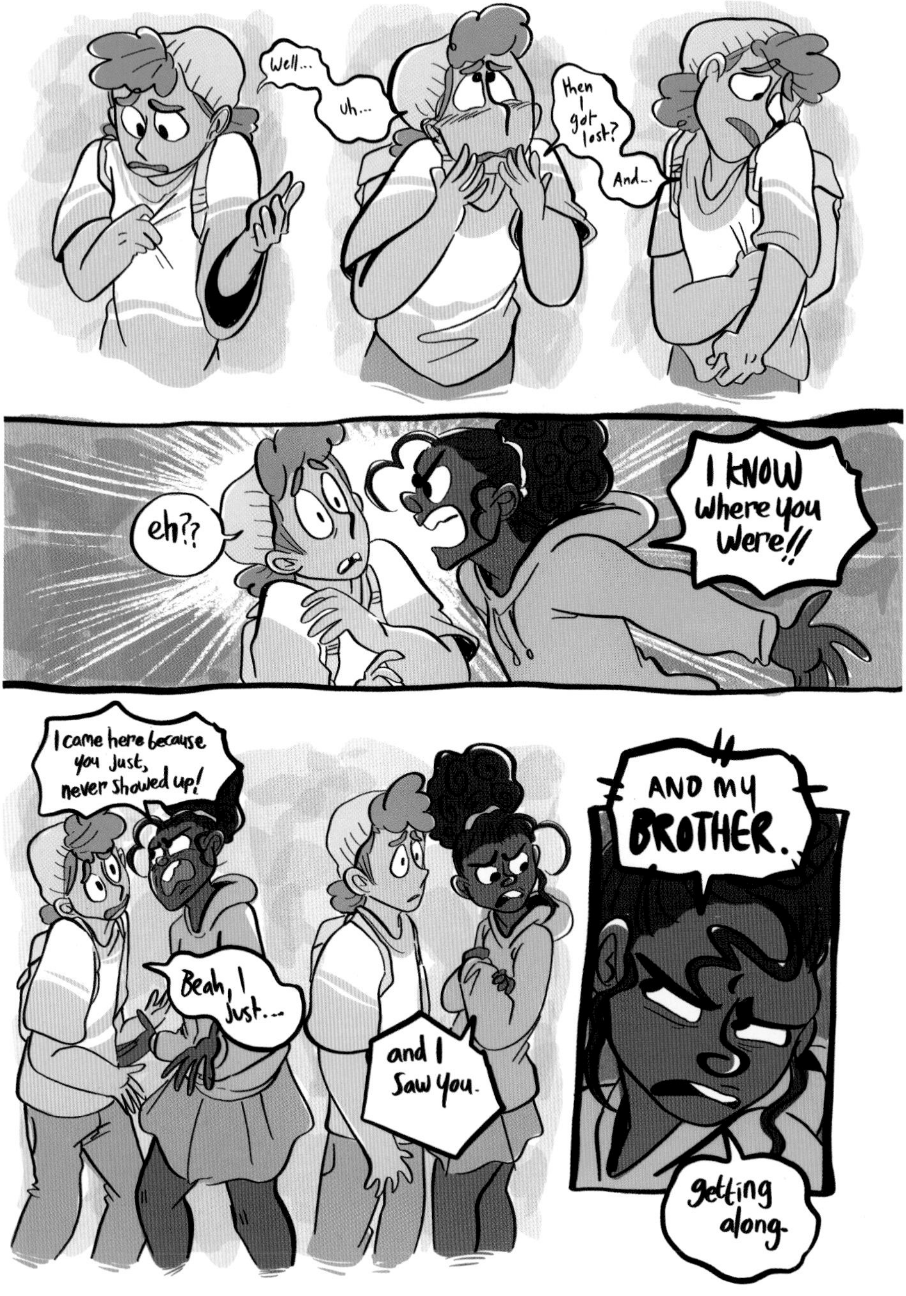
Well...
uh...
then I got lost?
And...
eh??
I KNOW where you were!!
I came here because you just, never showed up!
Beah, I just...
and I saw you.
AND MY BROTHER.
getting along.

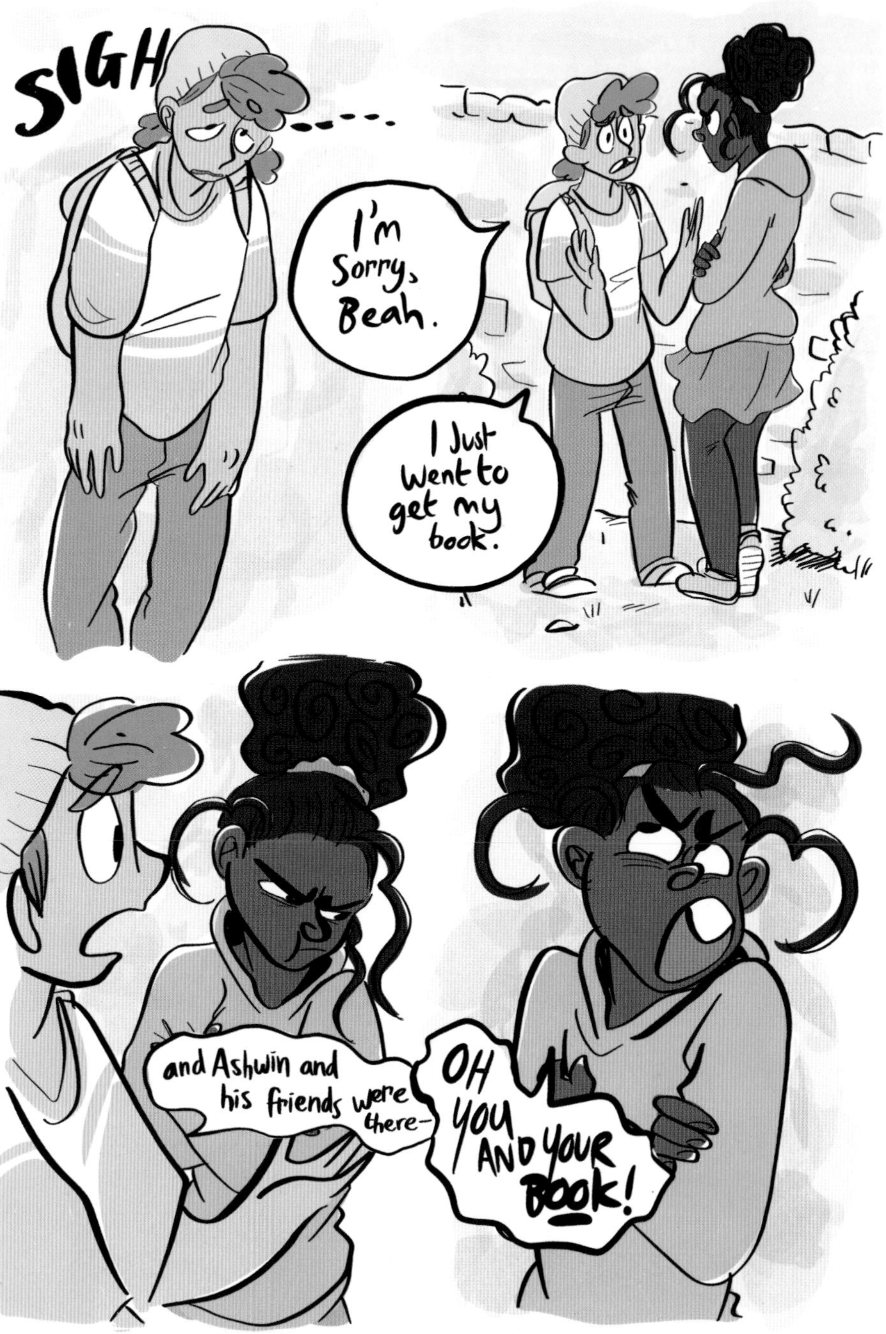
SIGH
I'm Sorry, Beah.
I Just Went to get my book.
and Ashwin and his friends were there-
OH YOU AND YOUR BOOK!

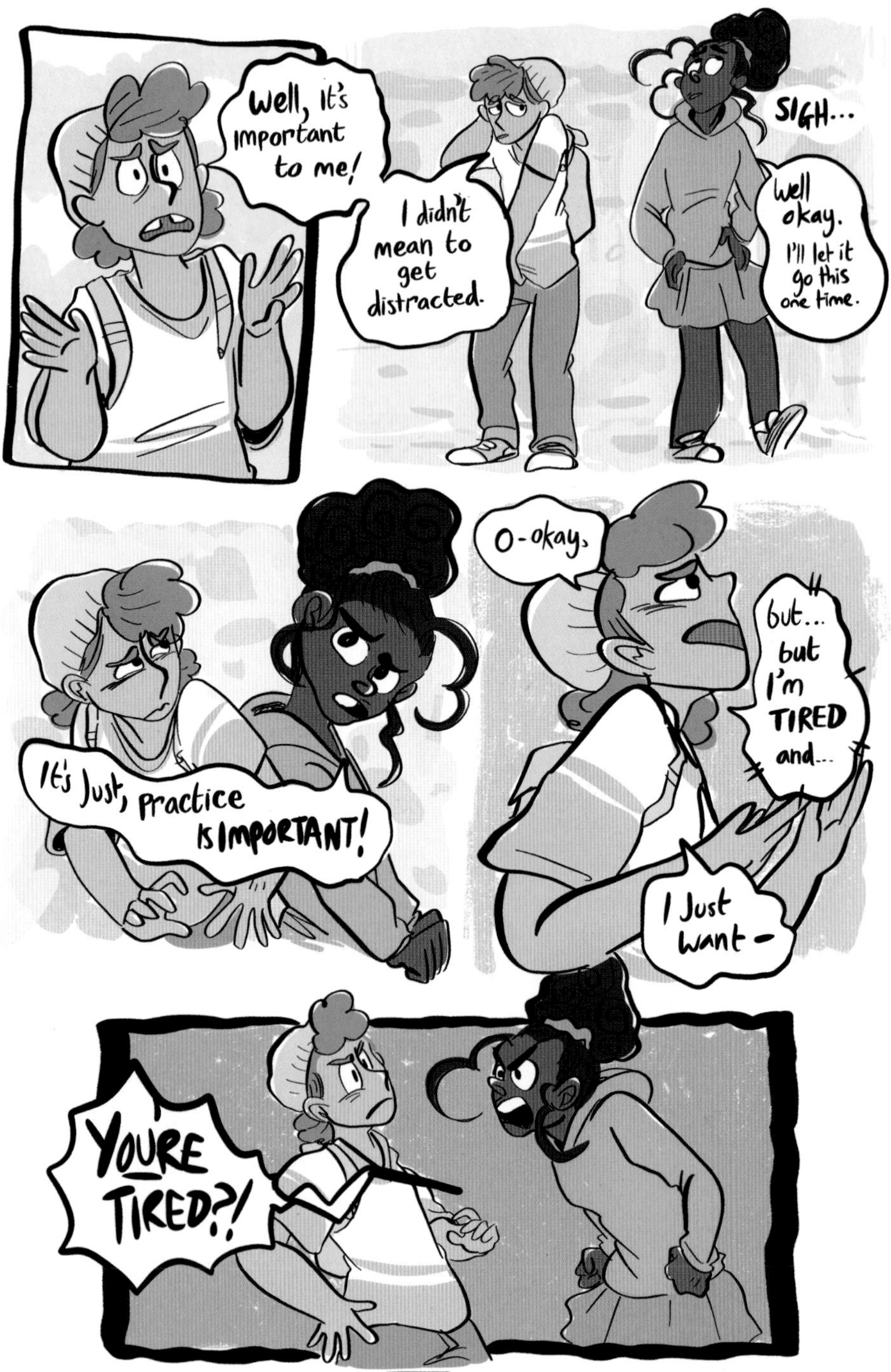

Well, It's important to me!
I didn't mean to get distracted.
SIGH...
Well okay. I'll let it go this one time.
It's Just, practice is IMPORTANT!
O-okay,
but... but I'm TIRED and...
I Just want-
YOURE TIRED?!

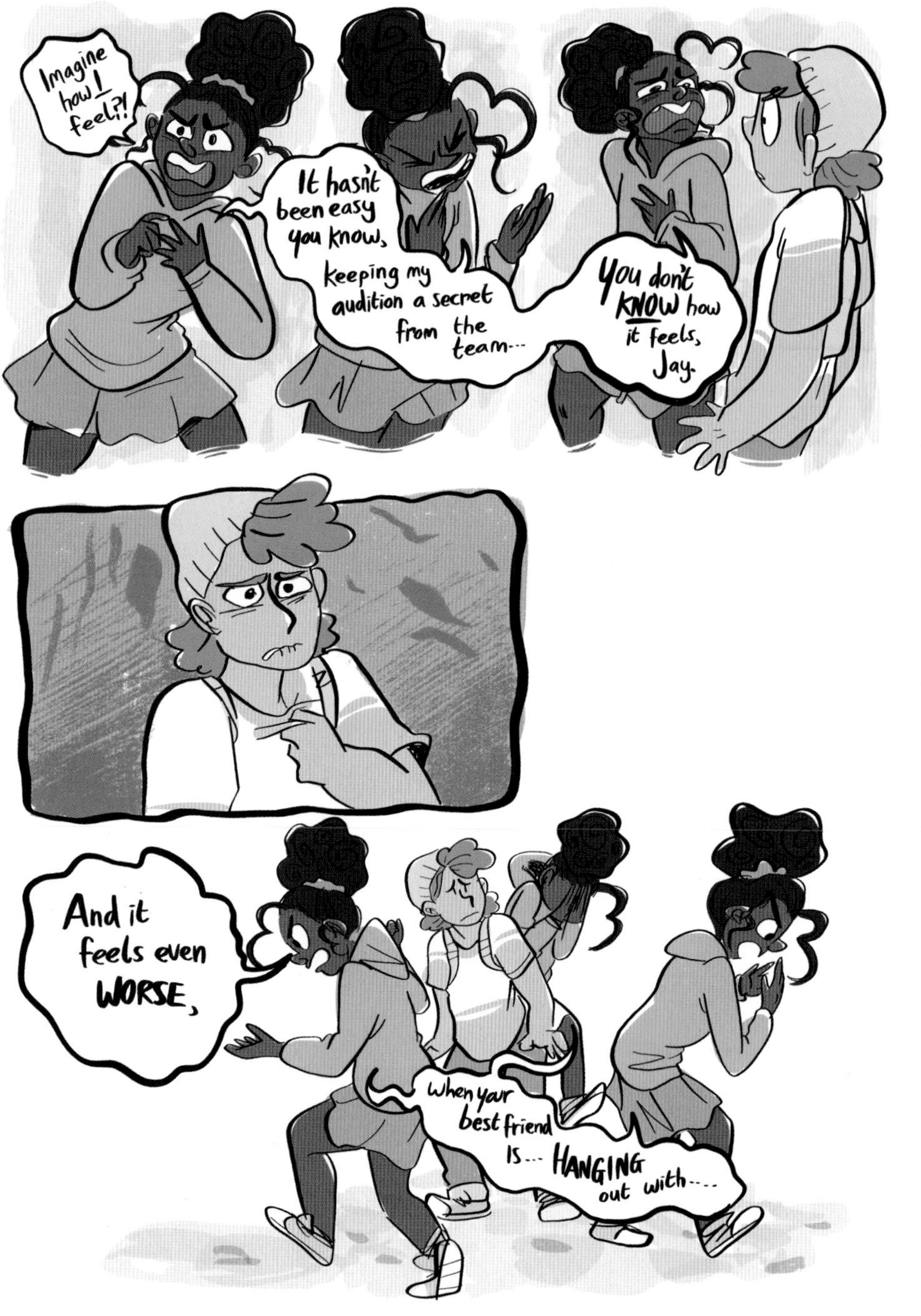
Imagine how I feel?!
It hasn't been easy you know,
keeping my audition a secret from the team...
You don't KNOW how it feels, Jay.
And it feels even WORSE,
when your best friend is... HANGING out with....

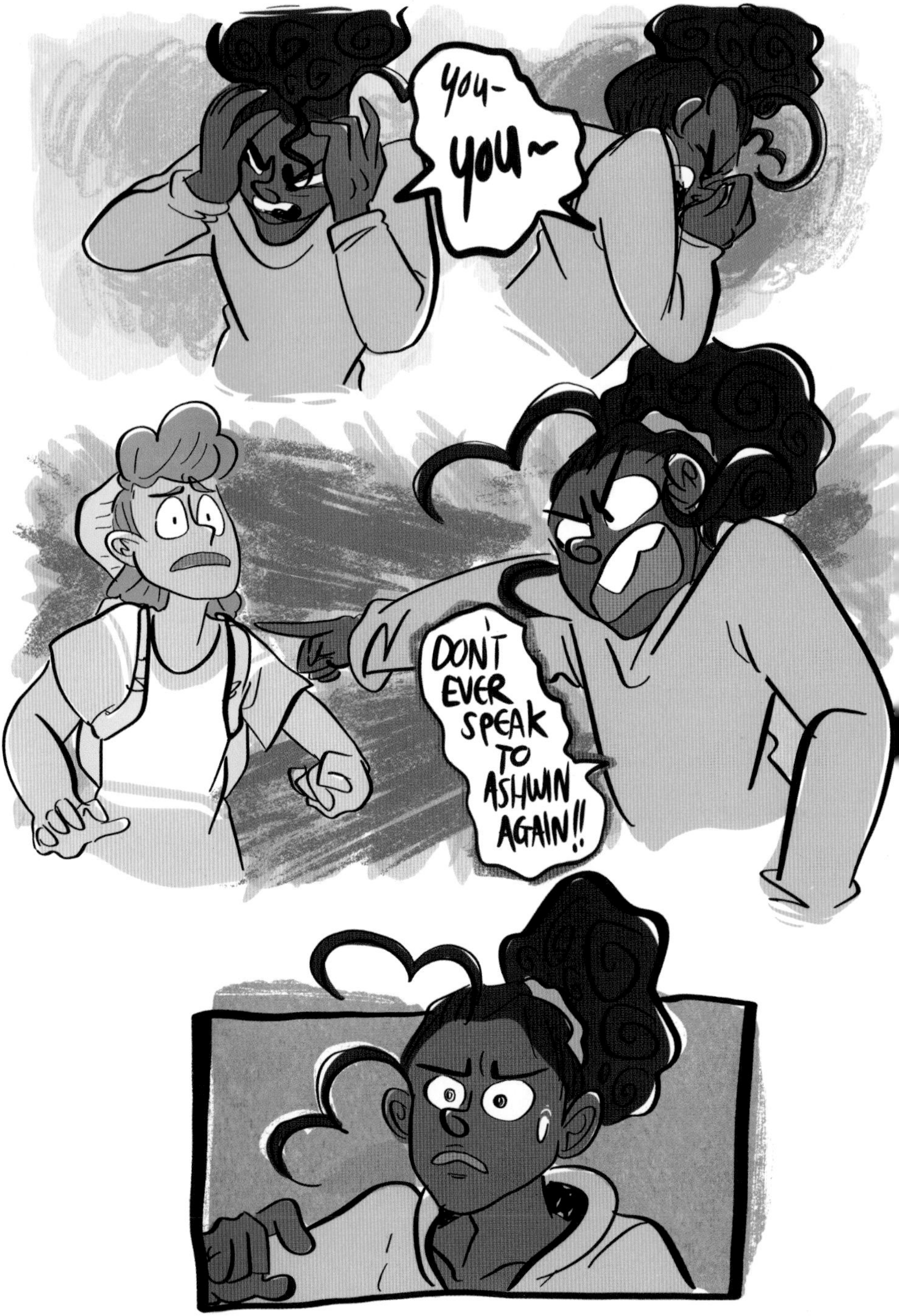
you-
you~
DON'T EVER SPEAK TO ASHWIN AGAIN!!

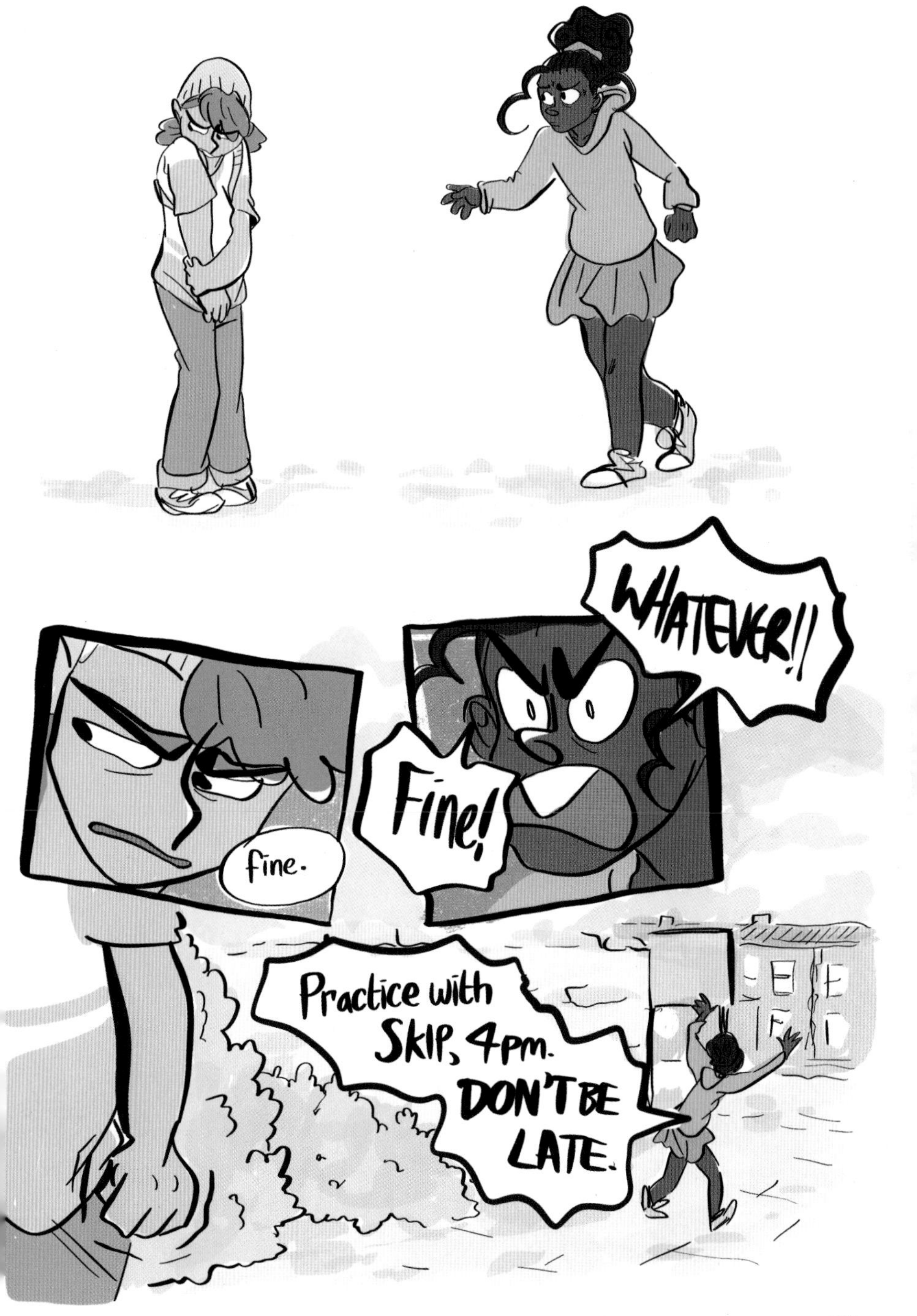
fine.
Fine!
WHATEVER!!
Practice with SKIP, 4pm. DON'T BE LATE.

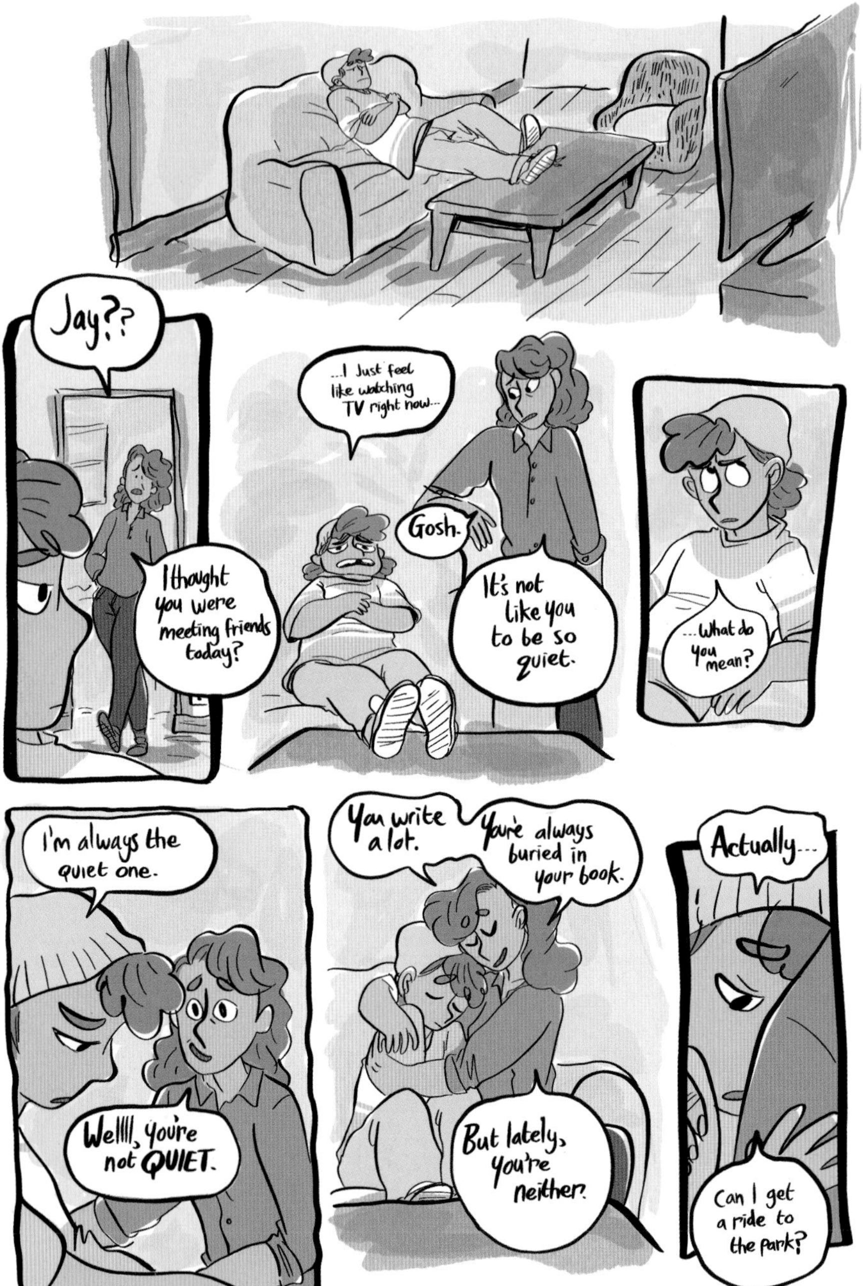

Jay??
I thought you were meeting friends today?
...I just feel like watching TV right now...
Gosh.
It's not like you to be so quiet.
...What do you mean?
I'm always the quiet one.
Wellll, you're not QUIET.
You write a lot.
You're always buried in your book.
But lately, you're neither.
Actually...
Can I get a ride to the park?

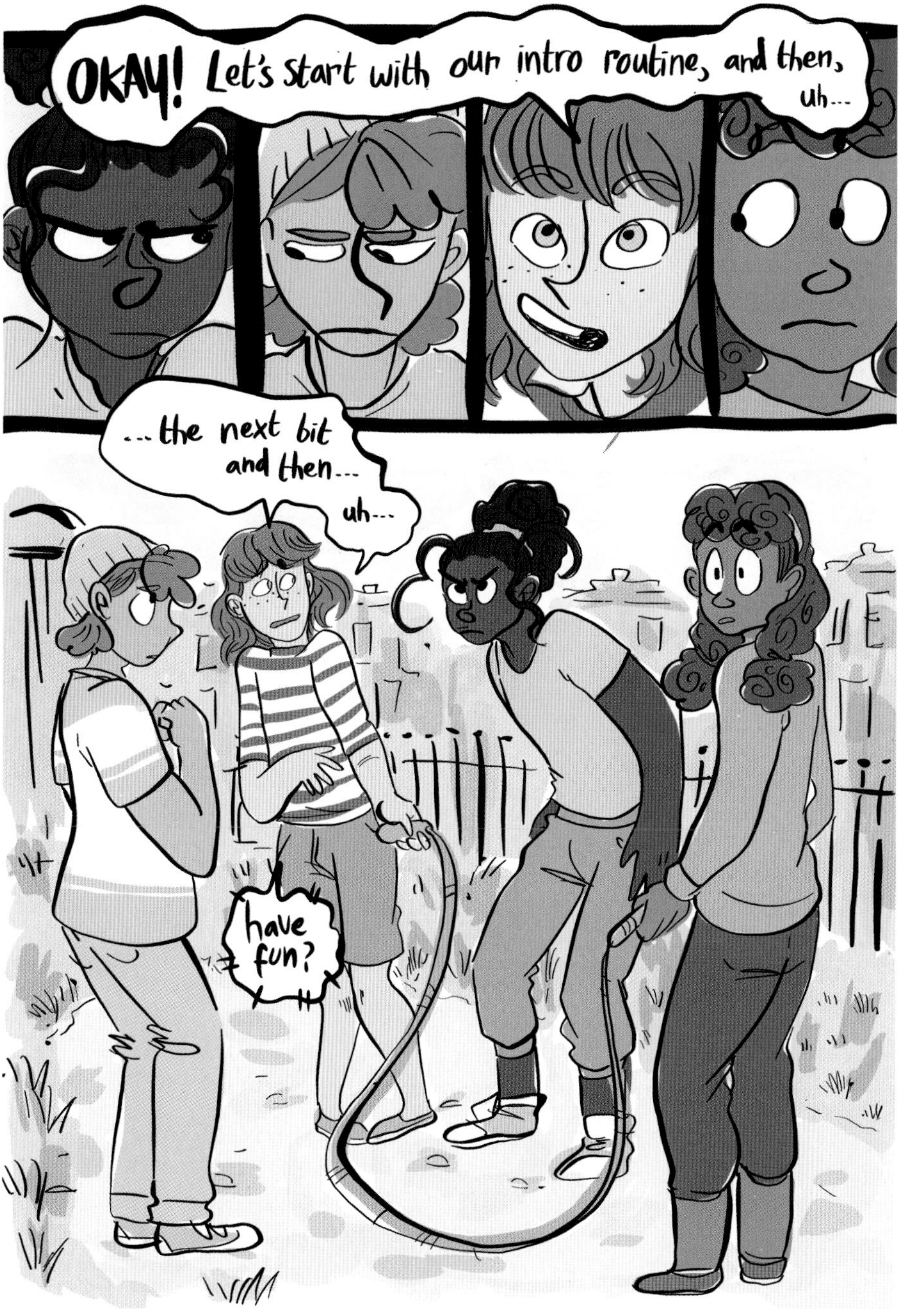
OKAY! Let's start with our intro routine, and then, uh...
...the next bit and then... uh...
have fun?

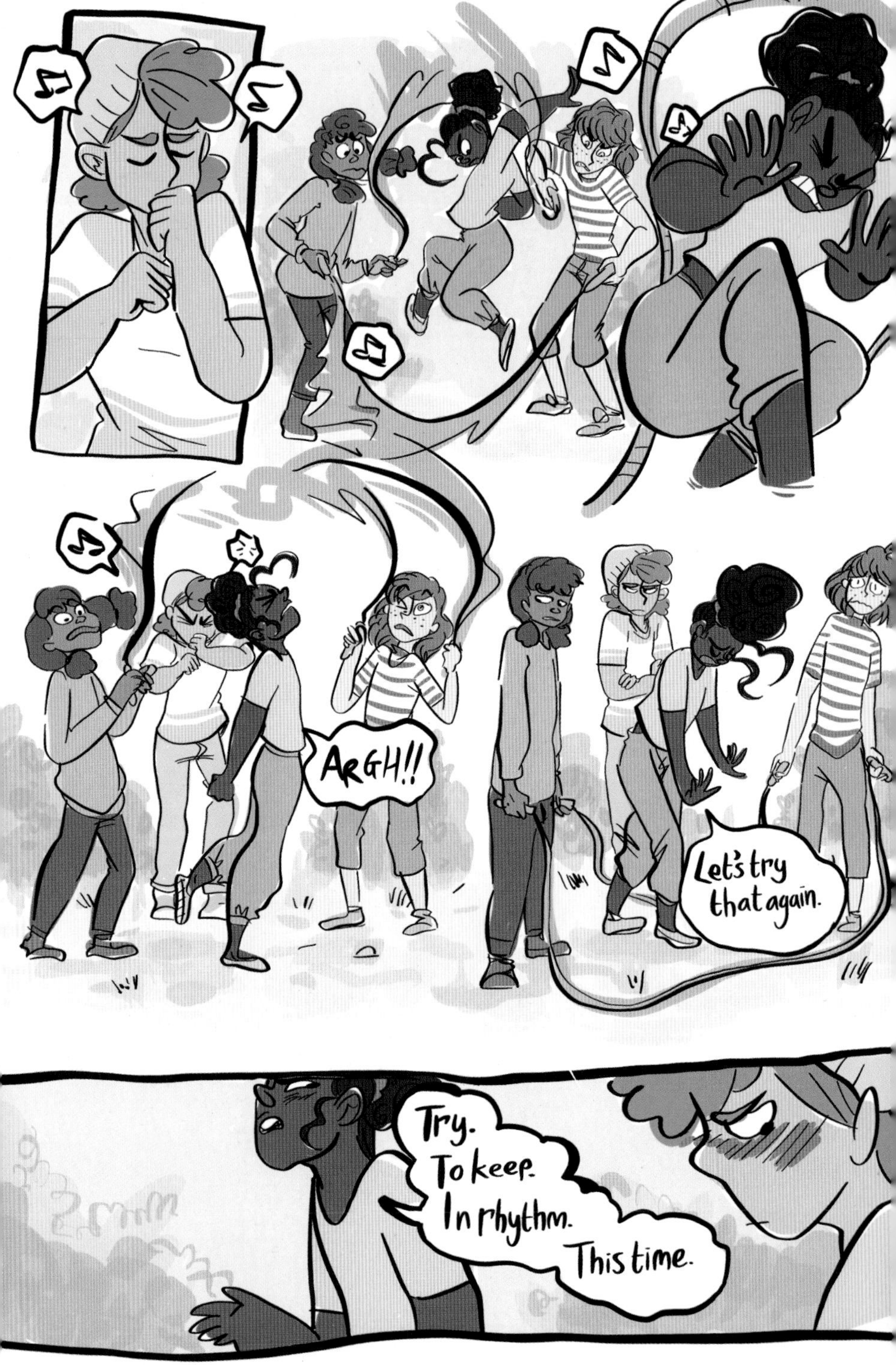
ARGH!!
Let's try that again.
Try.
To keep.
In rhythm.
This time.

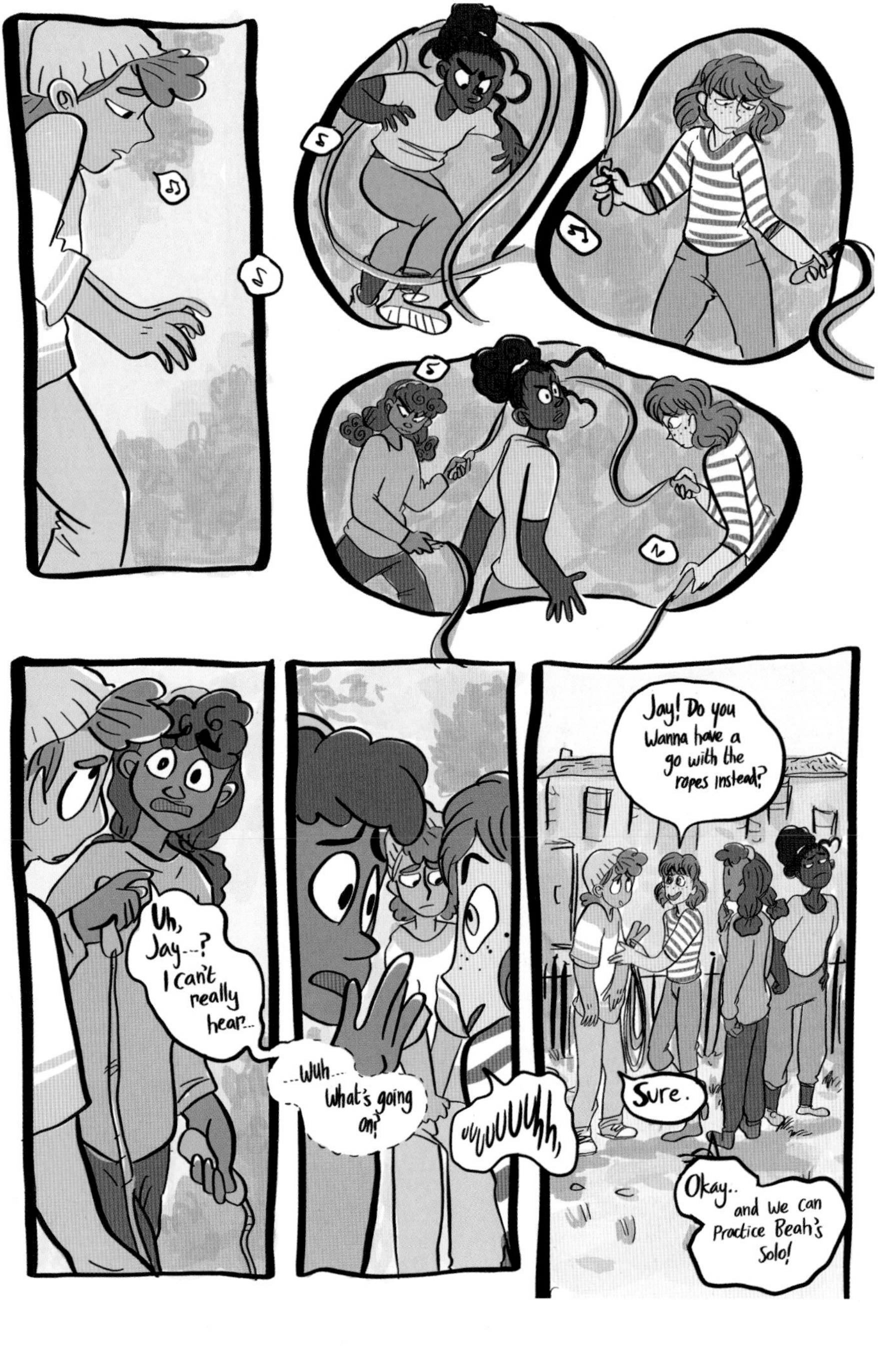
Jay! Do you Wanna have a go with the ropes instead?
Uh, Jay--? I can't really hear...
...Wuh... What's going on?
uuuUUhh,
Sure.
Okay.. and we can Practice Beah's Solo!

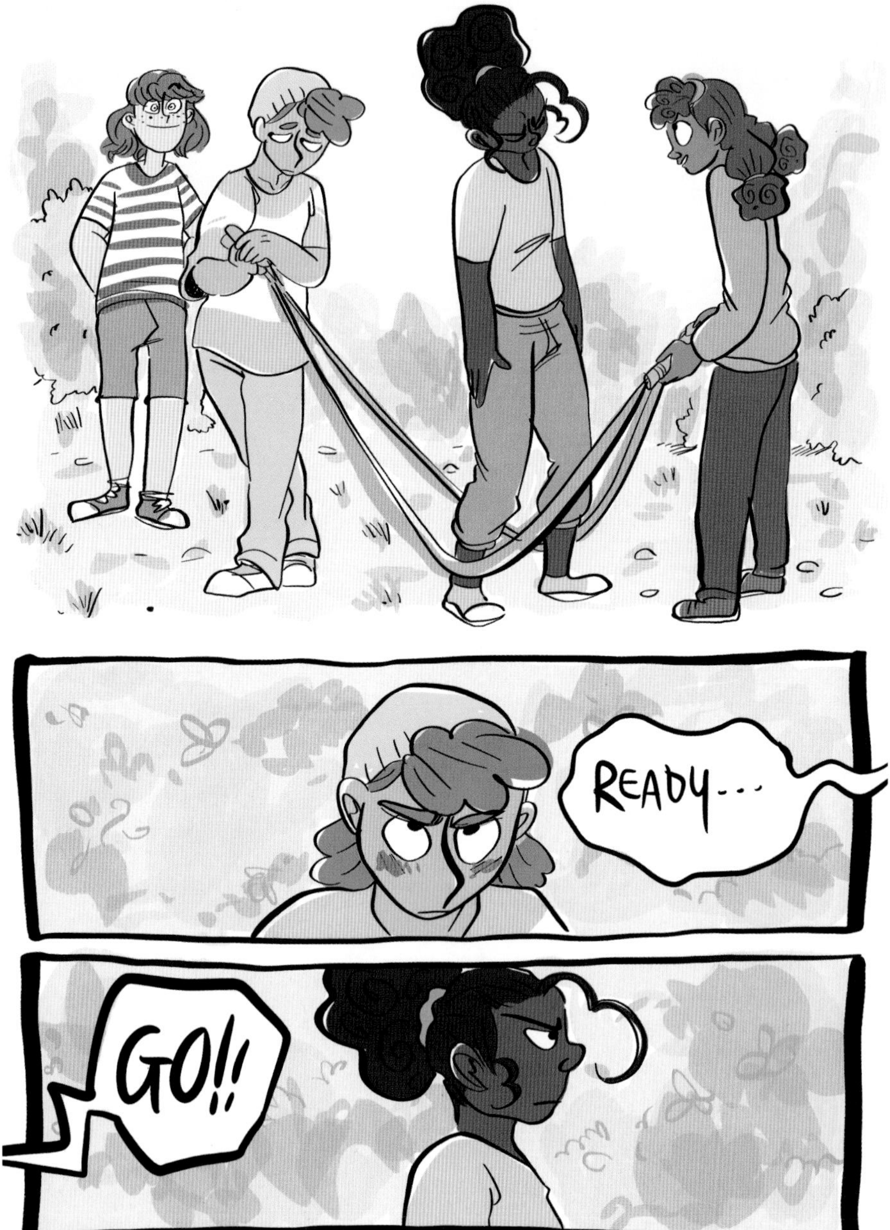
READY...
GO!!

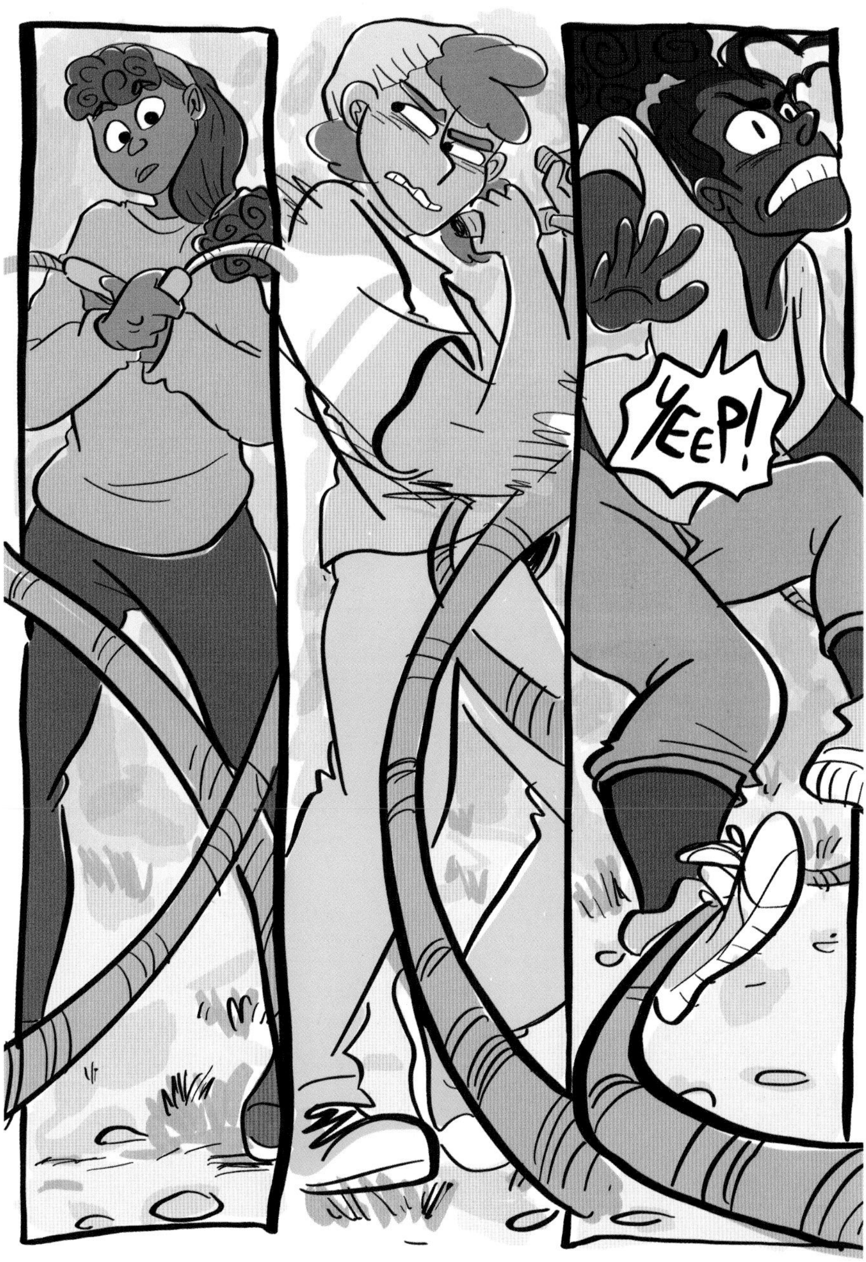
YEEP!

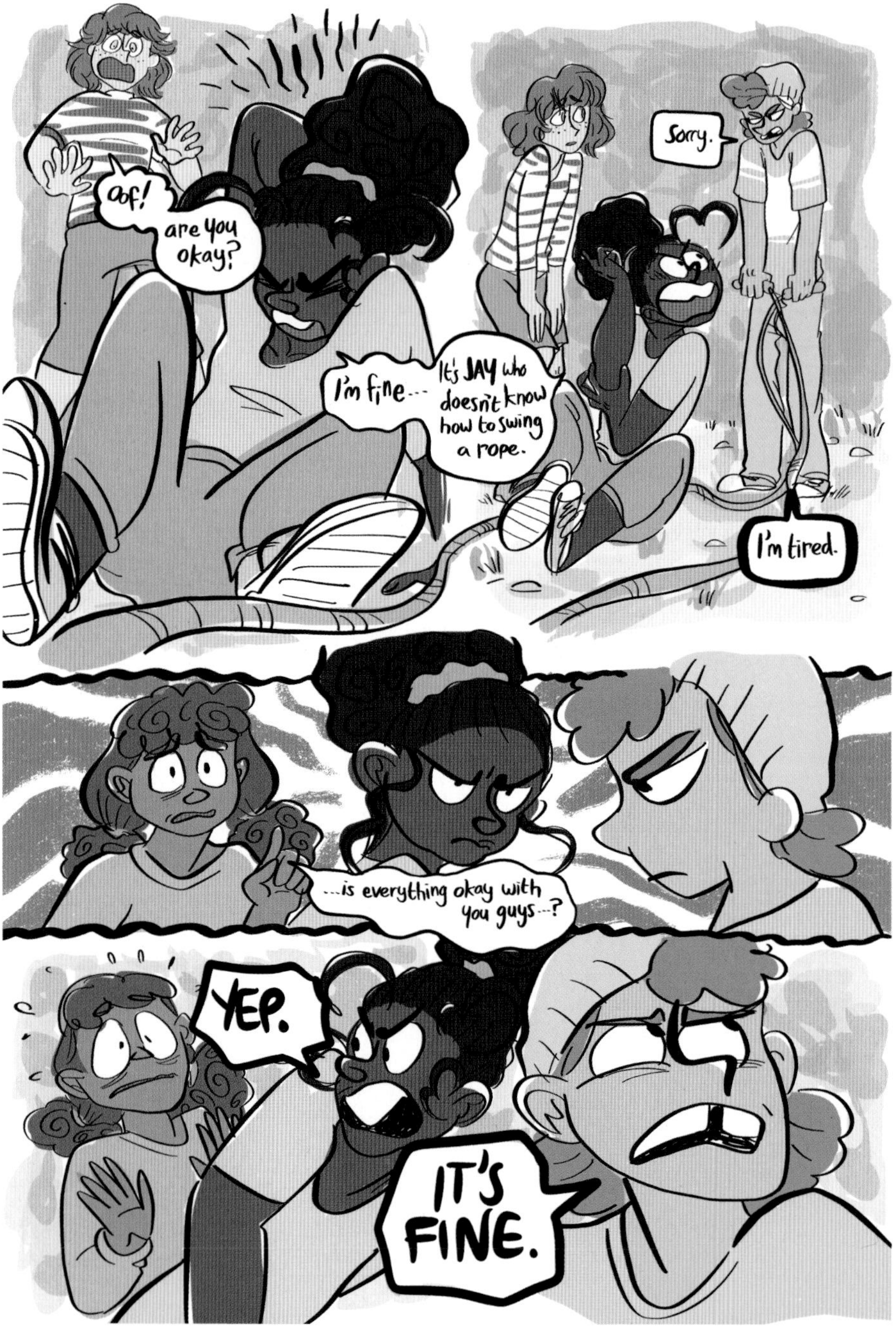
oof!
are you okay?
I'm fine... It's JAY who doesn't know how to swing a rope.
Sorry.
I'm tired.
...is everything okay with you guys...?
YEP.
IT'S FINE.

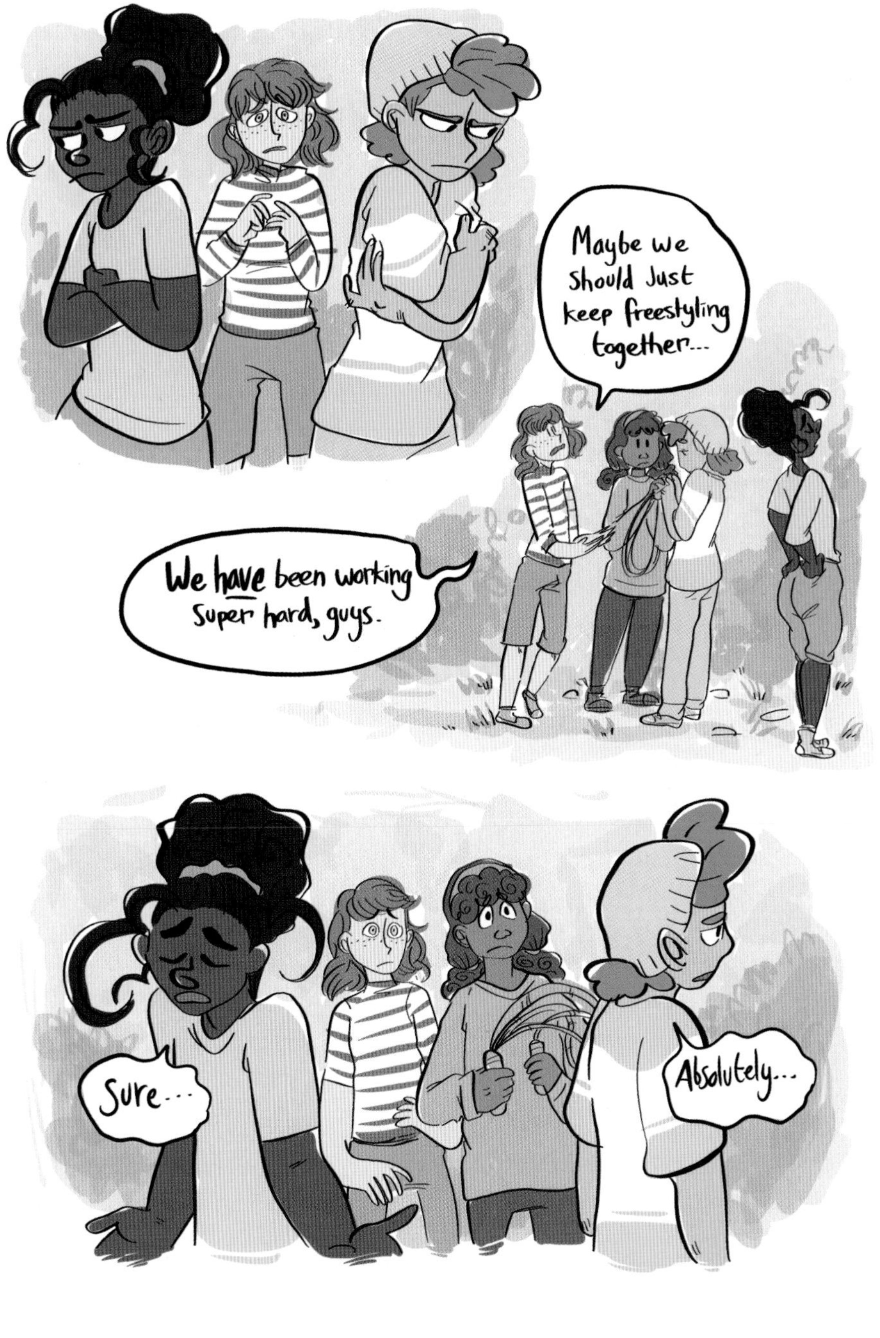
Maybe we should just keep freestyling together...
We have been working super hard, guys.
Sure...
Absolutely...

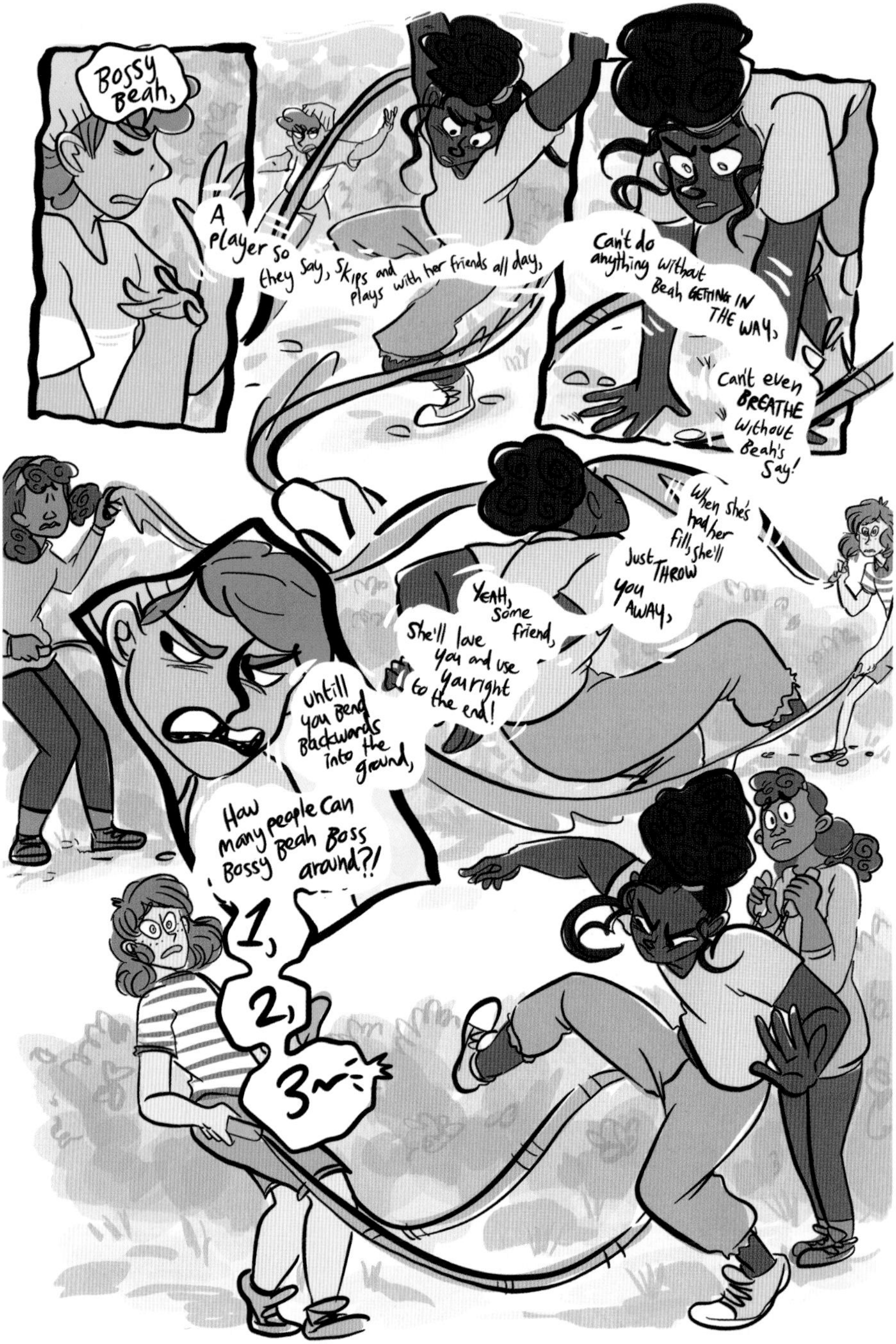
Bossy Beah,
A player so they say, Skips and plays with her friends all day,
Can't do anything without Beah GETTING IN THE WAY,
Can't even BREATHE without Beah's Say!
When she's had her fill, she'll Just THROW you AWAY,
YEAH, some friend,
She'll love you and use you right to the end!
Untill you Bend Backwards into the ground,
How many people Can Bossy Beah Boss around?!
1,
2,
3~

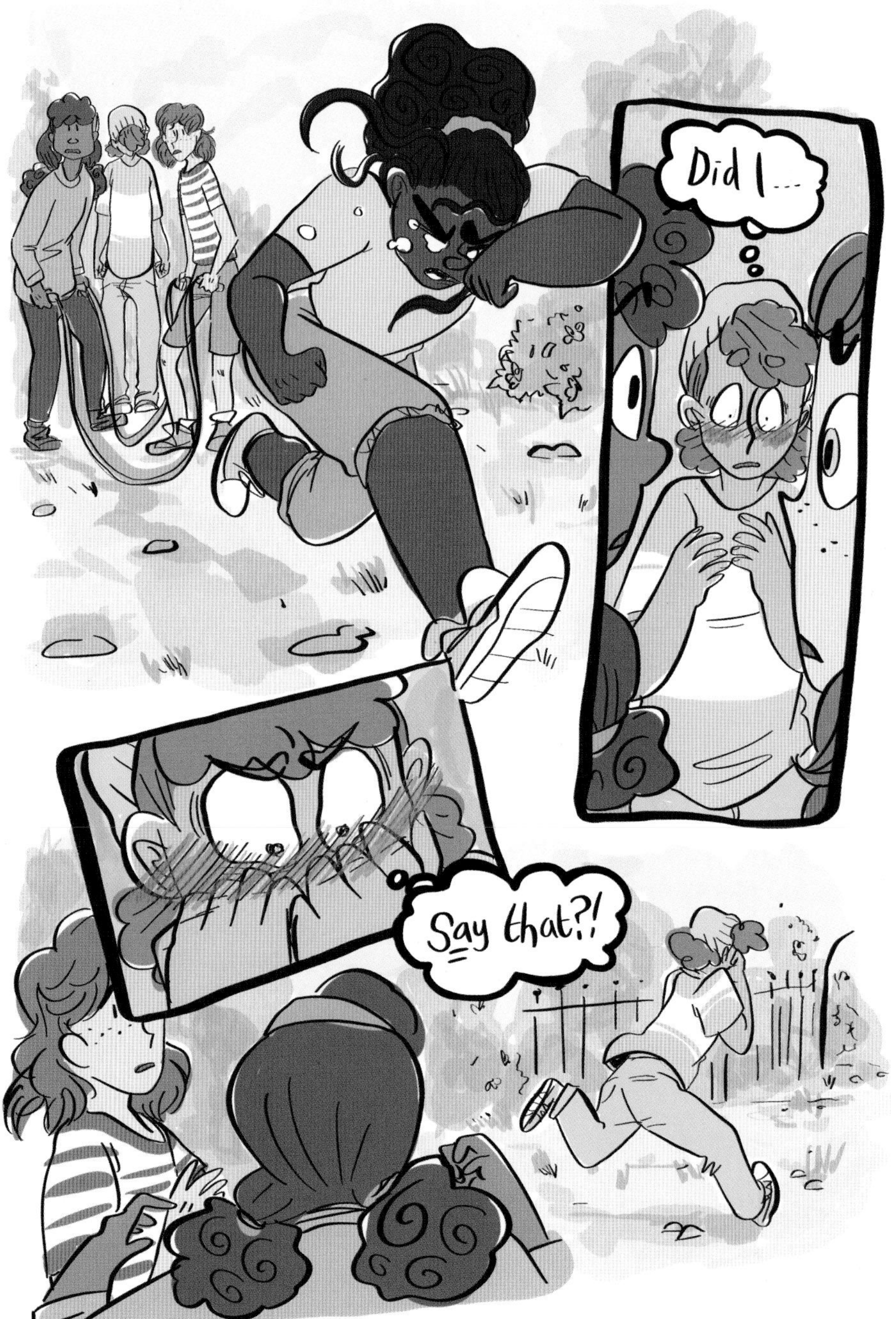
Did I...
Say that?!

CHAPTER NINE

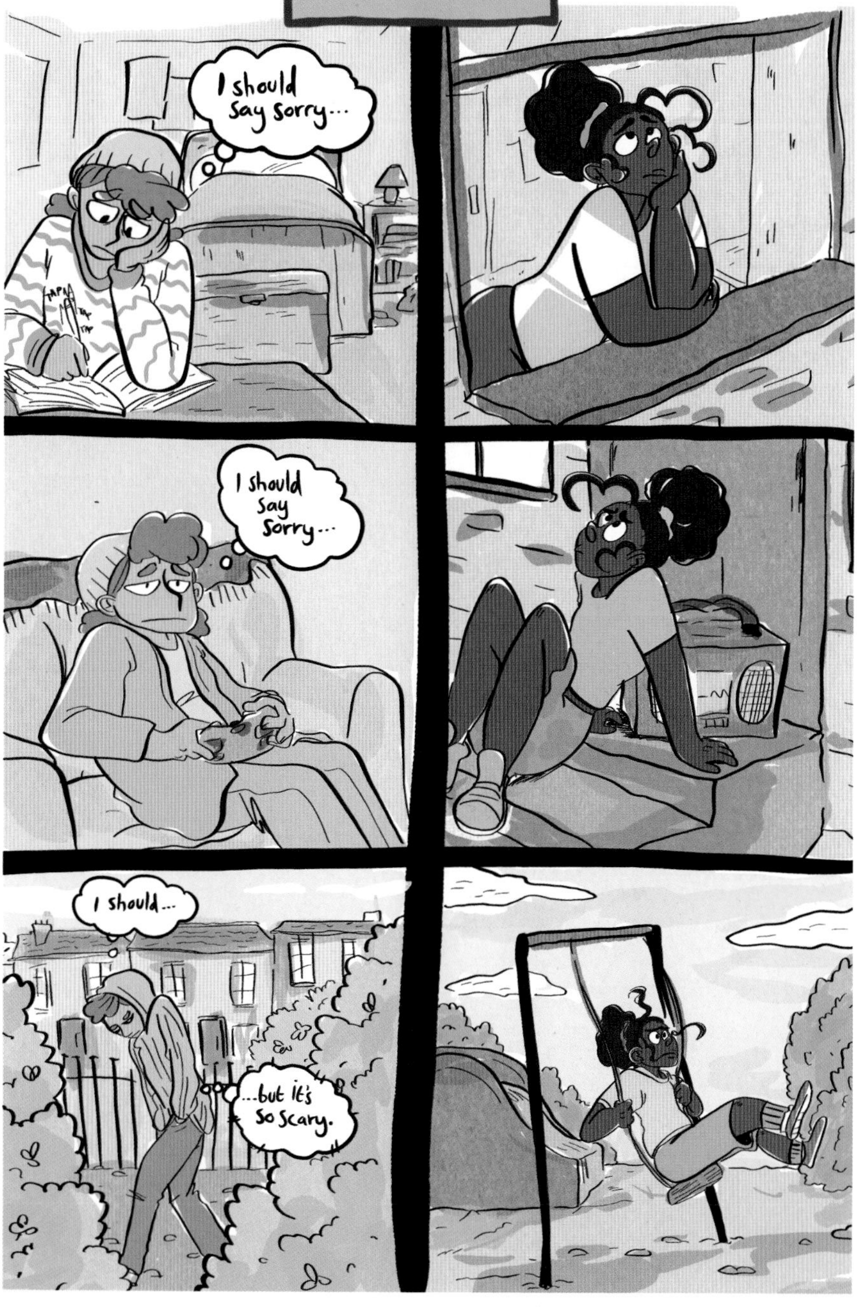
I should say sorry...
TAP TAP TAP
I should say sorry...
I should...
...but it's so scary.

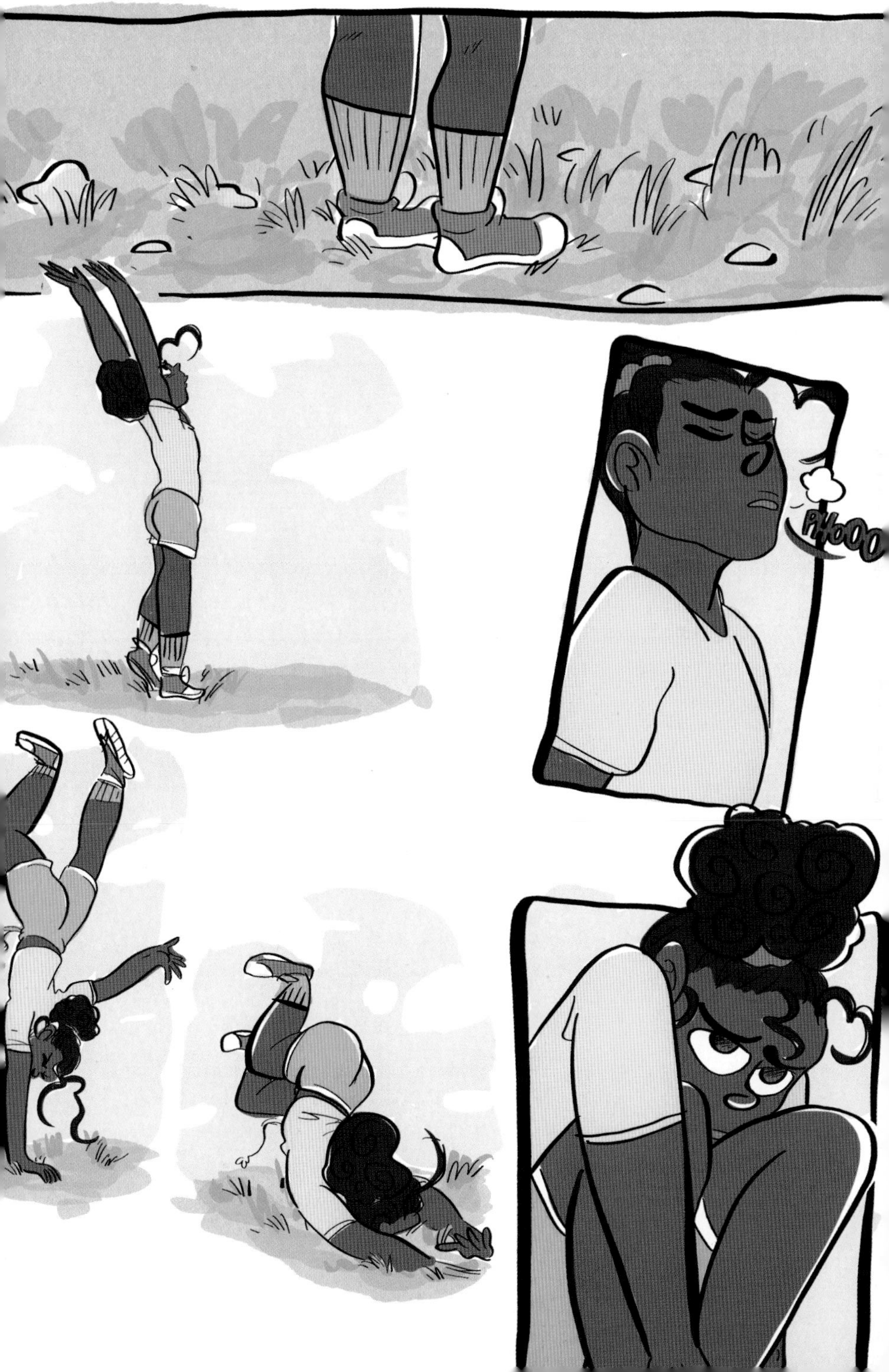
PHOOO

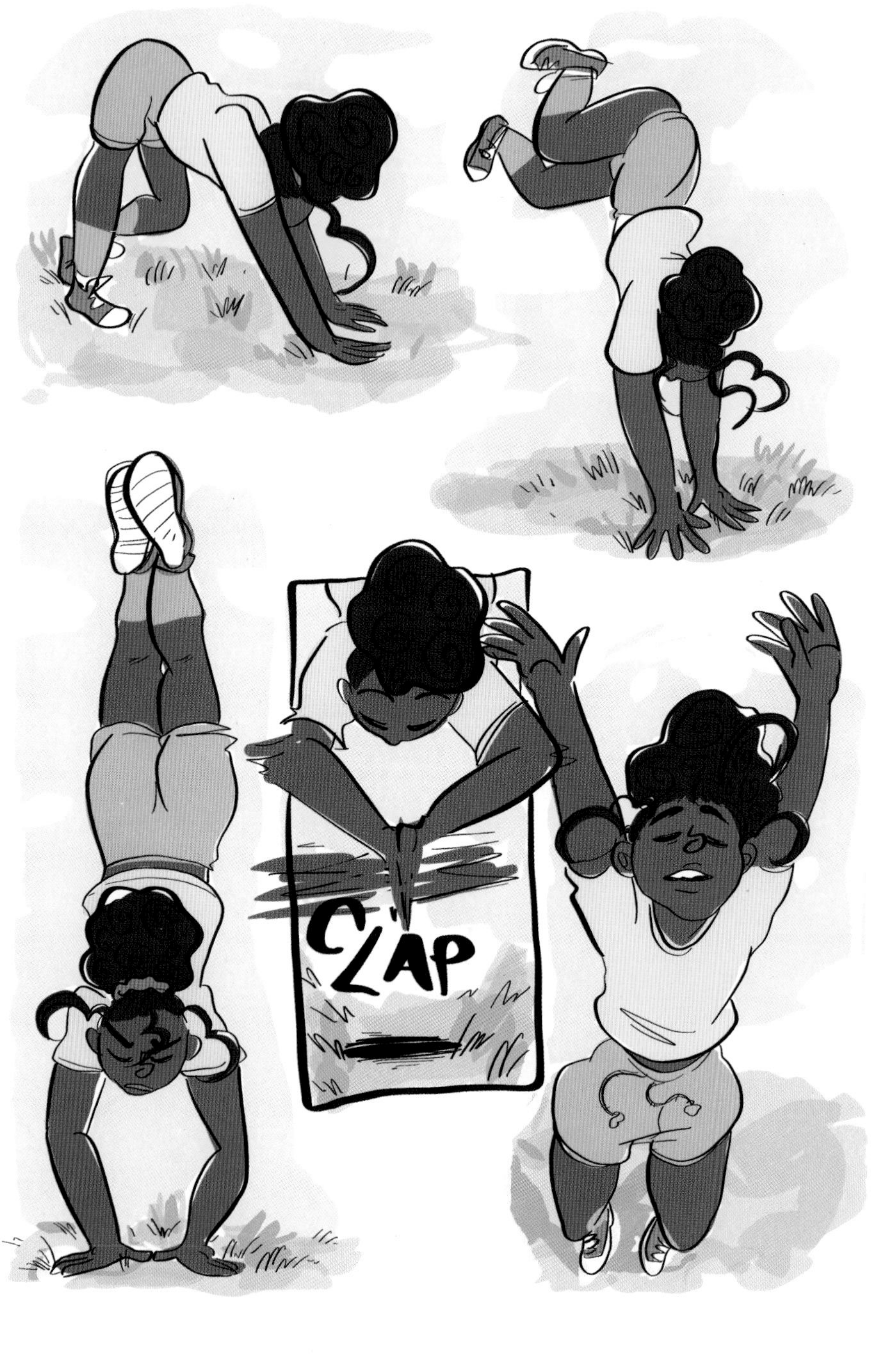
CLAP

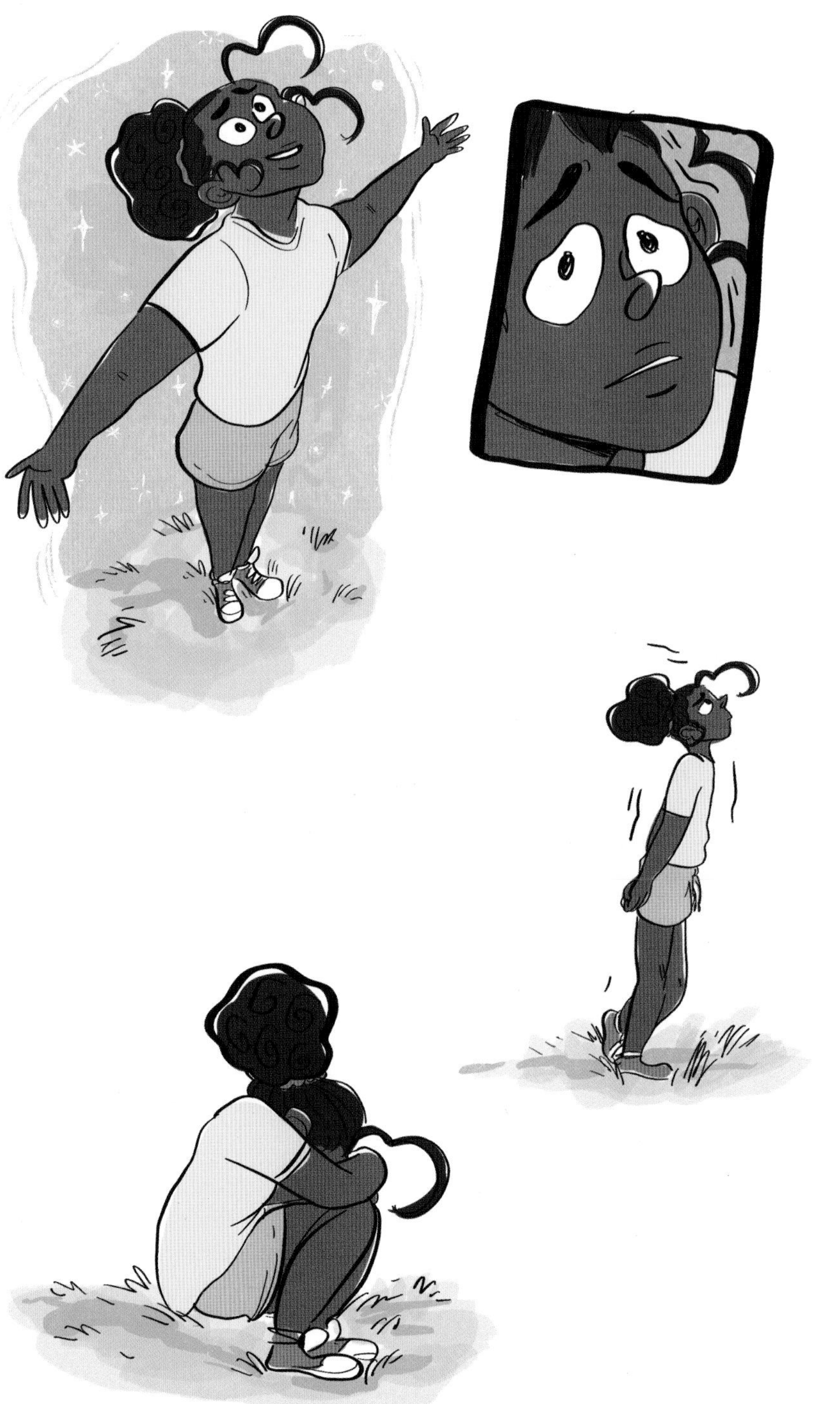

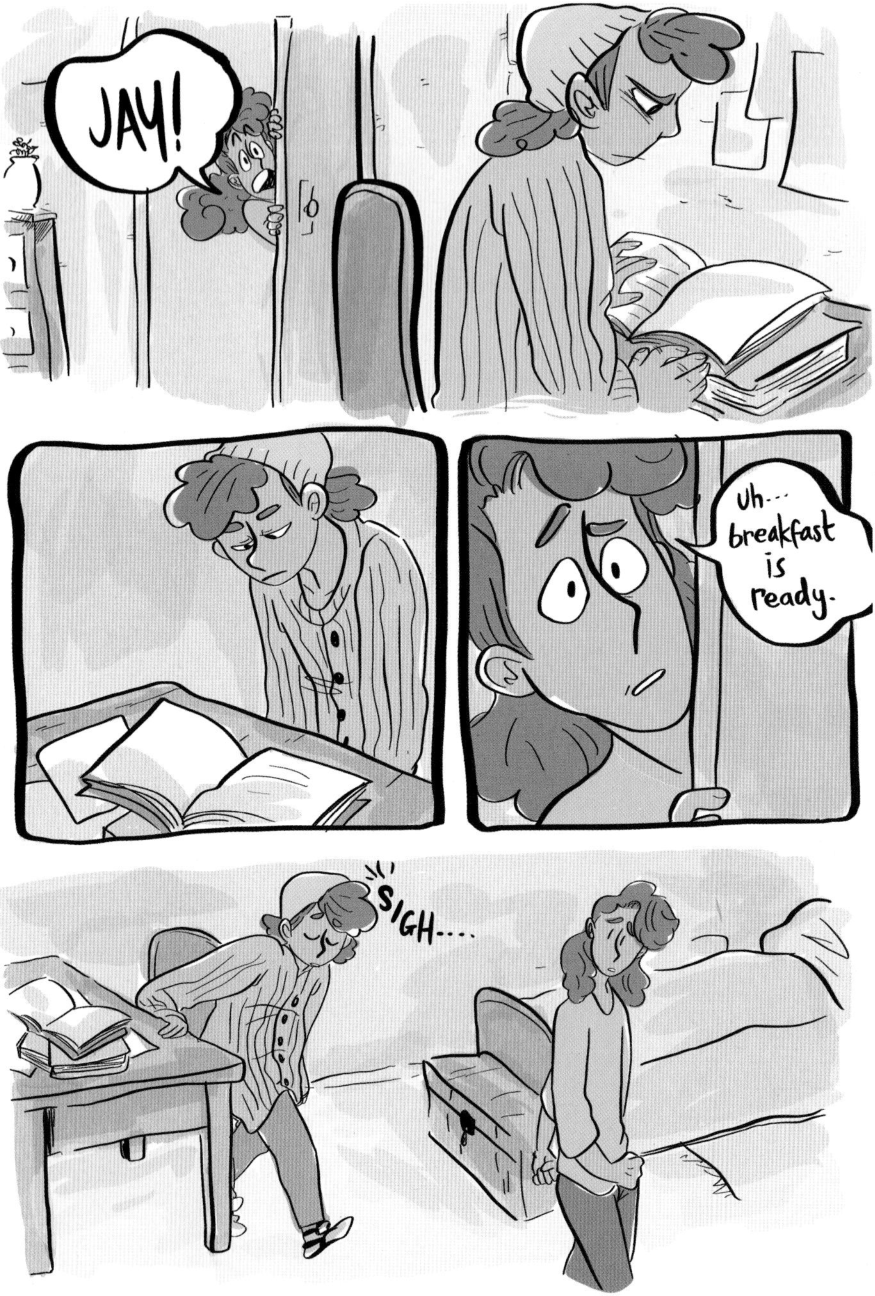
JAY!
Uh... breakfast is ready.
SIGH....

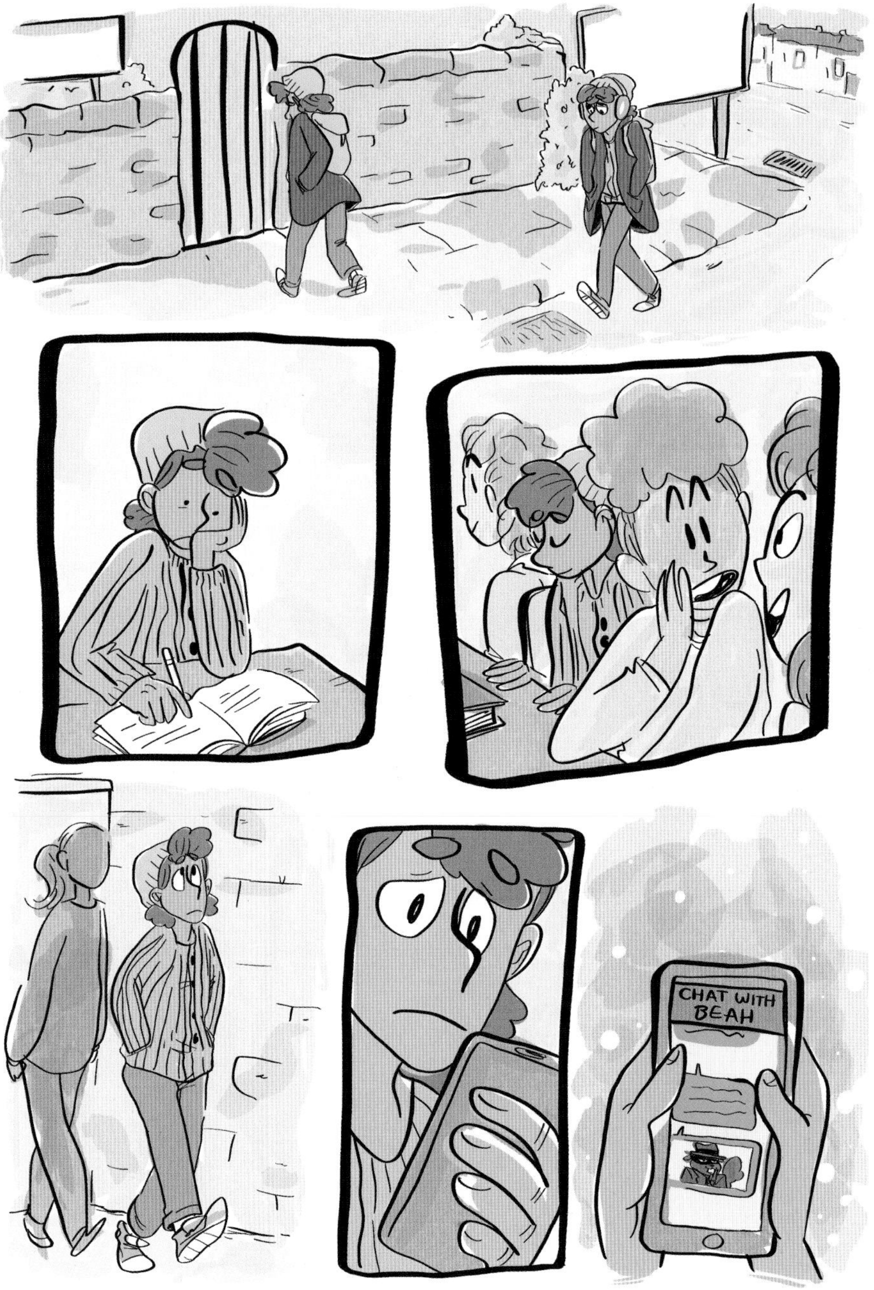
CHAT WITH BEAH

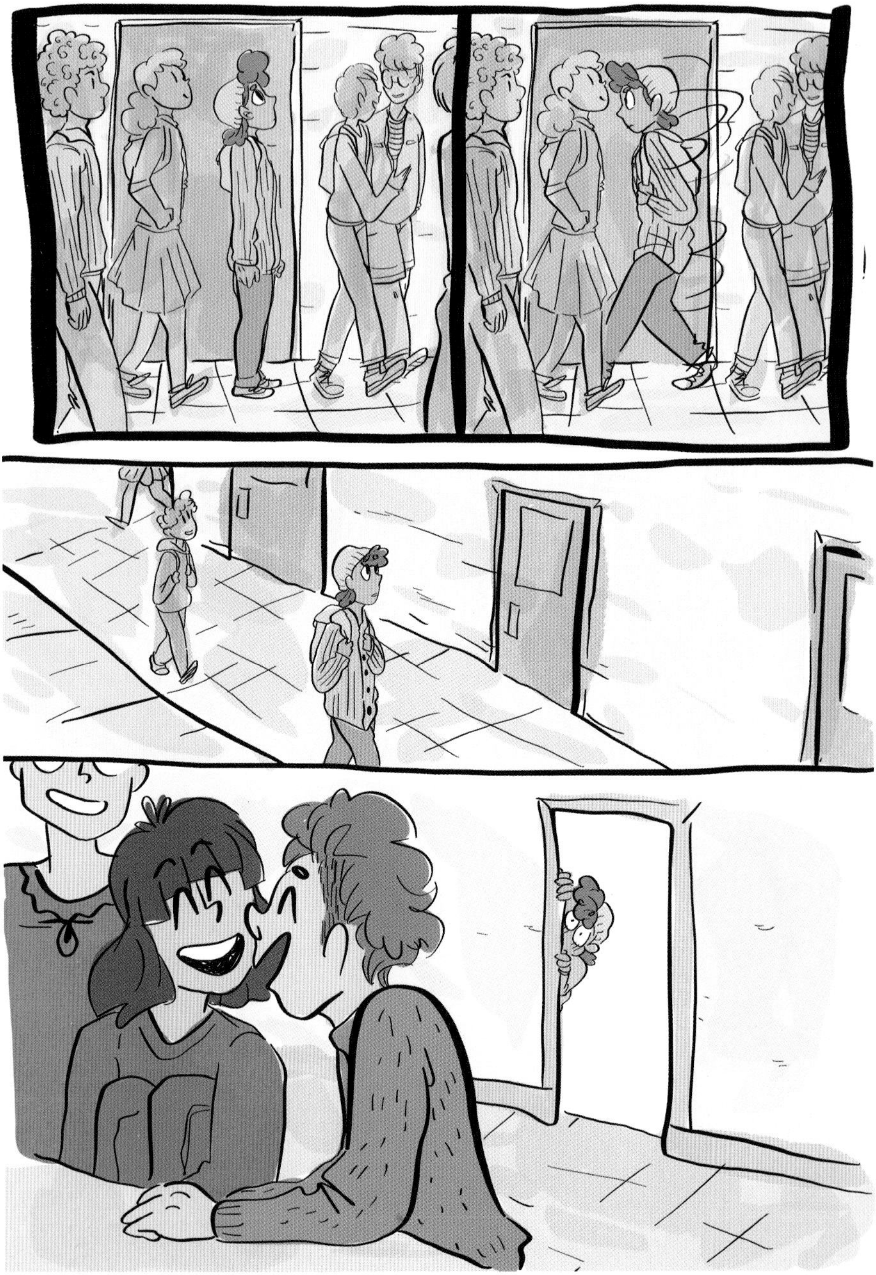

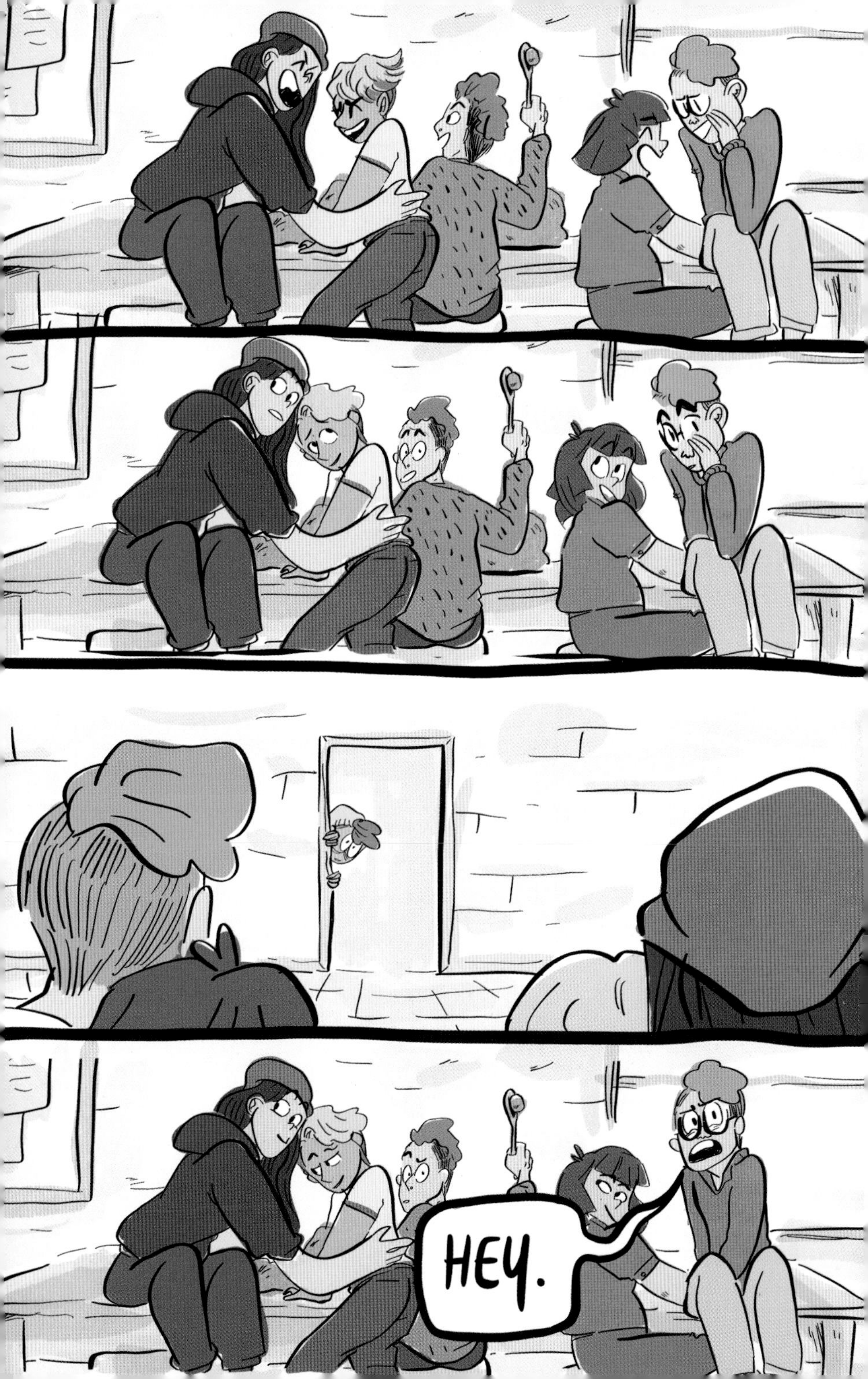
HEY.

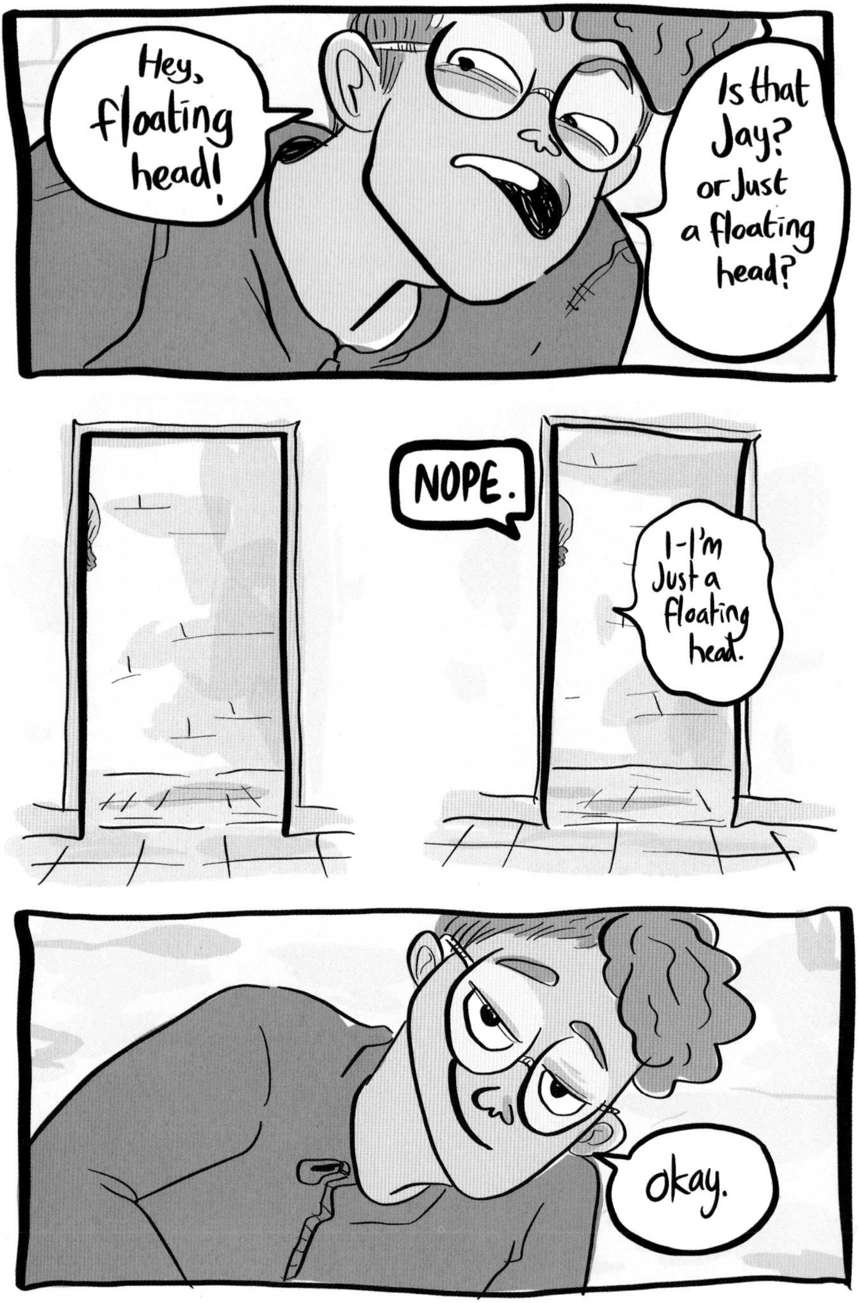
Hey, floating head!
Is that Jay? or Just a floating head?
NOPE.
I-I'm Just a floating head.
okay.

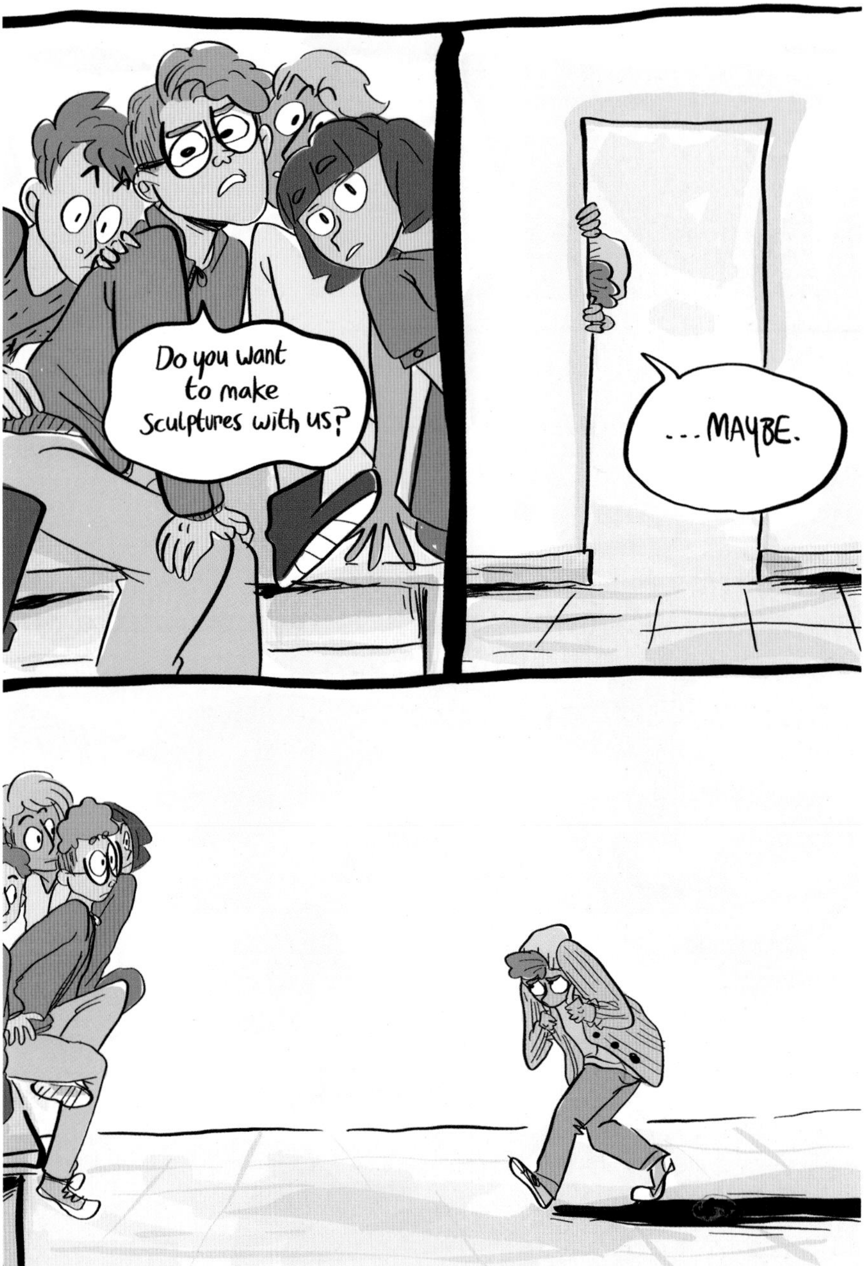
Do you want to make sculptures with us?
...MAYBE.

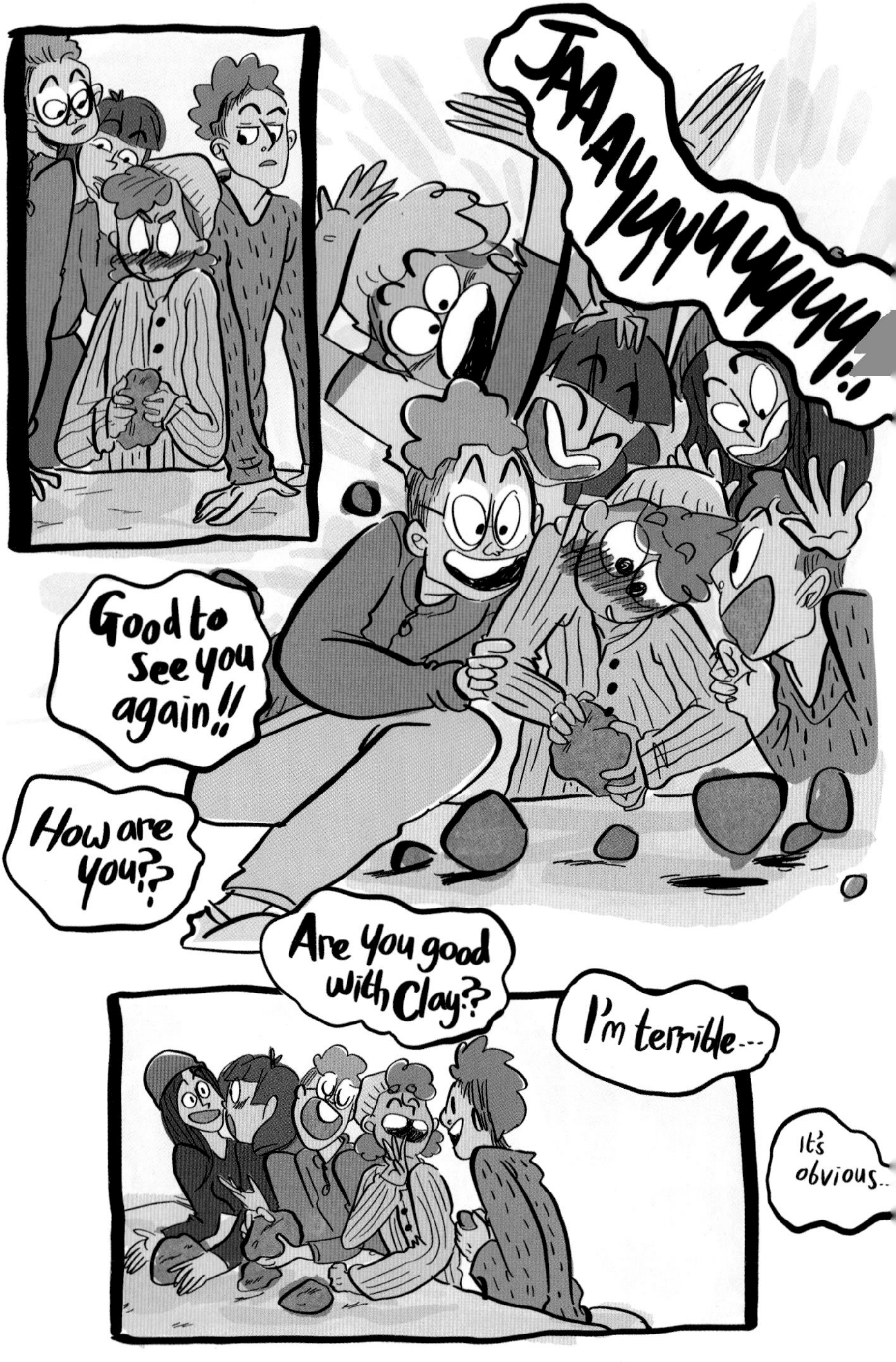
JAAAYYYYYYYYYY...
Good to see you again!!
How are you??
Are you good with Clay??
I'm terrible...
It's obvious...

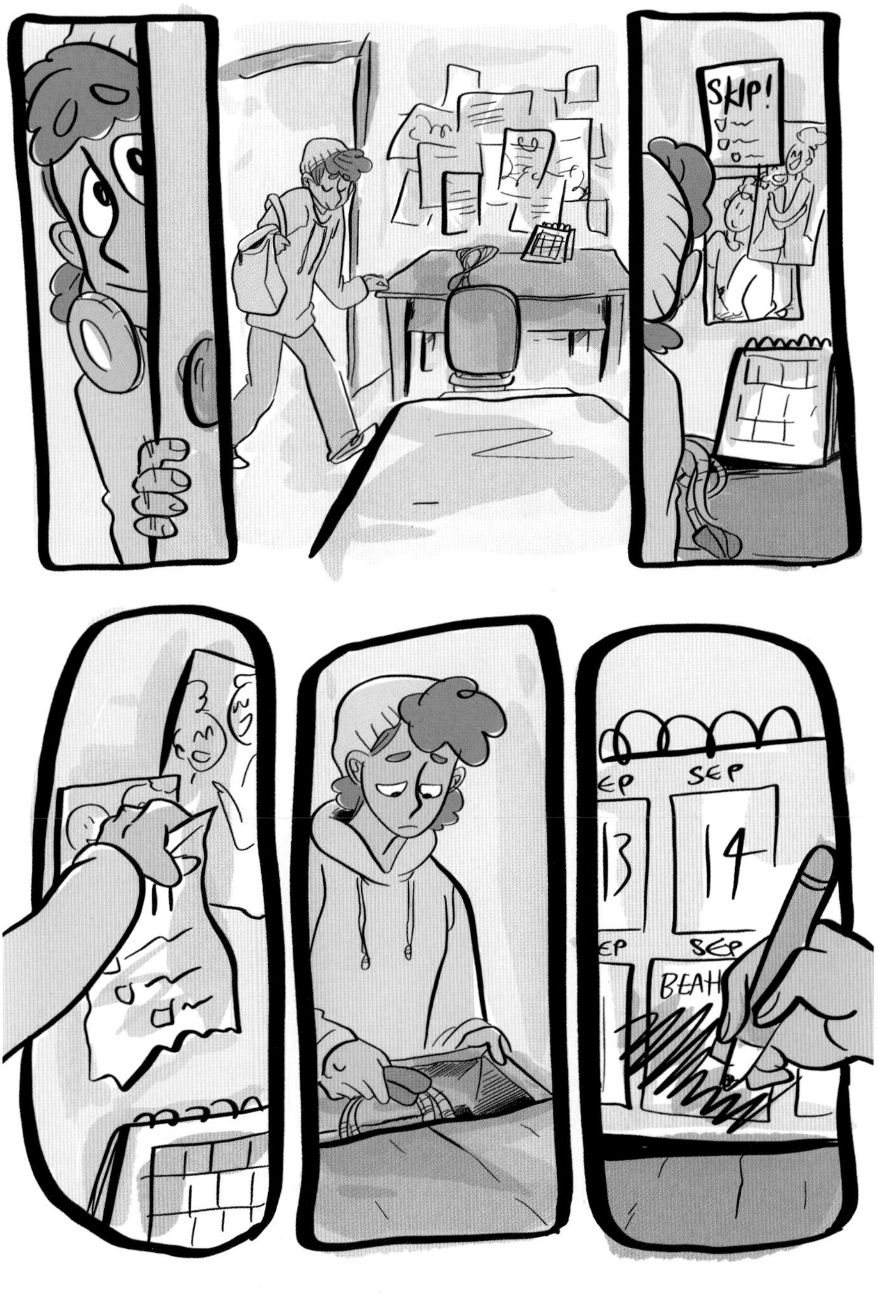
SKIP!
SEP
SEP
13
14
SEP
SEP
BEAH

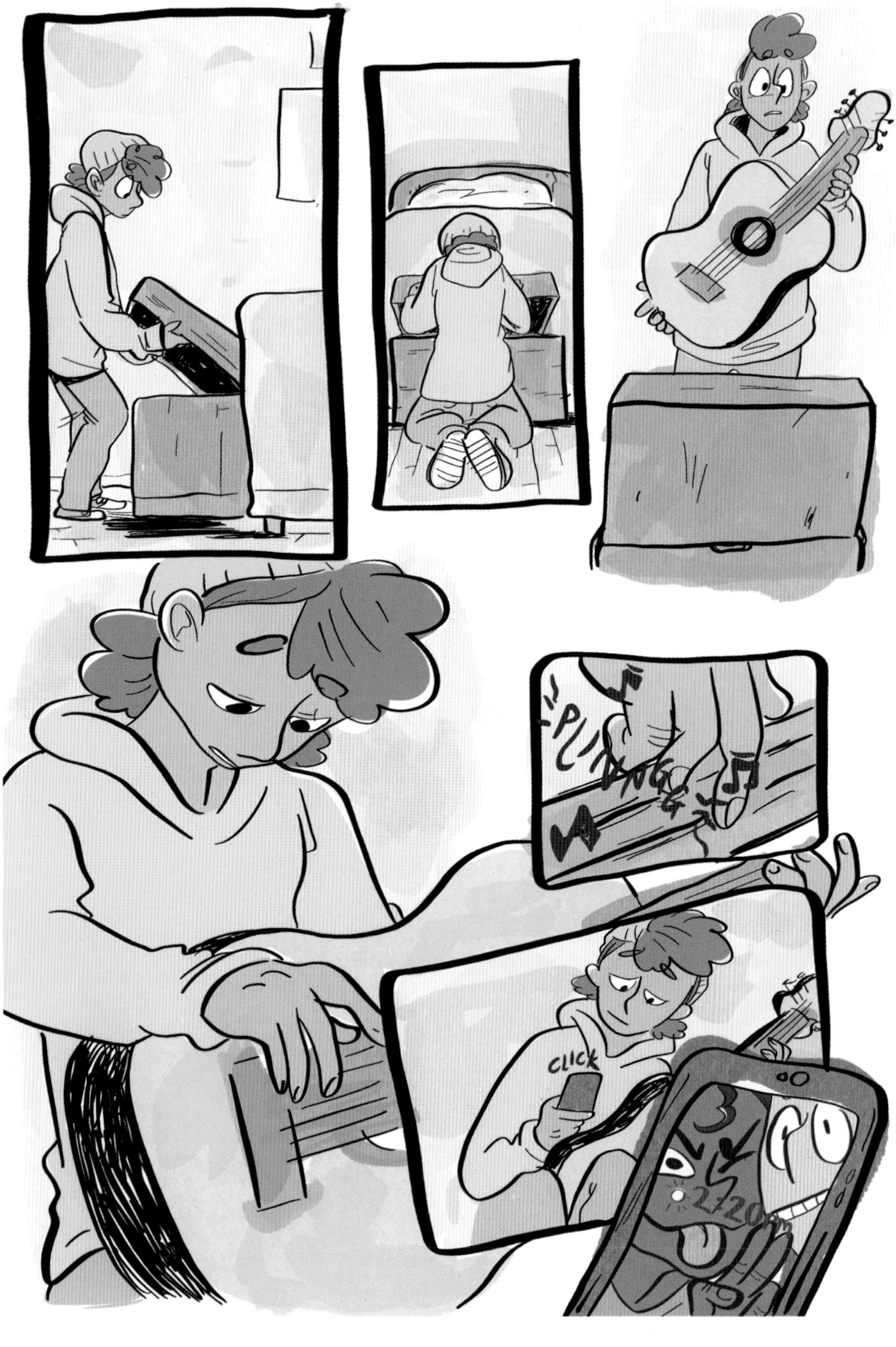
PLING
CLICK

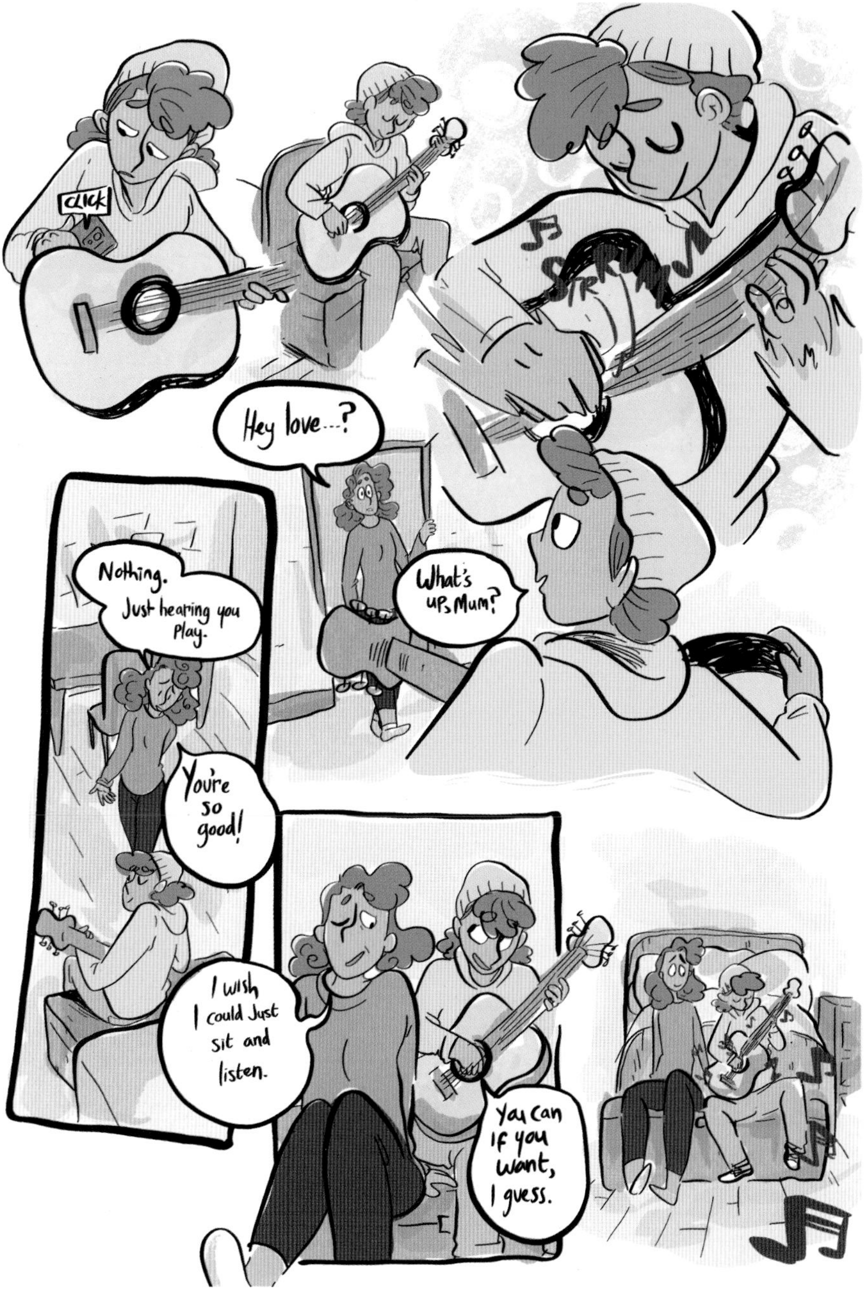
CLICK
STRUM
Hey love...?
What's up, Mum?
Nothing. Just hearing you play.
You're so good!
I wish I could just sit and listen.
You can if you want, I guess.

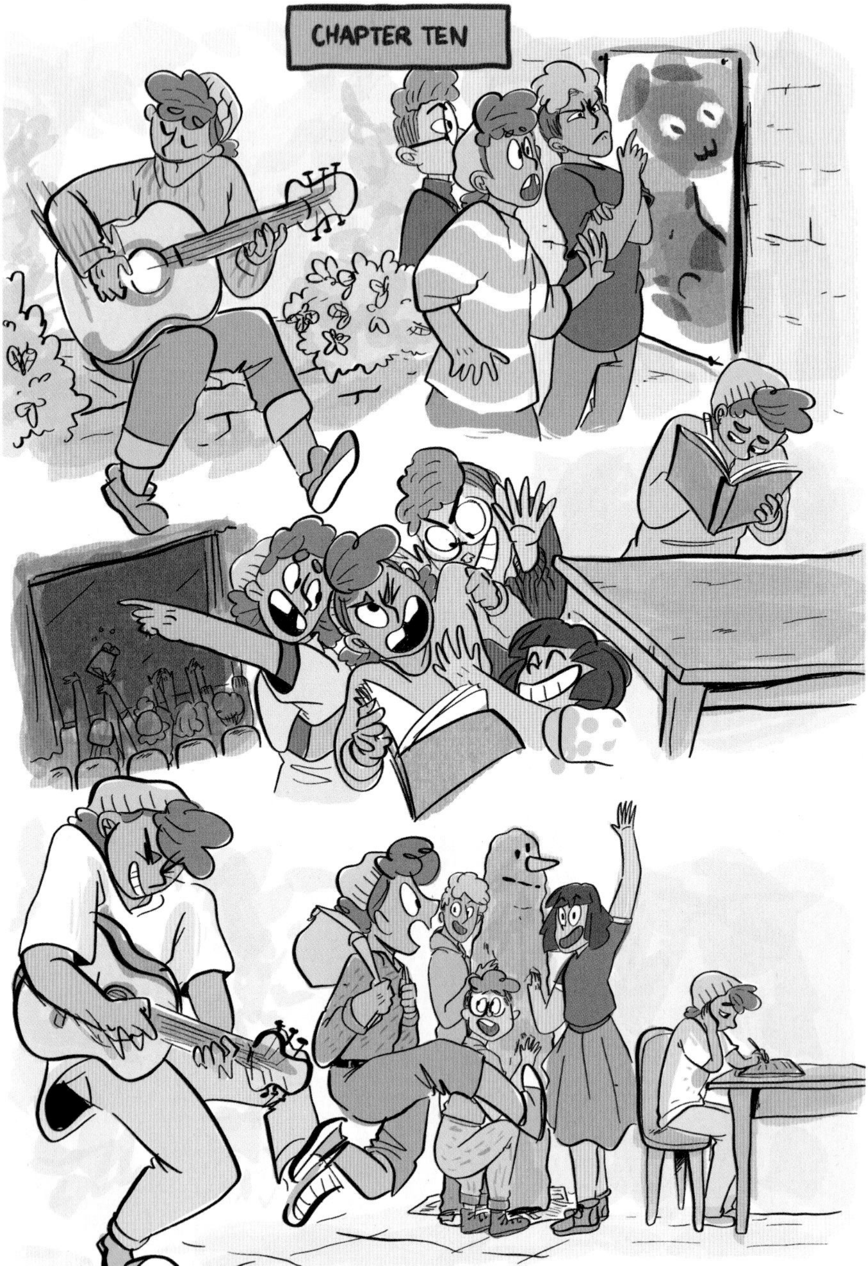
CHAPTER TEN

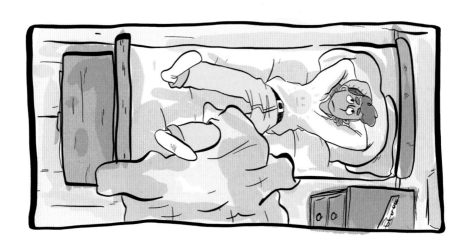

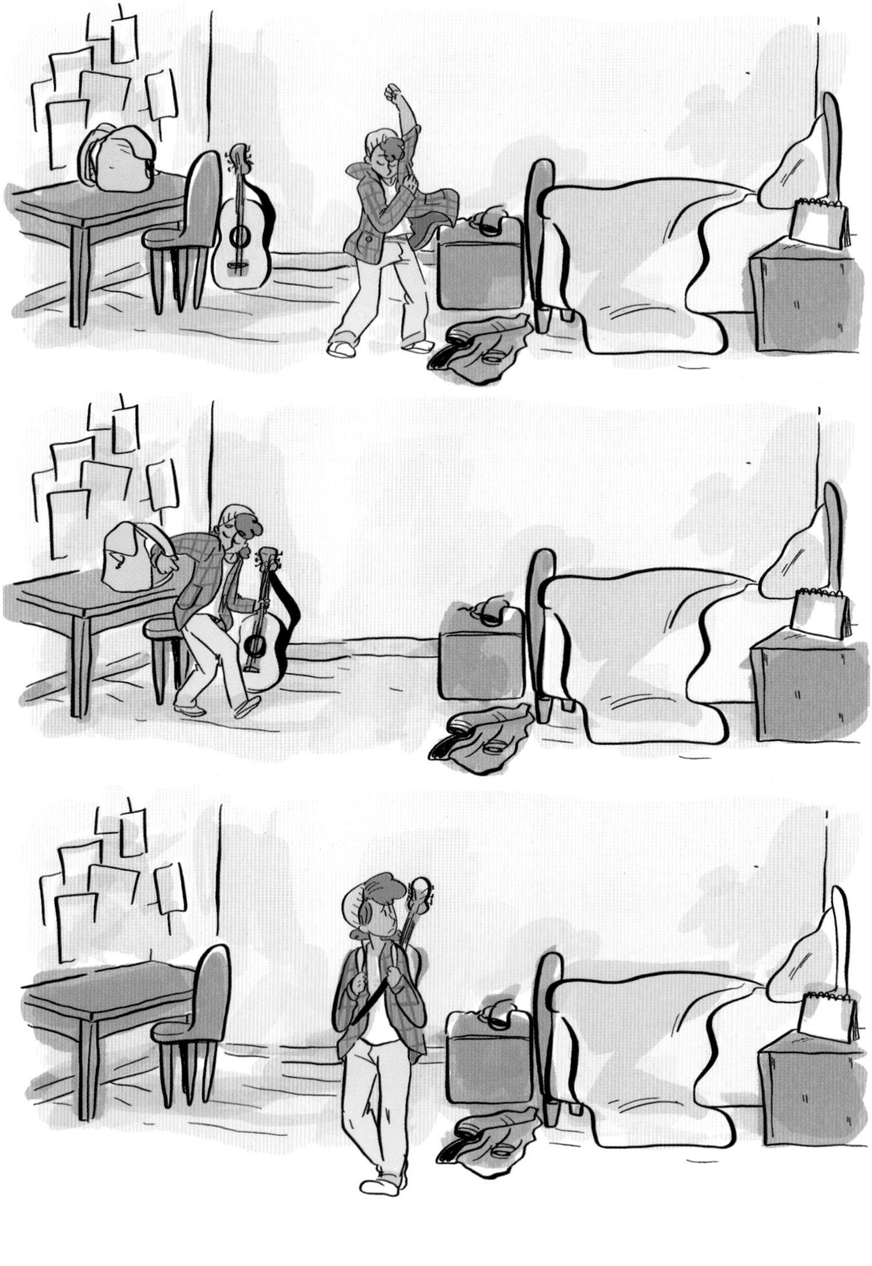

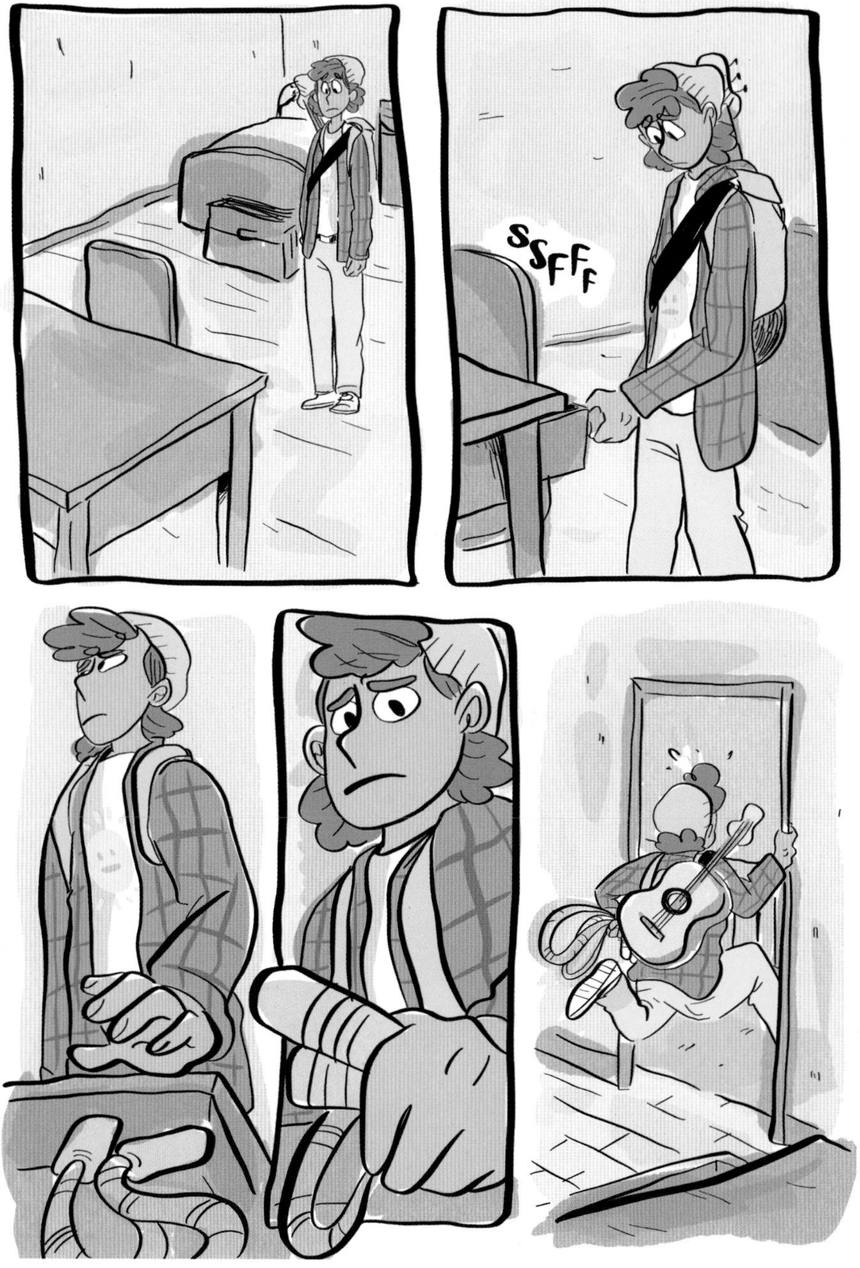
SSFFF

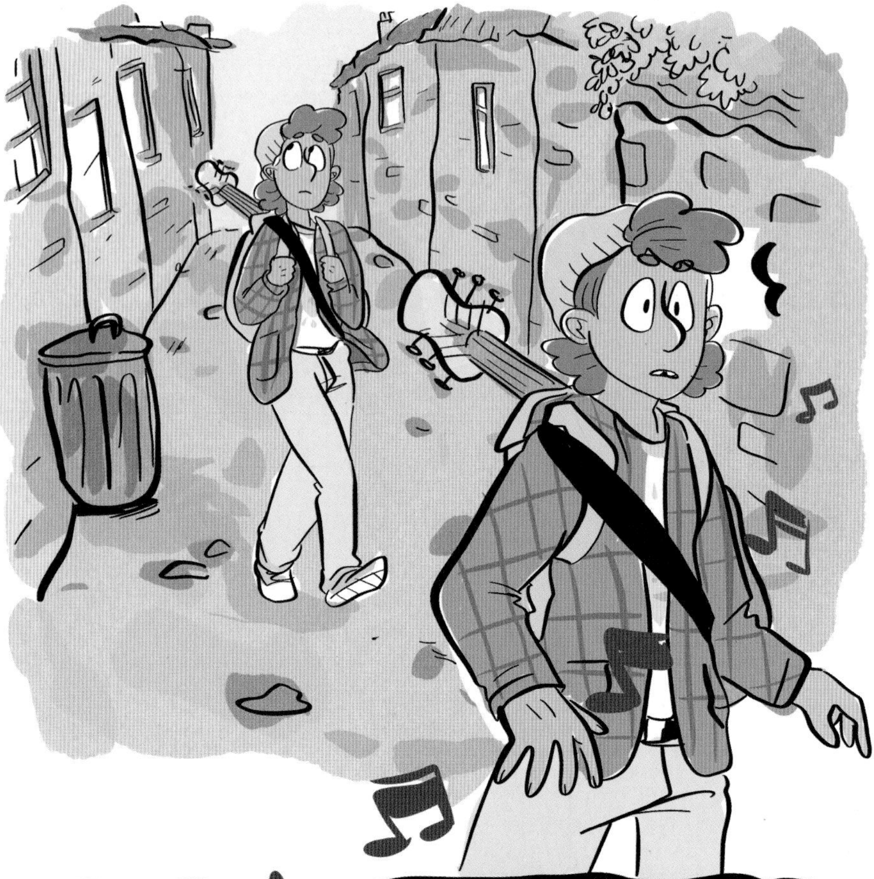

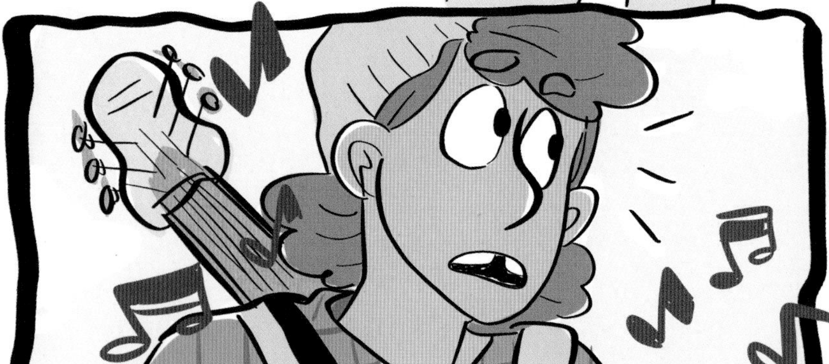

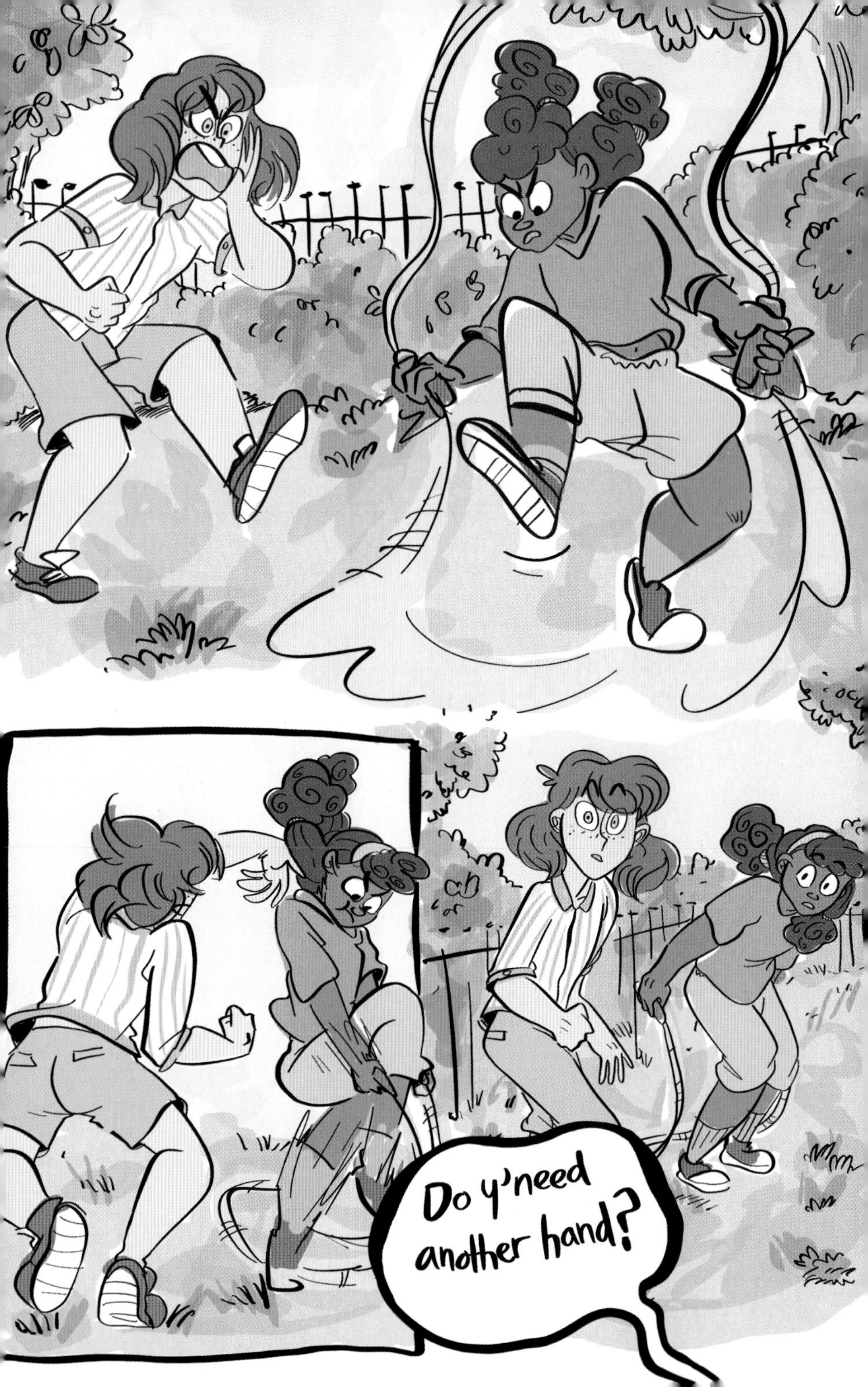
Do y'need another hand?

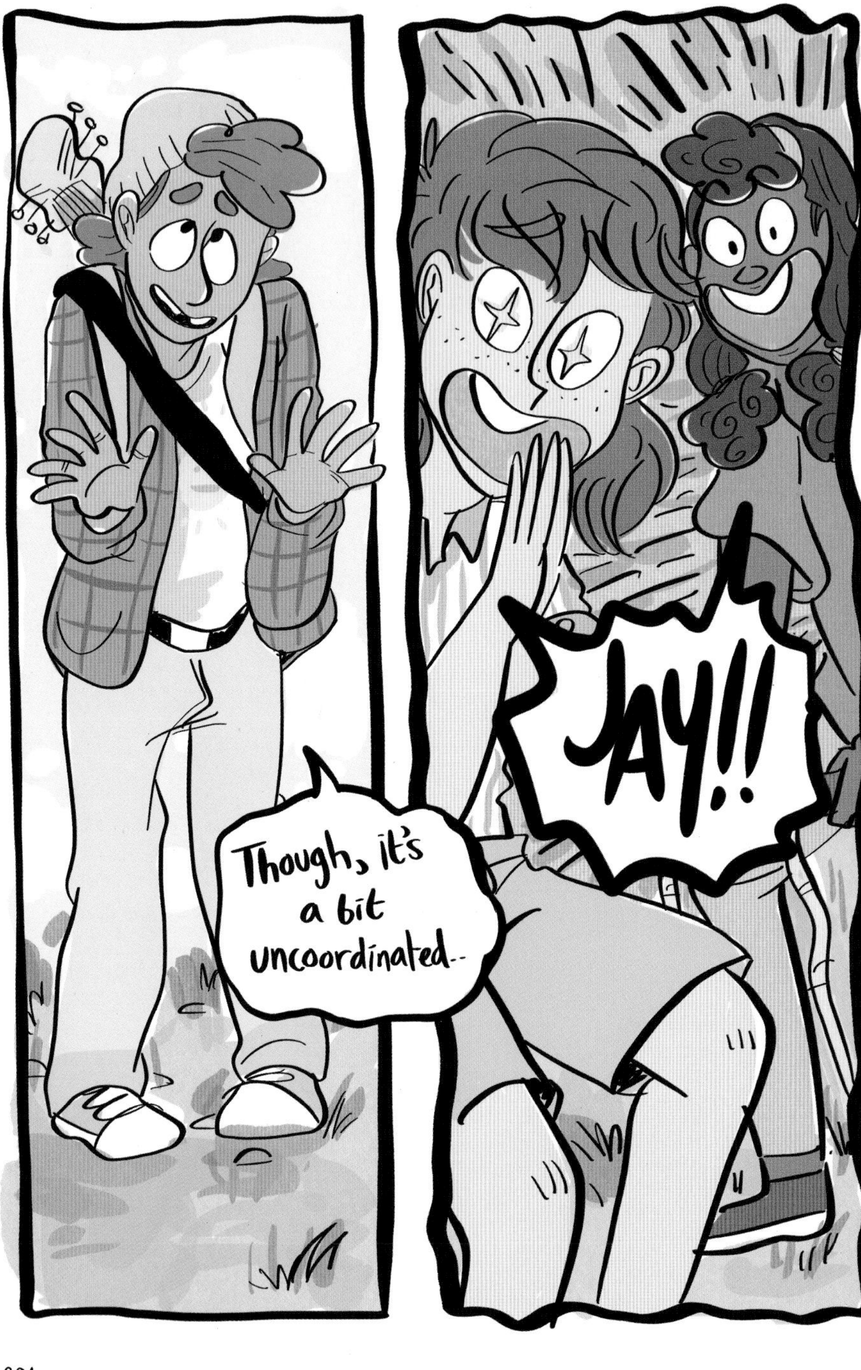
Though, it's a bit uncoordinated..
JAY!!

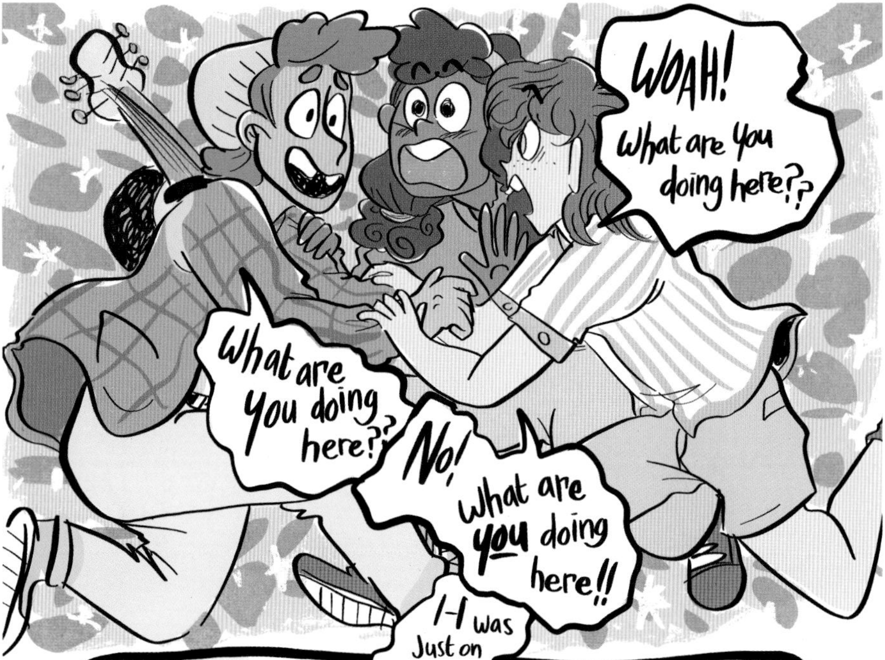
WOAH! What are you doing here?!?
What are you doing here?!?
No! what are YOU doing here!!
I-I was just on my way to...

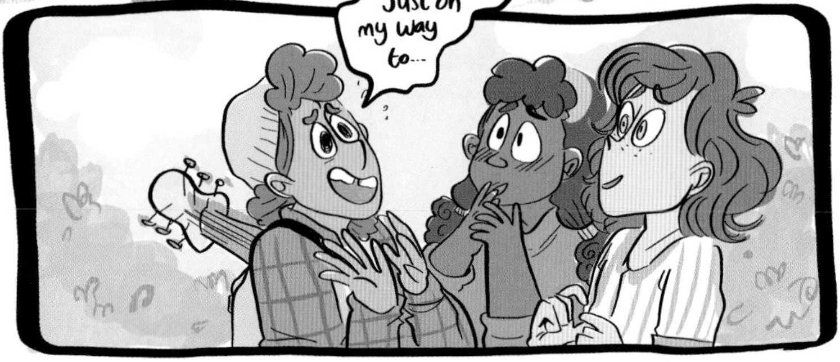

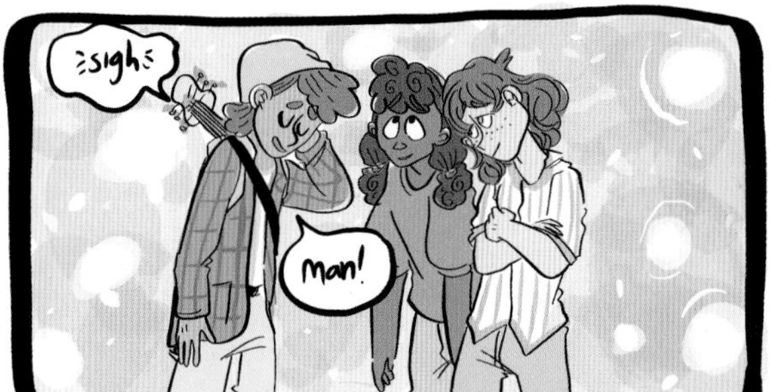
sigh
man!

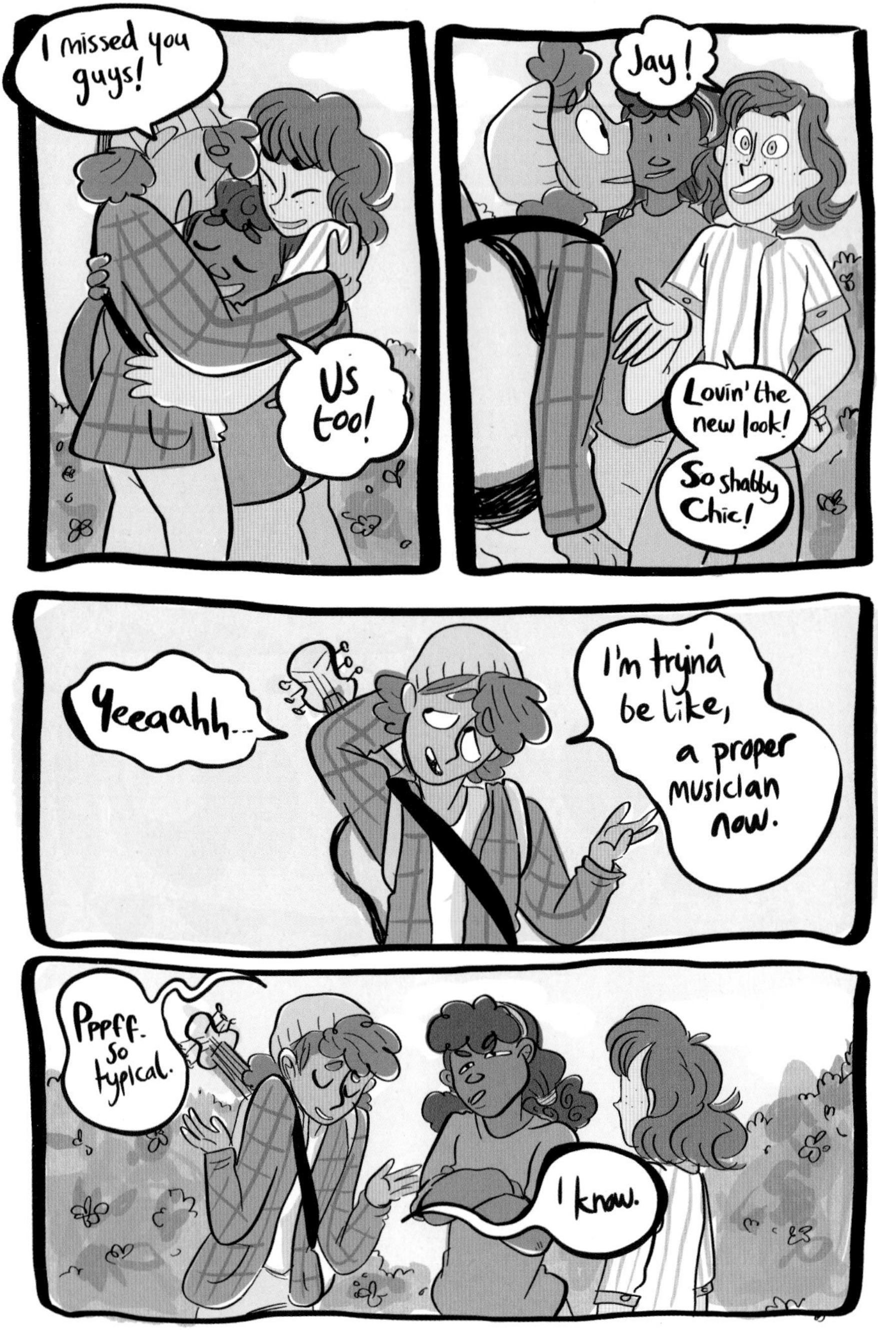
I missed you guys!
Us too!
Jay!
Lovin' the new look!
So shabby Chic!
Yeeaahh...
I'm tryna be like, a proper musician now.
Pppff. So typical.
I know.

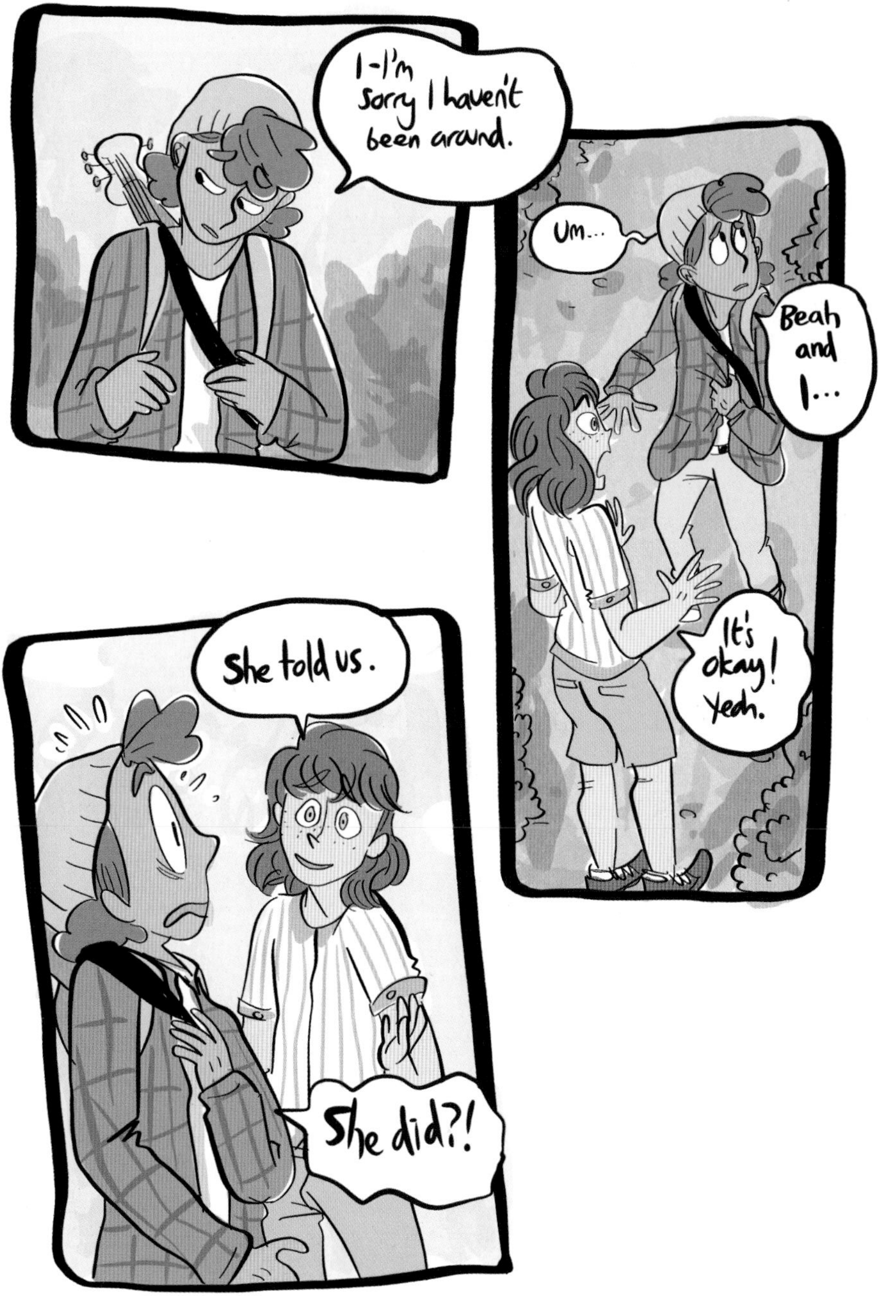
I-I'm sorry I haven't been around.
Um...
Beah and I...
It's okay! Yeah.
She told us.
She did?!

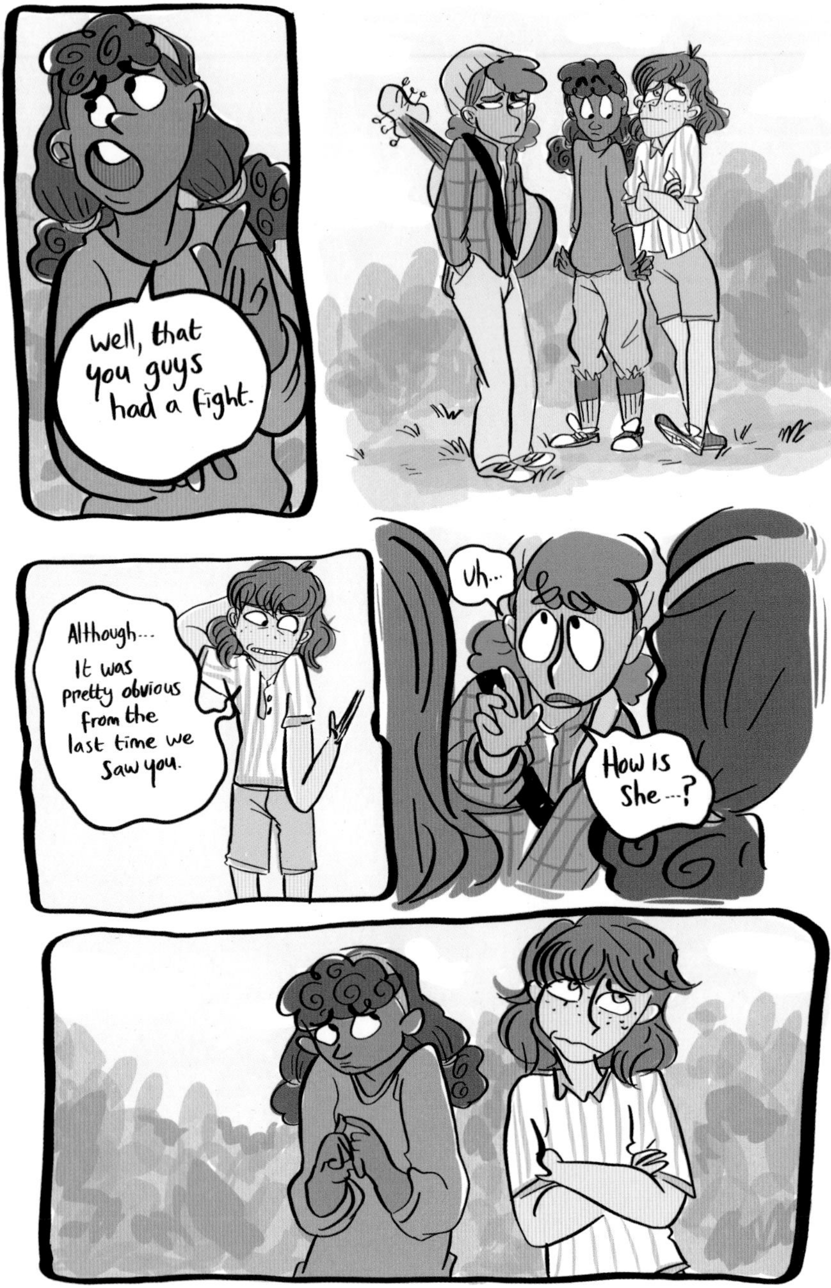
well, that you guys had a fight.
Although... It was pretty obvious from the last time we saw you.
Uh...
How is she...?

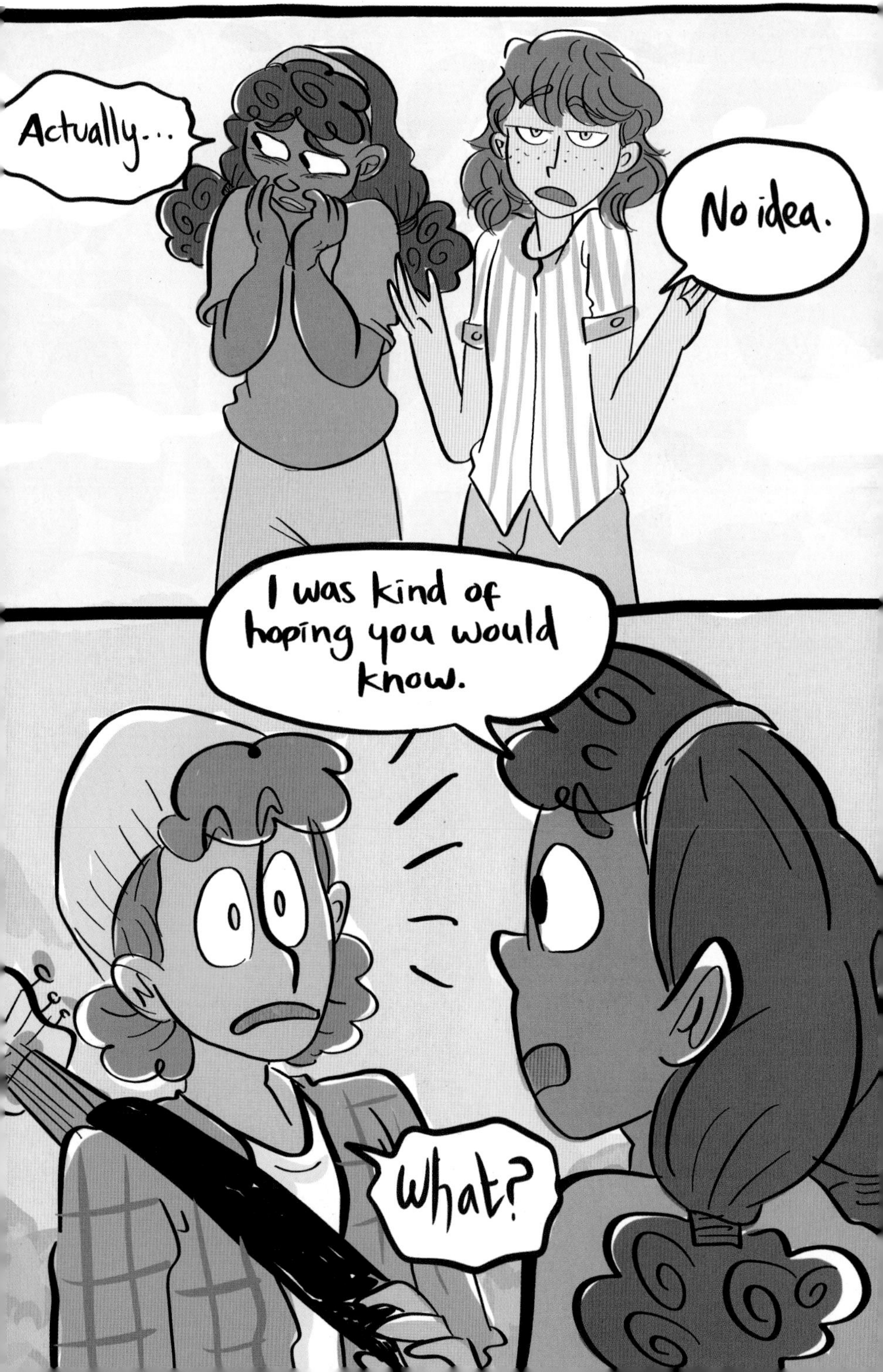
Actually...
No idea.
I was kind of hoping you would know.
What?

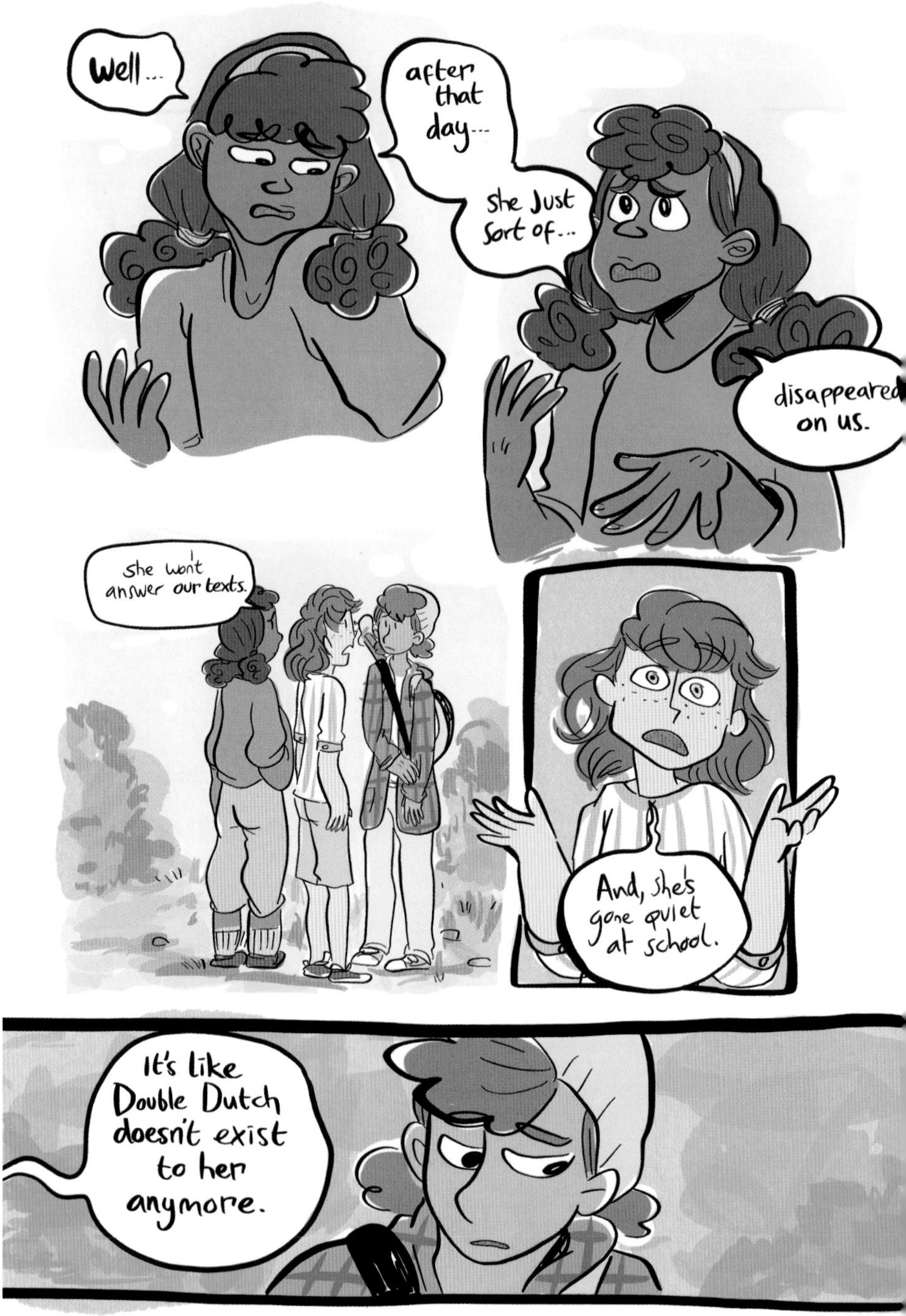
Well...
after that day...
she just sort of...
disappeared on us.
she won't answer our texts.
And, she's gone quiet at school.
It's like Double Dutch doesn't exist to her anymore.

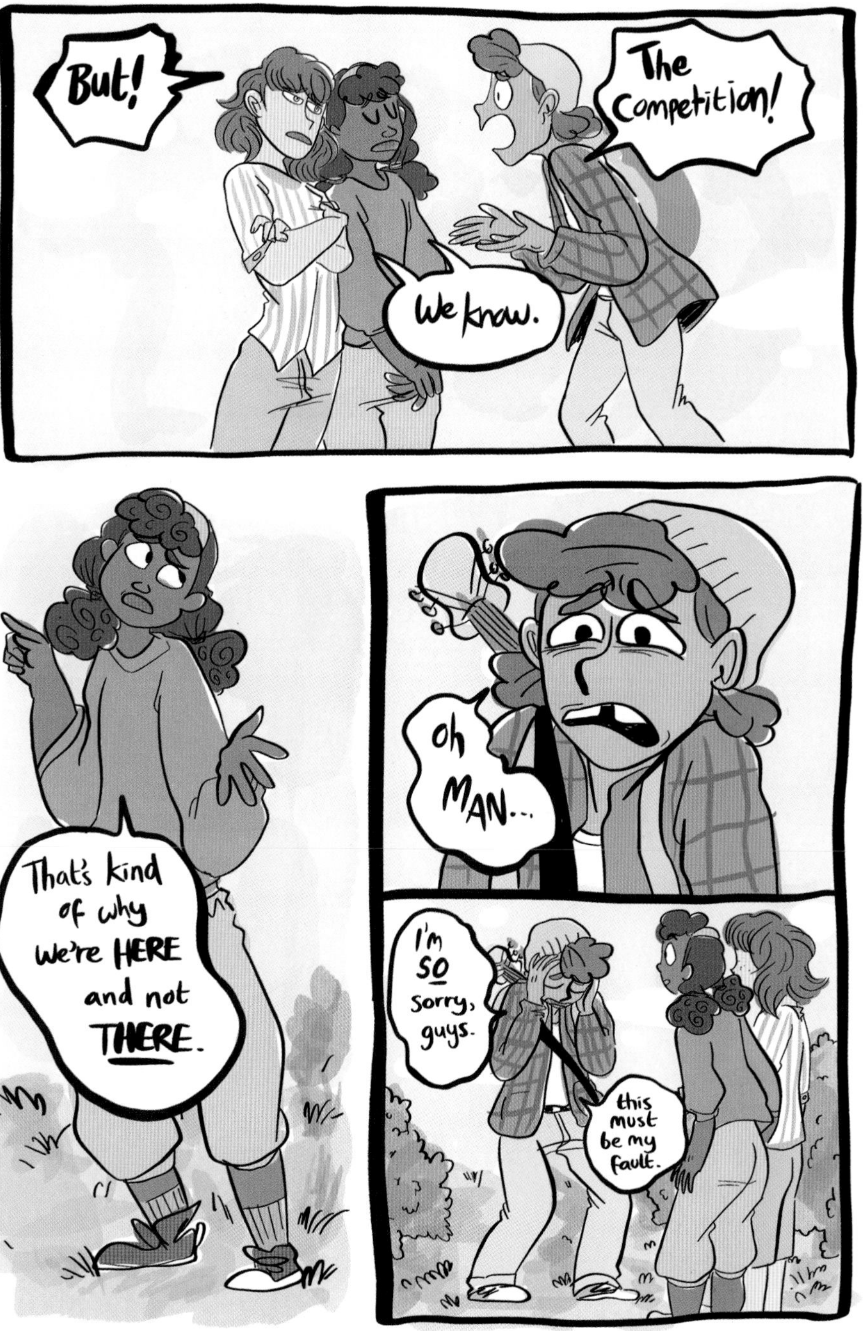
But!
The Competition!
We know.
That's kind of why we're HERE and not THERE.
Oh MAN...
I'm SO sorry, guys.
this must be my fault.

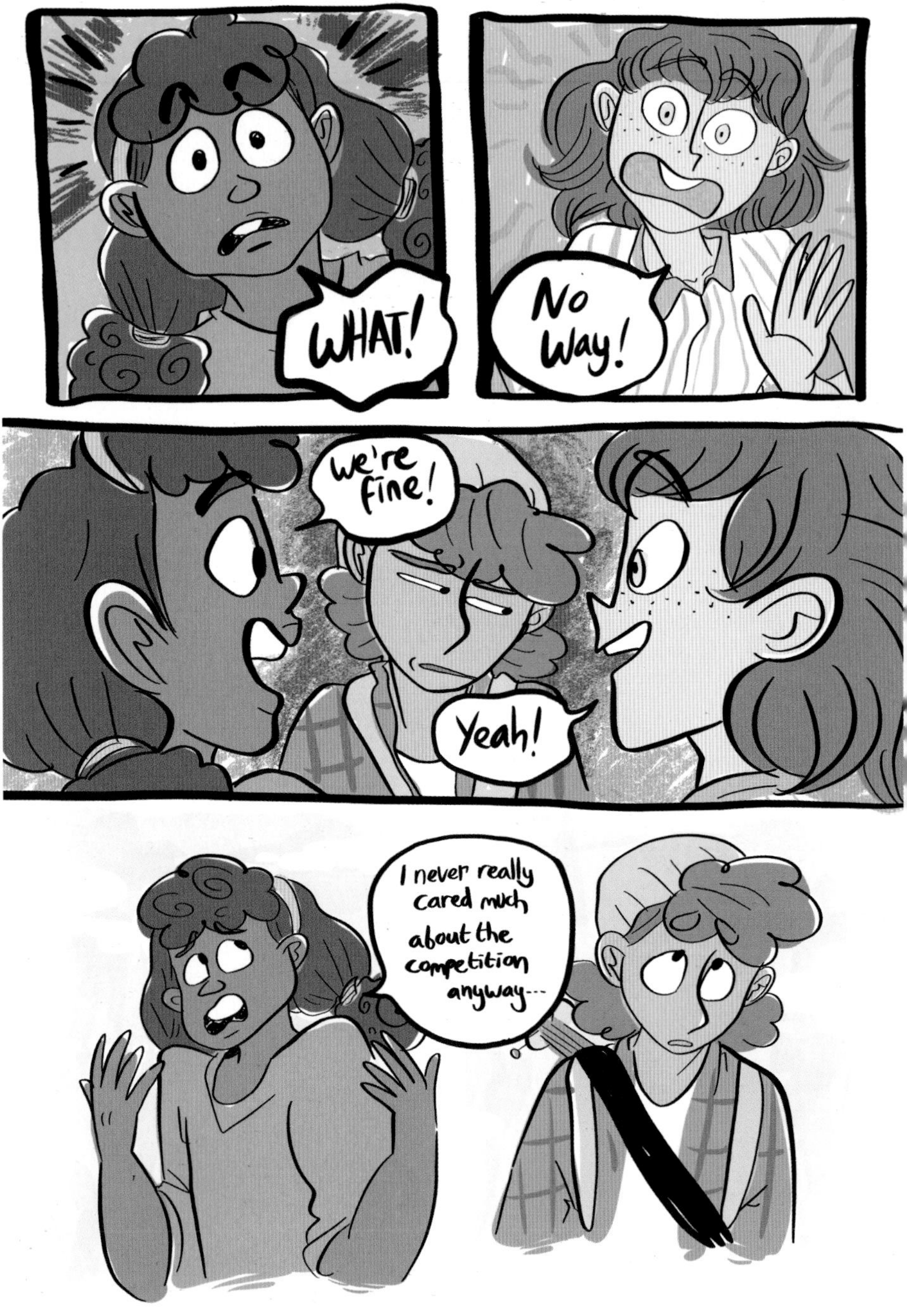
WHAT!
No way!
we're fine!
Yeah!
I never really cared much about the competition anyway...

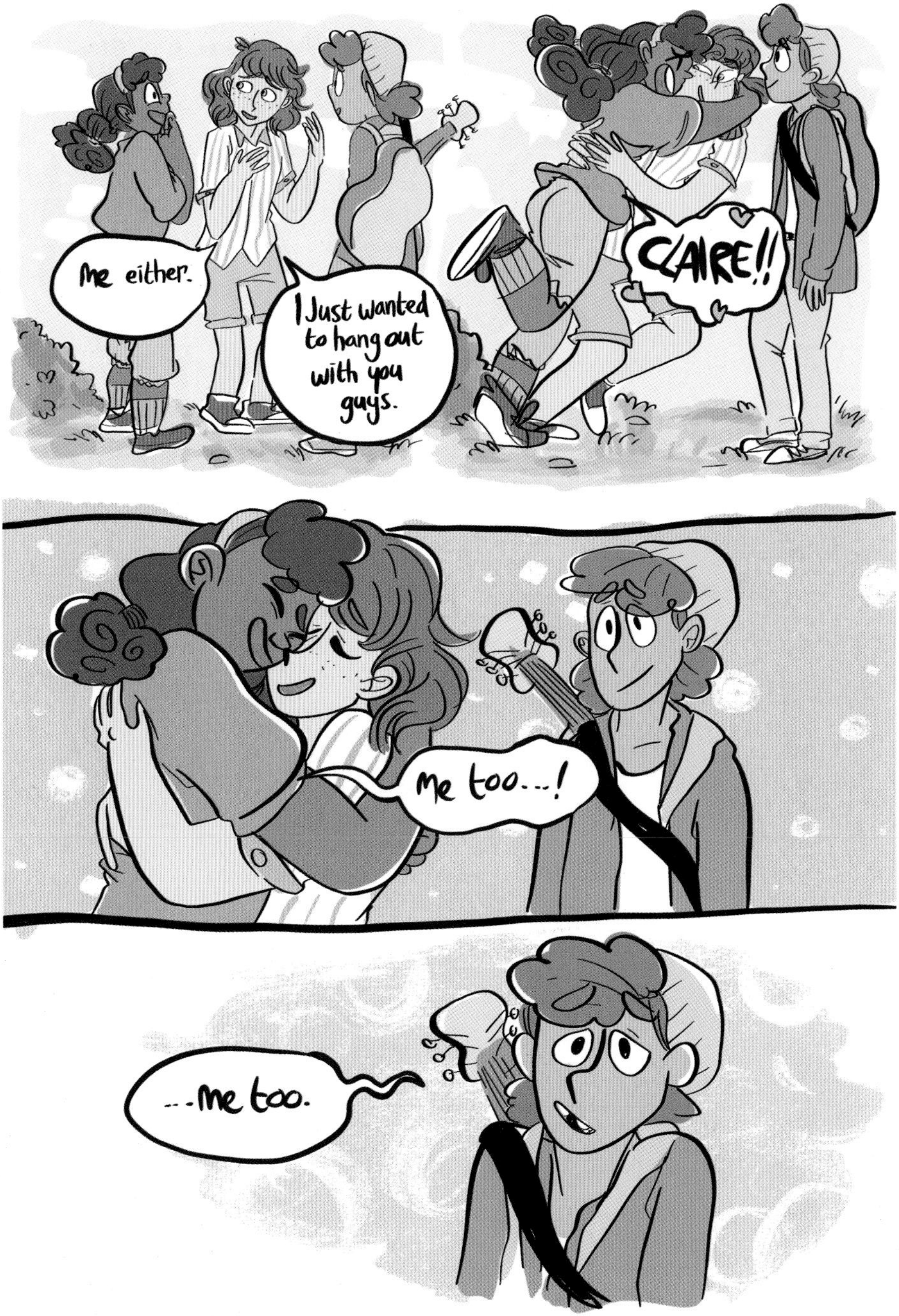
Me either.
I Just wanted to hang out with you guys.
CLAIRE!!
Me too...!
...Me too.

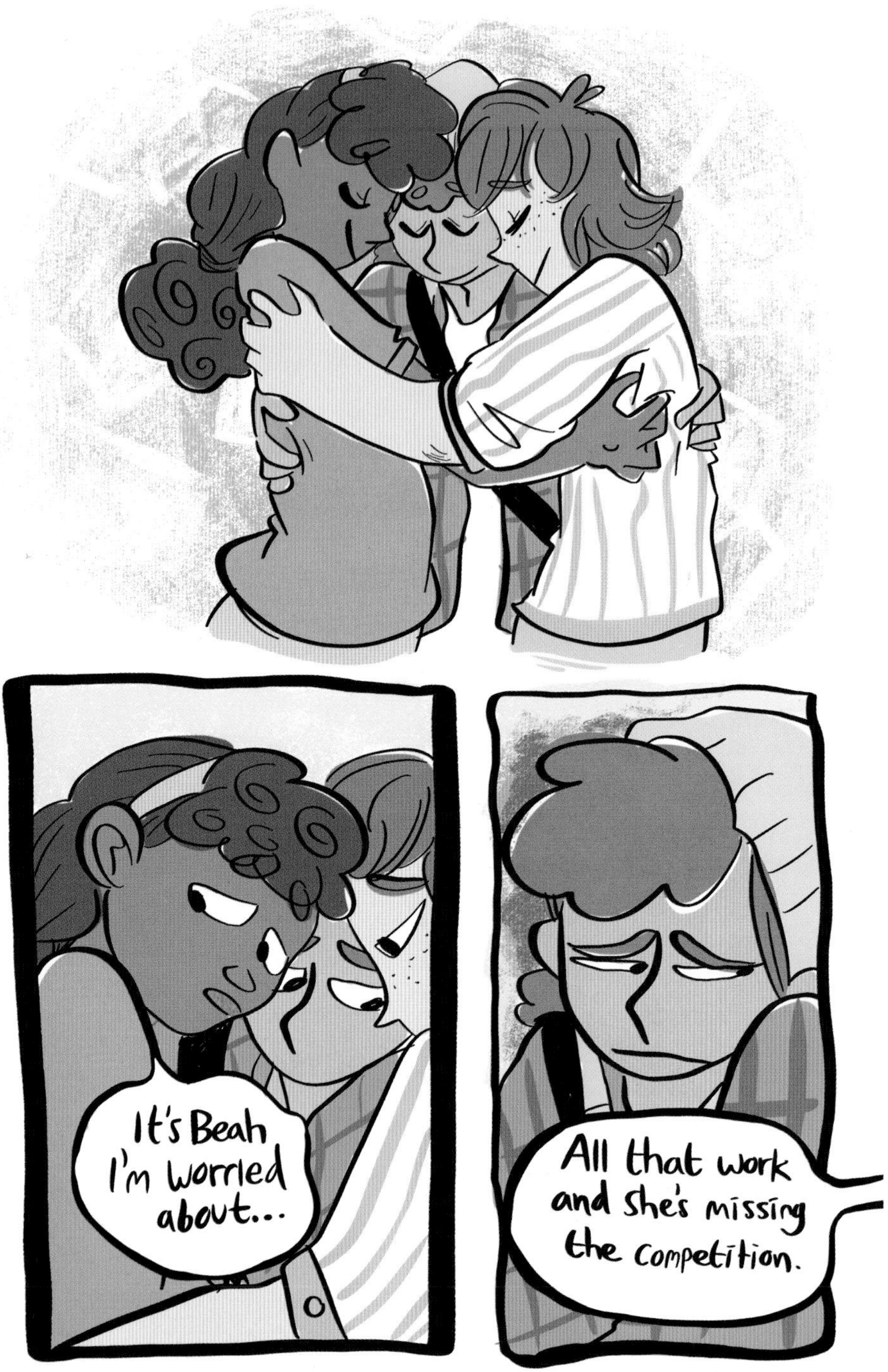
It's Beah I'm worried about...
All that work and she's missing the competition.

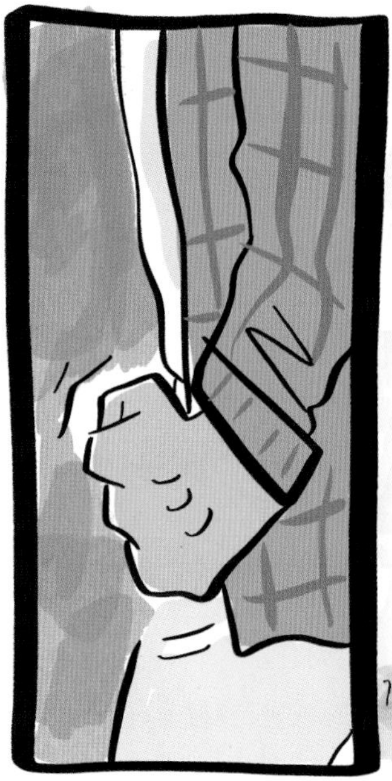

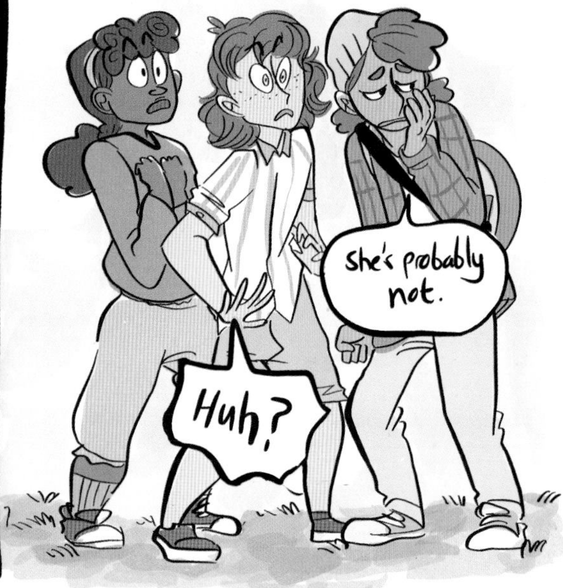
she's probably not.
Huh?

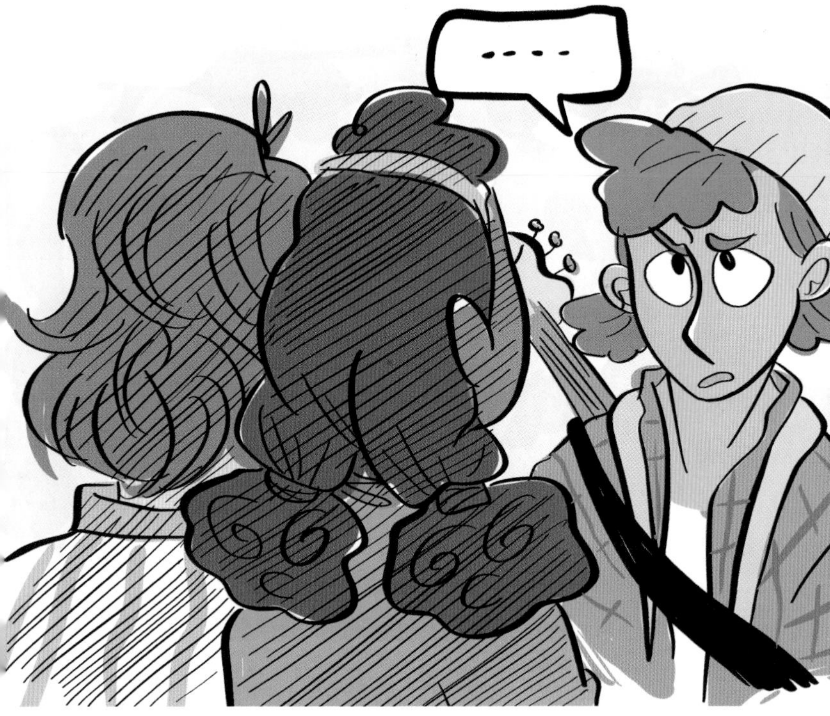
....

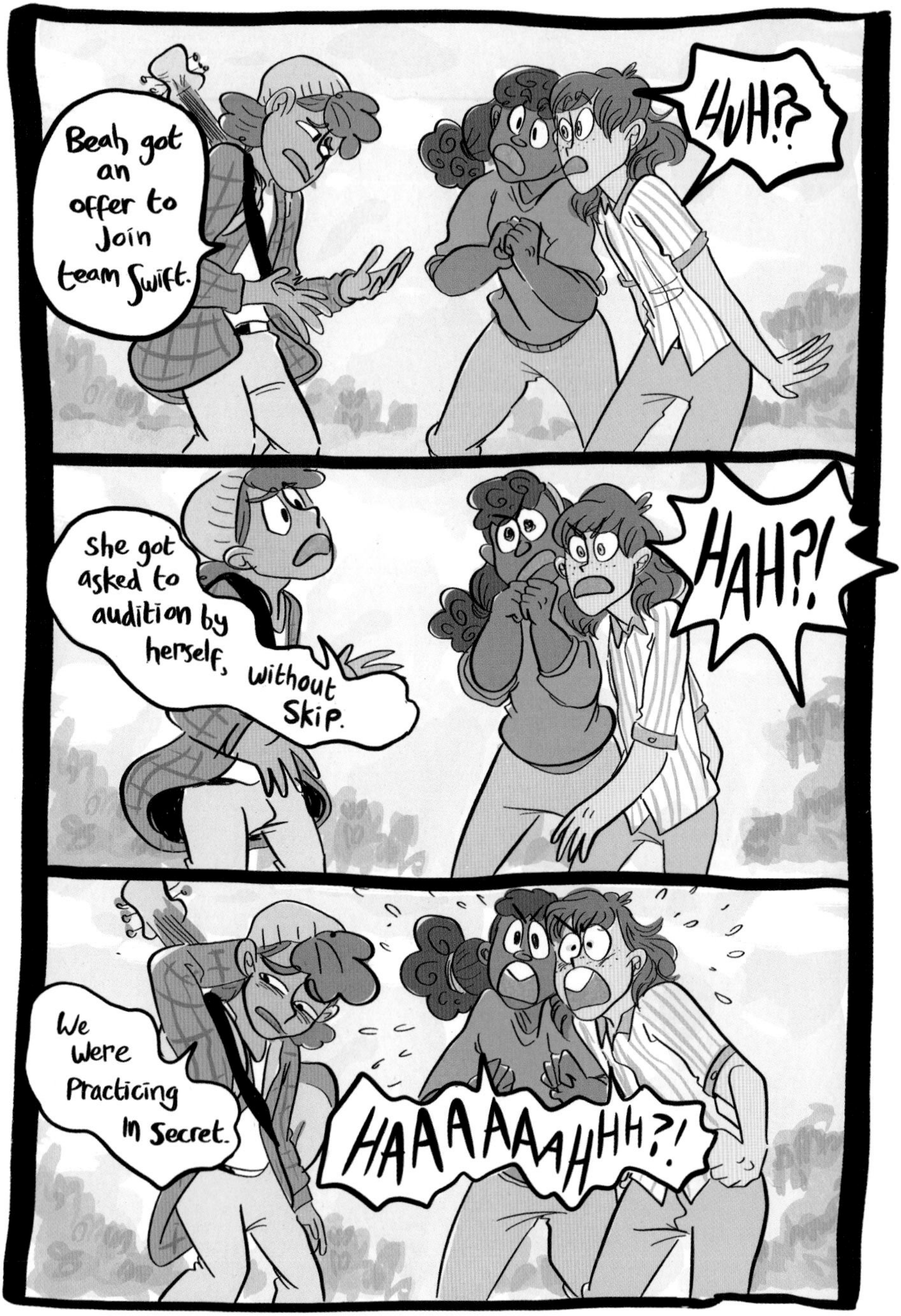
Beah got an offer to Join team Swift.
HUH?!
She got asked to audition by herself, without Skip.
HAH?!
We were Practicing in Secret.
HAAAAAAHHH?!

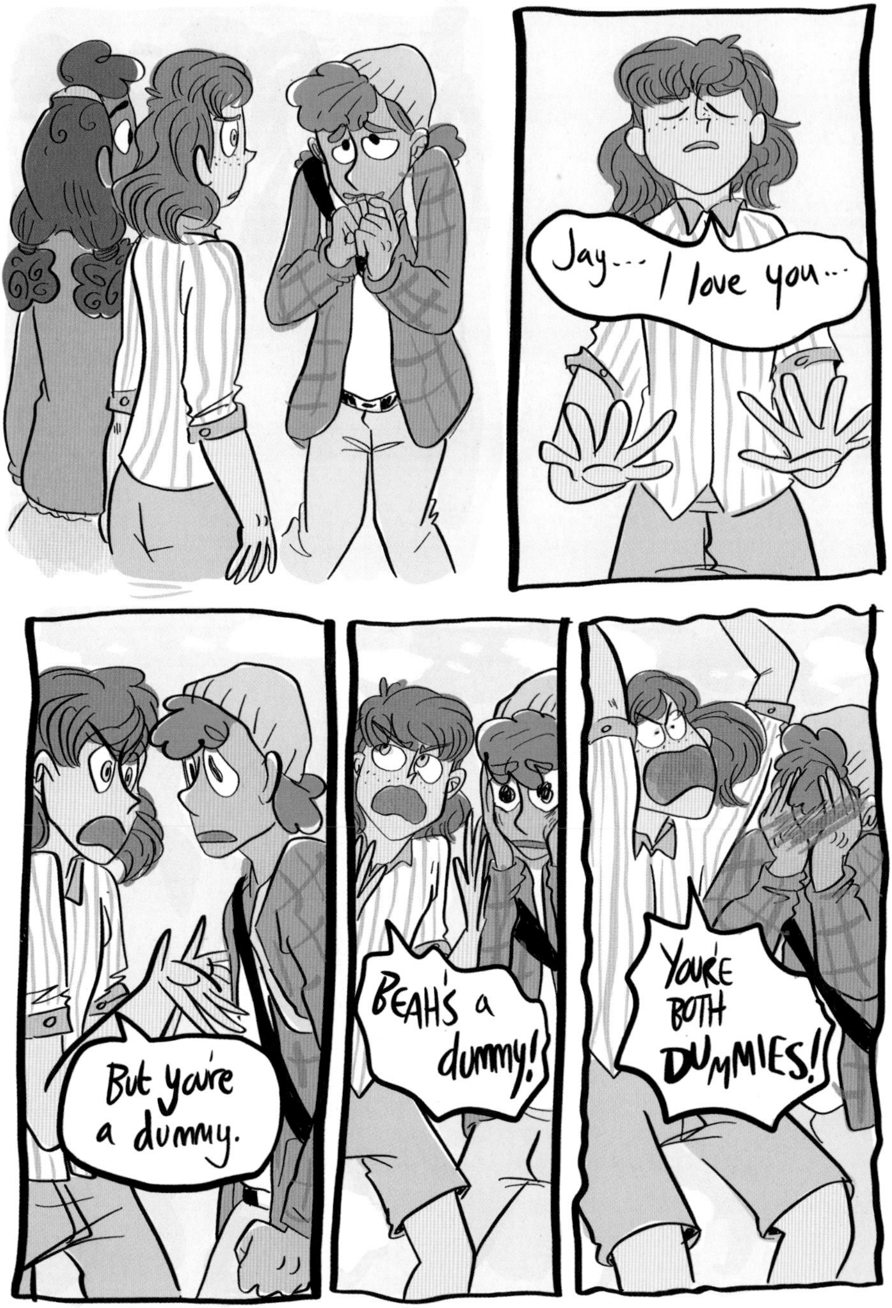
Jay... I love you...
But you're a dummy.
BEAH'S a dummy!
YOU'RE BOTH DUMMIES!

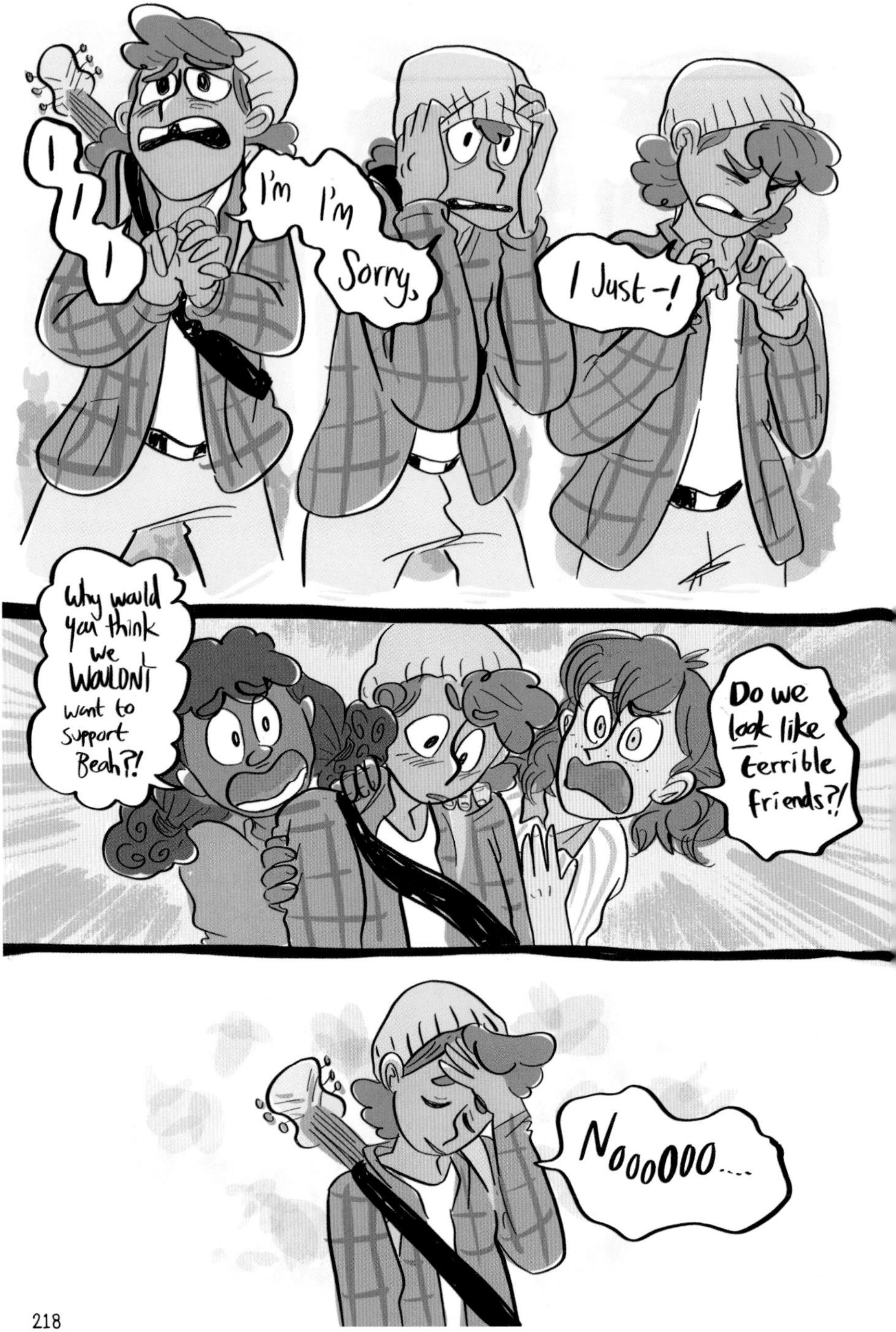
I- I- I
I'm I'm Sorry,
I Just-!
Why would you think we WOULDN'T want to support Beah?!
Do we look like terrible friends?!
NoooOOO....

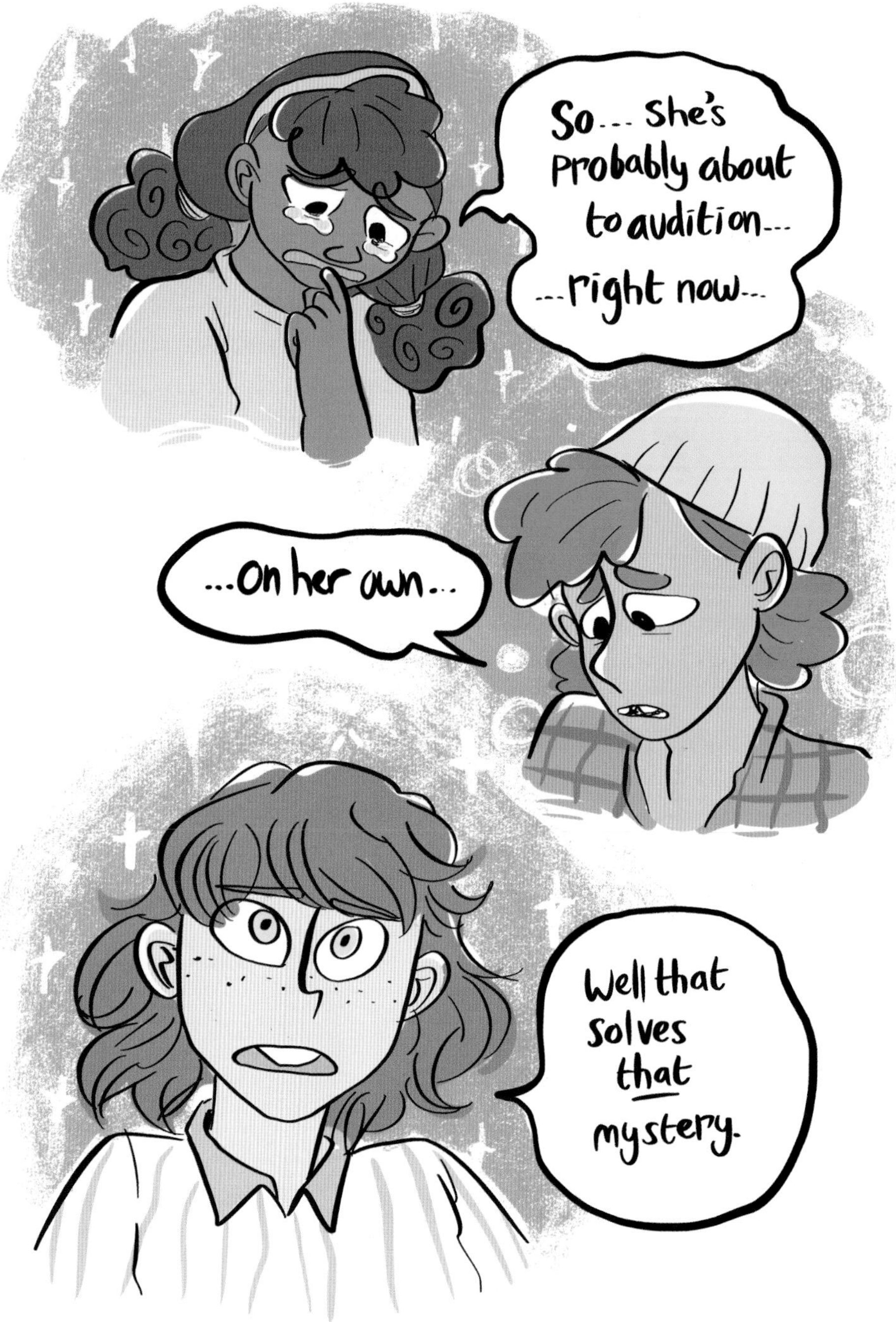
So... She's probably about to audition...
...right now...
...on her own...
Well that solves that mystery.

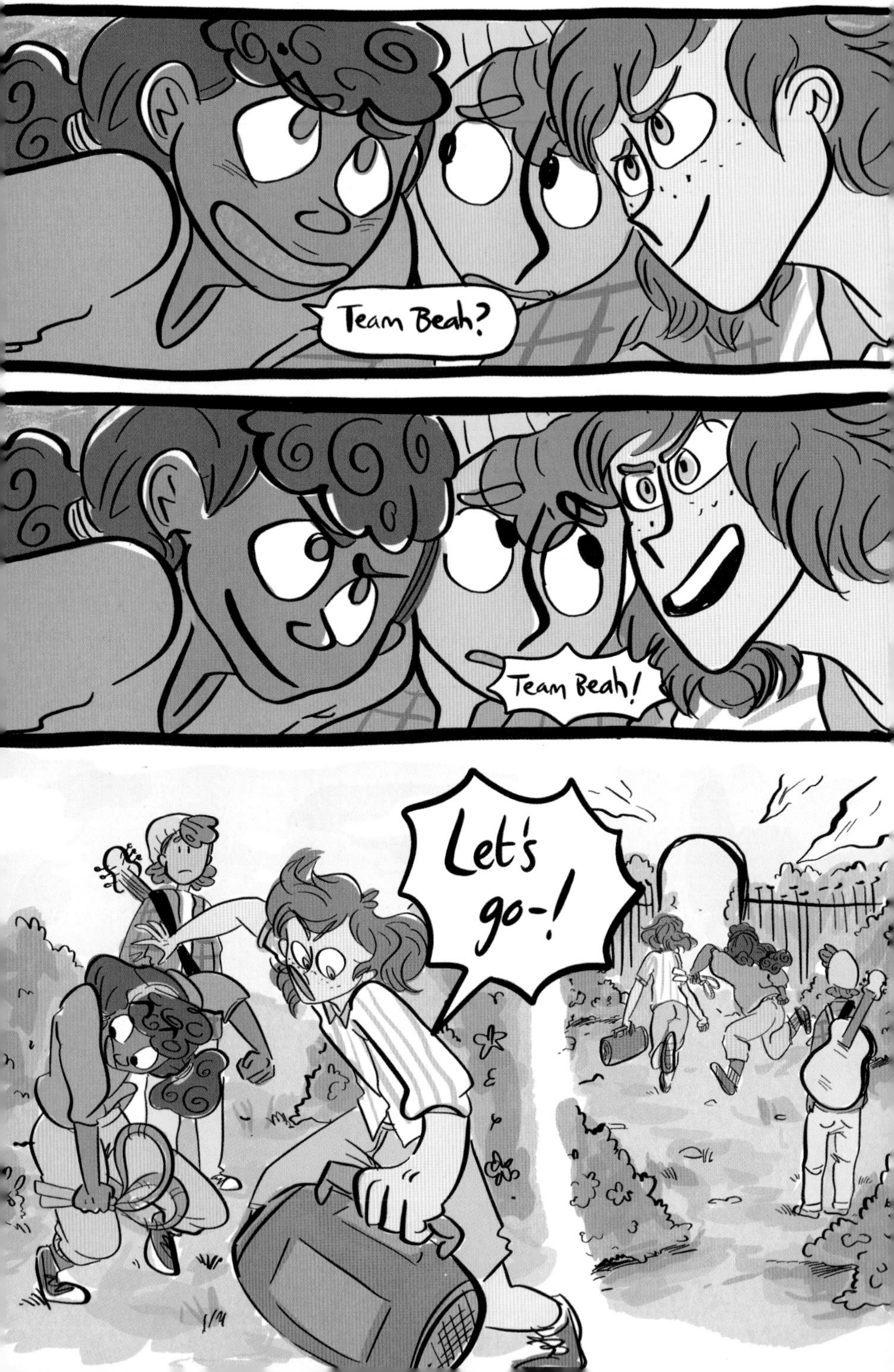
Team Beah?
Team Beah!
Let's go-!

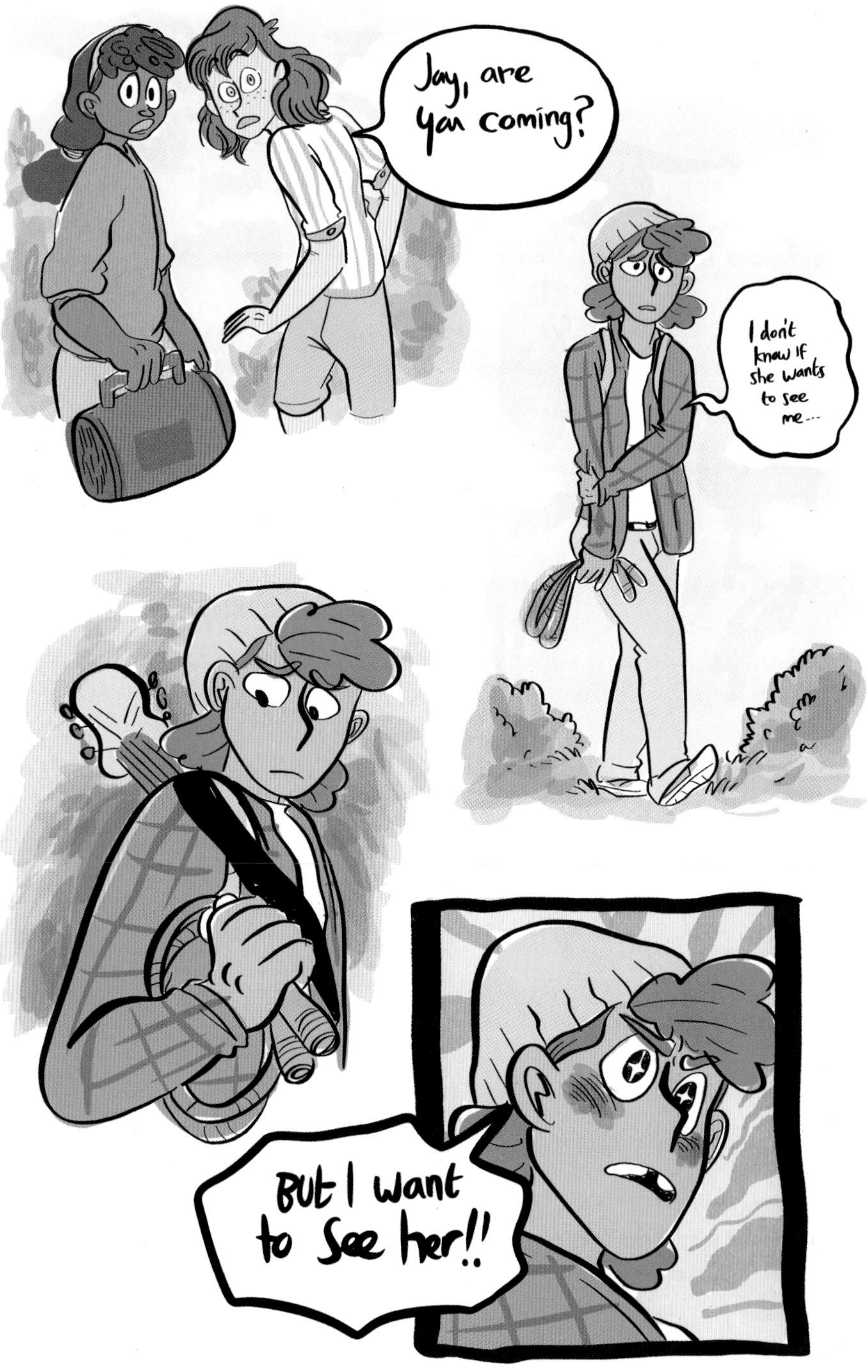
Jay, are you coming?
I don't know if she wants to see me...
But I want to see her!!

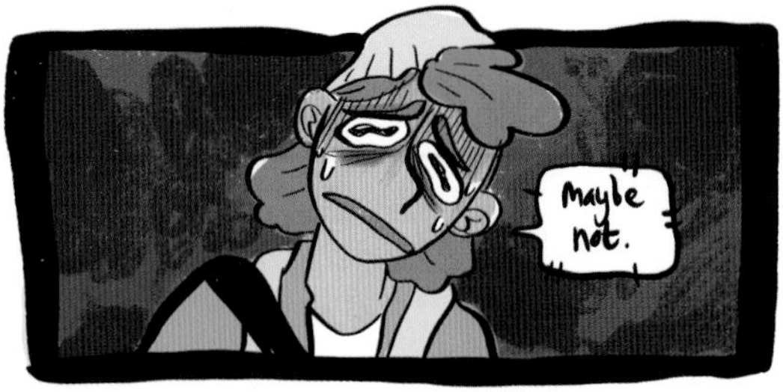
maybe not.

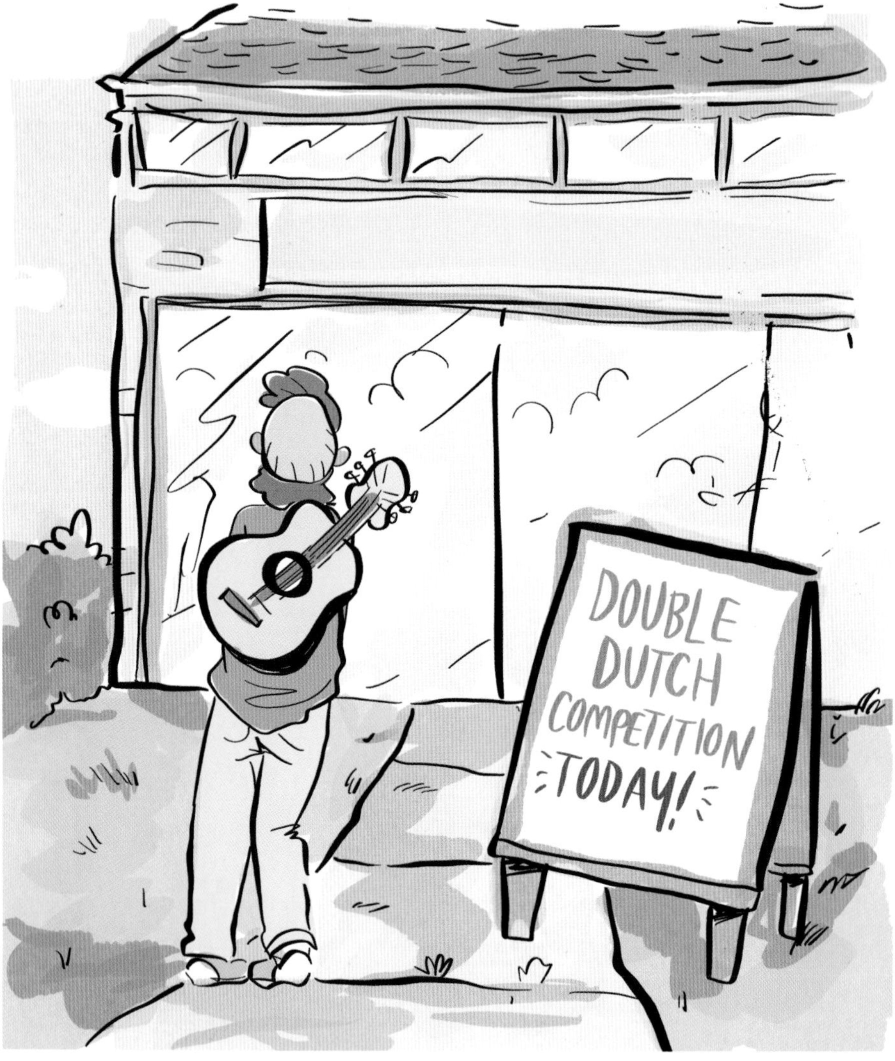
DOUBLE DUTCH COMPETITION TODAY!

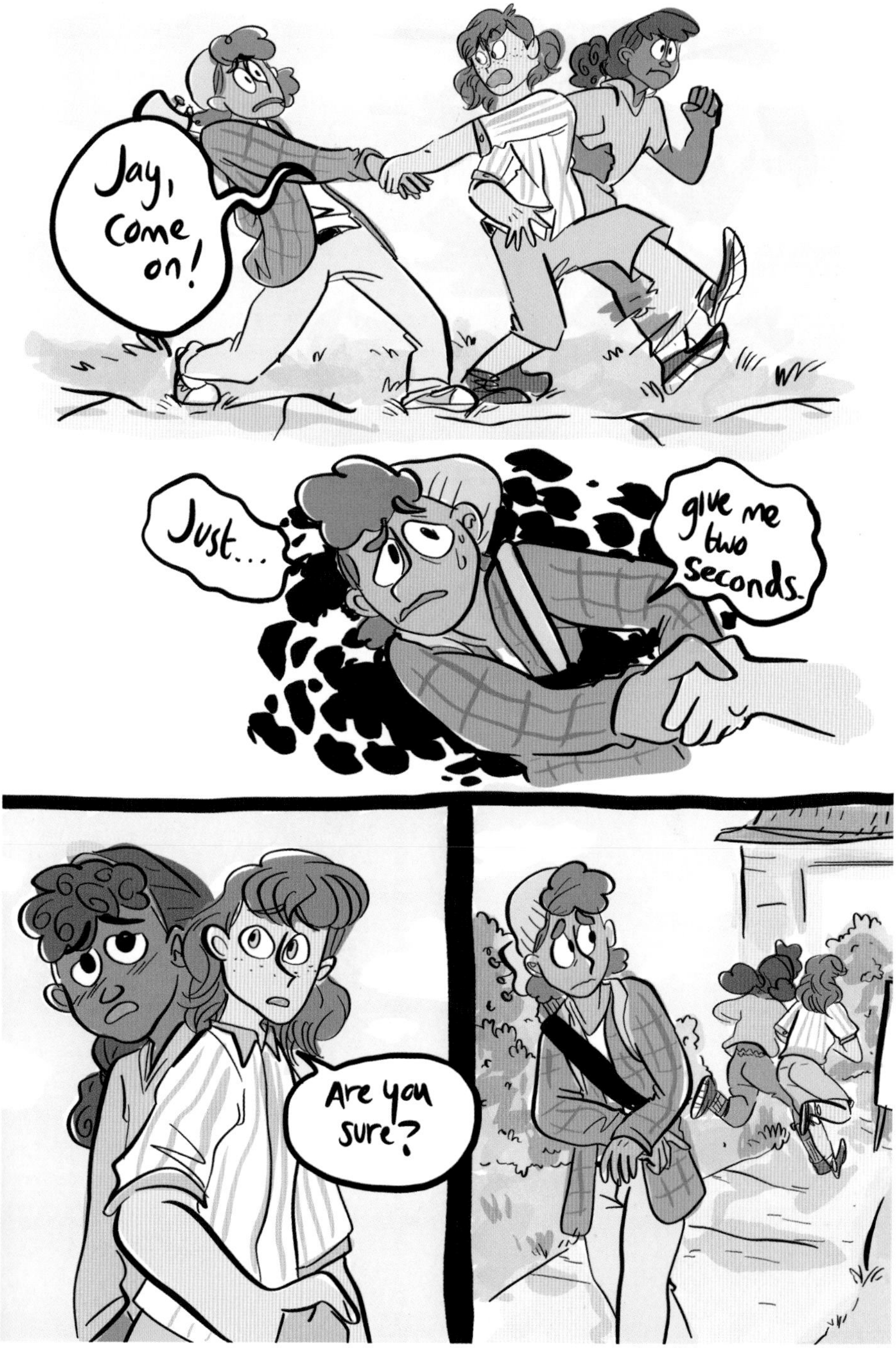
Jay, come on!
Just...
give me two seconds.
Are you sure?

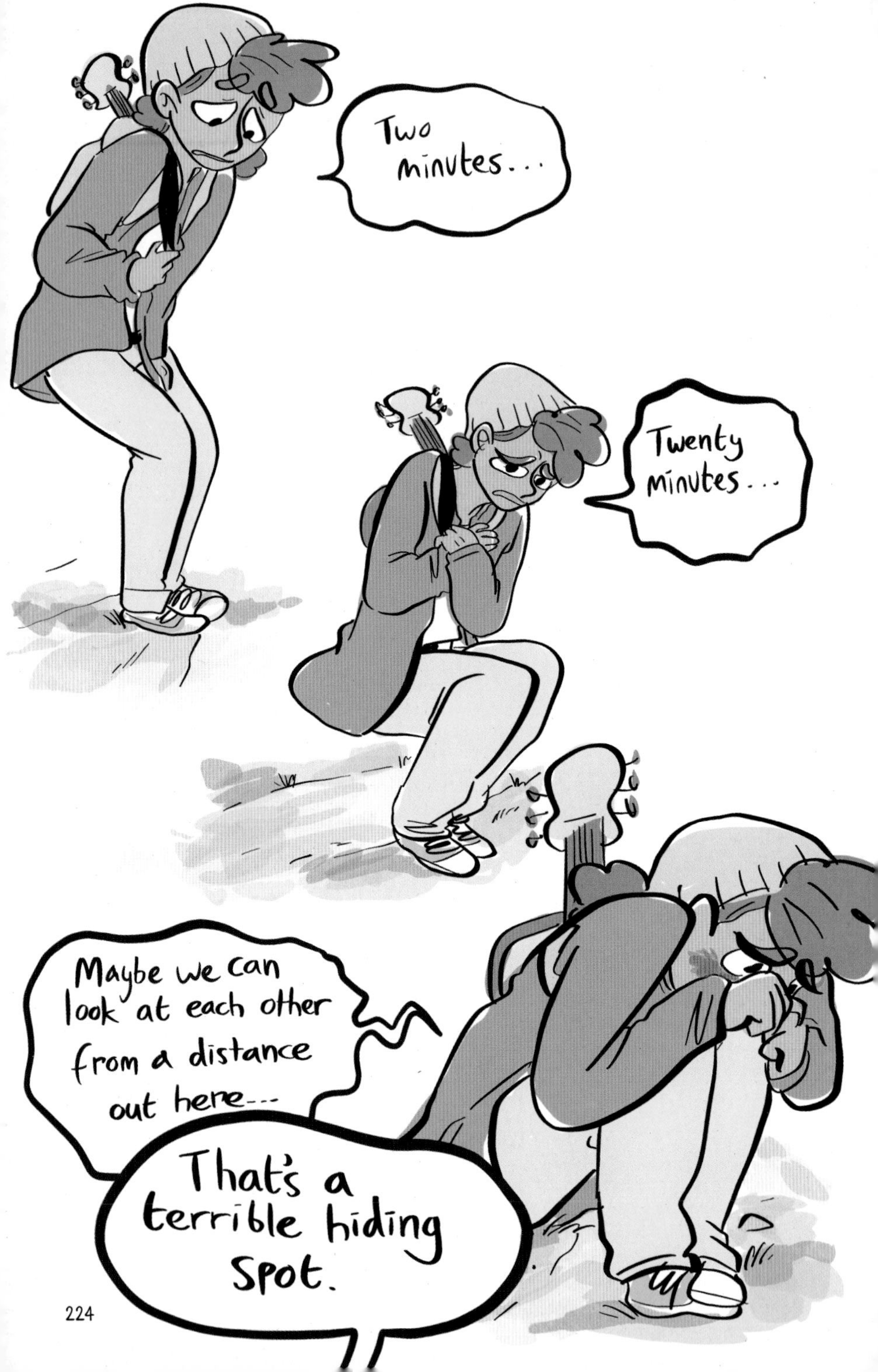
Two minutes...
Twenty minutes...
Maybe we can look at each other from a distance out here...
That's a terrible hiding spot.

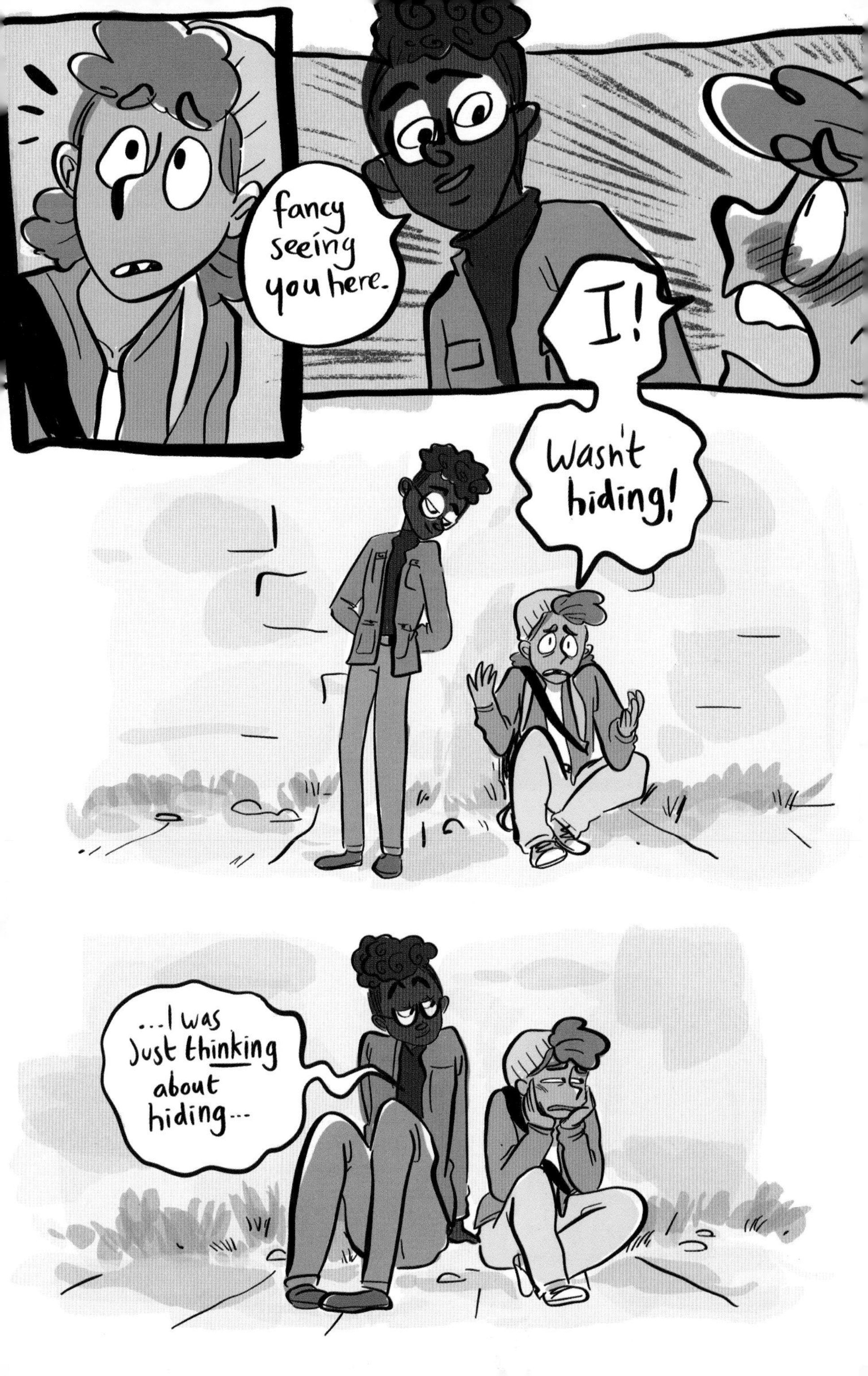
fancy seeing you here.
I! Wasn't hiding!
...I was just thinking about hiding...

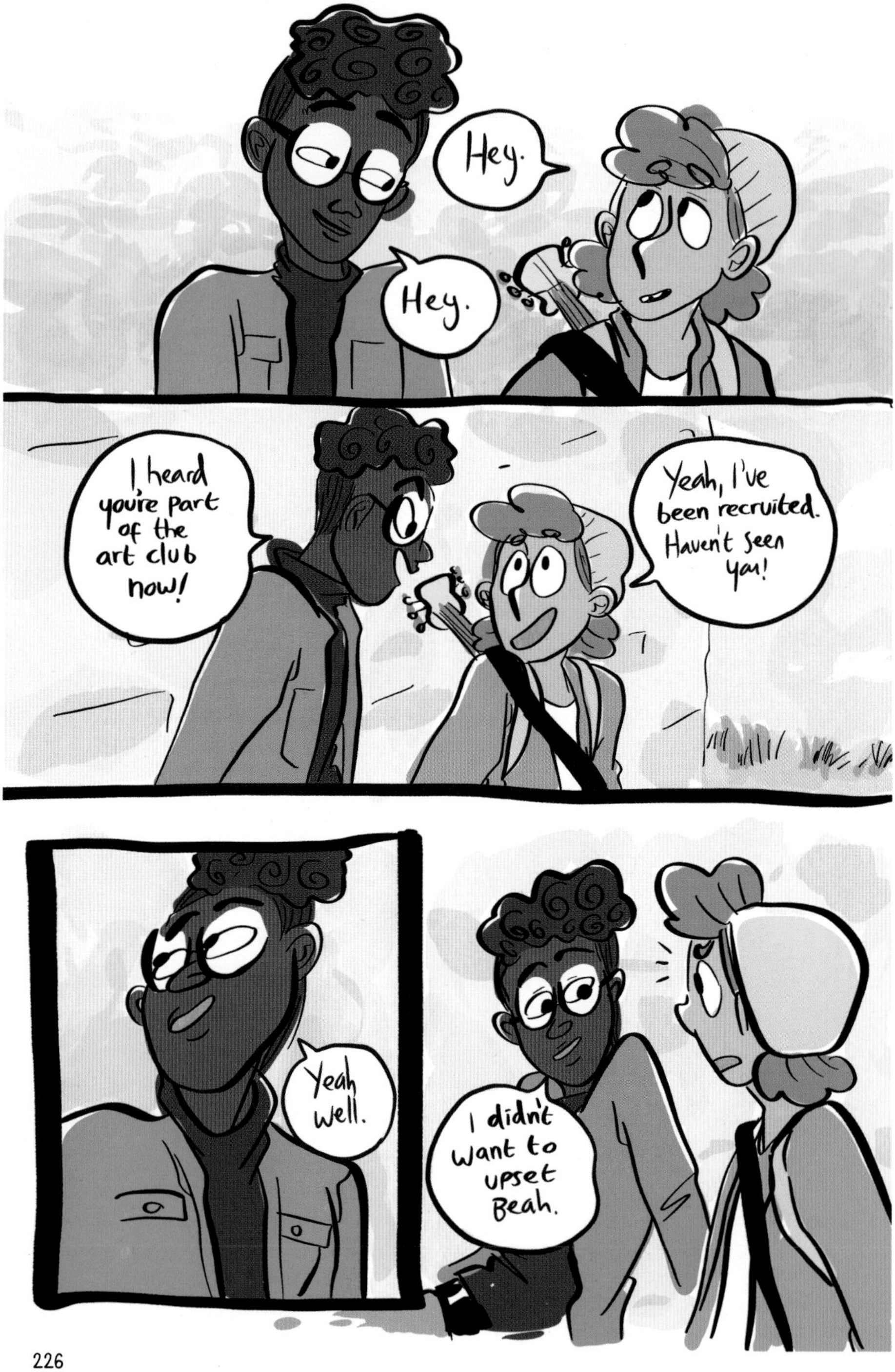
Hey.
Hey.
I heard you're part of the art club now!
Yeah, I've been recruited. Haven't seen you!
Yeah well.
I didn't want to upset Beah.

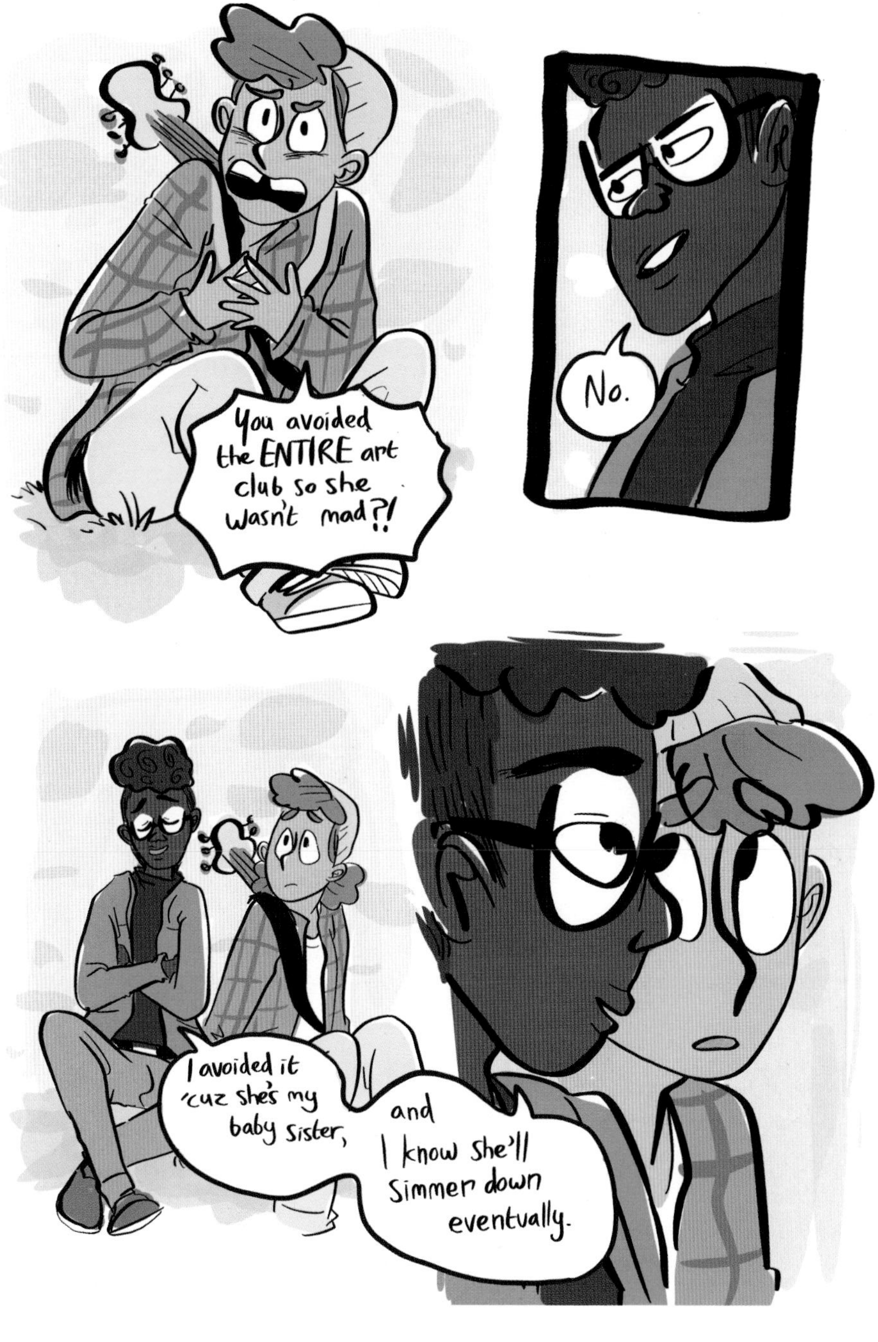
You avoided the ENTIRE art club so she wasn't mad?!
No.
I avoided it 'cuz she's my baby sister,
and I know she'll simmer down eventually.

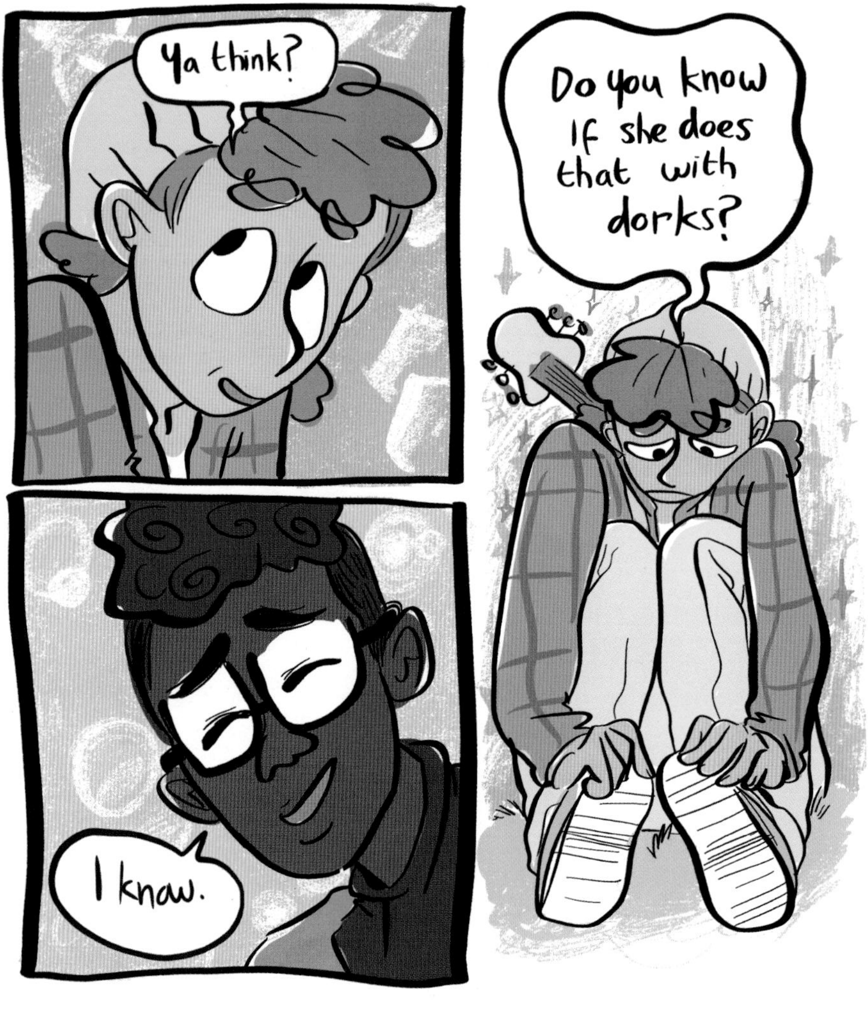
Ya think?
I know.
Do you know if she does that with dorks?

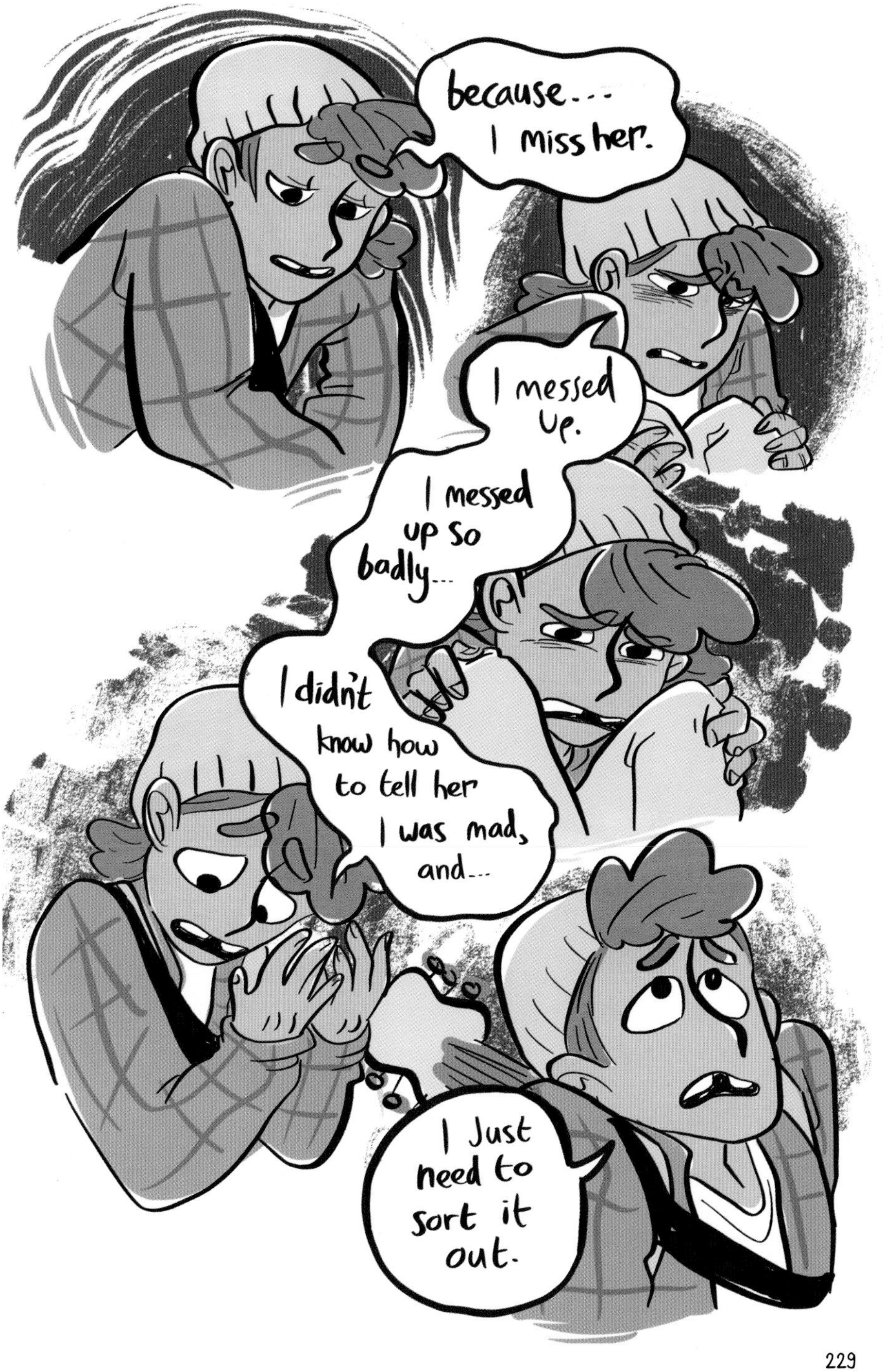
because... I miss her.
I messed up.
I messed up so badly...
I didn't know how to tell her I was mad, and...
I Just need to sort it out.

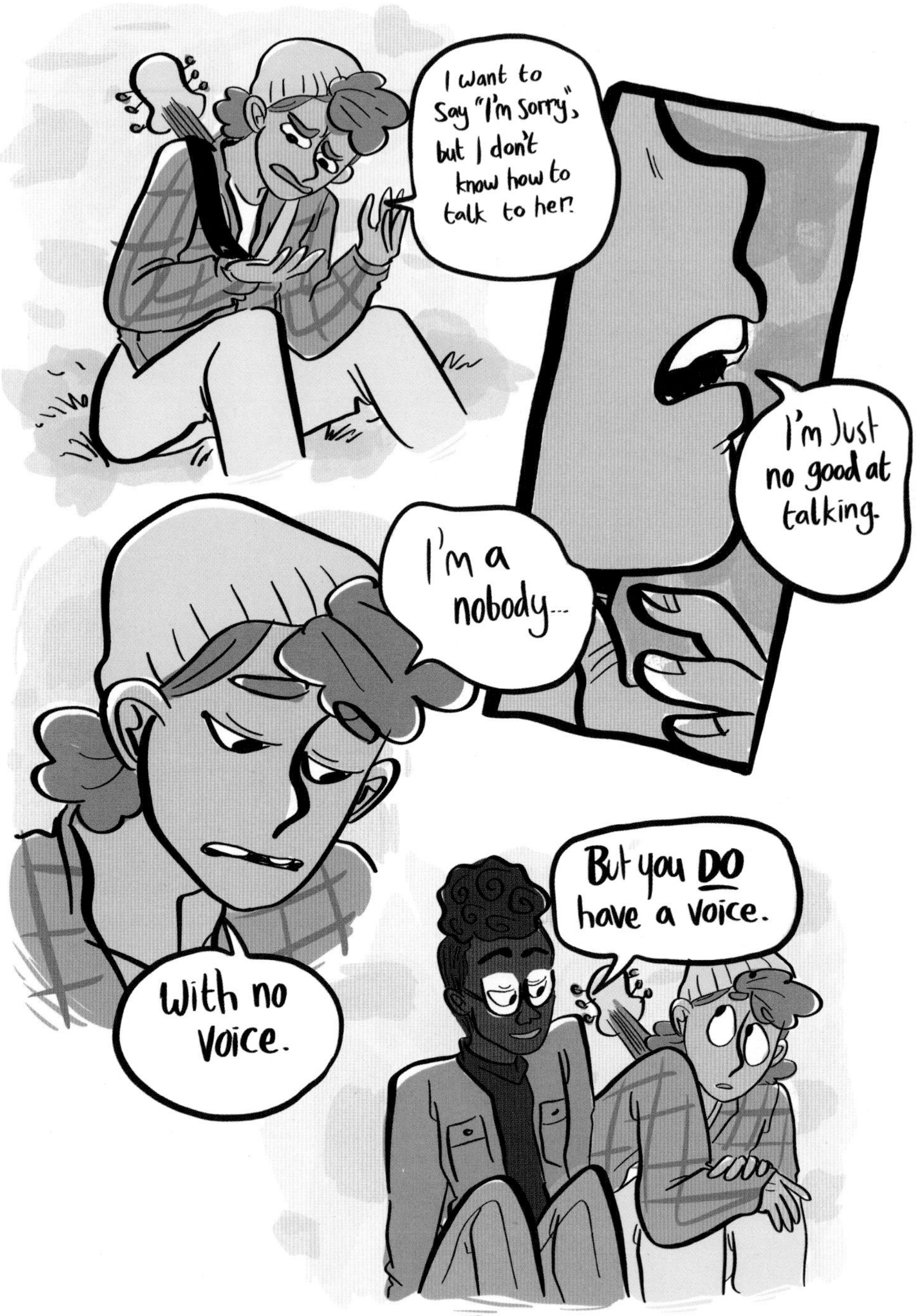
I want to say "I'm sorry", but I don't know how to talk to her!
I'm Just no good at talking.
I'm a nobody...
With no voice.
But you DO have a voice.

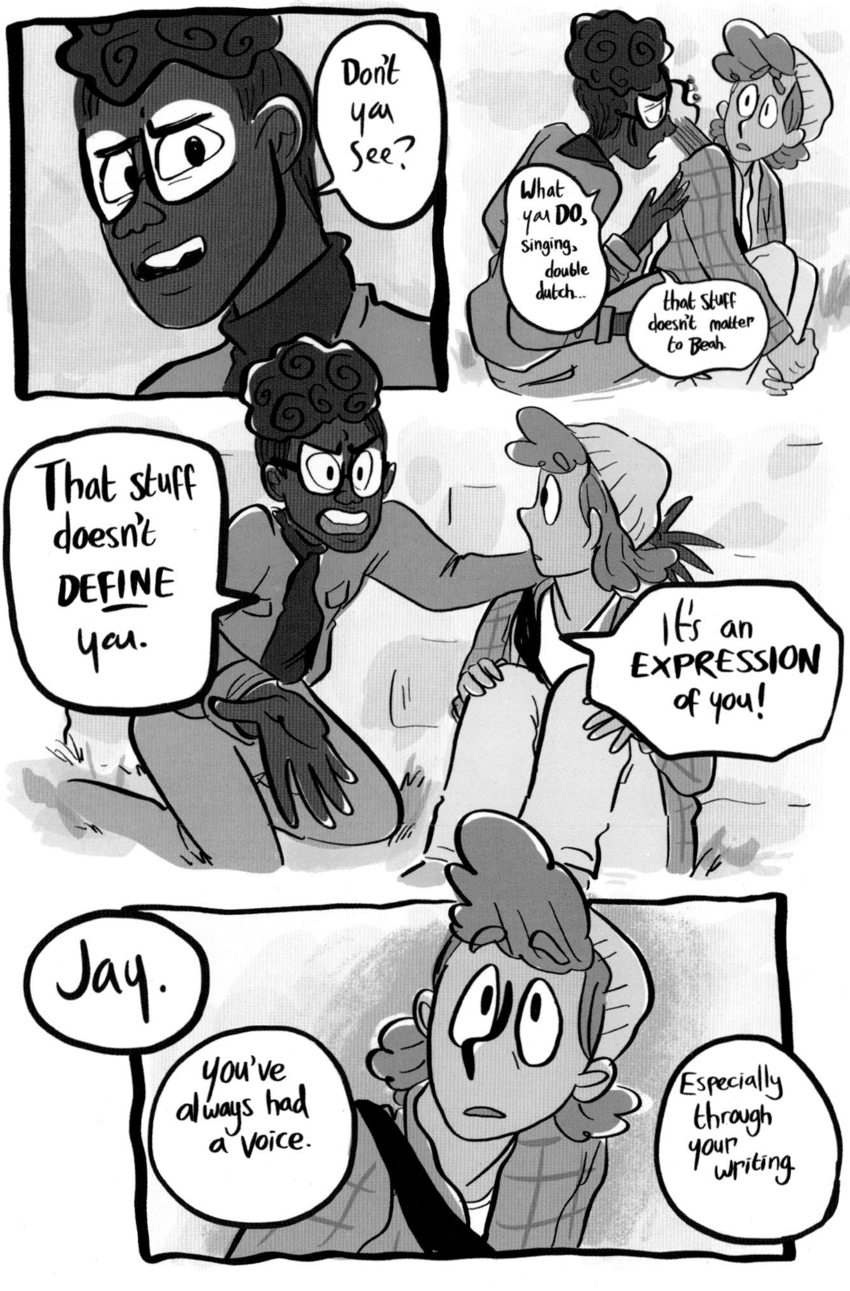
Don't you see?
What you DO, singing, double dutch...
that stuff doesn't matter to Beah.
That stuff doesn't DEFINE you.
It's an EXPRESSION of you!
Jay.
you've always had a voice.
Especially through your writing.

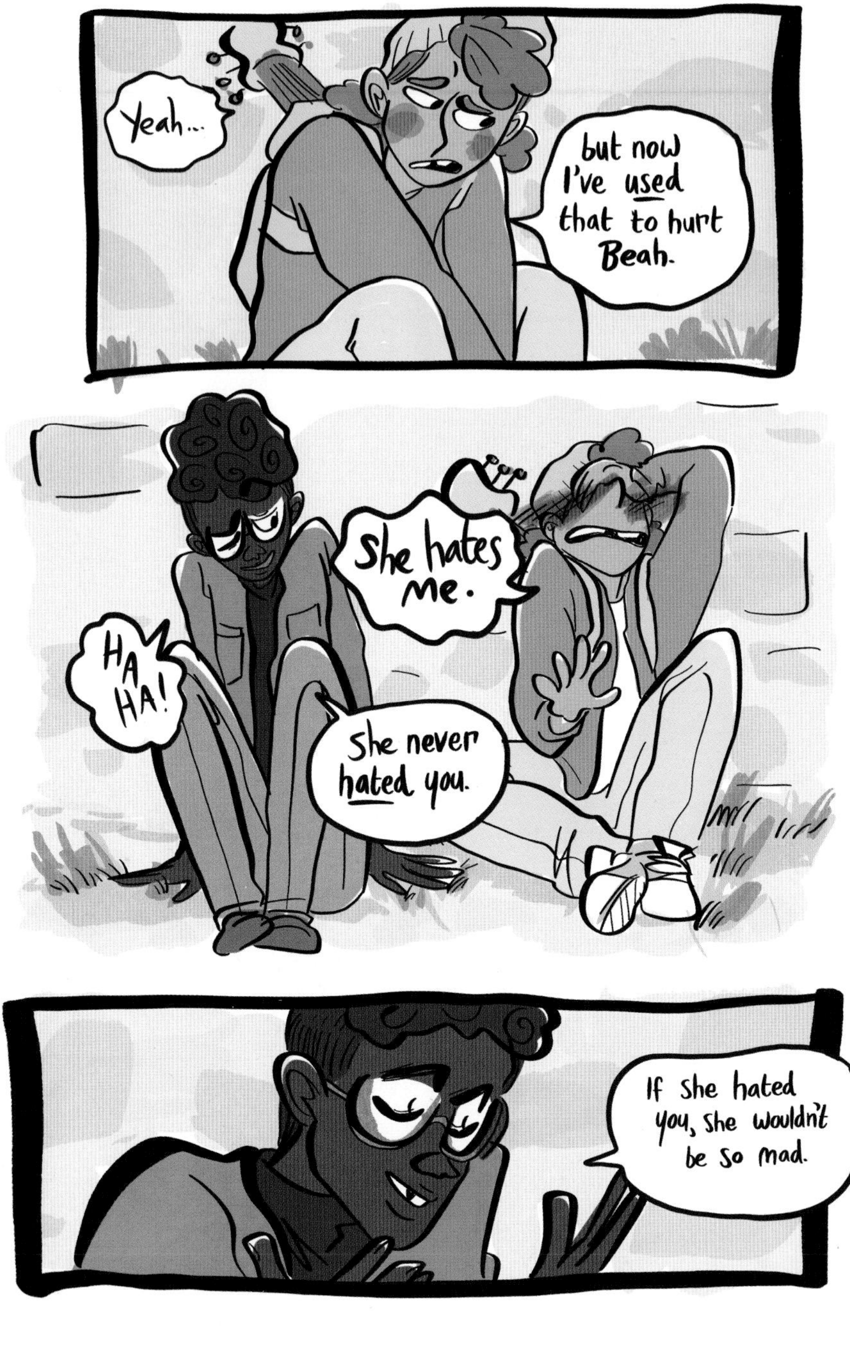
Yeah...
but now I've used that to hurt Beah.
She hates me.
HA HA!
She never hated you.
If she hated you, she wouldn't be so mad.

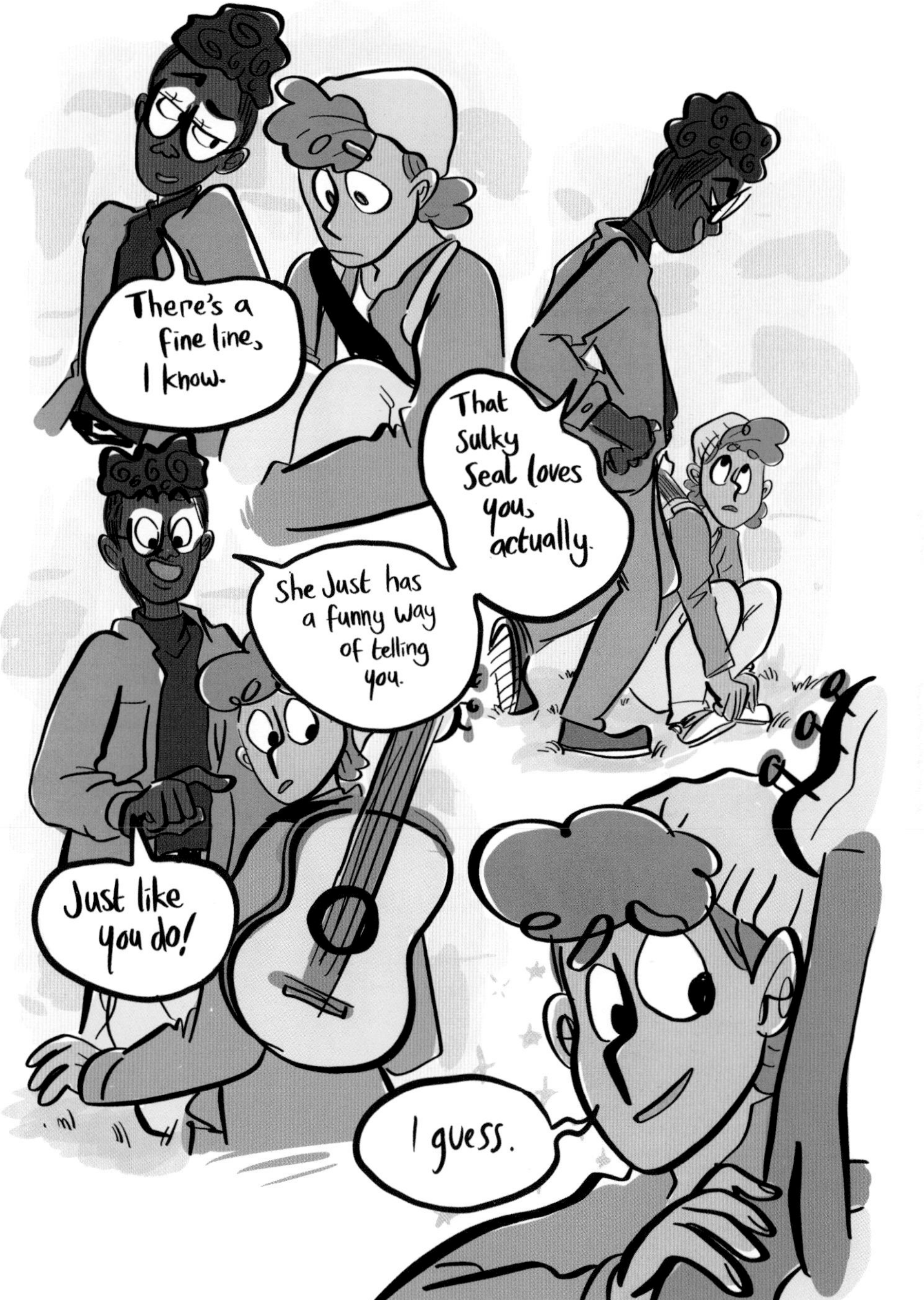
There's a fine line, I know.
That sulky Seal loves you, actually.
She Just has a funny way of telling you.
Just like you do!
I guess.

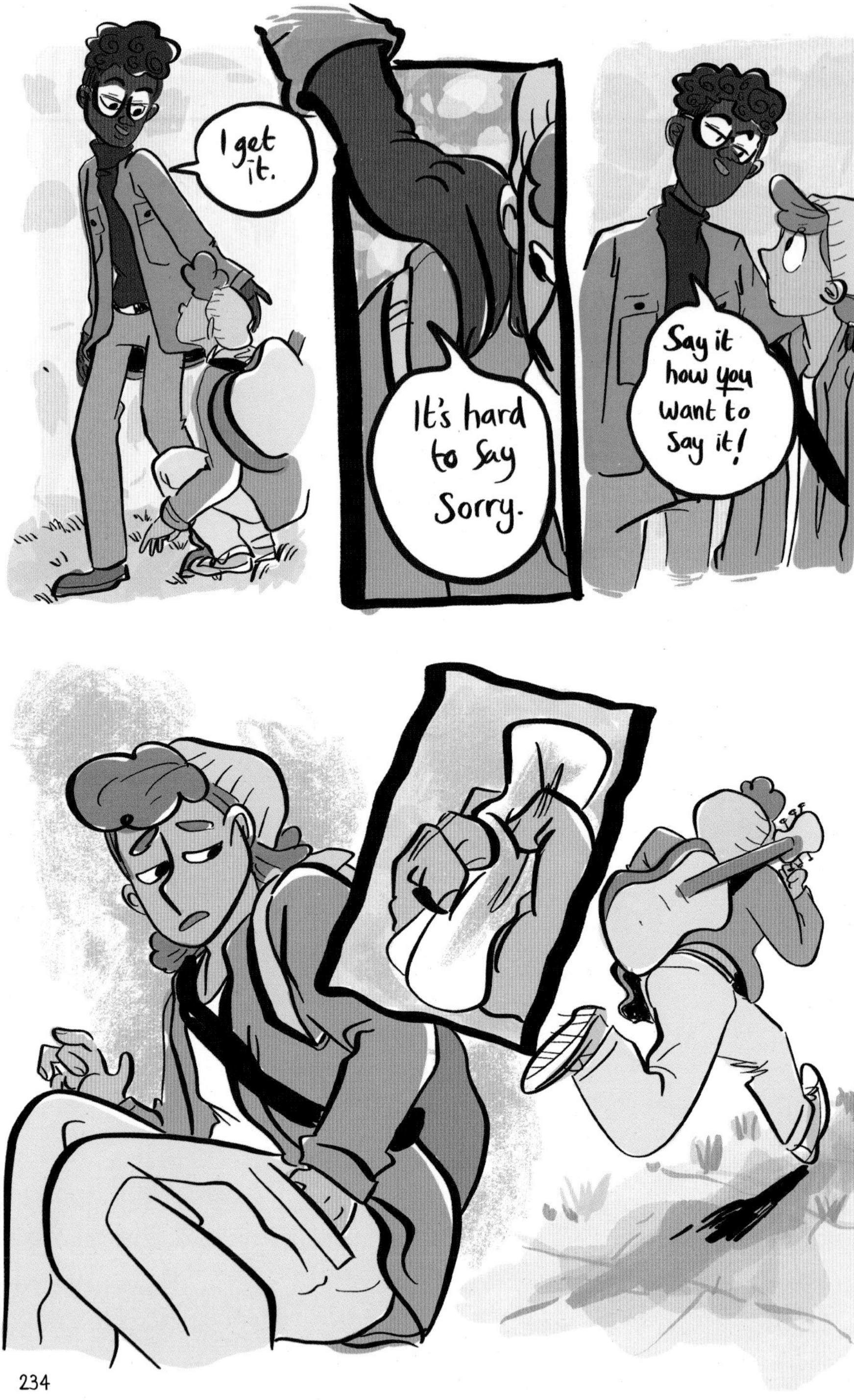
I get it.
It's hard to say sorry.
Say it how you want to say it!

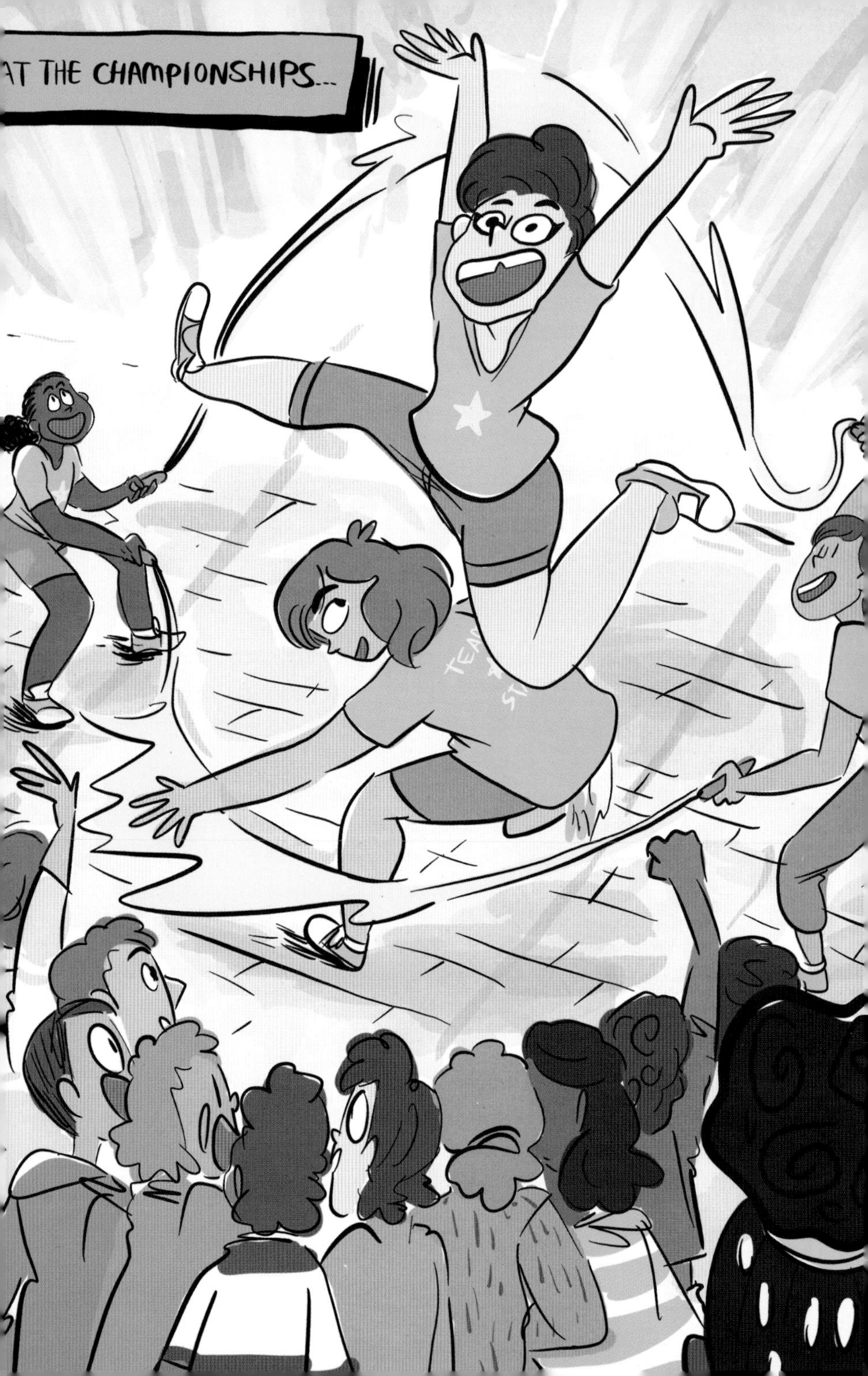
AT THE CHAMPIONSHIPS...

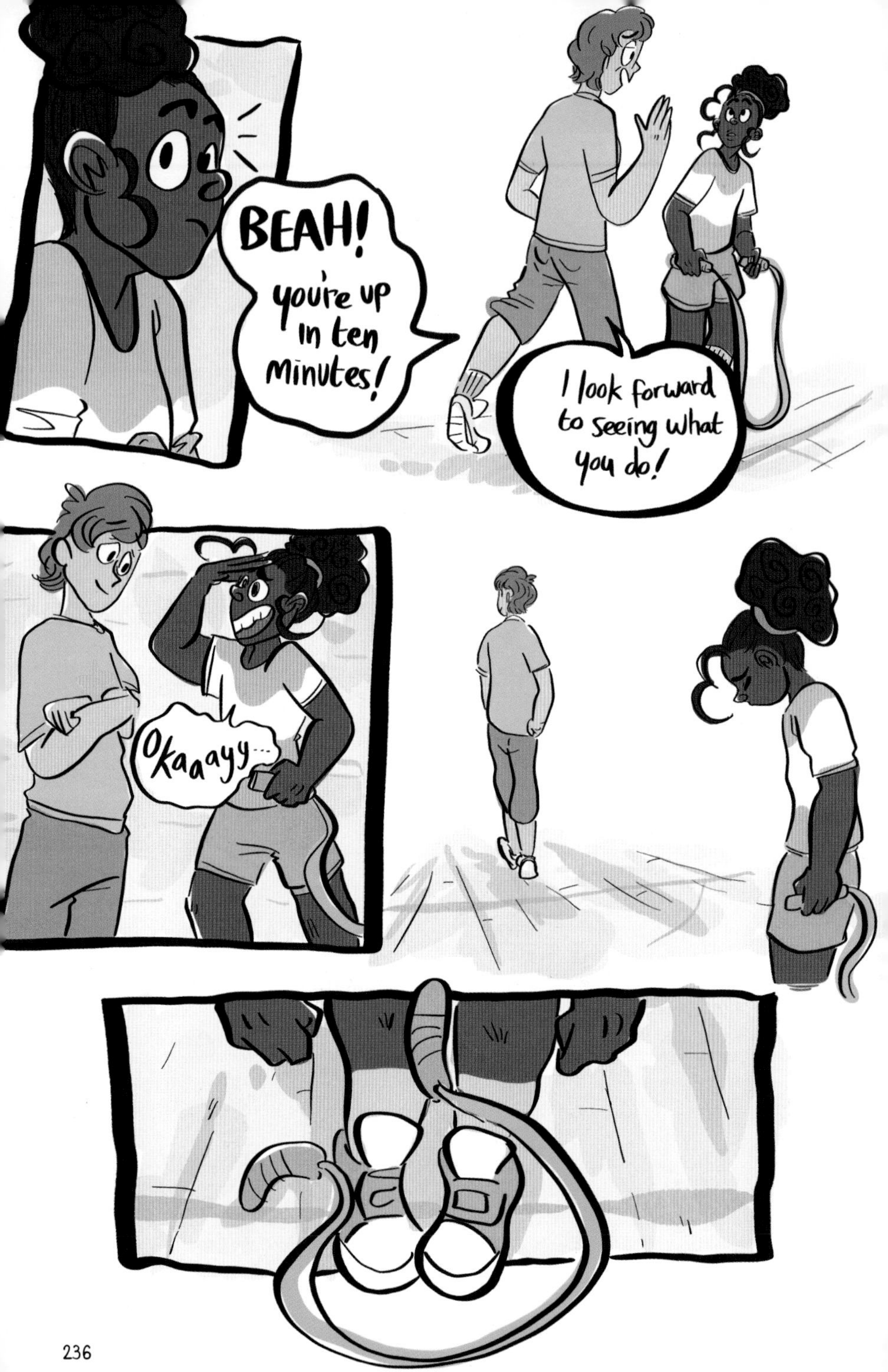
BEAH!
you're up in ten minutes!
I look forward to seeing what you do!
Okaaayy...

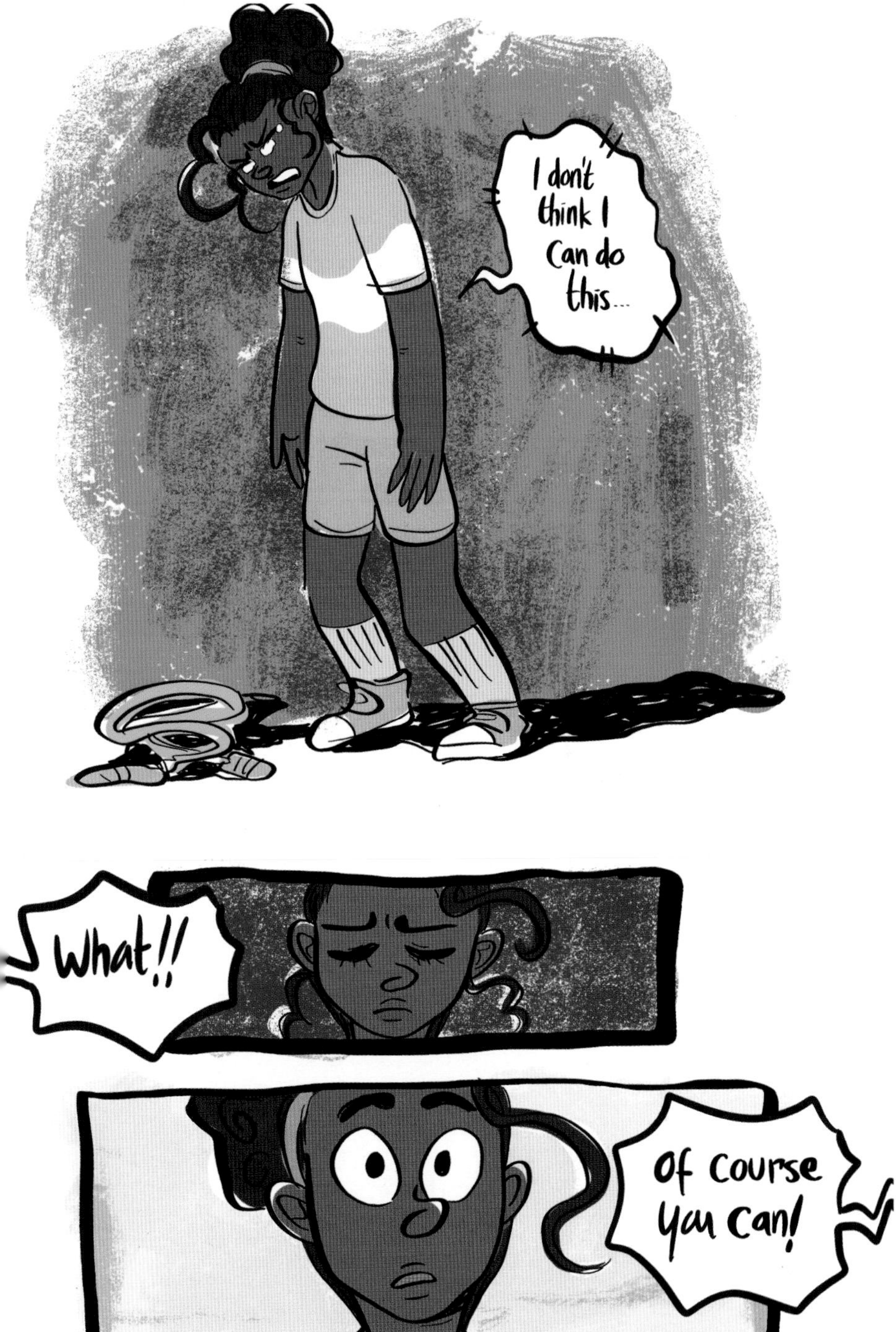
I don't think I can do this...
What!!
Of course you can!

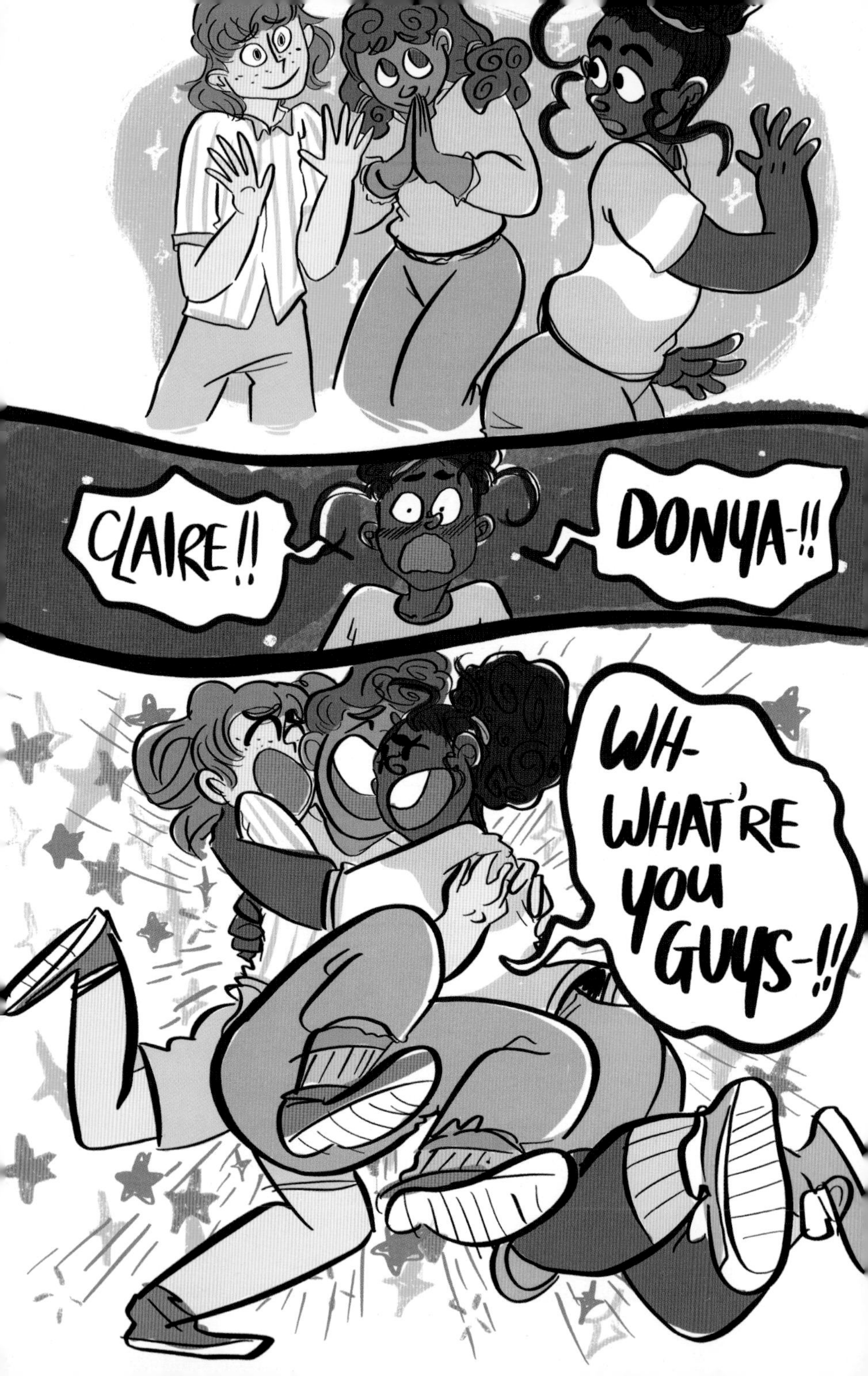
CLAIRE!!
DONYA-!!
WH- WHAT'RE YOU GUYS-!!

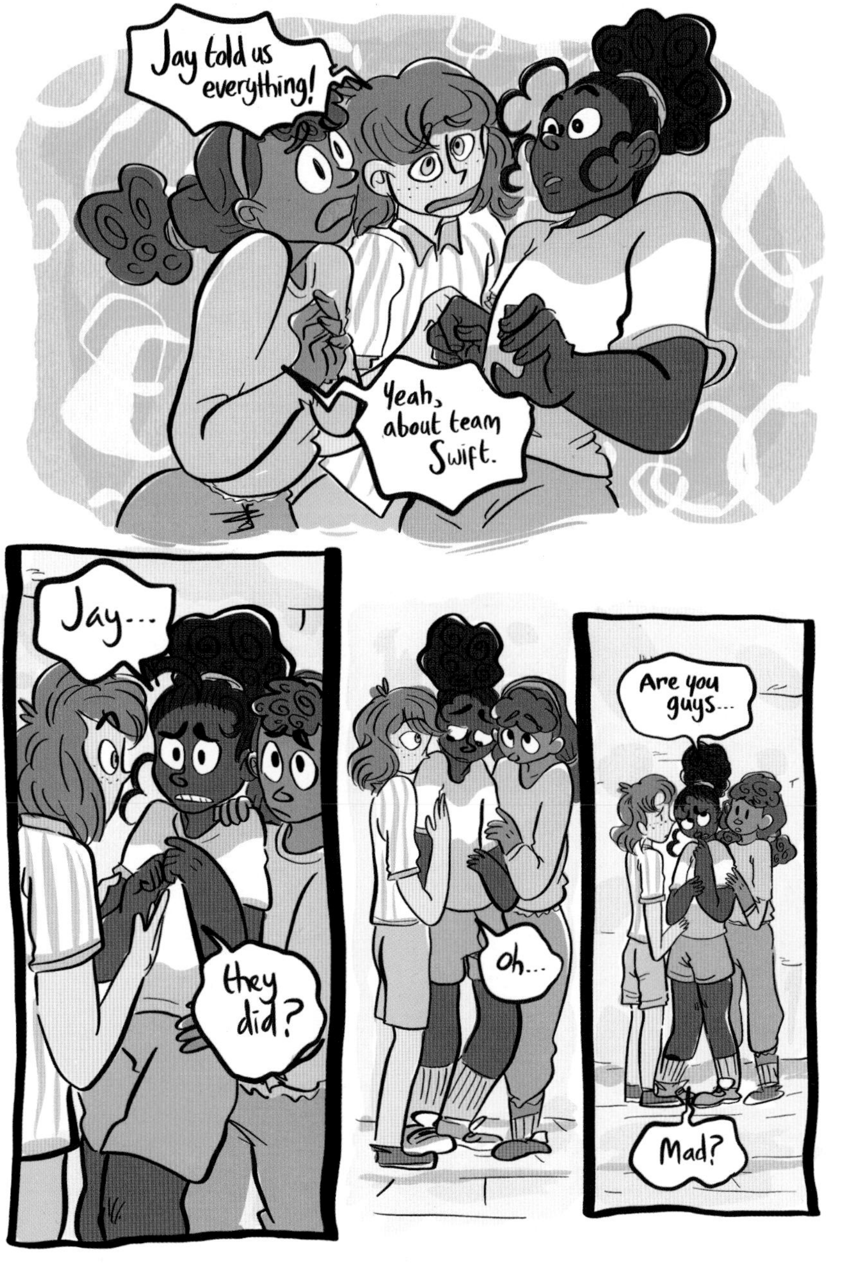
Jay told us everything!
Yeah, about team Swift.
Jay...
they did?
Oh...
Are you guys...
Mad?

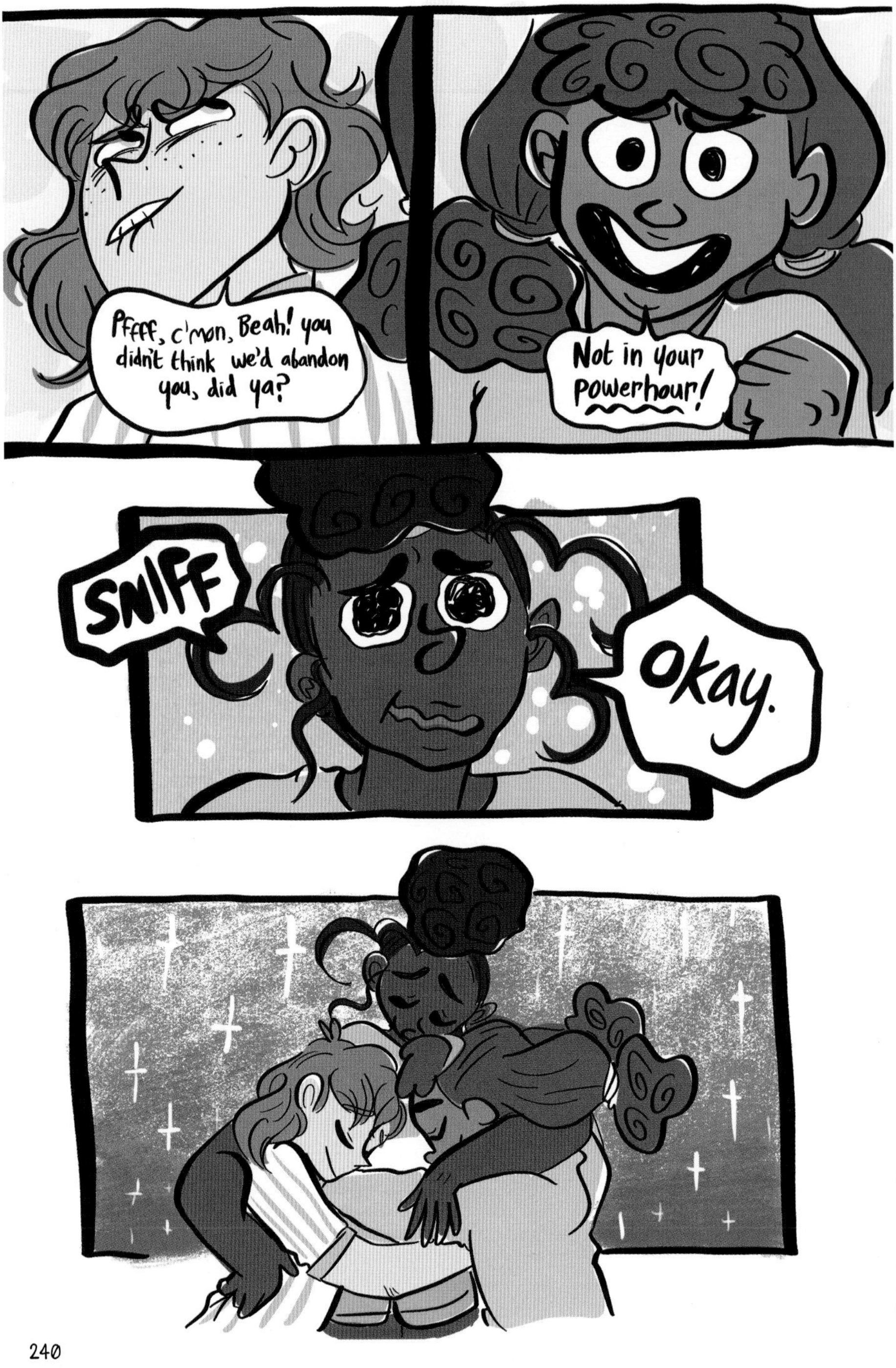
Pffff, c'mon, Beah! you didn't think we'd abandon you, did ya?
Not in your powerhour!
SNIFF
okay.

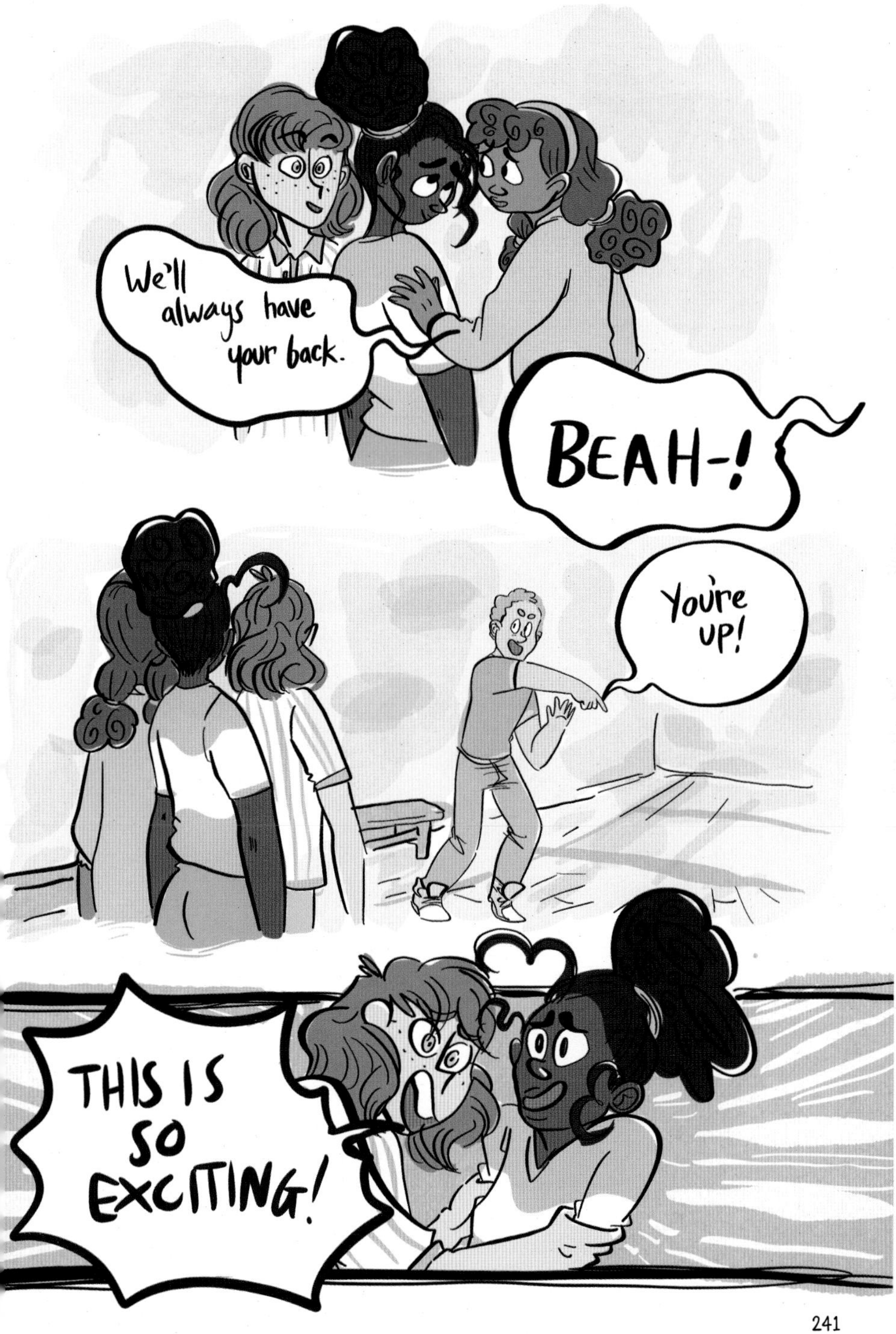
We'll always have your back.
BEAH-!
You're up!
THIS IS SO EXCITING!

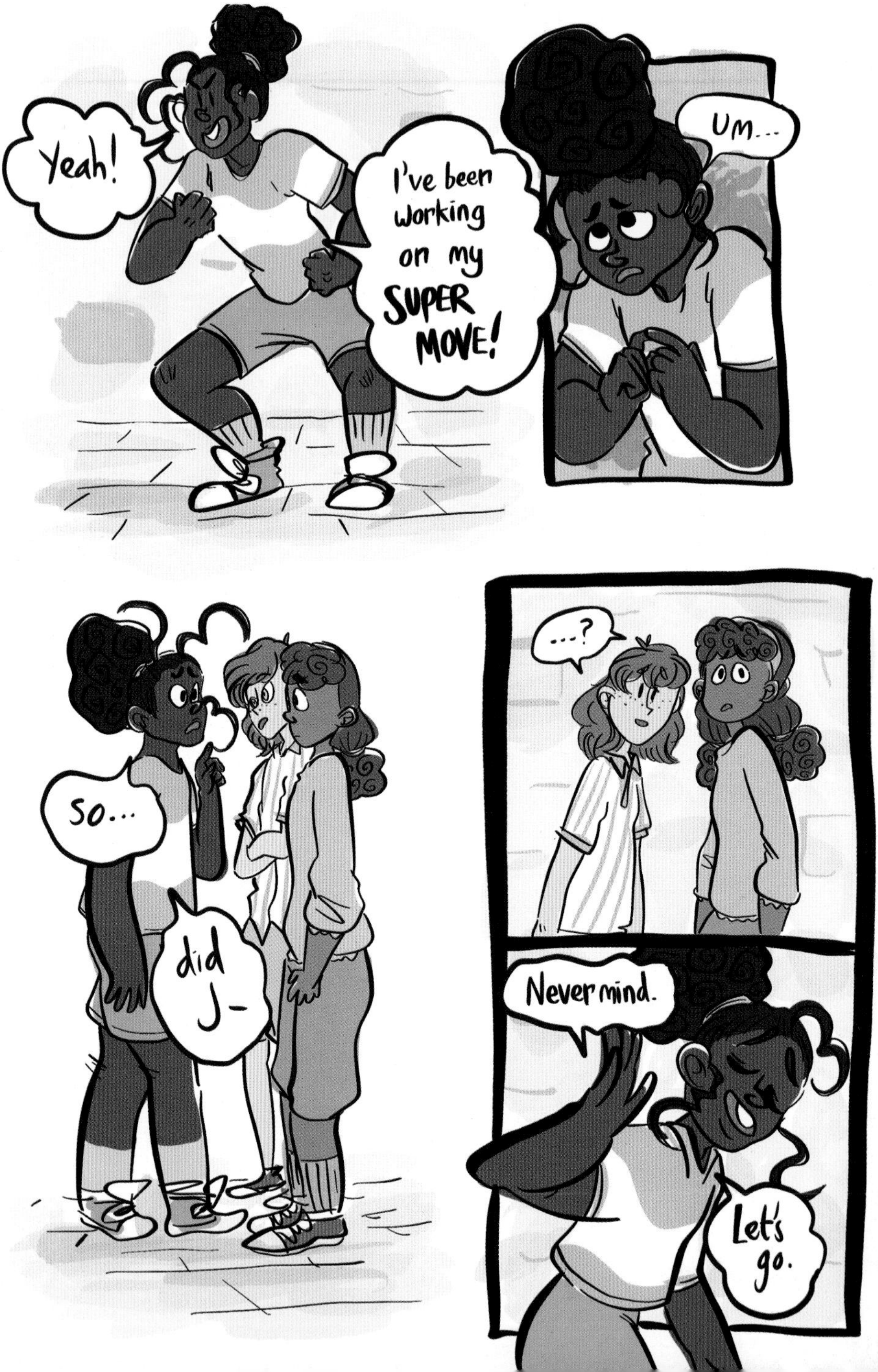
Yeah!
I've been working on my SUPER MOVE!
Um...
So...
did J-
...?
Never mind.
Let's go.

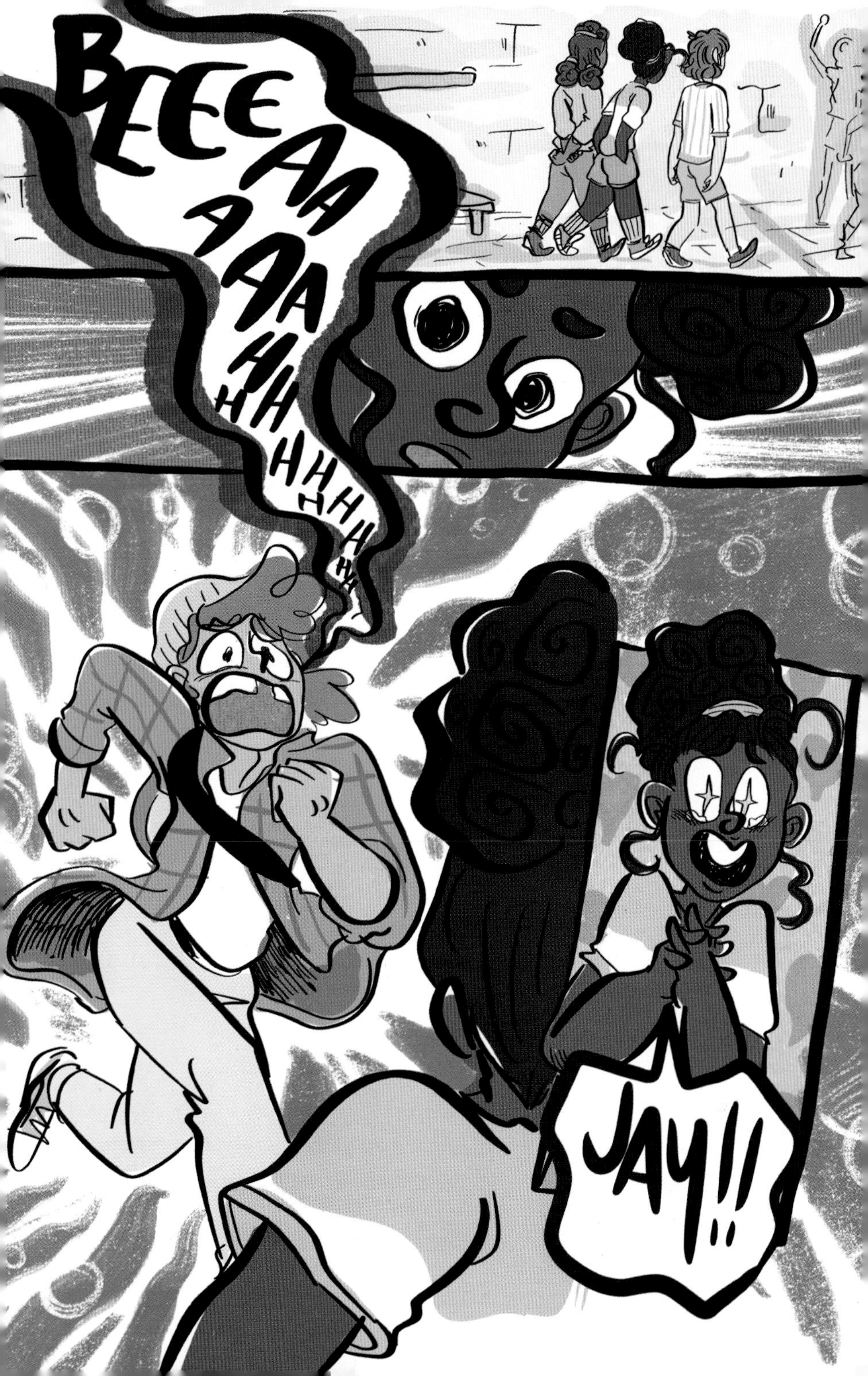
BEEEAAAAAAHHHHHHHHH
JAY!!

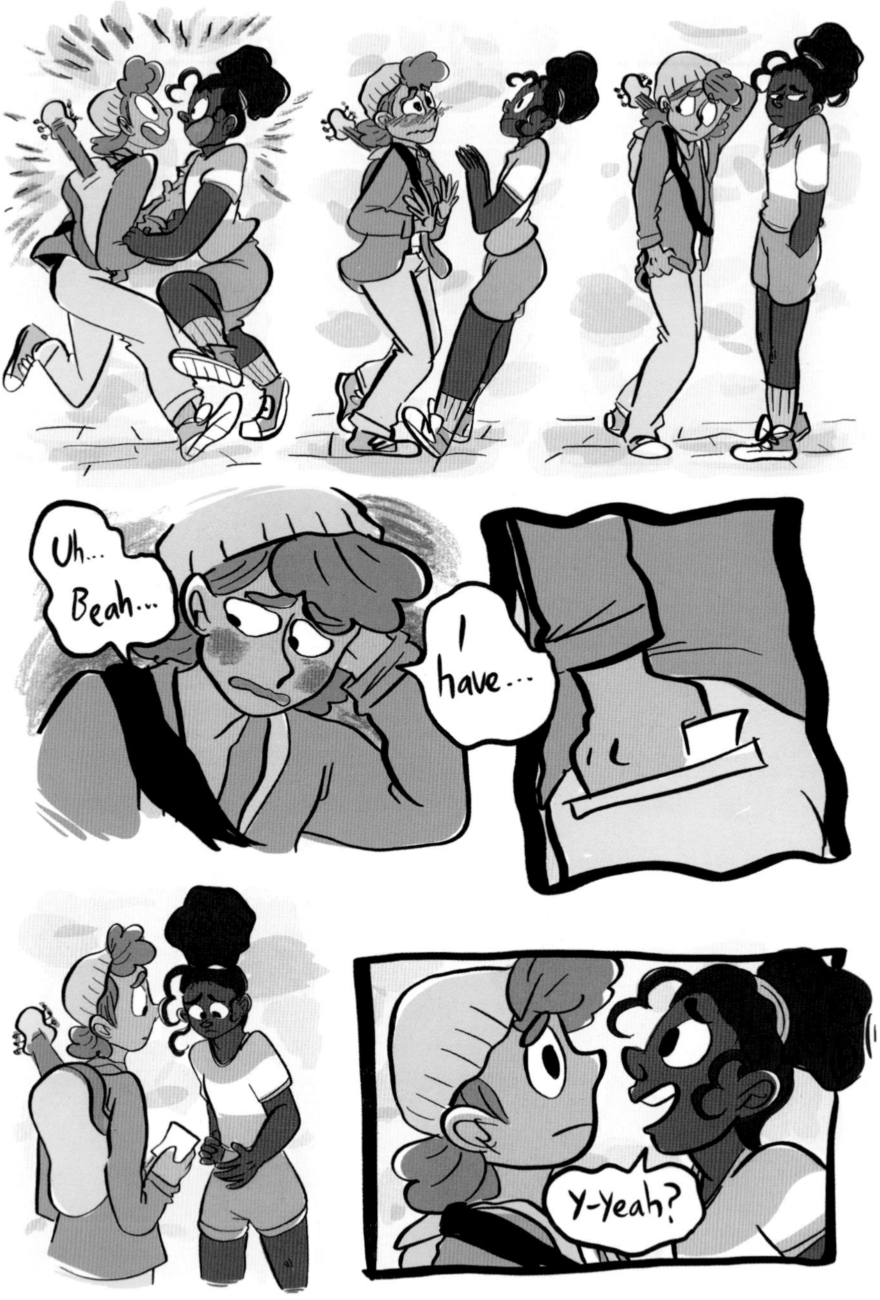
Uh... Beah...
I have...
Y-Yeah?

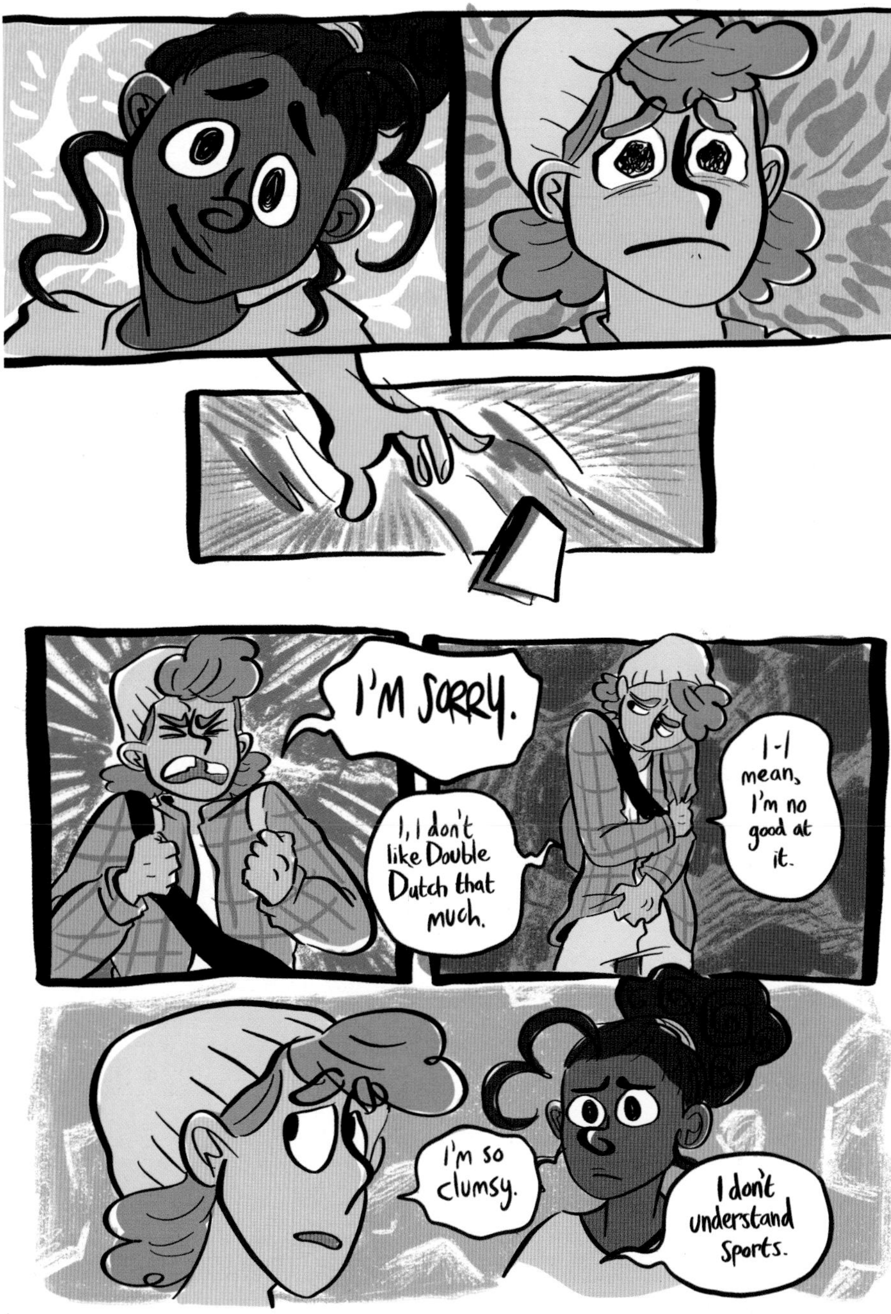
I'M SORRY.
I, I don't like Double Dutch that much.
I-I mean, I'm no good at it.
I'm so clumsy.
I don't understand sports.

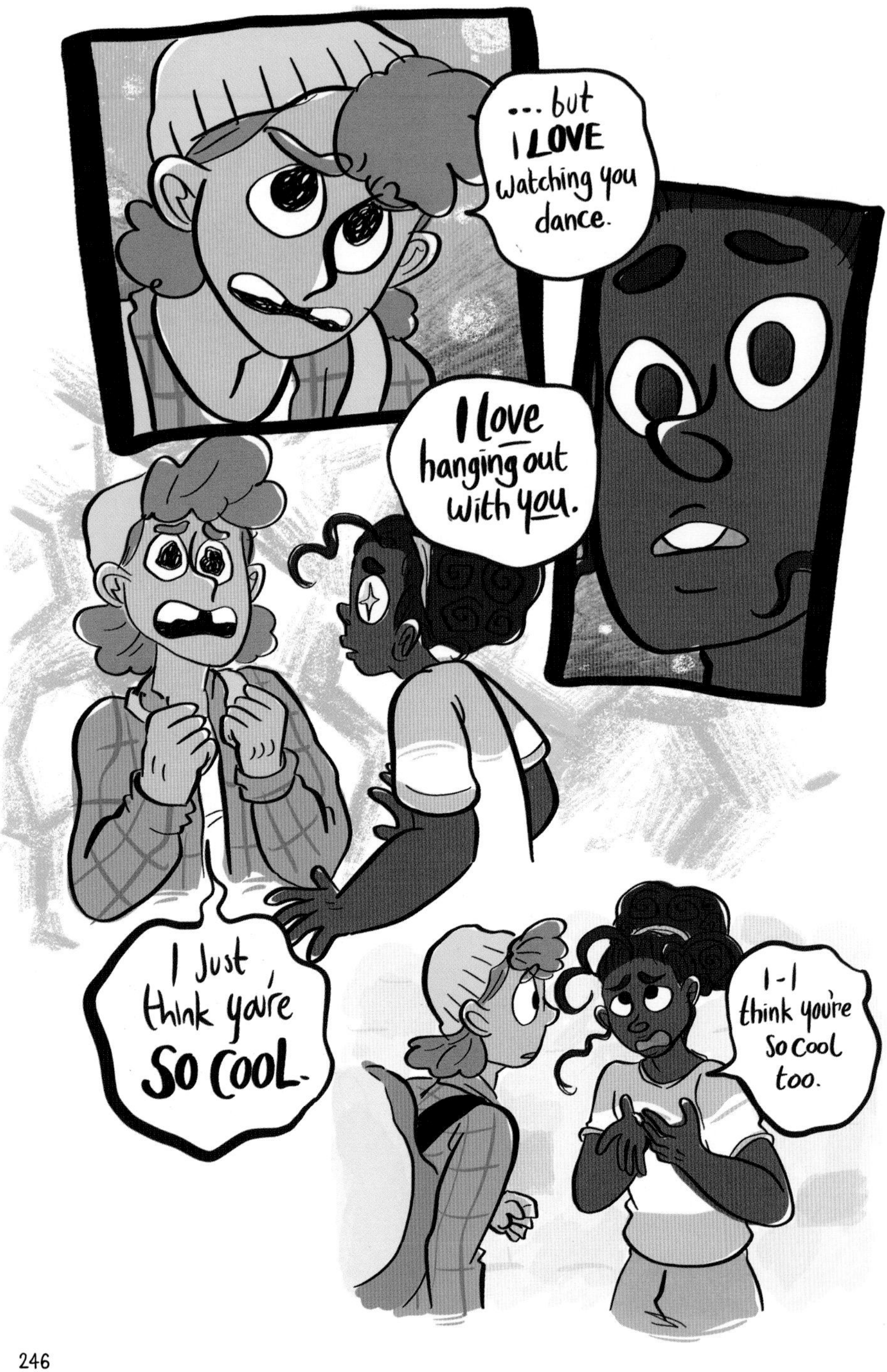
... but I LOVE watching you dance.
I love hanging out with you.
I just think you're SO COOL.
I-I think you're so cool too.

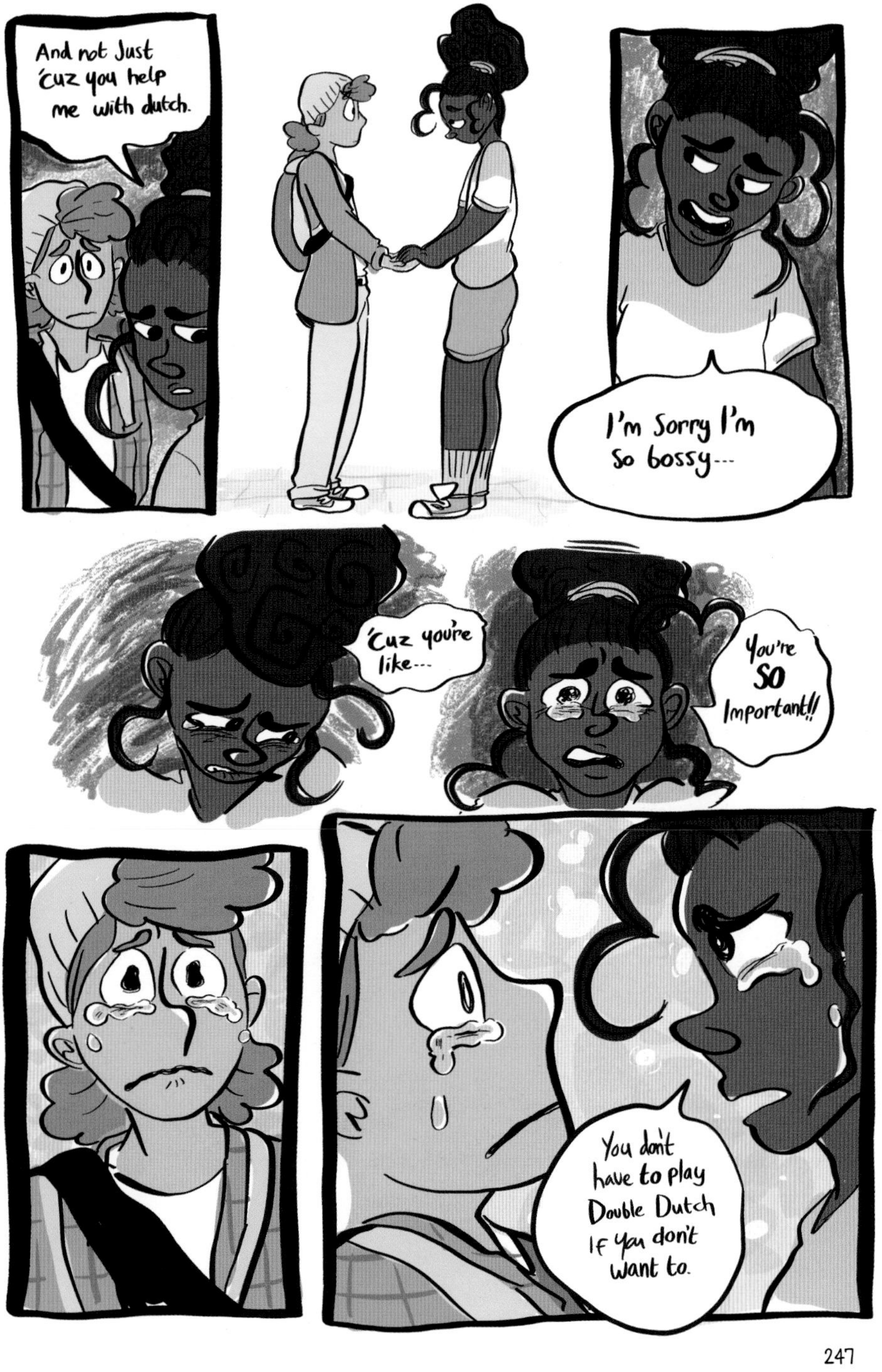
And not Just 'cuz you help me with dutch.
I'm Sorry I'm so bossy---
'Cuz you're like---
You're SO Important!!
You don't have to play Double Dutch If you don't want to.

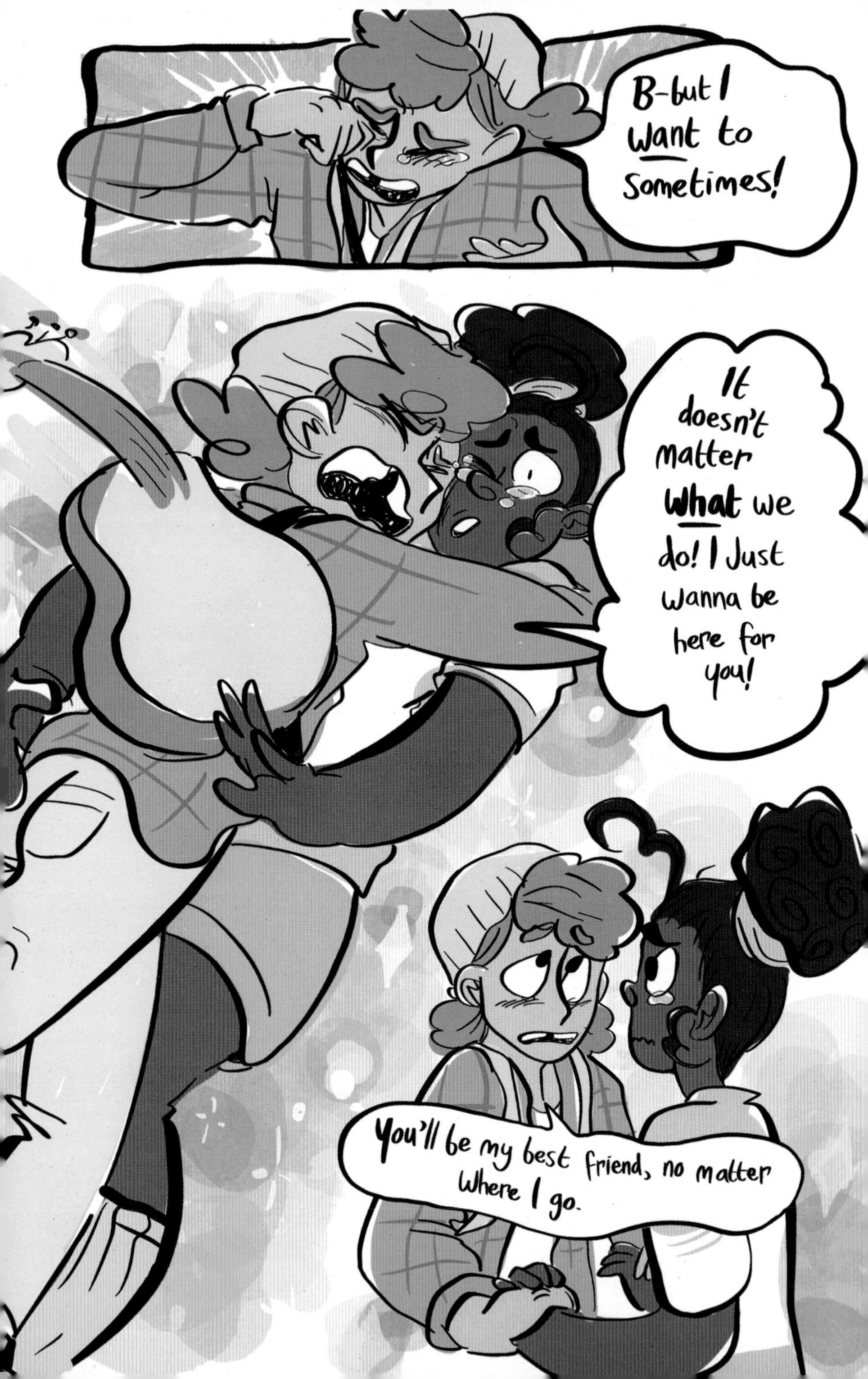
B-but I want to sometimes!
It doesn't matter what we do! I just wanna be here for you!
You'll be my best friend, no matter where I go.

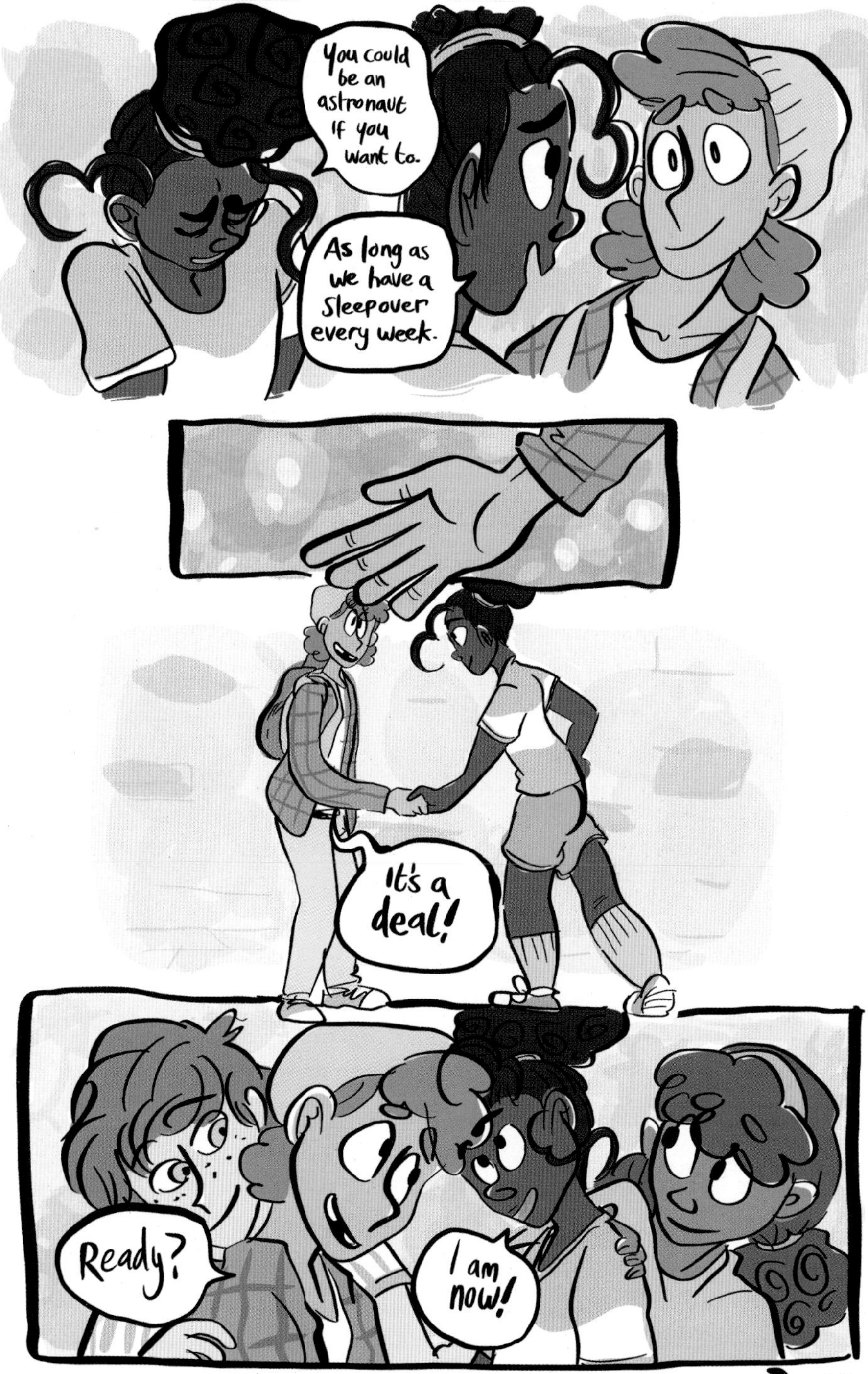
You could be an astronaut if you want to.
As long as we have a sleepover every week.
It's a deal!
Ready?
I am now!

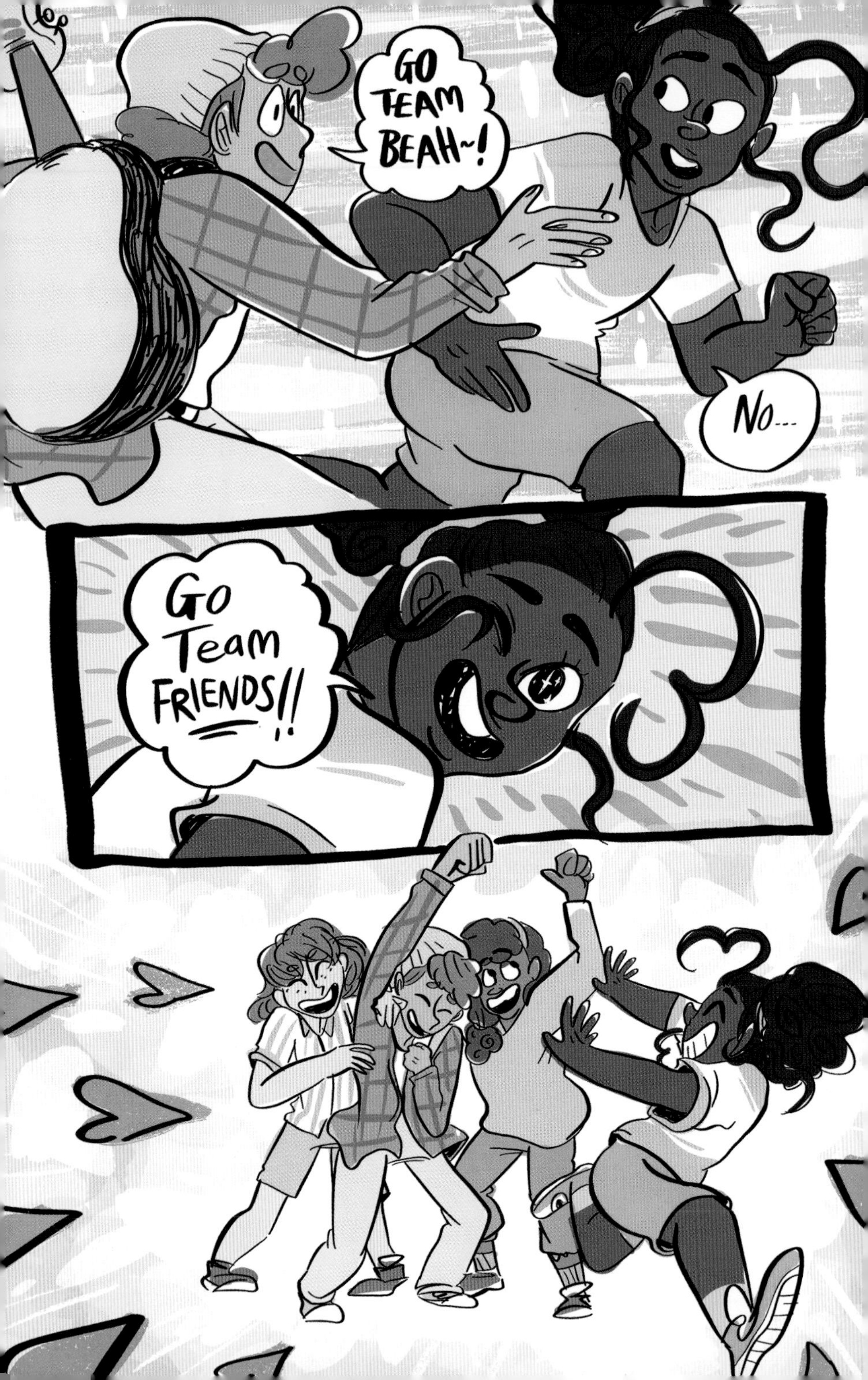
GO TEAM BEAH~!
No...
Go Team FRIENDS!!

THE END

For Liz, Zoe, Maddy, Rick, and James,
you guys had so much enthusiasm and interest for this
project, even when I felt invisible.

Thank you.

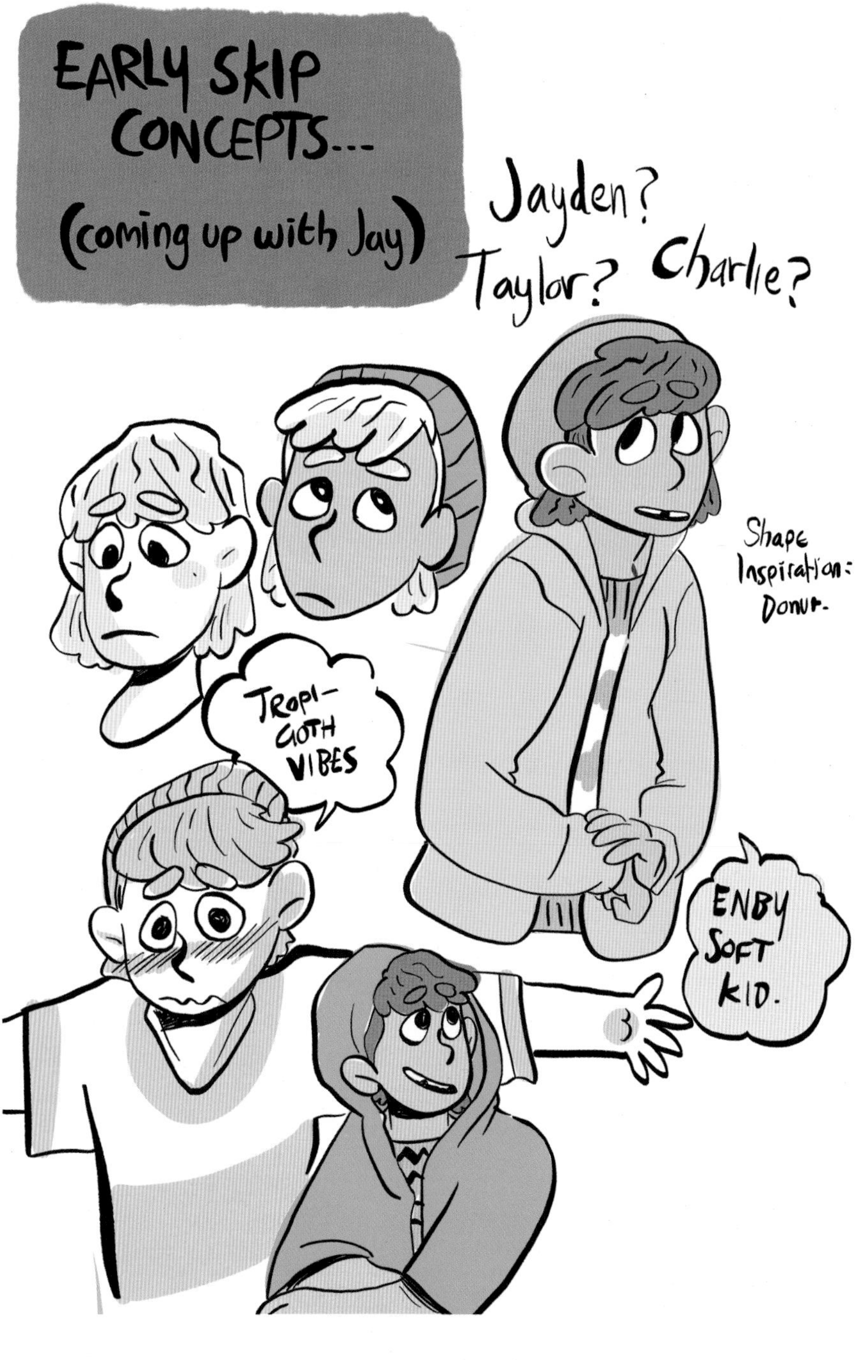
EARLY SKIP CONCEPTS...
(coming up with Jay)
Jayden?
Taylor?
Charlie?
Shape Inspiration: Donut.
TROPI-GOTH VIBES
ENBY SOFT KID.

MORE OLD SKIP CONCEPT ART...

First ever drawings of Beah!

SUPER OLD SKIP CONCEPT ART!

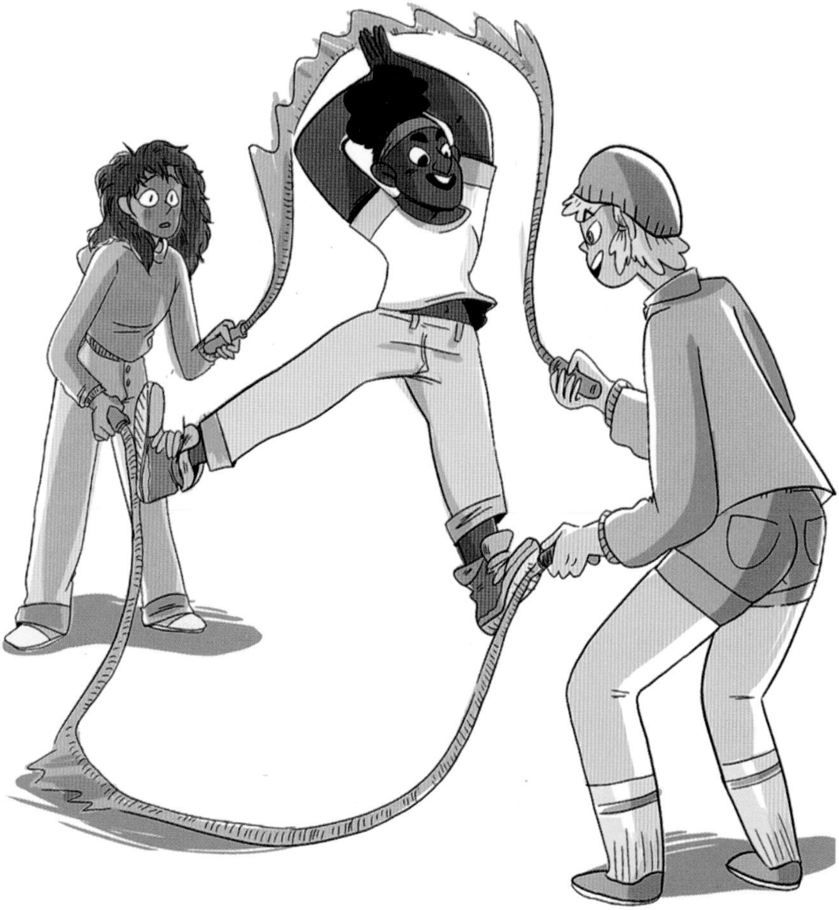

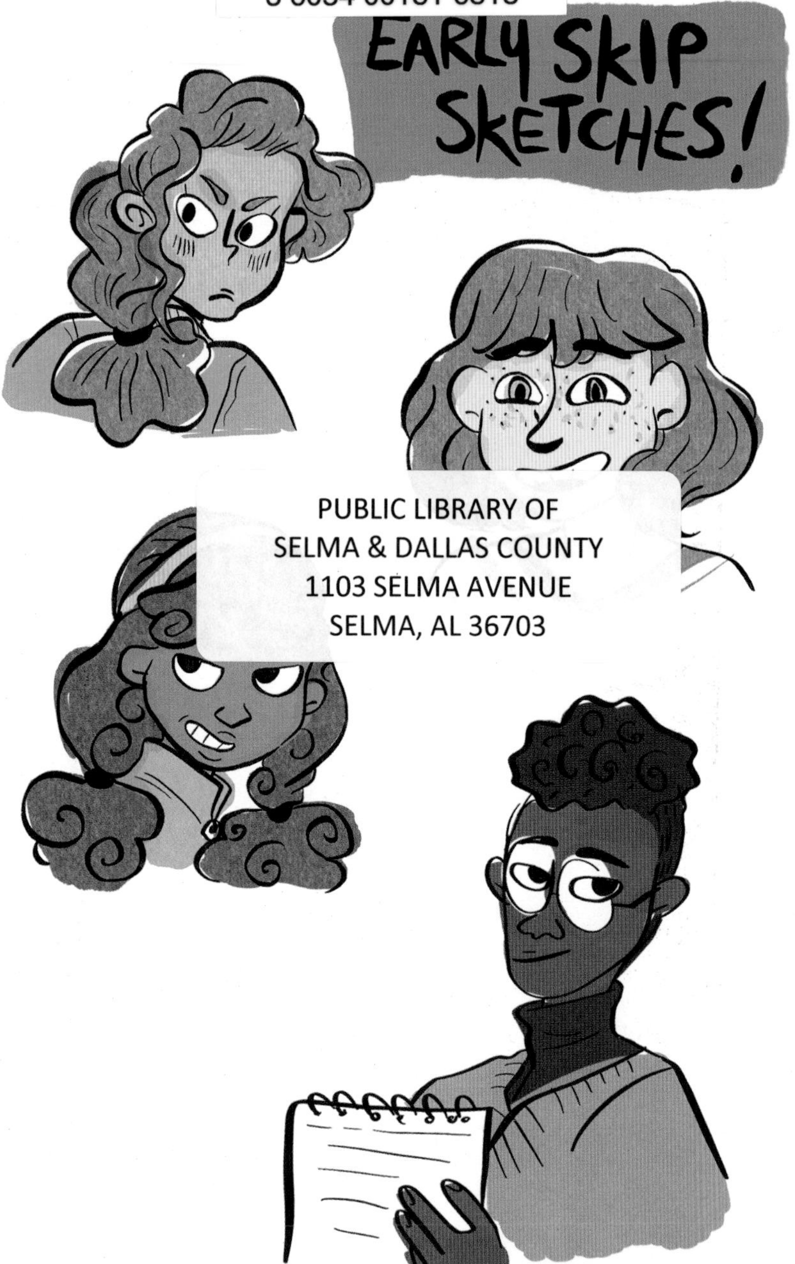
EARLY SKIP SKETCHES!